# GOTHIC

## ALGERNON BLACKWOOD
### HORROR STORIES

AN ANTHOLOGY OF CLASSIC TALES

Foreword by Ramsey Campbell

**FLAME TREE PUBLISHING**

## FANTASY

This is a FLAME TREE Book

Publisher & Creative Director: Nick Wells
Project Editor: Gillian Whitaker

Publisher's Note: Due to the historical nature of the classic text, we're aware that there may be some language used which has the potential to cause offence to the modern reader. However, wishing overall to preserve the integrity of the text, rather than imposing contemporary sensibilities, we have left it unaltered.

FLAME TREE PUBLISHING
6 Melbray Mews, Fulham,
London SW6 3NS, United Kingdom
www.flametreepublishing.com

First published 2023

Copyright © 2023 Flame Tree Publishing Ltd

23 25 27 26 24
1 3 5 7 9 10 8 6 4 2

ISBN: 978-1-80417-709-9
Special ISBN: 978-1-80417-711-2

All rights reserved. No part of this publication may be reproduced, stored in a retrieval system, or transmitted in any form or by any means, electronic, mechanical, photocopying, recording or otherwise, without the prior written permission of the publisher.

The cover image is created by Flame Tree Studio based on artwork by Slava Gerj, Gabor Ruszkai and Laurin Rinder and Samakai.

A copy of the CIP data for this book is available from the British Library.

Printed and bound in China

# GOTHIC

## ALGERNON BLACKWOOD
### HORROR STORIES

AN ANTHOLOGY OF CLASSIC TALES

Foreword by Ramsey Campbell

**FLAME TREE PUBLISHING**

# FANTASY

# Contents

Foreword by Ramsey Campbell ................................. 6
Publisher's Note ..................................................... 7

## Nature & The Wilderness

The Willows .......................................................... 11
The Sea Fit ........................................................... 41
The Wendigo ........................................................ 49
The Glamour of the Snow ..................................... 79
Ancient Lights ...................................................... 92
Special Delivery ................................................... 96
By Water ............................................................ 103
H.S.H. ................................................................ 108

## Tales of Transformation

May Day Eve ...................................................... 118
The Camp of the Dog .......................................... 132
The Terror of the Twins ....................................... 176
The Transfer ....................................................... 181
Strange Disappearance of a Baronet .................... 188
The Wings of Horus ............................................ 192
Tongues of Fire .................................................. 206
The Doll ............................................................. 213

## Weird Realities

Smith: An Episode in a Lodging House ............... 235
Ancient Sorceries ............................................. 246
Secret Worship ................................................ 275
The Man Who Found Out .................................. 296
A Victim of Higher Space .................................. 307
The Other Wing ................................................ 319
The Pikestaffe Case .......................................... 331

## Ghostly Visitations

A Haunted Island .............................................. 351
Keeping His Promise ......................................... 361
The Empty House ............................................. 371
The Listener ..................................................... 382
The Kit-Bag ...................................................... 400
The Occupant of the Room ............................... 408
The Damned ..................................................... 414
The Decoy ........................................................ 463

Biographies & Sources ...................................... 476

# Foreword: Algernon Blackwood Horror Stories

**ALGERNON BLACKWOOD** (1869–1951) is crucial to the development of supernatural fiction in English. His stories draw on varied aspects of his life: time spent in the Canadian and Alaskan wildernesses and in unsettled areas of Europe, a job as a New York reporter, his membership of the Order of the Golden Dawn, the Victorian occult society. He wrote new tales for more than forty years, frequently conveying uncanny dread but also often striving for awe if not to touch the mystical. He became an early television star, narrating some of his stories to the camera.

A few tales in our collection may appear conventional, perhaps because later writers have recycled their themes, but Blackwood's versions retain their vigour. 'Keeping His Promise' deals with a pact that is spectrally kept, while 'The Empty House' narrates a night spent in a haunted house, and 'The Occupant of the Room' evokes in daunting detail an encounter with the titular tenant. These and other Blackwood tales derive power from their close scrutiny of how such experiences would affect those undergoing them. This existential approach to the eerie remains at the core of his career, conferring the old vitality on late works like 'The Doll'. Other stories rival M.R. James in their gradual accretion of insidious detail, whether at ominous length ('The Listener') or refined to an absolute essence ('Ancient Lights').

If he occasionally touches on established religion, it's only to expand his conceptual largeness. Thus the diabolical visitation in 'H.S.H.' leads to a resolution bordering on the ecstatic, not to say encompassingly compassionate. His concept of an afterlife owes nothing to his early Lutheran upbringing, as 'The Damned' makes plain; indeed, the story reads like a conscious repudiation. Other aspects of childhood seem to have stayed with him throughout his life, in the unsullied wonder at the mysteries of nature he often communicated and a recurrent preoccupation with youthful experience: the fancies that may possess a child at night ('The Other Wing'), the unmediated insights adulthood may abandon ('The Transfer'). Not for nothing does 'The Pikestaffe Case' allude to 'those childhood alarms that pertain to the big unexplained mysteries no parent can elucidate because no parent knows'.

The professional psychic investigator had become a literary convention even in the Edwardian era, when Blackwood created John Silence. The central problem of any such series is the investigator's relative invulnerability, since we know they must survive to figure in another tale. Blackwood solves this by sometimes having Silence turn up only at the end, which is why I won't identify which four stories of him are included here. Savour their atmosphere and strangeness unprompted by me.

There's a moment in 'Smith: An Episode in a Lodging House' where the skeptical narrator regrets his own rationalism and yearns for the mystical. Soon he falters, but our author seldom does. Sometimes the searchers for higher experience whom Blackwood depicts seem to achieve a kind of cosmic elation, as in 'The Pikestaffe Case', whereas in 'The Man Who Found Out' the revealed truth is too devastating to be specified. The impulse to encompass or at least to encounter the wondrous inspires visions such as 'The Glamour of the Snow', where an apparition incarnates the lure of the wild, and 'The Sea

Fit', in which reminiscences of paganism may invoke 'immense Outer Beings', a phrase Lovecraft could have penned. At times his language stretches wonderfully wide in an attempt to contain a revelation, and in some stories the theme steeps the prose in the visionary – the avian intensity of 'The Wings of Horus', for instance, where the very words seem poised to take flight.

If I maintain that 'The Willows' and 'The Wendigo' epitomise Blackwood's aspiration to the marvellous and terrible as well as distilling his response to the awful mysteries of nature, this isn't to imply that his later work faltered; it's simply to claim those tales as twin summits of his achievement. The late Robert Aickman and I genially disagreed over their relative merits, with Robert according 'The Wendigo' the palm. In any case, Blackwood never surpassed this pair of tales for haunting weirdness, for the inexorable accumulation of details and glimpses that suggest a sense of the unknowably alien, for the construction of narratives that conjure up occult experiences and presences larger than they can directly show, instead functioning as metaphors for them. Yet these are just some of the dread delights and marvels on offer in these pages, and I hope to have imparted a few tastes of the feast. Let Blackwood into your imagination! You may find it enlarged and enriched.

*Ramsey Campbell*

# Publisher's Note

**WE'RE DELIGHTED** to have devoted an entire volume to the fiction of Algernon Blackwood, who has very much earned a place in our series of classic single-author collections. As one of the founding fathers of modern ghost and horror fiction, his influence can be felt in many of the speculative tales that we've published in our themed anthologies, including new work from authors writing today. Blackwood, who declared a fundamental interest in 'signs and proofs of other powers that lie hidden in us all', wrote stories that built on an older tradition but with an early modern edge; his tales concerned elemental forces, incomprehensible laws of physics and psychological exploration. He found a strain of horror in both urban landscapes and vast, remote wildernesses, as well as in the memories and dreams of the self.

No compendium of Blackwood's fiction would be complete without 'The Willows' and 'The Wendigo', but we have also sought to include some lesser-known tales alongside the popular choices. Frequently intense and atmospheric, they are also playful, whether it's in conjuring the terror of a haunted house, or in conveying the disconcerting prospect of other dimensions, being pulled into unfamiliar worlds and confronted with distorted versions of reality. The book is divided into thematic categories, and two recommended reads are provided at the end of each story for the reader's interest. While that we've been unable to include all of this prolific author's output, we hope this large sample of Blackwood's best horror stories provides an enjoyable treasure trove of his works.

# GOTHIC

## ALGERNON BLACKWOOD HORROR STORIES

AN ANTHOLOGY OF CLASSIC TALES

Foreword by Ramsey Campbell

**FLAME TREE PUBLISHING**

## FANTASY

# Nature & The Wilderness

# The Willows

## Chapter I

**AFTER LEAVING VIENNA**, and long before you come to Budapest, the Danube enters a region of singular loneliness and desolation, where its waters spread away on all sides regardless of a main channel, and the country becomes a swamp for miles upon miles, covered by a vast sea of low willow-bushes. On the big maps this deserted area is painted in a fluffy blue, growing fainter in colour as it leaves the banks, and across it may be seen in large straggling letters the word *Sümpfe*, meaning marshes.

In high flood this great acreage of sand, shingle-beds, and willow-grown islands is almost topped by the water, but in normal seasons the bushes bend and rustle in the free winds, showing their silver leaves to the sunshine in an ever-moving plain of bewildering beauty. These willows never attain to the dignity of trees; they have no rigid trunks; they remain humble bushes, with rounded tops and soft outline, swaying on slender stems that answer to the least pressure of the wind; supple as grasses, and so continually shifting that they somehow give the impression that the entire plain is moving and alive. For the wind sends waves rising and falling over the whole surface, waves of leaves instead of waves of water, green swells like the sea, too, until the branches turn and lift, and then silvery white as their underside turns to the sun.

Happy to slip beyond the control of the stern banks, the Danube here wanders about at will among the intricate network of channels intersecting the islands everywhere with broad avenues down which the waters pour with a shouting sound; making whirlpools, eddies, and foaming rapids; tearing at the sandy banks; carrying away masses of shore and willow-clumps; and forming new islands innumerably which shift daily in size and shape and possess at best an impermanent life, since the flood-time obliterates their very existence.

Properly speaking, this fascinating part of the river's life begins soon after leaving Pressburg, and we, in our Canadian canoe, with gipsy tent and frying-pan on board, reached it on the crest of a rising flood about mid-July. That very same morning, when the sky was reddening before sunrise, we had slipped swiftly through still-sleeping Vienna, leaving it a couple of hours later a mere patch of smoke against the blue hills of the Wienerwald on the horizon; we had breakfasted below Fischeramend under a grove of birch trees roaring in the wind; and had then swept on the tearing current past Orth, Hainburg, Petronell (the old Roman Carnuntum of Marcus Aurelius), and so under the frowning heights of Thelsen on a spur of the Carpathians, where the March steals in quietly from the left and the frontier is crossed between Austria and Hungary.

Racing along at twelve kilometers an hour soon took us well into Hungary, and the muddy waters – sure sign of flood – sent us aground on many a shingle-bed, and twisted us like a cork in many a sudden belching whirlpool before the towers of Pressburg (Hungarian, Poszóny) showed against the sky; and then the canoe, leaping like a spirited horse, flew at top speed under the grey walls, negotiated safely the sunken chain of the Fliegende Brucke ferry, turned the corner sharply to the left, and plunged on yellow foam into the wilderness of islands, sandbanks, and swamp-land beyond – the land of the willows.

The change came suddenly, as when a series of bioscope pictures snaps down on the streets of a town and shifts without warning into the scenery of lake and forest. We entered the land of desolation on wings, and in less than half an hour there was neither boat nor fishing-hut nor red roof, nor any single sign of human habitation and civilisation within sight. The sense of remoteness from the world of humankind, the utter isolation, the fascination of this singular world of willows, winds, and waters, instantly laid its spell upon us both, so that we allowed laughingly to one another that we ought by rights to have held some special kind of passport to admit us, and that we had, somewhat audaciously, come without asking leave into a separate little kingdom of wonder and magic – a kingdom that was reserved for the use of others who had a right to it, with everywhere unwritten warnings to trespassers for those who had the imagination to discover them.

Though still early in the afternoon, the ceaseless buffetings of a most tempestuous wind made us feel weary, and we at once began casting about for a suitable camping-ground for the night. But the bewildering character of the islands made landing difficult; the swirling flood carried us in shore and then swept us out again; the willow branches tore our hands as we seized them to stop the canoe, and we pulled many a yard of sandy bank into the water before at length we shot with a great sideways blow from the wind into a backwater and managed to beach the bows in a cloud of spray. Then we lay panting and laughing after our exertions on the hot yellow sand, sheltered from the wind, and in the full blaze of a scorching sun, a cloudless blue sky above, and an immense army of dancing, shouting willow bushes, closing in from all sides, shining with spray and clapping their thousand little hands as though to applaud the success of our efforts.

"What a river!" I said to my companion, thinking of all the way we had travelled from the source in the Black Forest, and how he had often been obliged to wade and push in the upper shallows at the beginning of June.

"Won't stand much nonsense now, will it?" he said, pulling the canoe a little farther into safety up the sand, and then composing himself for a nap.

I lay by his side, happy and peaceful in the bath of the elements – water, wind, sand, and the great fire of the sun – thinking of the long journey that lay behind us, and of the great stretch before us to the Black Sea, and how lucky I was to have such a delightful and charming travelling companion as my friend, the Swede.

We had made many similar journeys together, but the Danube, more than any other river I knew, impressed us from the very beginning with its aliveness. From its tiny bubbling entry into the world among the pinewood gardens of Donaueschingen, until this moment when it began to play the great river-game of losing itself among the deserted swamps, unobserved, unrestrained, it had seemed to us like following the growth of some living creature. Sleepy at first, but later developing violent desires as it became conscious of its deep soul, it rolled, like some huge fluid being, through all the countries we had passed, holding our little craft on its mighty shoulders, playing roughly with us sometimes, yet always friendly and well-meaning, till at length we had come inevitably to regard it as a Great Personage.

How, indeed, could it be otherwise, since it told us so much of its secret life? At night we heard it singing to the moon as we lay in our tent, uttering that odd sibilant note peculiar to itself and said to be caused by the rapid tearing of the pebbles along its bed, so great is its hurrying speed. We knew, too, the voice of its gurgling whirlpools, suddenly bubbling up on a surface previously quite calm; the roar of its shallows and swift rapids; its constant steady thundering below all mere surface sounds; and that ceaseless tearing of its icy waters at the banks. How it stood up and shouted when the rains fell flat upon its face! And how its laughter roared out when the wind blew up-stream and tried to stop its growing speed! We knew all its sounds and voices, its tumblings and foamings, its unnecessary splashing against the bridges; that self-conscious chatter when there were hills to look on; the affected dignity of its speech when it passed through the little towns, far too important to laugh; and all these faint, sweet whisperings when the sun caught it fairly in some slow curve and poured down upon it till the steam rose.

It was full of tricks, too, in its early life before the great world knew it. There were places in the upper reaches among the Swabian forests, when yet the first whispers of its destiny had not reached it, where it elected to disappear through holes in the ground, to appear again on the other side of the porous limestone hills and start a new river with another name; leaving, too, so little water in its own bed that we had to climb out and wade and push the canoe through miles of shallows.

And a chief pleasure, in those early days of its irresponsible youth, was to lie low, like Brer Fox, just before the little turbulent tributaries came to join it from the Alps, and to refuse to acknowledge them when in, but to run for miles side by side, the dividing line well marked, the very levels different, the Danube utterly declining to recognise the newcomer. Below Passau, however, it gave up this particular trick, for there the Inn comes in with a thundering power impossible to ignore, and so pushes and incommodes the parent river that there is hardly room for them in the long twisting gorge that follows, and the Danube is shoved this way and that against the cliffs, and forced to hurry itself with great waves and much dashing to and fro in order to get through in time. And during the fight our canoe slipped down from its shoulder to its breast, and had the time of its life among the struggling waves. But the Inn taught the old river a lesson, and after Passau it no longer pretended to ignore new arrivals.

This was many days back, of course, and since then we had come to know other aspects of the great creature, and across the Bavarian wheat plain of Straubing she wandered so slowly under the blazing June sun that we could well imagine only the surface inches were water, while below there moved, concealed as by a silken mantle, a whole army of Undines, passing silently and unseen down to the sea, and very leisurely too, lest they be discovered.

Much, too, we forgave her because of her friendliness to the birds and animals that haunted the shores. Cormorants lined the banks in lonely places in rows like short black palings; grey crows crowded the shingle-beds; storks stood fishing in the vistas of shallower water that opened up between the islands, and hawks, swans, and marsh birds of all sorts filled the air with glinting wings and singing, petulant cries. It was impossible to feel annoyed with the river's vagaries after seeing a deer leap with a splash into the water at sunrise and swim past the bows of the canoe; and often we saw fawns peering at us from the underbrush, or looked straight into the brown eyes of a stag as we charged full tilt round a corner and entered another reach of the river. Foxes, too, everywhere haunted the banks, tripping daintily among the driftwood and disappearing so suddenly that it was impossible to see how they managed it.

But now, after leaving Pressburg, everything changed a little, and the Danube became more serious. It ceased trifling. It was halfway to the Black Sea, within seeming distance almost of other, stranger countries where no tricks would be permitted or understood. It became suddenly grown-up, and claimed our respect and even our awe. It broke out into three arms, for one thing, that only met again a hundred kilometers farther down, and for a canoe there were no indications which one was intended to be followed.

"If you take a side channel," said the Hungarian officer we met in the Pressburg shop while buying provisions, "you may find yourselves, when the flood subsides, forty miles from anywhere, high and dry, and you may easily starve. There are no people, no farms, no fishermen. I warn you not to continue. The river, too, is still rising, and this wind will increase."

The rising river did not alarm us in the least, but the matter of being left high and dry by a sudden subsidence of the waters might be serious, and we had consequently laid in an extra stock of provisions. For the rest, the officer's prophecy held true, and the wind, blowing down a perfectly clear sky, increased steadily till it reached the dignity of a westerly gale.

It was earlier than usual when we camped, for the sun was a good hour or two from the horizon, and leaving my friend still asleep on the hot sand, I wandered about in desultory examination of our hotel. The island, I found, was less than an acre in extent, a mere sandy bank standing some two or three feet above the level of the river. The far end, pointing into the sunset, was covered with flying spray which the tremendous wind drove off the crests of the broken waves. It was triangular in shape, with the apex up stream.

I stood there for several minutes, watching the impetuous crimson flood bearing down with a shouting roar, dashing in waves against the bank as though to sweep it bodily away, and then swirling by in two foaming streams on either side. The ground seemed to shake with the shock and rush, while the furious movement of the willow bushes as the wind poured over them increased the curious illusion that the island itself actually moved. Above, for a mile or two, I could see the great river descending upon me; it was like looking up the slope of a sliding hill, white with foam, and leaping up everywhere to show itself to the sun.

The rest of the island was too thickly grown with willows to make walking pleasant, but I made the tour, nevertheless. From the lower end the light, of course, changed, and the river looked dark and angry. Only the backs of the flying waves were visible, streaked with foam, and pushed forcibly by the great puffs of wind that fell upon them from behind. For a short mile it was visible, pouring in and out among the islands, and then disappearing with a huge sweep into the willows, which closed about it like a herd of monstrous antediluvian creatures crowding down to drink. They made me think of gigantic sponge-like growths that sucked the river up into themselves. They caused it to vanish from sight. They herded there together in such overpowering numbers.

Altogether it was an impressive scene, with its utter loneliness, its bizarre suggestion; and as I gazed, long and curiously, a singular emotion began to stir somewhere in the depths of me. Midway in my delight of the wild beauty, there crept, unbidden and unexplained, a curious feeling of disquietude, almost of alarm.

A rising river, perhaps, always suggests something of the ominous; many of the little islands I saw before me would probably have been swept away by the morning; this resistless, thundering flood of water touched the sense of awe. Yet I was aware that my uneasiness lay far deeper than the emotions of awe and wonder. It was not that I felt. Nor had it directly to do with the power of the driving wind – this shouting hurricane that might almost carry up a few acres of willows into the air and scatter them like so much chaff over the landscape. The wind was simply enjoying itself, for nothing rose out of the flat landscape to stop it, and I was conscious of sharing its great game with a kind of pleasurable excitement. Yet this novel emotion had nothing to do with the wind. Indeed, so vague was the sense of distress I experienced, that it was impossible to trace it to its source and deal with it accordingly, though I was aware somehow that it had to do with my realisation of our utter insignificance before this unrestrained power of the elements about me. The huge-grown river had something to do with it too – a vague, unpleasant idea that we had somehow trifled with these great elemental forces in whose power we lay helpless every hour of the day and night. For here, indeed, they were gigantically at play together, and the sight appealed to the imagination.

But my emotion, so far as I could understand it, seemed to attach itself more particularly to the willow bushes, to these acres and acres of willows, crowding, so thickly growing there, swarming everywhere the eye could reach, pressing upon the river as though to suffocate it, standing in dense array mile after mile beneath the sky, watching, waiting, listening. And, apart quite from the elements, the willows connected themselves subtly with my malaise, attacking the mind insidiously somehow by reason of their vast numbers, and contriving in some way or other to represent to the imagination a new and mighty power, a power, moreover, not altogether friendly to us.

Great revelations of nature, of course, never fail to impress in one way or another, and I was no stranger to moods of the kind. Mountains overawe and oceans terrify, while the mystery of great forests exercises a spell peculiarly its own. But all these, at one point or another, somewhere link on intimately with human life and human experience. They stir comprehensible, even if alarming, emotions. They tend on the whole to exalt.

With this multitude of willows, however, it was something far different, I felt. Some essence emanated from them that besieged the heart. A sense of awe awakened, true, but of awe touched somewhere by a vague terror. Their serried ranks, growing everywhere darker about me as the shadows deepened, moving furiously yet softly in the wind, woke in me the curious and unwelcome suggestion that we had trespassed here upon the borders of an alien world, a world where we were intruders, a world where we were not wanted or invited to remain – where we ran grave risks perhaps!

The feeling, however, though it refused to yield its meaning entirely to analysis, did not at the time trouble me by passing into menace. Yet it never left me quite, even during the very practical business of putting up the tent in a hurricane of wind and building a fire for the stew-pot. It remained, just enough to bother and perplex, and to rob a most delightful camping-ground of a good portion of its charm. To my companion, however, I said nothing, for he was a man I considered devoid of imagination. In the first place, I could never have explained to him what I meant, and in the second, he would have laughed stupidly at me if I had.

There was a slight depression in the center of the island, and here we pitched the tent. The surrounding willows broke the wind a bit.

"A poor camp," observed the imperturbable Swede when at last the tent stood upright, "no stones and precious little firewood. I'm for moving on early tomorrow – eh? This sand won't hold anything."

But the experience of a collapsing tent at midnight had taught us many devices, and we made the cosy gipsy house as safe as possible, and then set about collecting a store of wood to last till bedtime. Willow bushes drop no branches, and driftwood was our only source of supply. We hunted the shores pretty thoroughly. Everywhere the banks were crumbling as the rising flood tore at them and carried away great portions with a splash and a gurgle.

"The island's much smaller than when we landed," said the accurate Swede. "It won't last long at this rate. We'd better drag the canoe close to the tent, and be ready to start at a moment's notice. I shall sleep in my clothes."

He was a little distance off, climbing along the bank, and I heard his rather jolly laugh as he spoke.

"By Jove!" I heard him call, a moment later, and turned to see what had caused his exclamation. But for the moment he was hidden by the willows, and I could not find him.

"What in the world's this?" I heard him cry again, and this time his voice had become serious.

I ran up quickly and joined him on the bank. He was looking over the river, pointing at something in the water.

"Good heavens, it's a man's body!" he cried excitedly. "Look!"

A black thing, turning over and over in the foaming waves, swept rapidly past. It kept disappearing and coming up to the surface again. It was about twenty feet from the shore, and just as it was opposite to where we stood it lurched round and looked straight at us. We saw its eyes reflecting the sunset, and gleaming an odd yellow as the body turned over. Then it gave a swift, gulping plunge, and dived out of sight in a flash.

"An otter, by gad!" we exclaimed in the same breath, laughing.

It was an otter, alive, and out on the hunt; yet it had looked exactly like the body of a drowned man turning helplessly in the current. Far below it came to the surface once again, and we saw its black skin, wet and shining in the sunlight.

Then, too, just as we turned back, our arms full of driftwood, another thing happened to recall us to the river bank. This time it really was a man, and what was more, a man in a boat. Now a small boat on the Danube was an unusual sight at any time, but here in this deserted region, and at flood time, it was so unexpected as to constitute a real event. We stood and stared.

Whether it was due to the slanting sunlight, or the refraction from the wonderfully illumined water, I cannot say, but, whatever the cause, I found it difficult to focus my sight properly upon the flying apparition. It seemed, however, to be a man standing upright in a sort of flat-bottomed boat, steering with a long oar, and being carried down the opposite shore at a tremendous pace. He apparently was looking across in our direction, but the distance was too great and the light too uncertain for us to make out very plainly what he was about. It seemed to me that he was gesticulating and making signs at us. His voice came across the water to us shouting something furiously, but the wind drowned it so that no single word was audible. There was something curious about the whole appearance – man, boat, signs, voice – that made an impression on me out of all proportion to its cause.

"He's crossing himself!" I cried. "Look, he's making the sign of the Cross!"

"I believe you're right," the Swede said, shading his eyes with his hand and watching the man out of sight. He seemed to be gone in a moment, melting away down there into the sea of willows where the sun caught them in the bend of the river and turned them into a great crimson wall of beauty. Mist, too, had begun to ruse, so that the air was hazy.

"But what in the world is he doing at nightfall on this flooded river?" I said, half to myself. "Where is he going at such a time, and what did he mean by his signs and shouting? D'you think he wished to warn us about something?"

"He saw our smoke, and thought we were spirits probably," laughed my companion. "These Hungarians believe in all sorts of rubbish; you remember the shopwoman at Pressburg warning us that no one ever landed here because it belonged to some sort of beings outside man's world! I suppose they believe in fairies and elementals, possibly demons, too. That peasant in the boat saw people on the islands for the first time in his life," he added, after a slight pause, "and it scared him, that's all."

The Swede's tone of voice was not convincing, and his manner lacked something that was usually there. I noted the change instantly while he talked, though without being able to label it precisely.

"If they had enough imagination," I laughed loudly – I remember trying to make as much *noise* as I could – "they might well people a place like this with the old gods of antiquity. The Romans must have haunted all this region more or less with their shrines and sacred groves and elemental deities."

The subject dropped and we returned to our stew-pot, for my friend was not given to imaginative conversation as a rule. Moreover, just then I remember feeling distinctly glad that he was not imaginative; his stolid, practical nature suddenly seemed to me welcome and comforting. It was an admirable temperament, I felt; he could steer down rapids like a red Indian, shoot dangerous bridges and whirlpools better than any white man I ever saw in a canoe. He was a grand fellow for an adventurous trip, a tower of strength when untoward things happened. I looked at his strong face and light curly hair as he staggered along under his pile of driftwood (twice the size of mine!), and I experienced a feeling of relief. Yes, I was distinctly glad just then that the Swede was – what he was, and that he never made remarks that suggested more than they said.

"The river's still rising, though," he added, as if following out some thoughts of his own, and dropping his load with a gasp. "This island will be under water in two days if it goes on."

"I wish the *wind* would go down," I said. "I don't care a fig for the river."

The flood, indeed, had no terrors for us; we could get off at ten minutes' notice, and the more water the better we liked it. It meant an increasing current and the obliteration of the treacherous shingle-beds that so often threatened to tear the bottom out of our canoe.

Contrary to our expectations, the wind did not go down with the sun. It seemed to increase with the darkness, howling overhead and shaking the willows round us like straws. Curious sounds accompanied it sometimes, like the explosion of heavy guns, and it fell upon the water and the island in great flat blows of immense power. It made me think of the sounds a planet must make, could we only hear it, driving along through space.

But the sky kept wholly clear of clouds, and soon after supper the full moon rose up in the east and covered the river and the plain of shouting willows with a light like the day.

We lay on the sandy patch beside the fire, smoking, listening to the noises of the night round us, and talking happily of the journey we had already made, and of our plans ahead. The map lay spread in the door of the tent, but the high wind made it hard to study, and presently we lowered the curtain and extinguished the lantern. The firelight was enough to smoke and see each other's faces by, and the sparks flew about overhead like fireworks. A few yards beyond, the river gurgled and hissed, and from time to time a heavy splash announced the falling away of further portions of the bank.

Our talk, I noticed, had to do with the faraway scenes and incidents of our first camps in the Black Forest, or of other subjects altogether remote from the present setting, for neither of us spoke of the actual moment more than was necessary – almost as though we had agreed tacitly to avoid discussion of the camp and its incidents. Neither the otter nor the boatman, for instance, received the honour of a single mention, though ordinarily these would have furnished discussion for the greater part of the evening. They were, of course, distinct events in such a place.

The scarcity of wood made it a business to keep the fire going, for the wind, that drove the smoke in our faces wherever we sat, helped at the same time to make a forced draught. We took it in turn to make some foraging expeditions into the darkness, and the quantity the Swede brought back always made me feel that he took an absurdly long time finding it; for the fact was I did not care much about being left alone, and yet it always seemed to be my turn to grub about among the bushes or scramble along the slippery banks in the moonlight. The long day's battle with wind and water – such wind and such water! – had tired us both, and an early bed was the obvious program. Yet neither of us made the move for the tent. We lay there, tending the fire, talking in desultory fashion, peering about us into the dense willow bushes, and listening to the thunder of wind and river. The loneliness of the place had entered our very bones, and silence seemed natural, for after a bit the sound of our voices became a trifle unreal and forced; whispering would have been the fitting mode of communication, I felt, and the human voice, always rather absurd amid the roar of the elements, now carried with it something almost illegitimate. It was like talking out loud in church, or in some place where it was not lawful, perhaps not quite *safe*, to be overheard.

The eeriness of this lonely island, set among a million willows, swept by a hurricane, and surrounded by hurrying deep waters, touched us both, I fancy. Untrodden by man, almost unknown to man, it lay there beneath the moon, remote from human influence, on the frontier of another world, an alien world, a world tenanted by willows only and the souls of willows. And we, in our rashness, had dared to invade it, even to make use of it! Something more than the power of its mystery stirred in me as I lay on the sand, feet to fire, and peered up through the leaves at the stars. For the last time I rose to get firewood.

"When this has burnt up," I said firmly, "I shall turn in," and my companion watched me lazily as I moved off into the surrounding shadows.

For an unimaginative man I thought he seemed unusually receptive that night, unusually open to suggestion of things other than sensory. He too was touched by the beauty and loneliness of the place. I was not altogether pleased, I remember, to recognise this slight change in him, and instead of immediately collecting sticks, I made my way to the far point of the island where the moonlight on plain and river could be seen to better advantage. The desire to be alone had come suddenly upon me; my former dread returned in force; there was a vague feeling in me I wished to face and probe to the bottom.

When I reached the point of sand jutting out among the waves, the spell of the place descended upon me with a positive shock. No mere 'scenery' could have produced such an effect. There was something more here, something to alarm.

I gazed across the waste of wild waters; I watched the whispering willows; I heard the ceaseless beating of the tireless wind; and, one and all, each in its own way, stirred in me this sensation of a strange distress. But the *willows* especially; for ever they went on chattering and talking among themselves, laughing a little, shrilly crying out, sometimes sighing – but what it was they made so much to-do about belonged to the secret life of the great plain they inhabited. And it was utterly alien to the world I knew, or to that of the wild yet kindly elements. They made me think of a host of beings from another plane of life, another evolution altogether, perhaps, all discussing a mystery known only to themselves. I watched them moving busily together, oddly shaking their big bushy heads, twirling their myriad leaves even when there was no wind. They moved of their own will as though alive, and they touched, by some incalculable method, my own keen sense of the *horrible*.

There they stood in the moonlight, like a vast army surrounding our camp, shaking their innumerable silver spears defiantly, formed all ready for an attack.

The psychology of places, for some imaginations at least, is very vivid; for the wanderer, especially, camps have their 'note' either of welcome or rejection. At first it may not always be apparent, because the busy preparations of tent and cooking prevent, but with the first pause – after supper usually – it comes and announces itself. And the note of this willow-camp now became unmistakably plain to me; we were interlopers, trespassers; we were not welcomed. The sense of unfamiliarity grew upon me as I stood there watching. We touched the frontier of a region where our presence was resented. For a night's lodging we might perhaps be tolerated; but for a prolonged and inquisitive stay – No! by all the gods of the trees and wilderness, no! We were the first human influences upon this island, and we were not wanted. *The willows were against us.*

Strange thoughts like these, bizarre fancies, borne I know not whence, found lodgment in my mind as I stood listening. What, I thought, if, after all, these crouching willows proved to be alive; if suddenly they should rise up, like a swarm of living creatures, marshalled by the gods whose territory we had invaded, sweep towards us off the vast swamps, booming overhead in the night – and then *settle down!* As I looked it was so easy to imagine they actually moved, crept nearer, retreated a little, huddled together in masses, hostile, waiting for the great wind that should finally start them a-running. I could have sworn their aspect changed a little, and their ranks deepened and pressed more closely together.

The melancholy shrill cry of a night-bird sounded overhead, and suddenly I nearly lost my balance as the piece of bank I stood upon fell with a great splash into the river, undermined by the flood. I stepped back just in time, and went on hunting for firewood again, half laughing at the odd fancies that crowded so thickly into my mind and cast their spell upon me. I recalled the Swede's remark about moving on next day, and I was just thinking that I fully agreed with him, when I turned with a start and saw the subject of my thoughts standing immediately in front of me. He was quite close. The roar of the elements had covered his approach.

"You've been gone so long," he shouted above the wind, "I thought something must have happened to you."

But there was that in his tone, and a certain look in his face as well, that conveyed to me more than his usual words, and in a flash I understood the real reason for his coming. It was because the spell of the place had entered his soul too, and he did not like being alone.

"River still rising," he cried, pointing to the flood in the moonlight, "and the wind's simply awful."

He always said the same things, but it was the cry for companionship that gave the real importance to his words.

"Lucky," I cried back, "our tent's in the hollow. I think it'll hold all right." I added something about the difficulty of finding wood, in order to explain my absence, but the wind caught my words and flung them across the river, so that he did not hear, but just looked at me through the branches, nodding his head.

"Lucky if we get away without disaster!" he shouted, or words to that effect; and I remember feeling half angry with him for putting the thought into words, for it was exactly what I felt myself. There was disaster impending somewhere, and the sense of presentiment lay unpleasantly upon me.

We went back to the fire and made a final blaze, poking it up with our feet. We took a last look round. But for the wind the heat would have been unpleasant. I put this thought into words, and I remember my friend's reply struck me oddly: that he would rather have the heat, the ordinary July weather, than this 'diabolical wind'.

Everything was snug for the night; the canoe lying turned over beside the tent, with both yellow paddles beneath her; the provision sack hanging from a willow-stem, and the washed-up dishes removed to a safe distance from the fire, all ready for the morning meal.

We smothered the embers of the fire with sand, and then turned in. The flap of the tent door was up, and I saw the branches and the stars and the white moonlight. The shaking willows and the heavy buffetings of the wind against our taut little house were the last things I remembered as sleep came down and covered all with its soft and delicious forgetfulness.

## Chapter II

**SUDDENLY** I found myself lying awake, peering from my sandy mattress through the door of the tent. I looked at my watch pinned against the canvas, and saw by the bright moonlight that it was past twelve o'clock – the threshold of a new day – and I had therefore slept a couple of hours. The Swede was asleep still beside me; the wind howled as before; something plucked at my heart and made me feel afraid. There was a sense of disturbance in my immediate neighbourhood.

I sat up quickly and looked out. The trees were swaying violently to and fro as the gusts smote them, but our little bit of green canvas lay snugly safe in the hollow, for the wind passed over it without meeting enough resistance to make it vicious. The feeling of disquietude did not pass, however, and I crawled quietly out of the tent to see if our belongings were safe. I moved carefully so as not to waken my companion. A curious excitement was on me.

I was halfway out, kneeling on all fours, when my eye first took in that the tops of the bushes opposite, with their moving tracery of leaves, made shapes against the sky. I sat back on my haunches and stared. It was incredible, surely, but there, opposite and slightly above me, were shapes of some indeterminate sort among the willows, and as the branches swayed in the wind they seemed to group themselves about these shapes, forming a series of monstrous outlines that shifted rapidly beneath the moon. Close, about fifty feet in front of me, I saw these things.

My first instinct was to waken my companion, that he too might see them, but something made me hesitate – the sudden realisation, probably, that I should not welcome corroboration; and meanwhile I crouched there staring in amazement with smarting eyes. I was wide awake. I remember saying to myself that I was not dreaming.

They first became properly visible, these huge figures, just within the tops of the bushes – immense, bronze-coloured, moving, and wholly independent of the swaying of the branches. I saw them plainly and noted, now I came to examine them more calmly, that they were very much larger than human, and indeed that something in their appearance proclaimed them to be not human at all. Certainly they were not merely the moving tracery of the branches against the moonlight. They shifted independently. They rose upwards in a continuous stream from earth to sky, vanishing utterly as soon as they reached the dark of the sky. They were interlaced one with another, making a great column, and I saw their limbs and huge bodies melting in and out of each other, forming this serpentine line that bent and swayed and twisted spirally with the contortions of the wind-tossed trees. They were nude, fluid shapes, passing up the bushes, within the leaves almost – rising up in a living column into the heavens. Their faces I never could see. Unceasingly they poured upwards, swaying in great bending curves, with a hue of dull bronze upon their skins.

I stared, trying to force every atom of vision from my eyes. For a long time I thought they must every moment disappear and resolve themselves into the movements of the branches and prove to be an optical illusion. I searched everywhere for a proof of reality, when all the while I understood quite well that the standard of reality had changed. For the longer I looked the more certain I became that these figures were real and living, though perhaps not according to the standards that the camera and the biologist would insist upon.

Far from feeling fear, I was possessed with a sense of awe and wonder such as I have never known. I seemed to be gazing at the personified elemental forces of this haunted and primeval region. Our intrusion had stirred the powers of the place into activity. It was we who were the cause of the disturbance, and my brain filled to bursting with stories and legends of the spirits and deities of places that have been acknowledged and worshipped by men in all ages of the world's history. But, before I could arrive at any possible explanation, something impelled me to go farther out, and I crept forward on the sand and stood upright. I felt the ground still warm under my bare feet; the wind tore at my hair and face; and the sound of the river burst upon my ears with a sudden roar. These things, I knew, were real, and proved that my senses were acting normally. Yet the figures still rose from earth to heaven, silent, majestically, in a great spiral of grace and strength that overwhelmed me at length with a genuine deep emotion of worship. I felt that I must fall down and worship – absolutely worship.

Perhaps in another minute I might have done so, when a gust of wind swept against me with such force that it blew me sideways, and I nearly stumbled and fell. It seemed to shake the dream violently out of me. At least it gave me another point of view somehow. The figures still remained, still ascended into heaven from the heart of the night, but my reason at last began to assert itself. It must be a subjective experience, I argued – none the less real for that, but still subjective. The moonlight and the branches combined to work out these pictures upon the mirror of my imagination, and for some reason I projected them outwards and made them appear objective. I knew this must be the case, of course. I took courage, and began to move forward across the open patches of sand. By Jove, though, was it all hallucination? Was it merely subjective? Did not my reason argue in the old futile way from the little standard of the known?

I only know that great column of figures ascended darkly into the sky for what seemed a very long period of time, and with a very complete measure of reality as most men are accustomed to gauge reality. Then suddenly they were gone!

And, once they were gone and the immediate wonder of their great presence had passed, fear came down upon me with a cold rush. The esoteric meaning of this lonely and haunted region suddenly flamed up within me, and I began to tremble dreadfully. I took a quick look round – a look of horror that came near to panic – calculating vainly ways of escape; and then, realising how helpless I was to achieve anything really effective,

I crept back silently into the tent and lay down again upon my sandy mattress, first lowering the door-curtain to shut out the sight of the willows in the moonlight, and then burying my head as deeply as possible beneath the blankets to deaden the sound of the terrifying wind.

## Chapter III

**AS THOUGH** further to convince me that I had not been dreaming, I remember that it was a long time before I fell again into a troubled and restless sleep; and even then only the upper crust of me slept, and underneath there was something that never quite lost consciousness, but lay alert and on the watch.

But this second time I jumped up with a genuine start of terror. It was neither the wind nor the river that woke me, but the slow approach of something that caused the sleeping portion of me to grow smaller and smaller till at last it vanished altogether, and I found myself sitting bolt upright – listening.

Outside there was a sound of multitudinous little patterings. They had been coming, I was aware, for a long time, and in my sleep they had first become audible. I sat there nervously wide awake as though I had not slept at all. It seemed to me that my breathing came with difficulty, and that there was a great weight upon the surface of my body. In spite of the hot night, I felt clammy with cold and shivered. Something surely was pressing steadily against the sides of the tent and weighing down upon it from above. Was it the body of the wind? Was this the pattering rain, the dripping of the leaves? The spray blown from the river by the wind and gathering in big drops? I thought quickly of a dozen things.

Then suddenly the explanation leaped into my mind: a bough from the poplar, the only large tree on the island, had fallen with the wind. Still half caught by the other branches, it would fall with the next gust and crush us, and meanwhile its leaves brushed and tapped upon the tight canvas surface of the tent. I raised a loose flap and rushed out, calling to the Swede to follow.

But when I got out and stood upright I saw that the tent was free. There was no hanging bough; there was no rain or spray; nothing approached.

A cold, grey light filtered down through the bushes and lay on the faintly gleaming sand. Stars still crowded the sky directly overhead, and the wind howled magnificently, but the fire no longer gave out any glow, and I saw the east reddening in streaks through the trees. Several hours must have passed since I stood there before watching the ascending figures, and the memory of it now came back to me horribly, like an evil dream. Oh, how tired it made me feel, that ceaseless raging wind! Yet, though the deep lassitude of a sleepless night was on me, my nerves were tingling with the activity of an equally tireless apprehension, and all idea of repose was out of the question. The river I saw had risen further. Its thunder filled the air, and a fine spray made itself felt through my thin sleeping shirt.

Yet nowhere did I discover the slightest evidence of anything to cause alarm. This deep, prolonged disturbance in my heart remained wholly unaccounted for.

My companion had not stirred when I called him, and there was no need to waken him now. I looked about me carefully, noting everything; the turned-over canoe; the yellow paddles – two of them, I'm certain; the provision sack and the extra lantern hanging together from the tree; and, crowding everywhere about me, enveloping all, the willows, those endless, shaking willows. A bird uttered its morning cry, and a string of ducks passed with whirring flight overhead in the twilight. The sand whirled, dry and stinging, about my bare feet in the wind.

I walked round the tent and then went out a little way into the bush, so that I could see across the river to the farther landscape, and the same profound yet indefinable emotion of distress seized upon me again as I saw the interminable sea of bushes stretching to the horizon, looking ghostly and unreal in the wan light of dawn. I walked softly here and there, still puzzling over that odd sound of infinite pattering, and of that pressure upon the tent that had wakened me. It *must* have been the wind, I reflected – the wind bearing upon the loose, hot sand, driving the dry particles smartly against the taut canvas – the wind dropping heavily upon our fragile roof.

Yet all the time my nervousness and malaise increased appreciably.

I crossed over to the farther shore and noted how the coastline had altered in the night, and what masses of sand the river had torn away. I dipped my hands and feet into the cool current, and bathed my forehead. Already there was a glow of sunrise in the sky and the exquisite freshness of coming day. On my way back I passed purposely beneath the very bushes where I had seen the column of figures rising into the air, and midway among the clumps I suddenly found myself overtaken by a sense of vast terror. From the shadows a large figure went swiftly by. Someone passed me, as sure as ever man did…

It was a great staggering blow from the wind that helped me forward again, and once out in the more open space, the sense of terror diminished strangely. The winds were about and walking, I remember saying to myself, for the winds often move like great presences under the trees. And altogether the fear that hovered about me was such an unknown and immense kind of fear, so unlike anything I had ever felt before, that it woke a sense of awe and wonder in me that did much to counteract its worst effects; and when I reached a high point in the middle of the island from which I could see the wide stretch of river, crimson in the sunrise, the whole magical beauty of it all was so overpowering that a sort of wild yearning woke in me and almost brought a cry up into the throat.

But this cry found no expression, for as my eyes wandered from the plain beyond to the island round me and noted our little tent half hidden among the willows, a dreadful discovery leaped out at me, compared to which my terror of the walking winds seemed as nothing at all.

For a change, I thought, had somehow come about in the arrangement of the landscape. It was not that my point of vantage gave me a different view, but that an alteration had apparently been effected in the relation of the tent to the willows, and of the willows to the tent. Surely the bushes now crowded much closer – unnecessarily, unpleasantly close. *They had moved nearer.*

Creeping with silent feet over the shifting sands, drawing imperceptibly nearer by soft, unhurried movements, the willows had come closer during the night. But had the wind moved them, or had they moved of themselves? I recalled the sound of infinite small patterings and the pressure upon the tent and upon my own heart that caused me to wake in terror. I swayed for a moment in the wind like a tree, finding it hard to keep my upright position on the sandy hillock. There was a suggestion here of personal agency, of deliberate intention, of aggressive hostility, and it terrified me into a sort of rigidity.

Then the reaction followed quickly. The idea was so bizarre, so absurd, that I felt inclined to laugh. But the laughter came no more readily than the cry, for the knowledge that my mind was so receptive to such dangerous imaginings brought the additional terror that it was through our minds and not through our physical bodies that the attack would come, and was coming.

The wind buffeted me about, and, very quickly it seemed, the sun came up over the horizon, for it was after four o'clock, and I must have stood on that little pinnacle of sand longer than I knew, afraid to come down to close quarters with the willows. I returned quietly, creepily, to the tent, first taking another exhaustive look round and – yes, I confess it – making a few measurements. I paced out on the warm sand the distances between the willows and the tent, making a note of the shortest distance particularly.

I crawled stealthily into my blankets. My companion, to all appearances, still slept soundly, and I was glad that this was so. Provided my experiences were not corroborated, I could find strength somehow to deny them, perhaps. With the daylight I could persuade myself that it was all a subjective hallucination, a fantasy of the night, a projection of the excited imagination.

Nothing further came in to disturb me, and I fell asleep almost at once, utterly exhausted, yet still in dread of hearing again that weird sound of multitudinous pattering, or of feeling the pressure upon my heart that had made it difficult to breathe.

## Chapter IV

**THE SUN** was high in the heavens when my companion woke me from a heavy sleep and announced that the porridge was cooked and there was just time to bathe. The grateful smell of frizzling bacon entered the tent door.

"River still rising," he said, "and several islands out in mid-stream have disappeared altogether. Our own island's much smaller."

"Any wood left?" I asked sleepily.

"The wood and the island will finish tomorrow in a dead heat," he laughed, "but there's enough to last us till then."

I plunged in from the point of the island, which had indeed altered a lot in size and shape during the night, and was swept down in a moment to the landing-place opposite the tent. The water was icy, and the banks flew by like the country from an express train. Bathing under such conditions was an exhilarating operation, and the terror of the night seemed cleansed out of me by a process of evaporation in the brain. The sun was blazing hot; not a cloud showed itself anywhere; the wind, however, had not abated one little jot.

Quite suddenly then the implied meaning of the Swede's words flashed across me, showing that he no longer wished to leave post-haste, and had changed his mind. "Enough to last till tomorrow" – he assumed we should stay on the island another night. It struck me as odd. The night before he was so positive the other way. How had the change come about?

Great crumblings of the banks occurred at breakfast, with heavy splashings and clouds of spray which the wind brought into our frying-pan, and my fellow-traveller talked incessantly about the difficulty the Vienna-Pesth steamers must have to find the channel in flood. But the state of his mind interested and impressed me far more than the state of the river or the difficulties of the steamers. He had changed somehow since the evening before. His manner was different – a trifle excited, a trifle shy, with a sort of suspicion about his voice and gestures. I hardly know how to describe it now in cold blood, but at the time I remember being quite certain of one thing – that he had become frightened?

He ate very little breakfast, and for once omitted to smoke his pipe. He had the map spread open beside him, and kept studying its markings.

"We'd better get off sharp in an hour," I said presently, feeling for an opening that must bring him indirectly to a partial confession at any rate. And his answer puzzled me uncomfortably: "Rather! If they'll let us."

"Who'll let us? The elements?" I asked quickly, with affected indifference.

"The powers of this awful place, whoever they are," he replied, keeping his eyes on the map. "The gods are here, if they are anywhere at all in the world."

"The elements are always the true immortals," I replied, laughing as naturally as I could manage, yet knowing quite well that my face reflected my true feelings when he looked up gravely at me and spoke across the smoke:

"We shall be fortunate if we get away without further disaster."

This was exactly what I had dreaded, and I screwed myself up to the point of the direct question. It was like agreeing to allow the dentist to extract the tooth; it *had* to come anyhow in the long run, and the rest was all pretence.

"Further disaster! Why, what's happened?"

"For one thing – the steering paddle's gone," he said quietly.

"The steering paddle gone!" I repeated, greatly excited, for this was our rudder, and the Danube in flood without a rudder was suicide. "But what—"

"And there's a tear in the bottom of the canoe," he added, with a genuine little tremor in his voice.

I continued staring at him, able only to repeat the words in his face somewhat foolishly. There, in the heat of the sun, and on this burning sand, I was aware of a freezing atmosphere descending round us. I got up to follow him, for he merely nodded his head gravely and led the way towards the tent a few yards on the other side of the fireplace. The canoe still lay there as I had last seen her in the night, ribs uppermost, the paddles, or rather, *the* paddle, on the sand beside her.

"There's only one," he said, stooping to pick it up. "And here's the rent in the base-board."

It was on the tip of my tongue to tell him that I had clearly noticed *two* paddles a few hours before, but a second impulse made me think better of it, and I said nothing. I approached to see.

There was a long, finely made tear in the bottom of the canoe where a little slither of wood had been neatly taken clean out; it looked as if the tooth of a sharp rock or snag had eaten down her length, and investigation showed that the hole went through. Had we launched out in her without observing it we must inevitably have foundered. At first the water would have made the wood swell so as to close the hole, but once out in midstream the water must have poured in, and the canoe, never more than two inches above the surface, would have filled and sunk very rapidly.

"There, you see an attempt to prepare a victim for the sacrifice," I heard him saying, more to himself than to me, "two victims rather," he added as he bent over and ran his fingers along the slit.

I began to whistle – a thing I always do unconsciously when utterly nonplussed – and purposely paid no attention to his words. I was determined to consider them foolish.

"It wasn't there last night," he said presently, straightening up from his examination and looking anywhere but at me.

"We must have scratched her in landing, of course," I stopped whistling to say. "The stones are very sharp."

I stopped abruptly, for at that moment he turned round and met my eye squarely. I knew just as well as he did how impossible my explanation was. There were no stones, to begin with.

"And then there's this to explain too," he added quietly, handing me the paddle and pointing to the blade.

A new and curious emotion spread freezingly over me as I took and examined it. The blade was scraped down all over, beautifully scraped, as though someone had sandpapered it with care, making it so thin that the first vigorous stroke must have snapped it off at the elbow.

"One of us walked in his sleep and did this thing," I said feebly, "or – or it has been filed by the constant stream of sand particles blown against it by the wind, perhaps."

"Ah," said the Swede, turning away, laughing a little, "you can explain everything."

"The same wind that caught the steering paddle and flung it so near the bank that it fell in with the next lump that crumbled," I called out after him, absolutely determined to find an explanation for everything he showed me.

"I see," he shouted back, turning his head to look at me before disappearing among the willow bushes.

Once alone with these perplexing evidences of personal agency, I think my first thoughts took the form of "One of us must have done this thing, and it certainly was not I." But my second thought decided how impossible it was to suppose, under all the circumstances, that either of us had done it. That my companion, the trusted friend of a dozen similar expeditions, could have knowingly had a hand in it, was a suggestion not to be entertained for a moment. Equally absurd seemed the explanation that this imperturbable and densely practical nature had suddenly become insane and was busied with insane purposes.

Yet the fact remained that what disturbed me most, and kept my fear actively alive even in this blaze of sunshine and wild beauty, was the clear certainty that some curious alteration had come about in his *mind* – that he was nervous, timid, suspicious, aware of goings on he did not speak about, watching a series of secret and hitherto unmentionable events – waiting, in a word, for a climax that he expected, and, I thought, expected very soon. This grew up in my mind intuitively – I hardly knew how.

I made a hurried examination of the tent and its surroundings, but the measurements of the night remained the same. There were deep hollows formed in the sand I now noticed for the first time, basin-shaped and of various depths and sizes, varying from that of a tea-cup to a large bowl. The wind, no doubt, was responsible for these miniature craters, just as it was for lifting the paddle and tossing it towards the water. The rent in the canoe was the only thing that seemed quite inexplicable; and, after all, it *was* conceivable that a sharp point had caught it when we landed. The examination I made of the shore did not assist this theory, but all the same I clung to it with that diminishing portion of my intelligence which I called my 'reason'. An explanation of some kind was an absolute necessity, just as some working explanation of the universe is necessary – however absurd – to the happiness of every individual who seeks to do his duty in the world and face the problems of life. The simile seemed to me at the time an exact parallel.

I at once set the pitch melting, and presently the Swede joined me at the work, though under the best conditions in the world the canoe could not be safe for travelling till the following day. I drew his attention casually to the hollows in the sand.

"Yes," he said, "I know. They're all over the island. But *you* can explain them, no doubt!"

"Wind, of course," I answered without hesitation. "Have you never watched those little whirlwinds in the street that twist and twirl everything into a circle? This sand's loose enough to yield, that's all."

He made no reply, and we worked on in silence for a bit. I watched him surreptitiously all the time, and I had an idea he was watching me. He seemed, too, to be always listening attentively to something I could not hear, or perhaps for something that he expected to hear, for he kept turning about and staring into the bushes, and up into the sky, and out across the water where it was visible through the openings among the willows. Sometimes he even put his hand to his ear and held it there for several minutes. He said nothing to me, however, about it, and I asked no questions. And meanwhile, as he mended that torn canoe with the skill and address of a red Indian, I was glad to notice his absorption in the work, for there was a vague dread in my heart that he would speak of the changed aspect of the willows. And, if he had noticed *that*, my imagination could no longer be held a sufficient explanation of it.

At length, after a long pause, he began to talk.

"Queer thing," he added in a hurried sort of voice, as though he wanted to say something and get it over. "Queer thing. I mean, about that otter last night."

I had expected something so totally different that he caught me with surprise, and I looked up sharply.

"Shows how lonely this place is. Otters are awfully shy things—"

"I don't mean that, of course," he interrupted. "I mean – do you think – did you think it really was an otter?"

"What else, in the name of Heaven, what else?"

"You know, I saw it before you did, and at first it seemed – so *much* bigger than an otter."

"The sunset as you looked up-stream magnified it, or something," I replied.

He looked at me absently a moment, as though his mind were busy with other thoughts.

"It had such extraordinary yellow eyes," he went on half to himself.

"That was the sun too," I laughed, a trifle boisterously. "I suppose you'll wonder next if that fellow in the boat—"

I suddenly decided not to finish the sentence. He was in the act again of listening, turning his head to the wind, and something in the expression of his face made me halt. The subject dropped, and we went on with our caulking. Apparently he had not noticed my unfinished sentence. Five minutes later, however, he looked at me across the canoe, the smoking pitch in his hand, his face exceedingly grave.

"I *did* rather wonder, if you want to know," he said slowly, "what that thing in the boat was. I remember thinking at the time it was not a man. The whole business seemed to rise quite suddenly out of the water."

I laughed again boisterously in his face, but this time there was impatience, and a strain of anger too, in my feeling.

"Look here now," I cried, "this place is quite queer enough without going out of our way to imagine things! That boat was an ordinary boat, and the man in it was an ordinary man, and they were both going down-stream as fast as they could lick. And that otter *was* an otter, so don't let's play the fool about it!"

He looked steadily at me with the same grave expression. He was not in the least annoyed. I took courage from his silence.

"And, for Heaven's sake," I went on, "don't keep pretending you hear things, because it only gives me the jumps, and there's nothing to hear but the river and this cursed old thundering wind."

"You *fool!*" he answered in a low, shocked voice, "you utter fool. That's just the way all victims talk. As if you didn't understand just as well as I do!" he sneered with scorn in his voice, and a sort of resignation. "The best thing you can do is to keep quiet and try to hold your mind as firm as possible. This feeble attempt at self-deception only makes the truth harder when you're forced to meet it."

My little effort was over, and I found nothing more to say, for I knew quite well his words were true, and that *I* was the fool, not *he*. Up to a certain stage in the adventure he kept ahead of me easily, and I think I felt annoyed to be out of it, to be thus proved less psychic, less sensitive than himself to these extraordinary happenings, and half ignorant all the time of what was going on under my very nose. *He knew* from the very beginning, apparently. But at the moment I wholly missed the point of his words about the necessity of there being a victim, and that we ourselves were destined to satisfy the want. I dropped all pretence thenceforward, but thenceforward likewise my fear increased steadily to the climax.

"But you're quite right about one thing," he added, before the subject passed, "and that is that we're wiser not to talk about it, or even to think about it, because what one *thinks* finds expression in words, and what one *says*, happens."

That afternoon, while the canoe dried and hardened, we spent trying to fish, testing the leak, collecting wood, and watching the enormous flood of rising water. Masses of driftwood swept near our shores sometimes, and we fished for them with long willow branches. The island grew perceptibly smaller as the banks were torn away with great gulps and splashes. The weather kept brilliantly fine till about four o'clock, and then for the first time for three days the wind showed signs of abating. Clouds began to gather in the south-west, spreading thence slowly over the sky.

This lessening of the wind came as a great relief, for the incessant roaring, banging, and thundering had irritated our nerves. Yet the silence that came about five o'clock with its sudden cessation was in a manner quite as oppressive. The booming of the river had everything in its own way then; it filled the air with deep murmurs, more musical than the wind noises, but infinitely more monotonous. The wind held many notes, rising, falling always beating out some sort of great elemental tune; whereas the river's song lay between three notes at most – dull pedal notes, that held a lugubrious quality foreign to the wind, and somehow seemed to me, in my then nervous state, to sound wonderfully well the music of doom.

It was extraordinary, too, how the withdrawal suddenly of bright sunlight took everything out of the landscape that made for cheerfulness; and since this particular landscape had already managed to convey the suggestion of something sinister, the change of course was all the more unwelcome and noticeable. For me, I know, the darkening outlook became distinctly more alarming, and I found myself more than once calculating how soon after sunset the full moon would get up in the east, and whether the gathering clouds would greatly interfere with her lighting of the little island.

With this general hush of the wind – though it still indulged in occasional brief gusts – the river seemed to me to grow blacker, the willows to stand more densely together. The latter, too, kept up a sort of independent movement of their own, rustling among themselves when no wind stirred, and shaking oddly from the roots upwards. When common objects in this way become charged with the suggestion of horror, they stimulate the imagination far more than things of unusual appearance; and these bushes, crowding huddled about us, assumed for me in the darkness a bizarre *grotesquerie* of appearance that lent to them somehow the aspect of purposeful and living creatures. Their very ordinariness, I felt, masked what was malignant and hostile to us. The forces of the region drew nearer with the coming of night. They were focusing upon our island, and more particularly upon ourselves. For thus, somehow, in the terms of the imagination, did my really indescribable sensations in this extraordinary place present themselves.

I had slept a good deal in the early afternoon, and had thus recovered somewhat from the exhaustion of a disturbed night, but this only served apparently to render me more susceptible than before to the obsessing spell of the haunting. I fought against it, laughing at my feelings as absurd and childish, with very obvious physiological explanations, yet, in spite of every effort, they gained in strength upon me so that I dreaded the night as a child lost in a forest must dread the approach of darkness.

The canoe we had carefully covered with a waterproof sheet during the day, and the one remaining paddle had been securely tied by the Swede to the base of a tree, lest the wind should rob us of that too. From five o'clock onwards I busied myself with the stew-pot and preparations for dinner, it being my turn to cook that night. We had potatoes, onions, bits of bacon fat to add flavour, and a general thick residue from former stews at the bottom of the pot; with black bread broken up into it the result was most excellent, and it was followed by a stew of plums with sugar and a brew of strong tea with dried milk. A good pile of wood lay close at hand, and the absence of wind made my duties easy. My companion sat lazily watching me, dividing his attentions between cleaning his pipe and giving useless advice – an admitted privilege of the off-duty man. He had been very quiet all the afternoon, engaged in re-caulking the canoe, strengthening the tent ropes, and fishing for driftwood while I slept. No more talk about undesirable things had passed between us, and I think his only remarks had to do with the gradual destruction of the island, which he declared was not fully a third smaller than when we first landed.

The pot had just begun to bubble when I heard his voice calling to me from the bank, where he had wandered away without my noticing. I ran up.

"Come and listen," he said, "and see what you make of it." He held his hand cupwise to his ear, as so often before.

"*Now* do you hear anything?" he asked, watching me curiously.

We stood there, listening attentively together. At first I heard only the deep note of the water and the hissings rising from its turbulent surface. The willows, for once, were motionless and silent. Then a sound began to reach my ears faintly, a peculiar sound – something like the humming of a distant gong. It seemed to come across to us in the darkness from the waste of swamps and willows opposite. It was repeated at regular intervals, but it was certainly neither the sound of a bell nor the hooting of a distant steamer. I can liken it to nothing so much as to the sound of an immense gong, suspended far up in the sky, repeating incessantly its muffled metallic note, soft and musical, as it was repeatedly struck. My heart quickened as I listened.

"I've heard it all day," said my companion. "While you slept this afternoon it came all round the island. I hunted it down, but could never get near enough to see – to localise it correctly. Sometimes it was overhead, and sometimes it seemed under the water. Once or twice, too, I could have sworn it was not outside at all, but *within myself* – you know – the way a sound in the fourth dimension is supposed to come."

I was too much puzzled to pay much attention to his words. I listened carefully, striving to associate it with any known familiar sound I could think of, but without success. It changed in the direction, too, coming nearer, and then sinking utterly away into remote distance. I cannot say that it was ominous in quality, because to me it seemed distinctly musical, yet I must admit it set going a distressing feeling that made me wish I had never heard it.

"The wind blowing in those sand-funnels," I said determined to find an explanation, "or the bushes rubbing together after the storm perhaps."

"It comes off the whole swamp," my friend answered. "It comes from everywhere at once." He ignored my explanations. "It comes from the willow bushes somehow—"

"But now the wind has dropped," I objected. "The willows can hardly make a noise by themselves, can they?"

His answer frightened me, first because I had dreaded it, and secondly, because I knew intuitively it was true.

"It is *because* the wind has dropped we now hear it. It was drowned before. It is the cry, I believe, of the—"

I dashed back to my fire, warned by the sound of bubbling that the stew was in danger, but determined at the same time to escape further conversation. I was resolute, if possible, to avoid the exchanging of views. I dreaded, too, that he would begin about the gods, or the elemental forces, or something else disquieting, and I wanted to keep myself well in hand for what might happen later. There was another night to be faced before we escaped from this distressing place, and there was no knowing yet what it might bring forth.

"Come and cut up bread for the pot," I called to him, vigorously stirring the appetising mixture. That stew-pot held sanity for us both, and the thought made me laugh.

He came over slowly and took the provision sack from the tree, fumbling in its mysterious depths, and then emptying the entire contents upon the ground-sheet at his feet.

"Hurry up!" I cried; "it's boiling."

The Swede burst out into a roar of laughter that startled me. It was forced laughter, not artificial exactly, but mirthless.

"There's nothing here!" he shouted, holding his sides.

"Bread, I mean."

"It's gone. There is no bread. They've taken it!"

I dropped the long spoon and ran up. Everything the sack had contained lay upon the ground-sheet, but there was no loaf.

The whole dead weight of my growing fear fell upon me and shook me. Then I burst out laughing too. It was the only thing to do: and the sound of my laughter also made me understand his. The strain of psychical pressure caused it – this explosion of unnatural laughter in both of us; it was an effort of repressed forces to seek relief; it was a temporary safety-valve. And with both of us it ceased quite suddenly.

"How criminally stupid of me!" I cried, still determined to be consistent and find an explanation. "I clean forgot to buy a loaf at Pressburg. That chattering woman put everything out of my head, and I must have left it lying on the counter or—"

"The oatmeal, too, is much less than it was this morning," the Swede interrupted.

Why in the world need he draw attention to it? I thought angrily.

"There's enough for tomorrow," I said, stirring vigorously, "and we can get lots more at Komorn or Gran. In twenty-four hours we shall be miles from here."

"I hope so – to God," he muttered, putting the things back into the sack, "unless we're claimed first as victims for the sacrifice," he added with a foolish laugh. He dragged the sack into the tent, for safety's sake, I suppose, and I heard him mumbling to himself, but so indistinctly that it seemed quite natural for me to ignore his words.

Our meal was beyond question a gloomy one, and we ate it almost in silence, avoiding one another's eyes, and keeping the fire bright. Then we washed up and prepared for the night, and, once smoking, our minds unoccupied with any definite duties, the apprehension I had felt all day long became more and more acute. It was not then active fear, I think, but the very vagueness of its origin distressed me far more that if I had been able to ticket and face it squarely. The curious sound I have likened to the note of a gong became now almost incessant, and filled the stillness of the night with a faint, continuous ringing rather than a series of distinct notes. At one time it was behind and at another time in front of us. Sometimes I fancied it came from the bushes on our left, and then again from the clumps on our right. More often it hovered directly overhead like the whirring of wings. It was really everywhere at once, behind, in front, at our sides and over our heads, completely surrounding us. The sound really defies description. But nothing within my knowledge is like that ceaseless muffled humming rising off the deserted world of swamps and willows.

We sat smoking in comparative silence, the strain growing every minute greater. The worst feature of the situation seemed to me that we did not know what to expect, and could therefore make no sort of preparation by way of defence. We could anticipate nothing. My explanations made in the sunshine, moreover, now came to haunt me with their foolish and wholly unsatisfactory nature, and it was more and more clear to us that some kind of plain talk with my companion was inevitable, whether I liked it or not. After all, we had to spend the night together, and to sleep in the same tent side by side. I saw that I could not get along much longer without the support of his mind, and for that, of course, plain talk was imperative. As long as possible, however, I postponed this little climax, and tried to ignore or laugh at the occasional sentences he flung into the emptiness.

Some of these sentences, moreover, were confoundedly disquieting to me, coming as they did to corroborate much that I felt myself; corroboration, too – which made it so much more convincing – from a totally different point of view. He composed such curious sentences, and hurled them at me in such an inconsequential sort of way, as though his main line of thought was secret to himself, and these fragments were mere bits he found it impossible to digest. He got rid of them by uttering them. Speech relieved him. It was like being sick.

"There are things about us, I'm sure, that make for disorder, disintegration, destruction, our destruction," he said once, while the fire blazed between us. "We've strayed out of a safe line somewhere."

And, another time, when the gong sounds had come nearer, ringing much louder than before, and directly over our heads, he said as though talking to himself:

"I don't think a gramophone would show any record of that. The sound doesn't come to me by the ears at all. The vibrations reach me in another manner altogether, and seem to be within me, which is precisely how a fourth dimensional sound might be supposed to make itself heard."

I purposely made no reply to this, but I sat up a little closer to the fire and peered about me into the darkness. The clouds were massed all over the sky, and no trace of moonlight came through. Very still, too, everything was, so that the river and the frogs had things all their own way.

"It has that about it," he went on, "which is utterly out of common experience. It is *unknown*. Only one thing describes it really; it is a non-human sound; I mean a sound outside humanity."

Having rid himself of this indigestible morsel, he lay quiet for a time, but he had so admirably expressed my own feeling that it was a relief to have the thought out, and to have confined it by the limitation of words from dangerous wandering to and fro in the mind.

The solitude of that Danube camping-place, can I ever forget it? The feeling of being utterly alone on an empty planet! My thoughts ran incessantly upon cities and the haunts of men. I would have given my soul, as the saying is, for the 'feel' of those Bavarian villages we had passed through by the score; for the normal, human commonplaces; peasants drinking beer, tables beneath the trees, hot sunshine, and a ruined castle on the rocks behind the red-roofed church. Even the tourists would have been welcome.

Yet what I felt of dread was no ordinary ghostly fear. It was infinitely greater, stranger, and seemed to arise from some dim ancestral sense of terror more profoundly disturbing than anything I had known or dreamed of. We had 'strayed', as the Swede put it, into some region or some set of conditions where the risks were great, yet unintelligible to us; where the frontiers of some unknown world lay close about us. It was a spot held by the dwellers in some outer space, a sort of peep-hole whence they could spy upon the earth, themselves unseen, a point where the veil between had worn a little thin. As the final result of too long a sojourn here, we should be carried over the border and deprived of what we called 'our lives', yet by mental, not physical, processes. In that sense, as he said, we should be the victims of our adventure – a sacrifice.

It took us in different fashion, each according to the measure of his sensitiveness and powers of resistance. I translated it vaguely into a personification of the mightily disturbed elements, investing them with the horror of a deliberate and malefic purpose, resentful of our audacious intrusion into their breeding-place; whereas my friend threw it into the unoriginal form at first of a trespass on some ancient shrine, some place where the old gods still held sway, where the emotional forces of former worshippers still clung, and the ancestral portion of him yielded to the old pagan spell.

At any rate, here was a place unpolluted by men, kept clean by the winds from coarsening human influences, a place where spiritual agencies were within reach and aggressive. Never, before or since, have I been so attacked by indescribable suggestions of a 'beyond region', of another scheme of life, another revolution not parallel to the human. And in the end our minds would succumb under the weight of the awful spell, and we should be drawn across the frontier into *their* world.

Small things testified to the amazing influence of the place, and now in the silence round the fire they allowed themselves to be noted by the mind. The very atmosphere had proved itself a magnifying medium to distort every indication: the otter rolling in the current, the hurrying boatman making signs, the shifting willows, one and all had been robbed of its natural character, and revealed in something of its other aspect – as it existed across the border to that other region. And this changed aspect I felt was now not merely to me, but to the race. The whole experience whose verge we touched was unknown to humanity at all. It was a new order of experience, and in the true sense of the word *unearthly*.

"It's the deliberate, calculating purpose that reduces one's courage to zero," the Swede said suddenly, as if he had been actually following my thoughts. "Otherwise imagination might count for much. But the paddle, the canoe, the lessening food—"

"Haven't I explained all that once?" I interrupted viciously.

"You have," he answered dryly; "you have indeed."

He made other remarks too, as usual, about what he called the "plain determination to provide a victim"; but, having now arranged my thoughts better, I recognised that this was simply the cry of his frightened soul against the knowledge that he was being attacked in a vital part, and that he would be somehow taken or destroyed. The situation called for a courage and calmness of reasoning that neither of us could compass, and I have never before been so clearly conscious of two persons in me – the one that explained everything, and the other that laughed at such foolish explanations, yet was horribly afraid.

Meanwhile, in the pitchy night the fire died down and the wood pile grew small. Neither of us moved to replenish the stock, and the darkness consequently came up very close to our faces. A few feet beyond the circle of firelight it was inky black. Occasionally a stray puff of wind set the willows shivering about us, but apart from this not very welcome sound a deep and depressing silence reigned, broken only by the gurgling of the river and the humming in the air overhead.

We both missed, I think, the shouting company of the winds.

At length, at a moment when a stray puff prolonged itself as though the wind were about to rise again, I reached the point for me of saturation, the point where it was absolutely necessary to find relief in plain speech, or else to betray myself by some hysterical extravagance that must have been far worse in its effect upon both of us. I kicked the fire into a blaze, and turned to my companion abruptly. He looked up with a start.

"I can't disguise it any longer," I said; "I don't like this place, and the darkness, and the noises, and the awful feelings I get. There's something here that beats me utterly. I'm in a blue funk, and that's the plain truth. If the other shore was – different, I swear I'd be inclined to swim for it!"

The Swede's face turned very white beneath the deep tan of sun and wind. He stared straight at me and answered quietly, but his voice betrayed his huge excitement by its unnatural calmness. For the moment, at any rate, he was the strong man of the two. He was more phlegmatic, for one thing.

"It's not a physical condition we can escape from by running away," he replied, in the tone of a doctor diagnosing some grave disease; "we must sit tight and wait. There are forces close here that could kill a herd of elephants in a second as easily as you or I could squash a fly. Our only chance is to keep perfectly still. Our insignificance perhaps may save us."

I put a dozen questions into my expression of face, but found no words. It was precisely like listening to an accurate description of a disease whose symptoms had puzzled me.

"I mean that so far, although aware of our disturbing presence, they have not *found* us – not 'located' us, as the Americans say," he went on. "They're blundering about like men hunting for a leak of gas. The paddle and canoe and provisions prove that. I think they *feel* us, but cannot actually see us. We must keep our minds quiet – it's our minds they feel. We must control our thoughts, or it's all up with us."

"Death, you mean?" I stammered, icy with the horror of his suggestion.

"Worse – by far," he said. "Death, according to one's belief, means either annihilation or release from the limitations of the senses, but it involves no change of character. *You* don't suddenly alter just because the body's gone. But this means a radical alteration, a complete change, a horrible loss of oneself by substitution – far worse than death, and not even annihilation. We happen to have camped in a spot where their region touches ours, where the veil between has worn thin" – horrors! he was using my very own phrase, my actual words – "so that they are aware of our being in their neighbourhood."

"But *who* are aware?" I asked.

I forgot the shaking of the willows in the windless calm, the humming overhead, everything except that I was waiting for an answer that I dreaded more than I can possibly explain.

He lowered his voice at once to reply, leaning forward a little over the fire, an indefinable change in his face that made me avoid his eyes and look down upon the ground.

"All my life," he said, "I have been strangely, vividly conscious of another region – not far removed from our own world in one sense, yet wholly different in kind – where great things go on unceasingly, where immense and terrible personalities hurry by, intent on vast purposes compared to which earthly affairs, the rise and fall of nations, the destinies of empires, the fate of armies and continents, are all as dust in the balance; vast purposes, I mean, that deal directly with the soul, and not indirectly with mere expressions of the soul—"

"I suggest just now—" I began, seeking to stop him, feeling as though I was face to face with a madman. But he instantly overbore me with his torrent that *had* to come.

"You think," he said, "it is the spirit of the elements, and I thought perhaps it was the old gods. But I tell you now it is – *neither*. These would be comprehensible entities, for they have relations with men, depending upon them for worship or sacrifice, whereas these beings who are now about us have absolutely nothing to do with mankind, and it is mere chance that their space happens just at this spot to touch our own."

The mere conception, which his words somehow made so convincing, as I listened to them there in the dark stillness of that lonely island, set me shaking a little all over. I found it impossible to control my movements.

"And what do you propose?" I began again.

"A sacrifice, a victim, might save us by distracting them until we could get away," he went on, "just as the wolves stop to devour the dogs and give the sleigh another start. But – I see no chance of any other victim now."

I stared blankly at him. The gleam in his eye was dreadful. Presently he continued.

"It's the willows, of course. The willows *mask* the others, but the others are feeling about for us. If we let our minds betray our fear, we're lost, lost utterly." He looked at me with an expression so calm, so determined, so sincere, that I no longer had any doubts as to his sanity. He was as sane as any man ever was. "If we can hold out through the night," he added, "we may get off in the daylight unnoticed, or rather, *undiscovered*."

"But you really think a sacrifice would—"

That gong-like humming came down very close over our heads as I spoke, but it was my friend's scared face that really stopped my mouth.

"Hush!" he whispered, holding up his hand. "Do not mention them more than you can help. Do not refer to them *by name*. To name is to reveal; it is the inevitable clue, and our only hope lies in ignoring them, in order that they may ignore us."

"Even in thought?" He was extraordinarily agitated.

"Especially in thought. Our thoughts make spirals in their world. We must keep them *out of our minds* at all costs if possible."

I raked the fire together to prevent the darkness having everything its own way. I never longed for the sun as I longed for it then in the awful blackness of that summer night.

"Were you awake all last night?" he went on suddenly.

"I slept badly a little after dawn," I replied evasively, trying to follow his instructions, which I knew instinctively were true, "but the wind, of course—"

"I know. But the wind won't account for all the noises."

"Then you heard it too?"

"The multiplying countless little footsteps I heard," he said, adding, after a moment's hesitation, "and that other sound—"

"You mean above the tent, and the pressing down upon us of something tremendous, gigantic?"

He nodded significantly.

"It was like the beginning of a sort of inner suffocation?" I said.

"Partly, yes. It seemed to me that the weight of the atmosphere had been altered – had increased enormously, so that we should have been crushed."

"And that," I went on, determined to have it all out, pointing upwards where the gong-like note hummed ceaselessly, rising and falling like wind. "What do you make of that?"

"It's *their* sound," he whispered gravely. "It's the sound of their world, the humming in their region. The division here is so thin that it leaks through somehow. But, if you listen carefully, you'll find it's not above so much as around us. It's in the willows. It's the willows themselves humming, because here the willows have been made symbols of the forces that are against us."

I could not follow exactly what he meant by this, yet the thought and idea in my mind were beyond question the thought and idea in his. I realised what he realised, only with less power of analysis than his. It was on the tip of my tongue to tell him at last about my hallucination of the ascending figures and the moving bushes, when he suddenly thrust his face again close into mine across the firelight and began to speak in a very earnest whisper. He amazed me by his calmness and pluck, his apparent control of the situation. This man I had for years deemed unimaginative, stolid!

"Now listen," he said. "The only thing for us to do is to go on as though nothing had happened, follow our usual habits, go to bed, and so forth; pretend we feel nothing and notice nothing. It is a question wholly of the mind, and the less we think about them the better our chance of escape. Above all, don't *think*, for what you think happens!"

"All right," I managed to reply, simply breathless with his words and the strangeness of it all; "all right, I'll try, but tell me one more thing first. Tell me what you make of those hollows in the ground all about us, those sand-funnels?"

"No!" he cried, forgetting to whisper in his excitement. "I dare not, simply dare not, put the thought into words. If you have not guessed I am glad. Don't try to. *They* have put it into my mind; try your hardest to prevent their putting it into yours."

He sank his voice again to a whisper before he finished, and I did not press him to explain. There was already just about as much horror in me as I could hold. The conversation came to an end, and we smoked our pipes busily in silence.

Then something happened, something unimportant apparently, as the way is when the nerves are in a very great state of tension, and this small thing for a brief space gave me an entirely different point of view. I chanced to look down at my sand-shoe – the sort we used for the canoe – and something to do with the hole at the toe suddenly recalled to me the London shop where I had bought them, the difficulty the man had in fitting me, and other details of the uninteresting but practical operation. At once, in its train, followed a wholesome view of the modern sceptical world I was accustomed to move in at home. I thought of roast beef, and ale, motor-cars, policemen, brass bands, and a dozen other things that proclaimed the soul of ordinariness or utility. The effect was immediate and astonishing even to myself. Psychologically, I suppose, it was simply a sudden and violent reaction after the strain of living in an atmosphere of things that to the normal consciousness must seem impossible and incredible. But, whatever the cause, it momentarily lifted the spell from my heart, and left me for the short space of a minute feeling free and utterly unafraid. I looked up at my friend opposite.

"You damned old pagan!" I cried, laughing aloud in his face. "You imaginative idiot! You superstitious idolater! You—"

I stopped in the middle, seized anew by the old horror. I tried to smother the sound of my voice as something sacrilegious. The Swede, of course, heard it too – the strange cry overhead in the darkness – and that sudden drop in the air as though something had come nearer.

He had turned ashen white under the tan. He stood bolt upright in front of the fire, stiff as a rod, staring at me.

"After that," he said in a sort of helpless, frantic way, "we must go! We can't stay now; we must strike camp this very instant and go on – down the river."

He was talking, I saw, quite wildly, his words dictated by abject terror – the terror he had resisted so long, but which had caught him at last.

"In the dark?" I exclaimed, shaking with fear after my hysterical outburst, but still realising our position better than he did. "Sheer madness! The river's in flood, and we've only got a single paddle. Besides, we only go deeper into their country! There's nothing ahead for fifty miles but willows, willows, willows!"

He sat down again in a state of semi-collapse. The positions, by one of those kaleidoscopic changes nature loves, were suddenly reversed, and the control of our forces passed over into my hands. His mind at last had reached the point where it was beginning to weaken.

"What on earth possessed you to do such a thing?" he whispered with the awe of genuine terror in his voice and face.

I crossed round to his side of the fire. I took both his hands in mine, kneeling down beside him and looking straight into his frightened eyes.

"We'll make one more blaze," I said firmly, "and then turn in for the night. At sunrise we'll be off full speed for Komorn. Now, pull yourself together a bit, and remember your own advice about *not thinking fear!*"

He said no more, and I saw that he would agree and obey. In some measure, too, it was a sort of relief to get up and make an excursion into the darkness for more wood. We kept close together, almost touching, groping among the bushes and along the bank. The humming overhead never ceased, but seemed to me to grow louder as we increased our distance from the fire. It was shivery work!

We were grubbing away in the middle of a thickish clump of willows where some driftwood from a former flood had caught high among the branches, when my body was seized in a grip that made me half drop upon the sand. It was the Swede. He had fallen against me, and was clutching me for support. I heard his breath coming and going in short gasps.

"Look! By my soul!" he whispered, and for the first time in my experience I knew what it was to hear tears of terror in a human voice. He was pointing to the fire, some fifty feet away. I followed the direction of his finger, and I swear my heart missed a beat.

There, in front of the dim glow, *something was moving.*

I saw it through a veil that hung before my eyes like the gauze drop-curtain used at the back of a theatre – hazily a little. It was neither a human figure nor an animal. To me it gave the strange impression of being as large as several animals grouped together, like horses, two or three, moving slowly. The Swede, too, got a similar result, though expressing it differently, for he thought it was shaped and sized like a clump of willow bushes, rounded at the top, and moving all over upon its surface – "coiling upon itself like smoke," he said afterwards.

"I watched it settle downwards through the bushes," he sobbed at me. "Look, by God! It's coming this way! Oh, oh!" – he gave a kind of whistling cry. *"They've found us."*

I gave one terrified glance, which just enabled me to see that the shadowy form was swinging towards us through the bushes, and then I collapsed backwards with a crash into the branches. These failed, of course, to support my weight, so that with the Swede on top of me we fell in a struggling heap upon the sand. I really hardly knew what was happening. I was conscious only of a sort of enveloping sensation of icy fear that plucked the nerves out of their fleshly covering, twisted them this way and that, and replaced them quivering. My eyes were tightly shut; something in my throat choked me; a feeling that my consciousness was expanding, extending out into space, swiftly gave way to another feeling that I was losing it altogether, and about to die.

An acute spasm of pain passed through me, and I was aware that the Swede had hold of me in such a way that he hurt me abominably. It was the way he caught at me in falling.

But it was the pain, he declared afterwards, that saved me; it caused me to *forget them* and think of something else at the very instant when they were about to find me. It concealed my mind from them at the moment of discovery, yet just in time to evade their terrible seizing of me. He himself, he says, actually swooned at the same moment, and that was what saved him.

I only know that at a later date, how long or short is impossible to say, I found myself scrambling up out of the slippery network of willow branches, and saw my companion standing in front of me holding out a hand to assist me. I stared at him in a dazed way, rubbing the arm he had twisted for me. Nothing came to me to say, somehow.

"I lost consciousness for a moment or two," I heard him say. "That's what saved me. It made me stop thinking about them."

"You nearly broke my arm in two," I said, uttering my only connected thought at the moment. A numbness came over me.

"That's what saved *you!*" he replied. "Between us, we've managed to set them off on a false tack somewhere. The humming has ceased. It's gone – for the moment at any rate!"

A wave of hysterical laughter seized me again, and this time spread to my friend too – great healing gusts of shaking laughter that brought a tremendous sense of relief in their train. We made our way back to the fire and put the wood on so that it blazed at once. Then we saw that the tent had fallen over and lay in a tangled heap upon the ground.

We picked it up, and during the process tripped more than once and caught our feet in sand.

"It's those sand-funnels," exclaimed the Swede, when the tent was up again and the firelight lit up the ground for several yards about us. "And look at the size of them!"

All round the tent and about the fireplace where we had seen the moving shadows there were deep funnel-shaped hollows in the sand, exactly similar to the ones we had already found over the island, only far bigger and deeper, beautifully formed, and wide enough in some instances to admit the whole of my foot and leg.

Neither of us said a word. We both knew that sleep was the safest thing we could do, and to bed we went accordingly without further delay, having first thrown sand on the fire and taken the provision sack and the paddle inside the tent with us. The canoe, too, we propped in such a way at the end of the tent that our feet touched it, and the least motion would disturb and wake us.

In case of emergency, too, we again went to bed in our clothes, ready for a sudden start.

## Chapter V

**IT WAS** my firm intention to lie awake all night and watch, but the exhaustion of nerves and body decreed otherwise, and sleep after a while came over me with a welcome blanket of oblivion. The fact that my companion also slept quickened its approach. At first he fidgeted and constantly sat up, asking me if I "heard this" or "heard that." He tossed about on his cork mattress, and said the tent was moving and the river had risen over the point of the island, but each time I went out to look I returned with the report that all was well, and finally he grew calmer and lay still. Then at length his breathing became regular and I heard unmistakable sounds of snoring – the first and only time in my life when snoring has been a welcome and calming influence.

This, I remember, was the last thought in my mind before dozing off.

A difficulty in breathing woke me, and I found the blanket over my face. But something else besides the blanket was pressing upon me, and my first thought was that my companion had rolled off his mattress on to my own in his sleep. I called to him and sat up, and at the same moment it came to me that the tent was *surrounded*. That sound of multitudinous soft pattering was again audible outside, filling the night with horror.

I called again to him, louder than before. He did not answer, but I missed the sound of his snoring, and also noticed that the flap of the tent was down. This was the unpardonable sin. I crawled out in the darkness to hook it back securely, and it was then for the first time I realised positively that the Swede was not here. He had gone.

I dashed out in a mad run, seized by a dreadful agitation, and the moment I was out I plunged into a sort of torrent of humming that surrounded me completely and came out of every quarter of the heavens at once. It was that same familiar humming – gone mad! A swarm of great invisible bees might have been about me in the air. The sound seemed to thicken the very atmosphere, and I felt that my lungs worked with difficulty.

But my friend was in danger, and I could not hesitate.

The dawn was just about to break, and a faint whitish light spread upwards over the clouds from a thin strip of clear horizon. No wind stirred. I could just make out the bushes and river beyond, and the pale sandy patches. In my excitement I ran frantically to and fro about the island, calling him by name, shouting at the top of my voice the first words that came into my head. But the willows smothered my voice, and the humming muffled it, so that the sound only travelled a few feet round me. I plunged among the bushes, tripping headlong, tumbling over roots, and scraping my face as I tore this way and that among the preventing branches.

Then, quite unexpectedly, I came out upon the island's point and saw a dark figure outlined between the water and the sky. It was the Swede. And already he had one foot in the river! A moment more and he would have taken the plunge.

I threw myself upon him, flinging my arms about his waist and dragging him shorewards with all my strength. Of course he struggled furiously, making a noise all the time just like that cursed humming, and using the most outlandish phrases in his anger about "going *inside* to Them," and "taking the way of the water and the wind," and God only knows what more besides, that I tried in vain to recall afterwards, but which turned me sick with horror and amazement as I listened. But in the end I managed to get him into the comparative safety of the tent, and flung him breathless and cursing upon the mattress where I held him until the fit had passed.

I think the suddenness with which it all went and he grew calm, coinciding as it did with the equally abrupt cessation of the humming and pattering outside – I think this was almost the strangest part of the whole business perhaps. For he had just opened his eyes and turned his tired face up to me so that the dawn threw a pale light upon it through the doorway, and said, for all the world just like a frightened child:

"My life, old man – it's my life I owe you. But it's all over now anyhow. They've found a victim in our place!"

Then he dropped back upon his blankets and went to sleep literally under my eyes. He simply collapsed, and began to snore again as healthily as though nothing had happened and he had never tried to offer his own life as a sacrifice by drowning. And when the sunlight woke him three hours later – hours of ceaseless vigil for me – it became so clear to me that he remembered absolutely nothing of what he had attempted to do, that I deemed it wise to hold my peace and ask no dangerous questions.

He woke naturally and easily, as I have said, when the sun was already high in a windless hot sky, and he at once got up and set about the preparation of the fire for breakfast. I followed him anxiously at bathing, but he did not attempt to plunge in, merely dipping his head and making some remark about the extra coldness of the water.

"River's falling at last," he said, "and I'm glad of it."

"The humming has stopped too," I said.

He looked up at me quietly with his normal expression. Evidently he remembered everything except his own attempt at suicide.

"Everything has stopped," he said, "because—"

He hesitated. But I knew some reference to that remark he had made just before he fainted was in his mind, and I was determined to know it.

"Because 'They've found another victim'?" I said, forcing a little laugh.

"Exactly," he answered, "exactly! I feel as positive of it as though – as though – I feel quite safe again, I mean," he finished.

He began to look curiously about him. The sunlight lay in hot patches on the sand. There was no wind. The willows were motionless. He slowly rose to feet.

"Come," he said; "I think if we look, we shall find it."

He started off on a run, and I followed him. He kept to the banks, poking with a stick among the sandy bays and caves and little back-waters, myself always close on his heels.

"Ah!" he exclaimed presently, "ah!"

The tone of his voice somehow brought back to me a vivid sense of the horror of the last twenty-four hours, and I hurried up to join him. He was pointing with his stick at a large black object that lay half in the water and half on the sand. It appeared to be caught by some twisted willow roots so that the river could not sweep it away. A few hours before the spot must have been under water.

"See," he said quietly, "the victim that made our escape possible!"

And when I peered across his shoulder I saw that his stick rested on the body of a man. He turned it over. It was the corpse of a peasant, and the face was hidden in the sand. Clearly the man had been drowned, but a few hours before, and his body must have been swept down upon our island somewhere about the hour of the dawn – *at the very time the fit had passed.*

"We must give it a decent burial, you know."

"I suppose so," I replied. I shuddered a little in spite of myself, for there was something about the appearance of that poor drowned man that turned me cold.

The Swede glanced up sharply at me, an undecipherable expression on his face, and began clambering down the bank. I followed him more leisurely. The current, I noticed, had torn away much of the clothing from the body, so that the neck and part of the chest lay bare.

Halfway down the bank my companion suddenly stopped and held up his hand in warning; but either my foot slipped, or I had gained too much momentum to bring myself quickly to a halt, for I bumped into him and sent him forward with a sort of leap to save himself. We tumbled together on to the hard sand so that our feet splashed into the water. And, before anything could be done, we had collided a little heavily against the corpse.

The Swede uttered a sharp cry. And I sprang back as if I had been shot.

At the moment we touched the body there rose from its surface the loud sound of humming – the sound of several hummings – which passed with a vast commotion as of winged things in the air about us and disappeared upwards into the sky, growing fainter and fainter till they finally ceased in the distance. It was exactly as though we had disturbed some living yet invisible creatures at work.

My companion clutched me, and I think I clutched him, but before either of us had time properly to recover from the unexpected shock, we saw that a movement of the current was turning the corpse round so that it became released from the grip of the willow roots. A moment later it had turned completely over, the dead face uppermost, staring at the sky. It lay on the edge of the main stream. In another moment it would be swept away.

The Swede started to save it, shouting again something I did not catch about a "proper burial" – and then abruptly dropped upon his knees on the sand and covered his eyes with his hands. I was beside him in an instant.

I saw what he had seen.

For just as the body swung round to the current the face and the exposed chest turned full towards us, and showed plainly how the skin and flesh were indented with small hollows, beautifully formed, and exactly similar in shape and kind to the sand-funnels that we had found all over the island.

"Their mark!" I heard my companion mutter under his breath. "Their awful mark!"

And when I turned my eyes again from his ghastly face to the river, the current had done its work, and the body had been swept away into mid-stream and was already beyond our reach and almost out of sight, turning over and over on the waves like an otter.

**If you enjoyed this, you might also like...**
The Wendigo, see page 49
A Haunted Island, see page 351

# The Sea Fit

**THE SEA** that night sang rather than chanted; all along the far-running shore a rising tide dropped thick foam, and the waves, white-crested, came steadily in with the swing of a deliberate purpose. Overhead, in a cloudless sky, that ancient Enchantress, the full moon, watched their dance across the sheeted sands, guiding them carefully while she drew them up. For through that moonlight, through that roar of surf, there penetrated a singular note of earnestness and meaning – almost as though these common processes of Nature were instinct with the flush of an unusual activity that sought audaciously to cross the borderland into some subtle degree of conscious life. A gauze of light vapour clung upon the surface of the sea, far out – a transparent carpet through which the rollers drove shorewards in a moving pattern.

In the low-roofed bungalow among the sand-dunes the three men sat. Foregathered for Easter, they spent the day fishing and sailing, and at night told yarns of the days when life was younger. It was fortunate that there were three – and later four – because in the mouths of several witnesses an extraordinary thing shall be established – when they agree. And although whisky stood upon the rough table made of planks nailed to barrels, it is childish to pretend that a few drinks invalidate evidence, for alcohol, up to a certain point, intensifies the consciousness, focuses the intellectual powers, sharpens observation; and two healthy men, certainly three, must have imbibed an absurd amount before they all see, or omit to see, the same things.

The other bungalows still awaited their summer occupants. Only the lonely tufted sand-dunes watched the sea, shaking their hair of coarse white grass to the winds. The men had the whole spit to themselves – with the wind, the spray, the flying gusts of sand, and that great Easter full moon. There was Major Reese of the Gunners and his half-brother, Dr. Malcolm Reese, and Captain Erricson, their host, all men whom the kaleidoscope of life had jostled together a decade ago in many adventures, then flung for years apart about the globe. There was also Erricson's body-servant, 'Sinbad', sailor of big seas, and a man who had shared on many a ship all the lust of strange adventure that distinguished his great blonde-haired owner – an ideal servant and dog-faithful, divining his master's moods almost before they were born. On the present occasion, besides crew of the fishing-smack, he was cook, valet, and steward of the bungalow smoking-room as well.

'Big Erricson', Norwegian by extraction, student by adoption, wanderer by blood, a Viking reincarnated if ever there was one, belonged to that type of primitive man in whom burns an inborn love and passion for the sea that amounts to positive worship – devouring tide, a lust and fever in the soul. "All genuine votaries of the old sea-gods have it," he used to say, by way of explaining his carelessness of worldly ambitions. "We're never at our best away from salt water – never quite right. I've got it bang in the heart myself. I'd do a bit before the mast sooner than make a million on shore. Simply can't help it, you see, and never could! It's our gods calling us to worship." And he had never tried to 'help it', which explains why he owned nothing in the world on land except this tumble-down, one-storey bungalow – more like a ship's cabin than anything else, to which he sometimes asked his bravest and most faithful friends – and a store of curious reading gathered in long, becalmed days at the ends of the world. Heart and mind, that is, carried a queer cargo. "I'm sorry if you poor devils are uncomfortable in her. You must ask Sinbad for anything you want and don't see, remember." As though Sinbad could have supplied comforts that were miles away, or converted a draughty wreck into a snug, taut, brand-new vessel.

Neither of the Reeses had cause for grumbling on the score of comfort, however, for they knew the keen joys of roughing it, and both weather and sport besides had been glorious. It was on another score this particular evening that they found cause for uneasiness, if not for actual grumbling. Erricson had one of his queer sea fits on – the Doctor was responsible for the term – and was in the thick of it, plunging like a straining boat at anchor, talking in a way that made them both feel vaguely uncomfortable and distressed. Neither of them knew exactly perhaps why he should have felt this growing *malaise*, and each was secretly vexed with the other for confirming his own unholy instinct that something uncommon was astir. The loneliness of the sand-spit and that melancholy singing of the sea before their very door may have had something to do with it, seeing that both were landsmen; for Imagination is ever Lord of the Lonely Places, and adventurous men remain children to the last. But, whatever it was that affected both men in different fashion, Malcolm Reese, the doctor, had not thought it necessary to mention to his brother that Sinbad had tugged his sleeve on entering and whispered in his ear significantly: "Full moon, sir, please, and he's better without too much! These high spring tides get him all caught off his feet sometimes – clean sea-crazy"; and the man had contrived to let the doctor see the hilt of a small pistol he carried in his hip-pocket.

For Erricson had got upon his old subject: that the gods were not dead, but merely withdrawn, and that even a single true worshipper was enough to draw them down again into touch with the world, into the sphere of humanity, even into active and visible manifestation. He spoke of queer things he had seen in queerer places. He was serious, vehement, voluble; and the others had let it pour out unchecked, hoping thereby for its speedier exhaustion. They puffed their pipes in comparative silence, nodding from time to time, shrugging their shoulders, the soldier mystified and bewildered, the doctor alert and keenly watchful.

"And I like the old idea," he had been saying, speaking of these departed pagan deities, "that sacrifice and ritual feed their great beings, and that death is only the final sacrifice by which the worshipper becomes absorbed into them. The devout worshipper" – and there was a singular drive and power behind the words – "should go to his death singing, as to a wedding the wedding of his soul with the particular deity he has loved and served all his life." He swept his tow-coloured beard with one hand, turning his shaggy head towards the window, where the moonlight lay upon the procession of shaking waves. "It's playing the whole game, I always think, man-fashion... I remember once, some years ago, down there off the coast by Yucatan—"

And then, before they could interfere, he told an extraordinary tale of something he had seen years ago, but told it with such a horrid earnestness of conviction – for it was dreadful, though fine, this adventure – that his listeners shifted in their wicker chairs, struck matches unnecessarily, pulled at their long glasses, and exchanged glances that attempted a smile yet did not quite achieve it. For the tale had to do with sacrifice of human life and a rather haunting pagan ceremonial of the sea, and at its close the room had changed in some indefinable manner – was not exactly as it had been before perhaps – as though the savage earnestness of the language had introduced some new element that made it less cosy, less cheerful, even less warm. A secret lust in the man's heart, born of the sea, and of his intense admiration of the pagan gods called a light into his eye not altogether pleasant.

"They were great Powers, at any rate, those ancient fellows," Erricson went on, refilling his huge pipe bowl; "too great to disappear altogether, though today they may walk the earth in another manner. I swear they're still going it – especially the—" (he hesitated for a mere second) "the old water Powers – the Sea Gods. Terrific beggars, every one of 'em."

"Still move the tides and raise the winds, eh?" from the Doctor.

Erricson spoke again after a moment's silence, with impressive dignity. "And I like, too, the way they manage to keep their names before us," he went on, with a curious eagerness that did not escape the Doctor's observation, while it clearly puzzled the soldier. "There's old Hu, the Druid god of justice, still alive in 'Hue and Cry'; there's Typhon hammering his way against us in the typhoon; there's the mighty Hurakar, serpent god of the winds, you know, shouting to us in hurricane and *ouragan*; and there's—"

"Venus still at it as hard as ever," interrupted the Major, facetiously, though his brother did not laugh because of their host's almost sacred earnestness of manner and uncanny grimness of face. Exactly how he managed to introduce that element of gravity – of conviction – into such talk neither of his listeners quite understood, for in discussing the affair later they were unable to pitch upon any definite detail that betrayed it. Yet there it was, alive and haunting, even distressingly so. All day he had been silent and morose, but since dusk, with the turn of the tide, in fact, these queer sentences, half mystical, half unintelligible, had begun to pour from him, till now that cabin-like room among the sand-dunes fairly vibrated with the man's emotion. And at last Major Reese, with blundering good intention, tried to shift the key from this portentous subject of sacrifice to something that might eventually lead towards comedy and laughter, and so relieve this growing pressure of melancholy and incredible things. The Viking fellow had just spoken of the possibility of the old gods manifesting themselves visibly, audibly, physically, and so the Major caught him up and made light mention of spiritualism and the so-called 'materialisation séances', where physical bodies were alleged to be built up out of the emanations of the medium and the sitters. This crude aspect of the Supernatural was the only possible link the soldier's mind could manage. He caught his brother's eye too late, it seems, for Malcolm Reese realised by this time that something untoward was afoot, and no longer needed the memory of Sinbad's warning to keep him sharply on the lookout. It was not the first time he had seen Erricson 'caught' by the sea; but he had never known him quite so bad, nor seen his face so flushed and white alternately, nor his eyes so oddly shining. So that Major Reese's well-intentioned allusion only brought wind to fire.

The man of the sea, once Viking, roared with a rush of boisterous laughter at the comic suggestion, then dropped his voice to a sudden hard whisper, awfully earnest, awfully intense. Anyone must have started at the abrupt change and the life-and-death manner of the big man. His listeners undeniably both did.

"Bunkum!" he shouted, "bunkum, and be damned to it all! There's only one real materialisation of these immense Outer Beings possible, and that's when the great embodied emotions, which are their sphere of action" – his words became wildly incoherent, painfully struggling to get out – "derived, you see, from their honest worshippers the world over constituting their Bodies, in fact – come down into matter and get condensed, crystallised into form – to claim that final sacrifice I spoke about just now, and to which any man might feel himself proud and honoured to be summoned... No dying in bed or fading out from old age, but to plunge full-blooded and alive into the great Body of the god who has deigned to descend and fetch you—"

The actual speech may have been even more rambling and incoherent than that. It came out in a torrent at white heat. Dr. Reese kicked his brother beneath the table, just in time. The soldier looked thoroughly uncomfortable and amazed, utterly at a loss to know how he had produced the storm. It rather frightened him.

"I know it because I've seen it," went on the sea man, his mind and speech slightly more under control. "Seen the ceremonies that brought these whopping old Nature gods down into form – seen 'em carry off a worshipper into themselves – seen that worshipper, too, go off singing and happy to his death, proud and honoured to be chosen."

"Have you really – by George!" the Major exclaimed. "You tell us a queer thing, Erricson"; and it was then for the fifth time that Sinbad cautiously opened the door, peeped in and silently withdrew after giving a swiftly comprehensive glance round the room.

The night outside was windless and serene, only the growing thunder of the tide near the full woke muffled echoes among the sand-dunes.

"Rites and ceremonies," continued the other, his voice booming with a singular enthusiasm, but ignoring the interruption, "are simply means of losing one's self by temporary ecstasy in the God of one's choice – the God one has worshipped all one's life – of being partially absorbed into his being. And sacrifice completes the process—"

"At death, you said?" asked Malcolm Reese, watching him keenly.

"Or voluntary," was the reply that came flash-like. "The devotee becomes wedded to his Deity – goes bang into him, you see, by fire or water or air – as by a drop from a height – according to the nature of the particular God; atonement, of course. A man's death that! Fine, you know!"

The man's inner soul was on fire now. He was talking at a fearful pace, his eyes alight, his voice turned somehow into a kind of singsong that chimed well, singularly well, with the booming of waves outside, and from time to time he turned to the window to stare at the sea and the moon-blanched sands. And then a look of triumph would come into his face – that giant face framed by slow-moving wreaths of pipe smoke.

Sinbad entered for the sixth time without any obvious purpose, busied himself unnecessarily with the glasses and went out again, lingeringly. In the room he kept his eye hard upon his master. This time he contrived to push a chair and a heap of netting between him and the window. No one but Dr. Reese observed the manoeuvre. And he took the hint.

"The portholes fit badly, Erricson," he laughed, but with a touch of authority. "There's a five-knot breeze coming through the cracks worse than an old wreck!" And he moved up to secure the fastening better.

"The room *is* confoundedly cold," Major Reese put in; "has been for the last half-hour, too." The soldier looked what he felt – cold – distressed – creepy. "But there's no wind really, you know," he added.

Captain Erricson turned his great bearded visage from one to the other before he answered; there was a gleam of sudden suspicion in his blue eyes. "The beggar's got that back door open again. If he's sent for anyone, as he did once before, I swear I'll drown him in fresh water for his impudence – or perhaps – can it be already that he expects—?" He left the sentence incomplete and rang the bell, laughing with a boisterousness that was clearly feigned. "Sinbad, what's this cold in the place? You've got the back door open. Not expecting anyone, are you—?"

"Everything's shut tight, Captain. There's a bit of a breeze coming up from the east. And the tide's drawing in at a raging pace—"

"We can all hear *that*. But are you expecting anyone? I asked," repeated his master, suspiciously, yet still laughing. One might have said he was trying to give the idea that the man had some land flirtation on hand. They looked one another square in the eye for a moment, these two. It was the straight stare of equals who understood each other well.

"Someone – might be – on the way, as it were, Captain. Couldn't say for certain."

The voice almost trembled. By a sharp twist of the eye, Sinbad managed to shoot a lightning and significant look at the Doctor.

"But this cold – this freezing, damp cold in the place? Are you sure no one's come – by the back ways?" insisted the master. He whispered it. "Across the dunes, for instance?" His voice conveyed awe and delight, both kept hard under.

"It's all over the house, Captain, already," replied the man, and moved across to put more sea-logs on the blazing fire. Even the soldier noticed then that their language was tight with allusion of another kind. To relieve the growing tension and uneasiness in his own mind he took up the word 'house' and made fun of it.

"As though it were a mansion," he observed, with a forced chuckle, "instead of a mere seashell!" Then, looking about him, he added: "But, all the same, you know, there *is* a kind of fog getting into the room – from the sea, I suppose; coming up with the tide, or something, eh?" The air had certainly in the last twenty minutes turned thickish; it was not all tobacco smoke, and there was a moisture that began to precipitate on the objects in tiny, fine globules. The cold, too, fairly bit.

"I'll take a look round," said Sinbad, significantly, and went out. Only the Doctor perhaps noticed that the man shook, and was white down to the gills. He said nothing, but moved his chair nearer to the window and to his host. It was really a little bit beyond comprehension how the wild words of this old sea-dog in the full sway of his 'sea fit' had altered the very air of the room as well as the personal equations of its occupants, for an extraordinary atmosphere of enthusiasm that was almost splendour pulsed about him, yet vilely close to something that suggested terror! Through the armour of everyday common sense that normally clothed the minds of these other two, had crept the faint wedges of a mood that made them vaguely wonder whether the incredible could perhaps sometimes – by way of bewildering exceptions – actually come to pass. The moods of their deepest life, that is to say, were already affected. An inner, and thoroughly unwelcome, change was in progress. And such psychic disturbances once started are hard to arrest. In this case it was well on the way before either the Army or Medicine had been willing to recognise the fact. There was something coming – coming from the sand-dunes or the sea. And it was invited, welcomed at any rate, by Erricson. His deep, volcanic enthusiasm and belief provided the channel. In lesser degree they, too, were caught in it. Moreover, it was terrific, irresistible.

And it was at this point – as the comparing of notes afterwards established – that Father Norden came in, Norden, the big man's nephew, having bicycled over from some point beyond Corfe Castle and raced along the hard Studland sand in the moonlight, and then hullood till a boat had ferried him across the narrow channel of Poole Harbour. Sinbad simply brought him in without any preliminary question or announcement. He could not resist the splendid night and the spring air, explained Norden. He felt sure his uncle could 'find a hammock' for him somewhere aft, as he put it. He did not add that Sinbad had telegraphed for him just before sundown from the coastguard hut. Dr. Reese already knew him, but he was introduced to the Major. Norden was a member of the Society of Jesus, an ardent, not clever, and unselfish soul.

Erricson greeted him with obviously mixed feelings, and with an extraordinary sentence: "It doesn't really matter," he exclaimed, after a few commonplaces of talk, "for all religions are the same if you go deep enough. All teach sacrifice, and, without exception, all seek final union by absorption into their Deity." And then, under his breath, turning sideways to peer out of the window, he added a swift rush of half-smothered words that only Dr. Reese caught: "The Army, the Church, the Medical Profession, and Labour – if they would only all come! What a fine result, what a grand offering! Alone – I seem so unworthy – insignificant…!"

But meanwhile young Norden was speaking before anyone could stop him, although the Major did make one or two blundering attempts. For once the Jesuit's tact was at fault. He evidently hoped to introduce a new mood – to shift the current already established by the single force of his own personality. And he was not quite man enough to carry it off.

It was an error of judgment on his part. For the forces he found established in the room were too heavy to lift and alter, their impetus being already acquired. He did his best, anyhow. He began moving with the current – it was not the first sea fit he had combated in this extraordinary personality – then found, too late, that he was carried along with it himself like the rest of them.

"Odd – but couldn't find the bungalow at first," he laughed, somewhat hardly. "It's got a bit of sea-fog all to itself that hides it. I thought perhaps my pagan uncle—"

The Doctor interrupted him hastily, with great energy. "The fog *does* lie caught in these sand hollows – like steam in a cup, you know," he put in. But the other, intent on his own procedure, missed the cue.

" – thought it was smoke at first, and that you were up to some heathen ceremony or other," laughing in Erricson's face; "sacrificing to the full moon or the sea, or the spirits of the desolate places that haunt sand-dunes, eh?"

No one spoke for a second, but Erricson's face turned quite radiant.

"My uncle's such a pagan, you know," continued the priest, "that as I flew along those deserted sands from Studland I almost expected to hear old Triton blow his wreathèd horn… or see fair Thetis's tinsel-slippered feet…"

Erricson, suppressing violent gestures, highly excited, face happy as a boy's, was combing his great yellow beard with both hands, and the other two men had begun to speak at once, intent on stopping the flow of unwise allusion. Norden, swallowing a mouthful of cold soda-water, had put the glass down, spluttering over its bubbles, when the sound was first heard at the window. And in the back room the manservant ran, calling something aloud that sounded like "It's coming, God save us, it's coming in…!" Though the Major swears some name was mentioned that he afterwards forgot – Glaucus – Proteus – Pontus or some such word. The sound itself, however, was plain enough – a kind of imperious tapping on the windowpanes as of a multitude of objects. Blown sand it might have been or heavy spray or, as Norden suggested later, a great water-soaked branch of giant seaweed. Everyone started up, but Erricson was first upon his feet, and had the window wide open in a twinkling. His voice roared forth over those moonlit sand-dunes and out towards the line of heavy surf ten yards below.

"All along the shore of the Aegean," he bellowed, with a kind of hoarse triumph that shook the heart, "that ancient cry once rang. But it was a lie, a thumping and audacious lie. And He is not the only one. Another still lives – and, by Poseidon, He comes! He knows His own and His own know Him – and His own shall go to meet Him…!"

That reference to the Aegean 'cry'! It was so wonderful. Everyone, of course, except the soldier, seized the allusion. It was a comprehensive, yet subtle, way of suggesting the idea. And meanwhile all spoke at once, shouted rather, for the Invasion was somehow – monstrous.

"Damn it – that's a bit too much. Something's caught my throat!" The Major, like a man drowning, fought with the furniture in his amazement and dismay. Fighting was his first instinct, of course. "Hurts so infernally – takes the breath," he cried, by way of explaining the extraordinarily violent impetus that moved him, yet half ashamed of himself for seeing nothing he could strike. But Malcolm Reese struggled to get between his host and the open window, saying in tense voice something like "Don't let him get out! Don't let him get out!" While the shouts of warning from Sinbad in the little cramped back offices added to the general confusion. Only Father Norden stood quiet – watching with a kind of admiring wonder the expression of magnificence that had flamed into the visage of Erricson.

"Hark, you fools! Hark!" boomed the Viking figure, standing erect and splendid.

And through that open window, along the far-drawn line of shore from Canford Cliffs to the chalk bluffs of Studland Bay, there certainly ran a sound that was no common roar of surf. It was articulate – a message from the sea – an announcement – a thunderous warning of approach. No mere surf breaking on sand could have compassed so deep and multitudinous a voice of dreadful roaring – far out over the entering tide, yet at the same time close in along the entire sweep of shore, shaking all the ocean, both depth and surface, with its deep vibrations. Into the bungalow chamber came – the *Sea*!

Out of the night, from the moonlit spaces where it had been steadily accumulating, into that little cabined room so full of humanity and tobacco smoke, came invisibly – the Power of the Sea. Invisible, yes, but mighty, pressed forward by the huge draw of the moon, soft-coated with brine and moisture – the great Sea. And with it, into the minds of those three other men, leaped instantaneously, not to be denied, overwhelming suggestions of waterpower, the tear and strain of thousand-mile currents, the irresistible pull and rush of tides, the suction of giant whirlpools – more, the massed and awful impetus of whole driven oceans. The air turned salt and briny, and a welter of seaweed clamped their very skins.

"Glaucus! I come to Thee, great God of the deep Waterways… Father and Master!" Erricson cried aloud in a voice that most marvellously conveyed supreme joy.

The little bungalow trembled as from a blow at the foundations, and the same second the big man was through the window and running down the moonlit sands towards the foam.

"God in Heaven! Did you all see *that*?" shouted Major Reese, for the manner in which the great body slipped through the tiny window-frame was incredible. And then, first tottering with a sudden weakness, he recovered himself and rushed round by the door, followed by his brother. Sinbad, invisible, but not inaudible, was calling aloud from the passage at the back. Father Norden, slimmer than the others – well controlled, too – was through the little window before either of them reached the fringe of beach beyond the sand-dunes. They joined forces halfway down to the water's edge. The figure of Erricson, towering in the moonlight, flew before them, coasting rapidly along the wave-line.

No one of them said a word; they tore along side by side, Norden a trifle in advance. In front of them, head turned seawards, bounded Erricson in great flying leaps, singing as he ran, impossible to overtake.

Then, what they witnessed all three witnessed; the weird grandeur of it in the moonshine was too splendid to allow the smaller emotions of personal alarm, it seems. At any rate, the divergence of opinion afterwards was unaccountably insignificant. For, on a sudden, that heavy roaring sound far out at sea came close in with a swift plunge of speed, followed simultaneously – accompanied, rather – by a dark line that was no mere wave moving: enormously, up and across, between the sea and sky it swept close in to shore. The moonlight caught it for a second as it passed, in a cliff of her bright silver.

And Erricson slowed down, bowed his great head and shoulders, spread his arms out and…

And what? For no one of those amazed witnesses could swear exactly what then came to pass. Upon this impossibility of telling it in language they all three agreed. Only those eyeless dunes of sand that watched, only the white and silent moon overhead, only that long, curved beach of empty and deserted shore retain the complete record, to be revealed some day perhaps when a later Science shall have learned to develop the photographs that Nature takes incessantly upon her secret plates. For Erricson's rough suit of tweed went out in ribbons across the air; his figure somehow turned dark like strips of tide-sucked seaweed; something enveloped and overcame him, half shrouding him from view. He stood for one instant upright, his hair wild in the moonshine, towering, with arms again outstretched; then bent forward, turned, drew out most curiously sideways, uttering the singing sound of tumbling waters. The next instant, curving over like a falling wave, he swept along the glistening surface of the sands – and was gone. In fluid form, wavelike, his being slipped away into the Being of the Sea. A violent tumult convulsed the surface of the tide near in, but at once, and with amazing speed, passed careering away into the deeper water – far out. To his singular death, as to a wedding, Erricson had gone, singing, and well content.

"May God, who holds the *sea* and all its powers in the hollow of His mighty hand, take them *both* into Himself!" Norden was on his knees, praying fervently.

The body was never recovered… and the most curious thing of all was that the interior of the cabin, where they found Sinbad shaking with terror when they at length returned, was splashed and sprayed, almost soaked, with salt water. Up into the bigger dunes beside the bungalow, and far beyond the reach of normal tides, lay, too, a great streak and furrow as of a large invading wave, caking the dry sand. A hundred tufts of the coarse grass tussocks had been torn away.

The high tide that night, drawn by the Easter full moon, of course, was known to have been exceptional, for it fairly flooded Poole Harbour, flushing all the coves and bays towards the mouth of the Frome. And the natives up at Arne Bay and Wych always declare that the noise of the sea was heard far inland even up to the nine Barrows of the Purbeck Hills – triumphantly singing.

**If you enjoyed this, you might also like…**
Ancient Sorceries, see page 246
The Wings of Horus, see page 192

# The Wendigo

## Chapter I

**A CONSIDERABLE** number of hunting parties were out that year without finding so much as a fresh trail; for the moose were uncommonly shy, and the various Nimrods returned to the bosoms of their respective families with the best excuses the facts of their imaginations could suggest. Dr. Cathcart, among others, came back without a trophy; but he brought instead the memory of an experience which he declares was worth all the bull moose that had ever been shot. But then Cathcart, of Aberdeen, was interested in other things besides moose – amongst them the vagaries of the human mind. This particular story, however, found no mention in his book on Collective Hallucination for the simple reason (so he confided once to a fellow colleague) that he himself played too intimate a part in it to form a competent judgment of the affair as a whole....

Besides himself and his guide, Hank Davis, there was young Simpson, his nephew, a divinity student destined for the 'Wee Kirk' (then on his first visit to Canadian backwoods), and the latter's guide, Défago. Joseph Défago was a French 'Canuck', who had strayed from his native Province of Quebec years before, and had got caught in Rat Portage when the Canadian Pacific Railway was a-building; a man who, in addition to his unparalleled knowledge of wood-craft and bush-lore, could also sing the old *voyageur* songs and tell a capital hunting yarn into the bargain. He was deeply susceptible, moreover, to that singular spell which the wilderness lays upon certain lonely natures, and he loved the wild solitudes with a kind of romantic passion that amounted almost to an obsession. The life of the backwoods fascinated him – whence, doubtless, his surpassing efficiency in dealing with their mysteries.

On this particular expedition he was Hank's choice. Hank knew him and swore by him. He also swore at him, "jest as a pal might", and since he had a vocabulary of picturesque, if utterly meaningless, oaths, the conversation between the two stalwart and hardy woodsmen was often of a rather lively description. This river of expletives, however, Hank agreed to dam a little out of respect for his old 'hunting boss', Dr. Cathcart, whom of course he addressed after the fashion of the country as 'Doc', and also because he understood that young Simpson was already a 'bit of a parson'. He had, however, one objection to Défago, and one only – which was, that the French Canadian sometimes exhibited what Hank described as 'the output of a cursed and dismal mind', meaning apparently that he sometimes was true to type, Latin type, and suffered fits of a kind of silent moroseness when nothing could induce him to utter speech. Défago, that is to say, was imaginative and melancholy. And, as a rule, it was too long a spell of 'civilisation' that induced the attacks, for a few days of the wilderness invariably cured them.

This, then, was the party of four that found themselves in camp the last week in October of that 'shy moose year' 'way up in the wilderness north of Rat Portage – a forsaken and desolate country. There was also Punk, an Indian, who had accompanied Dr. Cathcart and Hank on their hunting trips in previous years, and who acted as cook.

His duty was merely to stay in camp, catch fish, and prepare venison steaks and coffee at a few minutes' notice. He dressed in the worn-out clothes bequeathed to him by former patrons, and, except for his coarse black hair and dark skin, he looked in these city garments no more like a real redskin than a stage Negro looks like a real African. For all that, however, Punk had in him still the instincts of his dying race; his taciturn silence and his endurance survived; also his superstition.

The party round the blazing fire that night were despondent, for a week had passed without a single sign of recent moose discovering itself. Défago had sung his song and plunged into a story, but Hank, in bad humour, reminded him so often that "he kep' mussing-up the fac's so, that it was 'most all nothin' but a petered-out lie," that the Frenchman had finally subsided into a sulky silence which nothing seemed likely to break. Dr. Cathcart and his nephew were fairly done after an exhausting day. Punk was washing up the dishes, grunting to himself under the lean-to of branches, where he later also slept. No one troubled to stir the slowly dying fire. Overhead the stars were brilliant in a sky quite wintry, and there was so little wind that ice was already forming stealthily along the shores of the still lake behind them. The silence of the vast listening forest stole forward and enveloped them.

Hank broke in suddenly with his nasal voice.

"I'm in favour of breaking new ground tomorrow, Doc," he observed with energy, looking across at his employer. "We don't stand a dead Dago's chance around here."

"Agreed," said Cathcart, always a man of few words. "Think the idea's good."

"Sure pop, it's good," Hank resumed with confidence. "S'pose, now, you and I strike west, up Garden Lake way for a change! None of us ain't touched that quiet bit o' land yet—"

"I'm with you."

"And you, Défago, take Mr. Simpson along in the small canoe, skip across the lake, portage over into Fifty Island Water, and take a good squint down that thar southern shore. The moose 'yarded' there like hell last year, and for all we know they may be doin' it agin this year jest to spite us."

Défago, keeping his eyes on the fire, said nothing by way of reply. He was still offended, possibly, about his interrupted story.

"No one's been up that way this year, an' I'll lay my bottom dollar on *that!*" Hank added with emphasis, as though he had a reason for knowing. He looked over at his partner sharply. "Better take the little silk tent and stay away a couple o' nights," he concluded, as though the matter were definitely settled. For Hank was recognised as general organiser of the hunt, and in charge of the party.

It was obvious to anyone that Défago did not jump at the plan, but his silence seemed to convey something more than ordinary disapproval, and across his sensitive dark face there passed a curious expression like a flash of firelight – not so quickly, however, that the three men had not time to catch it.

"He funked for some reason, *I* thought," Simpson said afterwards in the tent he shared with his uncle. Dr. Cathcart made no immediate reply, although the look had interested him enough at the time for him to make a mental note of it. The expression had caused him a passing uneasiness he could not quite account for at the moment.

But Hank, of course, had been the first to notice it, and the odd thing was that instead of becoming explosive or angry over the other's reluctance, he at once began to humour him a bit.

"But there ain't no *speshul* reason why no one's been up there this year," he said with a perceptible hush in his tone; "not the reason you mean, anyway! Las' year it was the fires that kep' folks out, and this year I guess – I guess it jest happened so, that's all!" His manner was clearly meant to be encouraging.

Joseph Défago raised his eyes a moment, then dropped them again. A breath of wind stole out of the forest and stirred the embers into a passing blaze. Dr. Cathcart again noticed the expression in the guide's face, and again he did not like it. But this time the nature of the look betrayed itself. In those eyes, for an instant, he caught the gleam of a man scared in his very soul. It disquieted him more than he cared to admit.

"Bad Indians up that way?" he asked, with a laugh to ease matters a little, while Simpson, too sleepy to notice this subtle by-play, moved off to bed with a prodigious yawn; "or – or anything wrong with the country?" he added, when his nephew was out of hearing.

Hank met his eye with something less than his usual frankness.

"He's jest skeered," he replied good-humouredly. "Skeered stiff about some ole feery tale! That's all, ain't it, ole pard?" And he gave Défago a friendly kick on the moccasined foot that lay nearest the fire.

Défago looked up quickly, as from an interrupted reverie, a reverie, however, that had not prevented his seeing all that went on about him.

"Skeered – *nuthin'!*" he answered, with a flush of defiance. "There's nuthin' in the Bush that can skeer Joseph Défago, and don't you forget it!" And the natural energy with which he spoke made it impossible to know whether he told the whole truth or only a part of it.

Hank turned towards the doctor. He was just going to add something when he stopped abruptly and looked round. A sound close behind them in the darkness made all three start. It was old Punk, who had moved up from his lean-to while they talked and now stood there just beyond the circle of firelight – listening.

"'Nother time, Doc!" Hank whispered, with a wink, "when the gallery ain't stepped down into the stalls!" And, springing to his feet, he slapped the Indian on the back and cried noisily, "Come up t' the fire an' warm yer dirty red skin a bit." He dragged him towards the blaze and threw more wood on. "That was a mighty good feed you give us an hour or two back," he continued heartily, as though to set the man's thoughts on another scent, "and it ain't Christian to let you stand out there freezin' yer ole soul to hell while we're gettin' all good an' toasted!" Punk moved in and warmed his feet, smiling darkly at the other's volubility which he only half understood, but saying nothing. And presently Dr. Cathcart, seeing that further conversation was impossible, followed his nephew's example and moved off to the tent, leaving the three men smoking over the now blazing fire.

It is not easy to undress in a small tent without waking one's companion, and Cathcart, hardened and warm-blooded as he was in spite of his fifty odd years, did what Hank would have described as 'considerable of his twilight' in the open. He noticed, during the process, that Punk had meanwhile gone back to his lean-to, and that Hank and Défago were at it hammer and tongs, or, rather, hammer and anvil, the little French Canadian being the anvil. It was all very like the conventional stage picture of Western melodrama: the fire lighting up their faces with patches of alternate red and black; Défago, in slouch hat and moccasins in the part of the 'badlands' villain; Hank, open-faced and hatless, with that reckless fling of his shoulders, the honest and deceived hero; and old Punk, eavesdropping in the background, supplying the atmosphere of mystery. The doctor smiled as he noticed the details; but at the same time something deep within him – he hardly knew what – shrank a little, as though an almost imperceptible breath of warning had touched the surface of his soul and was gone again before he could seize it. Probably it was traceable to that 'scared expression' he had seen in the eyes of Défago; 'probably' – for this hint of fugitive emotion otherwise escaped his usually so keen analysis. Défago, he was vaguely aware, might cause trouble somehow... He was not as steady a guide as Hank, for instance... Further than that he could not get...

He watched the men a moment longer before diving into the stuffy tent where Simpson already slept soundly. Hank, he saw, was swearing like a mad African in a New York nigger saloon; but it was the swearing of 'affection'. The ridiculous oaths flew freely now that the cause of their obstruction was asleep. Presently he put his arm almost tenderly upon his comrade's shoulder, and they moved off together into the shadows where their tent stood faintly glimmering. Punk, too, a moment later followed their example and disappeared between his odorous blankets in the opposite direction.

Dr. Cathcart then likewise turned in, weariness and sleep still fighting in his mind with an obscure curiosity to know what it was that had scared Défago about the country up Fifty Island Water way, – wondering, too, why Punk's presence had prevented the completion of what Hank had to say. Then sleep overtook him. He would know tomorrow. Hank would tell him the story while they trudged after the elusive moose.

Deep silence fell about the little camp, planted there so audaciously in the jaws of the wilderness. The lake gleamed like a sheet of black glass beneath the stars. The cold air pricked. In the draughts of night that poured their silent tide from the depths of the forest, with messages from distant ridges and from lakes just beginning to freeze, there lay already the faint, bleak odours of coming winter. White men, with their dull scent, might never have divined them; the fragrance of the wood fire would have concealed from them these almost electrical hints of moss and bark and hardening swamp a hundred miles away. Even Hank and Défago, subtly in league with the soul of the woods as they were, would probably have spread their delicate nostrils in vain....

But an hour later, when all slept like the dead, old Punk crept from his blankets and went down to the shore of the lake like a shadow – silently, as only Indian blood can move. He raised his head and looked about him. The thick darkness rendered sight of small avail, but, like the animals, he possessed other senses that darkness could not mute. He listened – then sniffed the air. Motionless as a hemlock stem he stood there. After five minutes again he lifted his head and sniffed, and yet once again. A tingling of the wonderful nerves that betrayed itself by no outer sign, ran through him as he tasted the keen air. Then, merging his figure into the surrounding blackness in a way that only wild men and animals understand, he turned, still moving like a shadow, and went stealthily back to his lean-to and his bed.

And soon after he slept, the change of wind he had divined stirred gently the reflection of the stars within the lake. Rising among the far ridges of the country beyond Fifty Island Water, it came from the direction in which he had stared, and it passed over the sleeping camp with a faint and sighing murmur through the tops of the big trees that was almost too delicate to be audible. With it, down the desert paths of night, though too faint, too high even for the Indian's hair-like nerves, there passed a curious, thin odour, strangely disquieting, an odour of something that seemed unfamiliar – utterly unknown.

The French Canadian and the man of Indian blood each stirred uneasily in his sleep just about this time, though neither of them woke. Then the ghost of that unforgettably strange odour passed away and was lost among the leagues of tenantless forest beyond.

## Chapter II

**IN THE MORNING** the camp was astir before the sun. There had been a light fall of snow during the night and the air was sharp. Punk had done his duty betimes, for the odours of coffee and fried bacon reached every tent. All were in good spirits.

"Wind's shifted!" cried Hank vigorously, watching Simpson and his guide already loading the small canoe. "It's across the lake – dead right for you fellers. And the snow'll make bully trails! If there's any moose mussing around up thar, they'll not get so much as a tail-end scent of you with the wind as it is. Good luck, Monsieur Défago!" he added, facetiously giving the name its French pronunciation for once, "*bonne chance!*"

Défago returned the good wishes, apparently in the best of spirits, the silent mood gone. Before eight o'clock old Punk had the camp to himself, Cathcart and Hank were far along the trail that led westwards, while the canoe that carried Défago and Simpson, with silk tent and grub for two days, was already a dark speck bobbing on the bosom of the lake, going due east.

The wintry sharpness of the air was tempered now by a sun that topped the wooded ridges and blazed with a luxurious warmth upon the world of lake and forest below; loons flew skimming through the sparkling spray that the wind lifted; divers shook their dripping heads to the sun and popped smartly out of sight again; and as far as eye could reach rose the leagues of endless, crowding Bush, desolate in its lonely sweep and grandeur, untrodden by foot of man, and stretching its mighty and unbroken carpet right up to the frozen shores of Hudson Bay.

Simpson, who saw it all for the first time as he paddled hard in the bows of the dancing canoe, was enchanted by its austere beauty. His heart drank in the sense of freedom and great spaces just as his lungs drank in the cool and perfumed wind. Behind him in the stern seat, singing fragments of his native chanties, Défago steered the craft of birch bark like a thing of life, answering cheerfully all his companion's questions. Both were gay and light-hearted. On such occasions men lose the superficial, worldly distinctions; they become human beings working together for a common end. Simpson, the employer, and Défago the employed, among these primitive forces, were simply – two men, the 'guider' and the 'guided'. Superior knowledge, of course, assumed control, and the younger man fell without a second thought into the quasi-subordinate position. He never dreamed of objecting when Défago dropped the 'Mr.', and addressed him as "Say, Simpson," or "Simpson, boss," which was invariably the case before they reached the farther shore after a stiff paddle of twelve miles against a head wind. He only laughed, and liked it; then ceased to notice it at all.

For this 'divinity student' was a young man of parts and character, though as yet, of course, untravelled; and on this trip – the first time he had seen any country but his own and little Switzerland – the huge scale of things somewhat bewildered him. It was one thing, he realised, to hear about primeval forests, but quite another to see them. While to dwell in them and seek acquaintance with their wild life was, again, an initiation that no intelligent man could undergo without a certain shifting of personal values hitherto held for permanent and sacred.

Simpson knew the first faint indication of this emotion when he held the new .303 rifle in his hands and looked along its pair of faultless, gleaming barrels. The three days' journey to their headquarters, by lake and portage, had carried the process a stage farther. And now that he was about to plunge beyond even the fringe of wilderness where they were camped into the virgin heart of uninhabited regions as vast as Europe itself, the true nature of the situation stole upon him with an effect of delight and awe that his imagination was fully capable of appreciating. It was himself and Défago against a multitude – at least, against a Titan!

The bleak splendours of these remote and lonely forests rather overwhelmed him with the sense of his own littleness. That stern quality of the tangled backwoods which can only be described as merciless and terrible, rose out of these far blue woods swimming upon the horizon, and revealed itself. He understood the silent warning. He realised his own utter helplessness. Only Défago, as a symbol of a distant civilisation where man was master, stood between him and a pitiless death by exhaustion and starvation.

It was thrilling to him, therefore, to watch Défago turn over the canoe upon the shore, pack the paddles carefully underneath, and then proceed to 'blaze' the spruce stems for some distance on either side of an almost invisible trail, with the careless remark thrown in, "Say, Simpson, if anything happens to me, you'll find the canoe all correc' by these marks; – then strike doo west into the sun to hit the home camp agin, see?"

It was the most natural thing in the world to say, and he said it without any noticeable inflexion of the voice, only it happened to express the youth's emotions at the moment with an utterance that was symbolic of the situation and of his own helplessness as a factor in it. He was alone with Défago in a primitive world: that was all. The canoe, another symbol of man's ascendancy, was now to be left behind. Those small yellow patches, made on the trees by the axe, were the only indications of its hiding place.

Meanwhile, shouldering the packs between them, each man carrying his own rifle, they followed the slender trail over rocks and fallen trunks and across half-frozen swamps; skirting numerous lakes that fairly gemmed the forest, their borders fringed with mist; and towards five o'clock found themselves suddenly on the edge of the woods, looking out across a large sheet of water in front of them, dotted with pine-clad islands of all describable shapes and sizes.

"Fifty Island Water," announced Défago wearily, "and the sun jest goin' to dip his bald old head into it!" he added, with unconscious poetry; and immediately they set about pitching camp for the night.

In a very few minutes, under those skilful hands that never made a movement too much or a movement too little, the silk tent stood taut and cozy, the beds of balsam boughs ready laid, and a brisk cooking fire burned with the minimum of smoke. While the young Scotchman cleaned the fish they had caught trolling behind the canoe, Défago "guessed" he would "jest as soon" take a turn through the Bush for indications of moose. "*May* come across a trunk where they bin and rubbed horns," he said, as he moved off, "or feedin' on the last of the maple leaves" – and he was gone.

His small figure melted away like a shadow in the dusk, while Simpson noted with a kind of admiration how easily the forest absorbed him into herself. A few steps, it seemed, and he was no longer visible.

Yet there was little underbrush hereabouts; the trees stood somewhat apart, well spaced; and in the clearings grew silver birch and maple, spearlike and slender, against the immense stems of spruce and hemlock. But for occasional prostrate monsters, and the boulders of grey rock that thrust uncouth shoulders here and there out of the ground, it might well have been a bit of park in the Old Country. Almost, one might have seen in it the hand of man. A little to the right, however, began the great burnt section, miles in extent, proclaiming its real character – *brulé*, as it is called, where the fires of the previous year had raged for weeks, and the blackened stumps now rose gaunt and ugly, bereft of branches, like gigantic match heads stuck into the ground, savage and desolate beyond words. The perfume of charcoal and rain-soaked ashes still hung faintly about it.

The dusk rapidly deepened; the glades grew dark; the crackling of the fire and the wash of little waves along the rocky lake shore were the only sounds audible. The wind had dropped with the sun, and in all that vast world of branches nothing stirred. Any moment, it seemed, the woodland gods, who are to be worshipped in silence and loneliness, might stretch their mighty and terrific outlines among the trees. In front, through doorways pillared by huge straight stems, lay the stretch of Fifty Island Water, a crescent-shaped lake some fifteen miles from tip to tip, and perhaps five miles across where they were camped. A sky of rose and saffron, more clear than any atmosphere Simpson had ever known, still dropped its pale streaming fires across the waves, where the islands – a hundred, surely, rather than fifty – floated like the fairy barques of some enchanted fleet. Fringed with pines, whose crests fingered most delicately the sky, they almost seemed to move upwards as the light faded – about to weigh anchor and navigate the pathways of the heavens instead of the currents of their native and desolate lake.

And strips of coloured cloud, like flaunting pennons, signalled their departure to the stars....

The beauty of the scene was strangely uplifting. Simpson smoked the fish and burnt his fingers into the bargain in his efforts to enjoy it and at the same time tend the frying pan and the fire. Yet, ever at the back of his thoughts, lay that other aspect of the wilderness: the indifference to human life, the merciless spirit of desolation which took no note of man. The sense of his utter loneliness, now that even Défago had gone, came close as he looked about him and listened for the sound of his companion's returning footsteps.

There was pleasure in the sensation, yet with it a perfectly comprehensible alarm. And instinctively the thought stirred in him: "What should I – *could* I, do – if anything happened and he did not come back—?"

They enjoyed their well-earned supper, eating untold quantities of fish, and drinking unmilked tea strong enough to kill men who had not covered thirty miles of hard 'going', eating little on the way. And when it was over, they smoked and told stories round the blazing fire, laughing, stretching weary limbs, and discussing plans for the morrow. Défago was in excellent spirits, though disappointed at having no signs of moose to report. But it was dark and he had not gone far. The *brulé*, too, was bad. His clothes and hands were smeared with charcoal. Simpson, watching him, realised with renewed vividness their position – alone together in the wilderness.

"Défago," he said presently, "these woods, you know, are a bit too big to feel quite at home in – to feel comfortable in, I mean!... Eh?" He merely gave expression to the mood of the moment; he was hardly prepared for the earnestness, the solemnity even, with which the guide took him up.

"You've hit it right, Simpson, boss," he replied, fixing his searching brown eyes on his face, "and that's the truth, sure. There's no end to 'em – no end at all." Then he added in a lowered tone as if to himself, "There's lots found out *that*, and gone plumb to pieces!"

But the man's gravity of manner was not quite to the other's liking; it was a little too suggestive for this scenery and setting; he was sorry he had broached the subject. He remembered suddenly how his uncle had told him that men were sometimes stricken with a strange fever of the wilderness, when the seduction of the uninhabited wastes caught them so fiercely that they went forth, half fascinated, half deluded, to their death. And he had a shrewd idea that his companion held something in sympathy with that queer type. He led the conversation on to other topics, on to Hank and the doctor, for instance, and the natural rivalry as to who should get the first sight of moose.

"If they went doo west," observed Défago carelessly, "there's sixty miles between us now – with ole Punk at halfway house eatin' himself full to bustin' with fish and coffee." They laughed together over the picture. But the casual mention of those sixty miles again made Simpson realise the prodigious scale of this land where they hunted; sixty miles was a mere step; two hundred little more than a step. Stories of lost hunters rose persistently before his memory. The passion and mystery of homeless and wandering men, seduced by the beauty of great forests, swept his soul in a way too vivid to be quite pleasant. He wondered vaguely whether it was the mood of his companion that invited the unwelcome suggestion with such persistence.

"Sing us a song, Défago, if you're not too tired," he asked; "one of those old *voyageur* songs you sang the other night." He handed his tobacco pouch to the guide and then filled his own pipe, while the Canadian, nothing loth, sent his light voice across the lake in one of those plaintive, almost melancholy chanties with which lumbermen and trappers lessen the burden of their labour. There was an appealing and romantic flavour about it, something that recalled the atmosphere of the old pioneer days when Indians and wilderness were leagued together, battles frequent, and the Old Country farther off than it is today. The sound travelled pleasantly over the water, but the forest at their backs seemed to swallow it down with a single gulp that permitted neither echo nor resonance.

It was in the middle of the third verse that Simpson noticed something unusual – something that brought his thoughts back with a rush from faraway scenes. A curious change had come into the man's voice. Even before he knew what it was, uneasiness caught him, and looking up quickly, he saw that Défago, though still singing, was peering about him into the Bush, as though he heard or saw something. His voice grew fainter – dropped to a hush – then ceased altogether. The same instant, with a movement amazingly alert, he started to his feet and stood upright – *sniffing the air*. Like a dog scenting game, he drew the air into his nostrils in short, sharp breaths, turning quickly as he did so in all directions, and finally 'pointing' down the lake shore, eastwards. It was a performance unpleasantly suggestive and at the same time singularly dramatic. Simpson's heart fluttered disagreeably as he watched it.

"Lord, man! How you made me jump!" he exclaimed, on his feet beside him the same instant, and peering over his shoulder into the sea of darkness. "What's up? Are you frightened—?"

Even before the question was out of his mouth he knew it was foolish, for any man with a pair of eyes in his head could see that the Canadian had turned white down to his very gills. Not even sunburn and the glare of the fire could hide that.

The student felt himself trembling a little, weakish in the knees. "What's up?" he repeated quickly. "D'you smell moose? Or anything queer, anything – wrong?" He lowered his voice instinctively.

The forest pressed round them with its encircling wall; the nearer tree stems gleamed like bronze in the firelight; beyond that – blackness, and, so far as he could tell, a silence of death. Just behind them a passing puff of wind lifted a single leaf, looked at it, then laid it softly down again without disturbing the rest of the covey. It seemed as if a million invisible causes had combined just to produce that single visible effect. *Other* life pulsed about them – and was gone.

Défago turned abruptly; the livid hue of his face had turned to a dirty grey.

"I never said I heered – or smelt – nuthin'," he said slowly and emphatically, in an oddly altered voice that conveyed somehow a touch of defiance. "I was only – takin' a look round – so to speak. It's always a mistake to be too previous with yer questions." Then he added suddenly with obvious effort, in his more natural voice, "Have you got the matches, Boss Simpson?" and proceeded to light the pipe he had half filled just before he began to sing.

Without speaking another word they sat down again by the fire. Défago changing his side so that he could face the direction the wind came from. For even a tenderfoot could tell that. Défago changed his position in order to hear and smell – all there was to be heard and smelt. And, since he now faced the lake with his back to the trees it was evidently nothing in the forest that had sent so strange and sudden a warning to his marvellously trained nerves.

"Guess now I don't feel like singing any," he explained presently of his own accord. "That song kinder brings back memories that's troublesome to me; I never oughter've begun it. It sets me on t' imagining things, see?"

Clearly the man was still fighting with some profoundly moving emotion. He wished to excuse himself in the eyes of the other. But the explanation, in that it was only a part of the truth, was a lie, and he knew perfectly well that Simpson was not deceived by it. For nothing could explain away the livid terror that had dropped over his face while he stood there sniffing the air. And nothing – no amount of blazing fire, or chatting on ordinary subjects – could make that camp exactly as it had been before. The shadow of an unknown horror, naked if unguessed, that had flashed for an instant in the face and gestures of the guide, had also communicated itself, vaguely and therefore more potently, to his companion. The guide's visible efforts to dissemble the truth only made things worse. Moreover, to add to the younger man's uneasiness, was the difficulty, nay, the impossibility he felt of asking questions, and also his complete ignorance as to the cause...Indians, wild animals, forest fires – all these, he knew, were wholly out of the question. His imagination searched vigorously, but in vain....

* * *

Yet, somehow or other, after another long spell of smoking, talking and roasting themselves before the great fire, the shadow that had so suddenly invaded their peaceful camp began to shift. Perhaps Défago's efforts, or the return of his quiet and normal attitude accomplished this; perhaps Simpson himself had exaggerated the affair out of all proportion to the truth; or possibly the vigorous air of the wilderness brought its own powers of healing. Whatever the cause, the feeling of immediate horror seemed to have passed away as mysteriously as it had come, for nothing occurred to feed it. Simpson began to feel that he had permitted himself the unreasoning terror of a child. He put it down partly to a certain subconscious excitement that this wild and immense scenery generated in his blood, partly to the spell of solitude, and partly to overfatigue. That pallor in the guide's face was, of course, uncommonly hard to explain, yet it *might* have been due in some way to an effect of firelight, or his own imagination…He gave it the benefit of the doubt; he was Scotch.

When a somewhat unordinary emotion has disappeared, the mind always finds a dozen ways of explaining away its causes…Simpson lit a last pipe and tried to laugh to himself. On getting home to Scotland it would make quite a good story. He did not realise that this laughter was a sign that terror still lurked in the recesses of his soul – that, in fact, it was merely one of the conventional signs by which a man, seriously alarmed, tries to persuade himself that he is *not* so.

Défago, however, heard that low laughter and looked up with surprise on his face. The two men stood, side by side, kicking the embers about before going to bed. It was ten o'clock – a late hour for hunters to be still awake.

"What's ticklin' yer?" he asked in his ordinary tone, yet gravely.

"I – I was thinking of our little toy woods at home, just at that moment," stammered Simpson, coming back to what really dominated his mind, and startled by the question, "and comparing them to – to all this," and he swept his arm round to indicate the Bush.

A pause followed in which neither of them said anything.

"All the same I wouldn't laugh about it, if I was you," Défago added, looking over Simpson's shoulder into the shadows. "There's places in there nobody won't never see into – nobody knows what lives in there either."

"Too big – too far off?" The suggestion in the guide's manner was immense and horrible.

Défago nodded. The expression on his face was dark. He, too, felt uneasy. The younger man understood that in a *hinterland* of this size there might well be depths of wood that would never in the life of the world be known or trodden. The thought was not exactly the sort he welcomed. In a loud voice, cheerfully, he suggested that it was time for bed. But the guide lingered, tinkering with the fire, arranging the stones needlessly, doing a dozen things that did not really need doing. Evidently there was something he wanted to say, yet found it difficult to 'get at'.

"Say, you, Boss Simpson," he began suddenly, as the last shower of sparks went up into the air, "you don't – smell nothing, do you – nothing pertickler, I mean?" The commonplace question, Simpson realised, veiled a dreadfully serious thought in his mind. A shiver ran down his back.

"Nothing but burning wood," he replied firmly, kicking again at the embers. The sound of his own foot made him start.

"And all the evenin' you ain't smelt – nothing?" persisted the guide, peering at him through the gloom; "nothing extrordiny, and different to anything else you ever smelt before?"

"No, no, man; nothing at all!" he replied aggressively, half angrily.

Défago's face cleared. "That's good!" he exclaimed with evident relief. "That's good to hear."

"Have *you?*" asked Simpson sharply, and the same instant regretted the question.

The Canadian came closer in the darkness. He shook his head. "I guess not," he said, though without overwhelming conviction. "It must've been just that song of mine that did it. It's the song they sing in lumber camps and godforsaken places like that, when they're skeered the Wendigo's somewhere around, doin' a bit of swift travelling."

"And what's the Wendigo, pray?" Simpson asked quickly, irritated because again he could not prevent that sudden shiver of the nerves. He knew that he was close upon the man's terror and the cause of it. Yet a rushing passionate curiosity overcame his better judgment, and his fear.

Défago turned swiftly and looked at him as though he were suddenly about to shriek. His eyes shone, but his mouth was wide open. Yet all he said, or whispered rather, for his voice sank very low, was: "It's nuthin' – nuthin' but what those lousy fellers believe when they've bin hittin' the bottle too long – a sort of great animal that lives up yonder," he jerked his head northwards, "quick as lightning in its tracks, an' bigger'n anything else in the Bush, an' ain't supposed to be very good to look at – that's all!"

"A backwoods superstition—" began Simpson, moving hastily toward the tent in order to shake off the hand of the guide that clutched his arm. "Come, come, hurry up for God's sake, and get the lantern going! It's time we were in bed and asleep if we're going to be up with the sun tomorrow...."

The guide was close on his heels. "I'm coming," he answered out of the darkness, "I'm coming." And after a slight delay he appeared with the lantern and hung it from a nail in the front pole of the tent. The shadows of a hundred trees shifted their places quickly as he did so, and when he stumbled over the rope, diving swiftly inside, the whole tent trembled as though a gust of wind struck it.

The two men lay down, without undressing, upon their beds of soft balsam boughs, cunningly arranged. Inside, all was warm and cozy, but outside the world of crowding trees pressed close about them, marshalling their million shadows, and smothering the little tent that stood there like a wee white shell facing the ocean of tremendous forest.

Between the two lonely figures within, however, there pressed another shadow that was *not* a shadow from the night. It was the Shadow cast by the strange Fear, never wholly exorcised, that had leaped suddenly upon Défago in the middle of his singing. And Simpson, as he lay there, watching the darkness through the open flap of the tent, ready to plunge into the fragrant abyss of sleep, knew first that unique and profound stillness of a primeval forest when no wind stirs... and when the night has weight and substance that enters into the soul to bind a veil about it.... Then sleep took him....

## Chapter III

**THUS**, it seemed to him, at least. Yet it was true that the lap of the water, just beyond the tent door, still beat time with his lessening pulses when he realised that he was lying with his eyes open and that another sound had recently introduced itself with cunning softness between the splash and murmur of the little waves.

And, long before he understood what this sound was, it had stirred in him the centers of pity and alarm. He listened intently, though at first in vain, for the running blood beat all its drums too noisily in his ears. Did it come, he wondered, from the lake, or from the woods...?

Then, suddenly, with a rush and a flutter of the heart, he knew that it was close beside him in the tent; and, when he turned over for a better hearing, it focused itself unmistakably not two feet away. It was a sound of weeping; Défago upon his bed of branches was sobbing in the darkness as though his heart would break, the blankets evidently stuffed against his mouth to stifle it.

And his first feeling, before he could think or reflect, was the rush of a poignant and searching tenderness. This intimate, human sound, heard amid the desolation about them, woke pity. It was so incongruous, so pitifully incongruous – and so vain! Tears – in this vast and cruel wilderness: of what avail? He thought of a little child crying in mid-Atlantic.... Then, of course, with fuller realisation, and the memory of what had gone before, came the descent of the terror upon him, and his blood ran cold.

"Défago," he whispered quickly, "what's the matter?" He tried to make his voice very gentle. "Are you in pain – unhappy—?" There was no reply, but the sounds ceased abruptly. He stretched his hand out and touched him. The body did not stir.

"Are you awake?" for it occurred to him that the man was crying in his sleep. "Are you cold?" He noticed that his feet, which were uncovered, projected beyond the mouth of the tent. He spread an extra fold of his own blankets over them. The guide had slipped down in his bed, and the branches seemed to have been dragged with him. He was afraid to pull the body back again, for fear of waking him.

One or two tentative questions he ventured softly, but though he waited for several minutes there came no reply, nor any sign of movement. Presently he heard his regular and quiet breathing, and putting his hand again gently on the breast, felt the steady rise and fall beneath.

"Let me know if anything's wrong," he whispered, "or if I can do anything. Wake me at once if you feel – queer."

He hardly knew what to say. He lay down again, thinking and wondering what it all meant. Défago, of course, had been crying in his sleep. Some dream or other had afflicted him. Yet never in his life would he forget that pitiful sound of sobbing, and the feeling that the whole awful wilderness of woods listened....

His own mind busied itself for a long time with the recent events, of which *this* took its mysterious place as one, and though his reason successfully argued away all unwelcome suggestions, a sensation of uneasiness remained, resisting ejection, very deep-seated – peculiar beyond ordinary.

## Chapter IV

**BUT SLEEP**, in the long run, proves greater than all emotions. His thoughts soon wandered again; he lay there, warm as toast, exceedingly weary; the night soothed and comforted, blunting the edges of memory and alarm. Half an hour later he was oblivious of everything in the outer world about him.

Yet sleep, in this case, was his great enemy, concealing all approaches, smothering the warning of his nerves.

As, sometimes, in a nightmare events crowd upon each other's heels with a conviction of dreadfulest reality, yet some inconsistent detail accuses the whole display of incompleteness and disguise, so the events that now followed, though they actually happened, persuaded the mind somehow that the detail which could explain them had been overlooked in the confusion, and that therefore they were but partly true, the rest delusion. At the back of the sleeper's mind something remains awake, ready to let slip the judgment. "All this is not *quite* real; when you wake up you'll understand."

And thus, in a way, it was with Simpson. The events, not wholly inexplicable or incredible in themselves, yet remain for the man who saw and heard them a sequence of separate facts of cold horror, because the little piece that might have made the puzzle clear lay concealed or overlooked.

So far as he can recall, it was a violent movement, running downwards through the tent towards the door, that first woke him and made him aware that his companion was sitting bolt upright beside him – quivering. Hours must have passed, for it was the pale gleam of the dawn that revealed his outline against the canvas. This time the man was not crying; he was quaking like a leaf; the trembling he felt plainly through the blankets down the entire length of his own body. Défago had huddled down against him for protection, shrinking away from something that apparently concealed itself near the door flaps of the little tent.

Simpson thereupon called out in a loud voice some question or other – in the first bewilderment of waking he does not remember exactly what – and the man made no reply. The atmosphere and feeling of true nightmare lay horribly about him, making movement and speech both difficult. At first, indeed, he was not sure where he was – whether in one of the earlier camps, or at home in his bed at Aberdeen. The sense of confusion was very troubling.

And next – almost simultaneous with his waking, it seemed – the profound stillness of the dawn outside was shattered by a most uncommon sound. It came without warning, or audible approach; and it was unspeakably dreadful. It was a voice, Simpson declares, possibly a human voice; hoarse yet plaintive – a soft, roaring voice close outside the tent, overhead rather than upon the ground, of immense volume, while in some strange way most penetratingly and seductively sweet. It rang out, too, in three separate and distinct notes, or cries, that bore in some odd fashion a resemblance, farfetched yet recognisable, to the name of the guide: *"Dé-fa-go!"*

The student admits he is unable to describe it quite intelligently, for it was unlike any sound he had ever heard in his life, and combined a blending of such contrary qualities. "A sort of windy, crying voice," he calls it, "as of something lonely and untamed, wild and of abominable power...."

And, even before it ceased, dropping back into the great gulfs of silence, the guide beside him had sprung to his feet with an answering though unintelligible cry. He blundered against the tent pole with violence, shaking the whole structure, spreading his arms out frantically for more room, and kicking his legs impetuously free of the clinging blankets. For a second, perhaps two, he stood upright by the door, his outline dark against the pallor of the dawn; then, with a furious, rushing speed, before his companion could move a hand to stop him, he shot with a plunge through the flaps of canvas – and was gone. And as he went – so astonishingly fast that the voice could actually be heard dying in the distance – he called aloud in tones of anguished terror that at the same time held something strangely like the frenzied exultation of delight –

"Oh! oh! My feet of fire! My burning feet of fire! Oh! oh! This height and fiery speed!"

And then the distance quickly buried it, and the deep silence of very early morning descended upon the forest as before.

It had all come about with such rapidity that, but for the evidence of the empty bed beside him, Simpson could almost have believed it to have been the memory of a nightmare carried over from sleep. He still felt the warm pressure of that vanished body against his side; there lay the twisted blankets in a heap; the very tent yet trembled with the vehemence of the impetuous departure. The strange words rang in his ears, as though he still heard them in the distance – wild language of a suddenly stricken mind. Moreover, it was not only the senses of sight and hearing that reported uncommon things to his brain, for even while the man cried and ran, he had become aware that a strange perfume, faint yet pungent, pervaded the interior of the tent. And it was at this point, it seems, brought to himself by the consciousness that his nostrils were taking this distressing odour down into his throat, that he found his courage, sprang quickly to his feet – and went out.

The grey light of dawn that dropped, cold and glimmering, between the trees revealed the scene tolerably well. There stood the tent behind him, soaked with dew; the dark ashes of the fire, still warm; the lake, white beneath a coating of mist, the islands rising darkly out of it like objects packed in wool; and patches of snow beyond among the clearer spaces of the Bush – everything cold, still, waiting for the sun. But nowhere a sign of the vanished guide – still, doubtless, flying at frantic speed through the frozen woods. There was not even the sound of disappearing footsteps, nor the echoes of the dying voice. He had gone – utterly.

There was nothing; nothing but the sense of his recent presence, so strongly left behind about the camp; *and* – this penetrating, all-pervading odour.

And even this was now rapidly disappearing in its turn. In spite of his exceeding mental perturbation, Simpson struggled hard to detect its nature, and define it, but the ascertaining of an elusive scent, not recognised subconsciously and at once, is a very subtle operation of the mind. And he failed. It was gone before he could properly seize or name it. Approximate description, even, seems to have been difficult, for it was unlike any smell he knew. Acrid rather, not unlike the odour of a lion, he thinks, yet softer and not wholly unpleasing, with something almost sweet in it that reminded him of the scent of decaying garden leaves, earth, and the myriad, nameless perfumes that make up the odour of a big forest. Yet the 'odour of lions' is the phrase with which he usually sums it all up.

Then – it was wholly gone, and he found himself standing by the ashes of the fire in a state of amazement and stupid terror that left him the helpless prey of anything that chose to happen. Had a muskrat poked its pointed muzzle over a rock, or a squirrel scuttled in that instant down the bark of a tree, he would most likely have collapsed without more ado and fainted. For he felt about the whole affair the touch somewhere of a great Outer Horror... and his scattered powers had not as yet had time to collect themselves into a definite attitude of fighting self-control.

Nothing did happen, however. A great kiss of wind ran softly through the awakening forest, and a few maple leaves here and there rustled tremblingly to earth. The sky seemed to grow suddenly much lighter. Simpson felt the cool air upon his cheek and uncovered head; realised that he was shivering with the cold; and, making a great effort, realised next that he was alone in the Bush – *and* that he was called upon to take immediate steps to find and succour his vanished companion.

Make an effort, accordingly, he did, though an ill-calculated and futile one. With that wilderness of trees about him, the sheet of water cutting him off behind, and the horror of that wild cry in his blood, he did what any other inexperienced man would have done in similar bewilderment: he ran about, without any sense of direction, like a frantic child, and called loudly without ceasing the name of the guide:

"Défago! Défago! Défago!" he yelled, and the trees gave him back the name as often as he shouted, only a little softened – "Défago! Défago! Défago!"

He followed the trail that lay a short distance across the patches of snow, and then lost it again where the trees grew too thickly for snow to lie. He shouted till he was hoarse, and till the sound of his own voice in all that unanswering and listening world began to frighten him. His confusion increased in direct ratio to the violence of his efforts. His distress became formidably acute, till at length his exertions defeated their own object, and from sheer exhaustion he headed back to the camp again. It remains a wonder that he ever found his way. It was with great difficulty, and only after numberless false clues, that he at last saw the white tent between the trees, and so reached safety.

Exhaustion then applied its own remedy, and he grew calmer. He made the fire and breakfasted. Hot coffee and bacon put a little sense and judgment into him again, and he realised that he had been behaving like a boy. He now made another, and more successful attempt to face the situation collectedly, and, a nature naturally plucky coming to his assistance, he decided that he must first make as thorough a search as possible, failing success in which, he must find his way into the home camp as best he could and bring help.

And this was what he did. Taking food, matches and rifle with him, and a small axe to blaze the trees against his return journey, he set forth. It was eight o'clock when he started, the sun shining over the tops of the trees in a sky without clouds. Pinned to a stake by the fire he left a note in case Défago returned while he was away.

This time, according to a careful plan, he took a new direction, intending to make a wide sweep that must sooner or later cut into indications of the guide's trail; and, before he had gone a quarter of a mile he came across the tracks of a large animal in the snow, and beside it the light and smaller tracks of what were beyond question human feet – the feet of Défago. The relief he at once experienced was natural, though brief; for at first sight he saw in these tracks a simple explanation of the whole matter: these big marks had surely been left by a bull moose that, wind against it, had blundered upon the camp, and uttered its singular cry of warning and alarm the moment its mistake was apparent. Défago, in whom the hunting instinct was developed to the point of uncanny perfection, had scented the brute coming down the wind hours before. His excitement and disappearance were due, of course, to – to his—

Then the impossible explanation at which he grasped faded, as common sense showed him mercilessly that none of this was true. No guide, much less a guide like Défago, could have acted in so irrational a way, going off even without his rifle…! The whole affair demanded a far more complicated elucidation, when he remembered the details of it all – the cry of terror, the amazing language, the grey face of horror when his nostrils first caught the new odour; that muffled sobbing in the darkness, and – for this, too, now came back to him dimly – the man's original aversion for this particular bit of country….

Besides, now that he examined them closer, these were not the tracks of a bull moose at all! Hank had explained to him the outline of a bull's hoofs, of a cow's or calf's, too, for that matter; he had drawn them clearly on a strip of birch bark. And these were wholly different. They were big, round, ample, and with no pointed outline as of sharp hoofs. He wondered for a moment whether bear tracks were like that. There was no other animal he could think of, for caribou did not come so far south at this season, and, even if they did, would leave hoof marks.

They were ominous signs – these mysterious writings left in the snow by the unknown creature that had lured a human being away from safety – and when he coupled them in his imagination with that haunting sound that broke the stillness of the dawn, a momentary dizziness shook his mind, distressing him again beyond belief. He felt the *threatening* aspect of it all. And, stooping down to examine the marks more closely, he caught a faint whiff of that sweet yet pungent odour that made him instantly straighten up again, fighting a sensation almost of nausea.

Then his memory played him another evil trick. He suddenly recalled those uncovered feet projecting beyond the edge of the tent, and the body's appearance of having been dragged towards the opening; the man's shrinking from something by the door when he woke later. The details now beat against his trembling mind with concerted attack. They seemed to gather in those deep spaces of the silent forest about him, where the host of trees stood waiting, listening, watching to see what he would do. The woods were closing round him.

With the persistence of true pluck, however, Simpson went forward, following the tracks as best he could, smothering these ugly emotions that sought to weaken his will. He blazed innumerable trees as he went, ever fearful of being unable to find the way back, and calling aloud at intervals of a few seconds the name of the guide. The dull tapping of the axe upon the massive trunks, and the unnatural accents of his own voice became at length sounds that he even dreaded to make, dreaded to hear. For they drew attention without ceasing to his presence and exact whereabouts, and if it were really the case that something was hunting himself down in the same way that he was hunting down another –

With a strong effort, he crushed the thought out the instant it rose. It was the beginning, he realised, of a bewilderment utterly diabolical in kind that would speedily destroy him.

* * *

Although the snow was not continuous, lying merely in shallow flurries over the more open spaces, he found no difficulty in following the tracks for the first few miles. They went straight as a ruled line wherever the trees permitted. The stride soon began to increase in length, till it finally assumed proportions that seemed absolutely impossible for any ordinary animal to have made. Like huge flying leaps they became. One of these he measured, and though he knew that 'stretch' of eighteen feet must be somehow wrong, he was at a complete loss to understand why he found no signs on the snow between the extreme points. But what perplexed him even more, making him feel his vision had gone utterly awry, was that Défago's stride increased in the same manner, and finally covered the same incredible distances. It looked as if the great beast had lifted him with it and carried him across these astonishing intervals. Simpson, who was much longer in the limb, found that he could not compass even half the stretch by taking a running jump.

And the sight of these huge tracks, running side by side, silent evidence of a dreadful journey in which terror or madness had urged to impossible results, was profoundly moving. It shocked him in the secret depths of his soul. It was the most horrible thing his eyes had ever looked upon. He began to follow them mechanically, absentmindedly almost, ever peering over his shoulder to see if he, too, were being followed by something with a gigantic tread…. And soon it came about that he no longer quite realised what it was they signified – these impressions left upon the snow by something nameless and untamed, always accompanied by the footmarks of the little French Canadian, his guide, his comrade, the man who had shared his tent a few hours before, chatting, laughing, even singing by his side….

## Chapter V

**FOR A MAN** of his years and inexperience, only a canny Scot, perhaps, grounded in common sense and established in logic, could have preserved even that measure of balance that this youth somehow or other did manage to preserve through the whole adventure. Otherwise, two things he presently noticed, while forging pluckily ahead, must have sent him headlong back to the comparative safety of his tent, instead of only making his hands close more tightly upon the rifle stock, while his heart, trained for the Wee Kirk, sent a wordless prayer winging its way to heaven. Both tracks, he saw, had undergone a change, and this change, so far as it concerned the footsteps of the man, was in some undecipherable manner – appalling.

It was in the bigger tracks he first noticed this, and for a long time he could not quite believe his eyes. Was it the blown leaves that produced odd effects of light and shade, or that the dry snow, drifting like finely ground rice about the edges, cast shadows and high lights? Or was it actually the fact that the great marks had become faintly coloured? For round about the deep, plunging holes of the animal there now appeared a mysterious, reddish tinge that was more like an effect of light than of anything that dyed the substance of the snow itself. Every mark had it, and had it increasingly – this indistinct fiery tinge that painted a new touch of ghastliness into the picture.

But when, wholly unable to explain or to credit it, he turned his attention to the other tracks to discover if they, too, bore similar witness, he noticed that these had meanwhile undergone a change that was infinitely worse, and charged with far more horrible suggestion. For, in the last hundred yards or so, he saw that they had grown gradually into the semblance of the parent tread. Imperceptibly the change had come about, yet unmistakably. It was hard to see where the change first began. The result, however, was beyond question. Smaller, neater, more cleanly modeled, they formed now an exact and careful duplicate of the larger tracks beside them. The feet that produced them had, therefore, also changed. And something in his mind reared up with loathing and with terror as he saw it.

Simpson, for the first time, hesitated; then, ashamed of his alarm and indecision, took a few hurried steps ahead; the next instant stopped dead in his tracks. Immediately in front of him all signs of the trail ceased; both tracks came to an abrupt end. On all sides, for a hundred yards and more, he searched in vain for the least indication of their continuance. There was – nothing.

The trees were very thick just there, big trees all of them, spruce, cedar, hemlock; there was no underbrush. He stood, looking about him, all distraught; bereft of any power of judgment. Then he set to work to search again, and again, and yet again, but always with the same result: *nothing*. The feet that printed the surface of the snow thus far had now, apparently, left the ground!

And it was in that moment of distress and confusion that the whip of terror laid its most nicely calculated lash about his heart. It dropped with deadly effect upon the sorest spot of all, completely unnerving him. He had been secretly dreading all the time that it would come – and come it did.

Far overhead, muted by great height and distance, strangely thinned and wailing, he heard the crying voice of Défago, the guide.

The sound dropped upon him out of that still, wintry sky with an effect of dismay and terror unsurpassed. The rifle fell to his feet. He stood motionless an instant, listening as it were with his whole body, then staggered back against the nearest tree for support, disorganised hopelessly in mind and spirit. To him, in that moment, it seemed the most shattering and dislocating experience he had ever known, so that his heart emptied itself of all feeling whatsoever as by a sudden draught.

"Oh! oh! This fiery height! Oh, my feet of fire! My burning feet of fire…!" ran in far, beseeching accents of indescribable appeal this voice of anguish down the sky. Once it called – then silence through all the listening wilderness of trees.

And Simpson, scarcely knowing what he did, presently found himself running wildly to and fro, searching, calling, tripping over roots and boulders, and flinging himself in a frenzy of undirected pursuit after the Caller. Behind the screen of memory and emotion with which experience veils events, he plunged, distracted and half-deranged, picking up false lights like a ship at sea, terror in his eyes and heart and soul. For the Panic of the Wilderness had called to him in that far voice – the Power of untamed Distance – the Enticement of the Desolation that destroys. He knew in that moment all the pains of someone hopelessly and irretrievably lost, suffering the lust and travail of a soul in the final Loneliness. A vision of Défago, eternally hunted, driven and pursued across the skiey vastness of those ancient forests fled like a flame across the dark ruin of his thoughts…

It seemed ages before he could find anything in the chaos of his disorganised sensations to which he could anchor himself steady for a moment, and think…

The cry was not repeated; his own hoarse calling brought no response; the inscrutable forces of the Wild had summoned their victim beyond recall – and held him fast.

\* \* \*

Yet he searched and called, it seems, for hours afterwards, for it was late in the afternoon when at length he decided to abandon a useless pursuit and return to his camp on the shores of Fifty Island Water. Even then he went with reluctance, that crying voice still echoing in his ears. With difficulty he found his rifle and the homeward trail. The concentration necessary to follow the badly blazed trees, and a biting hunger that gnawed, helped to keep his mind steady. Otherwise, he admits, the temporary aberration he had suffered might have been prolonged to the point of positive disaster. Gradually the ballast shifted back again, and he regained something that approached his normal equilibrium.

But for all that the journey through the gathering dusk was miserably haunted. He heard innumerable following footsteps; voices that laughed and whispered; and saw figures crouching behind trees and boulders, making signs to one another for a concerted attack the moment he had passed. The creeping murmur of the wind made him start and listen. He went stealthily, trying to hide where possible, and making as little sound as he could. The shadows of the woods, hitherto protective or covering merely, had now become menacing, challenging; and the pageantry in his frightened mind masked a host of possibilities that were all the more ominous for being obscure. The presentiment of a nameless doom lurked ill-concealed behind every detail of what had happened.

It was really admirable how he emerged victor in the end; men of riper powers and experience might have come through the ordeal with less success. He had himself tolerably well in hand, all things considered, and his plan of action proves it. Sleep being absolutely out of the question and travelling an unknown trail in the darkness equally impracticable, he sat up the whole of that night, rifle in hand, before a fire he never for a single moment allowed to die down. The severity of the haunted vigil marked his soul for life; but it was successfully accomplished; and with the very first signs of dawn he set forth upon the long return journey to the home camp to get help. As before, he left a written note to explain his absence, and to indicate where he had left a plentiful *cache* of food and matches – though he had no expectation that any human hands would find them!

How Simpson found his way alone by the lake and forest might well make a story in itself, for to hear him tell it is to *know* the passionate loneliness of soul that a man can feel when the Wilderness holds him in the hollow of its illimitable hand – and laughs. It is also to admire his indomitable pluck.

He claims no skill, declaring that he followed the almost invisible trail mechanically, and without thinking. And this, doubtless, is the truth. He relied upon the guiding of the unconscious mind, which is instinct. Perhaps, too, some sense of orientation, known to animals and primitive men, may have helped as well, for through all that tangled region he succeeded in reaching the exact spot where Défago had hidden the canoe nearly three days before with the remark, "Strike doo west across the lake into the sun to find the camp."

There was not much sun left to guide him, but he used his compass to the best of his ability, embarking in the frail craft for the last twelve miles of his journey with a sensation of immense relief that the forest was at last behind him. And, fortunately, the water was calm; he took his line across the center of the lake instead of coasting round the shores for another twenty miles. Fortunately, too, the other hunters were back. The light of their fires furnished a steering point without which he might have searched all night long for the actual position of the camp.

It was close upon midnight all the same when his canoe grated on the sandy cove, and Hank, Punk and his uncle, disturbed in their sleep by his cries, ran quickly down and helped a very exhausted and broken specimen of Scotch humanity over the rocks toward a dying fire.

## Chapter VI

**THE SUDDEN** entrance of his prosaic uncle into this world of wizardry and horror that had haunted him without interruption now for two days and two nights, had the immediate effect of giving to the affair an entirely new aspect. The sound of that crisp "Hulloa, my boy! And what's up *now*?" and the grasp of that dry and vigorous hand introduced another standard of judgment. A revulsion of feeling washed through him. He realised that he had let himself 'go' rather badly. He even felt vaguely ashamed of himself. The native hard-headedness of his race reclaimed him.

And this doubtless explains why he found it so hard to tell that group round the fire – everything. He told enough, however, for the immediate decision to be arrived at that a relief party must start at the earliest possible moment, and that Simpson, in order to guide it capably, must first have food and, above all, sleep. Dr. Cathcart observing the lad's condition more shrewdly than his patient knew, gave him a very slight injection of morphine. For six hours he slept like the dead.

From the description carefully written out afterwards by this student of divinity, it appears that the account he gave to the astonished group omitted sundry vital and important details. He declares that, with his uncle's wholesome, matter-of-fact countenance staring him in the face, he simply had not the courage to mention them. Thus, all the search party gathered, it would seem, was that Défago had suffered in the night an acute and inexplicable attack of mania, had imagined himself 'called' by someone or something, and had plunged into the bush after it without food or rifle, where he must die a horrible and lingering death by cold and starvation unless he could be found and rescued in time. "In time," moreover, meant *at once*.

In the course of the following day, however – they were off by seven, leaving Punk in charge with instructions to have food and fire always ready – Simpson found it possible to tell his uncle a good deal more of the story's true inwardness, without divining that it was drawn out of him as a matter of fact by a very subtle form of cross examination. By the time they reached the beginning of the trail, where the canoe was laid up against the return journey, he had mentioned how Défago spoke vaguely of "something he called a 'Wendigo'"; how he cried in his sleep; how he imagined an unusual scent about the camp; and had betrayed other symptoms of mental excitement. He also admitted the bewildering effect of "that extraordinary odour" upon himself, "pungent and acrid like the odour of lions." And by the time they were within an easy hour of Fifty Island Water he had let slip the further fact – a foolish avowal of his own hysterical condition, as he felt afterwards – that he had heard the vanished guide call "for help." He omitted the singular phrases used, for he simply could not bring himself to repeat the preposterous language. Also, while describing how the man's footsteps in the snow had gradually assumed an exact miniature likeness of the animal's plunging tracks, he left out the fact that they measured a *wholly* incredible distance. It seemed a question, nicely balanced between individual pride and honesty, what he should reveal and what suppress. He mentioned the fiery tinge in the snow, for instance, yet shrank from telling that body and bed had been partly dragged out of the tent....

With the net result that Dr. Cathcart, adroit psychologist that he fancied himself to be, had assured him clearly enough exactly where his mind, influenced by loneliness, bewilderment and terror, had yielded to the strain and invited delusion. While praising his conduct, he managed at the same time to point out where, when, and how his mind had gone astray. He made his nephew think himself finer than he was by judicious praise, yet more foolish than he was by minimising the value of the evidence. Like many another materialist, that is, he lied cleverly on the basis of insufficient knowledge, *because* the knowledge supplied seemed to his own particular intelligence inadmissible.

"The spell of these terrible solitudes," he said, "cannot leave any mind untouched, any mind, that is, possessed of the higher imaginative qualities. It has worked upon yours exactly as it worked upon my own when I was your age. The animal that haunted your little camp was undoubtedly a moose, for the 'belling' of a moose may have, sometimes, a very peculiar quality of sound. The coloured appearance of the big tracks was obviously a defect of vision in your own eyes produced by excitement. The size and stretch of the tracks we shall prove when we come to them. But the hallucination of an audible voice, of course, is one of the commonest forms of delusion due to mental excitement – an excitement, my dear boy, perfectly excusable, and, let me add, wonderfully controlled by you under the circumstances. For the rest, I am bound to say, you have acted with a splendid courage, for the terror of feeling oneself lost in this wilderness is nothing short of awful, and, had I been in your place, I don't for a moment believe I could have behaved with one quarter of your wisdom and decision. The only thing I find it uncommonly difficult to explain is – that – damned odour."

"It made me feel sick, I assure you," declared his nephew, "positively dizzy!" His uncle's attitude of calm omniscience, merely because he knew more psychological formulae, made him slightly defiant. It was so easy to be wise in the explanation of an experience one has not personally witnessed. "A kind of desolate and terrible odour is the only way

I can describe it," he concluded, glancing at the features of the quiet, unemotional man beside him.

"I can only marvel," was the reply, "that under the circumstances it did not seem to you even worse." The dry words, Simpson knew, hovered between the truth, and his uncle's interpretation of 'the truth'.

\* \* \*

And so at last they came to the little camp and found the tent still standing, the remains of the fire, and the piece of paper pinned to a stake beside it – untouched. The cache, poorly contrived by inexperienced hands, however, had been discovered and opened – by musk rats, mink and squirrel. The matches lay scattered about the opening, but the food had been taken to the last crumb.

"Well, fellers, he ain't here," exclaimed Hank loudly after his fashion. "And that's as sartain as the coal supply down below! But whar he's got to by this time is 'bout as unsartain as the trade in crowns in t'other place." The presence of a divinity student was no barrier to his language at such a time, though for the reader's sake it may be severely edited. "I propose," he added, "that we start out at once an' hunt for'm like hell!"

The gloom of Défago's probable fate oppressed the whole party with a sense of dreadful gravity the moment they saw the familiar signs of recent occupancy. Especially the tent, with the bed of balsam branches still smoothed and flattened by the pressure of his body, seemed to bring his presence near to them. Simpson, feeling vaguely as if his world were somehow at stake, went about explaining particulars in a hushed tone. He was much calmer now, though overwearied with the strain of his many journeys. His uncle's method of explaining – 'explaining away', rather – the details still fresh in his haunted memory helped, too, to put ice upon his emotions.

"And that's the direction he ran off in," he said to his two companions, pointing in the direction where the guide had vanished that morning in the grey dawn. "Straight down there he ran like a deer, in between the birch and the hemlock...."

Hank and Dr. Cathcart exchanged glances.

"And it was about two miles down there, in a straight line," continued the other, speaking with something of the former terror in his voice, "that I followed his trail to the place where – it stopped – dead!"

"And where you heered him callin' an' caught the stench, an' all the rest of the wicked entertainment," cried Hank, with a volubility that betrayed his keen distress.

"And where your excitement overcame you to the point of producing illusions," added Dr. Cathcart under his breath, yet not so low that his nephew did not hear it.

\* \* \*

It was early in the afternoon, for they had travelled quickly, and there were still a good two hours of daylight left. Dr. Cathcart and Hank lost no time in beginning the search, but Simpson was too exhausted to accompany them. They would follow the blazed marks on the trees, and where possible, his footsteps. Meanwhile the best thing he could do was to keep a good fire going, and rest.

But after something like three hours' search, the darkness already down, the two men returned to camp with nothing to report. Fresh snow had covered all signs, and though they had followed the blazed trees to the spot where Simpson had turned back, they had not discovered the smallest indication of a human being – or for that matter, of an animal. There were no fresh tracks of any kind; the snow lay undisturbed.

It was difficult to know what was best to do, though in reality there was nothing more they *could* do. They might stay and search for weeks without much chance of success. The fresh snow destroyed their only hope, and they gathered round the fire for supper, a gloomy and despondent party. The facts, indeed, were sad enough, for Défago had a wife at Rat Portage, and his earnings were the family's sole means of support.

Now that the whole truth in all its ugliness was out, it seemed useless to deal in further disguise or pretence. They talked openly of the facts and probabilities. It was not the first time, even in the experience of Dr. Cathcart, that a man had yielded to the singular seduction of the Solitudes and gone out of his mind; Défago, moreover, was predisposed to something of the sort, for he already had a touch of melancholia in his blood, and his fiber was weakened by bouts of drinking that often lasted for weeks at a time. Something on this trip – one might never know precisely what – had sufficed to push him over the line, that was all. And he had gone, gone off into the great wilderness of trees and lakes to die by starvation and exhaustion. The chances against his finding camp again were overwhelming; the delirium that was upon him would also doubtless have increased, and it was quite likely he might do violence to himself and so hasten his cruel fate. Even while they talked, indeed, the end had probably come. On the suggestion of Hank, his old pal, however, they proposed to wait a little longer and devote the whole of the following day, from dawn to darkness, to the most systematic search they could devise. They would divide the territory between them. They discussed their plan in great detail. All that men could do they would do. And, meanwhile, they talked about the particular form in which the singular Panic of the Wilderness had made its attack upon the mind of the unfortunate guide. Hank, though familiar with the legend in its general outline, obviously did not welcome the turn the conversation had taken. He contributed little, though that little was illuminating. For he admitted that a story ran over all this section of country to the effect that several Indians had "seen the Wendigo" along the shores of Fifty Island Water in the "fall" of last year, and that this was the true reason of Défago's disinclination to hunt there. Hank doubtless felt that he had in a sense helped his old pal to death by overpersuading him. "When an Indian goes crazy," he explained, talking to himself more than to the others, it seemed, "it's always put that he's 'seen the Wendigo'. An' pore old Défaygo was superstitious down to the very heels...!"

And then Simpson, feeling the atmosphere more sympathetic, told over again the full story of his astonishing tale; he left out no details this time; he mentioned his own sensations and gripping fears. He only omitted the strange language used.

"But Défago surely had already told you all these details of the Wendigo legend, my dear fellow," insisted the doctor. "I mean, he had talked about it, and thus put into your mind the ideas which your own excitement afterwards developed?"

Whereupon Simpson again repeated the facts. Défago, he declared, had barely mentioned the beast. He, Simpson, knew nothing of the story, and, so far as he remembered, had never even read about it. Even the word was unfamiliar.

Of course he was telling the truth, and Dr. Cathcart was reluctantly compelled to admit the singular character of the whole affair. He did not do this in words so much as in manner, however. He kept his back against a good, stout tree; he poked the fire into a blaze the moment it showed signs of dying down; he was quicker than any of them to notice the least sound in the night about them – a fish jumping in the lake, a twig snapping in the bush, the dropping of occasional fragments of frozen snow from the branches overhead where the heat loosened them. His voice, too, changed a little in quality, becoming a shade less confident, lower also in tone. Fear, to put it plainly, hovered close about that little camp, and though all three would have been glad to speak of other matters, the only thing they seemed able to discuss was this – the source of their fear. They tried other subjects in vain; there was nothing to say about them. Hank was the most honest of the group; he said next to nothing. He never once, however, turned his back to the darkness. His face was always to the forest, and when wood was needed he didn't go farther than was necessary to get it.

## Chapter VII

**A WALL** of silence wrapped them in, for the snow, though not thick, was sufficient to deaden any noise, and the frost held things pretty tight besides. No sound but their voices and the soft roar of the flames made itself heard. Only, from time to time, something soft as the flutter of a pine moth's wings went past them through the air. No one seemed anxious to go to bed. The hours slipped towards midnight.

"The legend is picturesque enough," observed the doctor after one of the longer pauses, speaking to break it rather than because he had anything to say, "for the Wendigo is simply the Call of the Wild personified, which some natures hear to their own destruction."

"That's about it," Hank said presently. "An' there's no misunderstandin' when you hear it. It calls you by name right 'nough."

Another pause followed. Then Dr. Cathcart came back to the forbidden subject with a rush that made the others jump.

"The allegory *is* significant," he remarked, looking about him into the darkness, "for the Voice, they say, resembles all the minor sounds of the Bush – wind, falling water, cries of the animals, and so forth. And, once the victim hears *that* – he's off for good, of course! His most vulnerable points, moreover, are said to be the feet and the eyes; the feet, you see, for the lust of wandering, and the eyes for the lust of beauty. The poor beggar goes at such a dreadful speed that he bleeds beneath the eyes, and his feet burn."

Dr. Cathcart, as he spoke, continued to peer uneasily into the surrounding gloom. His voice sank to a hushed tone.

"The Wendigo," he added, "is said to burn his feet – owing to the friction, apparently caused by its tremendous velocity – till they drop off, and new ones form exactly like its own."

Simpson listened in horrified amazement; but it was the pallor on Hank's face that fascinated him most. He would willingly have stopped his ears and closed his eyes, had he dared.

"It don't always keep to the ground neither," came in Hank's slow, heavy drawl, "for it goes so high that he thinks the stars have set him all a-fire. An' it'll take great thumpin' jumps sometimes, an' run along the tops of the trees, carrying its partner with it, an' then droppin' him jest as a fish hawk'll drop a pickerel to kill it before eatin'. An' its food, of all the muck in the whole Bush is – moss!" And he laughed a short, unnatural laugh. "It's a moss-eater, is the Wendigo," he added, looking up excitedly into the faces of his companions. "Moss-eater," he repeated, with a string of the most outlandish oaths he could invent.

But Simpson now understood the true purpose of all this talk. What these two men, each strong and 'experienced' in his own way, dreaded more than anything else was – silence. They were talking against time. They were also talking against darkness, against the invasion of panic, against the admission reflection might bring that they were in an enemy's country – against anything, in fact, rather than allow their inmost thoughts to assume control. He himself, already initiated by the awful vigil with terror, was beyond both of them in this respect. He had reached the stage where he was immune. But these two, the scoffing, analytical doctor, and the honest, dogged backwoodsman, each sat trembling in the depths of his being.

Thus the hours passed; and thus, with lowered voices and a kind of taut inner resistance of spirit, this little group of humanity sat in the jaws of the wilderness and talked foolishly of the terrible and haunting legend. It was an unequal contest, all things considered, for the wilderness had already the advantage of first attack – and of a hostage. The fate of their comrade hung over them with a steadily increasing weight of oppression that finally became insupportable.

It was Hank, after a pause longer than the preceding ones that no one seemed able to break, who first let loose all this pent-up emotion in very unexpected fashion, by springing suddenly to his feet and letting out the most ear-shattering yell imaginable into the night. He could not contain himself any longer, it seemed. To make it carry even beyond an ordinary cry he interrupted its rhythm by shaking the palm of his hand before his mouth.

"That's for Défago," he said, looking down at the other two with a queer, defiant laugh, "for it's my belief" – the sandwiched oaths may be omitted – "that my ole partner's not far from us at this very minute."

There was a vehemence and recklessness about his performance that made Simpson, too, start to his feet in amazement, and betrayed even the doctor into letting the pipe slip from between his lips. Hank's face was ghastly, but Cathcart's showed a sudden weakness – a loosening of all his faculties, as it were. Then a momentary anger blazed into his eyes, and he too, though with deliberation born of habitual self-control, got upon his feet and faced the excited guide. For this was unpermissible, foolish, dangerous, and he meant to stop it in the bud.

What might have happened in the next minute or two one may speculate about, yet never definitely know, for in the instant of profound silence that followed Hank's roaring voice, and as though in answer to it, something went past through the darkness of the sky overhead at terrific speed – something of necessity very large, for it displaced much air, while down between the trees there fell a faint and windy cry of a human voice, calling in tones of indescribable anguish and appeal –

"Oh, oh! This fiery height! Oh, oh! My feet of fire! My burning feet of fire!"

White to the very edge of his shirt, Hank looked stupidly about him like a child. Dr. Cathcart uttered some kind of unintelligible cry, turning as he did so with an instinctive movement of blind terror towards the protection of the tent, then halting in the act as though frozen. Simpson, alone of the three, retained his presence of mind a little. His own horror was too deep to allow of any immediate reaction. He had heard that cry before.

Turning to his stricken companions, he said almost calmly –

"That's exactly the cry I heard – the very words he used!"

Then, lifting his face to the sky, he cried aloud, "Défago, Défago! Come down here to us! Come down—!"

And before there was time for anybody to take definite action one way or another, there came the sound of something dropping heavily between the trees, striking the branches on the way down, and landing with a dreadful thud upon the frozen earth below. The crash and thunder of it was really terrific.

"That's him, s'help me the good Gawd!" came from Hank in a whispering cry half choked, his hand going automatically toward the hunting knife in his belt. "And he's coming! He's coming!" he added, with an irrational laugh of horror, as the sounds of heavy footsteps crunching over the snow became distinctly audible, approaching through the blackness towards the circle of light.

And while the steps, with their stumbling motion, moved nearer and nearer upon them, the three men stood round that fire, motionless and dumb. Dr. Cathcart had the appearance of a man suddenly withered; even his eyes did not move. Hank, suffering shockingly, seemed on the verge again of violent action; yet did nothing. He, too, was hewn of stone. Like stricken children they seemed. The picture was hideous. And, meanwhile, their owner still invisible, the footsteps came closer, crunching the frozen snow. It was endless – too prolonged to be quite real – this measured and pitiless approach. It was accursed.

## Chapter VIII

**THEN** at length the darkness, having thus laboriously conceived, brought forth – a figure. It drew forward into the zone of uncertain light where fire and shadows mingled, not ten feet away; then halted, staring at them fixedly. The same instant it started forward again with the spasmodic motion as of a thing moved by wires, and coming up closer to them, full into the glare of the fire, they perceived then that – it was a man; and apparently that this man was – Défago.

Something like a skin of horror almost perceptibly drew down in that moment over every face, and three pairs of eyes shone through it as though they saw across the frontiers of normal vision into the Unknown.

Défago advanced, his tread faltering and uncertain; he made his way straight up to them as a group first, then turned sharply and peered close into the face of Simpson. The sound of a voice issued from his lips –

"Here I am, Boss Simpson. I heered someone calling me." It was a faint, dried up voice, made wheezy and breathless as by immense exertion. "I'm havin' a reg'lar hellfire kind of a trip, I am." And he laughed, thrusting his head forward into the other's face.

But that laugh started the machinery of the group of waxwork figures with the wax-white skins. Hank immediately sprang forward with a stream of oaths so farfetched that Simpson did not recognise them as English at all, but thought he had lapsed into Indian or some other lingo. He only realised that Hank's presence, thrust thus between them, was welcome – uncommonly welcome. Dr. Cathcart, though more calmly and leisurely, advanced behind him, heavily stumbling.

Simpson seems hazy as to what was actually said and done in those next few seconds, for the eyes of that detestable and blasted visage peering at such close quarters into his own utterly bewildered his senses at first. He merely stood still. He said nothing. He had not the trained will of the older men that forced them into action in defiance of all emotional stress. He watched them moving as behind a glass that half destroyed their reality; it was dreamlike; perverted. Yet, through the torrent of Hank's meaningless phrases, he remembers hearing his uncle's tone of authority – hard and forced – saying several things about food and warmth, blankets, whisky and the rest... and, further, that whiffs of that penetrating, unaccustomed odour, vile yet sweetly bewildering, assailed his nostrils during all that followed.

It was no less a person than himself, however – less experienced and adroit than the others though he was – who gave instinctive utterance to the sentence that brought a measure of relief into the ghastly situation by expressing the doubt and thought in each one's heart.

"It *is* – YOU, isn't it, Défago?" he asked under his breath, horror breaking his speech.

And at once Cathcart burst out with the loud answer before the other had time to move his lips. "Of course it is! Of course it is! Only – can't you see – he's nearly dead with exhaustion, cold and terror! Isn't *that* enough to change a man beyond all recognition?" It was said in order to convince himself as much as to convince the others. The overemphasis alone proved that. And continually, while he spoke and acted, he held a handkerchief to his nose. That odour pervaded the whole camp.

For the 'Défago' who sat huddled by the big fire, wrapped in blankets, drinking hot whisky and holding food in wasted hands, was no more like the guide they had last seen alive than the picture of a man of sixty is like a daguerreotype of his early youth in the costume of another generation. Nothing really can describe that ghastly caricature, that parody, masquerading there in the firelight as Défago. From the ruins of the dark and awful memories he still retains, Simpson declares that the face was more animal than human, the features drawn about into wrong proportions, the skin loose and hanging, as though he had been subjected to extraordinary pressures and tensions. It made him think vaguely of those bladder faces blown up by the hawkers on Ludgate Hill, that change their expression as they swell, and as they collapse emit a faint and wailing imitation of a voice. Both face and voice suggested some such abominable resemblance. But Cathcart long afterwards, seeking to describe the indescribable, asserts that thus might have looked a face and body that had been in air so rarified that, the weight of atmosphere being removed, the entire structure threatened to fly asunder and become – *incoherent*....

It was Hank, though all distraught and shaking with a tearing volume of emotion he could neither handle nor understand, who brought things to a head without much ado. He went off to a little distance from the fire, apparently so that the light should not dazzle him too much, and shading his eyes for a moment with both hands, shouted in a loud voice that held anger and affection dreadfully mingled:

"You ain't Défaygo! You ain't Défaygo at all! I don't give a – damn, but that ain't you, my ole pal of twenty years!" He glared upon the huddled figure as though he would destroy him with his eyes. "An' if it is I'll swab the floor of hell with a wad of cotton wool on a toothpick, s'help me the good Gawd!" he added, with a violent fling of horror and disgust.

It was impossible to silence him. He stood there shouting like one possessed, horrible to see, horrible to hear – *because it was the truth*. He repeated himself in fifty different ways, each more outlandish than the last. The woods rang with echoes. At one time it looked as if he meant to fling himself upon 'the intruder', for his hand continually jerked towards the long hunting knife in his belt.

But in the end he did nothing, and the whole tempest completed itself very shortly with tears. Hank's voice suddenly broke, he collapsed on the ground, and Cathcart somehow or other persuaded him at last to go into the tent and lie quiet. The remainder of the affair, indeed, was witnessed by him from behind the canvas, his white and terrified face peeping through the crack of the tent door flap.

Then Dr. Cathcart, closely followed by his nephew who so far had kept his courage better than all of them, went up with a determined air and stood opposite to the figure of Défago huddled over the fire. He looked him squarely in the face and spoke. At first his voice was firm.

"Défago, tell us what's happened – just a little, so that we can know how best to help you?" he asked in a tone of authority, almost of command. And at that point, it *was* command. At once afterwards, however, it changed in quality, for the figure turned up to him a face so piteous, so terrible and so little like humanity, that the doctor shrank back from him as from something spiritually unclean. Simpson, watching close behind him, says he got the impression of a mask that was on the verge of dropping off, and that underneath they would discover something black and diabolical, revealed in utter nakedness. "Out with it, man, out with it!" Cathcart cried, terror running neck and neck with entreaty. "None of us can stand this much longer…!" It was the cry of instinct over reason.

And then 'Défago', smiling *whitely*, answered in that thin and fading voice that already seemed passing over into a sound of quite another character –

"I seen that great Wendigo thing," he whispered, sniffing the air about him exactly like an animal. "I been with it too—"

Whether the poor devil would have said more, or whether Dr. Cathcart would have continued the impossible cross examination cannot be known, for at that moment the voice of Hank was heard yelling at the top of his voice from behind the canvas that concealed all but his terrified eyes. Such a howling was never heard.

"His feet! Oh, Gawd, his feet! Look at his great changed – feet!"

Défago, shuffling where he sat, had moved in such a way that for the first time his legs were in full light and his feet were visible. Yet Simpson had no time, himself, to see properly what Hank had seen. And Hank has never seen fit to tell. That same instant, with a leap like that of a frightened tiger, Cathcart was upon him, bundling the folds of blanket about his legs with such speed that the young student caught little more than a passing glimpse of something dark and oddly massed where moccasined feet ought to have been, and saw even that but with uncertain vision.

Then, before the doctor had time to do more, or Simpson time to even think a question, much less ask it, Défago was standing upright in front of them, balancing with pain and difficulty, and upon his shapeless and twisted visage an expression so dark and so malicious that it was, in the true sense, monstrous.

"Now *you* seen it too," he wheezed, "you seen my fiery, burning feet! And now – that is, unless you kin save me an' prevent – it's 'bout time for—"

His piteous and beseeching voice was interrupted by a sound that was like the roar of wind coming across the lake. The trees overhead shook their tangled branches. The blazing fire bent its flames as before a blast. And something swept with a terrific, rushing noise about the little camp and seemed to surround it entirely in a single moment of time. Défago shook the clinging blankets from his body, turned towards the woods behind, and with the same stumbling motion that had brought him – was gone: gone, before anyone could move muscle to prevent him, gone with an amazing, blundering swiftness that left no time to act. The darkness positively swallowed him; and less than a dozen seconds later, above the roar of the swaying trees and the shout of the sudden wind, all three men, watching and listening with stricken hearts, heard a cry that seemed to drop down upon them from a great height of sky and distance –

"Oh, oh! This fiery height! Oh, oh! My feet of fire! My burning feet of fire…!" then died away, into untold space and silence.

Dr. Cathcart – suddenly master of himself, and therefore of the others – was just able to seize Hank violently by the arm as he tried to dash headlong into the Bush.

"But I want ter know – you!" shrieked the guide. "I want ter see! That ain't him at all, but some – devil that's shunted into his place…!"

Somehow or other – he admits he never quite knew how he accomplished it – he managed to keep him in the tent and pacify him. The doctor, apparently, had reached the stage where reaction had set in and allowed his own innate force to conquer. Certainly he 'managed' Hank admirably. It was his nephew, however, hitherto so wonderfully controlled, who gave him most cause for anxiety, for the cumulative strain had now produced a condition of lachrymose hysteria which made it necessary to isolate him upon a bed of boughs and blankets as far removed from Hank as was possible under the circumstances.

And there he lay, as the watches of that haunted night passed over the lonely camp, crying startled sentences, and fragments of sentences, into the folds of his blanket. A quantity of gibberish about speed and height and fire mingled oddly with biblical memories of the classroom. "People with broken faces all on fire are coming at a most awful, awful, pace towards the camp!" he would moan one minute; and the next would sit up and stare into the woods, intently listening, and whisper, "How terrible in the wilderness are – are the feet of them that—" until his uncle came across to change the direction of his thoughts and comfort him.

The hysteria, fortunately, proved but temporary. Sleep cured him, just as it cured Hank.

Till the first signs of daylight came, soon after five o'clock, Dr. Cathcart kept his vigil. His face was the colour of chalk, and there were strange flushes beneath the eyes. An appalling terror of the soul battled with his will all through those silent hours. These were some of the outer signs…

At dawn he lit the fire himself, made breakfast, and woke the others, and by seven they were well on their way back to the home camp – three perplexed and afflicted men, but each in his own way having reduced his inner turmoil to a condition of more or less systematised order again.

## Chapter IX

**THEY** talked little, and then only of the most wholesome and common things, for their minds were charged with painful thoughts that clamoured for explanation, though no one dared refer to them. Hank, being nearest to primitive conditions, was the first to find himself, for he was also less complex. In Dr. Cathcart 'civilisation' championed his forces against an attack singular enough. To this day, perhaps, he is not *quite* sure of certain things. Anyhow, he took longer to 'find himself'.

Simpson, the student of divinity, it was who arranged his conclusions probably with the best, though not most scientific, appearance of order. Out there, in the heart of unreclaimed wilderness, they had surely witnessed something crudely and essentially primitive. Something that had survived somehow the advance of humanity had emerged terrifically, betraying a scale of life still monstrous and immature. He envisaged it rather as a glimpse into prehistoric ages, when superstitions, gigantic and uncouth, still oppressed the hearts of men; when the forces of nature were still untamed, the Powers that may have haunted a primeval universe not yet withdrawn. To this day he thinks of what he termed years later in a sermon "savage and formidable Potencies lurking behind the souls of men, not evil perhaps in themselves, yet instinctively hostile to humanity as it exists."

With his uncle he never discussed the matter in detail, for the barrier between the two types of mind made it difficult. Only once, years later, something led them to the frontier of the subject – of a single detail of the subject, rather –

"Can't you even tell me what – *they* were like?" he asked; and the reply, though conceived in wisdom, was not encouraging, "It is far better you should not try to know, or to find out."

"Well – that odour…?" persisted the nephew. "What do you make of that?"

Dr. Cathcart looked at him and raised his eyebrows.

"Odours," he replied, "are not so easy as sounds and sights of telepathic communication. I make as much, or as little, probably, as you do yourself."

He was not quite so glib as usual with his explanations. That was all.

\* \* \*

At the fall of day, cold, exhausted, famished, the party came to the end of the long portage and dragged themselves into a camp that at first glimpse seemed empty. Fire there was none, and no Punk came forward to welcome them. The emotional capacity of all three was too over-spent to recognise either surprise or annoyance; but the cry of spontaneous affection that burst from the lips of Hank, as he rushed ahead of them towards the fire-place, came probably as a warning that the end of the amazing affair was not quite yet. And both Cathcart and his nephew confessed afterwards that when they saw him kneel down in his excitement and embrace something that reclined, gently moving, beside the extinguished ashes, they felt in their very bones that this 'something' would prove to be Défago – the true Défago, returned.

And so, indeed, it was.

It is soon told. Exhausted to the point of emaciation, the French Canadian – what was left of him, that is – fumbled among the ashes, trying to make a fire. His body crouched there, the weak fingers obeying feebly the instinctive habit of a lifetime with twigs and matches. But there was no longer any mind to direct the simple operation. The mind had fled beyond recall. And with it, too, had fled memory. Not only recent events, but all previous life was a blank.

This time it was the real man, though incredibly and horribly shrunken. On his face was no expression of any kind whatever – fear, welcome, or recognition. He did not seem to know who it was that embraced him, or who it was that fed, warmed and spoke to him the words of comfort and relief. Forlorn and broken beyond all reach of human aid, the little man did meekly as he was bidden. The 'something' that had constituted him 'individual' had vanished for ever.

In some ways it was more terribly moving than anything they had yet seen – that idiot smile as he drew wads of coarse moss from his swollen cheeks and told them that he was "a damned moss-eater"; the continued vomiting of even the simplest food; and, worst of all, the piteous and childish voice of complaint in which he told them that his feet pained him – "burn like fire" – which was natural enough when Dr. Cathcart examined them and found that both were dreadfully frozen. Beneath the eyes there were faint indications of recent bleeding.

The details of how he survived the prolonged exposure, of where he had been, or of how he covered the great distance from one camp to the other, including an immense detour of the lake on foot since he had no canoe – all this remains unknown. His memory had vanished completely. And before the end of the winter whose beginning witnessed this strange occurrence, Défago, bereft of mind, memory and soul, had gone with it. He lingered only a few weeks.

And what Punk was able to contribute to the story throws no further light upon it. He was cleaning fish by the lake shore about five o'clock in the evening – an hour, that is, before the search party returned – when he saw this shadow of the guide picking its way weakly into camp. In advance of him, he declares, came the faint whiff of a certain singular odour.

That same instant old Punk started for home. He covered the entire journey of three days as only Indian blood could have covered it. The terror of a whole race drove him. He knew what it all meant. Défago had 'seen the Wendigo'.

**If you enjoyed this, you might also like...**
The Camp of the Dog, see page 132
The Willows, see page 11

# The Glamour of the Snow

## Chapter I

**HIBBERT**, always conscious of two worlds, was in this mountain village conscious of three. It lay on the slopes of the Valais Alps, and he had taken a room in the little post office, where he could be at peace to write his book, yet at the same time enjoy the winter sports and find companionship in the hotels when he wanted it.

The three worlds that met and mingled here seemed to his imaginative temperament very obvious, though it is doubtful if another mind less intuitively equipped would have seen them so well-defined. There was the world of tourist English, civilised, quasi-educated, to which he belonged by birth, at any rate; there was the world of peasants to which he felt himself drawn by sympathy – for he loved and admired their toiling, simple life; and there was this other – which he could only call the world of Nature. To this last, however, in virtue of a vehement poetic imagination, and a tumultuous pagan instinct fed by his very blood, he felt that most of him belonged. The others borrowed from it, as it were, for visits. Here, with the soul of Nature, hid his central life.

Between all three was conflict – potential conflict. On the skating-rink each Sunday the tourists regarded the natives as intruders; in the church the peasants plainly questioned: "Why do you come? We are here to worship; you to stare and whisper!" For neither of these two worlds accepted the other. And neither did Nature accept the tourists, for it took advantage of their least mistakes, and indeed, even of the peasant-world 'accepted' only those who were strong and bold enough to invade her savage domain with sufficient skill to protect themselves from several forms of – death.

Now Hibbert was keenly aware of this potential conflict and want of harmony; he felt outside, yet caught by it – torn in the three directions because he was partly of each world, but wholly in only one. There grew in him a constant, subtle effort – or, at least, desire – to unify them and decide positively to which he should belong and live in. The attempt, of course, was largely subconscious. It was the natural instinct of a richly imaginative nature seeking the point of equilibrium, so that the mind could feel at peace and his brain be free to do good work.

Among the guests no one especially claimed his interest. The men were nice but undistinguished – athletic schoolmasters, doctors snatching a holiday, good fellows all; the women, equally various – the clever, the would-be-fast, the dare-to-be-dull, the women 'who understood', and the usual pack of jolly dancing girls and 'flappers'. And Hibbert, with his forty odd years of thick experience behind him, got on well with the lot; he understood them all; they belonged to definite, predigested types that are the same the world over, and that he had met the world over long ago.

But to none of them did he belong. His nature was too 'multiple' to subscribe to the set of shibboleths of any one class. And, since all liked him, and felt that somehow he seemed outside of them – spectator, looker-on – all sought to claim him.

In a sense, therefore, the three worlds fought for him: natives, tourists, Nature....

It was thus began the singular conflict for the soul of Hibbert. *In* his own soul, however, it took place. Neither the peasants nor the tourists were conscious that they fought for anything. And Nature, they say, is merely blind and automatic.

The assault upon him of the peasants may be left out of account, for it is obvious that they stood no chance of success. The tourist world, however, made a gallant effort to subdue him to themselves. But the evenings in the hotel, when dancing was not in order, were – English. The provincial imagination was set upon a throne and worshipped heavily through incense of the stupidest conventions possible. Hibbert used to go back early to his room in the post office to work.

"It is a mistake on my part to have *realised* that there is any conflict at all," he thought, as he crunched home over the snow at midnight after one of the dances. "It would have been better to have kept outside it all and done my work. Better," he added, looking back down the silent village street to the church tower, "and – safer."

The adjective slipped from his mind before he was aware of it. He turned with an involuntary start and looked about him. He knew perfectly well what it meant – this thought that had thrust its head up from the instinctive region. He understood, without being able to express it fully, the meaning that betrayed itself in the choice of the adjective. For if he had ignored the existence of this conflict he would at the same time, have remained outside the arena. Whereas now he had entered the lists. Now this battle for his soul must have issue. And he knew that the spell of Nature was greater for him than all other spells in the world combined – greater than love, revelry, pleasure, greater even than study. He had always been afraid to let himself go. His pagan soul dreaded her terrific powers of witchery even while he worshipped.

The little village already slept. The world lay smothered in snow. The châlet roofs shone white beneath the moon, and pitch-black shadows gathered against the walls of the church. His eye rested a moment on the square stone tower with its frosted cross that pointed to the sky; then travelled with a leap of many thousand feet to the enormous mountains that brushed the brilliant stars. Like a forest rose the huge peaks above the slumbering village, measuring the night and heavens. They beckoned him. And something born of the snowy desolation, born of the midnight and the silent grandeur, born of the great listening hollows of the night, something that lay 'twixt terror and wonder, dropped from the vast wintry spaces down into his heart – and called him. Very softly, unrecorded in any word or thought his brain could compass, it laid its spell upon him. Fingers of snow brushed the surface of his heart. The power and quiet majesty of the winter's night appalled him....

Fumbling a moment with the big unwieldy key, he let himself in and went upstairs to bed. Two thoughts went with him – apparently quite ordinary and sensible ones:

"What fools these peasants are to sleep through such a night!" And the other:

"Those dances tire me. I'll never go again. My work only suffers in the morning." The claims of peasants and tourists upon him seemed thus in a single instant weakened.

The clash of battle troubled half his dreams. Nature had sent her Beauty of the Night and won the first assault. The others, routed and dismayed, fled far away.

## Chapter II

"**DON'T** go back to your dreary old post office. We're going to have supper in my room – something hot. Come and join us. Hurry up!"

There had been an ice carnival, and the last party, tailing up the snow-slope to the hotel, called him. The Chinese lanterns smoked and sputtered on the wires; the band had long since gone. The cold was bitter and the moon came only momentarily between high, driving clouds. From the shed where the people changed from skates to snow-boots he shouted something to the effect that he was 'following'; but no answer came; the moving shadows of those who had called were already merged high up against the village darkness. The voices died away. Doors slammed. Hibbert found himself alone on the deserted rink.

And it was then, quite suddenly, the impulse came to – stay and skate alone. The thought of the stuffy hotel room, and of those noisy people with their obvious jokes and laughter, oppressed him. He felt a longing to be alone with the night; to taste her wonder all by himself there beneath the stars, gliding over the ice. It was not yet midnight, and he could skate for half an hour. That supper party, if they noticed his absence at all, would merely think he had changed his mind and gone to bed.

It was an impulse, yes, and not an unnatural one; yet even at the time it struck him that something more than impulse lay concealed behind it. More than invitation, yet certainly less than command, there was a vague queer feeling that he stayed because he had to, almost as though there was something he had forgotten, overlooked, left undone. Imaginative temperaments are often thus; and impulse is ever weakness. For with such ill-considered opening of the doors to hasty action may come an invasion of other forces at the same time – forces merely waiting their opportunity perhaps!

He caught the fugitive warning even while he dismissed it as absurd, and the next minute he was whirling over the smooth ice in delightful curves and loops beneath the moon. There was no fear of collision. He could take his own speed and space as he willed. The shadows of the towering mountains fell across the rink, and a wind of ice came from the forests, where the snow lay ten feet deep. The hotel lights winked and went out. The village slept. The high wire netting could not keep out the wonder of the winter night that grew about him like a presence. He skated on and on, keen exhilarating pleasure in his tingling blood, and weariness all forgotten.

And then, midway in the delight of rushing movement, he saw a figure gliding behind the wire netting, watching him. With a start that almost made him lose his balance – for the abruptness of the new arrival was so unlooked for – he paused and stared. Although the light was dim he made out that it was the figure of a woman and that she was feeling her way along the netting, trying to get in. Against the white background of the snow-field he watched her rather stealthy efforts as she passed with a silent step over the banked-up snow. She was tall and slim and graceful; he could see that even in the dark. And then, of course, he understood. It was another adventurous skater like himself, stolen down unawares from hotel or châlet, and searching for the opening. At once, making a sign and pointing with one hand, he turned swiftly and skated over to the little entrance on the other side.

But, even before he got there, there was a sound on the ice behind him and, with an exclamation of amazement he could not suppress, he turned to see her swerving up to his side across the width of the rink. She had somehow found another way in.

Hibbert, as a rule, was punctilious, and in these free-and-easy places, perhaps, especially so. If only for his own protection he did not seek to make advances unless some kind of introduction paved the way. But for these two to skate together in the semi-darkness without speech, often of necessity brushing shoulders almost, was too absurd to think of. Accordingly he raised his cap and spoke. His actual words he seems unable to recall, nor what the girl said in reply, except that she answered him in accented English with some commonplace about doing figures at midnight on an empty rink. Quite natural it was, and right. She wore grey clothes of some kind, though not the customary long gloves or sweater, for indeed her hands were bare, and presently when he skated with her, he wondered with something like astonishment at their dry and icy coldness.

And she was delicious to skate with – supple, sure, and light, fast as a man yet with the freedom of a child, sinuous and steady at the same time. Her flexibility made him wonder, and when he asked where she had learned she murmured – he caught the breath against his ear and recalled later that it was singularly cold – that she could hardly tell, for she had been accustomed to the ice ever since she could remember.

But her face he never properly saw. A muffler of white fur buried her neck to the ears, and her cap came over the eyes. He only saw that she was young. Nor could he gather her hotel or châlet, for she pointed vaguely, when he asked her, up the slopes. "Just over there—" she said, quickly taking his hand again. He did not press her; no doubt she wished to hide her escapade. And the touch of her hand thrilled him more than anything he could remember; even through his thick glove he felt the softness of that cold and delicate softness.

The clouds thickened over the mountains. It grew darker. They talked very little, and did not always skate together. Often they separated, curving about in corners by themselves, but always coming together again in the centre of the rink; and when she left him thus Hibbert was conscious of – yes, of missing her. He found a peculiar satisfaction, almost a fascination, in skating by her side. It was quite an adventure – these two strangers with the ice and snow and night!

Midnight had long since sounded from the old church tower before they parted. She gave the sign, and he skated quickly to the shed, meaning to find a seat and help her take her skates off. Yet when he turned – she had already gone. He saw her slim figure gliding away across the snow… and hurrying for the last time round the rink alone he searched in vain for the opening she had twice used in this curious way.

"How very queer!" he thought, referring to the wire netting. "She must have lifted it and wriggled under…!"

Wondering how in the world she managed it, what in the world had possessed him to be so free with her, and who in the world she was, he went up the steep slope to the post office and so to bed, her promise to come again another night still ringing delightfully in his ears. And curious were the thoughts and sensations that accompanied him. Most of all, perhaps, was the half suggestion of some dim memory that he had known this girl before, had met her somewhere, more – that she knew him. For in her voice – a low, soft, windy little voice it was, tender and soothing for all its quiet coldness – there lay some faint reminder of two others he had known, both long since gone: the voice of the woman he had loved, and – the voice of his mother.

But this time through his dreams there ran no clash of battle. He was conscious, rather, of something cold and clinging that made him think of sifting snowflakes climbing slowly with entangling touch and thickness round his feet. The snow, coming without noise, each flake so light and tiny none can mark the spot whereon it settles, yet the mass of it able to smother whole villages, wove through the very texture of his mind – cold, bewildering, deadening effort with its clinging network of ten million feathery touches.

## Chapter III

**IN THE MORNING** Hibbert realised he had done, perhaps, a foolish thing. The brilliant sunshine that drenched the valley made him see this, and the sight of his work-table with its typewriter, books, papers, and the rest, brought additional conviction. To have skated with a girl alone at midnight, no matter how innocently the thing had come about, was unwise – unfair, especially to her. Gossip in these little winter resorts was worse than in a provincial town. He hoped no one had seen them. Luckily the night had been dark. Most likely none had heard the ring of skates.

Deciding that in future he would be more careful, he plunged into work, and sought to dismiss the matter from his mind.

But in his times of leisure the memory returned persistently to haunt him. When he 'ski-d', 'luged', or danced in the evenings, and especially when he skated on the little rink, he was aware that the eyes of his mind forever sought this strange companion of the night. A hundred times he fancied that he saw her, but always sight deceived him. Her face he might not know, but he could hardly fail to recognise her figure. Yet nowhere among the others did he catch a glimpse of that slim young creature he had skated with alone beneath the clouded stars. He searched in vain. Even his inquiries as to the occupants of the private châlets brought no results. He had lost her. But the queer thing was that he felt as though she were somewhere close; he *knew* she had not really gone. While people came and left with every day, it never once occurred to him that she had left. On the contrary, he felt assured that they would meet again.

This thought he never quite acknowledged. Perhaps it was the wish that fathered it only. And, even when he did meet her, it was a question how he would speak and claim acquaintance, or whether *she* would recognise himself. It might be awkward. He almost came to dread a meeting, though 'dread', of course, was far too strong a word to describe an emotion that was half delight, half wondering anticipation.

Meanwhile the season was in full swing. Hibbert felt in perfect health, worked hard, ski-d, skated, luged, and at night danced fairly often – in spite of his decision. This dancing was, however, an act of subconscious surrender; it really meant he hoped to find her among the whirling couples. He was searching for her without quite acknowledging it to himself; and the hotel-world, meanwhile, thinking it had won him over, teased and chaffed him. He made excuses in a similar vein; but all the time he watched and searched and – waited.

For several days the sky held clear and bright and frosty, bitterly cold, everything crisp and sparkling in the sun; but there was no sign of fresh snow, and the ski-ers began to grumble. On the mountains was an icy crust that made 'running' dangerous; they wanted the frozen, dry, and powdery snow that makes for speed, renders steering easier and falling less severe. But the keen east wind showed no signs of changing for a whole ten days. Then, suddenly, there came a touch of softer air and the weather-wise began to prophesy.

Hibbert, who was delicately sensitive to the least change in earth or sky, was perhaps the first to feel it. Only he did not prophesy. He knew through every nerve in his body that moisture had crept into the air, was accumulating, and that presently a fall would come. For he responded to the moods of Nature like a fine barometer.

And the knowledge, this time, brought into his heart a strange little wayward emotion that was hard to account for – a feeling of unexplained uneasiness and disquieting joy. For behind it, woven through it rather, ran a faint exhilaration that connected remotely somewhere with that touch of delicious alarm, that tiny anticipating 'dread', that so puzzled him when he thought of his next meeting with his skating companion of the night. It lay beyond all words, all telling, this queer relationship between the two; but somehow the girl and snow ran in a pair across his mind.

Perhaps for imaginative writing-men, more than for other workers, the smallest change of mood betrays itself at once. His work at any rate revealed this slight shifting of emotional values in his soul. Not that his writing suffered, but that it altered, subtly as those changes of sky or sea or landscape that come with the passing of afternoon into evening – imperceptibly. A subconscious excitement sought to push outwards and express itself... and, knowing the uneven effect such moods produced in his work, he laid his pen aside and took instead to reading that he had to do.

Meanwhile the brilliance passed from the sunshine, the sky grew slowly overcast; by dusk the mountain tops came singularly close and sharp; the distant valley rose into absurdly near perspective. The moisture increased, rapidly approaching saturation point, when it must fall in snow. Hibbert watched and waited.

And in the morning the world lay smothered beneath its fresh white carpet. It snowed heavily till noon, thickly, incessantly, chokingly, a foot or more; then the sky cleared, the sun came out in splendour, the wind shifted back to the east, and frost came down upon the mountains with its keenest and most biting tooth. The drop in the temperature was tremendous, but the ski-ers were jubilant. Next day the 'running' would be fast and perfect. Already the mass was settling, and the surface freezing into those moss-like, powdery crystals that make the ski run almost of their own accord with the faint 'sishing' as of a bird's wings through the air.

## Chapter IV

**THAT NIGHT** there was excitement in the little hotel-world, first because there was a *bal costumé*, but chiefly because the new snow had come. And Hibbert went – felt drawn to go; he did not go in costume, but he wanted to talk about the slopes and ski-ing with the other men, and at the same time....

Ah, there was the truth, the deeper necessity that called. For the singular connection between the stranger and the snow again betrayed itself, utterly beyond explanation as before, but vital and insistent. Some hidden instinct in his pagan soul – heaven knows how he phrased it even to himself, if he phrased it at all – whispered that with the snow the girl would be somewhere about, would emerge from her hiding place, would even look for him.

Absolutely unwarranted it was. He laughed while he stood before the little glass and trimmed his moustache, tried to make his black tie sit straight, and shook down his dinner jacket so that it should lie upon the shoulders without a crease. His brown eyes were very bright. "I look younger than I usually do," he thought. It was unusual, even significant, in a man who had no vanity about his appearance and certainly never questioned his age or tried to look younger than he was. Affairs of the heart, with one tumultuous exception that left no fuel for lesser subsequent fires, had never troubled him. The forces of his soul and mind not called upon for 'work' and obvious duties, all went to Nature. The desolate, wild places of the earth were what he loved; night, and the beauty of the stars and snow. And this evening he felt their claims upon him mightily stirring. A rising wildness caught his blood, quickened his pulse, woke longing and passion too. But chiefly snow. The snow whirred softly through his thoughts like white, seductive dreams…. For the snow had come; and She, it seemed, had somehow come with it – into his mind.

And yet he stood before that twisted mirror and pulled his tie and coat askew a dozen times, as though it mattered. "What in the world is up with me?" he thought. Then, laughing a little, he turned before leaving the room to put his private papers in order. The green morocco desk that held them he took down from the shelf and laid upon the table. Tied to the lid was the visiting card with his brother's London address 'in case of accident'. On the way down to the hotel he wondered why he had done this, for though imaginative, he was not the kind of man who dealt in presentiments. Moods with him were strong, but ever held in leash.

"It's almost like a warning," he thought, smiling. He drew his thick coat tightly round the throat as the freezing air bit at him. "Those warnings one reads of in stories sometimes…!"

A delicious happiness was in his blood. Over the edge of the hills across the valley rose the moon. He saw her silver sheet the world of snow. Snow covered all. It smothered sound and distance. It smothered houses, streets, and human beings. It smothered – life.

## Chapter V

**IN THE HALL** there was light and bustle; people were already arriving from the other hotels and châlets, their costumes hidden beneath many wraps. Groups of men in evening dress stood about smoking, talking 'snow' and 'ski-ing'. The band was tuning up. The claims of the hotel-world clashed about him faintly as of old. At the big glass windows of the verandah, peasants stopped a moment on their way home from the *café* to peer. Hibbert thought laughingly of that conflict he used to imagine. He laughed because it suddenly seemed so unreal. He belonged so utterly to Nature and the mountains, and especially to those desolate slopes where now the snow lay thick and fresh and sweet, that there was no question of a conflict at all. The power of the newly fallen snow had caught him, proving it without effort. Out there, upon those lonely reaches of the moonlit ridges, the snow lay ready – masses and masses of it – cool, soft, inviting. He longed for it. It awaited him. He thought of the intoxicating delight of ski-ing in the moonlight….

Thus, somehow, in vivid flashing vision, he thought of it while he stood there smoking with the other men and talking all the 'shop' of ski-ing.

And, ever mysteriously blended with this power of the snow, poured also through his inner being the power of the girl. He could not disabuse his mind of the insinuating presence of the two together. He remembered that queer skating-impulse of ten days ago, the impulse that had let her in. That any mind, even an imaginative one, could pass beneath the sway of such a fancy was strange enough; and Hibbert, while fully aware of the disorder, yet found a curious joy in yielding to it. This insubordinate centre that drew him towards old pagan beliefs had assumed command. With a kind of sensuous pleasure he let himself be conquered.

And snow that night seemed in everybody's thoughts. The dancing couples talked of it; the hotel proprietors congratulated one another; it meant good sport and satisfied their guests; everyone was planning trips and expeditions, talking of slopes and telemarks, of flying speed and distance, of drifts and crust and frost. Vitality and enthusiasm pulsed in the very air; all were alert and active, positive, radiating currents of creative life even into the stuffy atmosphere of that crowded ball-room. And the snow had caused it, the snow had brought it; all this discharge of eager sparkling energy was due primarily to the – Snow.

But in the mind of Hibbert, by some swift alchemy of his pagan yearnings, this energy became transmuted. It rarefied itself, gleaming in white and crystal currents of passionate anticipation, which he transferred, as by a species of electrical imagination, into the personality of the girl – the Girl of the Snow. She somewhere was waiting for him, expecting him, calling to him softly from those leagues of moonlit mountain. He remembered the touch of that cool, dry hand; the soft and icy breath against his cheek; the hush and softness of her presence in the way she came and the way she had gone again – like a flurry of snow the wind sent gliding up the slopes. She, like himself, belonged out there. He fancied that he heard her little windy voice come sifting to him through the snowy branches of the trees, calling his name... that haunting little voice that dived straight to the centre of his life as once, long years ago, two other voices used to do....

But nowhere among the costumed dancers did he see her slender figure. He danced with one and all, distrait and absent, a stupid partner as each girl discovered, his eyes ever turning towards the door and windows, hoping to catch the luring face, the vision that did not come... and at length, hoping even against hope. For the ball-room thinned; groups left one by one, going home to their hotels and châlets; the band tired obviously; people sat drinking lemon-squashes at the little tables, the men mopping their foreheads, everybody ready for bed.

It was close on midnight. As Hibbert passed through the hall to get his overcoat and snow-boots, he saw men in the passage by the 'sport-room', greasing their ski against an early start. Knapsack luncheons were being ordered by the kitchen swing doors. He sighed. Lighting a cigarette a friend offered him, he returned a confused reply to some question as to whether he could join their party in the morning. It seemed he did not hear it properly. He passed through the outer vestibule between the double glass doors, and went into the night.

The man who asked the question watched him go, an expression of anxiety momentarily in his eyes.

"Don't think he heard you," said another, laughing. "You've got to shout to Hibbert, his mind's so full of his work."

"He works too hard," suggested the first, "full of queer ideas and dreams."

But Hibbert's silence was not rudeness. He had not caught the invitation, that was all. The call of the hotel-world had faded. He no longer heard it. Another wilder call was sounding in his ears.

For up the street he had seen a little figure moving. Close against the shadows of the baker's shop it glided – white, slim, enticing.

## Chapter VI

**AND AT ONCE** into his mind passed the hush and softness of the snow – yet with it a searching, crying wildness for the heights. He knew by some incalculable, swift instinct she would not meet him in the village street. It was not there, amid crowding houses, she would speak to him. Indeed, already she had disappeared, melted from view up the white vista of the moonlit road. Yonder, he divined, she waited where the highway narrowed abruptly into the mountain path beyond the châlets.

It did not even occur to him to hesitate; mad though it seemed, and was – this sudden craving for the heights with her, at least for open spaces where the snow lay thick and fresh – it was too imperious to be denied. He does not remember going up to his room, putting the sweater over his evening clothes, and getting into the fur gauntlet gloves and the helmet cap of wool. Most certainly he has no recollection of fastening on his ski; he must have done it automatically. Some faculty of normal observation was in abeyance, as it were. His mind was out beyond the village – out with the snowy mountains and the moon.

Henri Défago, putting up the shutters over his *café* windows, saw him pass, and wondered mildly: "Un monsieur qui fait du ski à cette heure! Il est Anglais, donc…!" He shrugged his shoulders, as though a man had the right to choose his own way of death. And Marthe Perotti, the hunchback wife of the shoemaker, looking by chance from her window, caught his figure moving swiftly up the road. She had other thoughts, for she knew and believed the old traditions of the witches and snow-beings that steal the souls of men. She had even heard, 'twas said, the dreaded 'synagogue' pass roaring down the street at night, and now, as then, she hid her eyes. "They've called to him… and he must go," she murmured, making the sign of the cross.

But no one sought to stop him. Hibbert recalls only a single incident until he found himself beyond the houses, searching for her along the fringe of forest where the moonlight met the snow in a bewildering frieze of fantastic shadows. And the incident was simply this – that he remembered passing the church. Catching the outline of its tower against the stars, he was aware of a faint sense of hesitation. A vague uneasiness came and went – jarred unpleasantly across the flow of his excited feelings, chilling exhilaration. He caught the instant's discord, dismissed it, and – passed on. The seduction of the snow smothered the hint before he realised that it had brushed the skirts of warning.

And then he saw her. She stood there waiting in a little clear space of shining snow, dressed all in white, part of the moonlight and the glistening background, her slender figure just discernible.

"I waited, for I knew you would come," the silvery little voice of windy beauty floated down to him. "You *had* to come."

"I'm ready," he answered, "I knew it too."

The world of Nature caught him to its heart in those few words – the wonder and the glory of the night and snow. Life leaped within him. The passion of his pagan soul exulted, rose in joy, flowed out to her. He neither reflected nor considered, but let himself go like the veriest schoolboy in the wildness of first love.

"Give me your hand," he cried, "I'm coming…!"

"A little farther on, a little higher," came her delicious answer. "Here it is too near the village – and the church."

And the words seemed wholly right and natural; he did not dream of questioning them; he understood that, with this little touch of civilisation in sight, the familiarity he suggested was impossible. Once out upon the open mountains, 'mid the freedom of huge slopes and towering peaks, the stars and moon to witness and the wilderness of snow to watch, they could taste an innocence of happy intercourse free from the dead conventions that imprison literal minds.

He urged his pace, yet did not quite overtake her. The girl kept always just a little bit ahead of his best efforts…. And soon they left the trees behind and passed on to the enormous slopes of the sea of snow that rolled in mountainous terror and beauty to the stars. The wonder of the white world caught him away. Under the steady moonlight it was more than haunting. It was a living, white, bewildering power that deliciously confused the senses and laid a spell of wild perplexity upon the heart. It was a personality that cloaked, and yet revealed, itself through all this sheeted whiteness of snow. It rose, went with him, fled before, and followed after. Slowly it dropped lithe, gleaming arms about his neck, gathering him in....

Certainly some soft persuasion coaxed his very soul, urging him ever forwards, upwards, on towards the higher icy slopes. Judgment and reason left their throne, it seemed, completely, as in the madness of intoxication. The girl, slim and seductive, kept always just ahead, so that he never quite came up with her. He saw the white enchantment of her face and figure, something that streamed about her neck flying like a wreath of snow in the wind, and heard the alluring accents of her whispering voice that called from time to time: "A little farther on, a little higher.... Then we'll run home together!"

Sometimes he saw her hand stretched out to find his own, but each time, just as he came up with her, he saw her still in front, the hand and arm withdrawn. They took a gentle angle of ascent. The toil seemed nothing. In this crystal, wine-like air fatigue vanished. The sishing of the ski through the powdery surface of the snow was the only sound that broke the stillness; this, with his breathing and the rustle of her skirts, was all he heard. Cold moonshine, snow, and silence held the world. The sky was black, and the peaks beyond cut into it like frosted wedges of iron and steel. Far below the valley slept, the village long since hidden out of sight. He felt that he could never tire.... The sound of the church clock rose from time to time faintly through the air – more and more distant.

"Give me your hand. It's time now to turn back."

"Just one more slope," she laughed. "That ridge above us. Then we'll make for home." And her low voice mingled pleasantly with the purring of their ski. His own seemed harsh and ugly by comparison.

"But I have never come so high before. It's glorious! This world of silent snow and moonlight – and *you*. You're a child of the snow, I swear. Let me come up – closer – to see your face – and touch your little hand."

Her laughter answered him.

"Come on! A little higher. Here we're quite alone together."

"It's magnificent," he cried. "But why did you hide away so long? I've looked and searched for you in vain ever since we skated—" he was going to say "ten days ago," but the accurate memory of time had gone from him; he was not sure whether it was days or years or minutes. His thoughts of earth were scattered and confused.

"You looked for me in the wrong places," he heard her murmur just above him. "You looked in places where I never go. Hotels and houses kill me. I avoid them." She laughed – a fine, shrill, windy little laugh.

"I loathe them too—"

He stopped. The girl had suddenly come quite close. A breath of ice passed through his very soul. She had touched him.

"But this awful cold!" he cried out, sharply, "this freezing cold that takes me. The wind is rising; it's a wind of ice. Come, let us turn...!"

But when he plunged forward to hold her, or at least to look, the girl was gone again. And something in the way she stood there a few feet beyond, and stared down into his eyes so steadfastly in silence, made him shiver. The moonlight was behind her, but in some odd way he could not focus sight upon her face, although so close. The gleam of eyes he caught, but all the rest seemed white and snowy as though he looked beyond her – out into space....

The sound of the church bell came up faintly from the valley far below, and he counted the strokes – five. A sudden, curious weakness seized him as he listened. Deep within it was, deadly yet somehow sweet, and hard to resist. He felt like sinking down upon the snow and lying there.... They had been climbing for five hours.... It was, of course, the warning of complete exhaustion.

With a great effort he fought and overcame it. It passed away as suddenly as it came.

"We'll turn," he said with a decision he hardly felt. "It will be dawn before we reach the village again. Come at once. It's time for home."

The sense of exhilaration had utterly left him. An emotion that was akin to fear swept coldly through him. But her whispering answer turned it instantly to terror – a terror that gripped him horribly and turned him weak and unresisting.

"Our home is – *here*!" A burst of wild, high laughter, loud and shrill, accompanied the words. It was like a whistling wind. The wind *had* risen, and clouds obscured the moon. "A little higher – where we cannot hear the wicked bells," she cried, and for the first time seized him deliberately by the hand. She moved, was suddenly close against his face. Again she touched him.

And Hibbert tried to turn away in escape, and so trying, found for the first time that the power of the snow – that other power which does not exhilarate but deadens effort – was upon him. The suffocating weakness that it brings to exhausted men, luring them to the sleep of death in her clinging soft embrace, lulling the will and conquering all desire for life – this was awfully upon him. His feet were heavy and entangled. He could not turn or move.

The girl stood in front of him, very near; he felt her chilly breath upon his cheeks; her hair passed blindingly across his eyes; and that icy wind came with her. He saw her whiteness close; again, it seemed, his sight passed through her into space as though she had no face. Her arms were round his neck. She drew him softly downwards to his knees. He sank; he yielded utterly; he obeyed. Her weight was upon him, smothering, delicious. The snow was to his waist.... She kissed him softly on the lips, the eyes, all over his face. And then she spoke his name in that voice of love and wonder, the voice that held the accent of two others – both taken over long ago by Death – the voice of his mother, and of the woman he had loved.

He made one more feeble effort to resist. Then, realising even while he struggled that this soft weight about his heart was sweeter than anything life could ever bring, he let his muscles relax, and sank back into the soft oblivion of the covering snow. Her wintry kisses bore him into sleep.

## Chapter VII

They say that men who know the sleep of exhaustion in the snow find no awakening on the hither side of death.... The hours passed and the moon sank down below the white world's rim. Then, suddenly, there came a little crash upon his breast and neck, and Hibbert – woke.

He slowly turned bewildered, heavy eyes upon the desolate mountains, stared dizzily about him, tried to rise. At first his muscles would not act; a numbing, aching pain possessed him. He uttered a long, thin cry for help, and heard its faintness swallowed by the wind. And then he understood vaguely why he was only warm – not dead. For this very wind that took his cry had built up a sheltering mound of driven snow against his body while he slept. Like a curving wave it ran beside him. It was the breaking of its over-toppling edge that caused the crash, and the coldness of the mass against his neck that woke him.

Dawn kissed the eastern sky; pale gleams of gold shot every peak with splendour; but ice was in the air, and the dry and frozen snow blew like powder from the surface of the slopes. He saw the points of his ski projecting just below him. Then he – remembered. It seems he had just strength enough to realise that, could he but rise and stand, he might fly with terrific impetus towards the woods and village far beneath. The ski would carry him. But if he failed and fell…!

How he contrived it Hibbert never knew; this fear of death somehow called out his whole available reserve force. He rose slowly, balanced a moment, then, taking the angle of an immense zigzag, started down the awful slopes like an arrow from a bow. And automatically the splendid muscles of the practised ski-er and athlete saved and guided him, for he was hardly conscious of controlling either speed or direction. The snow stung face and eyes like fine steel shot; ridge after ridge flew past; the summits raced across the sky; the valley leaped up with bounds to meet him. He scarcely felt the ground beneath his feet as the huge slopes and distance melted before the lightning speed of that descent from death to life.

He took it in four mile-long zigzags, and it was the turning at each corner that nearly finished him, for then the strain of balancing taxed to the verge of collapse the remnants of his strength.

Slopes that have taken hours to climb can be descended in a short half-hour on ski, but Hibbert had lost all count of time. Quite other thoughts and feelings mastered him in that wild, swift dropping through the air that was like the flight of a bird. For ever close upon his heels came following forms and voices with the whirling snow-dust. He heard that little silvery voice of death and laughter at his back. Shrill and wild, with the whistling of the wind past his ears, he caught its pursuing tones; but in anger now, no longer soft and coaxing. And it was accompanied; she did not follow alone. It seemed a host of these flying figures of the snow chased madly just behind him. He felt them furiously smite his neck and cheeks, snatch at his hands and try to entangle his feet and ski in drifts. His eyes they blinded, and they caught his breath away.

The terror of the heights and snow and winter desolation urged him forward in the maddest race with death a human being ever knew; and so terrific was the speed that before the gold and crimson had left the summits to touch the ice-lips of the lower glaciers, he saw the friendly forest far beneath swing up and welcome him.

And it was then, moving slowly along the edge of the woods, he saw a light. A man was carrying it. A procession of human figures was passing in a dark line laboriously through the snow. And – he heard the sound of chanting.

Instinctively, without a second's hesitation, he changed his course. No longer flying at an angle as before, he pointed his ski straight down the mountain-side. The dreadful steepness did not frighten him. He knew full well it meant a crashing tumble at the bottom, but he also knew it meant a doubling of his speed – with safety at the end. For, though no definite thought passed through his mind, he understood that it was the village *curé* who carried that little gleaming lantern in the dawn, and that he was taking the Host to a châlet on the lower slopes – to some peasant *in extremis*. He remembered her terror of the church and bells. She feared the holy symbols.

There was one last wild cry in his ears as he started, a shriek of the wind before his face, and a rush of stinging snow against closed eyelids – and then he dropped through empty space. Speed took sight from him. It seemed he flew off the surface of the world.

* * *

Indistinctly he recalls the murmur of men's voices, the touch of strong arms that lifted him, and the shooting pains as the ski were unfastened from the twisted ankle... for when he opened his eyes again to normal life he found himself lying in his bed at the post office with the doctor at his side. But for years to come the story of 'mad Hibbert's' ski-ing at night is recounted in that mountain village. He went, it seems, up slopes, and to a height that no man in his senses ever tried before. The tourists were agog about it for the rest of the season, and the very same day two of the bolder men went over the actual ground and photographed the slopes. Later Hibbert saw these photographs. He noticed one curious thing about them – though he did not mention it to any one:

There was only a single track.

**If you enjoyed this, you might also like…**
H.S.H., see page 108
Ancient Sorceries, see page 246

# Ancient Lights

**FROM SOUTHWATER**, where he left the train, the road led due west. That he knew; for the rest he trusted to luck, being one of those born walkers who dislike asking the way. He had that instinct, and as a rule it served him well. "A mile or so due west along the sandy road till you come to a stile on the right; then across the fields. You'll see the red house straight before you." He glanced at the post-card's instructions once again, and once again he tried to decipher the scratched-out sentence – without success. It had been so elaborately inked over that no word was legible. Inked-out sentences in a letter were always enticing. He wondered what it was that had to be so very carefully obliterated.

The afternoon was boisterous, with a tearing, shouting wind that blew from the sea, across the Sussex weald. Massive clouds with rounded, piled-up edges, cannoned across gaping spaces of blue sky. Far away the line of Downs swept the horizon, like an arriving wave. Chanctonbury Ring rode their crest – a scudding ship, hull down before the wind. He took his hat off and walked rapidly, breathing great draughts of air with delight and exhilaration. The road was deserted; no horsemen, bicycles, or motors; not even a tradesman's cart; no single walker. But anyhow he would never have asked the way. Keeping a sharp eye for the stile, he pounded along, while the wind tossed the cloak against his face, and made waves across the blue puddles in the yellow road. The trees showed their under leaves of white. The bracken and the high new grass bent all one way. Great life was in the day, high spirits and dancing everywhere. And for a Croydon surveyor's clerk just out of an office this was like a holiday at the sea.

It was a day for high adventure, and his heart rose up to meet the mood of Nature. His umbrella with the silver ring ought to have been a sword, and his brown shoes should have been top-boots with spurs upon the heels. Where hid the enchanted Castle and the princess with the hair of sunny gold? His horse…

The stile came suddenly into view and nipped adventure in the bud. Everyday clothes took him prisoner again. He was a surveyor's clerk, middle-aged, earning three pounds a week, coming from Croydon to see about a client's proposed alterations in a wood – something to ensure a better view from the dining-room window. Across the fields, perhaps a mile away, he saw the red house gleaming in the sunshine; and resting on the stile a moment to get his breath he noticed a copse of oak and hornbeam on the right. "Aha," he told himself "so that must be the wood he wants to cut down to improve the view? I'll 'ave a look at it." There were boards up, of course, but there was an inviting little path as well. "I'm not a trespasser," he said; "it's part of my business, this is." He scrambled awkwardly over the gate and entered the copse. A little round would bring him to the field again.

But the moment he passed among the trees the wind ceased shouting and a stillness dropped upon the world. So dense was the growth that the sunshine only came through in isolated patches. The air was close. He mopped his forehead and put his green felt hat on, but a low branch knocked it off again at once, and as he stooped an elastic twig swung back and stung his face. There were flowers along both edges of the little path; glades opened on either side; ferns curved about in damper corners, and the smell of earth and foliage was rich and sweet. It was cooler here. What an enchanting little wood, he thought, turning down a small green glade where the sunshine flickered like silver wings. How it danced and fluttered and moved about! He put a dark blue flower in his buttonhole. Again his hat, caught by an oak branch as he rose, was knocked from his head, falling across his eyes. And this time he did not put it on again. Swinging his umbrella, he walked on with uncovered head, whistling rather loudly as he went. But the thickness of the trees hardly encouraged whistling, and something of his gaiety and high spirits seemed to leave him. He suddenly found himself treading circumspectly and with caution. The stillness in the wood was so peculiar.

There was a rustle among the ferns and leaves and something shot across the path ten yards ahead, stopped abruptly an instant with head cocked sideways to stare, then dived again beneath the underbrush with the speed of a shadow. He started like a frightened child, laughing the next second that a mere pheasant could have made him jump. In the distance he heard wheels upon the road, and wondered why the sound was pleasant. "Good old butcher's cart," he said to himself – then realised that he was going in the wrong direction and had somehow got turned round. For the road should be behind him, not in front.

And he hurriedly took another narrow glade that lost itself in greenness to the right. "That's my direction, of course," he said; "the trees has mixed me up a bit, it seems" – then found himself abruptly by the gate he had first climbed over. He had merely made a circle. Surprise became almost discomfiture then. And a man, dressed like a gamekeeper in browny green, leaned against the gate, hitting his legs with a switch. "I'm making for Mr. Lumley's farm," explained the walker. "This *is* his wood, I believe—" then stopped dead, because it was no man at all, but merely an effect of light and shade and foliage. He stepped back to reconstruct the singular illusion, but the wind shook the branches roughly here on the edge of the wood and the foliage refused to reconstruct the figure. The leaves all rustled strangely. And just then the sun went behind a cloud, making the whole wood look otherwise. Yet how the mind could be thus doubly deceived was indeed remarkable, for it almost seemed to him the man had answered, spoken – or was this the shuffling noise the branches made? – and had pointed with his switch to the notice-board upon the nearest tree. The words rang on in his head, but of course he had imagined them: "No, it's not his wood. It's ours." And some village wit, moreover, had changed the lettering on the weather-beaten board, for it read quite plainly, "Trespassers will be persecuted."

And while the astonished clerk read the words and chuckled, he said to himself, thinking what a tale he'd have to tell his wife and children later – "The blooming wood has tried to chuck me out. But I'll go in again. Why, it's only a matter of a square acre at most. I'm bound to reach the fields on the other side if I keep straight on." He remembered his position in the office. He had a certain dignity to maintain.

The cloud passed from below the sun, and light splashed suddenly in all manner of unlikely places. The man went straight on. He felt a touch of puzzling confusion somewhere; this way the copse had of shifting from sunshine into shadow doubtless troubled sight a little. To his relief at last, a new glade opened through the trees and disclosed the fields with a glimpse of the red house in the distance at the far end. But a little wicket gate that stood across the path had first to be climbed, and as he scrambled heavily over – for it would not open – he got the astonishing feeling that it slid off sideways beneath his weight, and towards the wood. Like the moving staircases at Harrod's and Earl's Court, it began to glide off with him. It was quite horrible. He made a violent effort to get down before it carried him into the trees, but his feet became entangled with the bars and umbrella, so that he fell heavily upon the farther side, arms spread across the grass and nettles, boots clutched between the first and second bars. He lay there a moment like a man crucified upside down, and while he struggled to get disentangled – feet, bars, and umbrella formed a regular net – he saw the little man in browny green go past him with extreme rapidity through the wood. The man was laughing. He passed across the glade some fifty yards away, and he was not alone this time. A companion like himself went with him. The clerk, now upon his feet again, watched them disappear into the gloom of green beyond. "They're tramps, not gamekeepers," he said to himself, half mortified, half angry. But his heart was thumping dreadfully, and he dared not utter all his thought.

He examined the wicket gate, convinced it was a trick gate somehow – then went hurriedly on again, disturbed beyond belief to see that the glade no longer opened into fields, but curved away to the right. What in the world had happened to him? His sight was so utterly at fault. Again the sun flamed out abruptly and lit the floor of the wood with pools of silver, and at the same moment a violent gust of wind passed shouting overhead. Drops fell clattering everywhere upon the leaves, making a sharp pattering as of many footsteps. The whole copse shuddered and went moving.

"Rain, by George," thought the clerk, and feeling for his umbrella, discovered he had lost it. He turned back to the gate and found it lying on the farther side. To his amazement he saw the fields at the far end of the glade, the red house, too, ashine in the sunset. He laughed then, for, of course, in his struggle with the gate, he had somehow got turned round – had fallen back instead of forwards. Climbing over, this time quite easily, he retraced his steps. The silver band, he saw, had been torn from the umbrella. No doubt his foot, a nail, or something had caught in it and ripped it off. The clerk began to run; he felt extraordinarily dismayed.

But, while he ran, the entire wood ran with him, round him, to and fro, trees shifting like living things, leaves folding and unfolding, trunks darting backwards and forwards, and branches disclosing enormous empty spaces, then closing up again before he could look into them. There were footsteps everywhere, and laughing, crying voices, and crowds of figures gathering just behind his back till the glade, he knew, was thick with moving life. The wind in his ears, of course, produced the voices and the laughter, while sun and clouds, plunging the copse alternately in shadow and bright dazzling light, created the figures. But he did not like it, and went as fast as ever his sturdy legs could take him. He was frightened now. This was no story for his wife and children. He ran like the wind. But his feet made no sound upon the soft mossy turf.

Then, to his horror, he saw that the glade grew narrow, nettles and weeds stood thick across it, it dwindled down into a tiny path, and twenty yards ahead it stopped finally and melted off among the trees. What the trick gate had failed to achieve, this twisting glade accomplished easily – carried him in bodily among the dense and crowding trees.

There was only one thing to do – turn sharply and dash back again, run headlong into the life that followed at his back, followed so closely too that now it almost touched him, pushing him in. And with reckless courage this was what he did. It seemed a fearful thing to do. He turned with a sort of violent spring, head down and shoulders forward, hands stretched before his face. He made the plunge; like a hunted creature he charged full tilt the other way, meeting the wind now in his face.

Good Lord! The glade behind him had closed up as well; there was no longer any path at all. Turning round and round, like an animal at bay, he searched for an opening, a way of escape, searched frantically, breathlessly, terrified now in his bones. But foliage surrounded him, branches blocked the way; the trees stood close and still, unshaken by a breath of wind; and the sun dipped that moment behind a great black cloud. The entire wood turned dark and silent. It watched him.

Perhaps it was this final touch of sudden blackness that made him act so foolishly, as though he had really lost his head. At any rate, without pausing to think, he dashed headlong in among the trees again. There was a sensation of being stiflingly surrounded and entangled, and that he *must* break out at all costs – out and away into the open of the blessed fields and air. He did this ill-considered thing, and apparently charged straight into an oak that deliberately moved into his path to stop him. He saw it shift across a good full yard, and being a measuring man, accustomed to theodolite and chain, he ought to know. He fell, saw stars, and felt a thousand tiny fingers tugging and pulling at his hands and neck and ankles. The stinging nettles, no doubt, were responsible for this. He thought of it later. At the moment it felt diabolically calculated.

But another remarkable illusion was not so easily explained. For all in a moment, it seemed, the entire wood went sliding past him with a thick deep rustling of leaves and laughter, myriad footsteps, and tiny little active, energetic shapes; two men in browny green gave him a mighty hoist – and he opened his eyes to find himself lying in the meadow beside the stile where first his incredible adventure had begun. The wood stood in its usual place and stared down upon him in the sunlight. There was the red house in the distance as before. Above him grinned the weather-beaten notice-board: "Trespassers will be prosecuted."

Dishevelled in mind and body, and a good deal shaken in his official soul, the clerk walked slowly across the fields. But on the way he glanced once more at the postcard of instructions, and saw with dull amazement that the inked-out sentence was quite legible after all beneath the scratches made across it: "There *is* a short cut through the wood – the wood I want cut down – if you care to take it." Only 'care' was so badly written, it looked more like another word; the 'c' was uncommonly like 'd'.

"That's the copse that spoils my view of the Downs, you see," his client explained to him later, pointing across the fields, and referring to the ordnance map beside him. "I want it cut down and a path made so and so." His finger indicated direction on the map. "The Fairy Wood – it's still called, and it's far older than this house. Come now, if you're ready, Mr. Thomas, we might go out and have a look at it…"

**If you enjoyed this, you might also like…**
May Day Eve, see page 118
The Other Wing, see page 319

# Special Delivery

MEIKLEJOHN, the curate, was walking through the Jura when this thing happened to him. There is only his word to vouch for it, for the inn and its proprietor are now both of the past, and the local record of the occurrence has long since assumed the proportions of a picturesque but inaccurate legend. As a true story, however, it stands out from those of its kidney by the fact that there seems to have been a deliberate intention in it. It saved a life – a life the world had need of. And this singular rescue of a man of value to the best order of things makes one feel that there was some sense, even logic, in the affair.

Moreover, Meiklejohn asserts that it was the only psychic experience he ever knew. Things of the sort were not a 'habit' with him. His rescue, thus, was not one of those meaningless interventions that puzzle the man in the street while they exhilarate the psychologist. It was a deliberate and very determined affair.

Meiklejohn found himself that hot August night in one of the valleys that slip like blue shadows hidden among pine-woods between the Swiss frontier and France. He had passed Ste. Croix earlier in the day; Les Rasses had been left behind about four o'clock; Buttes, and the Val de Travers, where the cement of many a London street comes from, was his goal. But the light failed long before he reached it, and he stopped at an inn that appeared unexpectedly round a corner of the dusty road, built literally against the great cliffs that formed one wall of the valley. He was so footsore, and his knapsack so heavy, that he turned in without more ado.

Le Guillaume Tell was the name of the inn – dirty white walls, with thin, almost mangy vines scrambling over the door, and the stream brawling beneath shuttered windows with green and white stripes all patched by sun and rain. His room was seven-pence, his dinner of soup, omelette, fruit, cheese, and coffee, a franc. The prices suited his pocket and made him feel comfortable and at home. Immediately behind the hotel – the only house visible, except the sawmill across the road, rose the ever-crumbling ridges and precipices that formed the flanks of Chasseront and ran on past La Sagne towards the grey Aiguilles de Baulmes. He was in the Jura fastnesses where tourists rarely penetrate.

Through the low doorway of the inn he carried with him the strong atmosphere of thoughts that had accompanied him all day – dreams of how he intended to spend his life, plans of sacrifice and effort. For his hopes of great achievement, even then at twenty-five, were a veritable passion in him, and his desire to spend himself for humanity a devouring flame. So occupied, indeed, was his mind with the emotions belonging to this line of thinking, that he hardly noticed the singular, though exceedingly faint, sense of alarm that stirred somewhere in the depths of his being as he passed within that doorway where the drooping vine-leaves clutched at his hat. He remembered it a little later. The sense of danger had been touched in him. He felt at the moment only a hint of discomfort, too vague to claim definite recognition. Yet it was there – the instant he stepped within the threshold – and afterwards he distinctly recalled its sudden and unaccountable advent.

His bedroom, though stuffy, as from windows long unopened, was clean; carpetless, of course, and primitive, with white pine floor and walls, and the short bed, smothered under its duvet, very creaky. And very short! For Meiklejohn was well over six feet.

"I shall have to curl up, as usual, in a knot," was his reflection as he measured the bed with his eye; "though tonight I think – after my twenty miles in this air—"

The thought refused to complete itself. He was going to add that he was tired enough to have slept on a stone floor, but for some undefined reason the same sense of alarm that had tapped him on the shoulder as he entered the inn returned now when he contemplated the bed. A sharp repugnance for that bed, as sudden and unaccountable as it was curious, swept into him – and was gone again before he had time to seize it wholly. It was in reality so slight that he dismissed it immediately as the merest fancy; yet, at the same time, he was aware that he would rather have slept on another bed, had there been one in the room – and then the queer feeling that, after all, perhaps, he would not sleep there in the end at all. How this idea came to him he never knew. He records it, however, as part of the occurrence.

After eight o'clock a few peasants, and workmen from the sawmill, came in to drink their demi-litre of red wine in the common room downstairs, to stare at the unexpected guest, and to smoke their vile tobacco. They were neither picturesque nor amusing – simply dirty and slightly malodorous. At nine o'clock Meiklejohn knocked the ashes from his briar pipe upon the limestone window-ledge, and went upstairs, overpowered with sleep. The sense of alarm had utterly disappeared; his mind was busy once more with his great dreams of the future – dreams that materialised themselves, as all the world knows, in the famous Meiklejohn Institutes…

Berthoud, the proprietor, short and sturdy, with his faded brown coat and no collar, slightly confused with red wine and a 'tourist' guest, showed him the way up. For, of course, there was no *femme de chambre*.

"You have the corridor all to yourself," the man said; showed him the best corner of the landing to shout from in case he wanted anything – there being no bell – eyed his boots, knapsack, and flask with considerable curiosity, wished him good night, and was gone. He went downstairs with a noise like a horse, thought the curate, as he locked the door after him.

The windows had been open now for a couple of hours, and the room smelt sweet with the odours of sawn wood and shavings, the resinous perfume of the surrounding hosts of pines, and the sharp, delicate touch of a lonely mountain valley where civilisation has not yet tainted the air. Whiffs of coarse tobacco, pungent without being offensive, came invisibly through the cracks of the floor. Primitive and simple it all was – a sort of vigorous 'backwoods' atmosphere. Yet, once again, as he turned to examine the room after Berthoud's steps had blundered down below into the passage, something rose faintly within him to set his nerves mysteriously a-quiver.

Out of these perfectly simple conditions, without the least apparent cause, the odd feeling again came over him that he was – in danger.

The curate was not much given to analysis. He was a man of action pure and simple, as a rule. But tonight, in spite of himself, his thoughts went plunging, searching, asking. For this singular message of dread that emanated as it were from the room, or from some article of furniture in the room perhaps – that bed still touched his mind with a peculiar repugnance – demanded somewhat insistently for an explanation. And the only explanation that suggested itself to his unimaginative mind was that the forces of nature hereabouts were – overpowering; that, after the slum streets and factory chimneys of the last twelve months, these towering cliffs and smothering pine-forests communicated to his soul a word of grandeur that amounted to awe. Inadequate and farfetched as the explanation seems, it was the only one that occurred to him; and its value in this remarkable adventure lies in the fact that he connected his sense of danger partly with the bed and partly with the mountains.

"I felt once or twice," he said afterwards, "as though some powerful agency of a spiritual kind were all the time trying to beat into my stupid brain a message of warning." And this way of expressing it is more true and graphic than many paragraphs of attempted analysis.

Meiklejohn hung his clothes by the open window to air, washed, read his Bible, looked several times over his shoulder without apparent cause, and then knelt down to pray. He was a simple and devout soul; his Self lost in the yearning, young but sincere, to live for humanity. He prayed, as usual, with intense earnestness that his life might be preserved for use in the world, when in the middle of his prayer – there came a knocking at the door.

Hastily rising from his knees, he opened. The sound of rushing water filled the corridor. He heard the voices of the workmen below in the drinking-room. But only darkness stood in the passages, filling the house to the very brim. No one was there. He returned to his interrupted devotions.

"I imagined it," he said to himself. He continued his prayers, however, longer than usual. At the back of his thoughts, dim, vague, half-defined only, lay this lurking sense of uneasiness – that he was in danger. He prayed earnestly and simply, as a child might pray, for the preservation of his life...

Again, just as he prepared to get into bed, struggling to make the heaped-up duvet spread all over, came that knocking at the bedroom door. It was soft, wonderfully soft, and something within him thrilled curiously in response. He crossed the floor to open – then hesitated. Suddenly he understood that that knocking at the door was connected with the sense of danger in his heart. In the region of subtle intuitions the two were linked. With this realisation there came over him, he declares, a singular mood in which, as in a revelation, he knew that Nature held forces that might somehow communicate directly and positively with – human beings. This thought rushed upon him out of the night, as it were. It arrested his movements. He stood there upon the bare pine boards, hesitating to open the door.

The delay thus described lasted actually only a few seconds, but in those few seconds these thoughts tore rapidly and like fire through his mind. The beauty of this lost and mysterious valley was certainly in his veins. He felt the strange presence of the encircling forests, soft and splendid, their million branches sighing in the night airs. The crying of the falling water touched him. He longed to transfer their peace and power to the hearts of suffering thousands of men and women and children. The towering precipices that literally dropped their pale walls over the roof of the inn lifted his thoughts to their own windswept heights; he longed to convey their message of inflexible strength to the weak-kneed folk in the slums where he worked. He was peculiarly conscious of the presence of these forces of Nature – the irresistible powers that regenerate as easily as they destroy.

All this, and far more, swept his soul like a huge wind as he stood there, waiting to open the door in answer to that mysterious soft knocking.

And there, when at length he opened, stood the figure of a man – staring at him and smiling.

Disappointment seized him instantly. He had expected, almost believed, that he would see something un-ordinary; and instead, there stood a man who had merely mistaken the door of his room, and was now bowing his apology for the interruption. Then, to his amazement, he saw that the man beckoned: the figure was someone who sought to draw him out.

"Come with me," it seemed to say.

But Meiklejohn only realised this afterwards, he says, when it was too late and he had already shut the door in the stranger's face. For the man had withdrawn into the darkness a little, and the curate had taken the movement for a mere acknowledgment of his mistake instead of – as he afterwards felt – a sign that he should follow.

"And the moment the door was shut," he says, "I felt that it would have been better for me to have gone out into the passage to see what he wanted. It came over me that the man had something important to say to me. I had missed it."

For some seconds, it seemed, he resisted the inclination to go after him. He argued with himself; then turned to his bed, pulled back the sheets and heavy duvet, and was met sharply again with the sense of repugnance, almost of fear, as before. It leaped out upon him – as though the drawing back of the blankets had set free some cold blast of wind that struck him across the face and made him shiver.

At the same moment a shadow fell from behind his shoulder and dropped across the pillow and upper half of the bed. It may, of course, have been the magnified shadow of the moth that buzzed about the pale-yellow electric light in the ceiling. He does not pretend to know. It passed swiftly, however, and was gone; and Meiklejohn, feeling less sure of himself than ever before in his life, crossed the floor quickly, almost running, and opened the door to go after the man who had knocked – twice. For in reality less than half a minute had passed since the shutting of the door and its reopening.

But the corridor was empty. He marched down the pine-board floor for some considerable distance. Below he saw the glimmer of the hall, and heard the voices of the peasants and workmen from the sawmill as they still talked and drank their red wine in the public room. That sound of falling water, as before, filled the air. Darkness reigned. But the person – the *messenger* – who had twice knocked at his door was gone utterly... Presently a door opened downstairs, and the peasants clattered out noisily. He turned and went back to bed. The electric light was switched off below. Silence fell. Conquering his strange repugnance, Meiklejohn, with a prayer on his lips, got into bed, and in less than ten minutes was sound asleep.

"I admit," he says, in telling the story, "that what happened afterwards came so swiftly and so confusingly, yet with such a storm of overwhelming conviction of its reality, that its sequence may be somewhat blurred in my memory, while, at the same time, I see it after all these years as though it was a thing of yesterday. But in my sleep, first of all, I again heard that soft, mysterious tapping – not in the course of a dream of any sort, but sudden and alone out of the dark blank of forgetfulness. I tried to wake. At first, however, the bonds of unconsciousness held me tight. I had to struggle in order to return to the waking world. There was a distinct effort before I opened my eyes; and in that slight interval I became aware that the person who had knocked at the door had meanwhile opened it and passed into the room. I had left the lock unturned. The person was close beside me in the darkness – not in utter darkness, however, for a rising three-quarter moon shed its faint silver upon the floor in patches, and, as I sprang swiftly from the bed, I noticed something alive moving towards me across the carpetless boards. Upon the edges of a patch of moonlight, where the fringe of silver and shadow mingled, it stopped. Three feet away from it I, too, stopped, shaking in every muscle. It lay there crouching at my very feet, staring up at me. But was it man or was it animal? For at first I took it certainly for a human being on all fours; but the next moment, with a spasm of genuine terror that half stopped my breath, it was borne in upon me that the creature was – nothing human. Only in this way can I describe it. It was identical with the human figure who had knocked before and beckoned to me to follow, but it was another presentation of that figure.

"And it held (or brought, if you will) some tremendous message for me – some message of tremendous importance, I mean. The first time I had argued, resisted, refused to listen. Now it had returned in a form that ensured obedience. Some quite terrific power emanated from it – a power that I understood instinctively belonged to the mountains and the forests and the untamed elemental forces of Nature. Amazing as it may sound in cold blood, I can only say that I felt as though the towering precipices outside had sent me a direct warning – that my life was in immediate danger.

"For a space that seemed minutes, but was probably less than a few seconds, I stood there trembling on the bare boards, my eyes riveted upon the dark, uncouth shape that covered all the floor beyond. I saw no limbs or features, no suggestion of outline that I could connect with any living form I know, animate or inanimate. Yet it moved and stirred all the time – *whirled within itself*, describes it best; and into my mind sprang a picture of an immense dark wheel, turning, spinning, whizzing so rapidly that it appears motionless, and uttering that low and ominous thunder that fills a great machinery-room of a factory. Then I thought of Ezekiel's vision of the Living Wheels...

"And it must have been at this instant, I think, that the muttering and deep note that issued from it formed itself into words within me. At any rate, I heard a voice that spoke with unmistakable intelligence:

"Come!" it said. "Come out – at once!" And the sense of power that accompanied the Voice was so splendid that my fear vanished and I obeyed instantly without thinking more. I followed; it led. It altered in shape. The door was *open*. It ran silently in a form that was more like a stream of deep black water than anything else I can think of – out of the room, down the stairs, across the hall, and up to the deep shadows that lay against the door leading into the road. There I lost sight of it."

Meiklejohn's only desire, he says, then was to rush after it – to escape. This he did. He understood that somehow it had passed through the door into the open air. Ten seconds later, perhaps even less, he, too, was in the open air. He acted almost automatically; reason, reflection, logic all swept away. Nowhere, however, in the soft moonlight about him was any sign of the extraordinary apparition that had succeeded in drawing him out of the inn, out of his bedroom, out of his – bed. He stared in a dazed way at everything – just beginning to get control of his faculties a bit – wondering what in the world it all meant. That huge spinning form, he felt convinced, lay hidden somewhere close beside him, waiting for the end. The danger it had enabled him to avoid was close at hand... He knew that, he says...

There lay the meadows, touched here and there with wisps of floating mist; the stream roared and tumbled down its rocky bed to his left; across the road the sawmill lifted its skeleton-like outline, moonlight shining on the dew-covered shingles of the roof, its lower part hidden in shadow. The cold air of the valley was exquisitely scented.

To the right, where his eye next wandered, he saw the thick black woods rising round the base of the precipices that soared into the sky, sheeted with silvery moonlight. His gaze ran up them to the far ridges that seemed to push the very stars farther into the heavens. Then, as he saw those stars crowding the night, he staggered suddenly backwards, seizing the wall of the road for support, and catching his breath. For the top of the cliff, he fancied, moved. A group of stars was for a fraction of a second – hidden. The earth – the scenery of the valley, at least – turned about him. Something prodigious was happening to the solid structure of the world. The precipices seemed to bend over upon the valley. The far, uppermost ridge of those beetling cliffs shifted downwards. Meiklejohn declares that the way its movement hid momentarily a group of stars was the most startling – for some reason horrible – thing he had ever witnessed.

Then came the roar and crash and thunder as the mass toppled, slid, and finally – took the frightful plunge. How long the forces of rain and frost had been chiselling out the slow detachment of the giant slabs that fell, or whence came the particular extra little push that drove the entire mass out from the parent rock, no one can know. Only one thing is certain: that it was due to no chance, but to the nicely and exactly calculated results of balanced cause and effect. From the beginning of time it had been known – it might have been accurately calculated, rather – that this particular thousand tons of rock would break away from the crumbling tops of the precipices and crash downwards with the roar of many tempests into the lost and mysterious mountain valley where Meiklejohn the curate spent such and such a night of such and such a holiday. It was just as sure as the return of Halley's comet.

"I watched it," he says, "because I couldn't do anything else. I would far rather have run – I was so frightfully close to it all – but I couldn't move a muscle. And in a few seconds it was over. A terrific wind knocked me backwards against the stone wall; there was a vast clattering of smaller stones, set rolling down the neighbouring couloirs; a steady roll of echoes ran thundering up and down the valley; and then all was still again exactly as it had been before. And the curious thing was – ascertained a little later, as you may imagine, and not at once – that the inn, being so closely built up against the cliffs, had almost entirely escaped. The great mass of rock and trees had taken a leap farther out, and filled the meadows, blocked the road, crushed the sawmill like a matchbox, and dammed up the stream; but the inn itself was almost untouched.

"*Almost* – for a single block of limestone, about the size of a grand piano, had dropped straight upon one corner of the roof and smashed its way through my bedroom, carrying everything it contained down to the level of the cellar, so terrific was the momentum of its crushing journey. Not a stick of the furniture was afterwards discoverable – as such. The bed seems to have been caught by the very middle of the fallen mass."

The confusion in Meiklejohn's mind may be imagined – the rush of feeling and emotion that swept over him. Berthoud and the peasants mustered in less than a dozen minutes, talking, crying, praying. Then the stream, dammed up by the accumulation of rock, carried off the debris of the broken roof and walls in less than half an hour. The rock, however, that swept the room and the *empty* bed of Meiklejohn the curate into dust, still lies in the valley where it fell.

"The only other thing that I remember," he says, in telling the story, "is that, as I stood there, shaking with excitement and the painful terror of it all, before Berthoud and the peasants had come to count over their number and learn that no one was missing – while

I stood there, leaning against the wall of the road, something rose out of the white dust at my feet, and, with a noise like the whirring of some immense projectile, passed swiftly and invisibly away up into space – so far as I could judge, towards the distant ridges that reared their motionless outline in moonlight beneath the stars."

**If you enjoyed this, you might also like...**
Keeping His Promise, see page 361
The Occupant of the Room, see page 408

# By Water

**THE NIGHT** before young Larsen left to take up his new appointment in Egypt he went to the clairvoyante. He neither believed nor disbelieved. He felt no interest, for he already knew his past and did not wish to know his future. "Just to please me, Jim," the girl pleaded. "The woman is wonderful. Before I had been five minutes with her she told me your initials, so there *must* be something in it." "She read your thought," he smiled indulgently. "Even I can do that!" But the girl was in earnest. He yielded; and that night at his farewell dinner he came to give his report of the interview.

The result was meagre and unconvincing: money was coming to him, he was soon to make a voyage, and – he would never marry. "So you see how silly it all is," he laughed, for they were to be married when his first promotion came. He gave the details, however, making a little story of it in the way he knew she loved.

"But was that all, Jim?" The girl asked it, looking rather hard into his face. "Aren't you hiding something from me?" He hesitated a moment, then burst out laughing at her clever discernment. "There *was* a little more," he confessed, "but you take it all so seriously; I—"

He had to tell it then, of course. The woman had told him a lot of gibberish about friendly and unfriendly elements. "She said water was unfriendly to me; I was to be careful of water, or else I should come to harm by it. *Fresh* water only," he hastened to add, seeing that the idea of shipwreck was in her mind.

"Drowning?" the girl asked quickly.

"Yes," he admitted with reluctance, but still laughing; "she did say drowning, though drowning in no ordinary way."

The girl's face showed uneasiness a moment. "What does that mean – drowning in no ordinary way?" she asked, a catch in her breath.

But that he could not tell her, because he did not know himself. He gave, therefore, the exact words: "You will drown, but will not know you drown."

It was unwise of him. He wished afterwards he had invented a happier report, or had kept this detail back. "I'm safe in Egypt, anyhow," he laughed. "I shall be a clever man if I can find enough water in the desert to do me harm!" And all the way from Trieste to Alexandria he remembered the promise she had extracted – that he would never once go on the Nile unless duty made it imperative for him to do so. He kept that promise like the literal, faithful soul he was. His love was equal to the somewhat quixotic sacrifice it occasionally involved. Fresh water in Egypt there was practically none other, and in any case the natrum works where his duty lay had their headquarters some distance out into the desert. The river, with its banks of welcome, refreshing verdure, was not even visible.

Months passed quickly, and the time for leave came within measurable distance. In the long interval luck had played the cards kindly for him, vacancies had occurred, early promotion seemed likely, and his letters were full of plans to bring her out to share a little house of their own. His health, however, had not improved; the dryness did not suit him; even in this short period his blood had thinned, his nervous system deteriorated, and, contrary to the doctor's prophecy, the waterless air had told upon his sleep. A damp climate liked him best, and once the sun had touched him with its fiery finger.

His letters made no mention of this. He described the life to her, the work, the sport, the pleasant people, and his chances of increased pay and early marriage. And a week before he sailed he rode out upon a final act of duty to inspect the latest diggings his company were making. His course lay some twenty miles into the desert behind El-Chobak and towards the limestone hills of Guebel Haidi, and he went alone, carrying lunch and tea, for it was the weekly holiday of Friday, and the men were not at work.

The accident was ordinary enough. On his way back in the heat of early afternoon his pony stumbled against a boulder on the treacherous desert film, threw him heavily, broke the girth, bolted before he could seize the reins again, and left him stranded some ten or twelve miles from home. There was a pain in his knee that made walking difficult, a buzzing in his head that troubled sight and made the landscape swim, while, worse than either, his provisions, fastened to the saddle, had vanished with the frightened pony into those blazing leagues of sand. He was alone in the Desert, beneath the pitiless afternoon sun, twelve miles of utterly exhausting country between him and safety.

Under normal conditions he could have covered the distance in four hours, reaching home by dark; but his knee pained him so that a mile an hour proved the best he could possibly do. He reflected a few minutes. The wisest course was to sit down and wait till the pony told its obvious story to the stable, and help should come. And this was what he did, for the scorching heat and glare were dangerous; they were terrible; he was shaken and bewildered by his fall, hungry and weak into the bargain; and an hour's painful scrambling over the baked and burning little gorges must have speedily caused complete prostration. He sat down and rubbed his aching knee. It was quite a little adventure. Yet, though he knew the Desert might not be lightly trifled with, he felt at the moment nothing more than this – and the amusing description of it he would give in his letter, or – intoxicating thought – by word of mouth. In the heat of the sun he began to feel drowsy. A soft torpor crept over him. He dozed. He fell asleep.

It was a long, a dreamless sleep… for when he woke at length the sun had just gone down, the dusk lay awfully upon the enormous desert, and the air was chilly. The cold had waked him. Quickly, as though on purpose, the red glow faded from the sky; the first stars shone; it was dark; the heavens were deep violet. He looked round and realised that his sense of direction had gone entirely. Great hunger was in him. The cold already was bitter as the wind rose, but the pain in his knee having eased, he got up and walked a little – and in a moment lost sight of the spot where he had been lying. The shadowy desert swallowed it. "Ah," he realised, "this is not an English field or moor. I'm in the Desert!" The safe thing to do was to remain exactly where he was; only thus could the rescuers find him; once he wandered he was done for. It was strange the search-party had not yet arrived. To keep warm, however, he was compelled to move, so he made a little pile of stones to mark the place, and walked round and round it in a circle of some dozen yards' diameter. He limped badly, and the hunger gnawed dreadfully; but, after all, the adventure was not so terrible. The amusing side of it kept uppermost still. Though fragile in body, his spirit was not unduly timid or imaginative; he *could* last out the night, or, if the worst came to the worst, the next day as well. But when he watched the little group of stones, he saw that there were dozens of them, scores, hundreds, thousands of these little groups of stones. The desert's face, of course, is thickly strewn with them. The original one was lost in the first five minutes. So he sat down again. But the biting cold, and the wind that licked his very skin beneath the light clothing, soon forced him up again. It was ominous; and the night huge and shelterless. The shaft of green zodiacal light that hung so strangely in the western sky for hours had faded away; the stars were out in their bright thousands; no guide was anywhere; the wind moaned and puffed among the sandy mounds; the vast sheet of desert stretched appallingly upon the world; he heard the jackals cry…

And with the jackals' cry came suddenly the unwelcome realisation that no play was in this adventure any more, but that a bleak reality stared at him through the surrounding darkness. He faced it – at bay. He was genuinely lost. Thought blocked in him. "I must be calm and think," he said aloud. His voice woke no echo; it was small and dead; something gigantic ate it instantly. He got up and walked again. Why did no one come? Hours had passed. The pony had long ago found its stable, or – had it run madly in another direction altogether? He worked out possibilities, tightening his belt. The cold was searching; he never had been, never could be warm again; the hot sunshine of a few hours ago seemed the merest dream. Unfamiliar with hardship, he knew not what to do, but he took his coat and shirt off, vigorously rubbed his skin where the dried perspiration of the afternoon still caused clammy shivers, swung his arms furiously like a London cabman, and quickly dressed again. Though the wind upon his bare back was fearful, he felt warmer a little. He lay down exhausted, sheltered by an overhanging limestone crag, and took snatches of fitful dog's-sleep, while the wind drove overhead and the dry sand pricked his skin. One face continually was near him; one pair of tender eyes; two dear hands smoothed him; he smelt the perfume of light brown hair. It was all natural enough. His whole thought, in his misery, ran to her in England – England where there were soft fresh grass, big sheltering trees, hemlock and honeysuckle in the hedges – while the hard black Desert guarded him, and consciousness dipped away at little intervals under this dry and pitiless Egyptian sky…

It was perhaps five in the morning when a voice spoke and he started up with a horrid jerk – the voice of that clairvoyante woman. The sentence died away into the darkness, but one word remained: *Water!* At first he wondered, but at once explanation came. Cause and effect were obvious. The clue was physical. His body needed water, and so the thought came up into his mind. He was thirsty.

This was the moment when fear first really touched him. Hunger was manageable, more or less – for a day or two, certainly. But thirst! Thirst and the Desert were an evil pair that, by cumulative suggestion gathering since childhood days, brought terror in. Once in the mind it could not be dislodged. In spite of his best efforts, the ghastly thing grew passionately – because his thirst grew too. He had smoked much; had eaten spiced things at lunch; had breathed in alkali with the dry, scorched air. He searched for a cool flint pebble to put into his burning mouth, but found only angular scraps of dusty limestone. There were no pebbles here. The cold helped a little to counteract, but already he knew in himself subconsciously the dread of something that was coming. What was it? He tried to hide the thought and bury it out of sight. The utter futility of his tiny strength against the power of the universe appalled him. And then he knew. The merciless sun was on the way, already rising. Its return was like the presage of execution to him…

It came. With true horror he watched the marvellous swift dawn break over the sandy sea. The eastern sky glowed hurriedly as from crimson fires. Ridges, not noticeable in the starlight, turned black in endless series, like flat-topped billows of a frozen ocean. Wide streaks of blue and yellow followed, as the sky dropped sheets of faint light upon the wind-eaten cliffs and showed their under sides. They did not advance; they waited till the sun was up – and then they moved; they rose and sank; they shifted as the sunshine lifted them and the shadows crept away. But in an hour there would be no shadows any more. There would be no shade...!

The little groups of stones began to dance. It was horrible. The unbroken, huge expanse lay round him, warming up, twelve hours of blazing hell to come. Already the monstrous Desert glared, each bit familiar, since each bit was a repetition of the bit before, behind, on either side. It laughed at guidance and direction. He rose and walked; for miles he walked, though how many, north, south, or west, he knew not. The frantic thing was in him now, the fury of the Desert; he took its pace, its endless, tireless stride, the stride of the burning, murderous Desert that is – waterless. He felt it alive – a blindly heaving desire in it to reduce him to its conditionless, awful dryness. He felt – yet knowing this was feverish and *not* to be believed – that his own small life lay on its mighty surface, a mere dot in space, a mere heap of little stones. His emotions, his fears, his hopes, his ambition, his love – mere bundled group of little unimportant stones that danced with apparent activity for a moment, then were merged in the undifferentiated surface underneath. He was included in a purpose greater than his own.

The will made a plucky effort then. "A night and a day," he laughed, while his lips cracked smartly with the stretching of the skin, "what is it? Many a chap has lasted days and days...!" Yes, only he was not of that rare company. He was ordinary, unaccustomed to privation, weak, untrained of spirit, unacquainted with stern resistance. He knew not how to spare himself. The Desert struck him where it pleased – all over. It played with him. His tongue was swollen; the parched throat could not swallow. He sank.... An hour he lay there, just wit enough in him to choose the top of a mound where he could be most easily seen. He lay two hours, three, four hours... The heat blazed down upon him like a furnace... The sky, when he opened his eyes once, was empty... then a speck became visible in the blue expanse; and presently another speck. They came from nowhere. They hovered very high, almost out of sight. They appeared, they disappeared, they – reappeared. Nearer and nearer they swung down, in sweeping stealthy circles... little dancing groups of them, miles away but ever drawing closer – the vultures...

He had strained his ears so long for sounds of feet and voices that it seemed he could no longer hear at all. Hearing had ceased within him. Then came the water-dreams, with their agonising torture. He heard *that*... heard it running in silvery streams and rivulets across green English meadows. It rippled with silvery music. He heard it splash. He dipped hands and feet and head in it – in deep, clear pools of generous depth. He drank; with his skin he drank, not with mouth and throat alone. Ice clinked in effervescent, sparkling water against a glass. He swam and plunged. Water gushed freely over back and shoulders, gallons and gallons of it, bathfuls and to spare, a flood of gushing, crystal, cool, life-giving liquid. ... And then he stood in a beech wood and felt the streaming deluge of delicious summer rain upon his face; heard it drip luxuriantly upon a million thirsty leaves. The wet trunks shone, the damp moss spread its perfume, ferns waved heavily in the moist atmosphere. He was soaked to the skin in it. A mountain torrent, fresh from fields of snow, foamed boiling past, and the spray fell in a shower upon his cheeks and hair. He dived – head foremost... Ah, he was up to the neck... and *she* was with him; they were under water together; he saw her eyes gleaming into his own beneath the copious flood.

The voice, however, was not hers... "You will drown, yet you will not know you drown...!" His swollen tongue called out a name. But no sound was audible. He closed his eyes. There came sweet unconsciousness...

A sound in that instant *was* audible, though. It was a voice – voices – and the thud of animal hoofs upon the sand. The specks had vanished from the sky as mysteriously as they came. And, as though in answer to the sound, he made a movement – an automatic, unconscious movement. He did not know he moved. And the body, uncontrolled, lost its precarious balance. He rolled; but he did not know he rolled. Slowly, over the edge of the sloping mound of sand, he turned sideways. Like a log of wood he slid gradually, turning over and over, nothing to stop him – to the bottom. A few feet only, and not even steep; just steep enough to keep rolling slowly. There was a – splash. But he did not know there was a splash.

They found him in a pool of water – one of these rare pools the Desert Bedouin mark preciously for their own. He had lain within three yards of it for hours. He was drowned... but he did not know he drowned...

**If you enjoyed this, you might also like...**
Ancient Sorceries, see page 246
The Wings of Horus, see page 192

# H.S.H.

**IN THE** mountain Club Hut, to which he had escaped after weeks of gaiety in the capital, Delane, young travelling Englishman, sat alone, and listened to the wind that beat the pines with violence. The firelight danced over the bare stone floor and raftered ceiling, giving the room an air of movement, and though the solid walls held steady against the wild spring hurricane, the cannonading of the wind seemed to threaten the foundations. For the mountain shook, the forest roared, and the shadows had a way of running everywhere as though the little building trembled. Delane watched and listened. He piled the logs on. From time to time he glanced nervously over his shoulder, restless, half uneasy, as a burst of spray from the branches dashed against the window, or a gust of unusual vehemence shook the door. Over-wearied with his long day's climb among impossible conditions, he now realised, in this mountain refuge, his utter loneliness; for his mind gave birth to that unwelcome symptom of true loneliness – that he was not, after all, alone. Continually he heard steps and voices in the storm. Another wanderer, another climber out of season like himself, would presently arrive, and sleep was out of the question until first he heard that knocking on the door. Almost – he expected some one.

He went for the tenth time to the little window. He peered forth into the thick darkness of the dropping night, shading his eyes against the streaming pane to screen the firelight in an attempt to see if another climber – perhaps a climber in distress – were visible. The surroundings were desolate and savage, well named the Devil's Saddle. Black-faced precipices, streaked with melting snow, rose towering to the north, where the heights were hidden in seas of vapour; waterfalls poured into abysses on two sides; a wall of impenetrable forest pressed up from the south; and the dangerous ridge he had climbed all day slid off wickedly into a sky of surging cloud. But no human figure was, of course, distinguishable, for both the lateness of the hour and the elemental fury of the night rendered it most unlikely. He turned away with a start, as the tempest delivered a blow with massive impact against his very face. Then, clearing the remnants of his frugal supper from the table, he hung his soaking clothes at a new angle before the fire, made sure the door was fastened on the inside, climbed into the bunk where white pillows and thick Austrian blankets looked so inviting, and prepared finally for sleep.

"I must be over-tired," he sighed, after half an hour's weary tossing, and went back to make up the sinking fire. Wood is plentiful in these climbers' huts; he heaped it on. But this time he lit the little oil lamp as well, realising – though unwilling to acknowledge it – that it was not over-fatigue that banished sleep, but this unwelcome sense of expecting some one, of being not quite alone. For the feeling persisted and increased. He drew the wooden bench close up to the fire, turned the lamp as high as it would go, and wished unaccountably for the morning. Light was a very pleasant thing; and darkness now, for the first time since childhood, troubled him. It was outside; but it might so easily come in and swamp, obliterate, extinguish. The darkness seemed a positive thing. Already, somehow, it was established in his mind – this sense of enormous, aggressive darkness that veiled an undesirable hint of personality. Some shadow from the peaks or from the forest, immense and threatening, pervaded all his thought. "This can't be entirely nerves," he whispered to himself. "I'm not so tired as all that!" And he made the fire roar. He shivered and drew closer to the blaze. "I'm out of condition; that's part of it," he realised, and remembered with loathing the weeks of luxurious indulgence just behind him.

For Delane had rather wasted his year of educational travel. Straight from Oxford, and well supplied with money, he had first saturated his mind in the latest Continental thought – the science of France, the metaphysics and philosophy of Germany – and had then been caught aside by the gaiety of capitals where the lights are not turned out at midnight by a Sunday School police. He had been surfeited, physically, emotionally, and intellectually, till his mind and body longed hungrily for simple living again and simple teaching – above all, the latter. The Road of Excess leads to the Palace of Wisdom – for certain temperaments (as Blake forgot to add), of which Delane was one. For there was stuff in the youth, and the reaction had set in with violent abruptness. His system rebelled. He cut loose energetically from all soft delights, and craved for severity, pure air, solitude and hardship. Clean and simple conditions he must have without delay, and the tonic of physical battling. It was too early in the year to climb seriously, for the snow was still dangerous and the weather wild, but he had chosen this most isolated of all the mountain huts in order to make sure of solitude, and had come, without guide or companion, for a week's strenuous life in wild surroundings, and to take stock of himself with a view to full recovery.

And all day long as he climbed the desolate, unsafe ridge, his mind – good, wholesome, natural symptom – had reverted to his childhood days, to the solid worldly wisdom of his church-going father, and to the early teaching (oh, how sweet and refreshing in its literal spirit!) at his mother's knee. Now, as he watched the blazing logs, it came back to him again with redoubled force; the simple, precious, old-world stories of heaven and hell, of a paternal Deity, and of a daring, subtle, personal devil –

The interruption to his thoughts came with startling suddenness, as the roaring night descended against the windows with a thundering violence that shook the walls and sucked the flame half-way up the wide stone chimney. The oil lamp flickered and went out. Darkness invaded the room for a second, and Delane sprang from his bench, thinking the wet snow had loosened far above and was about to sweep the hut into the depths. And he was still standing, trembling and uncertain, in the middle of the room, when a deep and sighing hush followed sharp upon the elemental outburst, and in the hush, like a whisper after thunder, he heard a curious steady sound that, at first, he thought must be a footstep by the door. It was then instantly repeated. But it was not a step. It was some one knocking on the heavy oaken panels – a firm, authoritative sound, as though the new arrival had the right to enter and was already impatient at the delay.

The Englishman recovered himself instantly, realising with keen relief the new arrival – at last.

"Another climber like myself, of course," he said, "or perhaps the man who comes to prepare the hut for others. The season has begun." And he went over quickly, without a further qualm, to unbolt the door.

"Forgive!" he exclaimed in German, as he threw it wide, "I was half asleep before the fire. It is a terrible night. Come in to food and shelter, for both are here, and you shall share such supper as I possess."

And a tall, cloaked figure passed him swiftly with a gust of angry wind from the impenetrable blackness of the world beyond. On the threshold, for a second, his outline stood full in the blaze of firelight with the sheet of darkness behind it, stately, erect, commanding, his cloak torn fiercely by the wind, but the face hidden by a low-brimmed hat; and an instant later the door shut with resounding clamour upon the hurricane, and the two men turned to confront one another in the little room.

Delane then realised two things sharply, both of them fleeting impressions, but acutely vivid: First, that the outside darkness seemed to have entered and established itself between him and the new arrival; and, secondly, that the stranger's face was difficult to focus for clear sight, although the covering hat was now removed. There was a blur upon it somewhere. And this the Englishman ascribed partly to the flickering effect of firelight, and partly to the lightning glare of the man's masterful and terrific eyes, which made his own sight waver in some curious fashion as he gazed upon him. These impressions, however, were but momentary and passing, due doubtless to the condition of his nerves and to the semi-shock of the dramatic, even theatrical entrance. Delane's senses, in this wild setting, were guilty of exaggeration. For now, while helping the man remove his cloak, speaking naturally of shelter, food, and the savage weather, he lost this first distortion and his mind recovered sane proportion. The stranger, after all, though striking, was not of appearance so uncommon as to cause alarm; the light and the low doorway had touched his stature with illusion. He dwindled. And the great eyes, upon calmer subsequent inspection, lost their original fierce lightning. The entering darkness, moreover, was but an effect of the upheaving night behind him as he strode across the threshold. The closed door proved it.

And yet, as Delane continued his quieter examination, there remained, he saw, the startling quality which had caused that first magnifying in his mind. His senses, while reporting accurately, insisted upon this arresting and uncommon touch: there was, about this late wanderer of the night, some evasive, lofty strangeness that set him utterly apart from ordinary men.

The Englishman examined him searchingly, surreptitiously, but with a touch of passionate curiosity he could not in the least account for nor explain. There were contradictions of perplexing character about him. For the first presentment had been of splendid youth, while on the face, though vigorous and gloriously handsome, he now discerned the stamp of tremendous age. It was worn and tired. While radiant with strength and health and power, it wore as well this certain signature of deep exhaustion that great experience rather than physical experience brings. Moreover, he discovered in it, in some way he could not hope to describe, man, woman, and child. There was a big, sad earnestness about it, yet a touch of humour too; patience, tenderness, and sweetness held the mouth; and behind the high pale forehead intellect sat enthroned and watchful. In it were both love and hatred, longing and despair; an expression of being ever on the defensive, yet hugely mutinous; an air both hunted and beseeching; great knowledge and great woe.

Delane gave up the search, aware that something unalterably splendid stood before him. Solemnity and beauty swept him too. His was never the grotesque assumption that man must be the highest being in the universe, nor that a thing is a miracle merely because it has never happened before. He groped, while explanation and analysis both halted. "A great teacher," thought fluttered through him, "or a mighty rebel! A distinguished personality beyond all question! Who can he be?" There was something regal that put respect upon his imagination instantly. And he remembered the legend of the country-side that Ludwig of Bavaria was said to be about when nights were very wild. He wondered. Into his speech and manner crept unawares an attitude of deference that was almost reverence, and with it – whence came this other quality? – a searching pity.

"You must be wearied out," he said respectfully, busying himself about the room, "as well as cold and wet. This fire will dry you, sir, and meanwhile I will prepare quickly such food as there is, if you will eat it." For the other carried no knapsack, nor was he clothed for the severity of mountain travel.

"I have already eaten," said the stranger courteously, "and, with my thanks to you, I am neither wet nor tired. The afflictions that I bear are of another kind, though ones that you shall more easily, I am sure, relieve."

He spoke as a man whose words set troops in action, and Delane glanced at him, deeply moved by the surprising phrase, yet hardly marvelling that it should be so. He found no ready answer. But there was evidently question in his look, for the other continued, and this time with a smile that betrayed sheer winning beauty as of a tender woman:

"I saw the light and came to it. It is unusual – at this time."

His voice was resonant, yet not deep. There was a ringing quality about it that the bare room emphasised. It charmed the young Englishman inexplicably. Also, it woke in him a sense of infinite pathos.

"You are a climber, sir, like myself," Delane resumed, lifting his eyes a moment uneasily from the coffee he brewed over a corner of the fire. "You know this neighbourhood, perhaps? Better, at any rate, than I can know it?" His German halted rather. He chose his words with difficulty. There was uncommon trouble in his mind.

"I know all wild and desolate places," replied the other, in perfect English, but with a wintry mournfulness in his voice and eyes, "for I feel at home in them, and their stern companionship my nature craves as solace. But, unlike yourself, I am no climber."

"The heights have no attraction for you?" asked Delane, as he mingled steaming milk and coffee in the wooden bowl, marvelling what brought him then so high above the valleys. "It is their difficulty and danger that fascinate me always. I find the loneliness of the summits intoxicating in a sense."

And, regardless of refusal, he set the bread and meat before him, the apple and the tiny packet of salt, then turned away to place the coffee pot beside the fire again. But as he did so a singular gesture of the other caught his eyes. Before touching bowl or plate, the stranger took the fruit and brushed his lips with it. He kissed it, then set it on the ground and crushed it into pulp beneath his heel. And, seeing this, the young Englishman knew something dreadfully arrested in his mind, for, as he looked away, pretending the act was unobserved, a thing of ice and darkness moved past him through the room, so that the pot trembled in his hand, rattling sharply against the hearthstone where he stooped. He could only interpret it as an act of madness, and the myth of the sad, drowned monarch wandering through this enchanted region, pressed into him again unsought and urgent. It was a full minute before he had control of his heart and hand again.

The bowl was half emptied, and the man was smiling – this time the smile of a child who implores the comfort of enveloping and understanding arms.

"I am a wanderer rather than a climber," he was saying, as though there had been no interval, "for, though the lonely summits suit me well, I now find in them only – terror. My feet lose their sureness, and my head its steady balance. I prefer the hidden gorges of these mountains, and the shadows of the covering forests. My days" – his voice drew the loneliness of uttermost space into its piteous accents – "are passed in darkness. I can never climb again."

He spoke this time, indeed, as a man whose nerve was gone for ever. It was pitiable almost to tears. And Delane, unable to explain the amazing contradictions, felt recklessly, furiously drawn to this trapped wanderer with the mien of a king yet the air and speech sometimes of a woman and sometimes of an outcast child.

"Ah, then you have known accidents," Delane replied with outer calmness, as he lit his pipe, trying in vain to keep his hand as steady as his voice. "You have been in one perhaps. The effect, I have been told, is—"

The power and sweetness in that resonant voice took his breath away as he heard it break in upon his own uncertain accents:

"I have – fallen," the stranger replied impressively, as the rain and wind wailed past the building mournfully, "yet a fall that was no part of any accident. For it was no common fall," the man added with a magnificent gesture of disdain, "while yet it broke my heart in two." He stooped a little as he uttered the next words with a crying pathos that an outcast woman might have used. "I am," he said, "engulfed in intolerable loneliness. I can never climb again."

With a shiver impossible to control, half of terror, half of pity, Delane moved a step nearer to the marvellous stranger. The spirit of Ludwig, exiled and distraught, had gripped his soul with a weakening terror; but now sheer beauty lifted him above all personal shrinking. There seemed some echo of lost divinity, worn, wild yet grandiose, through which this significant language strained towards a personal message – for himself.

"In loneliness?" he faltered, sympathy rising in a flood.

"For my Kingdom that is lost to me for ever," met him in deep, throbbing tones that set the air on fire. "For my imperial ancient heights that jealousy took from me—"

The stranger paused, with an indescribable air of broken dignity and pain.

Outside the tempest paused a moment before the awful elemental crash that followed. A bellowing of many winds descended like artillery upon the world. A burst of smoke rushed from the fireplace about them both, shrouding the stranger momentarily in a flying veil. And Delane stood up, uncomfortable in his very bones. "What can it be?" he asked himself sharply. "Who is this being that he should use such language?" He watched alarm chase pity, aware that the conversation held something beyond experience. But the pity returned in greater and ever greater flood. And love surged through him too. It was significant, he remembered afterwards, that he felt it incumbent upon himself to stand. Curious, too, how the thought of that mad, drowned monarch haunted memory with such persistence. Some vast emotion that he could not name drove out his subsequent words. The smoke had cleared, and a strange, high stillness held the world. The rain streamed down in torrents, isolating these two somehow from the haunts of men. And the Englishman stared then into a countenance grown mighty with woe and loneliness. There stood darkly in it this incommunicable magnificence of pain that mingled awe with the pity he had felt. The kingly eyes looked clear into his own, completing his subjugation out of time. "I would follow you," ran his thought upon its knees, "follow you with obedience for ever and ever, even into a last damnation. For you are sublime. You shall come again into your Kingdom, if my own small worship—"

Then blackness sponged the reckless thought away. He spoke in its place a more guarded, careful thing:

"I am aware," he faltered, yet conscious that he bowed, "of standing before a Great One of some world unknown to me. Who he may be I have but the privilege of wondering. He has spoken darkly of a Kingdom that is lost. Yet he is still, I see, a Monarch." And he lowered his head and shoulders involuntarily.

For an instant, then, as he said it, the eyes before him flashed their original terrific lightnings. The darkness of the common world faded before the entrance of an Outer Darkness. From gulfs of terror at his feet rose shadows out of the night of time, and a passionate anguish as of sudden madness seized his heart and shook it.

He listened breathlessly for the words that followed. It seemed some wind of unutterable despair passed in the breath from those non-human lips:

"I am still a Monarch, yes; but my Kingdom is taken from me, for I have no single subject. Lost in a loneliness that lies out of space and time, I am become a throneless Ruler, and my hopelessness is more than I can bear." The beseeching pathos of the voice tore him in two. The Deity himself, it seemed, stood there accused of jealousy, of sin and cruelty. The stranger rose. The power about him brought the picture of a planet, throned in mid-heaven and poised beyond assault. "Not otherwise," boomed the startling words as though an avalanche found syllables, "could I now show myself to – you."

Delane was trembling horribly. He felt the next words slip off his tongue unconsciously. The shattering truth had dawned upon his soul at last.

"Then the light you saw, and came to—?" he whispered.

"Was the light in your heart that guided me," came the answer, sweet, beguiling as the music in a woman's tones, "the light of your instant, brief desire that held love in it." He made an opening movement with his arms as he continued, smiling like stars in summer. "For you summoned me; summoned me by your dear and precious belief: how dear, how precious, none can know but I who stand before you."

His figure drew up with an imperial air of proud dominion. His feet were set among the constellations. The opening movement of his arms continued slowly. And the music in his tones seemed merged in distant thunder.

"For your single, brief belief," he smiled with the grandeur of a condescending Emperor, "shall give my vanished Kingdom back to me."

And with an air of native majesty he held his hand out – to be kissed.

The black hurricane of night, the terror of frozen peaks, the yawning horror of the great abyss outside – all three crowded into the Englishman's mind with a slashing impact that blocked delivery of any word or action. It was not that he refused, it was not that he withdrew, but that Life stood paralysed and rigid. The flow stopped dead for the first time since he had left his mother's womb. The God in him was turned to stone and rendered ineffective. For an appalling instant God was *not*.

He realised the stupendous moment. Before him, drinking his little soul out merely by his Presence, stood one whose habit of mind, not alone his external accidents, was imperial with black prerogative before the first man drew the breath of life. August procedure was native to his inner process of existence. The stars and confines of the universe owned his sway before he fell, to trifle away the dreary little centuries by haunting the minds of feeble men and women, by hiding himself in nursery cupboards, and by grinning with stained gargoyles from the roofs of city churches...

And the lad's life stammered, flickered, threatened to go out before the enveloping terror of the revelation.

"I called to you... but called to you in play," thought whispered somewhere deep below the level of any speech, yet not so low that the audacious sound of it did not crash above the elements outside; "for... till now... you have been to me but a... coated bogy... that my brain disowned with laughter... and my heart thought picturesque. If you are here... *alive*! May God forgive me for my..."

It seemed as though tears – the tears of love and profound commiseration – drowned the very seed of thought itself.

A sound stopped him that was like a collapse in heaven. Some crashing, as of a ruined world, passed splintering through his little timid heart. He did not yield, but he understood – with an understanding which seemed the delicate first sign of yielding – the seductiveness of evil, the sweet delight of surrendering the Will with utter recklessness to those swelling forces which disintegrate the heroic soul in man. He remembered. It was true. In the reaction from excess he *had* definitely called upon his childhood's teaching with a passing moment of genuine belief. And now that yearning of a fraction of a second bore its awful fruit. The luscious Capitals where he had rioted passed in a coloured stream before his eyes; the Wine, the Woman, and the Song stood there before him, clothed in that Power which lies insinuatingly disguised behind their little passing show of innocence. Their glamour donned this domino of regal and virile grandeur. He felt entangled beyond recovery. The idea of God seemed sterile and without reality. The one real thing, the one desirable thing, the one possible, strong and beautiful thing – was to bend his head and kiss those imperial fingers. He moved noiselessly towards the Hand. He raised his own to take it and lift it towards his mouth –

When there rose in his mind with startling vividness a small, soft picture of a child's nursery, a picture of a little boy, kneeling in scanty night-gown with pink upturned soles, and asking ridiculous, audacious things of a shining Figure seated on a summer cloud above the kitchen-garden walnut tree.

The tiny symbol flashed and went its way, yet not before it had lit the entire world with glory. For there came an absolutely routing power with it. In that half-forgotten instant's craving for the simple teaching of his childhood days, Belief had conjured with two immense traditions. This was the second of them. The appearance of the one had inevitably produced the passage of its opposite...

And the Hand that floated in the air before him to be kissed sank slowly down below the possible level of his lips. He shrank away. Though laughter tempted something in his brain, there still clung about his heart the first aching, pitying terror. But size retreated, dwindling somehow as it went. The wind and rain obliterated every other sound; yet in that bare, unfurnished room of a climber's mountain hut, there was a silence, above the roar, that drank in everything and broke the back of speech. In opposition to this masquerading splendour Delane had set up a personal, paternal Deity.

"I thought of you, perhaps," cried the voice of self-defence, "but I did not call to you with real belief. And, by the name of God, I did not summon you. For your sweetness, as your power, sickens me; and your hand is black with the curses of all the mothers in the world, whose prayers and tears—"

He stopped dead, overwhelmed by the cruelty of his reckless utterance.

And the Other moved towards him slowly. It was like the summit of some peaked and terrible height that moved. He spoke. He changed appallingly.

"But *I* claim," he roared, "your heart. I claim you by that instant of belief you felt. For by that alone you shall restore to me my vanished Kingdom. You shall worship me."

In the countenance was a sudden awful power; but behind the stupefying roar there was weakness in the voice as of an imploring and beseeching child. Again, deep love and searching pity seared the Englishman's heart as he replied in the gentlest accents he could find to master:

"And I claim *you*," he said, "by my understanding sympathy, and by my sorrow for your God-forsaken loneliness, and by my love. For no Kingdom built on hate can stand against the love you would deny—"

Words failed him then, as he saw the majesty fade slowly from the face, grown small and shadowy. One last expression of desperate energy in the eyes struck lightnings from the smoky air, as with an abandoned movement of the entire figure, he drew back, it seemed, towards the door behind him.

Delane moved slowly after him, opening his arms. Tenderness and big compassion flung wide the gates of love within him. He found strange language, too, although actual, spoken words did not produce them further than his entrails where they had their birth.

"Toys in the world are plentiful, Sire, and you may have them for your masterpiece of play. But you must seek them where they still survive; in the churches, and in isolated lands where thought lies unawakened. For they are the children's blocks of make-believe whose palaces, like your once tremendous kingdom, have no true existence for the thinking mind."

And he stretched his hands towards him with the gesture of one who sought to help and save, then paused as he realised that his arms enclosed sheer blackness, with the emptiness of wind and driving rain.

For the door of the hut stood open, and Delane balanced on the threshold, facing the sheet of night above the abyss. He heard the waterfalls in the valley far below. The forest flapped and tossed its myriad branches. Cold draughts swept down from spectral fields of melting snow above; and the blackness turned momentarily into the semblance of towers and bastions of thick beaten gloom. Above one soaring turret, then, a space of sky appeared, swept naked by a violent, lost wind – an opening of purple into limitless distance. For one second, amid the vapours, it was visible, empty and untenanted. The next, there sailed across its small diameter a falling Star. With an air of slow and endless leisure, yet at the same time with terrific speed, it dived behind the ragged curtain of the clouds, and the space closed up again. Blackness returned upon the heavens.

And through this blackness, plunging into that abyss of woe whence he had momentarily risen, the figure of the marvellous stranger melted utterly away. Delane, for a fleeting second, was aware of the earnestness in the sad, imploring countenance; of its sweetness and its power so strangely mingled; of it mysterious grandeur; and of its pathetic childishness. But, already, it was sunk into interminable distance. A star that would be baleful, yet was merely glorious, passed on its endless wandering among the teeming systems of the universe. Behind the fixed and steady stars, secure in their appointed places, it set. It vanished into the pit of unknown emptiness. It was gone.

"God help you!" sighed across the sea of wailing branches, echoing down the dark abyss below. "God give you rest at last!"

For he saw a princely, nay, an imperial Being, homeless for ever, and for ever wandering, hunted as by keen remorseless winds about a universe that held no corner for his feet, his majesty unworshipped, his reign a mockery, his Court unfurnished, and his courtiers mere shadows of deep space. . . .

And a thin, grey dawn, stealing up behind clearing summits in the east, crept then against the windows of the mountain hut. It brought with it a treacherous, sharp air that made the sleeper draw another blanket near to shelter him from the sudden cold. For the fire had died out, and an icy draught sucked steadily beneath the doorway.

**If you enjoyed this, you might also like...**
The Sea Fit, see page 41
The Glamour of the Snow, see page 79

# Tales of Transformation

# May Day Eve

## Chapter I

**IT WAS** in the spring when I at last found time from the hospital work to visit my friend, the old folklorist, in his country isolation, and I rather chuckled to myself, because in my bag I was taking down a book that utterly refuted all his tiresome pet theories of magic and the powers of the soul.

These theories were many and various, and had often troubled me. In the first place, I scorned them for professional reasons, and, in the second, because I had never been able to argue quite well enough to convince or to shake his faith, in even the smallest details, and any scientific knowledge I brought to bear only fed him with confirmatory data. To find such a book, therefore, and to know that it was safely in my bag, wrapped up in brown paper and addressed to him, was a deep and satisfactory joy, and I speculated a good deal during the journey how he would deal with the overwhelming arguments it contained against the existence of any important region outside the world of sensory perceptions.

Speculative, too, I was whether his visionary habits and absorbing experiments would permit him to remember my arrival at all, and I was accordingly relieved to hear from the solitary porter that the "professor" had sent a "veeckle" to meet me, and that I was thus free to send my bag and walk the four miles to the house across the hills.

It was a calm, windless evening, just after sunset, the air warm and scented, and delightfully still. The train, already sinking into distance, carried away with it the noise of crowds and cities and the last suggestions of the stressful life behind me, and from the little station on the moorland I stepped at once into the world of silent, growing things, tinkling sheep-bells, shepherds, and wild, desolate spaces.

My path lay diagonally across the turfy hills. It slanted a mile or so to the summit, wandered vaguely another two miles among gorse-bushes along the crest, passed Tom Bassett's cottage by the pines, and then dropped sharply down on the other side through rather thin woods to the ancient house where the old folklorist lived and dreamed himself into his impossible world of theory and fantasy. I fell to thinking busily about him during the first part of the ascent, and convinced myself, as usual, that, but for his generosity to the poor, and his benign aspect, the peasantry must undoubtedly have regarded him as a wizard who speculated in souls and had dark dealings with the world of faery.

The path I knew tolerably well. I had already walked it once before – a winter's day some years ago – and from the cottage onward felt sure of my way; but for the first mile or so there were so many cross cattle-tracks, and the light had become so dim that I felt it wise to inquire more particularly. And this I was fortunately able to do of a man who with astonishing suddenness rose from the grass where he had been lying behind a clump of bushes, and passed a few yards in front of me at a high pace downhill toward the darkening valley.

He was in such a state of hurry that I called out loudly to him, fearing to be too late, but on hearing my voice he turned sharply, and seemed to arrive almost at once beside me. In a single instant he was standing there, quite close, looking, with a smile and a certain expression of curiosity, I thought, into my face. I remember thinking that his features, pale and wholly untanned, were rather wonderful for a countryman, and that the eyes were those of a foreigner; his great swiftness, too, gave me a distinct sensation – something almost of a start – though I knew my vision was at fault at the best of times, and of course especially so in the deceptive twilight of the open hillside.

Moreover – as the way often is with such instructions – the words did not stay in my mind very clearly after he had uttered them, and the rapid, panther-like movements of the man as he quickly vanished down the hill again left me with little more than a sweeping gesture indicating the line I was to follow. No doubt his sudden rising from behind the gorse-bush, his curious swiftness, and the way he peered into my face, and even touched me on the shoulder, all combined to distract my attention somewhat from the actual words he used; and the fact that I was travelling at a wrong angle, and should have come out a mile too far to the right, helped to complete my feeling that his gesture, pointing the way, was sufficient.

On the crest of the ridge, panting a little with the unwonted exertion, I lay down to rest a moment on the grass beside a flaming yellow gorse-bush. There was still a good hour before I should be looked for at the house; the grass was very soft, the peace and silence soothing. I lingered, and lit a cigarette. And it was just then, I think, that my subconscious memory gave back the words, the actual words, the man had spoken, and the heavy significance of the personal pronoun, as he had emphasised it in his odd foreign voice, touched me with a sense of vague amusement: "The safest way for you now," he had said, as though I was so obviously a townsman and might be in danger on the lonely hills after dark. And the quick way he had reached my side, and then slipped off again like a shadow down the steep slope, completed a definite little picture in my mind. Then other thoughts and memories rose up and formed a series of pictures, following each other in rapid succession, and forming a chain of reflections undirected by the will and without purpose or meaning. I fell, that is, into a pleasant reverie.

Below me, and infinitely far away, it seemed, the valley lay silent under a veil of blue evening haze, the lower end losing itself among darkening hills whose peaks rose here and there like giant plumes that would surely nod their great heads and call to one another once the final shadows were down. The village lay, a misty patch, in which lights already twinkled. A sound of rooks faintly cawing, of seagulls crying far up in the sky, and of dogs barking at a great distance rose up out of the general murmur of evening voices. Odours of farm and field and open spaces stole to my nostrils, and everything contributed to the feeling that I lay on the top of the world, nothing between me and the stars, and that all the huge, free things of the earth – hills, valleys, woods, and sloping fields – lay breathing deeply about me.

A few seagulls – in daytime hereabouts they fill the air – still circled and wheeled within range of sight, uttering from time to time sharp, petulant cries; and far in the distance there was just visible a shadowy line that showed where the sea lay.

Then, as I lay gazing dreamily into this still pool of shadows at my feet, something rose up, something sheetlike, vast, imponderable, off the whole surface of the mapped-out country, moved with incredible swiftness down the valley, and in a single instant climbed the hill where I lay and swept by me, yet without hurry, and in a sense without speed.

Veils in this way rose one after another, filling the cups between the hills, shrouding alike fields, village, and hillside as they passed, and settled down somewhere into the gloom behind me over the ridge, or slipped off like vapour into the sky.

Whether it was actually mist rising from the surface of the fast-cooling ground, or merely the earth giving up her heat to the night, I could not determine. The coming of the darkness is ever a series of mysteries. I only know that this indescribable vast stirring of the landscape seemed to me as though the earth were unfolding immense sable wings from her sides, and lifting them for silent, gigantic strokes so that she might fly more swiftly from the sun into the night. The darkness, at any rate, did drop down over everything very soon afterward, and I rose up hastily to follow my pathway, realising with a degree of wonder strangely new to me the magic of twilight, the blue open depths into the valley below, and the pale yellow heights of the watery sky above.

I walked rapidly, a sense of chilliness about me, and soon lost sight of the valley altogether as I got upon the ridge proper of these lonely and desolate hills.

It could not have been more than fifteen minutes that I lay there in reverie, yet the weather, I at once noticed, had changed very abruptly, for mist was seething here and there about me, rising somewhere from smaller valleys in the hills beyond, and obscuring the path, while overhead there was plainly a sound of wind tearing past, far up, with a sound of high shouting. A moment before it had been the stillness of a warm spring night, yet now everything had changed; wet mist coated me, raindrops smartly stung my face, and a gusty wind, descending out of cool heights, began to strike and buffet me, so that I buttoned my coat and pressed my hat more firmly upon my head.

The change was really this – and it came to me for the first time in my life with the power of a real conviction – that everything about me seemed to have become suddenly alive.

It came oddly upon me – prosaic, matter-of-fact, materialistic doctor that I was – this realisation that the world about me had somehow stirred into life; oddly, I say, because Nature to me had always been merely a more or less definite arrangement of measurement, weight, and colour, and this new presentation of it was utterly foreign to my temperament. A valley to me was always a valley; a hill, merely a hill; a field, so many acres of flat surface, grass or ploughed, drained well or drained ill; whereas now, with startling vividness, came the strange, haunting idea that after all they could be something more than valley, hill, and field; that what I had hitherto perceived by these names were only the veils of something that lay concealed within, something alive. In a word, that the poetic sense I had always rather sneered at, in others, or explained away with some shallow physiological label, had apparently suddenly opened up in myself without any obvious cause.

And, the more I puzzled over it, the more I began to realise that its genesis dated from those few minutes of reverie lying under the gorse-bush (reverie, a thing I had never before in all my life indulged in!), or, now that I came to reflect more accurately, from my brief interview with that wild-eyed, swift-moving, shadowy man of whom I had first inquired the way.

I recalled my singular fancy that veils were lifting off the surface of the hills and fields, and a tremor of excitement accompanied the memory. Such a thing had never before been possible to my practical intelligence, and it made me feel suspicious – suspicious about myself. I stood still a moment – I looked about me into the gathering mist, above me to the vanishing stars, below me to the hidden valley, and then sent an urgent summons to my individuality, as I had always known it, to arrest and chase these undesirable fancies.

But I called in vain. No answer came. Anxiously, hurriedly, confusedly, too, I searched for my normal self, but could not find it; and this failure to respond induced in me a sense of uneasiness that touched very nearly upon the borders of alarm.

I pushed on faster and faster along the turfy track among the gorse-bushes with a dread that I might lose the way altogether, and a sudden desire to reach home as soon as might be. Then, without warning, I emerged unexpectedly into clear air again, and the vapour swept past me in a rushing wall and rose into the sky. Anew I saw the lights of the village behind me in the depths, here and there a line of smoke rising against the pale yellow sky, and stars overhead peering down through thin wispy clouds that stretched their wind-signs across the night.

After all, it had been nothing but a stray bit of sea-fog driving up from the coast, for the other side of the hills, I remembered, dipped their chalk cliffs straight into the sea, and strange lost winds must often come a-wandering this way with the sharp changes of temperature about sunset. Nonetheless, it was disconcerting to know that mist and storm lay hiding within possible reach, and I walked on smartly for a sight of Tom Bassett's cottage and the lights of the Manor House in the valley a short mile beyond.

The clearing of the air, however, lasted but a very brief while, and vapour was soon rising about me as before, hiding the path and making bushes and stone walls look like running shadows. It came, driven apparently, by little independent winds up the many side gullies, and it was very cold, touching my skin like a wet sheet. Curious great shapes, too, it assumed as the wind worked to and fro through it: forms of men and animals; grotesque, giant outlines; ever shifting and running along the ground with silent feet, or leaping into the air with sharp cries as the gusts twisted them inwardly and lent them voice. More and more I pushed my pace, and more and more darkness and vapour obliterated the landscape. The going was not otherwise difficult, and here and there cowslips glimmered in patches of dancing yellow, while the springy turf made it easy to keep up speed; yet in the gloom I frequently tripped and plunged into prickly gorse near the ground, so that from shin to knee was soon a-tingle with sharp pain. Odd puffs and spits of rain stung my face, and the periods of utter stillness were always followed by little shouting gusts of wind, each time from a new direction. Troubled is perhaps too strong a word, but flustered I certainly was; and though I recognised that it was due to my being in an environment so remote from the town life I was accustomed to, I found it impossible to stifle altogether the feeling of malaise that had crept into my heart, and I looked about with increasing eagerness for the lighted windows of Bassett's cottage.

More and more, little pinpricks of distress and confusion accumulated, adding to my realisation of being away from streets and shopwindows, and things I could classify and deal with. The mist, too, distorted as well as concealed, played tricks with sounds as well as with sights. And, once or twice, when I stumbled upon some crouching sheep, they got up without the customary alarm and hurry of sheep, and moved off slowly into the darkness, but in such a singular way that I could almost have sworn they were not sheep at all, but human beings crawling on all-fours, looking back and grimacing at me over their shoulders as they went. On these occasions – for there were more than one – I never could get close enough to feel their woolly wet backs, as I should have liked to do; and the sound of their tinkling bells came faintly through the mist, sometimes from one direction, sometimes from another, sometimes all round me as though a whole flock surrounded me; and I found it impossible to analyse or explain the idea I received that they were not sheep-bells at all, but something quite different.

But mist and darkness, and a certain confusion of the senses caused by the excitement of an utterly strange environment, can account for a great deal. I pushed on quickly. The conviction that I had strayed from the route grew, nevertheless, for occasionally there was a great commotion of seagulls about me, as though I had disturbed them in their sleeping-places. The air filled with their plaintive cries, and I heard the rushing of multitudinous wings, sometimes very close to my head, but always invisible owing to the mist. And once, above the swishing of the wet wind through the gorse-bushes, I was sure I caught the faint thunder of the sea and the distant crashing of waves rolling up some steep-throated gully in the cliffs. I went cautiously after this, and altered my course a little away from the direction of the sound.

Yet, increasingly all the time, it came to me how the cries of the seabirds sounded like laughter, and how the everlasting wind blew and drove about me with a purpose, and how the low bushes persistently took the shape of stooping people, moving stealthily past me, and how the mist more and more resembled huge protean figures escorting me across the desolate hills, silently, with immense footsteps. For the inanimate world now touched my awakened poetic sense in a manner hitherto unguided, and became fraught with the pregnant messages of a dimly concealed life. I readily understood, for the first time, how easily a superstitious peasantry might people their world, and how even an educated mind might favour an atmosphere of legend. I stumbled along, looking anxiously for the lights of the cottage.

Suddenly, as a shape of writhing mist whirled past, I received so direct a stroke of wind that it was palpably a blow in the face. Something swept by with a shrill cry into the darkness. It was impossible to prevent jumping to one side and raising an arm by way of protection, and I was only just quick enough to catch a glimpse of the seagull as it raced past, with suddenly altered flight, beating its powerful wings over my head. Its white body looked enormous as the mist swallowed it. At the same moment a gust tore my hat from my head and flung the flap of my coat across my eyes. But I was well-trained by this time, and made a quick dash after the retreating black object, only to find on overtaking it that I held a prickly branch of gorse. The wind combed my hair viciously. Then, out of a corner of my eye, I saw my hat still rolling, and grabbed swiftly at it; but just as I closed on it, the real hat passed in front of me, turning over in the wind like a ball, and I instantly released my first capture to chase it. Before it was within reach, another one shot between my feet so that I stepped on it. The grass seemed covered with moving hats, yet each one, when I seized it, turned into a piece of wood, or a tiny gorse-bush, or a black rabbit hole, till my hands were scored with prickles and running blood. In the darkness, I reflected, all objects looked alike, as though by general conspiracy.

I straightened up and took a long breath, mopping the blood with my handkerchief. Then something tapped at my feet, and on looking down, there was the hat within easy reach, and I stooped down and put it on my head again. Of course, there were a dozen ways of explaining my confusion and stupidity, and I walked along wondering which to select. My eyesight, for one thing – and under such conditions why seek further? It was nothing, after all, and the dizziness was a momentary effect caused by the effort and stooping.

But for all that, I shouted aloud, on the chance that a wandering shepherd might hear me; and of course no answer came, for it was like calling in a padded room, and the mist suffocated my voice and killed its resonance.

It was really very discouraging: I was cold and wet and hungry; my legs and clothes torn by the gorse, my hands scratched and bleeding; the wind brought water to my eyes by its constant buffeting, and my skin was numb from contact with the chill mist. Fortunately I had matches, and after some difficulty, by crouching under a wall, I caught a swift glimpse of my watch, and saw that it was but little after eight o'clock. Supper I knew was at nine, and I was surely over halfway by this time. But here again was another instance of the way everything seemed in a conspiracy against me to appear otherwise than ordinary, for in the gleam of the match my watch-glass showed as the face of a little old grey man, uncommonly like the folklorist himself, peering up at me with an expression of whimsical laughter. My own reflection it could not possibly have been, for I am clean-shaven, and this face looked up at me through a running tangle of grey hair. Yet a second and third match revealed only the white surface with the thin black hands moving across it.

## Chapter II

**AND** it was at this point, I well remember, that I reached what was for me the true heart of the adventure, the little fragment of real experience I learned from it and took back with me to my doctor's life in London, and that has remained with me ever since, and helped me to a new sympathetic insight into the intricacies of certain curious mental cases I had never before really understood.

For it was sufficiently obvious by now that a curious change had been going forward in me for some time, dating, so far as I could focus my thoughts sufficiently to analyse, from the moment of my speech with that hurrying man of shadow on the hillside. And the first deliberate manifestation of the change, now that I looked back, was surely the awakening in my prosaic being of the 'poetic thrill'; my sudden amazing appreciation of the world around me as something alive. From that moment the change in me had worked ahead subtly, swiftly. Yet, so natural had been the beginning of it, that although it was a radically new departure for my temperament, I was hardly aware at first of what had actually come about; and it was only now, after so many encounters, that I was forced at length to acknowledge it.

It came the more forcibly too, because my very commonplace ideas of beauty had hitherto always been associated with sunshine and crude effects; yet here this new revelation leaped to me out of wind and mist and desolation on a lonely hillside, out of night, darkness, and discomfort. New values rushed upon me from all sides. Everything had changed, and the very simplicity with which the new values presented themselves proved to me how profound the change, the readjustment, had been. In such trivial things the evidence had come that I was not aware of it until repetition forced my attention: the veils rising from valley and hill; the mountain tops as personalities that shout or murmur in the darkness; the crying of the sea birds and of the living, purposeful wind; above all, the feeling that Nature about me was instinct with a life differing from my own in degree rather than in kind; everything, from the conspiracy of the gorse-bushes to the disappearing hat, showed that a fundamental attitude of mind in me had changed – and changed, too, without my knowledge or consent.

Moreover, at the same time the deep sadness of beauty had entered my heart like a stroke; for all this mystery and loveliness, I realised poignantly was utterly independent and careless of me, as me; and that while I must pass, decay, grow old, these manifestations would remain forever young and unalterably potent. And thus gradually had I become permeated with the recognition of a region hitherto unknown to me, and that I had always depreciated in others and especially, it now occurred to me, in my friend the old folklorist.

Here surely, I thought, was the beginning of conditions which, carried a little further, must become pathogenic. That the change was real and pregnant I had no doubt whatever. My consciousness was expanding and I had caught it in the very act. I had of course read much concerning the changes of personality, swift, kaleidoscopic – had come across something of it in my practice – and had listened to the folklorist holding forth like a man inspired upon ways and means of reaching concealed regions of the human consciousness, and opening it to the knowledge of things called magical, so that one became free of a larger universe. But it was only now for the first time, on these bare hills, in touch with the wind and the rain, that I realised in how simple a fashion the frontiers of consciousness could shift this way and that, or with what touch of genuine awe the certainty might come that one stood on the borderland of new, untried, perhaps dangerous, experiences.

At any rate, it did now come to me that my consciousness had shifted its frontiers very considerably, and that whatever might happen must seem not abnormal, but quite simple and inevitable, and of course utterly true. This very simplicity, however, doing no violence to my being, brought with it nonetheless a sense of dread and discomfort; and my dim awareness that unknown possibilities were about me in the night puzzled and distressed me perhaps more than I cared to admit.

## Chapter III

**ALL THIS** that takes so long to describe became apparent to me in a few seconds. What I had always despised ascended the throne.

But with the finding of Bassett's cottage, as a signpost close to home, my former sangfroid, my stupidity, would doubtless return, and my relief was therefore considerable when at length a faint gleam of light appeared through the mist, against which the square dark shadow of the chimney-line pointed upwards. After all, I had not strayed so very far out of the way. Now I could definitely ascertain where I was wrong.

Quickening my pace, I scrambled over a broken stone wall, and almost ran across the open bit of grass to the door. One moment the black outline of the cottage was there in front of me, and the next, when I stood actually against it – there was nothing! I laughed to think how utterly I had been deceived. Yet not utterly, for as I groped back again over the wall, the cottage loomed up a little to the left, with its windows lighted and friendly, and I had only been mistaken in my angle of approach after all. Yet again, as I hurried to the door, the mist drove past and thickened a second time – and the cottage was not where I had seen it!

My confusion increased a lot after that. I scrambled about in all directions, rather foolishly hurried, and over countless stone walls it seemed, and completely dazed as to the true points of the compass. Then suddenly, just when a kind of despair came over me, the cottage stood there solidly before my eyes, and I found myself not two feet from the door. Was ever mist before so deceptive? And there, just behind it, I made out the row of pines like a dark wave breaking through the night. I sniffed the wet resinous odour with joy, and a genuine thrill ran through me as I saw the unmistakable yellow light of the windows. At last I was near home and my troubles would soon be over.

A cloud of birds rose with shrill cries off the roof and whirled into the darkness when I knocked with my stick on the door, and human voices, I was almost certain, mingled somewhere with them, though it was impossible to tell whether they were within the cottage or outside. It all sounded confusedly with a rush of air like a little whirlwind, and I stood there rather alarmed at the clamour of my knocking. By way, too, of further proof that my imagination had awakened, the significance of that knocking at the door set something vibrating within me that most surely had never vibrated before, so that I suddenly realised with what atmosphere of mystical suggestion is the mere act of knocking surrounded – knocking at a door – both for him who knocks, wondering what shall be revealed on opening, and for him who stands within, waiting for the summons of the knocker. I only know that I hesitated a lot before making up my mind to knock a second time.

And, anyhow, what happened subsequently came in a sort of haze. Words and memory both failed me when I try to record it truthfully, so that even the faces are difficult to visualise again, the words almost impossible to hear.

Before I knew it the door was open and before I could frame the words of my first brief question, I was within the threshold, and the door was shut behind me.

I had expected the little dark and narrow hallway of a cottage, oppressive of air and odour, but instead I came straight into a room that was full of light and full of – people. And the air tasted like the air about a mountain-top.

To the end I never saw what produced the light, nor understood how so many men and women found space to move comfortably to and fro, and pass each other as they did, within the confines of those four walls. An uncomfortable sense of having intruded upon some private gathering was, I think, my first emotion; though how the poverty-stricken countryside could have produced such an assemblage puzzled me beyond belief. And my second emotion – if there was any division at all in the wave of wonder that fairly drenched me – was feeling a sort of glory in the presence of such an atmosphere of splendid and vital youth. Everything vibrated, quivered, shook about me, and I almost felt myself as an aged and decrepit man by comparison.

I know my heart gave a great fiery leap as I saw them, for the faces that met me were fine, vigourous, and comely, while burning everywhere through their ripe maturity shone the ardours of youth and a kind of deathless enthusiasm. Old, yet eternally young they were, as rivers and mountains count their years by thousands, yet remain ever youthful; and the first effect of all those pairs of eyes lifted to meet my own was to send a whirlwind of unknown thrills about my heart and make me catch my breath with mingled terror and delight. A fear of death, and at the same time a sensation of touching something vast and eternal that could never die, surged through me.

A deep hush followed my entrance as all turned to look at me. They stood, men and women, grouped about a table, and something about them – not their size alone – conveyed the impression of being gigantic, giving me strangely novel realisations of freedom, power, and immense existence more or less than human.

I can only record my thoughts and impressions as they came to me and as I dimly now remember them. I had expected to see old Tom Bassett crouching half asleep over a peat fire, a dim lamp on the table beside him, and instead this assembly of tall and splendid men and women stood there to greet me, and stood in silence. It was little wonder that at first the ready question died upon my lips, and I almost forgot the words of my own language.

"I thought this was Tom Bassett's cottage!" I managed to ask at length, and looked straight at the man nearest me across the table. He had wild hair falling about his shoulders and a face of clear beauty. His eyes, too, like all the rest, seemed shrouded by something veil-like that reminded me of the shadowy man of whom I had first inquired the way. They were shaded – and for some reason I was glad they were.

At the sound of my voice, unreal and thin, there was a general movement throughout the room, as though everyone changed places, passing each other like those shapes of fluid sort I had seen outside in the mist. But no answer came. It seemed to me that the mist even penetrated into the room about me and spread inwardly over my thoughts.

"Is this the way to the Manor House?" I asked again, louder, fighting my inward confusion and weakness. "Can no one tell me?"

Then apparently everyone began to answer at once, or rather, not to answer directly, but to speak to each other in such a way that I could easily overhear. The voices of the men were deep, and of the women wonderfully musical, with a slow rhythm like that of the sea, or of the wind through the pine-trees outside. But the unsatisfactory nature of what they said only helped to increase my sense of confusion and dismay.

"Yes," said one; "Tom Bassett was here for a while with the sheep, but his home was not here."

"He asks the way to a house when he does not even know the way to his own mind!" another voice said, sounding overhead it seemed.

"And could he recognise the signs if we told him?" came in the singing tones of a woman's voice close behind me.

And then, with a noise more like running water, or wind in the wings of birds, than anything else I could liken it to, came several voices together:

"And what sort of way does he seek? The splendid way, or merely the easy?"

"Or the short way of fools!"

"But he must have some credentials, or he never could have got as far as this," came from another.

A laugh ran round the room at this, though what there was to laugh at I could not imagine. It sounded like wind rushing about the hills. I got the impression too that the roof was somehow open to the sky, for their laughter had such a spacious quality in it, and the air was so cool and fresh, and moving about in currents and waves.

"It was I who showed him the way," cried a voice belonging to someone who was looking straight into my face over the table. "It was the safest way for him once he had got so far—"

I looked up and met his eye, and the sentence remained unfinished. It was the hurrying, shadowy man of the hillside. He had the same shifting outline as the others now, and the same veiled and shaded eyes, and as I looked the sense of terror stirred and grew in me. I had come in to ask for help, but now I was only anxious to be free of them all and out again in the rain and darkness on the moor. Thoughts of escape filled my brain, and I searched quickly for the door through which I had entered. But nowhere could I discover it again. The walls were bare; not even the windows were visible. And the room seemed to fill and empty of these figures as the waves of the sea fill and empty a cavern, crowding one upon another, yet never occupying more space, or less. So the coming and going of these men and women always evaded me.

And my terror became simply a terror that the veils of their eyes might lift, and that they would look at me with their clear, naked sight. I became horribly aware of their eyes.

It was not that I felt them evil, but that I feared the new depths in me their merciless and terrible insight would stir into life. My consciousness had expanded quite enough for one night! I must escape at all costs and claim my own self again, however limited. I must have sanity, even if with limitations, but sanity at any price.

But meanwhile, though I tried hard to find my voice again, there came nothing but a thin piping sound that was like reeds whistling where winds meet about a corner. My throat was contracted, and I could only produce the smallest and most ridiculous of noises. The power of movement, too, was far less than when I first came in, and every moment it became more difficult to use my muscles, so that I stood there, stiff and awkward, face to face with this assemblage of shifting, wonderful people.

"And now," continued the voice of the man who had last spoken, "and now the safest way for him will be through the other door, where he shall see that which he may more easily understand."

With a great effort I regained the power of movement, while at the same time a burst of anger and a determination to be done with it all and to overcome my dreadful confusion drove me forward.

He saw me coming, of course, and the others indeed opened up and made a way for me, shifting to one side or the other whenever I came too near them, and never allowing me to touch them. But at last, when I was close in front of the man, ready both to speak and act, he was no longer there. I never saw the actual change – but instead of a man it was a woman! And when I turned with amazement, I saw that the other occupants walking like figures in some ancient ceremony, were moving slowly toward the far end of the room. One by one, as they filed past, they raised their calm, passionless faces to mine, immensely vital, proud, austere, and then, without further word or gesture, they opened the door I had lost and disappeared through it one by one into the darkness of the night beyond. And as they went it seemed that the mist swallowed them up and a gust of wind caught them away, and the light also went with them, leaving me alone with the figure who had last spoken.

Moreover it was just here that a most disquieting thought flashed through my brain with unreasoning conviction, shaking my personality, as it were, to the foundations: viz., that I had hitherto been spending my life in the pursuit of false knowledge, in the mere classifying and labelling of effects, the analysis of results, scientific so called; whereas it was the folklorist, and suchlike, who with their dreams and prayers were all the time on the path of real knowledge, the trail of causes; that the one was merely adding to the mechanical comfort and safety of the body, ultimately degrading the highest part of man, and never advancing the type, while the other – but then I had never yet believed in a soul – and now was no time to begin, terror or no terror. Clearly, my thoughts were wandering.

## Chapter IV

**IT WAS** at this moment the sound of the purring first reached me – deep, guttural purring – that made me think at once of some large concealed animal. It was precisely what I had heard many a time at the Zoological Gardens, and I had visions of cows chewing the cud, or horses munching hay in a stall outside the cottage. It was certainly an animal sound, and one of pleasure and contentment.

Semidarkness filled the room. Only a very faint moonlight, struggling through the mist, came through the window, and I moved back instinctively toward the support of the wall against my back. Somewhere, through openings, came the sound of the night driving over the roof, and far above I had visions of those everlasting winds streaming by with clouds as large as continents on their wings. Something in me wanted to sing and shout, but something else in me at the same time was in a very vivid state of unreasoning terror. I felt immense, yet tiny, confident, yet timid; a part of huge, universal forces, yet an utterly small, personal, and very limited being.

In the corner of the room on my right stood the woman. Her face was hid by a mass of tumbling hair, that made me think of living grasses on a field in June. Thus her head was partially turned from me, and the moonlight, catching her outline, just revealed it against the wall like an impressionist picture. Strange hidden memories stirred in the depths of me, and for a moment I felt that I knew all about her. I stared about me quickly, nervously, trying to take in everything at once. Then the purring sound grew much louder and closer, and I forgot my notion that this woman was no stranger to me and that I knew her as well as I knew myself. That purring thing was in the room close beside me. Between us two, indeed, it was, for I now saw that her arm nearest to me was raised, and that she was pointing to the wall in front of us.

Following the direction of her hand, I saw that the wall was transparent, and that I could see through a portion of it into a small square space beyond, as though I was looking through gauze instead of bricks. This small inner space was lighted, and on stooping down I saw that it was a sort of cupboard or cell-like cage let into the wall. The thing that purred was there in the centre of it.

I looked closer. It was a being, apparently a human being, crouched down in its narrow cage, feeding. I saw the body stooping over a quantity of coarse-looking, piled-up substance that was evidently food. It was like a man huddled up. There it squatted, happy and contented, with the minimum of air, light, and space, dully satisfied with its prisoned cage behind the bars, utterly unconscious of the vast world about it, grunting with pleasure, purring like a great cat, scornfully ignorant of what might lie beyond. The cell, moreover, I saw was a perfect masterpiece of mechanical contrivance and inventive ingenuity – the very last word in comfort, safety and scientific skill. I was in the act of trying to fit in my memory some of the details of its construction and arrangement, when I made a chance noise, and at once became too agitated to note carefully what I saw. For at the noise the creature turned, and I saw that it was a human being – a man. I was aware of a face close against my own as it pressed forward, but a face with embryonic features impossible to describe and utterly loathsome, with eyes, ears, nose and skin, only just sufficiently alive and developed to transfer the minimum of gross sensation to the brain. The mouth, however, was large and thick-lipped, and the jaws were still moving in the act of slow mastication.

I shrank back, shuddering with mingled pity and disgust, and at the same moment the woman beside me called me softly by my own name. She had moved forward a little so that she stood quite close to me, full in the thin stream of moonlight that fell across the floor, and I was conscious of a swift transition from hell to heaven as my gaze passed from that embryonic visage to a countenance so refined, so majestic, so divinely sensitive in its strength, that it was like turning from the face of a devil to look upon the features of a goddess.

At the same instant I was aware that both beings – the creature and the woman – were moving rapidly toward me.

A pain like a sharp sword dived deep down into me and twisted horribly through my heart, for as I saw them coming I realised in one swift moment of terrible intuition that they had their life in me, that they were born of my own being, and were indeed projections of myself. They were portions of my consciousness projected outwardly into objectivity, and their degree of reality was just as great as that of any other part of me.

With a dreadful swiftness they rushed toward me, and in a single second had merged themselves into my own being; and I understood in some marvellous manner beyond the possibility of doubt that they were symbolic of my own soul: the dull animal part of me that had hitherto acknowledged nothing beyond its cage of minute sensations, and the higher part, almost out of reach, and in touch with the stars, that for the first time had feebly awakened into life during my journey over the hill.

## Chapter V

**I FORGET** altogether how it was that I escaped, whether by the window or the door. I only know I found myself a moment later making great speed over the moor, followed by screaming birds and shouting winds, straight on the track downhill toward the Manor House. Something must have guided me, for I went with the instinct of an animal, having no uncertainties as to turnings, and saw the welcome lights of windows before I had covered another mile. And all the way I felt as though a great sluice gate had been opened to let a flood of new perceptions rush like a sea over my inner being, so that I was half ashamed and half delighted, partly angry, yet partly happy.

Servants met me at the door, several of them, and I was aware at once of an atmosphere of commotion in the house. I arrived breathless and hatless, wet to the skin, my hands scratched and my boots caked with mud.

"We made sure you were lost, sir," I heard the old butler say, and I heard my own reply, faintly, like the voice of someone else:

"I thought so too."

A minute later I found myself in the study, with the old folklorist standing opposite. In his hands he held the book I had brought down for him in my bag, ready addressed. There was a curious smile on his face.

"It never occurred to me that you would dare to walk – tonight of all nights," he was saying.

I stared without a word. I was bursting with the desire to tell him something of what had happened and try to be patient with his explanations, but when I sought for words and sentences my story seemed suddenly flat and pointless, and the details of my adventure began to evaporate and melt away, and seemed hard to remember.

"I had an exciting walk," I stammered, still a little breathless from running. "The weather was all right when I started from the station."

"The weather is all right still," he said, "though you may have found some evening mist on the top of the hills. But it's not that I meant."

"What then?"

"I meant," he said, still laughing quizzically, "that you were a very brave man to walk tonight over the enchanted hills, because this is May Day eve, and on May Day eve, you know, They have power over the minds of men, and can put glamour upon the imagination—"

"Who – 'they'? What do you mean?"

He put my book down on the table beside him and looked quietly for a moment into my eyes, and as he did so the memory of my adventure began to revive in detail, and I thought quickly of the shadowy man who had shown me the way first. What could it have been in the face of the old folklorist that made me think of this man? A dozen things ran like flashes through my excited mind, and while I attempted to seize them I heard the old man's voice continue. He seemed to be talking to himself as much as to me.

"The elemental beings you have always scoffed at, of course; they who operate ceaselessly behind the screen of appearances, and who fashion and mould the moods of the mind. And an extremist like you – for extremes are always dangerously weak – is their legitimate prey."

"Pshaw!" I interrupted him, knowing that my manner betrayed me hopelessly, and that he had guessed much. "Any man may have subjective experiences, I suppose—"

Then I broke off suddenly. The change in his face made me start; it had taken on for the moment so exactly the look of the man on the hillside. The eyes gazing so steadily into mine had shadows in them, I thought.

"Glamour!" he was saying, "all glamour! One of them must have come very close to you, or perhaps touched you." Then he asked sharply, "Did you meet anyone? Did you speak with anyone?"

"I came by Tom Bassett's cottage," I said. "I didn't feel quite sure of my way and I went in and asked."

"All glamour," he repeated to himself, and then aloud to me, "and as for Bassett's cottage, it was burnt down three years ago, and nothing stands there now but broken, roofless walls—"

He stopped because I had seized him by the arm. In the shadows of the lamp-lit room behind him I thought I caught sight of dim forms moving past the bookshelves. But when my eye tried to focus them they faded and slipped away again into ceiling and walls. The details of the hilltop cottage, however, started into life again at the sight, and I seized my friend's arm to tell him. But instantly, when I tried, it all faded away again as though it had been a dream, and I could recall nothing intelligible to repeat to him.

He looked at me and laughed.

"They always obliterate the memory afterwards," he said gently, "so that little remains beyond a mood, or an emotion, to show how profoundly deep their touch has been. Though sometimes part of the change remains and becomes permanent – as I hope in your case it may."

Then, before I had time to answer, to swear, or to remonstrate, he stepped briskly past me and closed the door into the hall, and then drew me aside farther into the room. The change that I could not understand was still working in his face and eyes.

"If you have courage enough left to come with me," he said, speaking very seriously, "we will go out again and see more. Up till midnight, you know, there is still the opportunity, and with me perhaps you won't feel so – so—"

It was impossible somehow to refuse; everything combined to make me go. We had a little food and then went out into the hall, and he clapped a wide-awake on his grey hairs. I took a cloak and seized a walking-stick from the stand. I really hardly knew what I was doing. The new world I had awakened to seemed still a-quiver about me.

As we passed out on to the gravel drive the light from the hall windows fell upon his face, and I saw that the change I had been so long observing was nearing its completeness, for there breathed about him that keen, wonderful atmosphere of eternal youth I had felt upon the inmates of the cottage. He seemed to have gone back forty years; a veil was gathering over his eyes; and I could have sworn that somehow his stature had increased, and that he moved beside me with a vigour and power I had never seen in him before.

And as we began to climb the hill together in silence I saw that the stars were clear overhead and there was no mist, that the trees stood motionless without wind, and that beyond us on the summit of the hills there were lights dancing to and fro, appearing and disappearing like the inflection of stars in water.

**If you enjoyed this, you might also like…**
Ancient Lights, see page 92
The Man Who Found Out, see page 296

# The Camp of the Dog

## Chapter I

**ISLANDS** of all shapes and sizes troop northward from Stockholm by the hundred, and the little steamer that threads their intricate mazes in summer leaves the traveller in a somewhat bewildered state as regards the points of the compass when it reaches the end of its journey at Waxholm. But it is only after Waxholm that the true islands begin, so to speak, to run wild, and start up the coast on their tangled course of a hundred miles of deserted loveliness, and it was in the very heart of this delightful confusion that we pitched our tents for a summer holiday. A veritable wilderness of islands lay about us: from the mere round button of a rock that bore a single fir, to the mountainous stretch of a square mile, densely wooded, and bounded by precipitous cliffs; so close together often that a strip of water ran between no wider than a country lane, or, again, so far that an expanse stretched like the open sea for miles.

Although the larger islands boasted farms and fishing stations, the majority were uninhabited. Carpeted with moss and heather, their coast-lines showed a series of ravines and clefts and little sandy bays, with a growth of splendid pine-woods that came down to the water's edge and led the eye through unknown depths of shadow and mystery into the very heart of primitive forest.

The particular islands to which we had camping rights by virtue of paying a nominal sum to a Stockholm merchant lay together in a picturesque group far beyond the reach of the steamer, one being a mere reef with a fringe of fairy-like birches, and two others, cliff-bound monsters rising with wooded heads out of the sea. The fourth, which we selected because it enclosed a little lagoon suitable for anchorage, bathing, night-lines, and what-not, shall have what description is necessary as the story proceeds; but, so far as paying rent was concerned, we might equally well have pitched our tents on any one of a hundred others that clustered about us as thickly as a swarm of bees.

It was in the blaze of an evening in July, the air clear as crystal, the sea a cobalt blue, when we left the steamer on the borders of civilisation and sailed away with maps, compasses, and provisions for the little group of dots in the Skägård that were to be our home for the next two months. The dinghy and my Canadian canoe trailed behind us, with tents and dunnage carefully piled aboard, and when the point of cliff intervened to hide the steamer and the Waxholm hotel we realised for the first time that the horror of trains and houses was far behind us, the fever of men and cities, the weariness of streets and confined spaces. The wilderness opened up on all sides into endless blue reaches, and the map and compasses were so frequently called into requisition that we went astray more often than not and progress was enchantingly slow. It took us, for instance, two whole days to find our crescent-shaped home, and the camps we made on the way were so fascinating that we left them with difficulty and regret, for each island seemed more desirable than the one before it, and over all lay the spell of haunting peace, remoteness from the turmoil of the world, and the freedom of open and desolate spaces.

And so many of these spots of world-beauty have I sought out and dwelt in, that in my mind remains only a composite memory of their faces, a true map of heaven, as it were, from which this particular one stands forth with unusual sharpness because of the strange things that happened there, and also, I think, because anything in which John Silence played a part has a habit of fixing itself in the mind with a living and lasting quality of vividness.

For the moment, however, Dr. Silence was not of the party. Some private case in the interior of Hungary claimed his attention, and it was not till later – the 15th of August, to be exact – that I had arranged to meet him in Berlin and then return to London together for our harvest of winter work. All the members of our party, however, were known to him more or less well, and on this third day as we sailed through the narrow opening into the lagoon and saw the circular ridge of trees in a gold and crimson sunset before us, his last words to me when we parted in London for some unaccountable reason came back very sharply to my memory, and recalled the curious impression of prophecy with which I had first heard them:

"Enjoy your holiday and store up all the force you can," he had said as the train slipped out of Victoria; "and we will meet in Berlin on the 15th – unless you should send for me sooner."

And now suddenly the words returned to me so clearly that it seemed I almost heard his voice in my ear: "Unless you should send for me sooner"; and returned, moreover, with a significance I was wholly at a loss to understand that touched somewhere in the depths of my mind a vague sense of apprehension that they had all along been intended in the nature of a prophecy.

In the lagoon, then, the wind failed us this July evening, as was only natural behind the shelter of the belt of woods, and we took to the oars, all breathless with the beauty of this first sight of our island home, yet all talking in somewhat hushed voices of the best place to land, the depth of water, the safest place to anchor, to put up the tents in, the most sheltered spot for the camp-fires, and a dozen things of importance that crop up when a home in the wilderness has actually to be made.

And during this busy sunset hour of unloading before the dark, the souls of my companions adopted the trick of presenting themselves very vividly anew before my mind, and introducing themselves afresh.

In reality, I suppose, our party was in no sense singular. In the conventional life at home they certainly seemed ordinary enough, but suddenly, as we passed through these gates of the wilderness, I saw them more sharply than before, with characters stripped of the atmosphere of men and cities. A complete change of setting often furnishes a startlingly new view of people hitherto held for well-known; they present another facet of their personalities. I seemed to see my own party almost as new people – people I had not known properly hitherto, people who would drop all disguises and henceforth reveal themselves as they really were. And each one seemed to say: "Now you will see me as I am. You will see me here in this primitive life of the wilderness without clothes. All my masks and veils I have left behind in the abodes of men. So, look out for surprises!"

The Reverend Timothy Maloney helped me to put up the tents, long practice making the process easy, and while he drove in pegs and tightened ropes, his coat off, his flannel collar flying open without a tie, it was impossible to avoid the conclusion that he was cut out for the life of a pioneer rather than the church. He was fifty years of age, muscular, blue-eyed and hearty, and he took his share of the work, and more, without shirking. The way he handled the axe in cutting down saplings for the tent-poles was a delight to see, and his eye in judging the level was unfailing.

Bullied as a young man into a lucrative family living, he had in turn bullied his mind into some semblance of orthodox beliefs, doing the honours of the little country church with an energy that made one think of a coal-heaver tending china; and it was only in the past few years that he had resigned the living and taken instead to cramming young men for their examinations. This suited him better. It enabled him, too, to indulge his passion for spells of 'wild life', and to spend the summer months of most years under canvas in one part of the world or another where he could take his young men with him and combine 'reading' with open air.

His wife usually accompanied him, and there was no doubt she enjoyed the trips, for she possessed, though in less degree, the same joy of the wilderness that was his own distinguishing characteristic. The only difference was that while he regarded it as the real life, she regarded it as an interlude. While he camped out with his heart and mind, she played at camping out with her clothes and body. None the less, she made a splendid companion, and to watch her busy cooking dinner over the fire we had built among the stones was to understand that her heart was in the business for the moment and that she was happy even with the detail.

Mrs. Maloney at home, knitting in the sun and believing that the world was made in six days, was one woman; but Mrs. Maloney, standing with bare arms over the smoke of a wood fire under the pine trees, was another; and Peter Sangree, the Canadian pupil, with his pale skin, and his loose, though not ungainly figure, stood beside her in very unfavourable contrast as he scraped potatoes and sliced bacon with slender white fingers that seemed better suited to hold a pen than a knife. She ordered him about like a slave, and he obeyed, too, with willing pleasure, for in spite of his general appearance of debility he was as happy to be in camp as any of them.

But more than any other member of the party, Joan Maloney, the daughter, was the one who seemed a natural and genuine part of the landscape, who belonged to it all just in the same way that the trees and the moss and the grey rocks running out into the water belonged to it. For she was obviously in her right and natural setting, a creature of the wilds, a gipsy in her own home.

To any one with a discerning eye this would have been more or less apparent, but to me, who had known her during all the twenty-two years of her life and was familiar with the ins and outs of her primitive, utterly un-modern type, it was strikingly clear. To see her there made it impossible to imagine her again in civilisation. I lost all recollection of how she looked in a town. The memory somehow evaporated. This slim creature before me, flitting to and fro with the grace of the woodland life, swift, supple, adroit, on her knees blowing the fire, or stirring the frying-pan through a veil of smoke, suddenly seemed the only way I had ever really seen her. Here she was at home; in London she became someone concealed by clothes, an artificial doll overdressed and moving by clockwork, only a portion of her alive. Here she was alive all over.

I forget altogether how she was dressed, just as I forget how any particular tree was dressed, or how the markings ran on any one of the boulders that lay about the Camp. She looked just as wild and natural and untamed as everything else that went to make up the scene, and more than that I cannot say.

Pretty, she was decidedly not. She was thin, skinny, dark-haired, and possessed of great physical strength in the form of endurance. She had, too, something of the force and vigorous purpose of a man, tempestuous sometimes and wild to passionate, frightening her mother, and puzzling her easy-going father with her storms of waywardness, while at the same time she stirred his admiration by her violence. A pagan of the pagans she was besides, and with some haunting suggestion of old-world pagan beauty about her dark face and eyes. Altogether an odd and difficult character, but with a generosity and high courage that made her very lovable.

In town life she always seemed to me to feel cramped, bored, a devil in a cage, in her eyes a hunted expression as though any moment she dreaded to be caught. But up in these spacious solitudes all this disappeared. Away from the limitations that plagued and stung her, she would show at her best, and as I watched her moving about the Camp I repeatedly found myself thinking of a wild creature that had just obtained its freedom and was trying its muscles.

Peter Sangree, of course, at once went down before her. But she was so obviously beyond his reach, and besides so well able to take care of herself, that I think her parents gave the matter but little thought, and he himself worshipped at a respectful distance, keeping admirable control of his passion in all respects save one; for at his age the eyes are difficult to master, and the yearning, almost the devouring, expression often visible in them was probably there unknown even to himself. He, better than anyone else, understood that he had fallen in love with something most hard of attainment, something that drew him to the very edge of life, and almost beyond it. It, no doubt, was a secret and terrible joy to him, this passionate worship from afar; only I think he suffered more than anyone guessed, and that his want of vitality was due in large measure to the constant stream of unsatisfied yearning that poured for ever from his soul and body. Moreover, it seemed to me, who now saw them for the first time together, that there was an unnamable something – an elusive quality of some kind – that marked them as belonging to the same world, and that although the girl ignored him she was secretly, and perhaps unknown to herself, drawn by some attribute very deep in her own nature to some quality equally deep in his.

This, then, was the party when we first settled down into our two months' camp on the island in the Baltic Sea. Other figures flitted from time to time across the scene, and sometimes one reading man, sometimes another, came to join us and spend his four hours a day in the clergyman's tent, but they came for short periods only, and they went without leaving much trace in my memory, and certainly they played no important part in what subsequently happened.

The weather favoured us that night, so that by sunset the tents were up, the boats unloaded, a store of wood collected and chopped into lengths, and the candle-lanterns hung round ready for lighting on the trees. Sangree, too, had picked deep mattresses of balsam boughs for the women's beds, and had cleared little paths of brushwood from their tents to the central fireplace. All was prepared for bad weather. It was a cosy supper and a well-cooked one that we sat down to and ate under the stars, and, according to the clergyman, the only meal fit to eat we had seen since we left London a week before.

The deep stillness, after that roar of steamers, trains, and tourists, held something that thrilled, for as we lay round the fire there was no sound but the faint sighing of the pines and the soft lapping of the waves along the shore and against the sides of the boat in the lagoon. The ghostly outline of her white sails was just visible through the trees, idly rocking to and fro in her calm anchorage, her sheets flapping gently against the mast. Beyond lay the dim blue shapes of other islands floating in the night, and from all the great spaces about us came the murmur of the sea and the soft breathing of great woods. The odours of the wilderness – smells of wind and earth, of trees and water, clean, vigorous, and mighty – were the true odours of a virgin world unspoilt by men, more penetrating and more subtly intoxicating than any other perfume in the whole world. Oh! – and dangerously strong, too, no doubt, for some natures!

"Ahhh!" breathed out the clergyman after supper, with an indescribable gesture of satisfaction and relief. "Here there is freedom, and room for body and mind to turn in. Here one can work and rest and play. Here one can be alive and absorb something of the earth-forces that never get within touching distance in the cities. By George, I shall make a permanent camp here and come when it is time to die!"

The good man was merely giving vent to his delight at being under canvas. He said the same thing every year, and he said it often. But it more or less expressed the superficial feelings of us all. And when, a little later, he turned to compliment his wife on the fried potatoes, and discovered that she was snoring, with her back against a tree, he grunted with content at the sight and put a ground-sheet over her feet, as if it were the most natural thing in the world for her to fall asleep after dinner, and then moved back to his own corner, smoking his pipe with great satisfaction.

And I, smoking mine too, lay and fought against the most delicious sleep imaginable, while my eyes wandered from the fire to the stars peeping through the branches, and then back again to the group about me. The Rev. Timothy soon let his pipe go out, and succumbed as his wife had done, for he had worked hard and eaten well. Sangree, also smoking, leaned against a tree with his gaze fixed on the girl, a depth of yearning in his face that he could not hide, and that really distressed me for him. And Joan herself, with wide staring eyes, alert, full of the new forces of the place, evidently keyed up by the magic of finding herself among all the things her soul recognised as 'home', sat rigid by the fire, her thoughts roaming through the spaces, the blood stirring about her heart. She was as unconscious of the Canadian's gaze as she was that her parents both slept. She looked to me more like a tree, or something that had grown out of the island, than a living girl of the century; and when I spoke across to her in a whisper and suggested a tour of investigation, she started and looked up at me as though she heard a voice in her dreams.

Sangree leaped up and joined us, and without waking the others we three went over the ridge of the island and made our way down to the shore behind. The water lay like a lake before us still coloured by the sunset. The air was keen and scented, wafting the smell of the wooded islands that hung about us in the darkening air. Very small waves tumbled softly on the sand. The sea was sown with stars, and everywhere breathed and pulsed the beauty of the northern summer night. I confess I speedily lost consciousness of the human presences beside me, and I have little doubt Joan did too. Only Sangree felt otherwise, I suppose, for presently we heard him sighing; and I can well imagine that he absorbed the whole wonder and passion of the scene into his aching heart, to swell the pain there that was more searching even than the pain at the sight of such matchless and incomprehensible beauty.

The splash of a fish jumping broke the spell.

"I wish we had the canoe now," remarked Joan; "we could paddle out to the other islands."

"Of course," I said; "wait here and I'll go across for it," and was turning to feel my way back through the darkness when she stopped me in a voice that meant what it said.

"No; Mr. Sangree will get it. We will wait here and cooee to guide him."

The Canadian was off in a moment, for she had only to hint of her wishes and he obeyed.

"Keep out from shore in case of rocks," I cried out as he went, "and turn to the right out of the lagoon. That's the shortest way round by the map."

My voice travelled across the still waters and woke echoes in the distant islands that came back to us like people calling out of space. It was only thirty or forty yards over the ridge and down the other side to the lagoon where the boats lay, but it was a good mile to coast round the shore in the dark to where we stood and waited. We heard him stumbling away among the boulders, and then the sounds suddenly ceased as he topped the ridge and went down past the fire on the other side.

"I didn't want to be left alone with him," the girl said presently in a low voice. "I'm always afraid he's going to say or do something—" She hesitated a moment, looking quickly over her shoulder towards the ridge where he had just disappeared – "something that might lead to unpleasantness."

She stopped abruptly.

"*You* frightened, Joan!" I exclaimed, with genuine surprise. "This is a new light on your wicked character. I thought the human being who could frighten you did not exist." Then I suddenly realised she was talking seriously – looking to me for help of some kind – and at once I dropped the teasing attitude.

"He's very far gone, I think, Joan," I added gravely. "You must be kind to him, whatever else you may feel. He's exceedingly fond of you."

"I know, but I can't help it," she whispered, lest her voice should carry in the stillness; "there's something about him that – that makes me feel creepy and half afraid."

"But, poor man, it's not his fault if he is delicate and sometimes looks like death," I laughed gently, by way of defending what I felt to be a very innocent member of my sex.

"Oh, but it's not that I mean," she answered quickly; "it's something I feel about him, something in his soul, something he hardly knows himself, but that may come out if we are much together. It draws me, I feel, tremendously. It stirs what is wild in me – deep down – oh, very deep down, – yet at the same time makes me feel afraid."

"I suppose his thoughts are always playing about you," I said, "but he's nice-minded and—"

"Yes, yes," she interrupted impatiently, "I can trust myself absolutely with him. He's gentle and singularly pure-minded. But there's something else that—" She stopped again sharply to listen. Then she came up close beside me in the darkness, whispering –

"You know, Mr. Hubbard, sometimes my intuitions warn me a little too strongly to be ignored. Oh, yes, you needn't tell me again that it's difficult to distinguish between fancy and intuition. I know all that. But I also know that there's something deep down in that man's soul that calls to something deep down in mine. And at present it frightens me. Because I cannot make out what it is; and I know, I *know*, he'll do something some day that – that will shake my life to the very bottom." She laughed a little at the strangeness of her own description.

I turned to look at her more closely, but the darkness was too great to show her face. There was an intensity, almost of suppressed passion, in her voice that took me completely by surprise.

"Nonsense, Joan," I said, a little severely; "you know him well. He's been with your father for months now."

"But that was in London; and up here it's different – I mean, I feel that it may be different. Life in a place like this blows away the restraints of the artificial life at home. I know, oh, I know what I'm saying. I feel all untied in a place like this; the rigidity of one's nature begins to melt and flow. Surely *you* must understand what I mean!"

"Of course I understand," I replied, yet not wishing to encourage her in her present line of thought, "and it's a grand experience – for a short time. But you're overtired tonight, Joan, like the rest of us. A few days in this air will set you above all fears of the kind you mention."

Then, after a moment's silence, I added, feeling I should estrange her confidence altogether if I blundered any more and treated her like a child –

"I think, perhaps, the true explanation is that you pity him for loving you, and at the same time you feel the repulsion of the healthy, vigorous animal for what is weak and timid. If he came up boldly and took you by the throat and shouted that he would force you to love him – well, then you would feel no fear at all. You would know exactly how to deal with him. Isn't it, perhaps, something of that kind?"

The girl made no reply, and when I took her hand I felt that it trembled a little and was cold.

"It's not his love that I'm afraid of," she said hurriedly, for at this moment we heard the dip of a paddle in the water, "it's something in his very soul that terrifies me in a way I have never been terrified before, – yet fascinates me. In town I was hardly conscious of his presence. But the moment we got away from civilisation, it began to come. He seems so – so *real* up here. I dread being alone with him. It makes me feel that something must burst and tear its way out – that he would do something – or I should do something – I don't know exactly what I mean, probably, – but that I should let myself go and scream—"

"Joan!"

"Don't be alarmed," she laughed shortly; "I shan't do anything silly, but I wanted to tell you my feelings in case I needed your help. When I have intuitions as strong as this they are never wrong, only I don't know yet what it means exactly."

"You must hold out for the month, at any rate," I said in as matter-of-fact a voice as I could manage, for her manner had somehow changed my surprise to a subtle sense of alarm. "Sangree only stays the month, you know. And, anyhow, you are such an odd creature yourself that you should feel generously towards other odd creatures," I ended lamely, with a forced laugh.

She gave my hand a sudden pressure. "I'm glad I've told you at any rate," she said quickly under her breath, for the canoe was now gliding up silently like a ghost to our feet, "and I'm glad you're here, too," she added as we moved down towards the water to meet it.

I made Sangree change into the bows and got into the steering seat myself, putting the girl between us so that I could watch them both by keeping their outlines against the sea and stars. For the intuitions of certain folk – women and children usually, I confess – I have always felt a great respect that has more often than not been justified by experience; and now the curious emotion stirred in me by the girl's words remained somewhat vividly in my consciousness. I explained it in some measure by the fact that the girl, tired out by the fatigue of many days' travel, had suffered a vigorous reaction of some kind from the strong, desolate scenery, and further, perhaps, that she had been treated to my own experience of seeing the members of the party in a new light – the Canadian, being partly a stranger, more vividly than the rest of us. But, at the same time, I felt it was quite possible that she had sensed some subtle link between his personality and her own, some quality that she had hitherto ignored and that the routine of town life had kept buried out of sight. The only thing that seemed difficult to explain was the fear she had spoken of, and this I hoped the wholesome effects of camp-life and exercise would sweep away naturally in the course of time.

We made the tour of the island without speaking. It was all too beautiful for speech. The trees crowded down to the shore to hear us pass. We saw their fine dark heads, bowed low with splendid dignity to watch us, forgetting for a moment that the stars were caught in the needled network of their hair. Against the sky in the west, where still lingered the sunset gold, we saw the wild toss of the horizon, shaggy with forest and cliff, gripping the heart like the motive in a symphony, and sending the sense of beauty all a-shiver through the mind – all these surrounding islands standing above the water like low clouds, and like them seeming to post along silently into the engulfing night. We heard the musical drip-drip of the paddle, and the little wash of our waves on the shore, and then suddenly we found ourselves at the opening of the lagoon again, having made the complete circuit of our home.

The Reverend Timothy had awakened from sleep and was singing to himself; and the sound of his voice as we glided down the fifty yards of enclosed water was pleasant to hear and undeniably wholesome. We saw the glow of the fire up among the trees on the ridge, and his shadow moving about as he threw on more wood.

"There you are!" he called aloud. "Good again! Been setting the night-lines, eh? Capital! And your mother's still fast asleep, Joan."

His cheery laugh floated across the water; he had not been in the least disturbed by our absence, for old campers are not easily alarmed.

"Now, remember," he went on, after we had told our little tale of travel by the fire, and Mrs. Maloney had asked for the fourth time exactly where her tent was and whether the door faced east or south, "every one takes their turn at cooking breakfast, and one of the men is always out at sunrise to catch it first. Hubbard, I'll toss you which you do in the morning and which I do!" He lost the toss. "Then I'll catch it," I said, laughing at his discomfiture, for I knew he loathed stirring porridge. "And mind you don't burn it as you did every blessed time last year on the Volga," I added by way of reminder.

Mrs. Maloney's fifth interruption about the door of her tent, and her further pointed observation that it was past nine o'clock, set us lighting lanterns and putting the fire out for safety.

But before we separated for the night the clergyman had a time-honoured little ritual of his own to go through that no one had the heart to deny him. He always did this. It was a relic of his pulpit habits. He glanced briefly from one to the other of us, his face grave and earnest, his hands lifted to the stars and his eyes all closed and puckered up beneath a momentary frown. Then he offered up a short, almost inaudible prayer, thanking Heaven for our safe arrival, begging for good weather, no illness or accidents, plenty of fish, and strong sailing winds.

And then, unexpectedly – no one knew why exactly – he ended up with an abrupt request that nothing from the kingdom of darkness should be allowed to afflict our peace, and no evil thing come near to disturb us in the night-time.

And while he uttered these last surprising words, so strangely unlike his usual ending, it chanced that I looked up and let my eyes wander round the group assembled about the dying fire. And it certainly seemed to me that Sangree's face underwent a sudden and visible alteration. He was staring at Joan, and as he stared the change ran over it like a shadow and was gone. I started in spite of myself, for something oddly concentrated, potent, collected, had come into the expression usually so scattered and feeble. But it was all swift as a passing meteor, and when I looked a second time his face was normal and he was looking among the trees.

And Joan, luckily, had not observed him, her head being bowed and her eyes tightly closed while her father prayed.

"The girl has a vivid imagination indeed," I thought, half laughing, as I lit the lanterns, "if her thoughts can put a glamour upon mine in this way"; and yet somehow, when we said good-night, I took occasion to give her a few vigorous words of encouragement, and went to her tent to make sure I could find it quickly in the night in case anything happened. In her quick way the girl understood and thanked me, and the last thing I heard as I moved off to the men's quarters was Mrs. Maloney crying that there were beetles in her tent, and Joan's laughter as she went to help her turn them out.

Half an hour later the island was silent as the grave, but for the mournful voices of the wind as it sighed up from the sea. Like white sentries stood the three tents of the men on one side of the ridge, and on the other side, half hidden by some birches, whose leaves just shivered as the breeze caught them, the women's tents, patches of ghostly grey, gathered more closely together for mutual shelter and protection. Something like fifty yards of broken ground, grey rock, moss and lichen, lay between, and over all lay the curtain of the night and the great whispering winds from the forests of Scandinavia.

And the very last thing, just before floating away on that mighty wave that carries one so softly off into the deeps of forgetfulness, I again heard the voice of John Silence as the train moved out of Victoria Station; and by some subtle connection that met me on the very threshold of consciousness there rose in my mind simultaneously the memory of the girl's half-given confidence, and of her distress. As by some wizardry of approaching dreams they seemed in that instant to be related; but before I could analyse the why and the wherefore, both sank away out of sight again, and I was off beyond recall.

"Unless you should send for me sooner."

## Chapter II

**WHETHER** Mrs. Maloney's tent door opened south or east I think she never discovered, for it is quite certain she always slept with the flap tightly fastened; I only know that my own little 'five by seven, all silk' faced due east, because next morning the sun, pouring in as only the wilderness sun knows how to pour, woke me early, and a moment later, with a short run over soft moss and a flying dive from the granite ledge, I was swimming in the most sparkling water imaginable.

It was barely four o'clock, and the sun came down a long vista of blue islands that led out to the open sea and Finland. Nearer by rose the wooded domes of our own property, still capped and wreathed with smoky trails of fast-melting mist, and looking as fresh as though it was the morning of Mrs. Maloney's Sixth Day and they had just issued, clean and brilliant, from the hands of the great Architect.

In the open spaces the ground was drenched with dew, and from the sea a cool salt wind stole in among the trees and set the branches trembling in an atmosphere of shimmering silver. The tents shone white where the sun caught them in patches. Below lay the lagoon, still dreaming of the summer night; in the open the fish were jumping busily, sending musical ripples towards the shore; and in the air hung the magic of dawn – silent, incommunicable.

I lit the fire, so that an hour later the clergyman should find good ashes to stir his porridge over, and then set forth upon an examination of the island, but hardly had I gone a dozen yards when I saw a figure standing a little in front of me where the sunlight fell in a pool among the trees.

It was Joan. She had already been up an hour, she told me, and had bathed before the last stars had left the sky. I saw at once that the new spirit of this solitary region had entered into her, banishing the fears of the night, for her face was like the face of a happy denizen of the wilderness, and her eyes stainless and shining. Her feet were bare, and drops of dew she had shaken from the branches hung in her loose-flying hair. Obviously she had come into her own.

"I've been all over the island," she announced laughingly, "and there are two things wanting."

"You're a good judge, Joan. What are they?"

"There's no animal life, and there's no – water."

"They go together," I said. "Animals don't bother with a rock like this unless there's a spring on it."

And as she led me from place to place, happy and excited, leaping adroitly from rock to rock, I was glad to note that my first impressions were correct. She made no reference to our conversation of the night before. The new spirit had driven out the old. There was no room in her heart for fear or anxiety, and Nature had everything her own way.

The island, we found, was some three-quarters of a mile from point to point, built in a circle, or wide horseshoe, with an opening of twenty feet at the mouth of the lagoon. Pine-trees grew thickly all over, but here and there were patches of silver birch, scrub oak, and considerable colonies of wild raspberry and gooseberry bushes. The two ends of the horseshoe formed bare slabs of smooth granite running into the sea and forming dangerous reefs just below the surface, but the rest of the island rose in a forty-foot ridge and sloped down steeply to the sea on either side, being nowhere more than a hundred yards wide.

The outer shore-line was much indented with numberless coves and bays and sandy beaches, with here and there caves and precipitous little cliffs against which the sea broke in spray and thunder. But the inner shore, the shore of the lagoon, was low and regular, and so well protected by the wall of trees along the ridge that no storm could ever send more than a passing ripple along its sandy marges. Eternal shelter reigned there.

On one of the other islands, a few hundred yards away – for the rest of the party slept late this first morning, and we took to the canoe – we discovered a spring of fresh water untainted by the brackish flavour of the Baltic, and having thus solved the most important problem of the Camp, we next proceeded to deal with the second – fish. And in half an hour we reeled in and turned homewards, for we had no means of storage, and to clean more fish than may be stored or eaten in a day is no wise occupation for experienced campers.

And as we landed towards six o'clock we heard the clergyman singing as usual and saw his wife and Sangree shaking out their blankets in the sun, and dressed in a fashion that finally dispelled all memories of streets and civilisation.

"The Little People lit the fire for me," cried Maloney, looking natural and at home in his ancient flannel suit and breaking off in the middle of his singing, "so I've got the porridge going – and this time it's *not* burnt."

We reported the discovery of water and held up the fish.

"Good! Good again!" he cried. "We'll have the first decent breakfast we've had this year. Sangree'll clean 'em in no time, and the Bo'sun's Mate—"

"Will fry them to a turn," laughed the voice of Mrs. Maloney, appearing on the scene in a tight blue jersey and sandals, and catching up the frying-pan. Her husband always called her the Bo'sun's Mate in Camp, because it was her duty, among others, to pipe all hands to meals.

"And as for you, Joan," went on the happy man, "you look like the spirit of the island, with moss in your hair and wind in your eyes, and sun and stars mixed in your face." He looked at her with delighted admiration. "Here, Sangree, take these twelve, there's a good fellow, they're the biggest; and we'll have 'em in butter in less time than you can say Baltic island!"

I watched the Canadian as he slowly moved off to the cleaning pail. His eyes were drinking in the girl's beauty, and a wave of passionate, almost feverish, joy passed over his face, expressive of the ecstasy of true worship more than anything else. Perhaps he was thinking that he still had three weeks to come with that vision always before his eyes; perhaps he was thinking of his dreams in the night. I cannot say. But I noticed the curious mingling of yearning and happiness in his eyes, and the strength of the impression touched my curiosity. Something in his face held my gaze for a second, something to do with its intensity. That so timid, so gentle a personality should conceal so virile a passion almost seemed to require explanation.

But the impression was momentary, for that first breakfast in Camp permitted no divided attentions, and I dare swear that the porridge, the tea, the Swedish 'flatbread', and the fried fish flavoured with points of frizzled bacon, were better than any meal eaten elsewhere that day in the whole world.

The first clear day in a new camp is always a furiously busy one, and we soon dropped into the routine upon which in large measure the real comfort of everyone depends. About the cooking-fire, greatly improved with stones from the shore, we built a high stockade consisting of upright poles thickly twined with branches, the roof lined with moss and lichen and weighted with rocks, and round the interior we made low wooden seats so that we could lie round the fire even in rain and eat our meals in peace. Paths, too, outlined themselves from tent to tent, from the bathing places and the landing stage, and a fair division of the island was decided upon between the quarters of the men and the women. Wood was stacked, awkward trees and boulders removed, hammocks slung, and tents strengthened. In a word, Camp was established, and duties were assigned and accepted as though we expected to live on this Baltic island for years to come and the smallest detail of the Community life was important.

Moreover, as the Camp came into being, this sense of a community developed, proving that we were a definite whole, and not merely separate human beings living for a while in tents upon a desert island. Each fell willingly into the routine. Sangree, as by natural selection, took upon himself the cleaning of the fish and the cutting of the wood into lengths sufficient for a day's use. And he did it well. The pan of water was never without a fish, cleaned and scaled, ready to fry for whoever was hungry; the nightly fire never died down for lack of material to throw on without going farther afield to search.

And Timothy, once reverend, caught the fish and chopped down the trees. He also assumed responsibility for the condition of the boat, and did it so thoroughly that nothing in the little cutter was ever found wanting. And when, for any reason, his presence was in demand, the first place to look for him was – in the boat, and there, too, he was usually found, tinkering away with sheets, sails, or rudder and singing as he tinkered.

Nor was the 'reading' neglected; for most mornings there came a sound of droning voices form the white tent by the raspberry bushes, which signified that Sangree, the tutor, and whatever other man chanced to be in the party at the time, were hard at it with history or the classics.

And while Mrs. Maloney, also by natural selection, took charge of the larder and the kitchen, the mending and general supervision of the rough comforts, she also made herself peculiarly mistress of the megaphone which summoned to meals and carried her voice easily from one end of the island to the other; and in her hours of leisure she daubed the surrounding scenery on to a sketching block with all the honesty and devotion of her determined but unreceptive soul.

Joan, meanwhile, Joan, elusive creature of the wilds, became I know not exactly what. She did plenty of work in the Camp, yet seemed to have no very precise duties. She was everywhere and anywhere. Sometimes she slept in her tent, sometimes under the stars with a blanket. She knew every inch of the island and kept turning up in places where she was least expected – for ever wandering about, reading her books in sheltered corners, making little fires on sunless days to "worship by to the gods", as she put it, ever finding new pools to dive and bathe in, and swimming day and night in the warm and waveless lagoon like a fish in a huge tank. She went bare-legged and bare-footed, with her hair down and her skirts caught up to the knees, and if ever a human being turned into a jolly savage within the compass of a single week, Joan Maloney was certainly that human being. She ran wild.

So completely, too, was she possessed by the strong spirit of the place that the little human fear she had yielded to so strangely on our arrival seemed to have been utterly dispossessed. As I hoped and expected, she made no reference to our conversation of the first evening. Sangree bothered her with no special attentions, and after all they were very little together. His behaviour was perfect in that respect, and I, for my part, hardly gave the matter another thought. Joan was ever a prey to vivid fancies of one kind or another, and this was one of them. Mercifully for the happiness of all concerned, it had melted away before the spirit of busy, active life and deep content that reigned over the island. Everyone was intensely alive, and peace was upon all.

\* \* \*

Meanwhile the effect of the camp-life began to tell. Always a searching test of character, its results, sooner or later, are infallible, for it acts upon the soul as swiftly and surely as the hypo bath upon the negative of a photograph. A readjustment of the personal forces takes place quickly; some parts of the personality go to sleep, others wake up: but the first sweeping change that the primitive life brings about is that the artificial portions of the character shed themselves one after another like dead skins. Attitudes and poses that seemed genuine in the city drop away. The mind, like the body, grows quickly hard, simple, uncomplex. And in a camp as primitive and close to nature as ours was, these effects became speedily visible.

Some folk, of course, who talk glibly about the simple life when it is safely out of reach, betray themselves in camp by for ever peering about for the artificial excitements of civilisation which they miss. Some get bored at once; some grow slovenly; some reveal the animal in most unexpected fashion; and some, the select few, find themselves in very short order and are happy.

And, in our little party, we could flatter ourselves that we all belonged to the last category, so far as the general effect was concerned. Only there were certain other changes as well, varying with each individual, and all interesting to note.

It was only after the first week or two that these changes became marked, although this is the proper place, I think, to speak of them. For, having myself no other duty than to enjoy a well-earned holiday, I used to load my canoe with blankets and provisions and journey forth on exploration trips among the islands of several days together; and it was on my return from the first of these – when I rediscovered the party, so to speak – that these changes first presented themselves vividly to me, and in one particular instance produced a rather curious impression.

In a word, then, while everyone had grown wilder, naturally wilder, Sangree, it seemed to me, had grown much wilder, and what I can only call unnaturally wilder. He made me think of a savage.

To begin with, he had changed immensely in mere physical appearance, and the full brown cheeks, the brighter eyes of absolute health, and the general air of vigour and robustness that had come to replace his customary lassitude and timidity, had worked such an improvement that I hardly knew him for the same man. His voice, too, was deeper and his manner bespoke for the first time a greater measure of confidence in himself. He now had some claims to be called nice-looking, or at least to a certain air of virility that would not lessen his value in the eyes of the opposite sex.

All this, of course, was natural enough, and most welcome. But, altogether apart from this physical change, which no doubt had also been going forward in the rest of us, there was a subtle note in his personality that came to me with a degree of surprise that almost amounted to shock.

And two things – as he came down to welcome me and pull up the canoe – leaped up in my mind unbidden, as though connected in some way I could not at the moment divine – first, the curious judgment formed of him by Joan; and secondly, that fugitive expression I had caught in his face while Maloney was offering up his strange prayer for special protection from Heaven.

The delicacy of manner and feature – to call it by no milder term – which had always been a distinguishing characteristic of the man, had been replaced by something far more vigorous and decided, that yet utterly eluded analysis. The change which impressed me so oddly was not easy to name. The others – singing Maloney, the bustling Bo'sun's Mate, and Joan, that fascinating half-breed of undine and salamander – all showed the effects of a life so close to nature; but in their case the change was perfectly natural and what was to be expected, whereas with Peter Sangree, the Canadian, it was something unusual and unexpected.

It is impossible to explain how he managed gradually to convey to my mind the impression that something in him had turned savage, yet this, more or less, is the impression that he did convey. It was not that he seemed really less civilised, or that his character had undergone any definite alteration, but rather that something in him, hitherto dormant, had awakened to life. Some quality, latent till now – so far, at least, as we were concerned, who, after all, knew him but slightly – had stirred into activity and risen to the surface of his being.

And while, for the moment, this seemed as far as I could get, it was but natural that my mind should continue the intuitive process and acknowledge that John Silence, owing to his peculiar faculties, and the girl, owing to her singularly receptive temperament, might each in a different way have divined this latent quality in his soul, and feared its manifestation later.

On looking back to this painful adventure, too, it now seems equally natural that the same process, carried to its logical conclusion, should have wakened some deep instinct in me that, wholly without direction from my will, set itself sharply and persistently upon the watch from that very moment. Thenceforward the personality of Sangree was never far from my thoughts, and I was for ever analysing and searching for the explanation that took so long in coming.

"I declare, Hubbard, you're tanned like an aboriginal, and you look like one, too," laughed Maloney.

"And I can return the compliment," was my reply, as we all gathered round a brew of tea to exchange news and compare notes.

And later, at supper, it amused me to observe that the distinguished tutor, once clergyman, did not eat his food quite as 'nicely' as he did at home – he devoured it; that Mrs. Maloney ate more, and, to say the least, with less delay, than was her custom in the select atmosphere of her English dining-room; and that while Joan attacked her tin plateful with genuine avidity, Sangree, the Canadian, bit and gnawed at his, laughing and talking and complimenting the cook all the while, and making me think with secret amusement of a starved animal at its first meal. While, from their remarks about myself, I judged that I had changed and grown wild as much as the rest of them.

In this and in a hundred other little ways the change showed, ways difficult to define in detail, but all proving – not the coarsening effect of leading the primitive life, but, let us say, the more direct and unvarnished methods that became prevalent. For all day long we were in the bath of the elements – wind, water, sun – and just as the body became insensible to cold and shed unnecessary clothing, the mind grew straightforward and shed many of the disguises required by the conventions of civilisation.

And in each, according to temperament and character, there stirred the life-instincts that were natural, untamed, and, in a sense – savage.

## Chapter III

**SO IT** came about that I stayed with our island party, putting off my second exploring trip from day to day, and I think that this far-fetched instinct to watch Sangree was really the cause of my postponement.

For another ten days the life of the Camp pursued its even and delightful way, blessed by perfect summer weather, a good harvest of fish, fine winds for sailing, and calm, starry nights. Maloney's selfish prayer had been favourably received. Nothing came to disturb or perplex. There was not even the prowling of night animals to vex the rest of Mrs. Maloney; for in previous camps it had often been her peculiar affliction that she heard the porcupines scratching against the canvas, or the squirrels dropping fir-cones in the early morning with a sound of miniature thunder upon the roof of her tent. But on this island there was not even a squirrel or a mouse. I think two toads and a small and harmless snake were the only living creatures that had been discovered during the whole of the first fortnight. And these two toads in all probability were not two toads, but one toad.

Then, suddenly, came the terror that changed the whole aspect of the place – the devastating terror.

It came, at first, gently, but from the very start it made me realise the unpleasant loneliness of our situation, our remote isolation in this wilderness of sea and rock, and how the islands in this tideless Baltic ocean lay about us like the advance guard of a vast besieging army. Its entry, as I say, was gentle, hardly noticeable, in fact, to most of us: singularly undramatic it certainly was. But, then, in actual life this is often the way the dreadful climaxes move upon us, leaving the heart undisturbed almost to the last minute, and then overwhelming it with a sudden rush of horror. For it was the custom at breakfast to listen patiently while each in turn related the trivial adventures of the night – how they slept, whether the wind shook their tent, whether the spider on the ridge pole had moved, whether they had heard the toad, and so forth – and on this particular morning Joan, in the middle of a little pause, made a truly novel announcement:

"In the night I heard the howling of a dog," she said, and then flushed up to the roots of her hair when we burst out laughing. For the idea of there being a dog on this forsaken island that was only able to support a snake and two toads was distinctly ludicrous, and I remember Maloney, half-way through his burnt porridge, capping the announcement by declaring that he had heard a 'Baltic turtle' in the lagoon, and his wife's expression of frantic alarm before the laughter undeceived her.

But the next morning Joan repeated the story with additional and convincing detail.

"Sounds of whining and growling woke me," she said, "and I distinctly heard sniffing under my tent, and the scratching of paws."

"Oh, Timothy! Can it be a porcupine?" exclaimed the Bo'sun's Mate with distress, forgetting that Sweden was not Canada.

But the girl's voice had sounded to me in quite another key, and looking up I saw that her father and Sangree were staring at her hard. They, too, understood that she was in earnest, and had been struck by the serious note in her voice.

"Rubbish, Joan! You are always dreaming something or other wild," her father said a little impatiently.

"There's not an animal of any size on the whole island," added Sangree with a puzzled expression. He never took his eyes from her face.

"But there's nothing to prevent one swimming over," I put in briskly, for somehow a sense of uneasiness that was not pleasant had woven itself into the talk and pauses. "A deer, for instance, might easily land in the night and take a look round—"

"Or a bear!" gasped the Bo'sun's Mate, with a look so portentous that we all welcomed the laugh.

But Joan did not laugh. Instead, she sprang up and called to us to follow.

"There," she said, pointing to the ground by her tent on the side farthest from her mother's; "there are the marks close to my head. You can see for yourselves."

We saw plainly. The moss and lichen – for earth there was hardly any – had been scratched up by paws. An animal about the size of a large dog it must have been, to judge by the marks. We stood and stared in a row.

"Close to my head," repeated the girl, looking round at us. Her face, I noticed, was very pale, and her lip seemed to quiver for an instant. Then she gave a sudden gulp – and burst into a flood of tears.

The whole thing had come about in the brief space of a few minutes, and with a curious sense of inevitableness, moreover, as though it had all been carefully planned from all time and nothing could have stopped it. It had all been rehearsed before – had actually happened before, as the strange feeling sometimes has it; it seemed like the opening movement in some ominous drama, and that I knew exactly what would happen next. Something of great moment was impending.

For this sinister sensation of coming disaster made itself felt from the very beginning, and an atmosphere of gloom and dismay pervaded the entire Camp from that moment forward.

I drew Sangree to one side and moved away, while Maloney took the distressed girl into her tent, and his wife followed them, energetic and greatly flustered.

For thus, in undramatic fashion, it was that the terror I have spoken of first attempted the invasion of our Camp, and, trivial and unimportant though it seemed, every little detail of this opening scene is photographed upon my mind with merciless accuracy and precision. It happened exactly as described. This was exactly the language used. I see it written before me in black and white. I see, too, the faces of all concerned with the sudden ugly signature of alarm where before had been peace. The terror had stretched out, so to speak, a first tentative feeler toward us and had touched the hearts of each with a horrid directness. And from this moment the Camp changed.

Sangree in particular was visibly upset. He could not bear to see the girl distressed, and to hear her actually cry was almost more than he could stand. The feeling that he had no right to protect her hurt him keenly, and I could see that he was itching to do something to help, and liked him for it. His expression said plainly that he would tear in a thousand pieces anything that dared to injure a hair of her head.

We lit our pipes and strolled over in silence to the men's quarters, and it was his odd Canadian expression "Gee whiz!" that drew my attention to a further discovery.

"The brute's been scratching round my tent too," he cried, as he pointed to similar marks by the door and I stooped down to examine them. We both stared in amazement for several minutes without speaking.

"Only I sleep like the dead," he added, straightening up again, "and so heard nothing, I suppose."

We traced the paw-marks from the mouth of his tent in a direct line across to the girl's, but nowhere else about the Camp was there a sign of the strange visitor. The deer, dog, or whatever it was that had twice favoured us with a visit in the night, had confined its attentions to these two tents. And, after all, there was really nothing out of the way about these visits of an unknown animal, for although our own island was destitute of life, we were in the heart of a wilderness, and the mainland and larger islands must be swarming with all kinds of four-footed creatures, and no very prolonged swimming was necessary to reach us. In any other country it would not have caused a moment's interest – interest of the kind we felt, that is. In our Canadian camps the bears were for ever grunting about among the provision bags at night, porcupines scratching unceasingly, and chipmunks scuttling over everything.

"My daughter is overtired, and that's the truth of it," explained Maloney presently when he rejoined us and had examined in turn the other paw-marks. "She's been overdoing it lately, and camp-life, you know, always means a great excitement to her. It's natural enough, if we take no notice she'll be all right." He paused to borrow my tobacco pouch and fill his pipe, and the blundering way he filled it and spilled the precious weed on the ground visibly belied the calm of his easy language. "You might take her out for a bit of fishing, Hubbard, like a good chap; she's hardly up to the long day in the cutter. Show her some of the other islands in your canoe, perhaps. Eh?"

And by lunch-time the cloud had passed away as suddenly, and as suspiciously, as it had come.

But in the canoe, on our way home, having till then purposely ignored the subject uppermost in our minds, she suddenly spoke to me in a way that again touched the note of sinister alarm – the note that kept on sounding and sounding until finally John Silence came with his great vibrating presence and relieved it; yes, and even after he came, too, for a while.

"I'm ashamed to ask it," she said abruptly, as she steered me home, her sleeves rolled up, her hair blowing in the wind, "and ashamed of my silly tears too, because I really can't make out what caused them; but, Mr. Hubbard, I want you to promise me not to go off for your long expeditions – just yet. I beg it of you." She was so in earnest that she forgot the canoe, and the wind caught it sideways and made us roll dangerously. "I have tried hard not to ask this," she added, bringing the canoe round again, "but I simply can't help myself."

It was a good deal to ask, and I suppose my hesitation was plain; for she went on before I could reply, and her beseeching expression and intensity of manner impressed me very forcibly.

"For another two weeks only—"

"Mr. Sangree leaves in a fortnight," I said, seeing at once what she was driving at, but wondering if it was best to encourage her or not.

"If I knew you were to be on the island till then," she said, her face alternately pale and blushing, and her voice trembling a little, "I should feel so much happier."

I looked at her steadily, waiting for her to finish.

"And safer," she added almost in a whisper; "especially – at night, I mean."

"Safer, Joan?" I repeated, thinking I had never seen her eyes so soft and tender. She nodded her head, keeping her gaze fixed on my face.

It was really difficult to refuse, whatever my thoughts and judgment may have been, and somehow I understood that she spoke with good reason, though for the life of me I could not have put it into words.

"Happier – and safer," she said gravely, the canoe giving a dangerous lurch as she leaned forward in her seat to catch my answer. Perhaps, after all, the wisest way was to grant her request and make light of it, easing her anxiety without too much encouraging its cause.

"All right, Joan, you queer creature; I promise," and the instant look of relief in her face, and the smile that came back like sunlight to her eyes, made me feel that, unknown to myself and the world, I was capable of considerable sacrifice after all.

"But, you know, there's nothing to be afraid of," I added sharply; and she looked up in my face with the smile women use when they know we are talking idly, yet do not wish to tell us so.

"*You* don't feel afraid, I know," she observed quietly.

"Of course not; why should I?"

"So, if you will just humour me this once I – I will never ask anything foolish of you again as long as I live," she said gratefully.

"You have my promise," was all I could find to say.

She headed the nose of the canoe for the lagoon lying a quarter of a mile ahead, and paddled swiftly; but a minute or two later she paused again and stared hard at me with the dripping paddle across the thwarts.

"You've not heard anything at night yourself, have you?" she asked.

"I never hear anything at night," I replied shortly, "from the moment I lie down till the moment I get up."

"That dismal howling, for instance," she went on, determined to get it out, "far away at first and then getting closer, and stopping just outside the Camp?"

"Certainly not."

"Because, sometimes I think I almost dreamed it."

"Most likely you did," was my unsympathetic response.

"And you don't think father has heard it either, then?"

"No. He would have told me if he had."

This seemed to relieve her mind a little. "I know mother hasn't," she added, as if speaking to herself, "for she hears nothing – ever."

\* \* \*

It was two nights after this conversation that I woke out of deep sleep and heard sounds of screaming. The voice was really horrible, breaking the peace and silence with its shrill clamour. In less than ten seconds I was half dressed and out of my tent. The screaming had stopped abruptly, but I knew the general direction, and ran as fast as the darkness would allow over to the women's quarters, and on getting close I heard sounds of suppressed weeping. It was Joan's voice. And just as I came up I saw Mrs. Maloney, marvellously attired, fumbling with a lantern. Other voices became audible in the same moment behind me, and Timothy Maloney arrived, breathless, less than half dressed, and carrying another lantern that had gone out on the way from being banged against a tree. Dawn was just breaking, and a chill wind blew in from the sea. Heavy black clouds drove low overhead.

The scene of confusion may be better imagined than described. Questions in frightened voices filled the air against this background of suppressed weeping. Briefly – Joan's silk tent had been torn, and the girl was in a state bordering upon hysterics. Somewhat reassured by our noisy presence, however – for she was plucky at heart – she pulled herself together and tried to explain what had happened; and her broken words, told there on the edge of night and morning upon this wild island ridge, were oddly thrilling and distressingly convincing.

"Something touched me and I woke," she said simply, but in a voice still hushed and broken with the terror of it, "something pushing against the tent; I felt it through the canvas. There was the same sniffing and scratching as before, and I felt the tent give a little as when wind shakes it. I heard breathing – very loud, very heavy breathing – and then came a sudden great tearing blow, and the canvas ripped open close to my face."

She had instantly dashed out through the open flap and screamed at the top of her voice, thinking the creature had actually got into the tent. But nothing was visible, she declared, and she heard not the faintest sound of an animal making off under cover of the darkness. The brief account seemed to exercise a paralysing effect upon us all as we listened to it. I can see the dishevelled group to this day, the wind blowing the women's hair, and Maloney craning his head forward to listen, and his wife, open-mouthed and gasping, leaning against a pine tree.

"Come over to the stockade and we'll get the fire going," I said; "that's the first thing," for we were all shaking with the cold in our scanty garments. And at that moment

Sangree arrived wrapped in a blanket and carrying his gun; he was still drunken with sleep.

"The dog again," Maloney explained briefly, forestalling his questions; "been at Joan's tent. Torn it, by Gad! this time. It's time we did something." He went on mumbling confusedly to himself.

Sangree gripped his gun and looked about swiftly in the darkness. I saw his eyes aflame in the glare of the flickering lanterns. He made a movement as though to start out and hunt – and kill. Then his glance fell on the girl crouching on the ground, her face hidden in her hands, and there leaped into his features an expression of savage anger that transformed them. He could have faced a dozen lions with a walking stick at that moment, and again I liked him for the strength of his anger, his self-control, and his hopeless devotion.

But I stopped him going off on a blind and useless chase.

"Come and help me start the fire, Sangree," I said, anxious also to relieve the girl of our presence; and a few minutes later the ashes, still growing from the night's fire, had kindled the fresh wood, and there was a blaze that warmed us well while it also lit up the surrounding trees within a radius of twenty yards.

"I heard nothing," he whispered; "what in the world do you think it is? It surely can't be only a dog!"

"We'll find that out later," I said, as the others came up to the grateful warmth; "the first thing is to make as big a fire as we can."

Joan was calmer now, and her mother had put on some warmer, and less miraculous, garments. And while they stood talking in low voices Maloney and I slipped off to examine the tent. There was little enough to see, but that little was unmistakable. Some animal had scratched up the ground at the head of the tent, and with a great blow of a powerful paw – a paw clearly provided with good claws – had struck the silk and torn it open. There was a hole large enough to pass a fist and arm through.

"It can't be far away," Maloney said excitedly. "We'll organise a hunt at once; this very minute."

We hurried back to the fire, Maloney talking boisterously about his proposed hunt. "There's nothing like prompt action to dispel alarm," he whispered in my ear; and then turned to the rest of us.

"We'll hunt the island from end to end at once," he said, with excitement; "that's what we'll do. The beast can't be far away. And the Bo'sun's Mate and Joan must come too, because they can't be left alone. Hubbard, you take the right shore, and you, Sangree, the left, and I'll go in the middle with the women. In this way we can stretch clean across the ridge, and nothing bigger than a rabbit can possibly escape us." He was extraordinarily excited, I thought. Anything affecting Joan, of course, stirred him prodigiously. "Get your guns and we'll start the drive at once," he cried. He lit another lantern and handed one each to his wife and Joan, and while I ran to fetch my gun I heard him singing to himself with the excitement of it all.

Meanwhile the dawn had come on quickly. It made the flickering lanterns look pale. The wind, too, was rising, and I heard the trees moaning overhead and the waves breaking with increasing clamour on the shore. In the lagoon the boat dipped and splashed, and the sparks from the fire were carried aloft in a stream and scattered far and wide.

We made our way to the extreme end of the island, measured our distances carefully, and then began to advance. None of us spoke. Sangree and I, with cocked guns, watched the shore lines, and all within easy touch and speaking distance. It was a slow and blundering drive, and there were many false alarms, but after the best part of half an hour we stood on the farther end, having made the complete tour, and without putting up so much as a squirrel. Certainly there was no living creature on that island but ourselves.

"I know what it is!" cried Maloney, looking out over the dim expanse of grey sea, and speaking with the air of a man making a discovery; "it's a dog from one of the farms on the larger islands" – he pointed seawards where the archipelago thickened – "and it's escaped and turned wild. Our fires and voices attracted it, and it's probably half starved as well as savage, poor brute!"

No one said anything in reply, and he began to sing again very low to himself.

The point where we stood – a huddled, shivering group – faced the wider channels that led to the open sea and Finland. The grey dawn had broken in earnest at last, and we could see the racing waves with their angry crests of white. The surrounding islands showed up as dark masses in the distance, and in the east, almost as Maloney spoke, the sun came up with a rush in a stormy and magnificent sky of red and gold. Against this splashed and gorgeous background black clouds, shaped like fantastic and legendary animals, filed past swiftly in a tearing stream, and to this day I have only to close my eyes to see again that vivid and hurrying procession in the air. All about us the pines made black splashes against the sky. It was an angry sunrise. Rain, indeed, had already begun to fall in big drops.

We turned, as by a common instinct, and, without speech, made our way back slowly to the stockade, Maloney humming snatches of his songs, Sangree in front with his gun, prepared to shoot at a moment's notice, and the women floundering in the rear with myself and the extinguished lanterns.

Yet it was only a dog!

Really, it was most singular when one came to reflect soberly upon it all. Events, say the occultists, have souls, or at least that agglomerate life due to the emotions and thoughts of all concerned in them, so that cities, and even whole countries, have great astral shapes which may become visible to the eye of vision; and certainly here, the soul of this drive – this vain, blundering, futile drive – stood somewhere between ourselves and – laughed.

All of us heard that laugh, and all of us tried hard to smother the sound, or at least to ignore it. Everyone talked at once, loudly, and with exaggerated decision, obviously trying to say something plausible against heavy odds, striving to explain naturally that an animal might so easily conceal itself from us, or swim away before we had time to light upon its trail. For we all spoke of that 'trail' as though it really existed, and we had more to go upon than the mere marks of paws about the tents of Joan and the Canadian. Indeed, but for these, and the torn tent, I think it would, of course, have been possible to ignore the existence of this beast intruder altogether.

And it was here, under this angry dawn, as we stood in the shelter of the stockade from the pouring rain, weary yet so strangely excited – it was here, out of this confusion of voices and explanations, that – very stealthily – the ghost of something horrible slipped in and stood among us. It made all our explanations seem childish and untrue; the false relation was instantly exposed. Eyes exchanged quick, anxious glances, questioning, expressive of dismay. There was a sense of wonder, of poignant distress, and of trepidation. Alarm stood waiting at our elbows. We shivered.

Then, suddenly, as we looked into each other's faces, came the long, unwelcome pause in which this new arrival established itself in our hearts.

And, without further speech, or attempt at explanation, Maloney moved off abruptly to mix the porridge for an early breakfast; Sangree to clean the fish; myself to chop wood and tend the fire; Joan and her mother to change their wet garments; and, most significant of all, to prepare her mother's tent for its future complement of two.

Each went to his duty, but hurriedly, awkwardly, silently; and this new arrival, this shape of terror and distress stalked, viewless, by the side of each.

"If only I could have traced that dog," I think was the thought in the minds of all.

But in Camp, where everyone realises how important the individual contribution is to the comfort and well-being of all, the mind speedily recovers tone and pulls itself together.

During the day, a day of heavy and ceaseless rain, we kept more or less to our tents, and though there were signs of mysterious conferences between the three members of the Maloney family, I think that most of us slept a good deal and stayed alone with his thoughts. Certainly, I did, because when Maloney came to say that his wife invited us all to a special 'tea' in her tent, he had to shake me awake before I realised that he was there at all.

And by supper-time we were more or less even-minded again, and almost jolly. I only noticed that there was an undercurrent of what is best described as 'jumpiness', and that the merest snapping of a twig, or plop of a fish in the lagoon, was sufficient to make us start and look over our shoulders. Pauses were rare in our talk, and the fire was never for one instant allowed to get low. The wind and rain had ceased, but the dripping of the branches still kept up an excellent imitation of a downpour. In particular, Maloney was vigilant and alert, telling us a series of tales in which the wholesome humorous element was especially strong. He lingered, too, behind with me after Sangree had gone to bed, and while I mixed myself a glass of hot Swedish punch, he did a thing I had never known him do before – he mixed one for himself, and then asked me to light him over to his tent. We said nothing on the way, but I felt that he was glad of my companionship.

I returned alone to the stockade, and for a long time after that kept the fire blazing, and sat up smoking and thinking. I hardly knew why; but sleep was far from me for one thing, and for another, an idea was taking form in my mind that required the comfort of tobacco and a bright fire for its growth. I lay against a corner of the stockade seat, listening to the wind whispering and to the ceaseless drip-drip of the trees. The night, otherwise, was very still, and the sea quiet as a lake. I remember that I was conscious, peculiarly conscious, of this host of desolate islands crowding about us in the darkness, and that we were the one little spot of humanity in a rather wonderful kind of wilderness.

But this, I think, was the only symptom that came to warn me of highly strung nerves, and it certainly was not sufficiently alarming to destroy my peace of mind. One thing, however, did come to disturb my peace, for just as I finally made ready to go, and had kicked the embers of the fire into a last effort, I fancied I saw, peering at me round the farther end of the stockade wall, a dark and shadowy mass that might have been – that strongly resembled, in fact – the body of a large animal. Two glowing eyes shone for an instant in the middle of it. But the next second I saw that it was merely a projecting mass of moss and lichen in the wall of our stockade, and the eyes were a couple of wandering sparks from the dying ashes I had kicked. It was easy enough, too, to imagine I saw an animal moving here and there between the trees, as I picked my way stealthily to my tent. Of course, the shadows tricked me.

And though it was after one o'clock, Maloney's light was still burning, for I saw his tent shining white among the pines.

It was, however, in the short space between consciousness and sleep – that time when the body is low and the voices of the submerged region tell sometimes true – that the idea which had been all this while maturing reached the point of an actual decision, and I suddenly realised that I had resolved to send word to Dr. Silence. For, with a sudden wonder that I had hitherto been so blind, the unwelcome conviction dawned upon me all at once that some dreadful thing was lurking about us on this island, and that the safety of at least one of us was threatened by something monstrous and unclean that was too horrible to contemplate. And, again remembering those last words of his as the train moved out of the platform, I understood that Dr. Silence would hold himself in readiness to come.

"Unless you should send for me sooner," he had said.

\* \* \*

I found myself suddenly wide awake. It is impossible to say what woke me, but it was no gradual process, seeing that I jumped from deep sleep to absolute alertness in a single instant. I had evidently slept for an hour and more, for the night had cleared, stars crowded the sky, and a pallid half-moon just sinking into the sea threw a spectral light between the trees.

I went outside to sniff the air, and stood upright. A curious impression that something was astir in the Camp came over me, and when I glanced across at Sangree's tent, some twenty feet away, I saw that it was moving. He too, then, was awake and restless, for I saw the canvas sides bulge this way and that as he moved within.

The flap pushed forward. He was coming out, like myself, to sniff the air; and I was not surprised, for its sweetness after the rain was intoxicating. And he came on all fours, just as I had done. I saw a head thrust round the edge of the tent.

And then I saw that it was not Sangree at all. It was an animal. And the same instant I realised something else too – it was *the* animal; and its whole presentment for some unaccountable reason was unutterably malefic.

A cry I was quite unable to suppress escaped me, and the creature turned on the instant and stared at me with baleful eyes. I could have dropped on the spot, for the strength all ran out of my body with a rush. Something about it touched in me the living terror that grips and paralyses. If the mind requires but the tenth of a second to form an impression, I must have stood there stockstill for several seconds while I seized the ropes for support and stared. Many and vivid impressions flashed through my mind, but not one of them resulted in action, because I was in instant dread that the beast any moment would leap in my direction and be upon me. Instead, however, after what seemed a vast period, it slowly turned its eyes from my face, uttered a low whining sound, and came out altogether into the open.

Then, for the first time, I saw it in its entirety and noted two things: it was about the size of a large dog, but at the same time it was utterly unlike any animal that I had ever seen. Also, that the quality that had impressed me first as being malefic was really only its singular and original strangeness. Foolish as it may sound, and impossible as it is for me to adduce proof, I can only say that the animal seemed to me then to be – not real.

But all this passed through my mind in a flash, almost subconsciously, and before I had time to check my impressions, or even properly verify them, I made an involuntary movement, catching the tight rope in my hand so that it twanged like a banjo string, and in that instant the creature turned the corner of Sangree's tent and was gone into the darkness.

Then, of course, my senses in some measure returned to me, and I realised only one thing: it had been inside his tent!

I dashed out, reached the door in half a dozen strides, and looked in. The Canadian, thank God! lay upon his bed of branches. His arm was stretched outside, across the blankets, the fist tightly clenched, and the body had an appearance of unusual rigidity that was alarming. On his face there was an expression of effort, almost of painful effort, so far as the uncertain light permitted me to see, and his sleep seemed to be very profound. He looked, I thought, so stiff, so unnaturally stiff, and in some indefinable way, too, he looked smaller – shrunken.

I called to him to wake, but called many times in vain. Then I decided to shake him, and had already moved forward to do so vigorously when there came a sound of footsteps padding softly behind me, and I felt a stream of hot breath burn my neck as I stooped. I turned sharply. The tent door was darkened and something silently swept in. I felt a rough and shaggy body push past me, and knew that the animal had returned. It seemed to leap forward between me and Sangree – in fact, to leap upon Sangree, for its dark body hid him momentarily from view, and in that moment my soul turned sick and coward with a horror that rose from the very dregs and depths of life, and gripped my existence at its central source.

The creature seemed somehow to melt away into him, almost as though it belonged to him and were a part of himself, but in the same instant – that instant of extraordinary confusion and terror in my mind – it seemed to pass over and behind him, and, in some utterly unaccountable fashion, it was gone. And the Canadian woke and sat up with a start.

"Quick! You fool!" I cried, in my excitement, "the beast has been in your tent, here at your very throat while you sleep like the dead. Up, man! Get your gun! Only this second it disappeared over there behind your head. Quick! or Joan—!"

And somehow the fact that he was there, wide-awake now, to corroborate me, brought the additional conviction to my own mind that this was no animal, but some perplexing and dreadful form of life that drew upon my deeper knowledge, that much reading had perhaps assented to, but that had never yet come within actual range of my senses.

He was up in a flash, and out. He was trembling, and very white. We searched hurriedly, feverishly, but found only the traces of paw-marks passing from the door of his own tent across the moss to the women's. And the sight of the tracks about Mrs. Maloney's tent, where Joan now slept, set him in a perfect fury.

"Do you know what it is, Hubbard, this beast?" he hissed under his breath at me; "it's a damned wolf, that's what it is – a wolf lost among the islands, and starving to death – desperate. So help me God, I believe it's that!"

He talked a lot of rubbish in his excitement. He declared he would sleep by day and sit up every night until he killed it. Again his rage touched my admiration; but I got him away before he made enough noise to wake the whole Camp.

"I have a better plan than that," I said, watching his face closely. "I don't think this is anything we can deal with. I'm going to send for the only man I know who can help. We'll go to Waxholm this very morning and get a telegram through."

Sangree stared at me with a curious expression as the fury died out of his face and a new look of alarm took its place.

"John Silence," I said, "will know—"

"You think it's something – of that sort?" he stammered.

"I am sure of it."

There was a moment's pause. "That's worse, far worse than anything material," he said, turning visibly paler. He looked from my face to the sky, and then added with sudden resolution, "Come; the wind's rising. Let's get off at once. From there you can telephone to Stockholm and get a telegram sent without delay."

I sent him down to get the boat ready, and seized the opportunity myself to run and wake Maloney. He was sleeping very lightly, and sprang up the moment I put my head inside his tent. I told him briefly what I had seen, and he showed so little surprise that I caught myself wondering for the first time whether he himself had seen more going on than he had deemed wise to communicate to the rest of us.

He agreed to my plan without a moment's hesitation, and my last words to him were to let his wife and daughter think that the great psychic doctor was coming merely as a chance visitor, and not with any professional interest.

So, with frying-pan, provisions, and blankets aboard, Sangree and I sailed out of the lagoon fifteen minutes later, and headed with a good breeze for the direction of Waxholm and the borders of civilisation.

## Chapter IV

**ALTHOUGH** nothing John Silence did ever took me, properly speaking, by surprise, it was certainly unexpected to find a letter from Stockholm waiting for me. "I have finished my Hungary business," he wrote, "and am here for ten days. Do not hesitate to send if you need me. If you telephone any morning from Waxholm I can catch the afternoon steamer."

My years of intercourse with him were full of 'coincidences' of this description, and although he never sought to explain them by claiming any magical system of communication with my mind, I have never doubted that there actually existed some secret telepathic method by which he knew my circumstances and gauged the degree of my need. And that this power was independent of time in the sense that it saw into the future, always seemed to me equally apparent.

Sangree was as much relieved as I was, and within an hour of sunset that very evening we met him on the arrival of the little coasting steamer, and carried him off in the dinghy to the camp we had prepared on a neighbouring island, meaning to start for home early next morning.

"Now," he said, when supper was over and we were smoking round the fire, "let me hear your story." He glanced from one to the other, smiling.

"You tell it, Mr. Hubbard," Sangree interrupted abruptly, and went off a little way to wash the dishes, yet not so far as to be out of earshot. And while he splashed with the hot water, and scraped the tin plates with sand and moss, my voice, unbroken by a single question from Dr. Silence, ran on for the next half-hour with the best account I could give of what had happened.

My listener lay on the other side of the fire, his face half hidden by a big sombrero; sometimes he glanced up questioningly when a point needed elaboration, but he uttered no single word till I had reached the end, and his manner all through the recital was grave and attentive. Overhead, the wash of the wind in the pine branches filled in the pauses; the darkness settled down over the sea, and the stars came out in thousands, and by the time I finished the moon had risen to flood the scene with silver. Yet, by his face and eyes, I knew quite well that the doctor was listening to something he had expected to hear, even if he had not actually anticipated all the details.

"You did well to send for me," he said very low, with a significant glance at me when I finished; "very well," – and for one swift second his eye took in Sangree, – "for what we have to deal with here is nothing more than a werewolf – rare enough, I am glad to say, but often very sad, and sometimes very terrible."

I jumped as though I had been shot, but the next second was heartily ashamed of my want of control; for this brief remark, confirming as it did my own worst suspicions, did more to convince me of the gravity of the adventure than any number of questions or explanations. It seemed to draw close the circle about us, shutting a door somewhere that locked us in with the animal and the horror, and turning the key. Whatever it was had now to be faced and dealt with.

"No one has been actually injured so far?" he asked aloud, but in a matter-of-fact tone that lent reality to grim possibilities.

"Good heavens, no!" cried the Canadian, throwing down his dishcloths and coming forward into the circle of firelight. "Surely there can be no question of this poor starved beast injuring anybody, can there?"

His hair straggled untidily over his forehead, and there was a gleam in his eyes that was not all reflection from the fire. His words made me turn sharply. We all laughed a little short, forced laugh.

"I trust not, indeed," Dr. Silence said quietly. "But what makes you think the creature is starved?" He asked the question with his eyes straight on the other's face. The prompt question explained to me why I had started, and I waited with just a tremor of excitement for the reply.

Sangree hesitated a moment, as though the question took him by surprise. But he met the doctor's gaze unflinchingly across the fire, and with complete honesty.

"Really," he faltered, with a little shrug of the shoulders, "I can hardly tell you. The phrase seemed to come out of its own accord. I have felt from the beginning that it was in pain and – starved, though why I felt this never occurred to me till you asked."

"You really know very little about it, then?" said the other, with a sudden gentleness in his voice.

"No more than that," Sangree replied, looking at him with a puzzled expression that was unmistakably genuine. "In fact, nothing at all, really," he added, by way of further explanation.

"I am glad of that," I heard the doctor murmur under his breath, but so low that I only just caught the words, and Sangree missed them altogether, as evidently he was meant to do.

"And now," he cried, getting on his feet and shaking himself with a characteristic gesture, as though to shake out the horror and the mystery, "let us leave the problem till tomorrow and enjoy this wind and sea and stars. I've been living lately in the atmosphere of many people, and feel that I want to wash and be clean. I propose a swim and then bed. Who'll second me?" And two minutes later we were all diving from the boat into cool, deep water, that reflected a thousand moons as the waves broke away from us in countless ripples.

We slept in blankets under the open sky, Sangree and I taking the outside places, and were up before sunrise to catch the dawn wind. Helped by this early start we were half-way home by noon, and then the wind shifted to a few points behind us so that we fairly ran. In and out among a thousand islands, down narrow channels where we lost the wind, out into open spaces where we had to take in a reef, racing along under a hot and cloudless sky, we flew through the very heart of the bewildering and lonely scenery.

"A real wilderness," cried Dr. Silence from his seat in the bows where he held the jib sheet. His hat was off, his hair tumbled in the wind, and his lean brown face gave him the touch of an Oriental. Presently he changed places with Sangree, and came down to talk with me by the tiller.

"A wonderful region, all this world of islands," he said, waving his hand to the scenery rushing past us, "but doesn't it strike you there's something lacking?"

"It's – hard," I answered, after a moment's reflection. "It has a superficial, glittering prettiness, without—" I hesitated to find the word I wanted.

John Silence nodded his head with approval.

"Exactly," he said. "The picturesqueness of stage scenery that is not real, not alive. It's like a landscape by a clever painter, yet without true imagination. Soulless – that's the word you wanted."

"Something like that," I answered, watching the gusts of wind on the sails. "Not dead so much, as without soul. That's it."

"Of course," he went on, in a voice calculated, it seemed to me, not to reach our companion in the bows, "to live long in a place like this – long and alone – might bring about a strange result in some men."

I suddenly realised he was talking with a purpose and pricked up my ears.

"There's no life here. These islands are mere dead rocks pushed up from below the sea – not living land; and there's nothing really alive on them. Even the sea, this tideless, brackish sea, neither salt water nor fresh, is dead. It's all a pretty image of life without the real heart and soul of life. To a man with too strong desires who came here and lived close to nature, strange things might happen."

"Let her out a bit," I shouted to Sangree, who was coming aft. "The wind's gusty and we've got hardly any ballast."

He went back to the bows, and Dr. Silence continued –

"Here, I mean, a long sojourn would lead to deterioration, to degeneration. The place is utterly unsoftened by human influences, by any humanising associations of history, good or bad. This landscape has never awakened into life; it's still dreaming in its primitive sleep."

"In time," I put in, "you mean a man living here might become brutal?"

"The passions would run wild, selfishness become supreme, the instincts coarsen and turn savage probably."

"But—"

"In other places just as wild, parts of Italy for instance, where there are other moderating influences, it could not happen. The character might grow wild, savage too in a sense, but with a human wildness one could understand and deal with. But here, in a hard place like this, it might be otherwise." He spoke slowly, weighing his words carefully.

I looked at him with many questions in my eyes, and a precautionary cry to Sangree to stay in the fore part of the boat, out of earshot.

"First of all there would come callousness to pain, and indifference to the rights of others. Then the soul would turn savage, not from passionate human causes, or with enthusiasm, but by deadening down into a kind of cold, primitive, emotionless savagery – by turning, like the landscape, soulless."

"And a man with strong desires, you say, might change?"

"Without being aware of it, yes; he might turn savage, his instincts and desires turn animal. And if" – he lowered his voice and turned for a moment towards the bows, and then continued in his most weighty manner – "owing to delicate health or other predisposing causes, his Double – you know what I mean, of course – his etheric Body of Desire, or astral body, as some term it – that part in which the emotions, passions and desires reside – if this, I say, were for some constitutional reason loosely joined to his physical organism, there might well take place an occasional projection—"

Sangree came aft with a sudden rush, his face aflame, but whether with wind or sun, or with what he had heard, I cannot say. In my surprise I let the tiller slip and the cutter gave a great plunge as she came sharply into the wind and flung us all together in a heap on the bottom. Sangree said nothing, but while he scrambled up and made the jib sheet fast my companion found a moment to add to his unfinished sentence the words, too low for any ear but mine –

"Entirely unknown to himself, however."

We righted the boat and laughed, and then Sangree produced the map and explained exactly where we were. Far away on the horizon, across an open stretch of water, lay a blue cluster of islands with our crescent-shaped home among them and the safe anchorage of the lagoon. An hour with this wind would get us there comfortably, and while Dr. Silence and Sangree fell into conversation, I sat and pondered over the strange suggestions that had just been put into my mind concerning the 'Double', and the possible form it might assume when dissociated temporarily from the physical body.

The whole way home these two chatted, and John Silence was as gentle and sympathetic as a woman. I did not hear much of their talk, for the wind grew occasionally to the force of a hurricane and the sails and tiller absorbed my attention; but I could see that Sangree was pleased and happy, and was pouring out intimate revelations to his companion in the way that most people did – when John Silence wished them to do so.

But it was quite suddenly, while I sat all intent upon wind and sails, that the true meaning of Sangree's remark about the animal flared up in me with its full import. For his admission that he knew it was in pain and starved was in reality nothing more or less than a revelation of his deeper self. It was in the nature of a confession. He was speaking of something that he knew positively, something that was beyond question or argument, something that had to do directly with himself. 'Poor starved beast' he had called it in words that had 'come out of their own accord', and there had not been the slightest evidence of any desire to conceal or explain away. He had spoken instinctively – from his heart, and as though about his own self.

And half an hour before sunset we raced through the narrow opening of the lagoon and saw the smoke of the dinner-fire blowing here and there among the trees, and the figures of Joan and the Bo'sun's Mate running down to meet us at the landing-stage.

## Chapter V

**EVERYTHING** changed from the moment John Silence set foot on that island; it was like the effect produced by calling in some big doctor, some great arbiter of life and death, for consultation. The sense of gravity increased a hundredfold. Even inanimate objects took upon themselves a subtle alteration, for the setting of the adventure – this deserted bit of sea with its hundreds of uninhabited islands – somehow turned sombre. An element that was mysterious, and in a sense disheartening, crept unbidden into the severity of grey rock and dark pine forest and took the sparkle from the sunshine and the sea.

I, at least, was keenly aware of the change, for my whole being shifted, as it were, a degree higher, becoming keyed up and alert. The figures from the background of the stage moved forward a little into the light – nearer to the inevitable action. In a word this man's arrival intensified the whole affair.

And, looking back down the years to the time when all this happened, it is clear to me that he had a pretty sharp idea of the meaning of it from the very beginning. How much he knew beforehand by his strange divining powers, it is impossible to say, but from the moment he came upon the scene and caught within himself the note of what was going on amongst us, he undoubtedly held the true solution of the puzzle and had no need to ask questions. And this certitude it was that set him in such an atmosphere of power and made us all look to him instinctively; for he took no tentative steps, made no false moves, and while the rest of us floundered he moved straight to the climax. He was indeed a true diviner of souls.

I can now read into his behaviour a good deal that puzzled me at the time, for though I had dimly guessed the solution, I had no idea how he would deal with it. And the conversations I can reproduce almost verbatim, for, according to my invariable habit, I kept full notes of all he said.

To Mrs. Maloney, foolish and dazed; to Joan, alarmed, yet plucky; and to the clergyman, moved by his daughter's distress below his usual shallow emotions, he gave the best possible treatment in the best possible way, yet all so easily and simply as to make it appear naturally spontaneous. For he dominated the Bo'sun's Mate, taking the measure of her ignorance with infinite patience; he keyed up Joan, stirring her courage and interest to the highest point for her own safety; and the Reverend Timothy he soothed and comforted, while obtaining his implicit obedience, by taking him into his confidence, and leading him gradually to a comprehension of the issue that was bound to follow.

And Sangree – here his wisdom was most wisely calculated – he neglected outwardly because inwardly he was the object of his unceasing and most concentrated attention. Under the guise of apparent indifference his mind kept the Canadian under constant observation.

There was a restless feeling in the Camp that evening and none of us lingered round the fire after supper as usual. Sangree and I busied ourselves with patching up the torn tent for our guest and with finding heavy stones to hold the ropes, for Dr. Silence insisted on having it pitched on the highest point of the island ridge, just where it was most rocky and there was no earth for pegs. The place, moreover, was midway between the men's and women's tents, and, of course, commanded the most comprehensive view of the Camp.

"So that if your dog comes," he said simply, "I may be able to catch him as he passes across."

The wind had gone down with the sun and an unusual warmth lay over the island that made sleep heavy, and in the morning we assembled at a late breakfast, rubbing our eyes and yawning. The cool north wind had given way to the warm southern air that sometimes came up with haze and moisture across the Baltic, bringing with it the relaxing sensations that produced enervation and listlessness.

And this may have been the reason why at first I failed to notice that anything unusual was about, and why I was less alert than normally; for it was not till after breakfast that the silence of our little party struck me and I discovered that Joan had not yet put in an appearance. And then, in a flash, the last heaviness of sleep vanished and I saw that Maloney was white and troubled and his wife could not hold a plate without trembling.

A desire to ask questions was stopped in me by a swift glance from Dr. Silence, and I suddenly understood in some vague way that they were waiting till Sangree should have gone. How this idea came to me I cannot determine, but the soundness of the intuition was soon proved, for the moment he moved off to his tent, Maloney looked up at me and began to speak in a low voice.

"You slept through it all," he half whispered.

"Through what?" I asked, suddenly thrilled with the knowledge that something dreadful had happened.

"We didn't wake you for fear of getting the whole Camp up," he went on, meaning, by the Camp, I supposed, Sangree. "It was just before dawn when the screams woke me."

"The dog again?" I asked, with a curious sinking of the heart.

"Got right into the tent," he went on, speaking passionately but very low, "and woke my wife by scrambling all over her. Then she realised that Joan was struggling beside her. And, by God! the beast had torn her arm; scratched all down the arm she was, and bleeding."

"Joan injured?" I gasped.

"Merely scratched – this time," put in John Silence, speaking for the first time; "suffering more from shock and fright than actual wounds."

"Isn't it a mercy the doctor was here?" said Mrs. Maloney, looking as if she would never know calmness again. "I think we should both have been killed."

"It has been a most merciful escape," Maloney said, his pulpit voice struggling with his emotion. "But, of course, we cannot risk another – we must strike Camp and get away at once—"

"Only poor Mr. Sangree must not know what has happened. He is so attached to Joan and would be so terribly upset," added the Bo'sun's Mate distractedly, looking all about in her terror.

"It is perhaps advisable that Mr. Sangree should not know what has occurred," Dr. Silence said with quiet authority, "but I think, for the safety of all concerned, it will be better not to leave the island just now." He spoke with great decision and Maloney looked up and followed his words closely.

"If you will agree to stay here a few days longer, I have no doubt we can put an end to the attentions of your strange visitor, and incidentally have the opportunity of observing a most singular and interesting phenomenon—"

"What!" gasped Mrs. Maloney, "a phenomenon? – you mean that you know what it is?"

"I am quite certain I know what it is," he replied very low, for we heard the footsteps of Sangree approaching, "though I am not so certain yet as to the best means of dealing with it. But in any case it is not wise to leave precipitately—"

"Oh, Timothy, does he think it's a devil—?" cried the Bo'sun's Mate in a voice that even the Canadian must have heard.

"In my opinion," continued John Silence, looking across at me and the clergyman, "it is a case of modern lycanthropy with other complications that may—" He left the sentence unfinished, for Mrs. Maloney got up with a jump and fled to her tent fearful she might hear a worse thing, and at that moment Sangree turned the corner of the stockade and came into view.

"There are footmarks all round the mouth of my tent," he said with excitement. "The animal has been here again in the night. Dr. Silence, you really must come and see them for yourself. They're as plain on the moss as tracks in snow."

But later in the day, while Sangree went off in the canoe to fish the pools near the larger islands, and Joan still lay, bandaged and resting, in her tent, Dr. Silence called me and the tutor and proposed a walk to the granite slabs at the far end. Mrs. Maloney sat on a stump near her daughter, and busied herself energetically with alternate nursing and painting.

"We'll leave you in charge," the doctor said with a smile that was meant to be encouraging, "and when you want us for lunch, or anything, the megaphone will always bring us back in time."

For, though the very air was charged with strange emotions, everyone talked quietly and naturally as with a definite desire to counteract unnecessary excitement.

"I'll keep watch," said the plucky Bo'sun's Mate, "and meanwhile I find comfort in my work." She was busy with the sketch she had begun on the day after our arrival. "For even a tree," she added proudly, pointing to her little easel, "is a symbol of the divine, and the thought makes me feel safer." We glanced for a moment at a daub which was more like the symptom of a disease than a symbol of the divine – and then took the path round the lagoon.

At the far end we made a little fire and lay round it in the shadow of a big boulder. Maloney stopped his humming suddenly and turned to his companion.

"And what do you make of it all?" he asked abruptly.

"In the first place," replied John Silence, making himself comfortable against the rock, "it is of human origin, this animal; it is undoubted lycanthropy."

His words had the effect precisely of a bombshell. Maloney listened as though he had been struck.

"You puzzle me utterly," he said, sitting up closer and staring at him.

"Perhaps," replied the other, "but if you'll listen to me for a few moments you may be less puzzled at the end – or more. It depends how much you know. Let me go further and say that you have underestimated, or miscalculated, the effect of this primitive wild life upon all of you."

"In what way?" asked the clergyman, bristling a trifle.

"It is strong medicine for any town-dweller, and for some of you it has been too strong. One of you has gone wild." He uttered these last words with great emphasis.

"Gone savage," he added, looking from one to the other.

Neither of us found anything to reply.

"To say that the brute has awakened in a man is not a mere metaphor always," he went on presently.

"Of course not!"

"But, in the sense I mean, may have a very literal and terrible significance," pursued Dr. Silence. "Ancient instincts that no one dreamed of, least of all their possessor, may leap forth—"

"Atavism can hardly explain a roaming animal with teeth and claws and sanguinary instincts," interrupted Maloney with impatience.

"The term is of your own choice," continued the doctor equably, "not mine, and it is a good example of a word that indicates a result while it conceals the process; but the explanation of this beast that haunts your island and attacks your daughter is of far deeper significance than mere atavistic tendencies, or throwing back to animal origin, which I suppose is the thought in your mind."

"You spoke just now of lycanthropy," said Maloney, looking bewildered and anxious to keep to plain facts evidently; "I think I have come across the word, but really – really – it can have no actual significance today, can it? These superstitions of medieval times can hardly—"

He looked round at me with his jolly red face, and the expression of astonishment and dismay on it would have made me shout with laughter at any other time. Laughter, however, was never farther from my mind than at this moment when I listened to Dr. Silence as he carefully suggested to the clergyman the very explanation that had gradually been forcing itself upon my own mind.

"However medieval ideas may have exaggerated the idea is not of much importance to us now," he said quietly, "when we are face to face with a modern example of what, I take it, has always been a profound fact. For the moment let us leave the name of any one in particular out of the matter and consider certain possibilities."

We all agreed with that at any rate. There was no need to speak of Sangree, or of any one else, until we knew a little more.

"The fundamental fact in this most curious case," he went on, "is that the 'Double' of a man—"

"You mean the astral body? I've heard of that, of course," broke in Maloney with a snort of triumph.

"No doubt," said the other, smiling, "no doubt you have; – that this Double, or fluidic body of a man, as I was saying, has the power under certain conditions of projecting itself and becoming visible to others. Certain training will accomplish this, and certain drugs likewise; illnesses, too, that ravage the body may produce temporarily the result that death produces permanently, and let loose this counterpart of a human being and render it visible to the sight of others.

"Everyone, of course, knows this more or less today; but it is not so generally known, and probably believed by none who have not witnessed it, that this fluidic body can, under certain conditions, assume other forms than human, and that such other forms may be determined by the dominating thought and wish of the owner. For this Double, or astral body as you call it, is really the seat of the passions, emotions and desires in the psychical economy. It is the Passion Body; and, in projecting itself, it can often assume a form that gives expression to the overmastering desire that moulds it; for it is composed of such tenuous matter that it lends itself readily to the moulding by thought and wish."

"I follow you perfectly," said Maloney, looking as if he would much rather be chopping firewood elsewhere and singing.

"And there are some persons so constituted," the doctor went on with increasing seriousness, "that the fluid body in them is but loosely associated with the physical, persons of poor health as a rule, yet often of strong desires and passions; and in these persons it is easy for the Double to dissociate itself during deep sleep from their system, and, driven forth by some consuming desire, to assume an animal form and seek the fulfilment of that desire."

There, in broad daylight, I saw Maloney deliberately creep closer to the fire and heap the wood on. We gathered in to the heat, and to each other, and listened to Dr. Silence's voice as it mingled with the swish and whirr of the wind about us, and the falling of the little waves.

"For instance, to take a concrete example," he resumed; "suppose some young man, with the delicate constitution I have spoken of, forms an overpowering attachment to a young woman, yet perceives that it is not welcomed, and is man enough to repress its outward manifestations. In such a case, supposing his Double be easily projected, the very repression of his love in the daytime would add to the intense force of his desire when released in deep sleep from the control of his will, and his fluidic body might issue forth in monstrous or animal shape and become actually visible to others. And, if his devotion were dog-like in its fidelity, yet concealing the fires of a fierce passion beneath, it might well assume the form of a creature that seemed to be half dog, half wolf—"

"A werewolf, you mean?" cried Maloney, pale to the lips as he listened.

John Silence held up a restraining hand. "A werewolf," he said, "is a true psychical fact of profound significance, however absurdly it may have been exaggerated by the imaginations of a superstitious peasantry in the days of unenlightenment, for a werewolf is nothing but the savage, and possibly sanguinary, instincts of a passionate man scouring the world in his fluidic body, his passion body, his body of desire. As in the case at hand, he may not know it—"

"It is not necessarily deliberate, then?" Maloney put in quickly, with relief.

" – It is hardly ever deliberate. It is the desires released in sleep from the control of the will finding a vent. In all savage races it has been recognised and dreaded, this phenomenon styled 'Wehr Wolf', but today it is rare. And it is becoming rarer still, for the world grows tame and civilised, emotions have become refined, desires lukewarm, and few men have savagery enough left in them to generate impulses of such intense force, and certainly not to project them in animal form."

"By Gad!" exclaimed the clergyman breathlessly, and with increasing excitement, "then I feel I must tell you – what has been given to me in confidence – that Sangree has in him an admixture of savage blood – of Red Indian ancestry—"

"Let us stick to our supposition of a man as described," the doctor stopped him calmly, "and let us imagine that he has in him this admixture of savage blood; and further, that he is wholly unaware of his dreadful physical and psychical infirmity; and that he suddenly finds himself leading the primitive life together with the object of his desires; with the result that the strain of the untamed wild-man in his blood—"

"Red Indian, for instance," from Maloney.

"Red Indian, perfectly," agreed the doctor; "the result, I say, that this savage strain in him is awakened and leaps into passionate life. What then?"

He looked hard at Timothy Maloney, and the clergyman looked hard at him.

"The wild life such as you lead here on this island, for instance, might quickly awaken his savage instincts – his buried instincts – and with profoundly disquieting results."

"You mean his Subtle Body, as you call it, might issue forth automatically in deep sleep and seek the object of its desire?" I said, coming to Maloney's aid, who was finding it more and more difficult to get words.

"Precisely; – yet the desire of the man remaining utterly unmalefic – pure and wholesome in every sense—"

"Ah!" I heard the clergyman gasp.

"The lover's desire for union run wild, run savage, tearing its way out in primitive, untamed fashion, I mean," continued the doctor, striving to make himself clear to a mind bounded by conventional thought and knowledge; "for the desire to possess, remember, may easily become importunate, and, embodied in this animal form of the Subtle Body which acts as its vehicle, may go forth to tear in pieces all that obstructs, to reach to the very heart of the loved object and seize it. *Au fond*, it is nothing more than the aspiration for union, as I said – the splendid and perfectly clean desire to absorb utterly into itself—"

He paused a moment and looked into Maloney's eyes.

"To bathe in the very heart's blood of the one desired," he added with grave emphasis.

The fire spurted and crackled and made me start, but Maloney found relief in a genuine shudder, and I saw him turn his head and look about him from the sea to the trees. The wind dropped just at that moment and the doctor's words rang sharply through the stillness.

"Then it might even kill?" stammered the clergyman presently in a hushed voice, and with a little forced laugh by way of protest that sounded quite ghastly.

"In the last resort it might kill," repeated Dr. Silence. Then, after another pause, during which he was clearly debating how much or how little it was wise to give to his audience, he continued: "And if the Double does not succeed in getting back to its physical body, that physical body would wake an imbecile – an idiot – or perhaps never wake at all."

Maloney sat up and found his tongue.

"You mean that if this fluid animal thing, or whatever it is, should be prevented getting back, the man might never wake again?" he asked, with shaking voice.

"He might be dead," replied the other calmly. The tremor of a positive sensation shivered in the air about us.

"Then isn't that the best way to cure the fool – the brute—?" thundered the clergyman, half rising to his feet.

"Certainly it would be an easy and undiscoverable form of murder," was the stern reply, spoken as calmly as though it were a remark about the weather.

Maloney collapsed visibly, and I gathered the wood over the fire and coaxed up a blaze.

"The greater part of the man's life – of his vital forces – goes out with this Double," Dr. Silence resumed, after a moment's consideration, "and a considerable portion of the actual material of his physical body. So the physical body that remains behind is depleted, not only of force, but of matter. You would see it small, shrunken, dropped together, just like the body of a materialising medium at a seance. Moreover, any mark or injury inflicted upon this Double will be found exactly reproduced by the phenomenon of repercussion upon the shrunken physical body lying in its trance—"

"An injury inflicted upon the one you say would be reproduced also on the other?" repeated Maloney, his excitement growing again.

"Undoubtedly," replied the other quietly; "for there exists all the time a continuous connection between the physical body and the Double – a connection of matter, though of exceedingly attenuated, possibly of etheric, matter. The wound *travels*, so to speak, from one to the other, and if this connection were broken the result would be death."

"Death," repeated Maloney to himself, "death!" He looked anxiously at our faces, his thoughts evidently beginning to clear.

"And this solidity?" he asked presently, after a general pause; "this tearing of tents and flesh; this howling, and the marks of paws? You mean that the Double—?"

"Has sufficient material drawn from the depleted body to produce physical results? Certainly!" the doctor took him up. "Although to explain at this moment such problems as the passage of matter through matter would be as difficult as to explain how the thought of a mother can actually break the bones of the child unborn."

Dr. Silence pointed out to sea, and Maloney, looking wildly about him, turned with a violent start. I saw a canoe, with Sangree in the stern-seat, slowly coming into view round the farther point. His hat was off, and his tanned face for the first time appeared to me – to us all, I think – as though it were the face of someone else. He looked like a wild man. Then he stood up in the canoe to make a cast with the rod, and he looked for all the world like an Indian. I recalled the expression of his face as I had seen it once or twice, notably on that occasion of the evening prayer, and an involuntary shudder ran down my spine.

At that very instant he turned and saw us where we lay, and his face broke into a smile, so that his teeth showed white in the sun. He looked in his element, and exceedingly attractive. He called out something about his fish, and soon after passed out of sight into the lagoon.

For a time none of us said a word.

"And the cure?" ventured Maloney at length.

"Is not to quench this savage force," replied Dr. Silence, "but to steer it better, and to provide other outlets. This is the solution of all these problems of accumulated force, for this force is the raw material of usefulness, and should be increased and cherished, not by separating it from the body by death, but by raising it to higher channels. The best and quickest cure of all," he went on, speaking very gently and with a hand upon the clergyman's arm, "is to lead it towards its object, provided that object is not unalterably hostile – to let it find rest where—"

He stopped abruptly, and the eyes of the two men met in a single glance of comprehension.

"Joan?" Maloney exclaimed, under his breath.

"Joan!" replied John Silence.

\* \* \*

We all went to bed early. The day had been unusually warm, and after sunset a curious hush descended on the island. Nothing was audible but that faint, ghostly singing which is inseparable from a pinewood even on the stillest day – a low, searching sound, as though the wind had hair and trailed it o'er the world.

With the sudden cooling of the atmosphere a sea fog began to form. It appeared in isolated patches over the water, and then these patches slid together and a white wall advanced upon us. Not a breath of air stirred; the firs stood like flat metal outlines; the sea became as oil. The whole scene lay as though held motionless by some huge weight in the air; and the flames from our fire – the largest we had ever made – rose upwards, straight as a church steeple.

As I followed the rest of our party tent-wards, having kicked the embers of the fire into safety, the advance guard of the fog was creeping slowly among the trees, like white arms feeling their way. Mingled with the smoke was the odour of moss and soil and bark, and the peculiar flavour of the Baltic, half salt, half brackish, like the smell of an estuary at low water.

It is difficult to say why it seemed to me that this deep stillness masked an intense activity; perhaps in every mood lies the suggestion of its opposite, so that I became aware of the contrast of furious energy, for it was like moving through the deep pause before a thunderstorm, and I trod gently lest by breaking a twig or moving a stone I might set the whole scene into some sort of tumultuous movement. Actually, no doubt, it was nothing more than a result of overstrung nerves.

There was no more question of undressing and going to bed than there was of undressing and going to bathe. Some sense in me was alert and expectant. I sat in my tent and waited. And at the end of half an hour or so my waiting was justified, for the canvas suddenly shivered, and someone tripped over the ropes that held it to the earth. John Silence came in.

The effect of his quiet entry was singular and prophetic: it was just as though the energy lying behind all this stillness had pressed forward to the edge of action. This, no doubt, was merely the quickening of my own mind, and had no other justification; for the presence of John Silence always suggested the near possibility of vigorous action, and as a matter of fact, he came in with nothing more than a nod and a significant gesture.

He sat down on a corner of my ground-sheet, and I pushed the blanket over so that he could cover his legs. He drew the flap of the tent after him and settled down, but hardly had he done so when the canvas shook a second time, and in blundered Maloney.

"Sitting in the dark?" he said self-consciously, pushing his head inside, and hanging up his lantern on the ridge-pole nail. "I just looked in for a smoke. I suppose—"

He glanced round, caught the eye of Dr. Silence, and stopped. He put his pipe back into his pocket and began to hum softly – that underbreath humming of a nondescript melody I knew so well and had come to hate.

Dr. Silence leaned forward, opened the lantern and blew the light out. "Speak low," he said, "and don't strike matches. Listen for sounds and movements about the Camp, and be ready to follow me at a moment's notice." There was light enough to distinguish our faces easily, and I saw Maloney glance again hurriedly at both of us.

"Is the Camp asleep?" the doctor asked presently, whispering.

"Sangree is," replied the clergyman, in a voice equally low. "I can't answer for the women; I think they're sitting up."

"That's for the best." And then he added: "I wish the fog would thin a bit and let the moon through; later – we may want it."

"It is lifting now, I think," Maloney whispered back. "It's over the tops of the trees already."

I cannot say what it was in this commonplace exchange of remarks that thrilled. Probably Maloney's swift acquiescence in the doctor's mood had something to do with it; for his quick obedience certainly impressed me a good deal. But, even without that slight evidence, it was clear that each recognised the gravity of the occasion, and understood that sleep was impossible and sentry duty was the order of the night.

"Report to me," repeated John Silence once again, "the least sound, and do nothing precipitately."

He shifted across to the mouth of the tent and raised the flap, fastening it against the pole so that he could see out. Maloney stopped humming and began to force the breath through his teeth with a kind of faint hissing, treating us to a medley of church hymns and popular songs of the day.

Then the tent trembled as though someone had touched it.

"That's the wind rising," whispered the clergyman, and pulled the flap open as far as it would go. A waft of cold damp air entered and made us shiver, and with it came a sound of the sea as the first wave washed its way softly along the shores.

"It's got round to the north," he added, and following his voice came a long-drawn whisper that rose from the whole island as the trees sent forth a sighing response. "The fog'll move a bit now. I can make out a lane across the sea already."

"Hush!" said Dr. Silence, for Maloney's voice had risen above a whisper, and we settled down again to another long period of watching and waiting, broken only by the occasional rubbing of shoulders against the canvas as we shifted our positions, and the increasing noise of waves on the outer coast-line of the island. And over all whirred the murmur of wind sweeping the tops of the trees like a great harp, and the faint tapping on the tent as drops fell from the branches with a sharp pinging sound.

We had sat for something over an hour in this way, and Maloney and I were finding it increasingly hard to keep awake, when suddenly Dr. Silence rose to his feet and peered out. The next minute he was gone.

Relieved of the dominating presence, the clergyman thrust his face close into mine. "I don't much care for this waiting game," he whispered, "but Silence wouldn't hear of my sitting up with the others; he said it would prevent anything happening if I did."

"He knows," I answered shortly.

"No doubt in the world about that," he whispered back; "it's this 'Double' business, as he calls it, or else it's obsession as the Bible describes it. But it's bad, whichever it is, and I've got my Winchester outside ready cocked, and I brought this too." He shoved a pocket Bible under my nose. At one time in his life it had been his inseparable companion.

"One's useless and the other's dangerous," I replied under my breath, conscious of a keen desire to laugh, and leaving him to choose. "Safety lies in following our leader—"

"I'm not thinking of myself," he interrupted sharply; "only, if anything happens to Joan tonight I'm going to shoot first – and pray afterwards!"

Maloney put the book back into his hip-pocket, and peered out of the doorway. "What is he up to now, in the devil's name, I wonder!" he added; "going round Sangree's tent and making gestures. How weird he looks disappearing in and out of the fog."

"Just trust him and wait," I said quickly, for the doctor was already on his way back. "Remember, he has the knowledge, and knows what he's about. I've been with him through worse cases than this."

Maloney moved back as Dr. Silence darkened the doorway and stooped to enter.

"His sleep is very deep," he whispered, seating himself by the door again. "He's in a cataleptic condition, and the Double may be released any minute now. But I've taken steps to imprison it in the tent, and it can't get out till I permit it. Be on the watch for signs of movement." Then he looked hard at Maloney. "But no violence, or shooting, remember, Mr. Maloney, unless you want a murder on your hands. Anything done to the Double acts by repercussion upon the physical body. You had better take out the cartridges at once."

His voice was stern. The clergyman went out, and I heard him emptying the magazine of his rifle. When he returned he sat nearer the door than before, and from that moment until we left the tent he never once took his eyes from the figure of Dr. Silence, silhouetted there against sky and canvas.

And, meanwhile, the wind came steadily over the sea and opened the mist into lanes and clearings, driving it about like a living thing.

It must have been well after midnight when a low booming sound drew my attention; but at first the sense of hearing was so strained that it was impossible exactly to locate it, and I imagined it was the thunder of big guns far out at sea carried to us by the rising wind. Then Maloney, catching hold of my arm and leaning forward, somehow brought the true relation, and I realised the next second that it was only a few feet away.

"Sangree's tent," he exclaimed in a loud and startled whisper.

I craned my head round the corner, but at first the effect of the fog was so confusing that every patch of white driving about before the wind looked like a moving tent and it was some seconds before I discovered the one patch that held steady. Then I saw that it was shaking all over, and the sides, flapping as much as the tightness of the ropes allowed, were the cause of the booming sound we had heard. Something alive was tearing frantically about inside, banging against the stretched canvas in a way that made me think of a great moth dashing against the walls and ceiling of a room. The tent bulged and rocked.

"It's trying to get out, by Jupiter!" muttered the clergyman, rising to his feet and turning to the side where the unloaded rifle lay. I sprang up too, hardly knowing what purpose was in my mind, but anxious to be prepared for anything. John Silence, however, was before us both, and his figure slipped past and blocked the doorway of the tent. And there was some quality in his voice next minute when he began to speak that brought our minds instantly to a state of calm obedience.

"First – the women's tent," he said low, looking sharply at Maloney, "and if I need your help, I'll call."

The clergyman needed no second bidding. He dived past me and was out in a moment. He was labouring evidently under intense excitement. I watched him picking his way silently over the slippery ground, giving the moving tent a wide berth, and presently disappearing among the floating shapes of fog.

Dr. Silence turned to me. "You heard those footsteps about half an hour ago?" he asked significantly.

"I heard nothing."

"They were extraordinarily soft – almost the soundless tread of a wild creature. But now, follow me closely," he added, "for we must waste no time if I am to save this poor man from his affliction and lead his werewolf Double to its rest. And, unless I am much mistaken" – he peered at me through the darkness, whispering with the utmost distinctness – "Joan and Sangree are absolutely made for one another. And I think she knows it too – just as well as he does."

My head swam a little as I listened, but at the same time something cleared in my brain and I saw that he was right. Yet it was all so weird and incredible, so remote from the commonplace facts of life as commonplace people know them; and more than once it flashed upon me that the whole scene – people, words, tents, and all the rest of it – were delusions created by the intense excitement of my own mind somehow, and that suddenly the sea-fog would clear off and the world become normal again.

The cold air from the sea stung our cheeks sharply as we left the close atmosphere of the little crowded tent. The sighing of the trees, the waves breaking below on the rocks, and the lines and patches of mist driving about us seemed to create the momentary illusion that the whole island had broken loose and was floating out to sea like a mighty raft.

The doctor moved just ahead of me, quickly and silently; he was making straight for the Canadian's tent where the sides still boomed and shook as the creature of sinister life raced and tore about impatiently within. A little distance from the door he paused and held up a hand to stop me. We were, perhaps, a dozen feet away.

"Before I release it, you shall see for yourself," he said, "that the reality of the werewolf is beyond all question. The matter of which it is composed is, of course, exceedingly attenuated, but you are partially clairvoyant – and even if it is not dense enough for normal sight you will see something."

He added a little more I could not catch. The fact was that the curiously strong vibrating atmosphere surrounding his person somewhat confused my senses. It was the result, of course, of his intense concentration of mind and forces, and pervaded the entire Camp and all the persons in it. And as I watched the canvas shake and heard it boom and flap I heartily welcomed it. For it was also protective.

At the back of Sangree's tent stood a thin group of pine trees, but in front and at the sides the ground was comparatively clear. The flap was wide open and any ordinary animal would have been out and away without the least trouble. Dr. Silence led me up to within a few feet, evidently careful not to advance beyond a certain limit, and then stooped down and signalled to me to do the same. And looking over his shoulder I saw the interior lit faintly by the spectral light reflected from the fog, and the dim blot upon the balsam boughs and blankets signifying Sangree; while over him, and round him, and up and down him, flew the dark mass of 'something' on four legs, with pointed muzzle and sharp ears plainly visible against the tent sides, and the occasional gleam of fiery eyes and white fangs.

I held my breath and kept utterly still, inwardly and outwardly, for fear, I suppose, that the creature would become conscious of my presence; but the distress I felt went far deeper than the mere sense of personal safety, or the fact of watching something so incredibly active and real. I became keenly aware of the dreadful psychic calamity it involved. The realisation that Sangree lay confined in that narrow space with this species of monstrous projection of himself – that he was wrapped there in the cataleptic sleep, all unconscious that this thing was masquerading with his own life and energies – added a distressing touch of horror to the scene. In all the cases of John Silence – and they were many and often terrible – no other psychic affliction has ever, before or since, impressed me so convincingly with the pathetic impermanence of the human personality, with its fluid nature, and with the alarming possibilities of its transformations.

"Come," he whispered, after we had watched for some minutes the frantic efforts to escape from the circle of thought and will that held it prisoner, "come a little farther away while I release it."

We moved back a dozen yards or so. It was like a scene in some impossible play, or in some ghastly and oppressive nightmare from which I should presently awake to find the blankets all heaped up upon my chest.

By some method undoubtedly mental, but which, in my confusion and excitement, I failed to understand, the doctor accomplished his purpose, and the next minute I heard him say sharply under his breath, "It's out! Now watch!"

At this very moment a sudden gust from the sea blew aside the mist, so that a lane opened to the sky, and the moon, ghastly and unnatural as the effect of stage limelight, dropped down in a momentary gleam upon the door of Sangree's tent, and I perceived that something had moved forward from the interior darkness and stood clearly defined upon the threshold. And, at the same moment, the tent ceased its shuddering and held still.

There, in the doorway, stood an animal, with neck and muzzle thrust forward, its head poking into the night, its whole body poised in that attitude of intense rigidity that precedes the spring into freedom, the running leap of attack. It seemed to be about the size of a calf, leaner than a mastiff, yet more squat than a wolf, and I can swear that I saw the fur ridged sharply upon its back. Then its upper lip slowly lifted, and I saw the whiteness of its teeth.

Surely no human being ever stared as hard as I did in those next few minutes. Yet, the harder I stared the clearer appeared the amazing and monstrous apparition. For, after all, it was Sangree – and yet it was not Sangree. It was the head and face of an animal, and yet it was the face of Sangree: the face of a wild dog, a wolf, and yet his face. The eyes were sharper, narrower, more fiery, yet they were his eyes – his eyes run wild; the teeth were longer, whiter, more pointed – yet they were his teeth, his teeth grown cruel; the expression was flaming, terrible, exultant – yet it was his expression carried to the border of savagery – his expression as I had already surprised it more than once, only dominant now, fully released from human constraint, with the mad yearning of a hungry and importunate soul. It was the soul of Sangree, the long suppressed, deeply loving Sangree, expressed in its single and intense desire – pure utterly and utterly wonderful.

Yet, at the same time, came the feeling that it was all an illusion. I suddenly remembered the extraordinary changes the human face can undergo in circular insanity, when it changes from melancholia to elation; and I recalled the effect of hascheesh, which shows the human countenance in the form of the bird or animal to which in character it most approximates; and for a moment I attributed this mingling of Sangree's face with a wolf to some kind of similar delusion of the senses. I was mad, deluded, dreaming! The excitement of the day, and this dim light of stars and bewildering mist combined to trick me. I had been amazingly imposed upon by some false wizardry of the senses. It was all absurd and fantastic; it would pass.

And then, sounding across this sea of mental confusion like a bell through a fog, came the voice of John Silence bringing me back to a consciousness of the reality of it all –

"Sangree – in his Double!"

And when I looked again more calmly, I plainly saw that it was indeed the face of the Canadian, but his face turned animal, yet mingled with the brute expression a curiously pathetic look like the soul seen sometimes in the yearning eyes of a dog – the face of an animal shot with vivid streaks of the human.

The doctor called to him softly under his breath –

"Sangree! Sangree, you poor afflicted creature! Do you know me? Can you understand what it is you're doing in your 'Body of Desire'?"

For the first time since its appearance the creature moved. Its ears twitched and it shifted the weight of its body on to the hind legs. Then, lifting its head and muzzle to the sky, it opened its long jaws and gave vent to a dismal and prolonged howling.

But, when I heard that howling rise to heaven, the breath caught and strangled in my throat and it seemed that my heart missed a beat; for, though the sound was entirely animal, it was at the same time entirely human. But, more than that, it was the cry I had so often heard in the Western States of America where the Indians still fight and hunt and struggle – it was the cry of the Redskin!

"The Indian blood!" whispered John Silence, when I caught his arm for support; "the ancestral cry."

And that poignant, beseeching cry, that broken human voice, mingling with the savage howl of the brute beast, pierced straight to my very heart and touched there something that no music, no voice, passionate or tender, of man, woman or child has ever stirred before or since for one second into life. It echoed away among the fog and the trees and lost itself somewhere out over the hidden sea. And some part of myself – something that was far more than the mere act of intense listening – went out with it, and for several minutes I lost consciousness of my surroundings and felt utterly absorbed in the pain of another stricken fellow-creature.

Again the voice of John Silence recalled me to myself.

"Hark!" he said aloud. "Hark!"

His tone galvanised me afresh. We stood listening side by side.

Far across the island, faintly sounding through the trees and brushwood, came a similar, answering cry. Shrill, yet wonderfully musical, shaking the heart with a singular wild sweetness that defies description, we heard it rise and fall upon the night air.

"It's across the lagoon," Dr. Silence cried, but this time in full tones that paid no tribute to caution. "It's Joan! She's answering him!"

Again the wonderful cry rose and fell, and that same instant the animal lowered its head, and, muzzle to earth, set off on a swift easy canter that took it off into the mist and out of our sight like a thing of wind and vision.

The doctor made a quick dash to the door of Sangree's tent, and, following close at his heels, I peered in and caught a momentary glimpse of the small, shrunken body lying upon the branches but half covered by the blankets – the cage from which most of the life, and not a little of the actual corporeal substance, had escaped into that other form of life and energy, the body of passion and desire.

By another of those swift, incalculable processes which at this stage of my apprenticeship I failed often to grasp, Dr. Silence reclosed the circle about the tent and body.

"Now it cannot return till I permit it," he said, and the next second was off at full speed into the woods, with myself close behind him. I had already had some experience of my companion's ability to run swiftly through a dense wood, and I now had the further proof of his power almost to see in the dark. For, once we left the open space about the tents, the trees seemed to absorb all the remaining vestiges of light, and I understood that special sensibility that is said to develop in the blind – the sense of obstacles.

And twice as we ran we heard the sound of that dismal howling drawing nearer and nearer to the answering faint cry from the point of the island whither we were going.

Then, suddenly, the trees fell away, and we emerged, hot and breathless, upon the rocky point where the granite slabs ran bare into the sea. It was like passing into the clearness of open day. And there, sharply defined against sea and sky, stood the figure of a human being. It was Joan.

I at once saw that there was something about her appearance that was singular and unusual, but it was only when we had moved quite close that I recognised what caused it. For while the lips wore a smile that lit the whole face with a happiness I had never seen there before, the eyes themselves were fixed in a steady, sightless stare as though they were lifeless and made of glass.

I made an impulsive forward movement, but Dr. Silence instantly dragged me back.

"No," he cried, "don't wake her!"

"What do you mean?" I replied aloud, struggling in his grasp.

"She's asleep. It's somnambulistic. The shock might injure her permanently."

I turned and peered closely into his face. He was absolutely calm. I began to understand a little more, catching, I suppose, something of his strong thinking.

"Walking in her sleep, you mean?"

He nodded. "She's on her way to meet him. From the very beginning he must have drawn her – irresistibly."

"But the torn tent and the wounded flesh?"

"When she did not sleep deep enough to enter the somnambulistic trance he missed her – he went instinctively and in all innocence to seek her out – with the result, of course, that she woke and was terrified—"

"Then in their heart of hearts they love?" I asked finally.

John Silence smiled his inscrutable smile. "Profoundly," he answered, "and as simply as only primitive souls can love. If only they both come to realise it in their normal waking states his Double will cease these nocturnal excursions. He will be cured, and at rest."

The words had hardly left his lips when there was a sound of rustling branches on our left, and the very next instant the dense brushwood parted where it was darkest and out rushed the swift form of an animal at full gallop. The noise of feet was scarcely audible, but in that utter stillness I heard the heavy panting breath and caught the swish of the low bushes against its sides. It went straight towards Joan – and as it went the girl lifted her head and turned to meet it. And the same instant a canoe that had been creeping silently and unobserved round the inner shore of the lagoon, emerged from the shadows and defined itself upon the water with a figure at the middle thwart. It was Maloney.

It was only afterwards I realised that we were invisible to him where we stood against the dark background of trees; the figures of Joan and the animal he saw plainly, but not Dr. Silence and myself standing just beyond them. He stood up in the canoe and pointed with his right arm. I saw something gleam in his hand.

"Stand aside, Joan girl, or you'll get hit," he shouted, his voice ringing horribly through the deep stillness, and the same instant a pistol-shot cracked out with a burst of flame and smoke, and the figure of the animal, with one tremendous leap into the air, fell back in the shadows and disappeared like a shape of night and fog. Instantly, then, Joan opened her eyes, looked in a dazed fashion about her, and pressing both hands against her heart, fell with a sharp cry into my arms that were just in time to catch her.

And an answering cry sounded across the lagoon – thin, wailing, piteous. It came from Sangree's tent.

"Fool!" cried Dr. Silence, "you've wounded him!" and before we could move or realise quite what it meant, he was in the canoe and half-way across the lagoon.

Some kind of similar abuse came in a torrent from my lips, too – though I cannot remember the actual words – as I cursed the man for his disobedience and tried to make the girl comfortable on the ground. But the clergyman was more practical. He was spreading his coat over her and dashing water on her face.

"It's not Joan I've killed at any rate," I heard him mutter as she turned and opened her eyes and smiled faintly up in his face. "I swear the bullet went straight."

Joan stared at him; she was still dazed and bewildered, and still imagined herself with the companion of her trance. The strange lucidity of the somnambulist still hung over her brain and mind, though outwardly she appeared troubled and confused.

"Where has he gone to? He disappeared so suddenly, crying that he was hurt," she asked, looking at her father as though she did not recognise him. "And if they've done anything to him – they have done it to me too – for he is more to me than—"

Her words grew vaguer and vaguer as she returned slowly to her normal waking state, and now she stopped altogether, as though suddenly aware that she had been surprised into telling secrets. But all the way back, as we carried her carefully through the trees, the girl smiled and murmured Sangree's name and asked if he was injured, until it finally became clear to me that the wild soul of the one had called to the wild soul of the other and in the secret depths of their beings the call had been heard and understood. John Silence was right. In the abyss of her heart, too deep at first for recognition, the girl loved him, and had loved him from the very beginning. Once her normal waking consciousness recognised the fact they would leap together like twin flames, and his affliction would be at an end; his intense desire would be satisfied; he would be cured.

And in Sangree's tent Dr. Silence and I sat up for the remainder of the night – this wonderful and haunted night that had shown us such strange glimpses of a new heaven and a new hell – for the Canadian tossed upon his balsam boughs with high fever in his blood, and upon each cheek a dark and curious contusion showed, throbbing with severe pain although the skin was not broken and there was no outward and visible sign of blood.

"Maloney shot straight, you see," whispered Dr. Silence to me after the clergyman had gone to his tent, and had put Joan to sleep beside her mother, who, by the way, had never once awakened. "The bullet must have passed clean through the face, for both cheeks are stained. He'll wear these marks all his life – smaller, but always there. They're the most curious scars in the world, these scars transferred by repercussion from an injured Double. They'll remain visible until just before his death, and then with the withdrawal of the subtle body they will disappear finally."

His words mingled in my dazed mind with the sighs of the troubled sleeper and the crying of the wind about the tent. Nothing seemed to paralyse my powers of realisation so much as these twin stains of mysterious significance upon the face before me.

It was odd, too, how speedily and easily the Camp resigned itself again to sleep and quietness, as though a stage curtain had suddenly dropped down upon the action and concealed it; and nothing contributed so vividly to the feeling that I had been a spectator of some kind of visionary drama as the dramatic nature of the change in the girl's attitude.

Yet, as a matter of fact, the change had not been so sudden and revolutionary as appeared. Underneath, in those remoter regions of consciousness where the emotions, unknown to their owners, do secretly mature, and owe thence their abrupt revelation to some abrupt psychological climax, there can be no doubt that Joan's love for the Canadian had been growing steadily and irresistibly all the time. It had now rushed to the surface so that she recognised it; that was all.

And it has always seemed to me that the presence of John Silence, so potent, so quietly efficacious, produced an effect, if one may say so, of a psychic forcing-house, and hastened incalculably the bringing together of these two 'wild' lovers. In that sudden awakening had occurred the very psychological climax required to reveal the passionate emotion accumulated below. The deeper knowledge had leaped across and transferred itself to her ordinary consciousness, and in that shock the collision of the personalities had shaken them to the depths and shown her the truth beyond all possibility of doubt.

"He's sleeping quietly now," the doctor said, interrupting my reflections. "If you will watch alone for a bit I'll go to Maloney's tent and help him to arrange his thoughts." He smiled in anticipation of that 'arrangement'. "He'll never quite understand how a wound on the Double can transfer itself to the physical body, but at least I can persuade him that the less he talks and 'explains' tomorrow, the sooner the forces will run their natural course now to peace and quietness."

He went away softly, and with the removal of his presence Sangree, sleeping heavily, turned over and groaned with the pain of his broken head.

And it was in the still hour just before the dawn, when all the islands were hushed, the wind and sea still dreaming, and the stars visible through clearing mists, that a figure crept silently over the ridge and reached the door of the tent where I dozed beside the sufferer, before I was aware of its presence. The flap was cautiously lifted a few inches and in looked – Joan.

That same instant Sangree woke and sat up on his bed of branches. He recognised her before I could say a word, and uttered a low cry. It was pain and joy mingled, and this time all human. And the girl too was no longer walking in her sleep, but fully aware of what she was doing. I was only just able to prevent him springing from his blankets.

"Joan, Joan!" he cried, and in a flash she answered him, "I'm here – I'm with you always now," and had pushed past me into the tent and flung herself upon his breast.

"I knew you would come to me in the end," I heard him whisper.

"It was all too big for me to understand at first," she murmured, "and for a long time I was frightened—"

"But not now!" he cried louder; "you don't feel afraid now of – of anything that's in me—"

"I fear nothing," she cried, "nothing, nothing!"

I led her outside again. She looked steadily into my face with eyes shining and her whole being transformed. In some intuitive way, surviving probably from the somnambulism, she knew or guessed as much as I knew.

"You must talk tomorrow with John Silence," I said gently, leading her towards her own tent. "He understands everything."

I left her at the door, and as I went back softly to take up my place of sentry again with the Canadian, I saw the first streaks of dawn lighting up the far rim of the sea behind the distant islands.

And, as though to emphasise the eternal closeness of comedy to tragedy, two small details rose out of the scene and impressed me so vividly that I remember them to this very day. For in the tent where I had just left Joan, all aquiver with her new happiness, there rose plainly to my ears the grotesque sounds of the Bo'sun's Mate heavily snoring, oblivious of all things in heaven or hell; and from Maloney's tent, so still was the night, where I looked across and saw the lantern's glow, there came to me, through the trees, the monotonous rising and falling of a human voice that was beyond question the sound of a man praying to his God.

**If you enjoyed this, you might also like…**
The Wendigo, see page 49
May Day Eve, see page 118

# The Terror of the Twins

THAT the man's hopes had built upon a son to inherit his name and estates – a single son, that is – was to be expected; but no one could have foreseen the depth and bitterness of his disappointment, the cold, implacable fury, when there arrived instead – twins. For, though the elder legally must inherit, that other ran him so deadly close. A daughter would have been a more reasonable defeat. But twins—! To miss his dream by so feeble a device—!

\* \* \*

The complete frustration of a hope deeply cherished for years may easily result in strange fevers of the soul, but the violence of the father's hatred, existing as it did side by side with a love he could not deny, was something to set psychologists thinking. More than unnatural, it was positively uncanny. Being a man of rigid self-control, however, it operated inwardly, and doubtless along some morbid line of weakness little suspected even by those nearest to him, preying upon his thought to such dreadful extent that finally the mind gave way. The suppressed rage and bitterness deprived him, so the family decided, of his reason, and he spent the last years of his life under restraint. He was possessed naturally of immense forces – of will, feeling, desire; his dynamic value truly tremendous, driving through life like a great engine; and the intensity of this concentrated and buried hatred was guessed by few. The twins themselves, however, knew it. They divined it, at least, for it operated ceaselessly against them side by side with the genuine soft love that occasionally sweetened it, to their great perplexity. They spoke of it only to each other, though.

"At twenty-one," Edward, the elder, would remark sometimes, unhappily, "we shall know more." "Too much," Ernest would reply, with a rush of unreasoning terror the thought never failed to evoke – *in him*. "Things father said always happened – in life." And they paled perceptibly. For the hatred, thus compressed into a veritable bomb of psychic energy, had found at the last a singular expression in the cry of the father's distraught mind. On the occasion of their final visit to the asylum, preceding his death by a few hours only, very calmly, but with an intensity that drove the words into their hearts like points of burning metal, he had spoken. In the presence of the attendant, at the door of the dreadful padded cell, he said it: "You are not two, but one. I still regard you as one. And at the coming of age, by h—, you shall find it out!"

The lads perhaps had never fully divined that icy hatred which lay so well concealed against them, but that this final sentence was a curse, backed by all the man's terrific force, they quite well realised; and accordingly, almost unknown to each other, they had come to dread the day inexpressibly. On the morning of that twenty-first birthday – their father gone these five years into the Unknown, yet still sometimes so strangely close to them – they shared the same biting, inner terror, just as they shared all other emotions of their life – intimately, without speech. During the daytime they managed to keep it at a distance; but when the dusk fell about the old house they knew the stealthy approach of a kind of panic sense. Their self-respect weakened swiftly... and they persuaded their old friend, and once tutor, the vicar, to sit up with them till midnight... He had humoured them to that extent, willing to forgo his sleep, and at the same time more than a little interested in their singular belief – that before the day was out, before midnight struck, that is, the curse of that terrible man would somehow come into operation against them.

Festivities over and the guests departed, they sat up in the library, the room usually occupied by their father, and little used since. Mr. Curtice, a robust man of fifty-five, and a firm believer in spiritual principalities and powers, dark as well as good, affected (for their own good) to regard the youths' obsession with a kindly cynicism. "I do not think it likely for one moment," he said gravely, "that such a thing would be permitted. All spirits are in the hands of God, and the violent ones more especially." To which Edward made the extraordinary reply: "Even if father does not come himself he will – *send!*" And Ernest agreed: "All this time he's been making preparations for this very day. We've both known it for a long time – by odd things that have happened, by our dreams, by nasty little dark hints of various kinds, and by these persistent attacks of terror that come from nowhere, especially of late. Haven't we, Edward?" Edward assenting with a shudder. "Father has been at us of late with renewed violence. Tonight it will be a regular assault upon our lives, or minds, or souls!"

"Strong personalities *may* possibly leave behind them forces that continue to act," observed Mr. Curtice with caution, while the brothers replied almost in the same breath: "That's exactly what we feel so curiously. Though – nothing has actually happened yet, you know, and it's a good many years now since—"

This was the way the twins spoke of it all. And it was their profound conviction that had touched their old friend's sense of duty. The experiment should justify itself – and cure them. Meanwhile none of the family knew. Everything was planned secretly.

The library was the quietest room in the house. It had shuttered bow-windows, thick carpets, heavy doors. Books lined the walls, and there was a capacious open fireplace of brick in which the wood logs blazed and roared, for the autumn night was chilly. Round this the three of them were grouped, the clergyman reading aloud from the Book of Job in low tones; Edward and Ernest, in dinner-jackets, occupying deep leather armchairs, listening. They looked exactly what they were – Cambridge 'undergrads', their faces pale against their dark hair, and alike as two peas. A shaded lamp behind the clergyman threw the rest of the room into shadow. The reading voice was steady, even monotonous, but something in it betrayed an underlying anxiety, and although the eyes rarely left the printed page, they took in every movement of the young men opposite, and noted every change upon their faces. It was his aim to produce an unexciting atmosphere, yet to miss nothing; if anything did occur to see it from the very beginning. Not to be taken by surprise was his main idea... And thus, upon this falsely peaceful scene, the minutes passed the hour of eleven and slipped rapidly along towards midnight.

The novel element in his account of this distressing and dreadful occurrence seems to be that what happened – happened without the slightest warning or preparation. There was no gradual presentiment of any horror; no strange blast of cold air; no dwindling of heat or light; no shaking of windows or mysterious tapping upon furniture. Without preliminaries it fell with its black trappings of terror upon the scene.

The clergyman had been reading aloud for some considerable time, one or other of the twins – Ernest usually – making occasional remarks, which proved that his sense of dread was disappearing. As the time grew short and nothing happened they grew more at their ease. Edward, indeed, actually nodded, dozed, and finally fell asleep. It was a few minutes before midnight. Ernest, slightly yawning, was stretching himself in the big chair. "Nothing's going to happen," he said aloud, in a pause. "Your good influence has prevented it." He even laughed now. "What superstitious asses we've been, sir; haven't we—?"

Curtice, then, dropping his Bible, looked hard at him under the lamp. For in that second, even while the words sounded, there had come about a most abrupt and dreadful change; and so swiftly that the clergyman, in spite of himself, was taken utterly by surprise and had no time to think. There had swooped down upon the quiet library – so he puts it – an immense hushing silence, so profound that the peace already reigning there seemed clamour by comparison; and out of this enveloping stillness there rose through the space about them a living and abominable Invasion – soft, motionless, terrific. It was as though vast engines, working at full speed and pressure, yet too swift and delicate to be appreciable to any definite sense, had suddenly dropped down upon them – from nowhere. "It made me think," the vicar used to say afterwards, "of the Mauretania machinery compressed into a nutshell, yet losing none of its awful power."

"… haven't we?" repeated Ernest, still laughing. And Curtice, making no audible reply, heard the true answer in his heart: "Because everything has *already happened* – even as you feared."

Yet, to the vicar's supreme astonishment, Ernest still noticed – nothing!

"Look," the boy added, "Eddy's sound asleep – sleeping like a pig. Doesn't say much for your reading, you know, sir!" And he laughed again – lightly, even foolishly. But that laughter jarred, for the clergyman understood now that the sleep of the elder twin was either feigned – or *unnatural*.

And while the easy words fell so lightly from his lips, the monstrous engines worked and pulsed against him and against his sleeping brother, all their huge energy concentrated down into points fine as Suggestion, delicate as Thought. The Invasion affected everything. The very objects in the room altered incredibly, revealing suddenly behind their normal exteriors horrid little hearts of darkness. It was truly amazing, this vile metamorphosis. Books, chairs, pictures, all yielded up their pleasant aspect, and betrayed, as with silent mocking laughter, their inner soul of blackness – their *decay*. This is how Curtice tries to body forth in words what he actually witnessed… And Ernest, yawning, talking lightly, half foolishly – still noticed nothing!

For all this, as described, came about in something like ten seconds; and with it swept into the clergyman's mind, like a blow, the memory of that sinister phrase used more than once by Edward: "If father doesn't come, he will certainly – send." And Curtice understood that he had done both – both sent and come himself… That violent mind, released from its spell of madness in the body, yet still retaining the old implacable hatred, was now directing the terrible, unseen assault. This silent room, so hushed and still, was charged to the brim. The horror of it, as he said later, "seemed to peel the very skin from my back." And, while Ernest noticed nothing, Edward slept…! The soul of the clergyman, strong with the desire to help or save, yet realising that he was alone against a Legion, poured out in wordless prayer to his Deity. The clock just then, whirring before it struck, made itself audible.

"By Jove! It's all right, you see!" exclaimed Ernest, his voice oddly fainter and lower than before. "There's midnight – and nothing's happened. Bally nonsense, all of it!" His voice had dwindled curiously in volume. "I'll get the whisky and soda from the hall." His relief was great and his manner showed it. But in him somewhere was a singular change. His voice, manner, gestures, his very tread as he moved over the thick carpet toward the door, all showed it. He seemed less real, less alive, reduced somehow to littleness, the voice without timbre or quality, the appearance of him diminished in some fashion quite ghastly. His presence, if not actually shrivelled, was at least impaired. Ernest had suffered a singular and horrible *decrease...*

The clock was still whirring before the strike. One heard the chain running up softly. Then the hammer fell upon the first stroke of midnight.

"I'm off," he laughed faintly from the door; "it's been pure funk – on my part, at least...!" He passed out of sight into the hall. *The Power that throbbed so mightily about the room followed him out.* Almost at the same moment Edward woke up. But he woke with a tearing and indescribable cry of pain and anguish on his lips: "Oh, oh, oh! But it hurts! It hurts! I can't hold you; leave me. It's breaking me asunder—"

The clergyman had sprung to his feet, but in the same instant everything had become normal once more – the room as it was before, the horror gone. There was nothing he could do or say, for there was no longer anything to put right, to defend, or to attack. Edward was speaking; his voice, deep and full as it never had been before: "By Jove, how that sleep has refreshed me! I feel twice the chap I was before – twice the chap. I feel quite splendid. Your voice, sir, must have hypnotised me to sleep..." He crossed the room with great vigour. "Where's – er – where's – Ernie, by the bye?" he asked casually, hesitating – almost searching – for the name. And a shadow as of a vanished memory crossed his face and was gone. The tone conveyed the most complete indifference where once the least word or movement of his twin had wakened solicitude, love. "Gone away, I suppose – gone to bed, I mean, of course."

Curtice has never been able to describe the dreadful conviction that overwhelmed him as he stood there staring, his heart in his mouth – the conviction, the positive certainty, that Edward had changed interiorly, had suffered an incredible accession to his existing personality. But he knew it as he watched. His mind, spirit, soul had most wonderfully increased. Something that hitherto the lad had known from the outside only, or by the magic of loving sympathy, had now passed, to be incorporated with his own being. And, being himself, it required no expression. Yet this visible increase was somehow terrible. Curtice shrank back from him. The instinct – he has never grasped the profound psychology of *that*, nor why it turned his soul dizzy with a kind of nausea – the instinct to strike him where he stood, passed, and a plaintive sound from the hall, stealing softly into the room between them, sent all that was left to him of self-possession into his feet. He turned and ran. Edward followed him – very leisurely.

They found Ernest, or what had been Ernest, crouching behind the table in the hall, weeping foolishly to himself. On his face lay blackness. The mouth was open, the jaw dropped; he dribbled hopelessly; and from the face had passed all signs of intelligence – of spirit.

For a few weeks he lingered on, regaining no sign of spiritual or mental life before the poor body, hopelessly disorganised, released what was left of him, from pure inertia – from complete and utter loss of vitality.

And the horrible thing – so the distressed family thought, at least – was that all those weeks Edward showed an indifference that was singularly brutal and complete. He rarely even went to visit him. I believe, too, it is true that he only once spoke of him by name; and that was when he said –

"Ernie? Oh, but Ernie is much better and happier where he is—!"

**If you enjoyed this, you might also like...**
The Transfer, see page 181
Strange Disappearance of a Baronet, see page 188

# The Transfer

**THE CHILD** began to cry in the early afternoon – about three o'clock, to be exact. I remember the hour, because I had been listening with secret relief to the sound of the departing carriage. Those wheels fading into the distance down the gravel drive with Mrs. Frene, and her daughter Gladys to whom I was governess, meant for me some hours' welcome rest, and the June day was oppressively hot. Moreover, there was this excitement in the little country household that had told upon us all, but especially upon myself. This excitement, running delicately behind all the events of the morning, was due to some mystery, and the mystery was of course kept concealed from the governess. I had exhausted myself with guessing and keeping on the watch. For some deep and unexplained anxiety possessed me, so that I kept thinking of my sister's dictum that I was really much too sensitive to make a good governess, and that I should have done far better as a professional clairvoyante.

Mr. Frene, senior, 'Uncle Frank', was expected for an unusual visit from town about teatime. That I knew. I also knew that his visit was concerned somehow with the future welfare of little Jamie, Gladys' seven-year-old brother. More than this, indeed, I never knew, and this missing link makes my story in a fashion incoherent – an important bit of the strange puzzle left out. I only gathered that the visit of Uncle Frank was of a condescending nature, that Jamie was told he must be upon his very best behaviour to make a good impression, and that Jamie, who had never seen his uncle, dreaded him horribly already in advance. Then, trailing thinly through the dying crunch of the carriage wheels this sultry afternoon, I heard the curious little wail of the child's crying, with the effect, wholly unaccountable, that every nerve in my body shot its bolt electrically, bringing me to my feet with a tingling of unequivocal alarm. Positively, the water ran into my eyes. I recalled his white distress that morning when told that Uncle Frank was motoring down for tea and that he was to be 'very nice indeed' to him. It had gone into me like a knife. All through the day, indeed, had run this nightmare quality of terror and vision.

"The man with the 'normous face?" he had asked in a little voice of awe, and then gone speechless from the room in tears that no amount of soothing management could calm. That was all I saw; and what he meant by 'the 'normous face' gave me only a sense of vague presentiment. But it came as anticlimax somehow – a sudden revelation of the mystery and excitement that pulsed beneath the quiet of the stifling summer day. I feared for him. For of all that commonplace household I loved Jamie best, though professionally I had nothing to do with him. He was a high-strung, ultra-sensitive child, and it seemed to me that no one understood him, least of all his honest, tender-hearted parents; so that his little wailing voice brought me from my bed to the window in a moment like a call for help.

The haze of June lay over that big garden like a blanket; the wonderful flowers, which were Mr. Frene's delight, hung motionless; the lawns, so soft and thick, cushioned all other sounds; only the limes and huge clumps of guelder roses hummed with bees.

Through this muted atmosphere of heat and haze the sound of the child's crying floated faintly to my ears – from a distance. Indeed, I wonder now that I heard it at all, for the next moment I saw him down beyond the garden, standing in his white sailor suit alone, two hundred yards away. He was down by the ugly patch where nothing grew – the Forbidden Corner. A faintness then came over me at once, a faintness as of death, when I saw him *there* of all places – where he never was allowed to go, and where, moreover, he was usually too terrified to go. To see him standing solitary in that singular spot, above all to hear him crying there, bereft me momentarily of the power to act. Then, before I could recover my composure sufficiently to call him in, Mr. Frene came round the corner from the Lower Farm with the dogs, and, seeing his son, performed that office for me. In his loud, good-natured, hearty voice he called him, and Jamie turned and ran as though some spell had broken just in time – ran into the open arms of his fond but uncomprehending father, who carried him indoors on his shoulder, while asking "what all this hubbub was about?" And, at their heels, the tailless sheepdogs followed, barking loudly, and performing what Jamie called their 'Gravel Dance', because they ploughed up the moist, rolled gravel with their feet.

I stepped back swiftly from the window lest I should be seen. Had I witnessed the saving of the child from fire or drowning the relief could hardly have been greater. Only Mr. Frene, I felt sure, would not say and do the right thing quite. He would protect the boy from his own vain imaginings, yet not with the explanation that could really heal. They disappeared behind the rose trees, making for the house. I saw no more till later, when Mr. Frene, senior, arrived.

To describe the ugly patch as 'singular' is hard to justify, perhaps, yet some such word is what the entire family sought, though never – oh, never! – used. To Jamie and myself, though equally we never mentioned it, that treeless, flowerless spot was more than singular. It stood at the far end of the magnificent rose garden, a bald, sore place, where the black earth showed uglily in winter, almost like a piece of dangerous bog, and in summer baked and cracked with fissures where green lizards shot their fire in passing. In contrast to the rich luxuriance of death amid life, a centre of disease that cried for healing lest it spread. But it never did spread. Behind it stood the thick wood of silver birches and, glimmering beyond, the orchard meadow, where the lambs played.

The gardeners had a very simple explanation of its barrenness – that the water all drained off it owing to the lie of the slopes immediately about it, holding no remnant to keep the soil alive. I cannot say. It was Jamie – Jamie who felt its spell and haunted it, who spent whole hours there, even while afraid, and for whom it was finally labelled 'strictly out of bounds' because it stimulated his already big imagination, not wisely but too darkly – it was Jamie who buried ogres there and heard it crying in an earthy voice, swore that it shook its surface sometimes while he watched it, and secretly gave it food in the form of birds or mice or rabbits he found dead upon his wanderings. And it was Jamie who put so extraordinarily into words the *feeling* that the horrid spot had given me from the moment I first saw it.

"It's bad, Miss Gould," he told me.

"But, Jamie, nothing in Nature is bad – exactly; only different from the rest sometimes."

"Miss Gould, if you please, then it's empty. It's not fed. It's dying because it can't get the food it wants." And when I stared into the little pale face where the eyes shone so dark and wonderful, seeking within myself for the right thing to say to him, he added, with an emphasis and conviction that made me suddenly turn cold: "Miss Gould" – he always used my name like this in all his sentences – "it's hungry, don't you see? But I know what would make it feel all right."

Only the conviction of an earnest child, perhaps, could have made so outrageous a suggestion worth listening to for an instant; but for me, who felt that things an imaginative child believed were important, it came with a vast disquieting shock of reality. Jamie, in this exaggerated way, had caught at the edge of a shocking fact – a hint of dark, undiscovered truth had leaped into that sensitive imagination. Why there lay horror in the words I cannot say, but I think some power of darkness trooped across the suggestion of that sentence at the end, "I know what would make it feel all right." I remember that I shrank from asking explanation. Small groups of other words, veiled fortunately by his silence, gave life to an unspeakable possibility that hitherto had lain at the back of my own consciousness. The way it sprang to life proves, I think, that my mind already contained it. The blood rushed from my heart as I listened. I remember that my knees shook. Jamie's idea was – had been all along – my own as well.

And now, as I lay down on my bed and thought about it all, I understood why the coming of his uncle involved somehow an experience that wrapped terror at its heart. With a sense of nightmare certainty that left me too weak to resist the preposterous idea, too shocked, indeed, to argue or reason it away, this certainty came with its full, black blast of conviction; and the only way I can put it into words, since nightmare horror really is not properly tellable at all, seems this: that there was something missing in that dying patch of garden; something lacking that it ever searched for; something, once found and taken, that would turn it rich and living as the rest; more – that there *was* some living person who could do this for it. Mr. Frene, senior, in a word, 'Uncle Frank', was this person who out of his abundant life could supply the lack – unwittingly.

For this connection between the dying, empty patch and the person of this vigorous, wealthy, and successful man had already lodged itself in my subconsciousness before I was aware of it. Clearly it must have lain there all along, though hidden. Jamie's words, his sudden pallor, his vibrating emotion of fearful anticipation had developed the plate, but it was his weeping alone there in the Forbidden Corner that had printed it. The photograph shone framed before me in the air. I hid my eyes. But for the redness – the charm of my face goes to pieces unless my eyes are clear – I could have cried. Jamie's words that morning about the "'normous face' came back upon me like a battering-ram.

Mr. Frene, senior, had been so frequently the subject of conversation in the family since I came, I had so often heard him discussed, and had then read so much about him in the papers – his energy, his philanthropy, his success with everything he laid his hand to – that a picture of the man had grown complete within me. I knew him as he was – within; or, as my sister would have said – clairvoyantly. And the only time I saw him (when I took Gladys to a meeting where he was chairman, and later *felt* his atmosphere and presence while for a moment he patronisingly spoke with her) had justified the portrait I had drawn. The rest, you may say, was a woman's wild imagining; but I think rather it was that kind of divining intuition which women share with children. If souls could be made visible, I would stake my life upon the truth and accuracy of my portrait.

For this Mr. Frene was a man who drooped alone, but grew vital in a crowd – because he used their vitality. He was a supreme, unconscious artist in the science of taking the fruits of others' work and living – for his own advantage. He vampired, unknowingly no doubt, everyone with whom he came in contact; left them exhausted, tired, listless. Others fed him, so that while in a full room he shone, alone by himself and with no life to draw upon he languished and declined. In the man's immediate neighbourhood you felt his presence draining you; he took your ideas, your strength, your very words, and later used them for his own benefit and aggrandisement. Not evilly, of course; the man was good enough; but you felt that he was dangerous owing to the facile way he absorbed into himself all loose vitality that was to be had. His eyes and voice and presence devitalised you. Life, it seemed, not highly organised enough to resist, must shrink from his too near approach and hide away for fear of being appropriated, for fear, that is, of – death.

Jamie, unknowingly, put in the finishing touch to my unconscious portrait. The man carried about with him some silent, compelling trick of drawing out all your reserves – then swiftly pocketing them. At first you would be conscious of taut resistance; this would slowly shade off into weariness; the will would become flaccid; then you either moved away or yielded – agreed to all he said with a sense of weakness pressing ever closer upon the edges of collapse. With a male antagonist it might be different, but even then the effort of resistance would generate force that *he* absorbed and not the other. He never gave out. Some instinct taught him how to protect himself from that. To human beings, I mean, he never gave out. This time it was a very different matter. He had no more chance than a fly before the wheels of a huge – what Jamie used to call – 'attraction' engine.

So this was how I saw him – a great human sponge, crammed and soaked with the life, or proceeds of life, absorbed from others – stolen. My idea of a human vampire was satisfied. He went about carrying these accumulations of the life of others. In this sense his 'life' was not really his own. For the same reason, I think, it was not so fully under his control as he imagined.

And in another hour this man would be here. I went to the window. My eye wandered to the empty patch, dull black there amid the rich luxuriance of the garden flowers. It struck me as a hideous bit of emptiness yawning to be filled and nourished. The idea of Jamie playing round its bare edge was loathsome. I watched the big summer clouds above, the stillness of the afternoon, the haze. The silence of the overheated garden was oppressive. I had never felt a day so stifling, motionless. It lay there waiting. The household, too, was waiting – waiting for the coming of Mr. Frene from London in his big motorcar.

And I shall never forget the sensation of icy shrinking and distress with which I heard the rumble of the car. He had arrived. Tea was all ready on the lawn beneath the lime trees, and Mrs. Frene and Gladys, back from their drive, were sitting in wicker chairs. Mr. Frene, junior, was in the hall to meet his brother, but Jamie, as I learned afterwards, had shown such hysterical alarm, offered such bold resistance, that it had been deemed wiser to keep him in his room. Perhaps, after all, his presence might not be necessary. The visit clearly had to do with something on the uglier side of life – money, settlements, or whatnot; I never knew exactly; only that his parents were anxious, and that Uncle Frank had to be propitiated. It does not matter. That has nothing to do with the affair. What has to do with it – or I should not be telling the story – is that Mrs. Frene sent for me to come down "in my nice white dress, if I didn't mind", and that I was terrified, yet pleased, because it meant that a pretty face would be considered a welcome addition to the visitor's landscape. Also, most odd it was, I felt my presence was somehow inevitable, that in some way it was intended that I should witness what I did witness. And the instant I came upon the lawn – I hesitate to set it down, it sounds so foolish, disconnected – I could have sworn, as my eyes met his, that a kind of sudden darkness came, taking the summer brilliance out of everything, and that it was caused by troops of small black horses that raced about us from his person – to attack.

After a first momentary approving glance he took no further notice of me. The tea and talk went smoothly; I helped to pass the plates and cups, filling in pauses with little under-talk to Gladys. Jamie was never mentioned. Outwardly all seemed well, but inwardly everything was awful – skirting the edge of things unspeakable, and so charged with danger that I could not keep my voice from trembling when I spoke.

I watched his hard, bleak face; I noticed how thin he was, and the curious, oily brightness of his steady eyes. They did not glitter, but they drew you with a sort of soft, creamy shine like Eastern eyes. And everything he said or did announced what I may dare to call the *suction* of his presence. His nature achieved this result automatically. He dominated us all, yet so gently that until it was accomplished no one noticed it.

Before five minutes had passed, however, I was aware of one thing only. My mind focused exclusively upon it, and so vividly that I marvelled the others did not scream, or run, or do something violent to prevent it. And it was this; that, separated merely by some dozen yards or so, this man, vibrating with the acquired vitality of others, stood within easy reach of that spot of yawning emptiness, waiting and eager to be filled. Earth scented her prey.

These two active 'centres' were within fighting distance; he so thin, so hard, so keen, yet really spreading large with the loose 'surround' of others' life he had appropriated, so practised and triumphant; that other so patient, deep, with so mighty a draw of the whole earth behind it, and – ugh! – so obviously aware that its opportunity at last had come.

I saw it all as plainly as though I watched two great animals prepare for battle, both unconsciously; yet in some inexplicable way I saw it, of course, within me, and not externally. The conflict would be hideously unequal. Each side had already sent out emissaries, how long before I could not tell, for the first evidence *he* gave that something was going wrong with him was when his voice grew suddenly confused, he missed his words, and his lips trembled a moment and turned flabby. The next second his face betrayed that singular and horrid change, growing somehow loose about the bones of the cheek, and larger, so that I remembered Jamie's miserable phrase. The emissaries of the two kingdoms, the human and the vegetable, had met, I make it out, in that very second. For the first time in his long career of battening on others, Mr. Frene found himself pitted against a vaster kingdom than he knew and, so finding, shook inwardly in that little part that was his definite actual self. He felt the huge disaster coming.

"Yes, John," he was saying, in his drawling, self-congratulating voice, "Sir George gave me that car – gave it to me as a present. Wasn't it char—?" and then broke off abruptly, stammered, drew breath, stood up, and looked uneasily about him. For a second there was a gaping pause. It was like the click which starts some huge machinery moving – that instant's pause before it actually starts. The whole thing, indeed, then went with the rapidity of machinery running down and beyond control. I thought of a giant dynamo working silently and invisible.

"What's that?" he cried, in a soft voice charged with alarm. "What's that horrid place? And someone's crying there – who is it?"

He pointed to the empty patch. Then, before anyone could answer, he started across the lawn towards it, going every minute faster. Before anyone could move he stood upon the edge. He leaned over – peering down into it.

It seemed a few hours passed, but really they were seconds, for time is measured by the quality and not the quantity of sensations it contains. I saw it all with merciless, photographic detail, sharply etched amid the general confusion. Each side was intensely active, but only one side, the human, exerted *all* its force – in resistance. The other merely stretched out a feeler, as it were, from its vast, potential strength; no more was necessary. It was such a soft and easy victory. Oh, it was rather pitiful! There was no bluster or great effort, on one side at least. Close by his side I witnessed it, for I, it seemed, alone had moved and followed him. No one else stirred, though Mrs. Frene clattered noisily with the cups, making some sudden impulsive gesture with her hands, and Gladys, I remember, gave a cry – it was like a little scream– "Oh, mother, it's the heat, isn't it?" Mr. Frene, her father, was speechless, pale as ashes.

But the instant I reached his side, it became clear what had drawn me there thus instinctively. Upon the other side, among the silver birches, stood little Jamie. He was watching. I experienced – for him – one of those moments that shake the heart; a liquid fear ran all over me, the more effective because unintelligible really. Yet I felt that if I could know all, and what lay actually behind, my fear would be more than justified; that the thing was awful, full of awe.

And then it happened – a truly wicked sight – like watching a universe in action, yet all contained within a small square foot of space. I think he understood vaguely that if someone could only take his place he might be saved, and that was why, discerning instinctively the easiest substitute within reach, he saw the child and called aloud to him across the empty patch, "James, my boy, come here!"

His voice was like a thin report, but somehow flat and lifeless, as when a rifle misses fire, sharp, yet weak; it had no 'crack' in it. It was really supplication. And, with amazement, I heard my own ring out imperious and strong, though I was not conscious of saying it, "Jamie, don't move. Stay where you are!" But Jamie, the little child, obeyed neither of us. Moving up nearer to the edge, he stood there – laughing! I heard that laughter, but could have sworn it did not come from him. The empty, yawning patch gave out that sound.

Mr. Frene turned sideways, throwing up his arms. I saw his hard, bleak face grow somehow wider, spread through the air, and downwards. A similar thing, I saw, was happening at the same time to his entire person, for it drew out into the atmosphere in a stream of movement. The face for a second made me think of those toys of green india-rubber that children pull. It grew enormous. But this was an external impression only. What actually happened, I clearly understood, was that all this vitality and life he had transferred from others to himself for years was now in turn being taken from him and transferred – elsewhere.

One moment on the edge he wobbled horribly, then with that queer sideways motion, rapid yet ungainly, he stepped forward into the middle of the patch and fell heavily upon his face. His eyes, as he dropped, faded shockingly, and across the countenance was written plainly what I can only call an expression of destruction. He looked utterly destroyed. I caught a sound – from Jamie? – but this time not of laughter. It was like a gulp; it was deep and muffled and it dipped away into the earth. Again I thought of a troop of small black horses galloping away down a subterranean passage beneath my feet – plunging into the depths – their tramping growing fainter and fainter into buried distance. In my nostrils was a pungent smell of earth.

And then – all passed. I came back into myself. Mr. Frene, junior, was lifting his brother's head from the lawn where he had fallen from the heat, close beside the tea-table.

He had never really moved from there. And Jamie, I learned afterwards, had been the whole time asleep upon his bed upstairs, worn out with his crying and unreasoning alarm. Gladys came running out with cold water, sponge and towel, brandy too – all kinds of things. "Mother, it *was* the heat, wasn't it?" I heard her whisper, but I did not catch Mrs. Frene's reply. From her face it struck me that she was bordering on collapse herself. Then the butler followed, and they just picked him up and carried him into the house. He recovered even before the doctor came.

But the queer thing to me is that I was convinced the others all had seen what I saw, only that no one said a word about it; and to this day no one *has* said a word. And that was, perhaps, the most horrid part of all.

From that day to this I have scarcely heard a mention of Mr. Frene, senior. It seemed as if he dropped suddenly out of life. The papers never mentioned him. His activities ceased, as it were. His afterlife, at any rate, became singularly ineffective. Certainly he achieved nothing worth public mention. But it may be only that, having left the employ of Mrs. Frene, there was no particular occasion for me to hear anything.

The afterlife of that empty patch of garden, however, was quite otherwise. Nothing, so far as I know, was done to it by gardeners, or in the way of draining it or bringing in new earth, but even before I left in the following summer it had changed. It lay untouched, full of great, luscious, driving weeds and creepers, very strong, full – fed, and bursting thick with life.

**If you enjoyed this, you might also like...**
The Damned, see page 414
Ancient Lights, see page 92

# Strange Disappearance of a Baronet

**HIS INTRINSIC VALUE** before the Eternities was exceedingly small, but he possessed most things the world sets store by – presence, name, wealth – and, above all, that high opinion of himself which saves it the bother of a separate and troublesome valuation. Outside these possessions he owned nothing of permanent value, or that could decently claim to be worthy of immortality. The fact was he had never even experienced that expansion of self commonly known as generosity. No apology, however, is necessary for his amazing adventure, for these same Eternities who judged him have made their affidavit that it was They who stripped him bare and showed himself to himself.

It all began with the receipt of that shattering letter from his solicitors. He read and reread it in his comfortable first-class compartment as the express hurried him to town, exceedingly comfortable among his rugs and furs, exceedingly distressed and ill at ease in his mind. And in his private sitting-room of the big hotel that same evening Mr. Smirles, more odious even than his letter, informed him plainly that this new and unexpected claimant to his title and estates was likely to be exceedingly troublesome "even dangerous, Sir Timothy! I am bound since you ask that it might be wise to regard the future – er – with a different scale of vision than the one you have been accustomed to."

Sir Timothy practically collapsed. Instinctively he perceived that the lawyer's manner already held less respect: the reflection was a shock to his vain and fatuous personality. "After all, then, it wasn't *me* he worshipped, but my position, and so forth...!" If this nonsense continued he would be no longer 'Sir Timothy', but simply 'Mister' Puffe, poor, a nobody. He seemed to shrink in size as he gazed at himself in the mirror of the gorgeous, flamboyantly decorated room. "It's too preposterous and absurd! There's nothing in it! Why, the whole County would go to pieces without me!" He even thought of making his secretary draft a letter to the *Times* a letter of violent, indignant protest.

He was a handsome, portly man, with a full-blown vanity justified by no single item of soul or mind; not unkind, so much as empty; created and kept alive by the small conventions and the ceaseless contemplation of himself, the withdrawal of which might be expected to leave him flat as a popped balloon... Such a mass of pompous conceit obscured his vision that he only slowly took in the fact that his very existence was at stake. His thoughts rumbled on without direction, the sense of loss, however, dreadfully sharp and painful all the time, till at length he sought relief in something he could really understand. He changed for dinner! He would dine in his sitting-room alone. And, meanwhile, he rang for the remainder of his voluminous luggage. But it was vastly annoying to his diminishing pride to discover that the gorgeous Head Porter (he remembered now having vaguely recognised him in the hall) was the same poor relation to whom he had denied help a year ago. The vicissitudes of life were indeed preposterous. He ought to have been protected from so ridiculous an encounter. For the moment, of course, he merely pretended not to see him – certainly he did not commend the excellently quick delivery of the luggage. And to praise the young fellow's pluck never occurred to him for one single instant.

"The house valet, please," he asked of the waiter who answered the bell soon afterwards – and then directed somewhat helplessly the unpacking of his emporium of exquisite clothes. "Yes, take everything out – everything," he said in reply to the man's question – rather an extraordinary, almost insolent question when he came to reflect upon it, surely: "Is it worth while, perhaps, sir…?" It flashed across his dazed mind that the Head Porter had made the very same remark to his subordinate in the passage when he asked if 'everything' was to come in. With a shrug of his gold-braided shoulders that poor relation had replied, "Seems hardly worth while, but they may as well all go in, yes."

And, with the double rejoinder perplexingly in his mind, Sir Timothy turned sharply upon the valet.

But the thing he was going to say faded on his lips. The man, holding out in his arms a heap of clothes, suits and whatnot, seemed so much taller than before. Sir Timothy had looked down upon him a moment ago, whereas now their eyes stared level. It was passing strange.

"Will you want these, sir?"

"Not tonight, of course."

"Want them at all, I meant, sir?"

Sir Timothy gasped. "Want them at all? Of course! What in the world are you talking about?"

"Beg pardon, sir. Didn't know if it was worth while now," the man said, with a quick flush. And, before the pompous and amazed baronet could get any words between his quivering lips, the man was gone. The waiter, Head Waiter it was, answered the bell almost immediately, and Sir Timothy found consolation for his injured feelings in discussing food and wine. He ordered an absurdly sumptuous meal for a man dining alone. He did so with a vague feeling that it would spite somebody, perhaps; he hardly knew whom. "The Pol Roger well iced, mind," he added with a false importance as the clever servant withdrew. But at the door the man paused and turned, as though he had not heard. "*Large* bottle, I said," repeated the other. The Head Waiter made an extraordinary gesture of indifference. "As you wish, Sir Timothy, as you wish!" And he was gone in his turn. But it was only the man's adroitness that had chosen the words instead of those others: "Is it really worth while?"

And at that very moment, while Sir Timothy stood there fuming inwardly over the extraordinary words and ways of these people – veiled insolence, he called it – the door opened, and a tall young woman poked her head inside, then followed it with her person. She was dignified, smart even for a hotel like this, and uncommonly pretty. It was the upper housemaid. Full in the eye she looked at him. In her face was a kind of swift sympathy and kindness; but her whole presentment betrayed more than anything else – terror.

"Make an effort, make an effort!" she whispered earnestly. "Before it's too late, make an effort!" And *she* was gone. Sir Timothy, hardly knowing what he meant to do, opened the door to dash after her and make her explain this latest insolence. But the passage was dark, and he heard the swish of skirts far away – too far away to overtake; while running along the walls, as in a whispering gallery, came the words, "Make an effort, make an effort!"

"Confound it all, then, I will!" he exclaimed to himself, as he stumbled back into the room, feeling horribly bewildered. "I will make an effort." And he dressed to go downstairs and show himself in the halls and drawing-rooms, give a few pompous orders, assert himself, and fuss about generally. But that process of dressing without his valet was chiefly and weirdly distressing because he had so amazingly – dwindled. His sight was, of course, awry; disordered nerves had played tricks with vision, proportion, perspective; something of the sort must explain why he seemed so small to himself in the reflection. The pier-glass, which showed him full length, he turned to the wall. But, none the less, to complete his toilet, he had to stand upon a footstool before the other mirror above the mantelpiece.

And go downstairs he did, his heart working with a strange and increasing perplexity. Yet, wherever he went, there came that poor relation, the Head Porter, to face him. Always big, he now looked bigger than ever. Sir Timothy Puffe felt somehow ridiculous in his presence. The young fellow had character, pluck, some touch of intrinsic value. For all his failure in life, the Eternities considered him real. He towered rather dreadfully in his gold braid and smart uniform – towered in his great height all about the hall, like some giant in his own palace. The other's head scarcely came up to his great black belt where the keys swung and jangled.

The Baronet went upstairs again to his room, strangely disconcerted. The first thing he did as he left the lift was to stumble over the step. The liftman picked him up as though he were a boy. Down the passage, now well lighted, he went quickly, his feet almost pattering, his tread light, and – so oddly short. His importance had gone. A voice behind each door he passed whispered to him through the narrow crack as it cautiously opened, "Make an effort, make an effort! Be yourself, be real, be alive before it's too late!" But he saw no one, and the first thing he did on entering his room was to hide the smaller mirror by turning it against the wall, just as he had done to the pier-glass. He was so painfully little and insignificant now. As the externals and the possessions dropped away one by one in his thoughts, the revelation of the tiny little centre of activity within was horrible. He puffed himself out in thought as of old, but there was no response. It was degrading.

The fact was – he began to understand it now – his mind had been pursuing possible results of his loss of title and estates to their logical conclusion. The idea in all its brutal nakedness, of course, hardly reached him – namely, that, without possessions, he was practically – nil! All he grasped was that he was – *less*. Still, the notion did prey upon him atrociously. He followed the advice of the strange housemaid and 'made an effort', but without marked success. So empty, indeed, was his life that, once stripped of the possessions, he would stand there as useless and insignificant as an ownerless street dog. And the thought appalled him. He had not even enough real interest in others to hold him upright, and certainly not enough sufficiency of self, good or evil, to stand alone before any tribunal. The discovery shocked him inexpressibly. But what distressed him still more was to find a fixed mirror in his sitting-room that he could *not* take down, for in its depths he saw himself shrunken and dwindled to the proportions of a...

The knock at the door and the arrival of his dinner broke the appalling train of thought, but rather than be seen in his present diminutive appearance – later, of course, he would surely grow again – he ran into the bedroom. And when he came out again after the waiter's departure he found that his dinner shared the same abominable change. The food upon the dishes was reduced to the minutest proportions – the toast like children's, the soup an egg-cupful, the tenderloin a little slice the size of a visiting-card, and the bird not much larger than a black-beetle. And yet more than he could eat; more than sufficient! He sat in the big chair positively lost, his feet dangling. Then, mortified, frightened, and angry beyond expression, he undressed and concealed himself beneath the sheets and blankets of his bed.

"Of course I'm going mad – that's what it all means," he exclaimed. "I'm no longer of any account in the world. I could never go into my Club, for instance, *like this*!" – and he surveyed the small outline that made a little lump beneath the surface of the bedclothes

– "or read the lessons having to stand upon a chair to reach the lectern." And tears of bleeding vanity and futile wrath mingled upon his pillow... The humiliation was agonising.

In the middle of which the door opened and in came the hotel valet, bearing before him upon a silver salver what at first appeared to be small, striped sandwiches, darkish in hue, but upon closer inspection were seen to be several wee suits of clothes, neatly pressed and folded for wearing. Glancing round the room and perceiving no one, the man proceeded to put them away in the chest of drawers, soliloquising from time to time as he did so.

"So the old buffer did go out after all!" he reflected, as he smoothed the tiny trousers in the drawer. "'E's nothing but a gasbag, anyway! Close with the coin, too – always was that! He whistled, spat in the grate, hunted about for a cigarette, and again found relief in speech. My little dawg's worth two of 'im all the time, and lots to spare. Tim's real...!" And other things, too, he said in similar vein. He was utterly oblivious of Sir Timothy's presence – serenely unconscious that the thin, fading line beneath the sheets was the very individual he was talking about. "Even hides his cigarettes, does he? He's right, though. Take away what he's got and there wouldn't be enough left over to stand upright at a poultry show!" And he guffawed merrily to himself. But what brought the final horror into that vanishing Personality on the bed was the singular fact that the valet made no remark about the absurd and horrible size of those tiny clothes. *This, then, was how others – even a hotel valet – saw him!*

All night long, it seemed, he lay in atrocious pain, the darkness mercifully hiding him, though never from himself, and only towards daylight did he pass off into a condition of unconsciousness. He must have slept very late indeed, too, for he woke to find sunlight in the room, and the housemaid – that tall, dignified girl who had tried to be kind – dusting and sweeping energetically. He screamed to her, but his voice was too feeble to make itself heard above the sweeping. The high-pitched squeak was scarcely audible even to himself. Presently she approached the bed and flung the sheets back. "That's funny," she observed, "could've sworn I saw something move!" She gave a hurried look, then went on sweeping. But in the process she had tossed his person, now no larger than a starved mouse, out on to the carpet. He cried aloud in his anguish, but the squeak was too faint to be audible. "Ugh!" exclaimed the girl, jumping to one side, "there's that 'orrid mouse again! Dead, too, I do declare!" And then, without being aware of the fact, she swept him up with the dust and bits of paper into her pan.

Whereupon Sir Timothy awoke with a bad start, and perceived that his train was running somewhat uneasily into King's Cross, and that he had slept nearly the whole way.

**If you enjoyed this, you might also like...**
A Victim of Higher Space, see page 307
The Pikestaffe Case, see page 331

# The Wings of Horus

**BINOVITCH** had the bird in him somewhere: in his features, certainly, with his piercing eye and hawk-like nose; in his movements, with his quick way of flitting, hopping, darting; in the way he perched on the edge of a chair; in the manner he pecked at his food; in his twittering, high-pitched voice as well; and, above all, in his mind. He skimmed all subjects and picked their heart out neatly, as a bird skims lawn or air to snatch its prey. He had the bird's-eye view of everything. He loved birds and understood them instinctively; could imitate their whistling notes with astonishing accuracy. Their one quality he had not was poise and balance. He was a nervous little man; he was neurasthenic. And he was in Egypt by doctor's orders.

Such imaginative, unnecessary ideas he had! Such uncommon beliefs!

"The old Egyptians," he said laughingly, yet with a touch of solemn conviction in his manner, "were a great people. Their consciousness was different from ours. The bird idea, for instance, conveyed a sense of deity to them – of bird deity, that is: they had sacred birds – hawks, ibis, and so forth – and worshipped them." And he put his tongue out as though to say with challenge, "Ha, ha!"

"They also worshipped cats and crocodiles and cows," grinned Palazov. Binovitch seemed to dart across the table at his adversary. His eyes flashed; his nose pecked the air. Almost one could imagine the beating of his angry wings.

"Because everything alive," he half screamed, "was a symbol of some spiritual power to them. Your mind is as literal as a dictionary and as incoherent. Pages of ink without connected meaning! Verb always in the infinitive! If you were an old Egyptian, you – you" – he flashed and spluttered, his tongue shot out again, his keen eyes blazed – "you might take all those words and spin them into a great interpretation of life, a cosmic romance, as they did. Instead, you get the bitter, dead taste of ink in your mouth, and spit it over us like that" – he made a quick movement of his whole body as a bird that shakes itself – "in empty phrases."

Khilkoff ordered another bottle of champagne, while Vera, his sister, said half nervously, "Let's go for a drive; it's moonlight." There was enthusiasm at once. Another of the party called the head waiter and told him to pack food and drink in baskets. It was only eleven o'clock. They would drive out into the desert, have a meal at two in the morning, tell stories, sing, and see the dawn.

It was in one of those cosmopolitan hotels in Egypt which attract the ordinary tourists as well as those who are doing a 'cure', and all these Russians were ill with one thing or another. All were ordered out for their health, and all were the despair of their doctors. They were as unmanageable as a bazaar and as incoherent. Excess and bed were their routine. They lived, but none of them got better. Equally, none of them got angry. They talked in this strange personal way without a shred of malice or offence. The English, French, and Germans in the hotel watched them with remote amazement, referring to them as 'that Russian lot'. Their energy was elemental. They never stopped. They merely disappeared when the pace became too fast, then reappeared again after a day or two, and resumed their 'living' as before. Binovitch, despite his neurasthenia, was the life of the party. He was also a special patient of Dr. Plitzinger, the famous psychiatrist, who took a peculiar interest in his case. It was not surprising. Binovitch was a man of unusual ability and of genuine, deep culture. But there was something more about him that stimulated curiosity. There was this striking originality. He said and did surprising things.

"I could fly if I wanted to," he said once when the airmen came to astonish the natives with their biplanes over the desert, "but without all that machinery and noise. It's only a question of believing and understanding—"

"Show us!" they cried. "Let's see you fly!"

"He's got it! He's off again! One of his impossible moments."

These occasions when Binovitch let himself go always proved wildly entertaining. He said monstrously incredible things as though he really did believe them. They loved his madness, for it gave them new sensations.

"It's only levitation, after all, this flying," he exclaimed, shooting out his tongue between the words, as his habit was when excited; "and what is levitation but a power of the air? None of you can hang an orange in space for a second, with all your scientific knowledge; but the moon is always levitated perfectly. And the stars. D'you think they swing on wires? What raised the enormous stones of ancient Egypt? D'you really believe it was heaped-up sand and ropes and clumsy leverage and all our weary and laborious mechanical contrivances? Bah! It was levitation. It was the powers of the air. Believe in those powers, and gravity becomes a mere nursery trick – true where it is, but true nowhere else. To know the fourth dimension is to step out of a locked room and appear instantly on the roof or in another country altogether. To know the powers of the air, similarly, is to annihilate what you call weight – and fly."

"Show us, show us!" they cried, roaring with delighted laughter.

"It's a question of belief," he repeated, his tongue appearing and disappearing like a pointed shadow. "It's in the heart; the power of the air gets into your whole being. Why should I show you? Why should I ask my deity to persuade your scoffing little minds by any miracle? For it is deity, I tell you, and nothing else. I *know* it. Follow one idea like that, as I follow my bird idea – follow it with the impetus and undeviating concentration of a projectile – and you arrive at power. You know deity – the bird idea of deity, that is. *They* knew that. The old Egyptians knew it."

"Oh, show us, show us!" they shouted impatiently, wearied of his nonsense-talk. "Get up and fly! Levitate yourself, as they did! Become a star!"

Binovitch turned suddenly very pale, and an odd light shone in his keen brown eyes. He rose slowly from the edge of the chair where he was perched. Something about him changed. There was silence instantly.

"I *will* show you," he said calmly, to their intense amazement; "not to convince your disbelief, but to prove it to myself. For the powers of the air are with me here. I believe. And Horus, great falcon-headed symbol, is my patron god."

The suppressed energy in his voice and manner was indescribable. There was a sense of lifting, upheaving power about him. He raised his arms; his face turned upward; he inflated his lungs with a deep, long breath, and his voice broke into a kind of singing cry, half prayer, half chant:

*"O Horus,*
*Bright-eyed deity of wind,*

> *Feather my soul*[*]
> *Though earth's thick air,*
> *To know thy awful swiftness—"*

[*The Russian is untranslatable. The phrase means, 'Give my life wings.']

He broke off suddenly. He climbed lightly and swiftly upon the nearest table – it was in a deserted card-room, after a game in which he had lost more pounds than there are days in the year – and leaped into the air. He hovered a second, spread his arms and legs in space, appeared to float a moment, then buckled, rushed down and forward, and dropped in a heap upon the floor, while everyone roared with laughter.

But the laughter died out quickly, for there was something in his wild performance that was peculiar and unusual. It was uncanny, not quite natural. His body had seemed, as with Mordkin and Nijinski, literally to hang upon the air a moment. For a second he gave the distressing impression of overcoming gravity. There was a touch in it of that faint horror which appals by its very vagueness. He picked himself up unhurt, and his face was as grave as a portrait in the academy, but with a new expression in it that everybody noticed with this strange, half-shocked amazement. And it was this expression that extinguished the claps of laughter as wind that takes away the sound of bells. Like many ugly men, he was an inimitable actor, and his facial repertory was endless and incredible. But this was neither acting nor clever manipulation of expressive features. There was something in his curious Russian physiognomy that made the heart beat slower. And that was why the laughter died away so suddenly.

"You ought to have flown farther," cried someone. It expressed what all had felt.

"Icarus didn't drink champagne," another replied, with a laugh; but nobody laughed with him.

"You went too near to Vera," said Palazov, "and passion melted the wax." But his face twitched oddly as he said it. There was something he did not understand, and so heartily disliked.

The strange expression on the features deepened. It was arresting in a disagreeable, almost in a horrible, way. The talk stopped dead; all stared; there was a feeling of dismay in everybody's heart, yet unexplained. Some lowered their eyes, or else looked stupidly elsewhere; but the women of the party felt a kind of fascination. Vera, in particular, could not move her sight away. The joking reference to his passionate admiration for her passed unnoticed. There was a general and individual sense of shock. And a chorus of whispers rose instantly:

"Look at Binovitch! What's happened to his face?"

"He's changed – he's changing!"

"God! Why he looks like a – bird!"

But no one laughed. Instead, they chose the names of birds – hawk, eagle, even owl. The figure of a man leaning against the edge of the door, watching them closely, they did not notice. He had been passing down the corridor, had looked in unobserved, and then had paused. He had seen the whole performance. He watched Binovitch narrowly, now with calm, discerning eyes. It was Dr. Plitzinger, the great psychiatrist.

For Binovitch had picked himself up from the floor in a way that was oddly self-possessed, and precluded the least possibility of the ludicrous. He looked neither foolish nor abashed. He looked surprised, but also he looked half angry and half frightened. As someone had said, he 'ought to have flown farther'. That was the incredible impression his acrobatics had produced – incredible, yet somehow actual. This uncanny idea prevailed, as at a séance where nothing genuine is expected to happen, and something genuine, after all, does happen. There was no pretence in this: Binovitch had flown.

And now he stood there, white in the face – with terror and with anger white. He looked extraordinary, this little, neurasthenic Russian, but he looked at the same time half terrific. Another thing, not commonly experienced by men, was in him, breaking out of him, affecting *directly* the minds of his companions. His mouth opened; blood and fury shone in his blazing eyes; his tongue shot out like an ant-eater's, though even in that the comic had no place. His arms were spread like flapping wings, and his voice rose dreadfully:

"He failed me, he failed me!" he tried to bellow. "Horus, my falcon-headed deity, my power of the air, deserted me! Hell take him! Hell burn his wings and blast his piercing sight! Hell scorch him into dust for his false prophecies! I curse him – I curse Horus!"

The voice that should have roared across the silent room emitted, instead, this high-pitched, bird-like scream. The added touch of sound, the reality it lent, was ghastly. Yet it was marvellously done and acted. The entire thing was a bit of instantaneous inspiration – his voice, his words, his gestures, his whole wild appearance. Only – here was the reality that caused the sense of shock – the expression on his altered features was genuine. *That* was not assumed. There was something new and alien in him, something cold and difficult to human life, something alert and swift and cruel, of another element than earth. A strange, rapacious grandeur had leaped upon the struggling features. The face looked hawk-like.

And he came forward suddenly and sharply toward Vera, whose fixed, staring eyes had never once ceased watching him with a kind of anxious and devouring pain in them. She was both drawn and beaten back. Binovitch advanced on tiptoe. No doubt he still was acting, still pretending this mad nonsense that he worshipped Horus, the falcon-headed deity of forgotten days, and that Horus had failed him in his hour of need; but somehow there was just a hint of too much reality in the way he moved and looked. The girl, a little creature, with fluffy golden hair, opened her lips; her cigarette fell to the floor; she shrank back; she looked for a moment like some smaller, coloured bird trying to escape from a great pursuing hawk; she screamed. Binovitch, his arms wide, his bird-like face thrust forward, had swooped upon her. He leaped. Almost he caught her.

No one could say exactly what happened. Play, become suddenly and unexpectedly too real, confuses the emotions. The change of key was swift. From fun to terror is a dislocating jolt upon the mind. Some one – it was Khilkoff, the brother – upset a chair; everybody spoke at once; everybody stood up. An unaccountable feeling of disaster was in the air, as with those drinkers' quarrels that blaze out from nothing, and end in a pistol-shot and death, no one able to explain clearly how it came about. It was the silent, watching figure in the doorway who saved the situation. Before anyone had noticed his approach, there he was among the group, laughing, talking, applauding – between Binovitch and Vera. He was vigorously patting his patient on the back, and his voice rose easily above the general clamour. He was a strong, quiet personality; even in his laughter there was authority. And his laughter now was the only sound in the room, as though by his mere presence peace and harmony were restored. Confidence came with him. The noise subsided; Vera was in her chair again. Khilkoff poured out a glass of wine for the great man.

"The Czar!" said Plitzinger, sipping his champagne, while all stood up, delighted with his compliment and tact. "And to your opening night with the Russian ballet," he added quickly a second toast, "or to your first performance at the Moscow Théâtre des Arts!" Smiling significantly, he glanced at Binovitch; he clinked glasses with him. Their arms were already linked, but it was Palazov who noticed that the doctor's fingers seemed rather tight upon the creased black coat. All drank, looking with laughter, yet with a touch of respect, toward Binovitch, who stood there dwarfed beside the stalwart Austrian, and suddenly as meek and subdued as any mole. Apparently the abrupt change of key had taken his mind successfully off something else.

"Of course – 'The Fire-Bird',") exclaimed the little man, mentioning the famous Russian ballet. "The very thing!" he exclaimed. "For *us*," he added, looking with devouring eyes at Vera. He was greatly pleased. He began talking vociferously about dancing and the rationale of dancing. They told him he was an undiscovered master. He was delighted. He winked at Vera and touched her glass again with his. "We'll make our début together," he cried. "We'll begin at Covent Garden, in London. I'll design the dresses and the posters 'The Hawk and the Dove!' *Magnifique!* I in dark grey, and you in blue and gold! Ah, dancing, you know, is sacred. The little self is lost, absorbed. It is ecstasy, it is divine. And dancing in air – the passion of the birds and stars – ah! they are the movements of the gods. You know deity that way – by living it."

He went on and on. His entire being had shifted with a leap upon this new subject. The idea of realising divinity by dancing it absorbed him. The party discussed it with him as though nothing else existed in the world, all sitting now and talking eagerly together. Vera took the cigarette he offered her, lighting it from his own; their fingers touched; he was as harmless and normal as a retired diplomat in a drawing-room. But it was Plitzinger whose subtle manoeuvring had accomplished the change so cleverly, and it was Plitzinger who presently suggested a game of billiards, and led him off, full now of a fresh enthusiasm for cannons, balls, and pockets, into another room. They departed arm in arm, laughing and talking together.

Their departure, it seemed, made no great difference at first. Vera's eyes watched him out of sight, then turned to listen to Baron Minski, who was describing with gusto how he caught wolves alive for coursing purposes. The speed and power of the wolf, he said, was impossible to realise; the force of their awful leap, the strength of their teeth, which could bite through metal stirrup-fastenings. He showed a scar on his arm and another on his lip. He was telling truth, and everybody listened with deep interest. The narrative lasted perhaps ten minutes or more, when Minski abruptly stopped. He had come to an end; he looked about him; he saw his glass, and emptied it. There was a general pause. Another subject did not at once present itself. Sighs were heard; several fidgeted; fresh cigarettes were lighted. But there was no sign of boredom, for where one or two Russians are gathered together there is always life. They produce gaiety and enthusiasm as wind produces waves. Like great children, they plunge whole-heartedly into whatever interest presents itself at the moment. There is a kind of uncouth gambolling in their way of taking life. It seems as if they are always fighting that deep, underlying, national sadness which creeps into their very blood.

"Midnight!" then exclaimed Palazov, abruptly, looking at his watch; and the others fell instantly to talking about that watch, admiring it and asking questions. For the moment that very ordinary timepiece became the centre of observation. Palazov mentioned the price. "It never stops," he said proudly, "not even under water." He looked up at everybody, challenging admiration. And he told how, at a country house, he made a bet that he would swim to a certain island in the lake, and won the bet. He and a girl were the winners, but as it was a horse they had bet, he got nothing out of it for himself, giving the horse to her. It was a genuine grievance in him. One felt he could have cried as he spoke of it. "But the watch went all the time," he said delightedly, holding the gun-metal object in his hand to show, "and I was twelve minutes in the water with my clothes on."

Yet this fragmentary talk was nothing but pretence. The sound of clicking billiard-balls was audible from the room at the end of the corridor. There was another pause. The pause, however, was intentional. It was not vacuity of mind or absence of ideas that caused it. There was another subject, an unfinished subject that each member of the group was still considering. Only no one cared to begin about it till at last, unable to resist the strain any longer, Palazov turned to Khilkoff, who was saying he would take a 'whisky-soda', as the champagne was too sweet, and whispered something beneath his breath; whereupon Khilkoff, forgetting his drink, glanced at his sister, shrugged his shoulders, and made a curious grimace. "He's all right now" – his reply was just audible – "he's with Plitzinger." He cocked his head sidewise to indicate that the clicking of the billiard-balls still was going on.

The subject was out: all turned their heads; voices hummed and buzzed; questions were asked and answered or half answered; eyebrows were raised, shoulders shrugged, hands spread out expressively. There came into the atmosphere a feeling of presentiment, of mystery, of things half understood; primitive, buried instinct stirred a little, the kind of racial dread of vague emotions that might gain the upper hand if encouraged. They shrank from looking something in the face, while yet this unwelcome influence drew closer round them all. They discussed Binovitch and his astonishing performance. Pretty little Vera listened with large and troubled eyes, though saying nothing. The Arab waiter had put out the lights in the corridor, and only a solitary cluster burned now above their heads, leaving their faces in shadow. In the distance the clicking of the billiard-balls still continued.

"It was not play; it was real," exclaimed Minski vehemently. "I can catch wolves," he blurted; "but birds – ugh! – and human birds!" He was half inarticulate. He had witnessed something he could not understand, and it had touched instinctive terror in him. "It was the way he leaped that put the wolf first into my mind, only it was not a wolf at all." The others agreed and disagreed. "It was play at first, but it was reality at the end," another whispered; "and it was no animal he mimicked, but a bird, and a bird of prey at that!"

Vera thrilled. In the Russian woman hides that touch of savagery which loves to be caught, mastered, swept helplessly away, captured utterly and deliciously by the one strong enough to do it thoroughly. She left her chair and sat down beside an older woman in the party, who took her arm quietly at once. Her little face wore a perplexed expression, mournful, yet somehow wild. It was clear that Binovitch was not indifferent to her.

"It's become an *idée fixe* with him," this older woman said. "The bird idea lives in his mind. He lives it in his imagination. Ever since that time at Edfu, when he pretended to worship the great stone falcons outside the temple – the Horus figures – he's been full of it." She stopped. The way Binovitch had behaved at Edfu was better left unmentioned at the moment, perhaps. A slight shiver ran round the listening group, each one waiting for someone else to focus their emotion, and so explain it by saying the convincing thing. Only no one ventured. Then Vera abruptly gave a little jump.

"Hark!" she exclaimed, in a staccato whisper, speaking for the first time. She sat bolt upright. She was listening. "Hark!" she repeated. "There it is again, but nearer than before. It's coming closer. I hear it." She trembled. Her voice, her manner, above all her great staring eyes, startled everybody. No one spoke for several seconds; all listened. The clicking of the billiard-balls had ceased. The halls and corridors lay in darkness, and gloom was over the big hotel. Everybody was in bed.

"Hear what?" asked the older woman soothingly, yet with a perceptible quaver in her voice, too. She was aware that the girl's arm shook upon her own.

"Do you not hear it, too?" the girl whispered.

All listened without speaking. All watched her paling face. Something wonderful, yet half terrible, seemed in the air about them. There was a dull murmur, audible, faint, remote, its direction hard to tell. It had come suddenly from nowhere. They shivered. That strange racial thrill again passed into the group, unwelcome, unexplained. It was aboriginal; it belonged to the unconscious primitive mind, half childish, half terrifying.

"*What* do you hear?" her brother asked angrily – the irritable anger of nervous fear.

"When he came at me," she answered very low, "I heard it first. I hear it now again. Listen! He's coming."

And at that minute, out of the dark mouth of the corridor, emerged two human figures, Plitzinger and Binovitch. Their game was over: they were going up to bed. They passed the open door of the card-room. But Binovitch was being half dragged, half restrained, for he was apparently attempting to run down the passage with flying, dancing leaps. He bounded. It was like a huge bird trying to rise for flight, while his companion kept him down by force upon the earth. As they entered the strip of light, Plitzinger changed his own position, placing himself swiftly between his companion and the group in the dark corner of the room. He hurried Binovitch along as though he sheltered him from view. They passed into the shadows down the passage. They disappeared. And everyone looked significantly, questioningly, at his neighbour, though at first saying no word. It seemed that a curious disturbance of the air had followed them audibly.

Vera was the first to open her lips. "You heard it *then*," she said breathlessly, her face whiter than the ceiling.

"Damn!" exclaimed her brother furiously. "It was wind against the outside walls – wind in the desert. The sand is driving."

Vera looked at him. She shrank closer against the side of the older woman, whose arm was tight about her.

"It was *not* wind," she whispered simply. She paused. All waited uneasily for the completion of her sentence. They stared into her face like peasants who expected a miracle.

"Wings," she whispered. "It was the sound of enormous wings."

\* \* \*

And at four o'clock in the morning, when they all returned exhausted from their excursion into the desert, little Binovitch was sleeping soundly and peacefully in his bed. They passed his door on tiptoe. But he did not hear them. He was dreaming. His spirit was at Edfu, experiencing with that ancient deity who was master of all flying life those strange enjoyments upon which his own troubled human heart was passionately set. Safe with that mighty falcon whose powers his lips had scorned a few hours before, his soul, released in vivid dream, went sweetly flying. It was amazing, it was gorgeous. He skimmed the Nile at lightning speed. Dashing down headlong from the height of the great Pyramid, he chased with faultless accuracy a little dove that sought vainly to hide from his terrific pursuit beneath the palm trees. For what he loved must worship where he worshipped, and the majesty of those tremendous effigies had fired his imagination to the creative point where expression was imperative.

Then suddenly, at the very moment of delicious capture, the dream turned horrible, becoming awful with the nightmare touch. The sky lost all its blue and sunshine. Far, far below him the little dove enticed him into nameless depths, so that he flew faster and faster, yet never fast enough to overtake it. Behind him came a great thing down the air, black, hovering, with gigantic wings outstretched. It had terrific eyes, and the beating of its feathers stole his wind away. It followed him, crowding space. He was aware of a colossal beak, curved like a scimitar and pointed wickedly like a tooth of iron. He dropped. He faltered. He tried to scream.

Through empty space he fell, caught by the neck. The huge spectral falcon was upon him. The talons were in his heart. And in sleep he remembered then that he had cursed. He recalled his reckless language. The curse of the ignorant is meaningless; that of the worshipper is real. This attack was on his soul. He had invoked it. He realised next, with a touch of ghastly horror, that the dove he chased was, after all, the bait that had lured him purposely to destruction, and awoke with a suffocating terror upon him, and his entire body bathed in icy perspiration. Outside the open window he heard a sound of wings retreating with powerful strokes into the surrounding darkness of the sky.

The nightmare made its impression upon Binovitch's impressionable and dramatic temperament. It aggravated his tendencies. He related it next day to Mme. de Drühn, the friend of Vera, telling it with that somewhat boisterous laughter some minds use to disguise less kind emotions. But he received no encouragement. The mood of the previous night was not recoverable; it was already ancient history. Russians never make the banal mistake of repeating a sensation till it is exhausted; they hurry on to novelties. Life flashes and rushes with them, never standing still for exposure before the cameras of their minds. Mme. de Drühn, however, took the trouble to mention the matter to Plitzinger, for Plitzinger, like Freud of Vienna, held that dreams revealed subconscious tendencies which sooner or later must betray themselves in action.

"Thank you for telling me," he smiled politely, "but I have already heard it from him." He watched her eyes for a moment, really examining her soul. "Binovitch, you see," he continued, apparently satisfied with what he saw, "I regard as that rare phenomenon – a genius without an outlet. His spirit, intensely creative, finds no adequate expression. His power of production is enormous and prolific; yet he accomplishes nothing." He paused an instant. "Binovitch, therefore, is in danger of poisoning – himself." He looked steadily into her face, as a man who weighs how much he may confide. "Now," he continued, "*if* we can find an outlet for him, a field wherein his bursting imaginative genius can produce results – above all, *visible* results" – he shrugged his shoulders – "the man is saved. Otherwise" – he looked extraordinarily impressive – "there is bound to be sooner or later—"

"Madness?" she asked very quietly.

"An explosion, let us say," he replied gravely. "For instance, take this Horus obsession of his, quite wrong archaeologically though it is. *Au fond* it is megalomania of a most unusual kind. His passionate interest, his love, his worship of birds, wholesome enough in itself, finds no satisfying outlet. A man who *really* loves birds neither keeps them in cages nor shoots them nor stuffs them. What, then, can he do? The commonplace bird-lover observes them through glasses, studies their habits, then writes a book about them. But a man like Binovitch, overflowing with this intense creative power of mind and imagination, is not content with that. He wants to know them from within. He wants to feel what they feel, to live their life. He wants to *become* them. You follow me? Not quite. Well, he seeks to be identified with the object of his sacred, passionate adoration. All genius seeks to know the thing itself from its own point of view. It desires union. That tendency, unrecognised by himself, perhaps, and therefore subconscious, hides in his very soul." He paused a moment. "And the sudden sight of those majestic figures at Edfu – that crystallisation of his *idée fixe* in granite – took hold of this excess in him, so to speak – and is now focusing it toward some definite act. Binovitch sometimes – feels himself a bird! You noticed what occurred last night?"

She nodded; a slight shiver passed over her.

"A most curious performance," she murmured; "an exhibition I never want to see again."

"The most curious part," replied the doctor coolly, "was its truth."

"Its truth!" she exclaimed beneath her breath. She was frightened by something in his voice and by the uncommon gravity in his eyes. It seemed to arrest her intelligence. She felt upon the edge of things beyond her. "You mean that Binovitch did for a moment – hang – in the air?" The other verb, the right one, she could not bring herself to use.

The great man's face was enigmatical. He talked to her sympathy, perhaps, rather than to her mind.

"Real genius," he said smilingly, "is as rare as talent, even great talent, is common. It means that the personality, if only for one second, becomes everything; becomes the universe; becomes the soul of the world. It gets the flash. It is identified with the universal life. Being everything and everywhere, all is possible to it – in that second of vivid realisation. It can brood with the crystal, grow with the plant, leap with the animal, fly with the bird: genius unifies all three. That is the meaning of 'creative'. It is faith. Knowing it, you can pass through fire and not be burned, walk on water and not sink, move a mountain, fly. Because you *are* fire, water, earth, air. Genius, you see, is madness in the magnificent sense of being superhuman. Binovitch has it."

He broke off abruptly, seeing he was not understood. Some great enthusiasm in him he deliberately suppressed.

"The point is," he resumed, speaking more carefully, "that we must try to lead this passionate constructive genius of the man into some human channel that will absorb it, and therefore render it harmless."

"He loves Vera," the woman said, bewildered, yet seizing this point correctly.

"But would he marry her?" asked Plitzinger at once.

"He is already married."

The doctor looked steadily at her a moment, hesitating whether he should utter all his thought.

"In that case," he said slowly after a pause, "it is better he or she should leave."

His tone and manner were exceedingly impressive.

"You mean there's danger?" she asked.

"I mean, rather," he replied earnestly, "that this great creative flood in him, so curiously focused now upon his Horus-falcon-bird idea, may result in some act of violence—"

"Which would be madness," she said, looking hard at him.

"Which would be disastrous," he corrected her. And then he added slowly: "Because in the mental moment of immense creation he might overlook material laws."

\* \* \*

The costume ball two nights later was a great success. Palazov was a Bedouin, and Khilkoff an Apache; Mme. de Drühn wore a national head-dress; Minski looked almost natural as Don Quixote; and the entire Russian 'set' was cleverly, if somewhat extravagantly, dressed. But Binovitch and Vera were the most successful of all the two hundred dancers who took part. Another figure, a big man dressed as a Pierrot, also claimed exceptional attention, for though the costume was commonplace enough, there was something of dignity in his appearance that drew the eyes of all upon him. But he wore a mask, and his identity was not discoverable.

It was Binovitch and Vera, however, who must have won the prize, if prize there had been, for they not only looked their parts, but acted them as well. The former in his dark grey feather tunic, and his falcon mask, complete even to the brown hooked beak and tufted talons, looked fierce and splendid. The disguise was so admirable, yet so entirely natural, that it was uncommonly seductive. Vera, in blue and gold, a charming head-dress of a dove upon her loosened hair, and a pair of little dove-pale wings fluttering from her shoulders, her tiny twinkling feet and slender ankles well visible, too, was equally successful and admired. Her large and timid eyes, her flitting movements, her light and dainty way of dancing – all added touches that made the picture perfect.

How Binovitch contrived his dress remained a mystery, for the layers of wings upon his back were real; the large black kites that haunt the Nile, soaring in their hundreds over Cairo and the bleak Mokattam Hills, had furnished them. He had procured them none knew how. They measured four feet across from tip to tip; they swished and rustled as he swept along; they were true falcons' wings. He danced with Nautch-girls and Egyptian princesses and Rumanian Gipsies; he danced well, with beauty, grace, and lightness. But with Vera he did not dance at all; with her he simply flew. A kind of passionate abandon was in him as he skimmed the floor with her in a way that made everybody turn to watch them. They seemed to leave the ground together. It was delightful, an amazing sight; but it was peculiar. The strangeness of it was on many lips. Somehow its queer extravagance communicated itself to the entire ball-room. They became the centre of observation. There were whispers.

"There's that extraordinary bird-man! Look! He goes by like a hawk. And he's always after that dove-girl. How marvellously he does it! It's rather awful. Who is he? I don't envy *her*."

People stood aside when he rushed past. They got out of his way. He seemed forever pursuing Vera, even when dancing with another partner. Word passed from mouth to mouth. A kind of telepathic interest was established everywhere. It was a shade too real sometimes, something unduly earnest in the chasing wildness, something unpleasant. There was even alarm.

"It's rowdy; I'd rather not see it; it's quite disgraceful," was heard. "*I* think it's horrible; you can see she's terrified."

And once there was a little scene, trivial enough, yet betraying this reality that many noticed and disliked. Binovitch came up to claim a dance, programme clutched in his great tufted claws, and at the same moment the big Pierrot appeared abruptly round the corner with a similar claim. Those who saw it assert he had been waiting, and came on purpose, and that there was something protective and authoritative in his bearing. The misunderstanding was ordinary enough – both men had written her name against the dance – but 'No. 13, Tango' also included the supper interval, and neither Hawk nor Pierrot would give way. They were very obstinate. Both men wanted her. It was awkward.

"The Dove shall decide between us," smiled the Hawk politely, yet his taloned fingers working nervously. Pierrot, however, more experienced in the ways of dealing with women, or more bold, said suavely:

"I am ready to abide by her decision" – his voice poorly cloaked this aggravating authority, as though he had the right to her – "only I engaged this dance before his Majesty Horus appeared upon the scene at all, and therefore it is clear that Pierrot has the right of way."

At once, with a masterful air, he took her off. There was no withstanding him. He meant to have her and he got her. She yielded meekly. They vanished among the maze of coloured dancers, leaving the Hawk, disconsolate and vanquished, amid the titters of the onlookers. His swiftness, as against this steady power, was of no avail.

It was then that the singular phenomenon was witnessed first. Those who saw it affirm that he changed absolutely into the part he played. It was dreadful; it was wicked. A frightened whisper ran about the rooms and corridors:

"An extraordinary thing is in the air!"

Some shrank away, while others flocked to see. There were those who swore that a curious, rushing sound was audible, the atmosphere visibly disturbed and shaken; that a shadow fell upon the spot the couple had vacated; that a cry was heard, a high, wild, searching cry: "Horus! bright deity of wind," it began, then died away. One man was positive that the windows had been opened and that something had flown in. It was the obvious explanation. The thing spread horribly. As in a fire-panic, there was consternation and excitement. Confusion caught the feet of all the dancers. The music fumbled and lost time. The leading pair of tango dancers halted and looked round. It seemed that everybody pressed back, hiding, shuffling, eager to see, yet more eager not to be seen, as though something dangerous, hostile, terrible, had broken loose. In rows against the wall they stood. For a great space had made itself in the middle of the ball-room, and into this empty space appeared suddenly the Pierrot and the Dove.

It was like a challenge. A sound of applause, half voices, half clapping of gloved hands, was heard. The couple danced exquisitely into the arena. All stared. There was an impression that a set piece had been prepared, and that this was its beginning. The music again took heart. Pierrot was strong and dignified, no whit nonplussed by this abrupt publicity. The Dove, though faltering, was deliciously obedient. They danced together like a single outline. She was captured utterly. And to the man who needed her the sight was naturally agonising – the protective way the Pierrot held her, the right and strength of it, the mastery, the complete possession.

"He's got her!" someone breathed too loud, uttering the thought of all. "Good thing it's not the Hawk!"

And, to the absolute amazement of the throng, this sight was then apparent. A figure dropped through space. That high, shrill cry again was heard:

"Feather my soul...to know thy awful swiftness!"

Its singing loveliness touched the heart, its appealing, passionate sweetness was marvellous, as from the gallery this figure of a man, dressed as a strong, dark bird, shot down with splendid grace and ease. The feathers swept; the swings spread out as sails that take the wind. Like a hawk that darts with unerring power and aim upon its prey, this thing of mighty wings rushed down into the empty space where the two danced. Observed by all, he entered, swooping beautifully, stretching his wings like any eagle. He dropped. He fixed his point of landing with consummate skill close beside the astonished dancers. He landed.

It happened with such swiftness it brought the dazzle and blindness as when lightning strikes. People in different parts of the room saw different details; a few saw nothing at all after the first startling shock, closing their eyes, or holding their arms before their faces as in self-protection. The touch of panic fear caught the entire room. The nameless thing that all the evening had been vaguely felt was come. It had suddenly materialised.

For this incredible thing occurred in the full blaze of light upon the open floor. Binovitch, grown in some sense formidable, opened his dark, big wings about the girl. The long grey feathers moved, causing powerful draughts of wind that made a rushing sound. An aspect of the terrible was about him, like an emanation. The great beaked head was poised to strike, the tufted claws were raised like fingers that shut and opened, and the whole presentment of his amazing figure focused in an attitude of attack that was magnificent and terrible. No one who saw it doubted. Yet there were those who swore that it was not Binovitch at all, but that another outline, monstrous and shadowy, towered above him, draping his lesser proportions with two colossal wings of darkness. That some touch of strange divinity lay in it may be claimed, however confused the wild descriptions afterward. For many lowered their heads and bowed their shoulders. There was terror. There was also awe. The onlookers swayed as though some power passed over them through the air.

A sound of wings was certainly in the room.

Then someone screamed; a shriek broke high and clear; and emotion, ordinary human emotion, unaccustomed to terrific things, swept loose. The Hawk and Vera flew. Beaten back against the wall as by a stroke of whirlwind, the Pierrot staggered. He watched them go. Out of the lighted room they flew, out of the crowded human atmosphere, out of the heat and artificial light, the walled-in, airless halls that were a cage. All this they left behind. They seemed things of wind and air, made free happily of another element. Earth held them not. Toward the open night they raced with this extraordinary lightness as of birds, down the long corridor and on to the southern terrace, where great coloured curtains were hung suspended from the columns. A moment they were visible. Then the fringe of one huge curtain, lifted by the wind, showed their dark outline for a second against the starry sky. There was a cry, a leap. The curtain flapped again and closed. They vanished. And into the ball-room swept the cold draught of night air from the desert.

But three figures instantly were close upon their heels. The throng of half-dazed, half-stupefied onlookers, it seemed, projected them as though by some explosive force. The general mass held back, but, like projectiles, these three flung themselves after the fugitives down the corridor at high speed – the Apache, Don Quixote, and, last of them, the Pierrot. For Khilkoff, the brother, and Baron Minski, the man who caught wolves alive, had been for some time keenly on the watch, while Dr. Plitzinger, reading the symptoms clearly, never far away, had been faithfully observant of every movement. His mask tossed aside, the great psychiatrist was now recognised by all. They reached the parapet just as the curtain flapped back heavily into place; the next second all three were out of sight behind it. Khilkoff was first, however, urged forward at frantic speed by the warning words the doctor had whispered as they ran. Some thirty yards beyond the terrace was the brink of the crumbling cliff on which the great hotel was built, and there was a drop of sixty feet to the desert floor below. Only a low stone wall marked the edge.

Accounts varied. Khilkoff, it seems, arrived in time – in the nick of time – to seize his sister, virtually hovering on the brink. He heard the loose stones strike the sand below. There was no struggle, though it appears she did not thank him for his interference at first. In a sense she was beside – outside – herself. And he did a characteristic thing: he not only brought her back into the ball-room, but he *danced* her back. It was admirable. Nothing could have calmed the general excitement better. The pair of them danced in together as though nothing was amiss. Accustomed to the strenuous practice of his Cossack regiment, this young cavalry officer's muscles were equal to the semi-dead weight in his arms. At most the onlookers thought her tired, perhaps. Confidence was restored – such is the psychology of a crowd – and in the middle of a thrilling Viennese waltz he easily smuggled her out of the room, administered brandy, and got her up to bed. The absence of the Hawk, meanwhile, was hardly noticed; comments were made and then forgotten; it was Vera in whom the strange, anxious sympathy had centred. And, with her obvious safety, the moment of primitive, childish panic passed away. Don Quixote, too, was presently seen dancing gaily as though nothing untoward had happened; supper intervened; the incident was over; it had melted into the general wildness of the evening's irresponsibility. The fact that Pierrot did not appear again was noticed by no single person.

But Dr. Plitzinger was otherwise engaged, his heart and mind and soul all deeply exercised. A death-certificate is not always made out quite so simply as the public thinks. That Binovitch had died of suffocation in his swift descent through merely sixty feet of air was not conceivable; yet that his body lay so neatly placed upon the desert after such a fall was stranger still. It was not crumpled, it was not torn; no single bone was broken, no muscle wrenched; there was no bruise. There was no indenture in the sand. The figure lay sidewise as though in sleep, no sign of violence visible anywhere, the dark wings folded as a great bird folds them when it creeps away to die in loneliness. Beneath the Horus mask the face was smiling. It seemed he had floated into death upon the element he loved. And only Vera had seen the enormous wings that, hovering invitingly above the dark abyss, bore him so softly into another world. Plitzinger, that is, saw them, too, but he said firmly that they belonged to the big black falcons that haunt the Mokattam Hills and roost upon these ridges, close beside the hotel, at night. Both he and Vera, however, agreed on one thing: the high, sharp cry in the air above them, wild and plaintive, was certainly the black kite's cry – the note of the falcon that passionately seeks its mate. It was the pause of a second, when she stood to listen, that made her rescue possible. A moment later and she, too, would have flown to death with Binovitch.

**If you enjoyed this, you might also like...**
The Glamour of the Snow, see page 79
The Camp of the Dog, see page 132

# Tongues of Fire

## Chapter I

**THE FRIENDLY** little dinner party was over, and Cecilia Lance had thoroughly enjoyed it; the Lindleys were kindly, simple people; the gramophone had been turned on and her dancing partner, Harold Sharpe, had been there. Cecilia and Harold knew one another's steps as intimately as they knew one another's minds.

"Odd that Cecilia doesn't marry," Lindley remarked, half to himself, half to his wife, as they sat over a cigarette when the last guest had driven away. "She's still pretty. Eveiybody likes her. And such a cheery soul." He puffed his cigarette reflectively. "She has charm, too – eh?" he inquired presently, as his wife offered no comment. He glanced up affectionately at her.

"Always full of life, yes," came the belated reply. "I think she enjoyed herself tonight. I think they all did. They liked the new records, too."

Her husband smiled and nodded. The new records had cost money. "I wish we could do it more often," he mentioned, sighing ruefully. The Lindleys were hospitably inclined, but they were poor, and even a dinner party had to be calculated. "Now, that fellow Sharpe" – he went back to his first line of thought – "I thought at one time – they seemed to understand each other pretty well."

His wife hesitated a moment, gazing into the gas fire. "They still do, I think," she said. "Their views of life are the same" – then, after a second's pause, as though the words slipped out against her kindlier judgment – "and of people."

Her husband, however, discerned neither the hesitation nor the effort at restraint that caused it. Both had their tongues well under control, he by a natural good nature, she by education. They were an affectionate, devoted, faithful couple to whom none but the most determined could impute deliberate evil. A little later, as they tidied away the records before going to bed, he remarked casually;

"Sharp as a needle, though, isn't she? By Jove, yes!" He laughed. "They both are, for that matter," and he chuckled again.

"They don't mean to be. I'm sure," was his wife's charitable comment.

Again, apparently, he did not notice anything. It was her usual way of talking, anyhow. The Lindleys invariably were kindly in their judgments of people. They did not criticise others – nastily.

"I'll put the lights out, Dolly," he said presently. "You pop up to bed. It's late, and you must be tired." He kissed her, patting her on the shoulder. Fifteen minutes afterwards the room, so lately filled with music, whirling couples and merry voices, had darkness and the atmosphere of faded scent and stale cigarette-smoke to itself.

Meanwhile Cecilia Lance and Harold Sharpe were also talking in their taxi as he drove her to the widowed sister she lived with in Chester Street. They were in merry mood, satisfied with the evening just over. They discussed it in their usual way. Both voted it 'ripping'.

"Yet I never really care for a gramophone," Cecilia mentioned.

"It's better than nothing, though," her dancing partner agreed, while he qualified.

"Yes, I suppose so," she submitted, "only the records were so rotten, weren't they?"

"Putrid," said Sharpe.

"Why don't they get a few good ones, I wonder." She mentioned a few names. "If people use a gramophone for dancing, the least they can do is to have the latest tunes." To this her companion also gave assent. They both felt aggrieved. In a few minutes there was nothing bad enough left to say about the music, the floor, the cooking of the little dinner, and the heat of the room. They selected all the least favourable points and emphasised them, yet in their easy, natural way and without calculated motives.

Next they turned their attention to the other dancers, Cecilia leading the way, as before, with faint praise. "Not a bad lot," observed Harold patronisingly. "Quite nice," Cecilia qualified, "only I wonder where in the world they pick up such people." Her companion, while agreeing, mentioned that a certain girl "looked all right, I thought."

"What! That dowdy creature!" Whereupon he swore he had really only noticed one girl, whose name was Cecilia, and so remedied his mistake. The criticism of the dresses which followed was largely a monologue, since Harold Sharpe merely approved her verdict with "awful, perfectly awful"; but when the taxi arrived after a drive of six minutes, the entire evening, including dinner, dance and dancers, had been so damned that no Recording Angel would have thought it worth even entering in his Book. The names of the destroyers, however, he possibly might have entered.

"Oh, come in for a minute and have a drink, my sister's sure to be up," invited Cecilia. Over his whisky and soda and her cigarette an opportunity was provided for chatting pleasantly about their late host and hostess, and without a chorus, since the sister had already gone to bed. "A good fellow, Jack Lindley," was Harold Sharpe's offhand opinion, "though what he sees in *her* I can't imagine." But Cecilia, feeling robbed of her accustomed right to start the line of criticism, assured him that he was quite mistaken, for Molly was the possessor of "such a good heart."

"It's what Molly sees in *him* that puzzles me! Still, she amuses herself with Sir Malcolm, the good-looking nerve specialist whom she's always going to see without the slightest reason."

"What! That quiet old frump Molly has a lover!"

"Why shouldn't she?" Cecilia championed her doubtfully.

Before her cigarette was half finished, Molly Lindley's character was demolished, and her husband, who was "gay enough when you got him alone," was insecurely balancing on one leg, which was certainly not fit to stand on. Husband and wife, a faithful, somewhat old-fashioned, devoted couple, who had just put themselves to trouble and expense to give the speakers a happy evening, had not a rag to their backs between them. Naked to the winds, vicious, false, and stupid, they were heading full speed for that hell in which the speakers, their detractors, did not, of course, believe. There was not a nastier couple than the Lindleys apparently in all Chelsea – and this result had been accomplished by faint praise, offered with a pleasant smile; by careless suggestion, presented with a shrug of the shoulders; and by a series of innocent questions sprinkled with adjectives and adverbs that carried dark hints of hidden wickedness and double lives – but without a single scrap of truth to support the entire case. The Recording Angel, if he entered anything, entered it, indeed, as evidence the destroyers unwittingly gave against themselves – a confession that what they had in their own hearts and minds they saw most easily in others.

The case, moreover, presented with the skill due to long practice, was completed in ten minutes at the most. Without motive, without malice, without conscious intention to do harm or wish to injure, but merely obeying a habit to say something startling perhaps, Mr. and Mrs. Lindley were left naked to the cruel winds and without a leg to stand on.

Incidentally, just before Harold took his leave – in the space of two minutes or so – Cecilia's sister, asleep upstairs, lay also without covering.

"One of the best," Cecilia replied, as he dropped a polite word of casual inquiry, "but oh, so queer and moody sometimes."

"She's jolly good to you, Ceci," Harold considered, knowing of the generous allowance.

"Oh, she's a perfect brick. It's only her moods that I find trying sometimes."

"Ah!" His ears were hungry at once. He glanced at her inquiringly.

Cecilia lowered her voice. "It's drugs probably," she mentioned.

Harold laughed, nodding understandingly. "They all do it," he said with a shrug, swallowing a gulp of the lady's excellent whisky, while the kindly soul they discussed lay dreaming peacefully on the floor above, a homoeopath ignorant of anything stronger than fairy doses of aconite for a cold or colocynth for indigestion. In future, however, whenever her name was mentioned in his presence, Harold Sharpe, with a looking of knowing sympathy, would say darkly, "Drugs, you know. Yes, I'm afraid it's drugs. Oh, her sister knows it…"

"Well, good night, Cecilia. I must be getting on. See you again soon."

"At the Lindleys probably. Molly said they'd give another gramophone hop before long. Good night."

An hour later both of them lay sound asleep, at peace with all the world and entirely pleased and satisfied with themselves, their hearts harbouring no malice, envy, or uncharitableness. Their tongues lay still. Their day, their evening, their conversation, had been an average sample of what occurred on the other 364 days of their year. Fallen reputations marked their course like birds before a skilful gun. These were not deliberately brought down, but when they aimed with deliberation they landed much bigger game, for they were both deadly shots.

Now, one of the latter, wounded but not killed it so happened, traced the shot that hit him to its source. He was not only big game, he was dangerous big game, a man of personality, a man of power, a man of strange knowledge, too. And he did not bring the action for slander he was justified in bringing, yet neither did he ignore the wicked snipers who used poisoned shafts in the darkness. He merely cursed them. He *cursed* them both. His curse, however, was perhaps no ordinary curse…

## Chapter II

**IT WAS** a lovely morning some weeks later that Cecilia sat alone in a taxi, examining her face uneasily in the narrow mirror, as she drove to Grosvenor Street. The sun shone brightly and old grimy London laughed with happiness. Flowers shone at every corner, in every buttonhole. Birds were singing gaily. The air was sweet and fresh, for it was summertime, and half-past ten was really half-past nine; but the pretty young face reflected in the taxi looking-glass betrayed no summertime. It was neither sweet nor fresh. A haunting anxiety lay in the otherwise bright eyes. The corners of the little mouth turned down. From time to time she crushed a small lace handkerchief against her lips with violence. Occasionally, removing it quickly, she drew in a deep draught of the sweet air from the open window, inhaling and exhaling with fixed concentration in her face, then swiftly placing the handkerchief on her lips again. One might have thought she suffered toothache, neuralgia; some nerve attack perhaps that affected the mouth or lips or gums. Her behaviour indicated extreme uneasiness, if not actual pain.

At the door of No. 100A she dismissed the taxi, and was admitted with scarcely a minute's delay. The butler with the sphinx-like face bowed her smoothly into the waiting-room, closing the door behind her silently. Evidently, since he did not ask her name, he knew it already. Finding herself alone, she ran to the big mirror quickly, but had only time to catch a glance of a white frightened face before the door reopened and her name was softly spoken. Biting her lips, her hands clenched tightly at her side, she followed the sphinx into the consulting-room of Sir Malcolm, the famous nerve specialist. With an instinctive movement, as she crossed the threshold and saw the tall, dark-faced figure rising to greet her, she crushed the small lace handkerchief tightly against her lips...

The interview was a long one. When she came out again the waiting-room was half-filled with fidgeting ladies who had been kept, they considered, unduly waiting. Her mind was too preoccupied to observe carefully, but she noticed, she fancied, one man among the women. Picking up her bag and parasol hastily, she looked into no single face. Her hands trembled, her breath came unevenly, her features were hard and aged, she kept the handkerchief pressed against her mouth. She hurried out; the sphinx called a taxi, she drove to her sister's house, ran quickly up to her room and locked herself in. The first thing she did on being alone was to collect several hand-mirrors and arrange them in such a way before the dressing-table that she could study her face from every possible angle. She studied herself thus for the best part of half an hour, her eyes too strained with intense anxiety for tears; her heart too overloaded with a strange biting dread for her breath to behave naturally; her mind gone too far beyond control for her to remain still a single instant.

Cecilia Lance was terrified. But she had force, she had courage, her personality was not negligible; she could face anything, provided she first had time to decide upon her attitude and line of conduct. By the lunch hour, when she came down to meet her sister's guests, she had found herself again. If the face was somewhat drawn, it was not noticeably so. Her breath was normal, her manner quiet yet not depressed, her voice betrayed no trembling. She had faced the situation and taken her line of conduct.

"Ah, there you are! You were out early, Thompson told me, I missed you." And her sister came forward with her usual affectionate embrace.

Cecilia drew back sharply. "You mustn't kiss me, Gerty. I've – got a cold. Oh, it's nothing. But I don't want to give it to you."

The luncheon party passed off pleasantly. No one could have said that Cecilia was not her gay and normal self, nor could anyone have guessed from her lighthearted manner the amount of nervous power she exerted to appear so. It was with difficulty, none the less, that she ate her food or swallowed her wine. She did not smoke. There was a sinking dread, a constant terror in her that required all her skill and courage to conceal successfully. That inner gnawing never ceased. The wolf of horror tore steadily at her very vitals. The handkerchief went from time to time to her mouth, but in such a way that the manoeuvre seemed quite natural. In her mind still echoed the words the specialist had used a few hours ago. Her visit that morning to Sir Malcolm was not the first. It was the tenth. And after she had left him, he made his next patient wait a little longer for her dreaded yet coveted ten minutes with him. In fact, he did a thing he rarely allowed himself to do – he saw another patient in her place, a man – and when the man had gone, he delayed the fuming lady still another ten minutes, while he made notes, consulted books, and looked generally more puzzled and interested, perhaps dismayed as well, than in the course of his strange practice he had ever looked before. With his subsequent visitors he was even a little absentminded, though he was certainly too skilful for this cardinal mistake to be discovered.

"It seems more than curious – it's incredible simply," he thought to himself, as he glanced over his notes that night before going to bed. It was a thing he had never done before – to think of a case when the day's work was done. He particularly examined a sheet of tissue paper which had a circular hole in it with rough uneven edges, tinged slightly yellow, red, and black. He wore an expression of bewilderment as he laid it down. He was evidently baffled. "I've never come across such a thing before. The books have no record of anything approaching it." He passed into a mood of deep reflection. "I'm damned!" he said aloud finally. "It's positively medieval. It's – it's uncanny." Sir Malcolm was baffled and admitted it – to himself only. "And two of them, by God!"

## Chapter III

**IT WAS JUST** as the last guests were leaving that Cecilia was called to the telephone by Harold Sharpe. He asked if he might look in for tea and whether she would be alone. His voice had an odd note of seriousness in it. But Cecilia excused herself on the plea that she was resting before the Lindley's dance that night.

"Aren't you well?" he asked sharply.

"Oh – I'm all right, yes," with a moment's hesitation before she said it. Then Harold insisted. He was very urgent, very determined. "I simply *must* see you," he declared, "and alone, Ciss." A quiver ran down her, making her voice tremble a little. "Oh, all right," she yielded. "Gerty's going out. Only you mustn't stay long. I'm dead tired." Her body swayed slightly. She dropped into a chair and hid her face in her hands. Ten minutes afterwards Harold was in the room with her alone.

"I haven't seen you for ages," he began. "What's up?" His manner was odd, it was strained and nervous. He spoke rapidly and his eyes had a hunted look. His skin was pale. Fingers and lips twitched badly. "What's been the matter, Ceci?" It was the form of her name he used when he was in earnest, which was not often. "You never turned up at Claridges last night either." He coughed. The girl started, and asked quickly if he would smoke, but he declined with a gesture of impatience. He coughed a second time. His handkerchief came out. The girl started again, worse than before.

"Harold—" she said abruptly, then stopped dead, and looked away. She had meant to say something else. "What does that cough mean?" she asked instead, keeping her face still turned from him. "I believe you're not – quite well. That wasn't a real cough."

His handkerchief was against his lips, and he did not answer.

"Harold!" she repeated, with a singular loudness, as though the word were produced by a shock. Slowly her head turned round towards him and their eyes met. "*Are* you?" she insisted in a tense whisper that had an ominous tremor in it – "*quite* – well?"

Instead of answering, he asked a point-blank question, staring fixedly at her: "What were *you* doing in Grosvenor Street this morning, Ceci?" And as he said it her memory worked vividly. She remembered. He, of course, had been the one man in the waiting-room. This flashed across her. Her hand went to her handkerchief, but she did not use it. His eye, however, she saw, detected the movement – and understood it. They knew one another's minds so intimately.

"So it was you, Harold!" She could only whisper now, it seemed. Control of her voice was gone.

Harold's face, already pale when he came in, turned a little paler. It went a shade more grey now. They stared hard into one another's eyes.

"I—" he began, then faltered. "What were you doing there?" he asked suddenly, and as he said it his eyes wandered down her face slowly, pausing at her lips. They were fixed in a dreadful stare. Unutterable questions, she knew, lay in them. Her handkerchief again flew upwards.

"Don't! Don't!" she cried vehemently, her voice muffled behind the pressing lace. "For God's sake, don't!"

He caught at her hand and wrenched it, so that the momentary pain gave her the energy to deflect her thoughts the least little bit. He was attempting – oh, she realised it quite clearly – attempting to look at her handkerchief and the knowledge gave her the power to try and hide it, to prevent him seeing it, to smother it away. Only he was too strong for her.

He forced her palm open.

"You were there," he said in a voice that was calm but oddly stupid, "for the same reason I was." He dropped her hand, while she thrust the crumpled scrap of lace with violence into her tiny bag, yet knowing it was a useless thing to do, because he had already seen the strange, discoloured patch.

"How d-dare you?" she cried, stammering in her fear and pain. "You forg-get yourself, Harold Sharpe!" But he made no attempt at either apology or explanation, merely sinking back with a faint sigh into his chair and leaving his own crumpled handkerchief open for her to see in the palm of his effortless hand.

It, too, bore the same dread signature – a discoloured patch.

For several minutes of silence the pair of them sat thus, each staring – as though bereft of any power to move or speak – at that ghastly and significant patch. It bore the appearance of having been burnt or scorched – by fire.

It was the girl who first recovered her self-control, though only in a measure. She rose from her chair and stood over him.

"Harold," she said in a very low voice, and as though it cost her enormous effort, "it's the same with both of us. And we've brought it on ourselves." Placing a hand on his smooth, thick hair, though he shrank from her touch, she continued in a whisper: "And do you realise – it's something not of this world – quite?" She paused, drew back a step, and stared down at him. "It's from the d-devil."

He made no sign, no answer, but his whole body shivered.

"Do you understand what it m-means?" she went on.

He sprang suddenly to his feet then, making strange gestures of futile violence with his hands.

"Ceci," he cried, "you're crazy! You're talking ihe damnedest nonsense in all the world. Pull yourself together—" and then his breath failed him and he collapsed in a stupid heap on his chair.

The girl shook him as though she could have struck his face for preference. There was great violence in her heart and mind. There was perhaps murder – or suicide, its equivalent.

"He told *you* – what he told *me*?" she asked in a voice that seemed without any emotion because its owner was beyond any feeling.

Harold nodded.

"He tried the tissue paper?"

He bowed his head.

"He told you what – what we have to expect?"

The only answer, the only sign that her words were heard, was a convulsive movement of the body that somehow communicated horror more than any words could possibly have done. It was without intelligence.

"Inc-c-curable," she said in level tones that conveyed even better than his convulsive gesture her blank, ultimate despair! The stammer added a touch of unintelligence similar to his own. It was dreadful.

He looked up then with an idiotic smile, while she responded, the mind in her obviously already clouded: "Flame that never d-dies."

"T-tongues of f-f-fire," he said with a feeble giggle. "We have t-tongues of f-fire – you and I—" He got up with a gesture as though to kiss her. In his hand fluttered his handkerchief, its awful patch apparent.

She did not move. "And afterwards, too," she whispered, the last gleam of reason fading from her eyes, "forever and ever…"

**If you enjoyed this, you might also like…**
By Water, see page 103
Strange Disappearance of a Baronet, see page 188

# The Doll

**SOME NIGHTS** are merely dark, others are dark in a suggestive way as though something ominous, mysterious, is going to happen. In certain remote outlying suburbs, at any rate, this seems true, where great spaces between the lamps go dead at night, where little happens, where a ring at the door is a summons almost, and people cry "Let's go to town!" In the villa gardens the mangy cedars sigh in the wind, but the hedges stiffen, there is a muffling of spontaneous activity.

On this particular November night a moist breeze barely stirred the silver pine in the narrow drive leading to the 'Laurels' where Colonel Masters lived. Colonel Hymber Masters, late of an Indian regiment, with many distinguished letters after his name. The housemaid in the limited staff being out, it was the cook who answered the bell when it rang with a sudden, sharp clang soon after ten o'clock – and gave an audible gasp half of surprise, half of fear. The bell's sudden clangour was an unpleasant and unwelcome sound. Monica, the Colonel's adored yet rather neglected child, was asleep upstairs, but the cook was not frightened lest Monica be disturbed, nor because it seemed a bit late for the bell to ring so violently; she was frightened because when she opened the door to let the fine rain drive in she saw a black man standing on the steps. There, in the wind and the rain, stood a tall, slim nigger holding a parcel.

Dark-skinned, at any rate, he was, she reflected afterwards, whether Negro, Hindu or Arab; the word 'nigger' describing any man not really white. Wearing a stained yellow mackintosh and dirty slouch hat, and "looking like a devil, so help me, God," he shoved the little parcel at her out of the gloom, the light from the hall flaring red into his gleaming eyes. "For Colonel Masters," he whispered rapidly, "and very special into his own personal touch and no one else." And he melted away into the night with his "strange foreign accent, his eyes of fire, and his nasty hissing voice."

He was gone, swallowed up in the wind and rain.

"But I saw his eyes," swore the cook the next morning to the housemaid, "his fiery eyes, and his nasty look and his black hands and long thin fingers, and his nails all shiny pink, and he looked to me – if you know wot I mean – he looked like – death..."

Thus the cook, so far as she was intelligently articulate next day, but standing now against the closed door with the small brown paper parcel in her hands, impressed by the orders that it was to be given into his personal touch, she was relieved by the fact that Colonel Masters never returned till after midnight and that she need not act at once. The reflection brought a certain comfort that restored her equanimity a little, though she still stood there, holding the parcel gingerly in her grimy hands, reluctant, hesitating, uneasy. A parcel, even brought by a mysterious dark stranger, was not in itself frightening, yet frightened she certainly felt. Instinct and superstition worked perhaps; the wind, the rain, the fact of being alone in the house, the unexpected black man, these also contributed to her discomfort. A vague sense of horror touched her, her Irish blood stirred ancient dreams, so that she began to shake a little, as though the parcel contained something alive, explosive, poisonous, unholy almost as though it moved, and, her fingers loosening their hold, the parcel – dropped. It fell on the tiled floor with a queer, sharp clack, but it lay motionless. She eyed it closely, cautiously, but, thank God, it did not move, an inert, brown-paper parcel. Brought by an errand boy in daylight, it might have been groceries, tobacco, even a mended shirt. She peeped and tinkered, that sharp clack puzzled her. Then, after a few minutes, remembering her duty, she picked it up gingerly even while she shivered. It was to be handed into the Colonel's 'personal touch'. She compromised, deciding to place it on his desk and to tell him about it in the morning; only Colonel Masters, with those mysterious years in the East behind him, his temper and his tyrannical orders, was not easy of direct approach at the best of times, in the morning least of all.

The cook left it at that – that is, she left it on the desk in his study, but left out all explanations about its arrival. She had decided to be vague about such unimportant details, for Mrs. O'Reilly was afraid of Colonel Masters, and only his professed love of Monica made her believe that he was quite human. He paid her well, oh yes, and sometimes he smiled, and he was a handsome man, if a bit too dark for her fancy, yet he also paid her an occasional compliment about her curry, and that soothed her for the moment. They suited one another, at any rate, and she stayed, robbing him comfortably, if cautiously.

"It ain't no good," she assured the housemaid next day, "wot with that 'personal touch into his hands, and no one else,' and that black man's eyes and that crack when it came away in my hands and fell on the floor. It ain't no good, not to us nor anybody. No man as black as he was means lucky stars to anybody. A parcel indeed – with those devil's eyes—"

"What did you do with it?" enquired the housemaid.

The cook looked her up and down. "Put it in the fire o' course," she replied. "On the stove if you want to know exact."

It was the housemaid's turn to look the cook up and down.

"I don't think," she remarked.

The cook reflected, probably because she found no immediate answer.

"Well," she puffed out presently, "D'you know wot I think? You don't. So I'll tell you. It was something the master's afraid of, that's wot it was. He's afraid of something – ever since I been here I've known that. And that's wot it was. He done somebody wrong in India long ago and that lanky nigger brought wot's coming to him, and that's why I says I put it on the stove – see?" She dropped her voice. "It was a bloody idol," she whispered, "that's wot it was, that parcel, and he – why, he's a bloody secret worshipper." And she crossed herself. "That's why I said I put it on the stove – see?"

The housemaid stared and gasped.

"And you mark my words, young Jane!" added the cook, turning to her dough.

And there the matter rested for a period, for the cook, being Irish, had more laughter in her than tears, and beyond admitting to the scared housemaid that she had not really burnt the parcel but had left it on the study table, she almost forgot the incident. It was not her job, in any case, to answer the front door. She had 'delivered' the parcel. Her conscience was quite clear.

Thus, nobody 'marked her words' apparently, for nothing untoward happened, as the way is in remote Suburbia, and Monica in her lonely play was happy, and Colonel Masters as tyrannical and grim as ever. The moist wintry wind blew through the silver pine, the rain beat against the bow window, and no one called. For a week this lasted, a longish time in uneventful Suburbia.

* * *

But suddenly one morning Colonel Masters rang his study bell and, the housemaid being upstairs, it was the cook who answered. He held a brown paper parcel in his hands, half opened, the string dangling.

"I found this on my desk. I haven't been in my room for a week. Who brought it? And when did it come?" His face, yellow as usual, held a fiery tinge.

Mrs. O'Reilly replied, post-dating the arrival vaguely.

"I asked *who* brought it?" he insisted sharply.

"A stranger," she fumbled. "Not anyone," she added nervously, "from hereabouts. No one I ever seen before. It was a man."

"What did he look like?" The question came like a bullet.

Mrs. O'Reilly was rather taken by surprise. "D-darkish," she stumbled. "Very darkish," she added, "if I saw him right. Only he came and went so quick I didn't get his face proper like, and…"

"Any message?" the Colonel cut her short.

She hesitated. "There was no answer," she began, remembering former occasions.

"Any *message*, I asked you?" he thundered.

"No message, sir, none at all. And he was gone before I could get his name and address, sir, but I think it was a sort of black man, or it may have been the darkness of the night – I couldn't reely say, sir…"

In another minute she would have burst into tears or dropped to the floor in a faint, such was her terror of her employer especially when she was lying blind. The Colonel, however, saved her both disasters by abruptly holding out the half opened parcel towards her. He neither cross-examined nor cursed her as she had expected. He spoke with the curtness that betrayed anger and anxiety, almost it occurred to her, distress.

"Take it away and burn it," he ordered in his army voice, passing it into her outstretched hands. "Burn it," he repeated it, "or chuck the damned thing away." He almost flung it at her as though he did not want to touch it. "If the man comes back," he ordered in a voice of steel, "tell him it's been destroyed – and say it *didn't reach me*," laying tremendous emphasis on the final words. "You understand?" He almost chucked it at her.

"Yes, sir. Exactly, sir," and she turned and stumbled out, holding the parcel gingerly in her arms rather than in her hands and fingers, as though it contained something that might bite or sting.

Yet her fear had somehow lessened, for if he, Colonel Masters, could treat the parcel so contemptuously, why should she feel afraid of it. And, once alone in her kitchen among her household gods, she opened it. Turning back the thick paper wrappings, she started, and to her rather disappointed amazement, she found herself staring at nothing but a fair, waxen faced doll that could be bought in any toyshop for one shilling and sixpence. A commonplace little cheap doll! Its face was pallid, white, expressionless, its flaxen hair was dirty, its tiny ill-shaped hands and fingers lay motionless by its side, its mouth was closed, though somehow grinning, no teeth visible, its eyelashes ridiculously like a worn tooth brush, its entire presentment in its flimsy skirt, contemptible, harmless, even ugly.

A doll! She giggled to herself, all fear evaporated.

"Gawd!" she thought. "The master must have a conscience like the floor of a parrot's cage! And worse than that!" She was too afraid of him to despise him, her feeling was probably more like pity. "At any rate," she reflected, "he had the wind up pretty bad. It was something else he expected – not a two-penny halfpenny doll!" Her warm heart felt almost sorry for him.

Instead of 'chucking the damned thing away or burning it', however – for it was quite a nice looking doll, she presented it to Monica, and Monica, having few new toys, instantly adored it, promising faithfully, as gravely warned by Mrs. O'Reilly, that she would never *never* let her father know she had it.

Her father. Colonel Hymber Masters, was, it seems, what's called a 'disappointed' man, a man whose fate forced him to live in surroundings he detested, disappointed in his career probably, possibly in love as well, Monica a love-child doubtless, and limited by his pension to face daily conditions that he loathed.

He was a silent, bitter sort of fellow, no more than that, and not so much disliked in the neighbourhood, as misunderstood. A sombre man they reckoned him, with his dark, furrowed face and silent ways. Yet 'dark' in the suburbs meant mysterious, and 'silent' invited female fantasy to fill the vacuum. It's the frank, corn-haired man who invites sympathy and generous comment. He enjoyed his Bridge, however, and was accepted as a first-class player. Thus, he went out nightly, and rarely came back before midnight. He was welcome among the gamblers evidently, while the fact that he had an adored child at home softened the picture of this 'mysterious' man. Monica, though rarely seen, appealed to the women of the neighbourhood, and "whatever her origin" said the gossips, "he loves her."

To Monica, meanwhile, in her rather play-less, toy-less life, the doll, her new treasure, was a spot of gold. The fact that it was a 'secret' present from her father, added to its value. Many other presents had come to her like that; she thought nothing of it; only, he had never given her a doll before, and it spelt rapture. Never, never, would she betray her pleasure and delight; it should remain her secret and his; and that made her love it all the more. She loved her father too, his taciturn silence was something she vaguely respected and adored. "That's just like father," she always said, when a strange new present came, and she knew instinctively that she must never say Thank you for it, for that was part of the lovely game between them. But this doll was exceptionally marvellous.

"It's much more real and alive than my teddy bears," she told the cook, after examining it critically. "Whatever made him think of it? Why, it even talks to me!" and she cuddled and fondled the half misshapened toy. "It's my baby," she cried taking it against her cheek.

For no teddy-bear could really be a child; cuddly bears were not offspring, whereas a doll was a potential baby. It brought sweetness, as both cook and governess realised, into a rather grim house, hope and tenderness, a maternal flavour almost, something anyhow that no young bear could possibly bring. A child, a human baby! And yet both cook and governess – for both were present at the actual delivery – recalled later that Monica opened the parcel and recognised the doll with a yell of wild delight that seemed almost a scream of pain. There was this too high note of delirious exultation as though some instinctive horror of revulsion were instantly smothered and obliterated in a whirl of overmastering joy. It was Madame Jodzka who recalled – long afterwards – this singular contradiction.

"I did think she shrieked at it a bit, now you ask me," admitted Mrs. O'Reilly later, though at the actual moment all she said was "Oh, lovely, darling, ain't it a pet!" While all

Madame Jodzka said was a cautionary "If you squash its mouth like that, Monica, it won't be able to breathe!"

While Monica, paying no attention to either of them, fell to cuddling the doll with ecstasy.

A cheap little flaxen-haired, waxen-faced doll.

That so strange a case should come to us at second hand is, admittedly, a pity; that so much of the information should reach us largely through a cook and housemaid and through a foreigner of questionable validity, is equally unfortunate. Where precisely the reported facts creep across the feathery frontier into the incredible and thence into the fantastic would need the spider's thread of the big telescopes to define. With the eye to the telescope, the thread of that New Zealand spider seems thick as a rope; but with the eye examining secondhand reports the thread becomes elusive gossamer.

\* \* \*

The Polish governess, Madame Todzka, left the house rather abruptly. Though adored by Monica and accepted by Colonel Masters, she left not long after the arrival of the doll. She was a comely, youngish widow of birth and breeding, tactful, discreet, understanding. She adored Monica, and Monica was happy with her; she feared her employer, yet perhaps secretly admired him as the strong, silent, dominating Englishman. He gave her great freedom, she never took liberties, everything went smoothly. The pay was good and she needed it. Then, suddenly, she left. In the suddenness of her departure, as in the odd reason she gave for leaving, lie doubtless the first hints of this remarkable affair, creeping across that 'feathery frontier' into the incredible and fantastic. An understandable reason she gave for leaving was that she was too frightened to stay in the house another night. She left at twenty-four hours' notice. Her reason was absurd, even if understandable, because any woman might find herself so frightened in a certain building that it has become intolerable to her nerves. Foolish or otherwise, this is understandable. An idée fixe, an obsession, once lodged in the mind of a superstitious, therefore hysterically-favoured woman, cannot be dislodged by argument. It may be absurd, yet it is 'understandable'.

The story behind the reason for Madame Jodzka's sudden terror is another matter, and it is best given quite simply. It relates to the doll. She swears by all her gods that she saw the doll 'walking by itself'. It was walking in a disjointed, hoppity, hideous fashion across the bed in which Monica lay sleeping.

In the gleam of the night-light, Madame Jodzka swears she saw this happen. She was half inside the opened door, peeping in, as her habit, and duty decreed, to see if all was well with the child before going up to bed herself. The light, if faint, was clear. A jerky movement on the counterpane first caught her attention, for a smallish object seemed blundering awkwardly across its slippery silken surface. Something rolling, possibly, some object Monica had left outside on falling asleep rolling mechanically as the child shifted or turned over.

After staring for some seconds, she then saw that it was not merely an 'object', since it had a living outline, nor was it rolling mechanically, or sliding, as she had first imagined. It was horribly taking steps, small but quite deliberate steps as though alive. It had a tiny, dreadful face, it had an expressionless tiny face, and the face had eyes – small, brightly shining eyes, and the eyes looked straight at Madame Jodzka.

She watched for a few seconds thunderstruck, and then suddenly realised with a shock of utter horror that this small, purposive monster was the doll, Monica's doll! And this doll was moving towards her across the tumbled surface of the counterpane. It was coming in her direction – straight at her.

Madame Jodzka gripped herself, physically and mentally, making a great effort, it seems, to deny the abnormal, the incredible. She denied the ice in her veins and down her spine. She prayed. She thought frantically of her priest in Warsaw. Making no audible sound, she screamed in her mind. But the doll, quickening its pace, came hobbling straight towards her, its glassy eyes fixed hard upon her own.

Then Madame Jodzka fainted.

\* \* \*

That she was, in some ways, a remarkable woman, with a sense of values, is clear from the fact that she realised this story 'wouldn't wash', for she confided it only to the cook in cautious whispers, while giving her employer some more 'washable' tale about a family death that obliged her to hurry home to Warsaw. Nor was there the slightest attempt at embroidery, for on recovering consciousness she had recovered her courage, too – and done a remarkable thing; she had compelled herself to investigate. Aided and fortified by her religion, she compelled herself to make an examination. She had tiptoed further into the room, had made sure that Monica was sleeping peacefully, and that the doll lay – motionless – half way down the counterpane. She gave it a long, concentrated look. Its lidless eyes, fringed by hideously ridiculous black lashes were fixed on space. Its expression was not so much innocent, as blankly stupid, idiotic, a mask of death that aped cheaply a pretence of life, where life could never be. Not ugly merely, it was revolting.

Madame Jodzka however, did more than study this visage with concentration, for with admirable pluck she forced herself to touch the little horror. She actually picked it up. Her faith, her deep religious conviction denied the former evidence of her senses. She had not seen movement. It was incredible, impossible. The fault lay somewhere in herself. This persuasion, at any rate, lasted long enough to enable her to touch the repulsive little toy, to pick it up, to lift it. She placed it steadily on the table near the bed between the bowl of flowers and the night-light, where it lay on its back helpless, innocent, yet horrible, and only then on shaking legs did she leave the room and go up to her own bed. That her fingers remained ice-cold until eventually she fell asleep can be explained, of course, too easily and naturally to claim examination.

\* \* \*

Whether imagined or actual, it must have been, none the less, a horrifying spectacle – a mechanical outline from a commercial factory walking like a living thing with a purpose. It holds the nightmare touch. To Madame Jodzka, protected since youth within cast-iron tenets, it came as a shock. And a shock dislocates. The sight smashed everything she knew as possible and real. The flow of her blood was interrupted, it froze, there came icy terror into her heart, her normal mechanism failed for a moment, she fainted. And fainting seemed a natural result. Yet it was the shock of the incredible masquerade that gave her the courage to act. She loved Monica, apart from any consideration of paid duty. The sight of this tiny monstrosity strutting across the counterpane not far from the child's sleeping face and folded hands – it was this that enabled her to pick it up with naked fingers and set it out of reach....

For hours, before falling asleep, she reviewed the incredible thing, alternately denying the facts, then accepting them, yet taking into sleep finally the assured conviction that her senses had not deceived her. There seems little, indeed, that in a court of law could have been advanced against her character for reliability, for sincerity, for the logic of her detailed account.

"I'm sorry," said Colonel Masters quietly, referring to her bereavement. He looked searchingly at her. "And Monica will miss you," he added with one of his rare smiles. "She needs you." Then just as she turned away, he suddenly extended his hand. "If perhaps later you can come back – do let me know. Your influence is – so helpful – and good."

She mumbled some phrase with a promise in it, yet she left with a queer, deep impression that it was not merely, not chiefly perhaps, Monica who needed her. She wished he had not used quite those words. A sense of shame lay in her, almost as though she were running away from duty, or at least from a chance to help God had put in her way. "Your influence is – so good."

\* \* \*

Already in the train and on the boat conscience attacked her, biting, scratching, gnawing. She had deserted a child she loved, a child who needed her, because she was scared out of her wits. No, that was a one-sided statement. She had left a house because the Devil had come into it. No, that was only partially true. When a hysterical temperament, engrained since early childhood in fixed dogmas, begins to sift facts and analyse reactions, logic and common sense themselves become confused. Thought led one way, emotion another, and no honest conclusion dawned on her mind.

She hurried on to Warsaw, to a stepfather, a retired General whose gay life had no place for her and who would not welcome her return. It was a derogatory prospect for this youngish widow who had taken a job in order to escape from his vulgar activities to return now empty-handed. Yet it was easier, perhaps, to face a stepfather's selfish anger than to go and tell Colonel Masters her real reason for leaving his service. Her conscience, too, troubled her on another score as thoughts and memories travelled backwards and half-forgotten details emerged.

Those spots of blood, for instance, mentioned by Mrs. O'Reilly, the superstitious Irish cook. She had made it a rule to ignore Mrs. O'Reilly's silly fairy tales, yet now she recalled suddenly those ridiculous discussions about the laundry list and the foolish remarks that the cook and housemaid had let fall.

"But there ain't no paint in a doll, I tell you. It's all sawdust and wax and muck," from the housemaid. "I know red paint when I sees it, and that ain't paint, it's blood." And from Mrs. O'Reilly later: "Mother o' God! Another red blob! She's biting her fingernails – and that's not *my* job...!"

The red stains on sheets and pillow cases were puzzling certainly, but Madame Jodzka, hearing these remarks by chance as it were, had paid no particular attention to them at the moment. The laundry lists were hardly her affair. These ridiculous servants anyhow...! And yet, now in the train, those spots of red, be they paint or blood, crept back to trouble her.

Another thing, oddly enough, also troubled her – the ill-defined feeling that she was deserting a man who needed help, help that she could give. It was too vague to put into words. Was it based on his remark that her influence was 'good' perhaps? She could not say. It was an intuition, and few intuitions bear analysis. Supporting it, however, was a conviction she had felt since first she entered the service of Colonel Masters, the conviction, namely, that he had a Past that frightened him. There was something he had done, something he regretted and was probably ashamed of, something at any rate, for which he feared retribution. A retribution, moreover, he expected; a punishment that would come like a thief in the night and seize him by the throat.

It was against this dreaded vengeance that her influence was 'good', a protective influence possibly that her religion supplied, something on the side of the angels, in any case, that her personality provided.

Her mind worked thus, it seems; and whether a concealed admiration for this sombre and mysterious man, an admiration and protective instinct never admitted even to her inmost self, existed below the surface, hidden yet urgent, remains the secret of her own heart.

* * *

It was naturally and according to human nature, at any rate, that after a few weeks of her stepfather's outrageous behaviour in the house, his cruelty too, she decided to return. She prayed to her gods incessantly, also she found oppressive her sense of neglected duty and failure of self-respect. She returned to the soulless suburban villa. It was understandable; the welcome from Monica was also understandable, the relief and pleasure of Colonel Masters still more so. It was expressed, this latter, in a courteous message only, tactfully worded, as though she had merely left for brief necessity, for it was some days before she actually saw him to speak to. From cook and housemaid the welcome was voluble and – disquieting. There were no more inexplicable 'spots of red', but there were other unaccountable happenings even more distressing.

"She's missed you something terrible," said Mrs. O'Reilly, "though she's found something else to keep her quiet – if you like to put it that way." And she made the sign of the cross.

"The doll?" asked Madame Jodzka with a start of shocked horror, forcing herself to come straight to the point and forcing herself also io speak lightly, casually.

"That's it, Madame. The bleeding doll."

The governess had heard the strange adjective many times already, but did not know whether to take it figuratively or not. She chose the latter.

"Blood?" she asked in a lowered voice.

The cook's body gave an odd jerk. "Well," she explained. "I meant more the way it goes on. Like a thing of flesh and blood, if you get me. And the way she treats it and plays with it," and her voice, while loud, had a hush of fear in it somewhere. She held her arms before her in a protective, shielding way, as though to ward off aggression.

"Scratches ain't proof of nothing," interjected the housemaid scornfully.

"You mean," asked Madame Jodzka gravely, "there's a question of – of injury – to someone?" She suppressed an involuntary gasp, but paid no attention to the maid's interruption otherwise.

Mrs. O'Reilly seemed to mismanage her breath for a moment.

"It ain't Miss Monica it's after," she announced in a defiant whisper as soon as she recovered herself, "it's someone else. *That's* what I mean. And no man as black as he was," she let herself go, "ever brought no good into a house, not since I was born."

"Someone else—?" repeated Madame Jodzka almost to herself, seizing the vital words.

"You and yer black man!" interjected the housemaid. "Get along with yer! Thank God I ain't a Christian or anything like that! But I did 'ear them sort of jerky shuffling footsteps one night, I admit, and the doll did look bigger – swollen like – when I peeked in and looked—"

"Stop it!" cried Mrs. O'Reilly, "for you ain't saying what's true or what you reely know." She turned to the governess.

"There's more talk what means nothing about this doll," she said by way of apology, "than all the fairy tales I was brought up with as a child in Mayo, and I – I wouldn't be believing anything of it."

Turning her back contemptuously on the chattering housemaid, she came close to Madame Jodzka.

"There's no harm coming to Miss Monica, Madame," she whispered vehemently, "you can be quite sure about her. Any trouble there may be is for someone else." And again she crossed herself.

Madame Jodzka, in the privacy of her room, reflected between her prayers. She felt a deep, a dreadful uneasiness.

A doll! A cheap, tawdry little toy made in factories by the hundred, by the thousand, a manufactured article of commerce for children to play with... But...

"The way she treats it and plays with it..." rang on in her disturbed mind.

A doll! But for the maternal suggestion, a doll was a pathetic, even horrible plaything, yet to watch a child busy with it involved deep reflections, since here the future mother prophesied. The child fondles and caresses her doll with passionate love, cares for it, seeks its welfare, yet stuffs it down into the perambulator, its head and neck twisted, its limbs broken and contorted, leaving it atrociously upside down so that blood and breathing cannot possibly function, while she runs to the window to see if the rain has stopped or the sun has come out. A blind and hideous automatism dictated by the Race, provided nothing of more immediate interest interferes, yet a herd-instinct that overcomes all obstacles, its vitality insuperable. The maternity instinct defies, even denies death. The doll, whether left upside down on the floor with broken teeth and ruined eyes, or lovingly arranged to be overlaid in the night, squashed, tortured, mutilated, survives all cruelties and disasters, and asserts finally its immortal qualities. It is unkillable. It is beyond death.

A child with her doll, reflected Madame Jodzka, is an epitome of nature's remorseless and unconquerable passion, of her dominant purpose – the survival of the race...

Such thoughts, influenced perhaps by her bitter subconscious grievance against nature for depriving her of a child of her own, were unable to hold that level for long; they soon dropped back to the concrete case that perplexed and frightened her – Monica and her flaxen haired, sightless, idiotic doll. In the middle of her prayers, falling asleep incontinently, she did not even dream of it, and she woke refreshed and vigorous, facing the fact that sooner or later, sooner probably, she would have to speak to her employer.

She watched and listened. She watched Monica; she watched the doll. All seemed as normal as in a thousand other homes. Her mind reviewed the position, and where mind and superstition clashed, the former held its own easily. During her evening off she enjoyed the local cinema, leaving the heated building with the conviction that coloured fantasy benumbed the faculties, and that ordinary life was in itself prosaic. Yet before she had covered the half-mile to the house, her deep, unaccountable uneasiness returned with overmastering power.

Mrs. O'Reilly had seen Monica to bed for her, and it was Mrs. O'Reilly who let her in. Her face was like the dead.

"It's been talking," whispered the cook, even before she closed the door. She was white about the gills.

"Talking! *Who's* been talking? What do you mean?"

Mrs. O'Reilly closed the door softly. "Both," she stated with dramatic emphasis, then sat down and wiped her face. She looked distraught with fear.

Madame took command, if only a command based on dreadful insecurity.

"Both?" she repeated, in a voice deliberately loud so as to counteract the other's whisper. "What are you talking about?"

"They've *both* been talking – talking together," stated the cook.

The governess kept silent for a moment, fighting to deny a shrinking heart.

"You've heard them talking together, you mean?" she asked presently in a shaking voice that tried to be ordinary.

Mrs. O'Reilly nodded looking over her shoulder as she did so. Her nerves were, obviously, in rags. "I thought you'd never come back," she whimpered. "I could hardly stay in the house."

Madame looked intently into her frightened eyes.

"You *heard*...?" she asked quietly.

"I listened at the door. There were two voices. Different voices."

Madame Jodzka did not insist or cross-examine, as though acute fear helped her to a greater wisdom.

"You mean, Mrs. O'Reilly," she said in flat, quiet tones, "that you heard Miss Monica talking to her doll as she always does, and herself inventing the doll's answers in a changed voice? Isn't that what you mean you heard?"

But Mrs. O'Reilly was not to be shaken. By way of answer she crossed herself and shook her head.

She spoke in a low whisper. "Come up now and listen with me, Madame, and judge for yourself."

Thus, soon after midnight, and Monica long since asleep, these two, the cook and governess in a suburban villa, took up their places in the dark corridor outside a child's bedroom door. It was a quiet windless night; Colonel Masters, whom they both feared, doubtless long since gone to his room in another corner of the ungainly villa. It must have been a long dreary wait before sounds in the child's bedroom first became audible – the low quiet sound of voices talking audibly – two voices. A hushed, secretive, unpleasant sound in the room where Monica slept peacefully with her beloved doll beside her. Yet two voices assuredly, it was.

Both women sat erect, both crossed themselves involuntarily, exchanging glances. Both were bewildered, terrified. Both sat aghast.

What lay in Mrs. O'Reilly's superstitious mind, only the gods of 'ould Oireland' can tell, but what the Polish woman's contained was clear as a bell; it was not two voices talking, it was only one. Her ear was pressed against the crack in the door. She listened intently; shaking to the bone, she listened. Voices in sleep-talking, she remembered, changed oddly.

"The child's talking to herself in sleep," she whispered firmly, "and that's all it is, Mrs. O'Reilly. She's just talking in her sleep," she repeated with emphasis to the woman crowding against her shoulder as though in need of support. "Can't you hear it," she added loudly, half angrily, "isn't it the same voice always? Listen carefully and you'll see I'm right."

She listened herself more closely than before.

"Listen! Hark...!" she repeated in a breathless whisper, concentrating her mind upon the curious sound, "isn't that the same voice – answering itself?"

Yet, as she listened, another sound disturbed her concentration, and this time it seemed a sound behind her – a faint, rustling, shuffling sound rather like footsteps hurrying away on tiptoe. She turned her head sharply and found that she had been whispering to no one. There was no one beside her. She was alone in the darkened corridor. Mrs. O'Reilly was gone. From the well of the house below a voice came up in a smothered cry beneath the darkened stairs: "Mother o' God and all the Saints..." and more besides.

A gasp of surprise and alarm escaped her doubtless at finding herself deserted and alone but in the same instant, exactly as in the story books, came another sound that caught her breath still more aghast – the rattle of a key in the front door below. Colonel Masters, after all, had not yet come in and gone to bed as expected: he was coming in now. Would Mrs. O'Reilly have time to slip across the hall before he caught her? More – and worse – would he come up and peep into Monica's bedroom on his way up to bed, as he rarely did? Madame Jodzka listened, her nerves in rags. She heard him fling dowm his coat. He was a man quick in such actions. The stick or umbrella was banged down noisily, hastily. The same instant his step sounded on the stairs. He was coming up. Another minute and he would start into the passage where she crouched against Monica's door.

He was mounting rapidly, two stairs at a time.

She, too, was quick in action and decision. She thought in a flash. To be caught crouching outside the door was ludicrous, but to be caught inside the door would be natural and explicable. She acted at once.

With a palpitating heart, she opened the bedroom door and stepped inside. A second later she heard Colonel Masters' tread, as he stumped along the corridor up to bed. He passed the door. He went on. She heard this with intense relief.

Now, inside the room, the door closed behind her, she saw the picture clearly.

Monica, sound asleep, was playing with her beloved doll, but in her sleep. She was indubitably in deep slumber. Her fingers, however, were roughing the doll this way and that, as though some dream perplexed her. The child was mumbling in her sleep, though no words were distinguishable. Muffled sighs and groans issued from her lips. Yet another sound there certainly was, though it could not have issued from the child's mouth. Whence, then, did it come?

Madame Jodzka paused, holding her breath, her heart panting. She watched and listened intently. She heard squeaks and grunts, but a moment's examination convinced her whence these noises came. They did not come from Monica's lips. They issued indubitably from the doll she clutched and twisted in her dream. The joints, as Monica twisted them emitted these odd sounds, as though the sawdust in knees and elbows wheezed and squeaked against the unnatural rubbing. Monica obviously was wholly unconscious of these noises. As the doll's neck screwed round, the material – wax, thread, sawdust – produced this curious grating sound that was almost like syllables of a word or words.

Madame Jodzka stared and listened. She felt icy cold. Seeking for a natural explanation she found none. Prayer and terror raced in her helter-skelter. Her skin began to sweat.

Then, suddenly Monica, her expression peaceful and composed, turned over in her sleep, and the dreadful doll, released from the dream-clutch, fell to one side on the bed and lay apparently lifeless and inert. In which moment, to Madame Jodzka's unbelieving yet horrified ears, it continued to squeak and utter. It went on mouthing itself. Worse than that, the next instant it stood abruptly upright, rising on its twisted legs. It started moving. It began to move, walking crookedly, across the counterpane. Its glassy, sightless eyes, seemed to look straight at her. It presented an inhuman and appalling picture, a picture of the utterly incredible. With a queer, hoppity motion of its broken legs and joints, it came fumbling and tumbling across the rough unevenness of the slippery counterpane towards her. Its appearance was deliberate and aggressive. The sounds, as of syllables, came with it – strange, meaningless syllables that yet managed to convey anger. It stumbled towards her like a living thing. Its whole presentment conveyed attack.

Once again, this effect of a mere child's toy, aping the life of some awful monstrosity with purpose and passion in its hideous tiny outline, brought collapse to the plucky Polish governess. The rush of blood without control drained her heart, and a moment of unconsciousness supervened so that everything, as it were, turned black.

This time, however, the moment of dark unconsciousness passed instantly: it came and went, almost like a moment of forgetfulness in passion. Passionate it certainly was, for the reaction came upon her like a storm. With recovered consciousness a sudden rage rushed into her woman heart – perhaps a coward's rage, an exaggerated fury against her own weakness? It rushed, in any case, to help her. She staggered, caught her breath, clutched violently at the cupboard next her, and – recovered her self-control. A fury of resentment blazed through her, fury against this utterly incredible exhibition of a wax doll walking and squawking as though it were something intelligently alive that could utter syllables. Syllables, she felt convinced, in a language she did not know.

If the monstrous can paralyse, it also can affront. The sight and sound of this cheap factory toy behaving with a will and heart of its own stung her into an act of violence that became imperative. For it was more than she could stand. Irresistibly, she rushed forward. She hurled herself against it, her only available weapon the high-heeled shoe her foot kicked loose on the instant, determined to smash down the frightful apparition into fragments and annihilate it. Hysterical, no doubt, she was at the moment, and yet logical: the godless horror must be blotted out of visible existence. This one thing obsessed her – to destroy beyond all possibility of survival. It must be smashed into fragments, into dust.

They stood close, face to face, the glassy eyes staring into her own, her hand held high for the destruction she craved – but the hand did not fall. A stinging pain, sharp as a serpent's bite, darted suddenly through her fingers, wrist and arm, her grip was broken, the shoe spun sideways across the room, and in the flickering light of the candle, it seemed to her, the whole room quivered. Paralysed and helpless, she stood utterly aghast. What gods or saints could come to aid her? None. Her own will alone could help her. Some effort, at any rate, she made, trembling, on the edge of collapse: "My God!" she heard her half whispering, strangled voice cry out. "It is not true! You are a lie! My God denies you! I call upon my God…!"

Whereupon, to her added horror, the dreadful little doll, waving a broken arm, squawked back at her, as though in definite answer the strange disjointed syllables she could not understand, syllables as though in another tongue. The same instant it collapsed abruptly on the counterpane like a toy balloon that had been pricked. It shrank down in a mutilated mess before her eyes, when Monica – added touch of horror – stirred uneasily in her sleep, turning over and stretching out her hands as though feeling blindly for something that she missed. And this sight of the innocent sleeping child fumbling instinctively towards an incomprehensible evil and dangerous something that attracted her proved again too strong for the Polish woman to control.

The blackness intervened a second time.

It was undoubtedly a blur in memory that followed, emotion and superstition proving too much for common sense to deal with. She just remembers violent, unreasoned action on her part before she came back to clearer consciousness in her own room, praying volubly on her knees against her own bed. The interval of transit down the corridor and upstairs remained a blank. Yet her shoe was with her, clutched tightly in her hand. And she remembered also having clutched an inert, waxen doll with frantic fingers, clutched and crushed and crumpled its awful little frame till the sawdust came spurting from its broken joints and its tiny body was mutilated beyond recognition, if not annihilated… then stuffing it down ruthlessly on a table far out of Monica's reach, Monica lying peacefully in deepest sleep. She remembered that. She also saw the clear picture of the small monster lying upside down, grossly untidy, an obscene attitude in the disorder of its flimsy dress and exposed limbs, lying motionless, its eyes crookedly aglint, motionless, yet alive still, alive moreover with intense and malignant purpose.

No duration or intensity of prayer could obliterate the picture.

*　*　*

She knew now that a plain, face to face talk with her employer was essential; her conscience, her peace of mind, her sanity, her sense of duty all demanded this. Deliberately, and she was sure, rightly, she had never once risked a word with the child herself. Danger lay that way, the danger of emphasising something in the child's mind that was best left ignored. But with Colonel Masters, who paid her for her services, believed in her integrity, trusted her, with him there must be an immediate explanation.

An interview was absurdly difficult; in the first place because he loathed and avoided such occasions; secondly because he was so exceedingly impervious to approach, being so rarely even visible at all. At night he came home late, in the mornings no one dared go near him. He expected the little household, once its routine established, to run itself. The only inmate who dared beard him was Mrs. O'Reilly, who periodically, once every six months, walked straight into his study, gave notice, received an addition to her wages, and then left him alone for another six months.

Madame Jodzka, knowing his habits, waylaid him in the hall next morning while Monica was lying down before lunch, as usual. He was on his way out and she had been watching from the upper landing. She had hardly set eyes on him since her return from Warsaw. His lean, upright figure, his dark, emotionless face, she thought magnificent. He was the perfect expression of the soldier. Her heart fluttered as she raced downstairs. Her carefully prepared sentences, however, evaporated when he stopped and looked at her, a jumble of wild words pouring from her in confused English instead. He cut her rigmarole short, though he listened politely enough at first.

"I'm so glad you were able to come back to us, as I told you. Monica missed you very much—"

"She has something now she plays with—"

"The very thing," he interrupted. "No doubt the kind of toy she needs... Your excellent judgment... Please tell me if there's anything else you think..." and he half turned as though to move away.

"But I didn't get it. It's a horrible – horrible—"

Colonel Masters uttered one of his rare laughs. "Of course, all children's toys are horrible, but if she's pleased with it... I haven't seen it. I'm no judge... If you can buy something better—" and he shrugged his shoulders.

"I didn't buy it," she cried desperately. "It was brought. It makes sounds by itself – syllables. I've seen it move – move by itself. It's a doll."

He turned from the front door which he had just reached as though he had been shot; the skin held a sudden pallor beneath the flush and something contradicted the blazing eyes, something that seemed to shrink.

"A doll," he repeated in a very quiet voice. "You said – a doll?"

But his eyes and face disconcerted her, so that she merely gave a fumbling account of a parcel that had been brought. His question about a parcel he had ordered strictly to be destroyed added to her confusion.

"Wasn't it?" he asked in a rasping whisper, as though a disobeyed order seemed incredible.

"It was thrown away, I believe," she prevaricated, unable to meet his eyes, anxious to protect the cook as well. "I think Monica – perhaps found it." She despised her lack of courage, but his intensity scattered her wits; she was conscious, moreover, of a strange desire not to give him pain, as though his safety and happiness, not Monica's, were at stake. "It – talks! – as well as *moves*," she cried desperately, forcing herself at last to look at him.

Colonel Masters seemed to stiffen; his breath caught oddly.

"You say Monica has it? Plays with it? You've seen movement and heard sounds like syllables?" He asked the questions in a low voice, almost as though talking to himself. "You've – listened?" he whispered.

Unable to find convincing words, she bowed her head, while some terror in him came across to her like a blast of icy wind. The man was afraid in his heart. Instead, however, of some explosive reply by way of blame or criticism, he spoke quietly, even calmly: "You did right to come and tell me this – quite right," adding then in so low a tone that she barely caught the ominous words, "for I have been expecting something of the sort... sooner or later... it was bound to come..." the voice dying away into the handkerchief he put to his face.

And abruptly then, as though aware of an appeal for sympathy, an emotional reaction swept her fear away. Stepping closer, she looked her employer straight in the eyes.

"See the child for yourself," she said with sudden firmness. "Come and listen with me. Come into the bedroom."

She saw him stagger. For a moment he said nothing.

"Who," he then asked, the low voice unsteady, "who brought that parcel?"

"A man, I believe."

There was a pause that seemed like minutes before his next question.

"White," he asked, "or – black?"

"Dark," she told him, "very dark."

He was shaking like a leaf, the skin of his face blanched; he leaned against the door, wilted, limp; unless she somehow took command there threatened a collapse she did not wish to witness.

"You shall come with me tonight," she said firmly, "and we shall listen together. Wait till I return now. I go for brandy," and a minute later as she came back breathless and watched him gulp down half a tumbler full, she knew that she had done right in telling him. His obedience proved it, though it seemed strange that cowardice should borrow from its like to produce courage.

"Tonight," she repeated, "tonight after your Bridge. We meet in the corridor outside the bedroom. I shall be there. At half-past twelve."

He pulled himself into an upright position, staring at her fixedly, making a movement of his head, half bow, half nod.

"Twelve thirty," he muttered, "in the passage outside the bedroom door," and using his stick heavily rather, he opened che door and passed out into the drive. She watched him go, aware that her fear had changed to pity, aware also that she watched the stumbling gait of a man too conscience-stricken to know a moment's peace, too frightened even to think of God.

Madame Jodzka kept the appointment; she had eaten no supper, but had stayed in her room – praying. She had first put Monica to bed.

"My doll," the child pleaded, good as gold, after being tucked up. "I must have my doll or else I'll never get to sleep," and Madame Jodzka had brought it with reluctant fingers, placing it on the night-table beside the bed,

"She'll sleep quite comfortably here, Monica, darling. Why not leave her outside the sheets?" It had been carefully mended, she noticed, patched together with pins and stitches.

The child grabbed at it. "I want her in bed beside me, close against me," she said with a happy smile. "We tell each other stories. If she's too far away I can't hear what she says." And she seized it with a cuddling pleasure that made the woman's heart turn cold.

"Of course, darling – if it helps you to fall asleep quickly, you shall have it," and Monica did not see the trembling fingers, not notice the horror in the face and voice. Indeed, hardly was the doll against her cheek on the pillow, her fingers half stroking the flaxen hair and pink wax cheeks, than her eyes closed, a sigh of deep content breathed out, and Monica was asleep.

Madame Jodzka, fearful of looking behind her, tiptoed to the door, and left the room. In the passage she wiped a cold sweat from her forehead. "God bless her and protect her," her heart murmured, "and may God forgive me if I've sinned."

She kept the appointment; she knew Colonel Masters would keep it, too.

It had been a long wait from eight o'clock till after midnight. With great determination she had kept away from the bedroom door, fearful lest she might hear a sound that would necessitate action on her part: she went to her room and stayed there. But praying exhausted itself, for it both excited and betrayed her. If her God could help, a brief request alone was needed. To go on praying for help hour by hour was not only an insult to her deity, but it also wore her out physically. She stopped, therefore, and read some pages of a Polish saint which she did not understand. Later she fell into a state of horrified nervous drowse. In due course, she slept...

A noise awoke her – steps going softly past her door. A glance at her watch showed eleven o'clock. The steps, though stealthy, were familiar. Mrs. O'Reilly was waddling up to bed. The sounds died away. Madame Jodzka, a trifle ashamed, though she hardly knew why, returned to her Polish saint, yet determined to keep her ears open. Then slept again...

What woke her a second time she could not tell. She was startled. She listened. The night was unpleasantly still, the house quiet as the grave. No casual traffic passed No wind stirred the gloomy evergreens in the drive. The world outside was silent. And then, as she saw by her watch that it was some minutes after midnight, a sharp click became audible that acted like a pistol shot to her keyed-up nerves. It was the front door closing softly. Steps followed across the hall below, then up the stairs, unsteadily a little. Colonel Masters had come in. He was coming up slowly, unwillingly she felt, to keep the appointment. Madame Jodzka started from her chair, looked in the glass, mumbled a quick confused prayer, and opened her door into the dark passage.

She stiffened, physically and mentally. "Now, he'll hear and perhaps see – for himself," she thought. "And God help him!"

She marched along the passage and reached the door of Monica's bedroom, listening with such intentness that she seemed to hear only the confused running murmur of her own blood. Having reached the appointed spot, she stood stock still and waited while his steps approached. A moment later his bulk blocked the passage, shown up as a dark shadow by the light in the hall below. This bulk came nearer, came right up to her. She believed she said "Good evening," and that he mumbled something about "I said I'd come… damned nonsense…" or words to that effect, whereupon the couple stood side by side in the darkened silence of the corridor, remote from the rest of the house, and waited without further words. They stood shoulder to shoulder outside the door of Monica's bedroom. Her heart was knocking against her side.

She heard his breathing, there came a whiff of spirits, of stale tobacco smoke, his outline seemed to shift against the wall unsteadily, he moved his feet; and a sudden, extraordinary wave of emotion swept over her, half of protective maternal yearning, half almost of sexual desire, so that for a passing instant she burned to take him in her arms and kiss him savagely, and at the same time shield him from some appalling danger his blunt ignorance laid him open to. With revulsion, pity, and a sense of sin and passion, she acknowledged this odd sudden weakness in herself, but the face of the Warsaw priest flashed across her fuddled mind the next instant. There was evil in the air. This meant the Devil. She felt herself trembling dreadfully, shaking in her shoes, losing her balance, her whole body leaning over, but leaning in his direction. A moment more and she must have fallen towards him, dropped into his arms.

A sound broke the silence, and she drew up just in time. It came from beyond the door, from inside the bedroom.

"Hark!" she whispered, her hand upon his arm, and while he made no movement, spoke no word, she saw his head and shoulders bend down toward the panel of the closed door. There was a noise, upon the other side, there were noises, Monica's voice distinctly recognisable, another slighter, shriller sound accompanying it, breaking in upon it, answering it. Two voices.

"Listen," she repeated in a whisper scarcely audible, and felt his warm hand grip her own so fiercely that it hurt her.

No words were distinguishable at first, just these odd broken sounds of two separate voices in that dark corridor of the silent house – the voice of a child, and the other a strange faint, hardly a human sound, while yet a voice.

"*Que le bon Dieu—*" she began, then faltered, breath failing her, for she saw Colonel Masters stoop down suddenly and do the last thing that would have occurred to her as likely: he put his eye to the keyhole and kept it there steadily, for the best part of a minute, his hand still gripping her own firmly. He knelt on one knee to keep his balance.

The sounds had ceased, no movement now stirred inside the room. The night-light, she knew, would show him clearly the pillows of the bed, Monica's head, the doll in her arms. Colonel Masters must see clearly anything there was to see, and he yet gave no sign that he saw anything. She experienced a queer sensation for a few seconds – almost as though she had perhaps imagined everything and proved herself a consummate, idiotic, hysterical fool. For a few seconds this ghastly thought flashed over her, the odd silence emphasising it. Had she been after all, just a crazy lunatic? Had her senses all deceived her? Why should he see nothing, make no sign? Why had the voice, the voices, ceased? Not a murmur of any sort was audible in the room.

Then Colonel Masters, suddenly releasing his grip of her hand, shuffled on to both feet and stood up straight, while in the same instant she herself stiffened, trying to prepare for the angry scorn, the contemptuous abuse he was about to pour upon her. Protecting herself against this attack, expecting it, she was the more amazed at what she did hear:

"I saw it," came in a strangled whisper. "I saw it walk!"

She stood paralysed.

"It's watching me," he added, scarcely audible. "Me!"

The revulsion of feeling at first left her speechless; it was the sheer terror in his strangled whisper that restored a measure of self possession to her. Yet it was he who found words first, awful whispered words, words spoken to himself, it seemed, more than to her.

"It's what I've always feared – I knew it must come some day – yet not like this. Not this way."

Then immediately the voice in the room became audible, and it was a sweet and gentle voice, sincere and natural, with feeling in it – Monica's childish voice, pleading:

"Don't go, don't leave me! Come back into bed – please."

An incomprehensible sound followed, as though by way of answer. There were syllables in that faint, creaky tone Madame Jodzka recognised, but syllables she could not comprehend. They seemed to enter her like points of ice. She froze. And facing her stood the motionless, inanimate bulk of him, his outline, then leaned leaned over towards her, his lips so close to her own face that, as he spoke, she felt the breath upon her cheek.

"*Buth laga...*" she heard him repeat the syllables to himself again and again. "*Revenge...* in Hindustani...!" He drew a long, anguished breath. The sounds sank into her like drops of poison, the syllables she had heard several times already but had not understood. At last she understood their meaning. Revenge!

"I must go in, go in," he was mumbling to himself. "I must go in and face it." Her intuition was justified: the danger was not for Monica but for himself. Her sudden protective maternal instinct found its explanation too. The lethal power concentrated in that hideous puppet was aimed at *him*. He began to edge impetuously past her.

"No!" she cried. "I'll go? Let me go in!" pushing him aside with all her strength. But his hand was already on the knob and the next instant the door was open and he was inside the room. On the threshold they stood still a second side by side, though she was slightly behind, struggling to shove past him and stand protectively in front.

She stared across his shoulder, her eyes so wide open that the intense strain to note everything at once threatened to defeat its own end. Sight, none the less, worked normally; she saw all there was to see, and that was – nothing; nothing unusual, that is, nothing abnormal, nothing terrifying, so that this second time the threat of anticlimax rose to her mind. Had she worked herself up to this peak of horror merely to behold Monica lying sound asleep in a safe and quiet room? The flickering night-light revealed no more than a child in natural slumber without a toy of any sort against her pillow. There stood the glass of water beside the flowers in their saucer, the picture-book on the sill of the window within reach, the window opened a little at the bottom, and there also lay the calm face of Monica with eyes tight shut upon the pillow. Her breathing was deep and regular, no sign of disquiet anywhere, no hint of disturbance that might have accompanied that pleading sentence of two minutes ago, except that the bedclothes were perhaps somewhat tumbled. The counterpane humped itself in folds towards the foot of the bed, she noticed, as though Monica, finding it too warm, had tossed it away in sleep. No more than that.

In that first moment Colonel Masters and the governess took in this whole pretty picture complete. The room was so still that the child's breathing was distinctly audible. Their eyes roved all over. Nothing was anywhere in movement. Yet the same instant Madame Jodzka became aware that there was movement. Something stirred. The report came, perhaps, through her skin, for no sense announced it. It was undeniable; in that still, silent room there was movement somewhere, and with that unreported movement there was danger.

Certain, rightly or wrongly, that she herself was safe, also that the quietly sleeping child was safe, she was equally certain that Colonel Masters was the one in danger. She knew that in her very bones.

"Wait here by the door," she said almost peremptorily, as she felt him pushing past her further into the quiet room. "You saw it watching you. It's somewhere – Take care!"

She clutched at him, but he was already beyond her.

"Damned nonsense," he muttered and strode forward.

Never before in her whole life had she admired a man more than in this instant when she saw him moving towards what she knew to be physical and spiritual danger – never before, and never again, was such a hideous and dreadful sight to be repeatable in a woman's life. Pity and horror drowned her in a sea of passionate, futile longing. A man going to meet his fate, it flashed over her, was something none, without power to help, should witness. No human power can stay the course of the stars.

Her eye rested, as it were by chance, on the crumpled ridges and hollows of the discarded counterpane. These lay by the foot of the bed in shadow, confused a little in their contours and their masses. Had Monica not moved, they must have lain thus till morning. But Monica did move. At this particular moment she turned over in her sleep. She stretched her little legs before settling down in the new position, and this stretching squeezed and twisted the contours of the heavy counterpane at the foot of the bed. The tiny landscape altered thus a fraction, its immediate detail shifted. And an outline – a very small outline – emerged. Hitherto, it had lain concealed among the shadows. It emerged now with disconcerting rapidity, as though a spring released it. Out of its nest of darkness it seemed almost to leap forward. Fast it came, supernaturally fast, its velocity actually shocking, for a shock came with it. It was exceedingly small, it was exceedingly dreadful, its head erect and venomous and the movement of its legs and arms, as of its bitter, glittering eyes, aping humanity. Malignant evil, personified and aggressive, shaped itself in this otherwise ridiculous outline.

It was the doll.

Racing with incredible security across the slippery surface of the crumpled silk counterpane, it dived and climbed and shot forward with an appearance of complete control and deliberate purpose. That it had a definite aim was overwhelmingly obvious. Its fixed, glassy eyes were concentrated upon a point beyond and behind the terrified governess, the point precisely where Colonel Masters, her employer, stood against her shoulder.

A frantic, half protective movement on her part, seemed lost in the air...

She turned instinctively, putting an arm about his shoulders, which he instantly flung off.

"Let the bloody thing come," he cried. "I'll deal with it...!" He thrust her violently aside.

The doll came at him. The hinges of its diminutive broken arms and its jointed legs emitted a thin, creaking sound as it came darting – the syllables Madame Jodzka had already heard more than once. Syllables she had heard without understanding – "*buth laga*" – but syllables now packed with awful meaning: *Revenge*.

The sounds hissed and squeaked, yet clear as a bell as the beast advanced at this miraculous speed.

Before Colonel Masters could move an inch backwards or forwards in self protection, before he could command himself to any sort of action, or contrive the smallest measure of self defence, it was off the bed and at him. It settled. Savagely, its little jaws of tiny make-believe were bitten deep into Colonel Masters' throat, fastened tightly.

In a flash this happened, in a flash it was over. In Madame Jodzka's memory it remained like the impression of a lightning flash, simultaneously etched in black and white. It had happened in the present as though it had no past. It came and was gone again. Her faculties, as after a vivid lightning flash, were momentarily paralysed, without past or present. She had witnessed these awful things, but had not realised them. It was this lack of realisation that struck her motionless and dumb.

Colonel Masters, on the other hand, stood beside her quietly as though nothing unusual had happened, wholly master of himself, calm, collected. At the moment of attack no sound had left his lips, there had been no gesture even of defence. Whatever had come, he had apparently accepted. The words that now fell from his lips were, thus, all the more dreadful in their appalling commonplaceness.

"Hadn't you better put that counterpane, straight a bit... Perhaps?"

Common sense, as always, enables the gas of hysteria to escape. Madame Jodzka gasped, but she obeyed. Automatically she moved across to do his bidding, yet aware, even as she thus moved, that he flicked something from his neck, as though a wasp, a mosquito, or some poisonous insect, had tried to sting him. She remembered no more than that, for he, in his calmness, had contributed nothing else.

Fumbling with the folds of slippery counterpane she tried to straighten out, she was startled to find that Monica was sitting up in bed, awake.

"Oh, Doska – you here!" the child exclaimed innocently, straight out of sleep and using the affectionate nickname. "And Daddy, too! Oh, my goodness...!"

"Sm-moothing your bed, darling," she stammered, hardly aware of what she said. "You ought to be asleep. I just looked in to see..." She mumbled a few other automatic words.

"And Daddy with you!" repeated the child excitedly, sleep still about her, wondering what it all meant. "Ooh! Ooh!" holding out her arms.

This brief exchange of spoken words, though it takes a minute to describe, occurred simultaneously with the action – perhaps ten seconds all told, for while the governess fumbled with the counter-pane, Colonel Masters was in the act of brushing something from his neck. Nothing else was audible, nothing but his quick gasp and sudden intake of breath: but something else – she swears it on her Warsaw priest – was visible. Madame Jodzka maintains by all her gods she saw this other thing.

In moments of paralysing stress it is not the senses that act less speedily nor with less precision; their action, on the contrary, is intensified and speeded up: what takes longer is the registration of their reports. The numbed brain causes the apparent delay; realisation is slowed down.

Madame Jodzka thus only realised a fraction of a second later what her eyes had indubitably witnessed; a dark-skinned arm slanting in through the open window by the bed and snatching at a small object that lay on the floor after dropping from Colonel Masters' throat, then withdrawing again at lightning speed into the darkness of the night outside.

No one but herself, apparently, had seen this – it was almost supernaturally swift.

"And now you'll be asleep again in two minutes, lucky Monica," Colonel Masters was whispering over by the bed. "I just peeped in to see that you were all right…" His voice was thin, dreadfully soundless.

Madame Jodzka, against the door, frozen, terrified, looked on and listened.

"Are you quite well, Daddy? Sure? I had a dream, but it's gone now."

"Splendid. Never better in my life. But better still if I saw you sound asleep. Come now. I'll blow out this silly night-light, for that's what woke you up, I'll be bound."

He blew it out, he and the child blew it out together, the latter with sleepy laughter that then hushed. And Colonel Masters tiptoed to join Madame Jodzka at the door. "A lot of damned fuss about nothing," she heard him muttering in that same thin dreadful voice, and then, as they closed the door and stood a moment in the darkened passage, he did suddenly an unexpected thing. He took the Polish woman in his arms, held her fiercely to him for a second, kissed her vehemently, and flung her away.

"Bless you and thank you," he said in a low, angry voice. "You did your best. You made a great fight. But I got what I deserved. I've been waiting years for it." And he was off down the stairs to his own quarters. Half way down he stopped and looked up to where she stood against the rails. "Tell the doctor," he whispered hoarsely, "that I took a sleeping draught – an overdose." And he was gone.

* * *

And this was, roughly, what she did tell the doctor next morning when a hurried telephone summons brought him to the bed whereon a dead man lay with a swollen, blackened tongue. She told the same tale at the inquest too and an emptied bottle of a powerful sleeping-draught supported her…

And Monica, too young to realise grief beyond its trumpery meaning of a selfishly felt loss, never once – oddly enough – referred to the absence of her lovely doll that had comforted so many hours, proved such an intimate companion day and night in a life that held no other playmates. It seemed forgotten, expunged utterly, from her memory, as though it had never existed at all. She stared blankly, stupidly, when a doll was mentioned: she preferred her worn-out teddy bears. The slate of memory in this particular, was wiped clean.

"They're so warm and comfy," she described her bears, "and they cuddle without tickling. Besides," she added innocently, "they don't squeak and try to slip away…"

Thus in the suburbs, where great spaces between the lamps go dead at night, where the moist wind comes whispering through the mournful branches of the silver-pines, where nothing happens and people cry "Let's go to town!" there are occasional stirrings among the dead dry bones that hide behind respectable villa walls...

**If you enjoyed this, you might also like...**
The Kit-Bag, see page 400
The Damned, see page 414

# Weird Realities

# Smith: An Episode in a Lodging House

"WHEN I was a medical student," began the doctor, half turning towards his circle of listeners in the firelight, "I came across one or two very curious human beings; but there was one fellow I remember particularly, for he caused me the most vivid, and I think the most uncomfortable, emotions I have ever known.

"For many months I knew Smith only by name as the occupant of the floor above me. Obviously his name meant nothing to me. Moreover I was busy with lectures, reading, cliniques and the like, and had little leisure to devise plans for scraping acquaintance with any of the other lodgers in the house. Then chance brought us curiously together, and this fellow Smith left a deep impression upon me as the result of our first meeting. At the time the strength of this first impression seemed quite inexplicable to me, but looking back at the episode now from a stand-point of greater knowledge I judge the fact to have been that he stirred my curiosity to an unusual degree, and at the same time awakened my sense of horror – whatever that may be in a medical student – about as deeply and permanently as these two emotions were capable of being stirred at all in the particular system and set of nerves called *me*.

"How he knew that I was interested in the study of languages was something I could never explain, but one day, quite unannounced, he came quietly into my room in the evening and asked me point-blank if I knew enough Hebrew to help him in the pronunciation of certain words.

"He caught me along the line of least resistance, and I was greatly flattered to be able to give him the desired information; but it was only when he had thanked me and was gone that I realised I had been in the presence of an unusual individuality. For the life of me I could not quite seize and label the peculiarities of what I felt to be a very striking personality, but it was borne in upon me that he was a man apart from his fellows, a mind that followed a line leading away from ordinary human intercourse and human interests, and into regions that left in his atmosphere something remote, rarefied, chilling.

"The moment he was gone I became conscious of two things – an intense curiosity to know more about this man and what his real interests were, and secondly, the fact that my skin was crawling and that my hair had a tendency to rise."

The doctor paused a moment here to puff hard at his pipe, which, however, had gone out beyond recall without the assistance of a match; and in the deep silence, which testified to the genuine interest of his listeners, someone poked the fire up into a little blaze, and one or two others glanced over their shoulders into the dark distances of the big hall.

"On looking back," he went on, watching the momentary flames in the grate, "I see a short, thick-set man of perhaps forty-five, with immense shoulders and small, slender hands. The contrast was noticeable, for I remember thinking that such a giant frame and such slim finger bones hardly belonged together. His head, too, was large and very long, the head of an idealist beyond all question, yet with an unusually strong development of the jaw and chin. Here again was a singular contradiction, though I am better able now to appreciate its full meaning, with a greater experience in judging the values of physiognomy. For this meant, of course, an enthusiastic idealism balanced and kept in check by will and judgment – elements usually deficient in dreamers and visionaries.

"At any rate, here was a being with probably a very wide range of possibilities, a machine with a pendulum that most likely had an unusual length of swing.

"The man's hair was exceedingly fine, and the lines about his nose and mouth were cut as with a delicate steel instrument in wax. His eyes I have left to the last. They were large and quite changeable, not in colour only, but in character, size, and shape. Occasionally they seemed the eyes of someone else, if you can understand what I mean, and at the same time, in their shifting shades of blue, green, and a nameless sort of dark grey, there was a sinister light in them that lent to the whole face an aspect almost alarming. Moreover, they were the most luminous optics I think I have ever seen in any human being.

"There, then, at the risk of a wearisome description, is Smith as I saw him for the first time that winter's evening in my shabby student's rooms in Edinburgh. And yet the real part of him, of course, I have left untouched, for it is both indescribable and un-get-atable. I have spoken already of an atmosphere of warning and aloofness he carried about with him. It is impossible further to analyse the series of little shocks his presence always communicated to my being; but there was that about him which made me instantly on the *qui vive* in his presence, every nerve alert, every sense strained and on the watch. I do not mean that he deliberately suggested danger, but rather that he brought forces in his wake which automatically warned the nervous centres of my system to be on their guard and alert.

"Since the days of my first acquaintance with this man I have lived through other experiences and have seen much I cannot pretend to explain or understand; but, so far in my life, I have only once come across a human being who suggested a disagreeable familiarity with unholy things, and who made me feel uncanny and 'creepy' in his presence; and that unenviable individual was Mr. Smith.

"What his occupation was during the day I never knew. I think he slept until the sun set. No one ever saw him on the stairs, or heard him move in his room during the day. He was a creature of the shadows, who apparently preferred darkness to light. Our landlady either knew nothing, or would say nothing. At any rate she found no fault, and I have since wondered often by what magic this fellow was able to convert a common landlady of a common lodging-house into a discreet and uncommunicative person. This alone was a sign of genius of some sort.

"'He's been here with me for years – long before you come, an' I don't interfere or ask no questions of what doesn't concern me, as long as people pays their rent,' was the only remark on the subject that I ever succeeded in winning from that quarter, and it certainly told me nothing nor gave me any encouragement to ask for further information.

"Examinations, however, and the general excitement of a medical student's life for a time put Mr. Smith completely out of my head. For a long period he did not call upon me again, and for my part, I felt no courage to return his unsolicited visit.

"Just then, however, there came a change in the fortunes of those who controlled my very limited income, and I was obliged to give up my ground-floor and move aloft to more modest chambers on the top of the house. Here I was directly over Smith, and had to pass his door to reach my own.

"It so happened that about this time I was frequently called out at all hours of the night for the maternity cases which a fourth-year student takes at a certain period of his studies, and on returning from one of these visits at about two o'clock in the morning I was surprised to hear the sound of voices as I passed his door. A peculiar sweet odour, too, not unlike the smell of incense, penetrated into the passage.

"I went upstairs very quietly, wondering what was going on there at this hour of the morning. To my knowledge Smith never had visitors. For a moment I hesitated outside the door with one foot on the stairs. All my interest in this strange man revived, and my curiosity rose to a point not far from action. At last I might learn something of the habits of this lover of the night and the darkness.

"The sound of voices was plainly audible, Smith's predominating so much that I never could catch more than points of sound from the other, penetrating now and then the steady stream of his voice. Not a single word reached me, at least, not a word that I could understand, though the voice was loud and distinct, and it was only afterwards that I realised he must have been speaking in a foreign language.

"The sound of footsteps, too, was equally distinct. Two persons were moving about the room, passing and repassing the door, one of them a light, agile person, and the other ponderous and somewhat awkward. Smith's voice went on incessantly with its odd, monotonous droning, now loud, now soft, as he crossed and re-crossed the floor. The other person was also on the move, but in a different and less regular fashion, for I heard rapid steps that seemed to end sometimes in stumbling, and quick sudden movements that brought up with a violent lurching against the wall or furniture.

"As I listened to Smith's voice, moreover, I began to feel afraid. There was something in the sound that made me feel intuitively he was in a tight place, and an impulse stirred faintly in me – very faintly, I admit – to knock at the door and inquire if he needed help.

"But long before the impulse could translate itself into an act, or even before it had been properly weighed and considered by the mind, I heard a voice close beside me in the air, a sort of hushed whisper which I am certain was Smith speaking, though the sound did not seem to have come to me through the door. It was close in my very ear, as though he stood beside me, and it gave me such a start, that I clutched the banisters to save myself from stepping backwards and making a clatter on the stairs.

"'There is nothing you can do to help me,' it said distinctly, 'and you will be much safer in your own room.'

"I am ashamed to this day of the pace at which I covered the flight of stairs in the darkness to the top floor, and of the shaking hand with which I lit my candles and bolted the door. But, there it is, just as it happened.

"This midnight episode, so odd and yet so trivial in itself, fired me with more curiosity than ever about my fellow-lodger. It also made me connect him in my mind with a sense of fear and distrust. I never saw him, yet I was often, and uncomfortably, aware of his presence in the upper regions of that gloomy lodging-house. Smith and his secret mode of life and mysterious pursuits, somehow contrived to awaken in my being a line of reflection that disturbed my comfortable condition of ignorance. I never saw him, as I have said, and exchanged no sort of communication with him, yet it seemed to me that his mind was in contact with mine, and some of the strange forces of his atmosphere filtered through into my being and disturbed my equilibrium. Those upper floors became haunted for me after dark, and, though outwardly our lives never came into contact, I became unwillingly involved in certain pursuits on which his mind was centred. I felt that he was somehow making use of me against my will, and by methods which passed my comprehension.

"I was at that time, moreover, in the heavy, unquestioning state of materialism which is common to medical students when they begin to understand something of the human anatomy and nervous system, and jump at once to the conclusion that they control the universe and hold in their forceps the last word of life and death. I 'knew it all', and regarded a belief in anything beyond matter as the wanderings of weak, or at best, untrained minds. And this condition of mind, of course, added to the strength of this upsetting fear which emanated from the floor below and began slowly to take possession of me.

"Though I kept no notes of the subsequent events in this matter, they made too deep an impression for me ever to forget the sequence in which they occurred. Without difficulty I can recall the next step in the adventure with Smith, for adventure it rapidly grew to be."

The doctor stopped a moment and laid his pipe on the table behind him before continuing. The fire had burned low, and no one stirred to poke it. The silence in the great hall was so deep that when the speaker's pipe touched the table the sound woke audible echoes at the far end among the shadows.

"One evening, while I was reading, the door of my room opened and Smith came in. He made no attempt at ceremony. It was after ten o'clock and I was tired, but the presence of the man immediately galvanised me into activity. My attempts at ordinary politeness he thrust on one side at once, and began asking me to vocalise, and then pronounce for him, certain Hebrew words; and when this was done he abruptly inquired if I was not the fortunate possessor of a very rare Rabbinical Treatise, which he named.

"How he knew that I possessed this book puzzled me exceedingly; but I was still more surprised to see him cross the room and take it out of my book-shelf almost before I had had time to answer in the affirmative. Evidently he knew exactly where it was kept. This excited my curiosity beyond all bounds, and I immediately began asking him questions; and though, out of sheer respect for the man, I put them very delicately to him, and almost by way of mere conversation, he had only one reply for the lot. He would look up at me from the pages of the book with an expression of complete comprehension on his extraordinary features, would bow his head a little and say very gravely –

"'That, of course, is a perfectly proper question,' – which was absolutely all I could ever get out of him.

"On this particular occasion he stayed with me perhaps ten or fifteen minutes. Then he went quickly downstairs to his room with my Hebrew Treatise in his hand, and I heard him close and bolt his door.

"But a few moments later, before I had time to settle down to my book again, or to recover from the surprise his visit had caused me, I heard the door open, and there stood Smith once again beside my chair. He made no excuse for his second interruption, but bent his head down to the level of my reading lamp and peered across the flame straight into my eyes.

"'I hope,' he whispered, 'I hope you are never disturbed at night?'

"'Eh?' I stammered, 'disturbed at night? Oh no, thanks, at least, not that I know of—'

"'I'm glad,' he replied gravely, appearing not to notice my confusion and surprise at his question. 'But, remember, should it ever be the case, please let me know at once.'

"And he was gone down the stairs and into his room again.

"For some minutes I sat reflecting upon his strange behaviour. He was not mad, I argued, but was the victim of some harmless delusion that had gradually grown upon him as a result of his solitary mode of life; and from the books he used, I judged that it had something to do with medieval magic, or some system of ancient Hebrew mysticism. The words he asked me to pronounce for him were probably 'Words of Power', which, when uttered with the vehemence of a strong will behind them, were supposed to produce physical results, or set up vibrations in one's own inner being that had the effect of a partial lifting of the veil.

"I sat thinking about the man, and his way of living, and the probable effects in the long-run of his dangerous experiments, and I can recall perfectly well the sensation of disappointment that crept over me when I realised that I had labelled his particular form of aberration, and that my curiosity would therefore no longer be excited.

"For some time I had been sitting alone with these reflections – it may have been ten minutes or it may have been half an hour – when I was aroused from my reverie by the knowledge that someone was again in the room standing close beside my chair. My first thought was that Smith had come back again in his swift, unaccountable manner, but almost at the same moment I realised that this could not be the case at all. For the door faced my position, and it certainly had not been opened again.

"Yet, someone was in the room, moving cautiously to and fro, watching me, almost touching me. I was as sure of it as I was of myself, and though at the moment I do not think I was actually afraid, I am bound to admit that a certain weakness came over me and that I felt that strange disinclination for action which is probably the beginning of the horrible paralysis of real terror. I should have been glad to hide myself, if that had been possible, to cower into a corner, or behind a door, or anywhere so that I could not be watched and observed.

"But, overcoming my nervousness with an effort of the will, I got up quickly out of my chair and held the reading lamp aloft so that it shone into all the corners like a searchlight.

"The room was utterly empty! It was utterly empty, at least, to the *eye*, but to the nerves, and especially to that combination of sense perception which is made up by all the senses acting together, and by no one in particular, there was a person standing there at my very elbow.

"I say 'person', for I can think of no appropriate word. For, if it *was* a human being, I can only affirm that I had the overwhelming conviction that it was *not*, but that it was some form of life wholly unknown to me both as to its essence and its nature. A sensation of gigantic force and power came with it, and I remember vividly to this day my terror on realising that I was close to an invisible being who could crush me as easily as I could crush a fly, and who could see my every movement while itself remaining invisible.

"To this terror was added the certain knowledge that the 'being' kept in my proximity for a definite purpose. And that this purpose had some direct bearing upon my well-being, indeed upon my life, I was equally convinced; for I became aware of a sensation of growing lassitude as though the vitality were being steadily drained out of my body. My heart began to beat irregularly at first, then faintly. I was conscious, even within a few minutes, of a general drooping of the powers of life in the whole system, an ebbing away of self-control, and a distinct approach of drowsiness and torpor.

"The power to move, or to think out any mode of resistance, was fast leaving me, when there rose, in the distance as it were, a tremendous commotion. A door opened with a clatter, and I heard the peremptory and commanding tones of a human voice calling aloud in a language I could not comprehend. It was Smith, my fellow-lodger, calling up the stairs; and his voice had not sounded for more than a few seconds, when I felt something withdrawn from my presence, from my person, indeed from my *very skin*. It seemed as if there was a rushing of air and some large creature swept by me at about the level of my shoulders. Instantly the pressure on my heart was relieved, and the atmosphere seemed to resume its normal condition.

"Smith's door closed quietly downstairs, as I put the lamp down with trembling hands. What had happened I do not know; only, I was alone again and my strength was returning as rapidly as it had left me.

"I went across the room and examined myself in the glass. The skin was very pale, and the eyes dull. My temperature, I found, was a little below normal and my pulse faint and irregular. But these smaller signs of disturbance were as nothing compared with the feeling I had – though no outward signs bore testimony to the fact – that I had narrowly escaped a real and ghastly catastrophe. I felt shaken, somehow, shaken to the very roots of my being."

The doctor rose from his chair and crossed over to the dying fire, so that no one could see the expression on his face as he stood with his back to the grate, and continued his weird tale.

"It would be wearisome," he went on in a lower voice, looking over our heads as though he still saw the dingy top floor of that haunted Edinburgh lodging-house; "it would be tedious for me at this length of time to analyse my feelings, or attempt to reproduce for you the thorough examination to which I endeavoured then to subject my whole being, intellectual, emotional, and physical. I need only mention the dominant emotion with which this curious episode left me – the indignant anger against myself that I could ever have lost my self-control enough to come under the sway of so gross and absurd a delusion. This protest, however, I remember making with all the emphasis possible. And I also remember noting that it brought me very little satisfaction, for it was the protest of my reason only, when all the rest of my being was up in arms against its conclusions.

"My dealings with the 'delusion', however, were not yet over for the night; for very early next morning, somewhere about three o'clock, I was awakened by a curiously stealthy noise in the room, and the next minute there followed a crash as if all my books had been swept bodily from their shelf on to the floor.

"But this time I was not frightened. Cursing the disturbance with all the resounding and harmless words I could accumulate, I jumped out of bed and lit the candle in a second, and in the first dazzle of the flaring match – but before the wick had time to catch – I was certain I *saw* a dark grey shadow, of ungainly shape, and with something more or less like a human head, drive rapidly past the side of the wall farthest from me and disappear into the gloom by the angle of the door.

"I waited one single second to be sure the candle was alight, and then dashed after it, but before I had gone two steps, my foot stumbled against something hard piled up on the carpet and I only just saved myself from falling headlong. I picked myself up and found that all the books from what I called my 'language shelf' were strewn across the floor. The room, meanwhile, as a minute's search revealed, was quite empty. I looked in every corner and behind every stick of furniture, and a student's bedroom on a top floor, costing twelve shillings a week, did not hold many available hiding-places, as you may imagine.

"The crash, however, was explained. Some very practical and physical force had thrown the books from their resting-place. That, at least, was beyond all doubt. And as I replaced them on the shelf and noted that not one was missing, I busied myself mentally with the sore problem of how the agent of this little practical joke had gained access to my room, and then escaped again. *For my door was locked and bolted.*

"Smith's odd question as to whether I was disturbed in the night, and his warning injunction to let him know at once if such were the case, now of course returned to affect me as I stood there in the early morning, cold and shivering on the carpet; but I realised at the same moment how impossible it would be for me to admit that a more than usually vivid nightmare could have any connection with himself. I would rather stand a hundred of these mysterious visitations than consult such a man as to their possible cause.

"A knock at the door interrupted my reflections, and I gave a start that sent the candle grease flying.

"'Let me in,' came in Smith's voice.

"I unlocked the door. He came in fully dressed. His face wore a curious pallor. It seemed to me to be under the skin and to shine through and almost make it luminous. His eyes were exceedingly bright.

"I was wondering what in the world to say to him, or how he would explain his visit at such an hour, when he closed the door behind him and came close up to me – uncomfortably close.

"'You should have called me at once,' he said in his whispering voice, fixing his great eyes on my face.

"I stammered something about an awful dream, but he ignored my remark utterly, and I caught his eye wandering next – if any movement of those optics can be described as 'wandering' – to the book-shelf. I watched him, unable to move my gaze from his person. The man fascinated me horribly for some reason. Why, in the devil's name, was he up and dressed at three in the morning? How did he know anything had happened unusual in my room? Then his whisper began again.

"'It's your amazing vitality that causes you this annoyance,' he said, shifting his eyes back to mine.

"I gasped. Something in his voice or manner turned my blood into ice.

"'That's the real attraction,' he went on. 'But if this continues one of us will have to leave, you know.'

"I positively could not find a word to say in reply. The channels of speech dried up within me. I simply stared and wondered what he would say next. I watched him in a sort of dream, and as far as I can remember, he asked me to promise to call him sooner another time, and then began to walk round the room, uttering strange sounds, and making signs with his arms and hands until he reached the door. Then he was gone in a second, and I had closed and locked the door behind him.

"After this, the Smith adventure drew rapidly to a climax. It was a week or two later, and I was coming home between two and three in the morning from a maternity case, certain features of which for the time being had very much taken possession of my mind, so much so, indeed, that I passed Smith's door without giving him a single thought.

"The gas jet on the landing was still burning, but so low that it made little impression on the waves of deep shadow that lay across the stairs. Overhead, the faintest possible gleam of grey showed that the morning was not far away. A few stars shone down through the sky-light. The house was still as the grave, and the only sound to break the silence was the rushing of the wind round the walls and over the roof. But this was a fitful sound, suddenly rising and as suddenly falling away again, and it only served to intensify the silence.

"I had already reached my own landing when I gave a violent start. It was automatic, almost a reflex action in fact, for it was only when I caught myself fumbling at the door handle and thinking where I could conceal myself quickest that I realised a voice had sounded close beside me in the air. It was the same voice I had heard before, and it seemed to me to be calling for help. And yet the very same minute I pushed on into the room, determined to disregard it, and seeking to persuade myself it was the creaking of the boards under my weight or the rushing noise of the wind that had deceived me.

"But hardly had I reached the table where the candles stood when the sound was unmistakably repeated: 'Help! help!' And this time it was accompanied by what I can only describe as a vivid tactile hallucination. I was touched: the *skin* of my arm was clutched by fingers.

"Some compelling force sent me headlong downstairs as if the haunting forces of the whole world were at my heels. At Smith's door I paused. The force of his previous warning injunction to seek his aid without delay acted suddenly and I leant my whole weight against the panels, little dreaming that I should be called upon to give help rather than to receive it.

"The door yielded at once, and I burst into a room that was so full of a choking vapour, moving in slow clouds, that at first I could distinguish nothing at all but a set of what seemed to be huge shadows passing in and out of the mist. Then, gradually, I perceived that a red lamp on the mantelpiece gave all the light there was, and that the room which I now entered for the first time was almost empty of furniture.

"The carpet was rolled back and piled in a heap in the corner, and upon the white boards of the floor I noticed a large circle drawn in black of some material that emitted a faint glowing light and was apparently smoking. Inside this circle, as well as at regular intervals outside it, were curious-looking designs, also traced in the same black, smoking substance. These, too, seemed to emit a feeble light of their own.

"My first impression on entering the room had been that it was full of – *people*, I was going to say; but that hardly expresses my meaning. *Beings*, they certainly were, but it was borne in upon me beyond the possibility of doubt, that they were not human beings. That I had caught a momentary glimpse of living, intelligent entities I can never doubt, but I am equally convinced, though I cannot prove it, that these entities were from some other scheme of evolution altogether, and had nothing to do with the ordinary human life, either incarnate or discarnate.

"But, whatever they were, the visible appearance of them was exceedingly fleeting. I no longer saw anything, though I still felt convinced of their immediate presence. They were, moreover, of the same order of life as the visitant in my bedroom of a few nights before, and their proximity to my atmosphere in numbers, instead of singly as before, conveyed to my mind something that was quite terrible and overwhelming. I fell into a violent trembling, and the perspiration poured from my face in streams.

"They were in constant motion about me. They stood close to my side; moved behind me; brushed past my shoulder; stirred the hair on my forehead; and circled round me without ever actually touching me, yet always pressing closer and closer. Especially in the air just over my head there seemed ceaseless movement, and it was accompanied by a confused noise of whispering and sighing that threatened every moment to become articulate in words. To my intense relief, however, I heard no distinct words, and the noise continued more like the rising and falling of the wind than anything else I can imagine.

"But the characteristic of these 'Beings' that impressed me most strongly at the time, and of which I have carried away the most permanent recollection, was that each one of them possessed what seemed to be a *vibrating centre* which impelled it with tremendous force and caused a rapid whirling motion of the atmosphere as it passed me. The air was full of these little vortices of whirring, rotating force, and whenever one of them pressed me too closely I felt as if the nerves in that particular portion of my body had been literally drawn out, absolutely depleted of vitality, and then immediately replaced – but replaced dead, flabby, useless.

"Then, suddenly, for the first time my eyes fell upon Smith. He was crouching against the wall on my right, in an attitude that was obviously defensive, and it was plain he was in extremities. The terror on his face was pitiable, but at the same time there was another expression about the tightly clenched teeth and mouth which showed that he had not lost all control of himself. He wore the most resolute expression I have ever seen on a human countenance, and, though for the moment at a fearful disadvantage, he looked like a man who had confidence in himself, and, in spite of the working of fear, was waiting his opportunity.

"For my part, I was face to face with a situation so utterly beyond my knowledge and comprehension, that I felt as helpless as a child, and as useless.

"'Help me back – quick – into that circle,' I heard him half cry, half whisper to me across the moving vapours.

"My only value appears to have been that I was not afraid to act. Knowing nothing of the forces I was dealing with I had no idea of the deadly perils risked, and I sprang forward and caught him by the arms. He threw all his weight in my direction, and by our combined efforts his body left the wall and lurched across the floor towards the circle.

"Instantly there descended upon us, out of the empty air of that smoke-laden room, a force which I can only compare to the pushing, driving power of a great wind pent up within a narrow space. It was almost explosive in its effect, and it seemed to operate upon all parts of my body equally. It fell upon us with a rushing noise that filled my ears and made me think for a moment the very walls and roof of the building had been torn asunder. Under its first blow we staggered back against the wall, and I understood plainly that its purpose was to prevent us getting back into the circle in the middle of the floor.

"Pouring with perspiration, and breathless, with every muscle strained to the very utmost, we at length managed to get to the edge of the circle, and at this moment, so great was the opposing force, that I felt myself actually torn from Smith's arms, lifted from my feet, and twirled round in the direction of the windows as if the wheel of some great machine had caught my clothes and was tearing me to destruction in its revolution.

"But, even as I fell, bruised and breathless, against the wall, I saw Smith firmly upon his feet in the circle and slowly rising again to an upright position. My eyes never left his figure once in the next few minutes.

"He drew himself up to his full height. His great shoulders squared themselves. His head was thrown back a little, and as I looked I saw the expression on his face change swiftly from fear to one of absolute command. He looked steadily round the room and then his voice began to *vibrate*. At first in a low tone, it gradually rose till it assumed the same volume and intensity I had heard that night when he called up the stairs into my room.

"It was a curiously increasing sound, more like the swelling of an instrument than a human voice; and as it grew in power and filled the room, I became aware that a great change was being effected slowly and surely. The confusion of noise and rushings of air fell into the roll of long, steady vibrations not unlike those caused by the deeper pedals of an organ. The movements in the air became less violent, then grew decidedly weaker, and finally ceased altogether. The whisperings and sighings became fainter and fainter, till at last I could not hear them at all; and, strangest of all, the light emitted by the circle, as well as by the designs round it, increased to a steady glow, casting their radiance upwards with the weirdest possible effect upon his features. Slowly, by the power of his voice, behind which lay undoubtedly a genuine knowledge of the occult manipulation of sound, this man dominated the forces that had escaped from their proper sphere, until at length the room was reduced to silence and perfect order again.

"Judging by the immense relief which also communicated itself to my nerves I then felt that the crisis was over and Smith was wholly master of the situation.

"But hardly had I begun to congratulate myself upon this result, and to gather my scattered senses about me, when, uttering a loud cry, I saw him leap out of the circle and fling himself into the air – as it seemed to me, into the empty air. Then, even while holding my breath for dread of the crash he was bound to come upon the floor, I saw him strike with a dull thud against a solid body in mid-air, and the next instant he was wrestling with some ponderous thing that was absolutely invisible to me, and the room shook with the struggle.

"To and fro *they* swayed, sometimes lurching in one direction, sometimes in another, and always in horrible proximity to myself, as I leaned trembling against the wall and watched the encounter.

"It lasted at most but a short minute or two, ending as suddenly as it had begun. Smith, with an unexpected movement, threw up his arms with a cry of relief. At the same instant there was a wild, tearing shriek in the air beside me and something rushed past us with a noise like the passage of a flock of big birds. Both windows rattled as if they would break away from their sashes. Then a sense of emptiness and peace suddenly came over the room, and I knew that all was over.

"Smith, his face exceedingly white, but otherwise strangely composed, turned to me at once.

"'God! – if you hadn't come – You deflected the stream; broke it up—' he whispered. 'You saved me.'"

The doctor made a long pause. Presently he felt for his pipe in the darkness, groping over the table behind us with both hands. No one spoke for a bit, but all dreaded the sudden glare that would come when he struck the match. The fire was nearly out and the great hall was pitch dark.

But the story-teller did not strike that match. He was merely gaining time for some hidden reason of his own. And presently he went on with his tale in a more subdued voice.

"I quite forget," he said, "how I got back to my own room. I only know that I lay with two lighted candles for the rest of the night, and the first thing I did in the morning was to let the landlady know I was leaving her house at the end of the week.

"Smith still has my Rabbinical Treatise. At least he did not return it to me at the time, and I have never seen him since to ask for it."

**If you enjoyed this, you might also like...**
The Listener, see page 382
Secret Worship, see page 275

# Ancient Sorceries

## Chapter I

**THERE ARE**, it would appear, certain wholly unremarkable persons, with none of the characteristics that invite adventure, who yet once or twice in the course of their smooth lives undergo an experience so strange that the world catches its breath – and looks the other way! And it was cases of this kind, perhaps, more than any other, that fell into the wide-spread net of John Silence, the psychic doctor, and, appealing to his deep humanity, to his patience, and to his great qualities of spiritual sympathy, led often to the revelation of problems of the strangest complexity, and of the profoundest possible human interest.

Matters that seemed almost too curious and fantastic for belief he loved to trace to their hidden sources. To unravel a tangle in the very soul of things – and to release a suffering human soul in the process – was with him a veritable passion. And the knots he untied were, indeed, after passing strange.

The world, of course, asks for some plausible basis to which it can attach credence – something it can, at least, pretend to explain. The adventurous type it can understand: such people carry about with them an adequate explanation of their exciting lives, and their characters obviously drive them into the circumstances which produce the adventures. It expects nothing else from them, and is satisfied. But dull, ordinary folk have no right to out-of-the-way experiences, and the world having been led to expect otherwise, is disappointed with them, not to say shocked. Its complacent judgment has been rudely disturbed.

"Such a thing happened to *that* man!" it cries – "a commonplace person like that! It is too absurd! There must be something wrong!"

Yet there could be no question that something did actually happen to little Arthur Vezin, something of the curious nature he described to Dr. Silence. Outwardly or inwardly, it happened beyond a doubt, and in spite of the jeers of his few friends who heard the tale, and observed wisely that "such a thing might perhaps have come to Iszard, that crack-brained Iszard, or to that odd fish Minski, but it could never have happened to commonplace little Vezin, who was fore-ordained to live and die according to scale."

But, whatever his method of death was, Vezin certainly did not 'live according to scale' so far as this particular event in his otherwise uneventful life was concerned; and to hear him recount it, and watch his pale delicate features change, and hear his voice grow softer and more hushed as he proceeded, was to know the conviction that his halting words perhaps failed sometimes to convey. He lived the thing over again each time he told it. His whole personality became muffled in the recital. It subdued him more than ever, so that the tale became a lengthy apology for an experience that he deprecated. He appeared to excuse himself and ask your pardon for having dared to take part in so fantastic an episode. For little Vezin was a timid, gentle, sensitive soul, rarely able to assert himself, tender to man and beast, and almost constitutionally unable to say No, or to claim many things that should rightly have been his. His whole scheme of life seemed utterly remote from anything more exciting than missing a train or losing an umbrella on an omnibus. And when this curious event came upon him he was already more years beyond forty than his friends suspected or he cared to admit.

John Silence, who heard him speak of his experience more than once, said that he sometimes left out certain details and put in others; yet they were all obviously true. The whole scene was unforgettably cinematographed on to his mind. None of the details were imagined or invented. And when he told the story with them all complete, the effect was undeniable. His appealing brown eyes shone, and much of the charming personality, usually so carefully repressed, came forward and revealed itself. His modesty was always there, of course, but in the telling he forgot the present and allowed himself to appear almost vividly as he lived again in the past of his adventure.

He was on the way home when it happened, crossing northern France from some mountain trip or other where he buried himself solitary-wise every summer. He had nothing but an unregistered bag in the rack, and the train was jammed to suffocation, most of the passengers being unredeemed holiday English. He disliked them, not because they were his fellow-countrymen, but because they were noisy and obtrusive, obliterating with their big limbs and tweed clothing all the quieter tints of the day that brought him satisfaction and enabled him to melt into insignificance and forget that he was anybody. These English clashed about him like a brass band, making him feel vaguely that he ought to be more self-assertive and obstreperous, and that he did not claim insistently enough all kinds of things that he didn't want and that were really valueless, such as corner seats, windows up or down, and so forth.

So that he felt uncomfortable in the train, and wished the journey were over and he was back again living with his unmarried sister in Surbiton.

And when the train stopped for ten panting minutes at the little station in northern France, and he got out to stretch his legs on the platform, and saw to his dismay a further batch of the British Isles debouching from another train, it suddenly seemed impossible to him to continue the journey. Even *his* flabby soul revolted, and the idea of staying a night in the little town and going on next day by a slower, emptier train, flashed into his mind. The guard was already shouting "*en voiture*" and the corridor of his compartment was already packed when the thought came to him. And, for once, he acted with decision and rushed to snatch his bag.

Finding the corridor and steps impassable, he tapped at the window (for he had a corner seat) and begged the Frenchman who sat opposite to hand his luggage out to him, explaining in his wretched French that he intended to break the journey there. And this elderly Frenchman, he declared, gave him a look, half of warning, half of reproach, that to his dying day he could never forget; handed the bag through the window of the moving train; and at the same time poured into his ears a long sentence, spoken rapidly and low, of which he was able to comprehend only the last few words: "*à cause du sommeil et à cause des chats.*"

In reply to Dr. Silence, whose singular psychic acuteness at once seized upon this Frenchman as a vital point in the adventure, Vezin admitted that the man had impressed him favourably from the beginning, though without being able to explain why. They had sat facing one another during the four hours of the journey, and though no conversation had passed between them – Vezin was timid about his stuttering French – he confessed that his eyes were being continually drawn to his face, almost, he felt, to rudeness, and that each, by a dozen nameless little politenesses and attentions, had evinced the desire to be kind. The men liked each other and their personalities did not clash, or would not have clashed had they chanced to come to terms of acquaintance. The Frenchman, indeed, seemed to have exercised a silent protective influence over the insignificant little Englishman, and without words or gestures betrayed that he wished him well and would gladly have been of service to him.

"And this sentence that he hurled at you after the bag?" asked John Silence, smiling that peculiarly sympathetic smile that always melted the prejudices of his patient, "were you unable to follow it exactly?"

"It was so quick and low and vehement," explained Vezin, in his small voice, "that I missed practically the whole of it. I only caught the few words at the very end, because he spoke them so clearly, and his face was bent down out of the carriage window so near to mine."

"'À cause du sommeil et à cause des chats'?" repeated Dr. Silence, as though half speaking to himself.

"That's it exactly," said Vezin; "which, I take it, means something like 'because of sleep and because of the cats', doesn't it?"

"Certainly, that's how I should translate it," the doctor observed shortly, evidently not wishing to interrupt more than necessary.

"And the rest of the sentence – all the first part I couldn't understand, I mean – was a warning not to do something – not to stop in the town, or at some particular place in the town, perhaps. That was the impression it made on me."

Then, of course, the train rushed off, and left Vezin standing on the platform alone and rather forlorn.

The little town climbed in straggling fashion up a sharp hill rising out of the plain at the back of the station, and was crowned by the twin towers of the ruined cathedral peeping over the summit. From the station itself it looked uninteresting and modern, but the fact was that the medieval position lay out of sight just beyond the crest. And once he reached the top and entered the old streets, he stepped clean out of modern life into a bygone century. The noise and bustle of the crowded train seemed days away. The spirit of this silent hill-town, remote from tourists and motor-cars, dreaming its own quiet life under the autumn sun, rose up and cast its spell upon him. Long before he recognised this spell he acted under it. He walked softly, almost on tiptoe, down the winding narrow streets where the gables all but met over his head, and he entered the doorway of the solitary inn with a deprecating and modest demeanour that was in itself an apology for intruding upon the place and disturbing its dream.

At first, however, Vezin said, he noticed very little of all this. The attempt at analysis came much later. What struck him then was only the delightful contrast of the silence and peace after the dust and noisy rattle of the train. He felt soothed and stroked like a cat.

"Like a cat, you said?" interrupted John Silence, quickly catching him up.

"Yes. At the very start I felt that." He laughed apologetically. "I felt as though the warmth and the stillness and the comfort made me purr. It seemed to be the general mood of the whole place – then."

The inn, a rambling ancient house, the atmosphere of the old coaching days still about it, apparently did not welcome him too warmly. He felt he was only tolerated, he said. But it was cheap and comfortable, and the delicious cup of afternoon tea he ordered at once made him feel really very pleased with himself for leaving the train in this bold, original way. For to him it had seemed bold and original. He felt something of a dog. His room, too, soothed him with its dark panelling and low irregular ceiling, and the long sloping passage that led to it seemed the natural pathway to a real Chamber of Sleep – a little dim cubby hole out of the world where noise could not enter. It looked upon the courtyard at the back. It was all very charming, and made him think of himself as dressed in very soft velvet somehow, and the floors seemed padded, the walls provided with cushions. The sounds of the streets could not penetrate there. It was an atmosphere of absolute rest that surrounded him.

On engaging the two-franc room he had interviewed the only person who seemed to be about that sleepy afternoon, an elderly waiter with Dundreary whiskers and a drowsy courtesy, who had ambled lazily towards him across the stone yard; but on coming downstairs again for a little promenade in the town before dinner he encountered the proprietress herself. She was a large woman whose hands, feet, and features seemed to swim towards him out of a sea of person. They emerged, so to speak. But she had great dark, vivacious eyes that counteracted the bulk of her body, and betrayed the fact that in reality she was both vigorous and alert. When he first caught sight of her she was knitting in a low chair against the sunlight of the wall, and something at once made him see her as a great tabby cat, dozing, yet awake, heavily sleepy, and yet at the same time prepared for instantaneous action. A great mouser on the watch occurred to him.

She took him in with a single comprehensive glance that was polite without being cordial. Her neck, he noticed, was extraordinarily supple in spite of its proportions, for it turned so easily to follow him, and the head it carried bowed so very flexibly.

"But when she looked at me, you know," said Vezin, with that little apologetic smile in his brown eyes, and that faintly deprecating gesture of the shoulders that was characteristic of him, "the odd notion came to me that really she had intended to make quite a different movement, and that with a single bound she could have leaped at me across the width of that stone yard and pounced upon me like some huge cat upon a mouse."

He laughed a little soft laugh, and Dr. Silence made a note in his book without interrupting, while Vezin proceeded in a tone as though he feared he had already told too much and more than we could believe.

"Very soft, yet very active she was, for all her size and mass, and I felt she knew what I was doing even after I had passed and was behind her back. She spoke to me, and her voice was smooth and running. She asked if I had my luggage, and was comfortable in my room, and then added that dinner was at seven o'clock, and that they were very early people in this little country town. Clearly, she intended to convey that late hours were not encouraged."

Evidently, she contrived by voice and manner to give him the impression that here he would be 'managed', that everything would be arranged and planned for him, and that he had nothing to do but fall into the groove and obey. No decided action or sharp personal effort would be looked for from him. It was the very reverse of the train. He walked quietly out into the street feeling soothed and peaceful. He realised that he was in a *milieu* that suited him and stroked him the right way. It was so much easier to be obedient. He began to purr again, and to feel that all the town purred with him.

About the streets of that little town he meandered gently, falling deeper and deeper into the spirit of repose that characterised it. With no special aim he wandered up and down, and to and fro. The September sunshine fell slantingly over the roofs. Down winding alleyways, fringed with tumbling gables and open casements, he caught fairylike glimpses of the great plain below, and of the meadows and yellow copses lying like a dream-map in the haze. The spell of the past held very potently here, he felt.

The streets were full of picturesquely garbed men and women, all busy enough, going their respective ways; but no one took any notice of him or turned to stare at his obviously English appearance. He was even able to forget that with his tourist appearance he was a false note in a charming picture, and he melted more and more into the scene, feeling delightfully insignificant and unimportant and unselfconscious. It was like becoming part of a softly coloured dream which he did not even realise to be a dream.

On the eastern side the hill fell away more sharply, and the plain below ran off rather suddenly into a sea of gathering shadows in which the little patches of woodland looked like islands and the stubble fields like deep water. Here he strolled along the old ramparts of ancient fortifications that once had been formidable, but now were only vision-like with their charming mingling of broken grey walls and wayward vine and ivy. From the broad coping on which he sat for a moment, level with the rounded tops of clipped plane trees, he saw the esplanade far below lying in shadow. Here and there a yellow sunbeam crept in and lay upon the fallen yellow leaves, and from the height he looked down and saw that the townsfolk were walking to and fro in the cool of the evening. He could just hear the sound of their slow footfalls, and the murmur of their voices floated up to him through the gaps between the trees. The figures looked like shadows as he caught glimpses of their quiet movements far below.

He sat there for some time pondering, bathed in the waves of murmurs and half-lost echoes that rose to his ears, muffled by the leaves of the plane trees. The whole town, and the little hill out of which it grew as naturally as an ancient wood, seemed to him like a being lying there half asleep on the plain and crooning to itself as it dozed.

And, presently, as he sat lazily melting into its dream, a sound of horns and strings and wood instruments rose to his ears, and the town band began to play at the far end of the crowded terrace below to the accompaniment of a very soft, deep-throated drum. Vezin was very sensitive to music, knew about it intelligently, and had even ventured, unknown to his friends, upon the composition of quiet melodies with low-running chords which he played to himself with the soft pedal when no one was about. And this music floating up through the trees from an invisible and doubtless very picturesque band of the townspeople wholly charmed him. He recognised nothing that they played, and it sounded as though they were simply improvising without a conductor. No definitely marked time ran through the pieces, which ended and began oddly after the fashion of wind through an Aeolian harp. It was part of the place and scene, just as the dying sunlight and faintly breathing wind were part of the scene and hour, and the mellow notes of old-fashioned plaintive horns, pierced here and there by the sharper strings, all half smothered by the continuous booming of the deep drum, touched his soul with a curiously potent spell that was almost too engrossing to be quite pleasant.

There was a certain queer sense of bewitchment in it all. The music seemed to him oddly unartificial. It made him think of trees swept by the wind, of night breezes singing among wires and chimney-stacks, or in the rigging of invisible ships; or – and the simile leaped up in his thoughts with a sudden sharpness of suggestion – a chorus of animals, of wild creatures, somewhere in desolate places of the world, crying and singing as animals will, to the moon. He could fancy he heard the wailing, half-human cries of cats upon the tiles at night, rising and falling with weird intervals of sound, and this music, muffled by distance and the trees, made him think of a queer company of these creatures on some roof far away in the sky, uttering their solemn music to one another and the moon in chorus.

It was, he felt at the time, a singular image to occur to him, yet it expressed his sensation pictorially better than anything else. The instruments played such impossibly odd intervals, and the crescendos and diminuendos were so very suggestive of cat-land on the tiles at night, rising swiftly, dropping without warning to deep notes again, and all in such strange confusion of discords and accords. But, at the same time a plaintive sweetness resulted on the whole, and the discords of these half-broken instruments were so singular that they did not distress his musical soul like fiddles out of tune.

He listened a long time, wholly surrendering himself as his character was, and then strolled homewards in the dusk as the air grew chilly.

"There was nothing to alarm?" put in Dr. Silence briefly.

"Absolutely nothing," said Vezin; "but you know it was all so fantastical and charming that my imagination was profoundly impressed. Perhaps, too," he continued, gently explanatory, "it was this stirring of my imagination that caused other impressions; for, as I walked back, the spell of the place began to steal over me in a dozen ways, though all intelligible ways. But there were other things I could not account for in the least, even then."

"Incidents, you mean?"

"Hardly incidents, I think. A lot of vivid sensations crowded themselves upon my mind and I could trace them to no causes. It was just after sunset and the tumbled old buildings traced magical outlines against an opalescent sky of gold and red. The dusk was running down the twisted streets. All round the hill the plain pressed in like a dim sea, its level rising with the darkness. The spell of this kind of scene, you know, can be very moving, and it was so that night. Yet I felt that what came to me had nothing directly to do with the mystery and wonder of the scene."

"Not merely the subtle transformations of the spirit that come with beauty," put in the doctor, noticing his hesitation.

"Exactly," Vezin went on, duly encouraged and no longer so fearful of our smiles at his expense. "The impressions came from somewhere else. For instance, down the busy main street where men and women were bustling home from work, shopping at stalls and barrows, idly gossiping in groups, and all the rest of it, I saw that I aroused no interest and that no one turned to stare at me as a foreigner and stranger. I was utterly ignored, and my presence among them excited no special interest or attention.

"And then, quite suddenly, it dawned upon me with conviction that all the time this indifference and inattention were merely feigned. Everybody as a matter of fact was watching me closely. Every movement I made was known and observed. Ignoring me was all a pretence – an elaborate pretence."

He paused a moment and looked at us to see if we were smiling, and then continued, reassured –

"It is useless to ask me how I noticed this, because I simply cannot explain it. But the discovery gave me something of a shock. Before I got back to the inn, however, another curious thing rose up strongly in my mind and forced my recognition of it as true. And this, too, I may as well say at once, was equally inexplicable to me. I mean I can only give you the fact, as fact it was to me."

The little man left his chair and stood on the mat before the fire. His diffidence lessened from now onwards, as he lost himself again in the magic of the old adventure. His eyes shone a little already as he talked.

"Well," he went on, his soft voice rising somewhat with his excitement, "I was in a shop when it came to me first – though the idea must have been at work for a long time subconsciously to appear in so complete a form all at once. I was buying socks, I think," he laughed, "and struggling with my dreadful French, when it struck me that the woman in the shop did not care two pins whether I bought anything or not. She was indifferent whether she made a sale or did not make a sale. She was only pretending to sell.

"This sounds a very small and fanciful incident to build upon what follows. But really it was not small. I mean it was the spark that lit the line of powder and ran along to the big blaze in my mind.

"For the whole town, I suddenly realised, was something other than I so far saw it. The real activities and interests of the people were elsewhere and otherwise than appeared. Their true lives lay somewhere out of sight behind the scenes. Their busy-ness was but the outward semblance that masked their actual purposes. They bought and sold, and ate and drank, and walked about the streets, yet all the while the main stream of their existence lay somewhere beyond my ken, underground, in secret places. In the shops and at the stalls they did not care whether I purchased their articles or not; at the inn, they were indifferent to my staying or going; their life lay remote from my own, springing from hidden, mysterious sources, coursing out of sight, unknown. It was all a great elaborate pretence, assumed possibly for my benefit, or possibly for purposes of their own. But the main current of their energies ran elsewhere. I almost felt as an unwelcome foreign substance might be expected to feel when it has found its way into the human system and the whole body organises itself to eject it or to absorb it. The town was doing this very thing to me.

"This bizarre notion presented itself forcibly to my mind as I walked home to the inn, and I began busily to wonder wherein the true life of this town could lie and what were the actual interests and activities of its hidden life.

"And, now that my eyes were partly opened, I noticed other things too that puzzled me, first of which, I think, was the extraordinary silence of the whole place. Positively, the town was muffled. Although the streets were paved with cobbles the people moved about silently, softly, with padded feet, like cats. Nothing made noise. All was hushed, subdued, muted. The very voices were quiet, low-pitched like purring. Nothing clamorous, vehement or emphatic seemed able to live in the drowsy atmosphere of soft dreaming that soothed this little hill-town into its sleep. It was like the woman at the inn – an outward repose screening intense inner activity and purpose.

"Yet there was no sign of lethargy or sluggishness anywhere about it. The people were active and alert. Only a magical and uncanny softness lay over them all like a spell."

Vezin passed his hand across his eyes for a moment as though the memory had become very vivid. His voice had run off into a whisper so that we heard the last part with difficulty. He was telling a true thing obviously, yet something that he both liked and hated telling.

"I went back to the inn," he continued presently in a louder voice, "and dined. I felt a new strange world about me. My old world of reality receded. Here, whether I liked it or no, was something new and incomprehensible. I regretted having left the train so impulsively. An adventure was upon me, and I loathed adventures as foreign to my nature. Moreover, this was the beginning apparently of an adventure somewhere deep within me, in a region I could not check or measure, and a feeling of alarm mingled itself with my wonder – alarm for the stability of what I had for forty years recognised as my 'personality'.

"I went upstairs to bed, my mind teeming with thoughts that were unusual to me, and of rather a haunting description. By way of relief I kept thinking of that nice, prosaic noisy train and all those wholesome, blustering passengers. I almost wished I were with them again. But my dreams took me elsewhere. I dreamed of cats, and soft-moving creatures, and the silence of life in a dim muffled world beyond the senses."

## Chapter II

**VEZIN** stayed on from day to day, indefinitely, much longer than he had intended. He felt in a kind of dazed, somnolent condition. He did nothing in particular, but the place fascinated him and he could not decide to leave. Decisions were always very difficult for him and he sometimes wondered how he had ever brought himself to the point of leaving the train. It seemed as though someone else must have arranged it for him, and once or twice his thoughts ran to the swarthy Frenchman who had sat opposite. If only he could have understood that long sentence ending so strangely with "*à cause du sommeil et à cause des chats.*" He wondered what it all meant.

Meanwhile the hushed softness of the town held him prisoner and he sought in his muddling, gentle way to find out where the mystery lay, and what it was all about. But his limited French and his constitutional hatred of active investigation made it hard for him to buttonhole anybody and ask questions. He was content to observe, and watch, and remain negative.

The weather held on calm and hazy, and this just suited him. He wandered about the town till he knew every street and alley. The people suffered him to come and go without let or hindrance, though it became clearer to him every day that he was never free himself from observation. The town watched him as a cat watches a mouse. And he got no nearer to finding out what they were all so busy with or where the main stream of their activities lay. This remained hidden. The people were as soft and mysterious as cats.

But that he was continually under observation became more evident from day to day.

For instance, when he strolled to the end of the town and entered a little green public garden beneath the ramparts and seated himself upon one of the empty benches in the sun, he was quite alone – at first. Not another seat was occupied; the little park was empty, the paths deserted. Yet, within ten minutes of his coming, there must have been fully twenty persons scattered about him, some strolling aimlessly along the gravel walks, staring at the flowers, and others seated on the wooden benches enjoying the sun like himself. None of them appeared to take any notice of him; yet he understood quite well they had all come there to watch. They kept him under close observation. In the street they had seemed busy enough, hurrying upon various errands; yet these were suddenly all forgotten and they had nothing to do but loll and laze in the sun, their duties unremembered. Five minutes after he left, the garden was again deserted, the seats vacant. But in the crowded street it was the same thing again; he was never alone. He was ever in their thoughts.

By degrees, too, he began to see how it was he was so cleverly watched, yet without the appearance of it. The people did nothing *directly*. They behaved *obliquely*. He laughed in his mind as the thought thus clothed itself in words, but the phrase exactly described it. They looked at him from angles which naturally should have led their sight in another direction altogether. Their movements were oblique, too, so far as these concerned himself. The straight, direct thing was not their way evidently. They did nothing obviously. If he entered a shop to buy, the woman walked instantly away and busied herself with something at the farther end of the counter, though answering at once when he spoke, showing that she knew he was there and that this was only her way of attending to him. It was the fashion of the cat she followed. Even in the dining-room of the inn, the be-whiskered and courteous waiter, lithe and silent in all his movements, never seemed able to come straight to his table for an order or a dish. He came by zigzags, indirectly, vaguely, so that he appeared to be going to another table altogether, and only turned suddenly at the last moment, and was there beside him.

Vezin smiled curiously to himself as he described how he began to realise these things. Other tourists there were none in the hostel, but he recalled the figures of one or two old men, inhabitants, who took their *déjeuner* and dinner there, and remembered how fantastically they entered the room in similar fashion. First, they paused in the doorway, peering about the room, and then, after a temporary inspection, they came in, as it were, sideways, keeping close to the walls so that he wondered which table they were making for, and at the last minute making almost a little quick run to their particular seats. And again he thought of the ways and methods of cats.

Other small incidents, too, impressed him as all part of this queer, soft town with its muffled, indirect life, for the way some of the people appeared and disappeared with extraordinary swiftness puzzled him exceedingly. It may have been all perfectly natural, he knew, yet he could not make it out how the alleys swallowed them up and shot them forth in a second of time when there were no visible doorways or openings near enough to explain the phenomenon. Once he followed two elderly women who, he felt, had been particularly examining him from across the street – quite near the inn this was – and saw them turn the corner a few feet only in front of him. Yet when he sharply followed on their heels he saw nothing but an utterly deserted alley stretching in front of him with no sign of a living thing. And the only opening through which they could have escaped was a porch some fifty yards away, which not the swiftest human runner could have reached in time.

And in just such sudden fashion people appeared, when he never expected them. Once when he heard a great noise of fighting going on behind a low wall, and hurried up to see what was going on, what should he see but a group of girls and women engaged in vociferous conversation which instantly hushed itself to the normal whispering note of the town when his head appeared over the wall. And even then none of them turned to look at him directly, but slunk off with the most unaccountable rapidity into doors and sheds across the yard. And their voices, he thought, had sounded so like, so strangely like, the angry snarling of fighting animals, almost of cats.

The whole spirit of the town, however, continued to evade him as something elusive, protean, screened from the outer world, and at the same time intensely, genuinely vital; and, since he now formed part of its life, this concealment puzzled and irritated him; more – it began rather to frighten him.

Out of the mists that slowly gathered about his ordinary surface thoughts, there rose again the idea that the inhabitants were waiting for him to declare himself, to take an attitude, to do this, or to do that; and that when he had done so they in their turn would at length make some direct response, accepting or rejecting him. Yet the vital matter concerning which his decision was awaited came no nearer to him.

Once or twice he purposely followed little processions or groups of the citizens in order to find out, if possible, on what purpose they were bent; but they always discovered him in time and dwindled away, each individual going his or her own way. It was always the same: he never could learn what their main interest was. The cathedral was ever empty, the old church of St. Martin, at the other end of the town, deserted. They shopped because they had to, and not because they wished to. The booths stood neglected, the stalls unvisited, the little *cafés* desolate. Yet the streets were always full, the townsfolk ever on the bustle.

"Can it be," he thought to himself, yet with a deprecating laugh that he should have dared to think anything so odd, "can it be that these people are people of the twilight, that they live only at night their real life, and come out honestly only with the dusk? That during the day they make a sham though brave pretence, and after the sun is down their true life begins? Have they the souls of night-things, and is the whole blessed town in the hands of the cats?"

The fancy somehow electrified him with little shocks of shrinking and dismay. Yet, though he affected to laugh, he knew that he was beginning to feel more than uneasy, and that strange forces were tugging with a thousand invisible cords at the very centre of his being. Something utterly remote from his ordinary life, something that had not waked for years, began faintly to stir in his soul, sending feelers abroad into his brain and heart, shaping queer thoughts and penetrating even into certain of his minor actions. Something exceedingly vital to himself, to his soul, hung in the balance.

And, always when he returned to the inn about the hour of sunset, he saw the figures of the townsfolk stealing through the dusk from their shop doors, moving sentry-wise to and fro at the corners of the streets, yet always vanishing silently like shadows at his near approach. And as the inn invariably closed its doors at ten o'clock he had never yet found the opportunity he rather half-heartedly sought to see for himself what account the town could give of itself at night.

" – *à cause du sommeil et à cause des chats*" – the words now rang in his ears more and more often, though still as yet without any definite meaning.

Moreover, something made him sleep like the dead.

## Chapter III

**IT WAS**, I think, on the fifth day – though in this detail his story sometimes varied – that he made a definite discovery which increased his alarm and brought him up to a rather sharp climax. Before that he had already noticed that a change was going forward and certain subtle transformations being brought about in his character which modified several of his minor habits. And he had affected to ignore them. Here, however, was something he could no longer ignore; and it startled him.

At the best of times he was never very positive, always negative rather, compliant and acquiescent; yet, when necessity arose he was capable of reasonably vigorous action and could take a strongish decision. The discovery he now made that brought him up with such a sharp turn was that this power had positively dwindled to nothing. He found it impossible to make up his mind. For, on this fifth day, he realised that he had stayed long enough in the town and that for reasons he could only vaguely define to himself it was wiser *and safer* that he should leave.

And he found that he could not leave!

This is difficult to describe in words, and it was more by gesture and the expression of his face that he conveyed to Dr. Silence the state of impotence he had reached. All this spying and watching, he said, had as it were spun a net about his feet so that he was trapped and powerless to escape; he felt like a fly that had blundered into the intricacies of a great web; he was caught, imprisoned, and could not get away. It was a distressing sensation. A numbness had crept over his will till it had become almost incapable of decision. The mere thought of vigorous action – action towards escape – began to terrify him. All the currents of his life had turned inwards upon himself, striving to bring to the surface something that lay buried almost beyond reach, determined to force his recognition of something he had long forgotten – forgotten years upon years, centuries almost ago. It seemed as though a window deep within his being would presently open and reveal an entirely new world, yet somehow a world that was not unfamiliar. Beyond that, again, he fancied a great curtain hung; and when that too rolled up he would see still farther into this region and at last understand something of the secret life of these extraordinary people.

"Is this why they wait and watch?" he asked himself with rather a shaking heart, "for the time when I shall join them – or refuse to join them? Does the decision rest with me after all, and not with them?"

And it was at this point that the sinister character of the adventure first really declared itself, and he became genuinely alarmed. The stability of his rather fluid little personality was at stake, he felt, and something in his heart turned coward.

Why otherwise should he have suddenly taken to walking stealthily, silently, making as little sound as possible, for ever looking behind him? Why else should he have moved almost on tiptoe about the passages of the practically deserted inn, and when he was abroad have found himself deliberately taking advantage of what cover presented itself? And why, if he was not afraid, should the wisdom of staying indoors after sundown have suddenly occurred to him as eminently desirable? Why, indeed?

And, when John Silence gently pressed him for an explanation of these things, he admitted apologetically that he had none to give.

"It was simply that I feared something might happen to me unless I kept a sharp lookout. I felt afraid. It was instinctive," was all he could say. "I got the impression that the whole town was after me – wanted me for something; and that if it got me I should lose myself, or at least the Self I knew, in some unfamiliar state of consciousness. But I am not a psychologist, you know," he added meekly, "and I cannot define it better than that."

It was while lounging in the courtyard half an hour before the evening meal that Vezin made this discovery, and he at once went upstairs to his quiet room at the end of the winding passage to think it over alone. In the yard it was empty enough, true, but there was always the possibility that the big woman whom he dreaded would come out of some door, with her pretence of knitting, to sit and watch him. This had happened several times, and he could not endure the sight of her. He still remembered his original fancy, bizarre though it was, that she would spring upon him the moment his back was turned and land with one single crushing leap upon his neck. Of course it was nonsense, but then it haunted him, and once an idea begins to do that it ceases to be nonsense. It has clothed itself in reality.

He went upstairs accordingly. It was dusk, and the oil lamps had not yet been lit in the passages. He stumbled over the uneven surface of the ancient flooring, passing the dim outlines of doors along the corridor – doors that he had never once seen opened – rooms that seemed never occupied. He moved, as his habit now was, stealthily and on tiptoe.

Half-way down the last passage to his own chamber there was a sharp turn, and it was just here, while groping round the walls with outstretched hands, that his fingers touched something that was not wall – something that moved. It was soft and warm in texture, indescribably fragrant, and about the height of his shoulder; and he immediately thought of a furry, sweet-smelling kitten. The next minute he knew it was something quite different.

Instead of investigating, however, – his nerves must have been too overwrought for that, he said, – he shrank back as closely as possible against the wall on the other side. The thing, whatever it was, slipped past him with a sound of rustling and, retreating with light footsteps down the passage behind him, was gone. A breath of warm, scented air was wafted to his nostrils.

Vezin caught his breath for an instant and paused, stockstill, half leaning against the wall – and then almost ran down the remaining distance and entered his room with a rush, locking the door hurriedly behind him. Yet it was not fear that made him run: it was excitement, pleasurable excitement. His nerves were tingling, and a delicious glow made itself felt all over his body. In a flash it came to him that this was just what he had felt twenty-five years ago as a boy when he was in love for the first time. Warm currents of life ran all over him and mounted to his brain in a whirl of soft delight. His mood was suddenly become tender, melting, loving.

The room was quite dark, and he collapsed upon the sofa by the window, wondering what had happened to him and what it all meant. But the only thing he understood clearly in that instant was that something in him had swiftly, magically changed: he no longer wished to leave, or to argue with himself about leaving. The encounter in the passage-way had changed all that. The strange perfume of it still hung about him, bemusing his heart and mind. For he knew that it was a girl who had passed him, a girl's face that his fingers had brushed in the darkness, and he felt in some extraordinary way as though he had been actually kissed by her, kissed full upon the lips.

Trembling, he sat upon the sofa by the window and struggled to collect his thoughts. He was utterly unable to understand how the mere passing of a girl in the darkness of a narrow passage-way could communicate so electric a thrill to his whole being that he still shook with the sweetness of it. Yet, there it was! And he found it as useless to deny as to attempt analysis. Some ancient fire had entered his veins, and now ran coursing through his blood; and that he was forty-five instead of twenty did not matter one little jot. Out of all the inner turmoil and confusion emerged the one salient fact that the mere atmosphere, the merest casual touch, of this girl, unseen, unknown in the darkness, had been sufficient to stir dormant fires in the centre of his heart, and rouse his whole being from a state of feeble sluggishness to one of tearing and tumultuous excitement.

After a time, however, the number of Vezin's years began to assert their cumulative power; he grew calmer, and when a knock came at length upon his door and he heard the waiter's voice suggesting that dinner was nearly over, he pulled himself together and slowly made his way downstairs into the dining-room.

Everyone looked up as he entered, for he was very late, but he took his customary seat in the far corner and began to eat. The trepidation was still in his nerves, but the fact that he had passed through the courtyard and hall without catching sight of a petticoat served to calm him a little. He ate so fast that he had almost caught up with the current stage of the table d'hôte, when a slight commotion in the room drew his attention.

His chair was so placed that the door and the greater portion of the long *salle à manger* were behind him, yet it was not necessary to turn round to know that the same person he had passed in the dark passage had now come into the room. He felt the presence long before he heard or saw any one. Then he became aware that the old men, the only other guests, were rising one by one in their places, and exchanging greetings with someone who passed among them from table to table. And when at length he turned with his heart beating furiously to ascertain for himself, he saw the form of a young girl, lithe and slim, moving down the centre of the room and making straight for his own table in the corner. She moved wonderfully, with sinuous grace, like a young panther, and her approach filled him with such delicious bewilderment that he was utterly unable to tell at first what her face was like, or discover what it was about the whole presentment of the creature that filled him anew with trepidation and delight.

"Ah, Ma'mselle est de retour!" he heard the old waiter murmur at his side, and he was just able to take in that she was the daughter of the proprietress, when she was upon him, and he heard her voice. She was addressing him. Something of red lips he saw and laughing white teeth, and stray wisps of fine dark hair about the temples; but all the rest was a dream in which his own emotion rose like a thick cloud before his eyes and prevented his seeing accurately, or knowing exactly what he did. He was aware that she greeted him with a charming little bow; that her beautiful large eyes looked searchingly into his own; that the perfume he had noticed in the dark passage again assailed his nostrils, and that she was bending a little towards him and leaning with one hand on the table at this side. She was quite close to him – that was the chief thing he knew – explaining that she had been asking after the comfort of her mother's guests, and now was introducing herself to the latest arrival – himself.

"M'sieur has already been here a few days," he heard the waiter say; and then her own voice, sweet as singing, replied –

"Ah, but M'sieur is not going to leave us just yet, I hope. My mother is too old to look after the comfort of our guests properly, but now I am here I will remedy all that." She laughed deliciously. "M'sieur shall be well looked after."

Vezin, struggling with his emotion and desire to be polite, half rose to acknowledge the pretty speech, and to stammer some sort of reply, but as he did so his hand by chance touched her own that was resting upon the table, and a shock that was for all the world like a shock of electricity, passed from her skin into his body. His soul wavered and shook deep within him. He caught her eyes fixed upon his own with a look of most curious intentness, and the next moment he knew that he had sat down wordless again on his chair, that the girl was already half-way across the room, and that he was trying to eat his salad with a dessert-spoon and a knife.

Longing for her return, and yet dreading it, he gulped down the remainder of his dinner, and then went at once to his bedroom to be alone with his thoughts. This time the passages were lighted, and he suffered no exciting contretemps; yet the winding corridor was dim with shadows, and the last portion, from the bend of the walls onwards, seemed longer than he had ever known it. It ran downhill like the pathway on a mountain side, and as he tiptoed softly down it he felt that by rights it ought to have led him clean out of the house into the heart of a great forest. The world was singing with him. Strange fancies filled his brain, and once in the room, with the door securely locked, he did not light the candles, but sat by the open window thinking long, long thoughts that came unbidden in troops to his mind.

## Chapter IV

**THIS PART** of the story he told to Dr. Silence, without special coaxing, it is true, yet with much stammering embarrassment. He could not in the least understand, he said, how the girl had managed to affect him so profoundly, and even before he had set eyes upon her. For her mere proximity in the darkness had been sufficient to set him on fire. He knew nothing of enchantments, and for years had been a stranger to anything approaching tender relations with any member of the opposite sex, for he was encased in shyness, and realised his overwhelming defects only too well. Yet this bewitching young creature came to him deliberately. Her manner was unmistakable, and she sought him out on every possible occasion. Chaste and sweet she was undoubtedly, yet frankly inviting; and she won him utterly with the first glance of her shining eyes, even if she had not already done so in the dark merely by the magic of her invisible presence.

"You felt she was altogether wholesome and good!" queried the doctor. "You had no reaction of any sort – for instance, of alarm?"

Vezin looked up sharply with one of his inimitable little apologetic smiles. It was some time before he replied. The mere memory of the adventure had suffused his shy face with blushes, and his brown eyes sought the floor again before he answered.

"I don't think I can quite say that," he explained presently. "I acknowledged certain qualms, sitting up in my room afterwards. A conviction grew upon me that there was something about her – how shall I express it? – well, something unholy. It is not impurity in any sense, physical or mental, that I mean, but something quite indefinable that gave me a vague sensation of the creeps. She drew me, and at the same time repelled me, more than – than—"

He hesitated, blushing furiously, and unable to finish the sentence.

"Nothing like it has ever come to me before or since," he concluded, with lame confusion. "I suppose it was, as you suggested just now, something of an enchantment. At any rate, it was strong enough to make me feel that I would stay in that awful little haunted town for years if only I could see her every day, hear her voice, watch her wonderful movements, and sometimes, perhaps, touch her hand."

"Can you explain to me what you felt was the source of her power?" John Silence asked, looking purposely anywhere but at the narrator.

"I am surprised that you should ask me such a question," answered Vezin, with the nearest approach to dignity he could manage. "I think no man can describe to another convincingly wherein lies the magic of the woman who ensnares him. I certainly cannot. I can only say this slip of a girl bewitched me, and the mere knowledge that she was living and sleeping in the same house filled me with an extraordinary sense of delight.

"But there's one thing I can tell you," he went on earnestly, his eyes aglow, "namely, that she seemed to sum up and synthesise in herself all the strange hidden forces that operated so mysteriously in the town and its inhabitants. She had the silken movements of the panther, going smoothly, silently to and fro, and the same indirect, oblique methods as the townsfolk, screening, like them, secret purposes of her own – purposes that I was sure had *me* for their objective. She kept me, to my terror and delight, ceaselessly under observation, yet so carelessly, so consummately, that another man less sensitive, if I may say so" – he made a deprecating gesture – "or less prepared by what had gone before, would never have noticed it at all. She was always still, always reposeful, yet she seemed to be everywhere at once, so that I never could escape from her. I was continually meeting the stare and laughter of her great eyes, in the corners of the rooms, in the passages, calmly looking at me through the windows, or in the busiest parts of the public streets."

Their intimacy, it seems, grew very rapidly after this first encounter which had so violently disturbed the little man's equilibrium. He was naturally very prim, and prim folk live mostly in so small a world that anything violently unusual may shake them clean out of it, and they therefore instinctively distrust originality. But Vezin began to forget his primness after awhile. The girl was always modestly behaved, and as her mother's representative she naturally had to do with the guests in the hotel. It was not out of the way that a spirit of camaraderie should spring up. Besides, she was young, she was charmingly pretty, she was French, and – she obviously liked him.

At the same time, there was something indescribable – a certain indefinable atmosphere of other places, other times – that made him try hard to remain on his guard, and sometimes made him catch his breath with a sudden start. It was all rather like a delirious dream, half delight, half dread, he confided in a whisper to Dr. Silence; and more than once he hardly knew quite what he was doing or saying, as though he were driven forward by impulses he scarcely recognised as his own.

And though the thought of leaving presented itself again and again to his mind, it was each time with less insistence, so that he stayed on from day to day, becoming more and more a part of the sleepy life of this dreamy medieval town, losing more and more of his recognisable personality. Soon, he felt, the Curtain within would roll up with an awful rush, and he would find himself suddenly admitted into the secret purposes of the hidden life that lay behind it all. Only, by that time, he would have become transformed into an entirely different being.

And, meanwhile, he noticed various little signs of the intention to make his stay attractive to him: flowers in his bedroom, a more comfortable arm-chair in the corner, and even special little extra dishes on his private table in the dining-room. Conversations, too, with 'Mademoiselle Ilsé' became more and more frequent and pleasant, and although they seldom travelled beyond the weather, or the details of the town, the girl, he noticed, was never in a hurry to bring them to an end, and often contrived to interject little odd sentences that he never properly understood, yet felt to be significant.

And it was these stray remarks, full of a meaning that evaded him, that pointed to some hidden purpose of her own and made him feel uneasy. They all had to do, he felt sure, with reasons for his staying on in the town indefinitely.

"And has M'sieur not even yet come to a decision?" she said softly in his ear, sitting beside him in the sunny yard before *déjeuner*, the acquaintance having progressed with significant rapidity. "Because, if it's so difficult, we must all try together to help him!"

The question startled him, following upon his own thoughts. It was spoken with a pretty laugh, and a stray bit of hair across one eye, as she turned and peered at him half roguishly. Possibly he did not quite understand the French of it, for her near presence always confused his small knowledge of the language distressingly. Yet the words, and her manner, and something else that lay behind it all in her mind, frightened him. It gave such point to his feeling that the town was waiting for him to make his mind up on some important matter.

At the same time, her voice, and the fact that she was there so close beside him in her soft dark dress, thrilled him inexpressibly.

"It is true I find it difficult to leave," he stammered, losing his way deliciously in the depths of her eyes, "and especially now that Mademoiselle Ilsé has come."

He was surprised at the success of his sentence, and quite delighted with the little gallantry of it. But at the same time he could have bitten his tongue off for having said it.

"Then after all you like our little town, or you would not be pleased to stay on," she said, ignoring the compliment.

"I am enchanted with it, and enchanted with you," he cried, feeling that his tongue was somehow slipping beyond the control of his brain. And he was on the verge of saying all manner of other things of the wildest description, when the girl sprang lightly up from her chair beside him, and made to go.

"It is *soupe à l'onion* today!" she cried, laughing back at him through the sunlight, "and I must go and see about it. Otherwise, you know, M'sieur will not enjoy his dinner, and then, perhaps, he will leave us!"

He watched her cross the courtyard, moving with all the grace and lightness of the feline race, and her simple black dress clothed her, he thought, exactly like the fur of the same supple species. She turned once to laugh at him from the porch with the glass door, and then stopped a moment to speak to her mother, who sat knitting as usual in her corner seat just inside the hall-way.

But how was it, then, that the moment his eye fell upon this ungainly woman, the pair of them appeared suddenly as other than they were? Whence came that transforming dignity and sense of power that enveloped them both as by magic? What was it about that massive woman that made her appear instantly regal, and set her on a throne in some dark and dreadful scenery, wielding a sceptre over the red glare of some tempestuous orgy? And why did this slender stripling of a girl, graceful as a willow, lithe as a young leopard, assume suddenly an air of sinister majesty, and move with flame and smoke about her head, and the darkness of night beneath her feet?

Vezin caught his breath and sat there transfixed. Then, almost simultaneously with its appearance, the queer notion vanished again, and the sunlight of day caught them both, and he heard her laughing to her mother about the *soupe à l'onion*, and saw her glancing back at him over her dear little shoulder with a smile that made him think of a dew-kissed rose bending lightly before summer airs.

And, indeed, the onion soup was particularly excellent that day, because he saw another cover laid at his small table, and, with fluttering heart, heard the waiter murmur by way of explanation that "Ma'mselle Ilsé would honour M'sieur today at *déjeuner*, as her custom sometimes is with her mother's guests."

So actually she sat by him all through that delirious meal, talking quietly to him in easy French, seeing that he was well looked after, mixing the salad-dressing, and even helping him with her own hand. And, later in the afternoon, while he was smoking in the courtyard, longing for a sight of her as soon as her duties were done, she came again to his side, and when he rose to meet her, she stood facing him a moment, full of a perplexing sweet shyness before she spoke –

"My mother thinks you ought to know more of the beauties of our little town, and *I* think so too! Would M'sieur like me to be his guide, perhaps? I can show him everything, for our family has lived here for many generations."

She had him by the hand, indeed, before he could find a single word to express his pleasure, and led him, all unresisting, out into the street, yet in such a way that it seemed perfectly natural she should do so, and without the faintest suggestion of boldness or immodesty. Her face glowed with the pleasure and interest of it, and with her short dress and tumbled hair she looked every bit the charming child of seventeen that she was, innocent and playful, proud of her native town, and alive beyond her years to the sense of its ancient beauty.

So they went over the town together, and she showed him what she considered its chief interest: the tumble-down old house where her forebears had lived; the sombre, aristocratic-looking mansion where her mother's family dwelt for centuries, and the ancient market-place where several hundred years before the witches had been burnt by the score. She kept up a lively running stream of talk about it all, of which he understood not a fiftieth part as he trudged along by her side, cursing his forty-five years and feeling all the yearnings of his early manhood revive and jeer at him. And, as she talked, England and Surbiton seemed very far away indeed, almost in another age of the world's history. Her voice touched something immeasurably old in him, something that slept deep. It lulled the surface parts of his consciousness to sleep, allowing what was far more ancient to awaken. Like the town, with its elaborate pretence of modern active life, the upper layers of his being became dulled, soothed, muffled, and what lay underneath began to stir in its sleep. That big Curtain swayed a little to and fro. Presently it might lift altogether....

He began to understand a little better at last. The mood of the town was reproducing itself in him. In proportion as his ordinary external self became muffled, that inner secret life, that was far more real and vital, asserted itself. And this girl was surely the high-priestess of it all, the chief instrument of its accomplishment. New thoughts, with new interpretations, flooded his mind as she walked beside him through the winding streets, while the picturesque old gabled town, softly coloured in the sunset, had never appeared to him so wholly wonderful and seductive.

And only one curious incident came to disturb and puzzle him, slight in itself, but utterly inexplicable, bringing white terror into the child's face and a scream to her laughing lips. He had merely pointed to a column of blue smoke that rose from the burning autumn leaves and made a picture against the red roofs, and had then run to the wall and called her to his side to watch the flames shooting here and there through the heap of rubbish. Yet, at the sight of it, as though taken by surprise, her face had altered dreadfully, and she had turned and run like the wind, calling out wild sentences to him as she ran, of which he had not understood a single word, except that the fire apparently frightened her, and she wanted to get quickly away from it, and to get him away too.

Yet five minutes later she was as calm and happy again as though nothing had happened to alarm or waken troubled thoughts in her, and they had both forgotten the incident.

They were leaning over the ruined ramparts together listening to the weird music of the band as he had heard it the first day of his arrival. It moved him again profoundly as it had done before, and somehow he managed to find his tongue and his best French. The girl leaned across the stones close beside him. No one was about. Driven by some remorseless engine within he began to stammer something – he hardly knew what – of his strange admiration for her. Almost at the first word she sprang lightly off the wall and came up smiling in front of him, just touching his knees as he sat there. She was hatless as usual, and the sun caught her hair and one side of her cheek and throat.

"Oh, I'm so glad!" she cried, clapping her little hands softly in his face, "so very glad, because that means that if you like me you must also like what I do, and what I belong to."

Already he regretted bitterly having lost control of himself. Something in the phrasing of her sentence chilled him. He knew the fear of embarking upon an unknown and dangerous sea.

"You will take part in our real life, I mean," she added softly, with an indescribable coaxing of manner, as though she noticed his shrinking. "You will come back to us."

Already this slip of a child seemed to dominate him; he felt her power coming over him more and more; something emanated from her that stole over his senses and made him aware that her personality, for all its simple grace, held forces that were stately, imposing, august. He saw her again moving through smoke and flame amid broken and tempestuous scenery, alarmingly strong, her terrible mother by her side. Dimly this shone through her smile and appearance of charming innocence.

"You will, I know," she repeated, holding him with her eyes.

They were quite alone up there on the ramparts, and the sensation that she was overmastering him stirred a wild sensuousness in his blood. The mingled abandon and reserve in her attracted him furiously, and all of him that was man rose up and resisted the creeping influence, at the same time acclaiming it with the full delight of his forgotten youth. An irresistible desire came to him to question her, to summon what still remained to him of his own little personality in an effort to retain the right to his normal self.

The girl had grown quiet again, and was now leaning on the broad wall close beside him, gazing out across the darkening plain, her elbows on the coping, motionless as a figure carved in stone. He took his courage in both hands.

"Tell me, Ilsé," he said, unconsciously imitating her own purring softness of voice, yet aware that he was utterly in earnest, "what is the meaning of this town, and what is this real life you speak of? And why is it that the people watch me from morning to night? Tell me what it all means? And, tell me," he added more quickly with passion in his voice, "what you really are – yourself?"

She turned her head and looked at him through half-closed eyelids, her growing inner excitement betraying itself by the faint colour that ran like a shadow across her face.

"It seems to me," – he faltered oddly under her gaze – "that I have some right to know—"

Suddenly she opened her eyes to the full. "You love me, then?" she asked softly.

"I swear," he cried impetuously, moved as by the force of a rising tide, "I never felt before – I have never known any other girl who—"

"Then you *have* the right to know," she calmly interrupted his confused confession, "for love shares all secrets."

She paused, and a thrill like fire ran swiftly through him. Her words lifted him off the earth, and he felt a radiant happiness, followed almost the same instant in horrible contrast by the thought of death. He became aware that she had turned her eyes upon his own and was speaking again.

"The real life I speak of," she whispered, "is the old, old life within, the life of long ago, the life to which you, too, once belonged, and to which you still belong."

A faint wave of memory troubled the deeps of his soul as her low voice sank into him. What she was saying he knew instinctively to be true, even though he could not as yet understand its full purport. His present life seemed slipping from him as he listened, merging his personality in one that was far older and greater. It was this loss of his present self that brought to him the thought of death.

"You came here," she went on, "with the purpose of seeking it, and the people felt your presence and are waiting to know what you decide, whether you will leave them without having found it, or whether—"

Her eyes remained fixed upon his own, but her face began to change, growing larger and darker with an expression of age.

"It is their thoughts constantly playing about your soul that makes you feel they watch you. They do not watch you with their eyes. The purposes of their inner life are calling to you, seeking to claim you. You were all part of the same life long, long ago, and now they want you back again among them."

Vezin's timid heart sank with dread as he listened; but the girl's eyes held him with a net of joy so that he had no wish to escape. She fascinated him, as it were, clean out of his normal self.

"Alone, however, the people could never have caught and held you," she resumed. "The motive force was not strong enough; it has faded through all these years. But I" – she paused a moment and looked at him with complete confidence in her splendid eyes – "I possess the spell to conquer you and hold you: the spell of old love. I can win you back again and make you live the old life with me, for the force of the ancient tie between us, if I choose to use it, is irresistible. And I do choose to use it. I still want you. And you, dear soul of my dim past" – she pressed closer to him so that her breath passed across his eyes, and her voice positively sang – "I mean to have you, for you love me and are utterly at my mercy."

Vezin heard, and yet did not hear; understood, yet did not understand. He had passed into a condition of exaltation. The world was beneath his feet, made of music and flowers, and he was flying somewhere far above it through the sunshine of pure delight. He was breathless and giddy with the wonder of her words. They intoxicated him. And, still, the terror of it all, the dreadful thought of death, pressed ever behind her sentences. For flames shot through her voice out of black smoke and licked at his soul.

And they communicated with one another, it seemed to him, by a process of swift telepathy, for his French could never have compassed all he said to her. Yet she understood perfectly, and what she said to him was like the recital of verses long since known. And the mingled pain and sweetness of it as he listened were almost more than his little soul could hold.

"Yet I came here wholly by chance—" he heard himself saying.

"No," she cried with passion, "you came here because I called to you. I have called to you for years, and you came with the whole force of the past behind you. You had to come, for I own you, and I claim you."

She rose again and moved closer, looking at him with a certain insolence in the face – the insolence of power.

The sun had set behind the towers of the old cathedral and the darkness rose up from the plain and enveloped them. The music of the band had ceased. The leaves of the plane trees hung motionless, but the chill of the autumn evening rose about them and made Vezin shiver. There was no sound but the sound of their voices and the occasional soft rustle of the girl's dress. He could hear the blood rushing in his ears. He scarcely realised where he was or what he was doing. Some terrible magic of the imagination drew him deeply down into the tombs of his own being, telling him in no unfaltering voice that her words shadowed forth the truth. And this simple little French maid, speaking beside him with so strange authority, he saw curiously alter into quite another being. As he stared into her eyes, the picture in his mind grew and lived, dressing itself vividly to his inner vision with a degree of reality he was compelled to acknowledge. As once before, he saw her tall and stately, moving through wild and broken scenery of forests and mountain caverns, the glare of flames behind her head and clouds of shifting smoke about her feet. Dark leaves encircled her hair, flying loosely in the wind, and her limbs shone through the merest rags of clothing. Others were about her, too, and ardent eyes on all sides cast delirious glances upon her, but her own eyes were always for One only, one whom she held by the hand. For she was leading the dance in some tempestuous orgy to the music of chanting voices, and the dance she led circled about a great and awful Figure on a throne, brooding over the scene through lurid vapours, while innumerable other wild faces and forms crowded furiously about her in the dance. But the one she held by the hand he knew to be himself, and the monstrous shape upon the throne he knew to be her mother.

The vision rose within him, rushing to him down the long years of buried time, crying aloud to him with the voice of memory reawakened…. And then the scene faded away and he saw the clear circle of the girl's eyes gazing steadfastly into his own, and she became once more the pretty little daughter of the innkeeper, and he found his voice again.

"And you," he whispered tremblingly – "you child of visions and enchantment, how is it that you so bewitch me that I loved you even before I saw?"

She drew herself up beside him with an air of rare dignity.

"The call of the Past," she said; "and besides," she added proudly, "in the real life I am a princess—"

"A princess!" he cried.

" – and my mother is a queen!"

At this, little Vezin utterly lost his head. Delight tore at his heart and swept him into sheer ecstasy. To hear that sweet singing voice, and to see those adorable little lips utter such things, upset his balance beyond all hope of control. He took her in his arms and covered her unresisting face with kisses.

But even while he did so, and while the hot passion swept him, he felt that she was soft and loathsome, and that her answering kisses stained his very soul…. And when, presently, she had freed herself and vanished into the darkness, he stood there, leaning against the wall in a state of collapse, creeping with horror from the touch of her yielding body, and inwardly raging at the weakness that he already dimly realised must prove his undoing.

And from the shadows of the old buildings into which she disappeared there rose in the stillness of the night a singular, long-drawn cry, which at first he took for laughter, but which later he was sure he recognised as the almost human wailing of a cat.

## Chapter V

**FOR A LONG TIME** Vezin leant there against the wall, alone with his surging thoughts and emotions. He understood at length that he had done the one thing necessary to call down upon him the whole force of this ancient Past. For in those passionate kisses he had acknowledged the tie of olden days, and had revived it. And the memory of that soft impalpable caress in the darkness of the inn corridor came back to him with a shudder. The girl had first mastered him, and then led him to the one act that was necessary for her purpose. He had been waylaid, after the lapse of centuries – caught, and conquered.

Dimly he realised this, and sought to make plans for his escape. But, for the moment at any rate, he was powerless to manage his thoughts or will, for the sweet, fantastic madness of the whole adventure mounted to his brain like a spell, and he gloried in the feeling that he was utterly enchanted and moving in a world so much larger and wilder than the one he had ever been accustomed to.

The moon, pale and enormous, was just rising over the sea-like plain, when at last he rose to go. Her slanting rays drew all the houses into new perspective, so that their roofs, already glistening with dew, seemed to stretch much higher into the sky than usual, and their gables and quaint old towers lay far away in its purple reaches.

The cathedral appeared unreal in a silver mist. He moved softly, keeping to the shadows; but the streets were all deserted and very silent; the doors were closed, the shutters fastened. Not a soul was astir. The hush of night lay over everything; it was like a town of the dead, a churchyard with gigantic and grotesque tombstones.

Wondering where all the busy life of the day had so utterly disappeared to, he made his way to a back door that entered the inn by means of the stables, thinking thus to reach his room unobserved. He reached the courtyard safely and crossed it by keeping close to the shadow of the wall. He sidled down it, mincing along on tiptoe, just as the old men did when they entered the *salle à manger*. He was horrified to find himself doing this instinctively. A strange impulse came to him, catching him somehow in the centre of his body – an impulse to drop upon all fours and run swiftly and silently. He glanced upwards and the idea came to him to leap up upon his window-sill overhead instead of going round by the stairs. This occurred to him as the easiest, and most natural way. It was like the beginning of some horrible transformation of himself into something else. He was fearfully strung up.

The moon was higher now, and the shadows very dark along the side of the street where he moved. He kept among the deepest of them, and reached the porch with the glass doors.

But here there was light; the inmates, unfortunately, were still about. Hoping to slip across the hall unobserved and reach the stairs, he opened the door carefully and stole in. Then he saw that the hall was not empty. A large dark thing lay against the wall on his left. At first he thought it must be household articles. Then it moved, and he thought it was an immense cat, distorted in some way by the play of light and shadow. Then it rose straight up before him and he saw that it was the proprietress.

What she had been doing in this position he could only venture a dreadful guess, but the moment she stood up and faced him he was aware of some terrible dignity clothing her about that instantly recalled the girl's strange saying that she was a queen. Huge and sinister she stood there under the little oil lamp; alone with him in the empty hall. Awe stirred in his heart, and the roots of some ancient fear. He felt that he must bow to her and make some kind of obeisance. The impulse was fierce and irresistible, as of long habit. He glanced quickly about him. There was no one there. Then he deliberately inclined his head toward her. He bowed.

"Enfin! M'sieur s'est donc décidé. C'est bien alors. J'en suis contente."

Her words came to him sonorously as through a great open space.

Then the great figure came suddenly across the flagged hall at him and seized his trembling hands. Some overpowering force moved with her and caught him.

"On pourrait faire un p'tit tour ensemble, n'est-ce pas? Nous y allons cette nuit et il faut s'exercer un peu d'avance pour cela. Ilsé, Ilsé, viens donc ici. Viens vite!"

And she whirled him round in the opening steps of some dance that seemed oddly and horribly familiar. They made no sound on the stones, this strangely assorted couple. It was all soft and stealthy. And presently, when the air seemed to thicken like smoke, and a red glare as of flame shot through it, he was aware that some one else had joined them and that his hand the mother had released was now tightly held by the daughter. Ilsé had come in answer to the call, and he saw her with leaves of vervain twined in her dark hair, clothed in tattered vestiges of some curious garment, beautiful as the night, and horribly, odiously, loathsomely seductive.

"To the Sabbath! To the Sabbath!" they cried. "On to the Witches' Sabbath!"

Up and down that narrow hall they danced, the women on each side of him, to the wildest measure he had ever imagined, yet which he dimly, dreadfully remembered, till the lamp on the wall flickered and went out, and they were left in total darkness. And the devil woke in his heart with a thousand vile suggestions and made him afraid.

Suddenly they released his hands and he heard the voice of the mother cry that it was time, and they must go. Which way they went he did not pause to see. He only realised that he was free, and he blundered through the darkness till he found the stairs and then tore up them to his room as though all hell was at his heels.

He flung himself on the sofa, with his face in his hands, and groaned. Swiftly reviewing a dozen ways of immediate escape, all equally impossible, he finally decided that the only thing to do for the moment was to sit quiet and wait. He must see what was going to happen. At least in the privacy of his own bedroom he would be fairly safe. The door was locked. He crossed over and softly opened the window which gave upon the courtyard and also permitted a partial view of the hall through the glass doors.

As he did so the hum and murmur of a great activity reached his ears from the streets beyond – the sound of footsteps and voices muffled by distance. He leaned out cautiously and listened. The moonlight was clear and strong now, but his own window was in shadow, the silver disc being still behind the house. It came to him irresistibly that the inhabitants of the town, who a little while before had all been invisible behind closed doors, were now issuing forth, busy upon some secret and unholy errand. He listened intently.

At first everything about him was silent, but soon he became aware of movements going on in the house itself. Rustlings and cheepings came to him across that still, moonlit yard. A concourse of living beings sent the hum of their activity into the night. Things were on the move everywhere. A biting, pungent odour rose through the air, coming he knew not whence. Presently his eyes became glued to the windows of the opposite wall where the moonshine fell in a soft blaze. The roof overhead, and behind him, was reflected clearly in the panes of glass, and he saw the outlines of dark bodies moving with long footsteps over the tiles and along the coping. They passed swiftly and silently, shaped like immense cats, in an endless procession across the pictured glass, and then appeared to leap down to a lower level where he lost sight of them. He just caught the soft thudding of their leaps. Sometimes their shadows fell upon the white wall opposite, and then he could not make out whether they were the shadows of human beings or of cats. They seemed to change swiftly from one to the other. The transformation looked horribly real, for they leaped like human beings, yet changed swiftly in the air immediately afterwards, and dropped like animals.

The yard, too, beneath him, was now alive with the creeping movements of dark forms all stealthily drawing towards the porch with the glass doors. They kept so closely to the wall that he could not determine their actual shape, but when he saw that they passed on to the great congregation that was gathering in the hall, he understood that these were the creatures whose leaping shadows he had first seen reflected in the windowpanes opposite. They were coming from all parts of the town, reaching the appointed meeting-place across the roofs and tiles, and springing from level to level till they came to the yard.

Then a new sound caught his ear, and he saw that the windows all about him were being softly opened, and that to each window came a face. A moment later figures began dropping hurriedly down into the yard. And these figures, as they lowered themselves down from the windows, were human, he saw; but once safely in the yard they fell upon all fours and changed in the swiftest possible second into – cats – huge, silent cats. They ran in streams to join the main body in the hall beyond.

So, after all, the rooms in the house had not been empty and unoccupied.

Moreover, what he saw no longer filled him with amazement. For he remembered it all. It was familiar. It had all happened before just so, hundreds of times, and he himself had taken part in it and known the wild madness of it all. The outline of the old building changed, the yard grew larger, and he seemed to be staring down upon it from a much greater height through smoky vapours. And, as he looked, half remembering, the old pains of long ago, fierce and sweet, furiously assailed him, and the blood stirred horribly as he heard the Call of the Dance again in his heart and tasted the ancient magic of Ilsé whirling by his side.

Suddenly he started back. A great lithe cat had leaped softly up from the shadows below on to the sill close to his face, and was staring fixedly at him with the eyes of a human. "Come," it seemed to say, "come with us to the Dance! Change as of old! Transform yourself swiftly and come!" Only too well he understood the creature's soundless call.

It was gone again in a flash with scarcely a sound of its padded feet on the stones, and then others dropped by the score down the side of the house, past his very eyes, all changing as they fell and darting away rapidly, softly, towards the gathering point. And again he felt the dreadful desire to do likewise; to murmur the old incantation, and then drop upon hands and knees and run swiftly for the great flying leap into the air. Oh, how the passion of it rose within him like a flood, twisting his very entrails, sending his heart's desire flaming forth into the night for the old, old Dance of the Sorcerers at the Witches' Sabbath! The whirl of the stars was about him; once more he met the magic of the moon. The power of the wind, rushing from precipice and forest, leaping from cliff to cliff across the valleys, tore him away.... He heard the cries of the dancers and their wild laughter, and with this savage girl in his embrace he danced furiously about the dim Throne where sat the Figure with the sceptre of majesty....

Then, suddenly, all became hushed and still, and the fever died down a little in his heart. The calm moonlight flooded a courtyard empty and deserted. They had started. The procession was off into the sky. And he was left behind – alone.

Vezin tiptoed softly across the room and unlocked the door. The murmur from the streets, growing momentarily as he advanced, met his ears. He made his way with the utmost caution down the corridor. At the head of the stairs he paused and listened. Below him, the hall where they had gathered was dark and still, but through opened doors and windows on the far side of the building came the sound of a great throng moving farther and farther into the distance.

He made his way down the creaking wooden stairs, dreading yet longing to meet some straggler who should point the way, but finding no one; across the dark hall, so lately thronged with living, moving things, and out through the opened front doors into the street. He could not believe that he was really left behind, really forgotten, that he had been purposely permitted to escape. It perplexed him.

Nervously he peered about him, and up and down the street; then, seeing nothing, advanced slowly down the pavement.

The whole town, as he went, showed itself empty and deserted, as though a great wind had blown everything alive out of it. The doors and windows of the houses stood open to the night; nothing stirred; moonlight and silence lay over all. The night lay about him like a cloak. The air, soft and cool, caressed his cheek like the touch of a great furry paw. He gained confidence and began to walk quickly, though still keeping to the shadowed side. Nowhere could he discover the faintest sign of the great unholy exodus he knew had just taken place. The moon sailed high over all in a sky cloudless and serene.

Hardly realising where he was going, he crossed the open market-place and so came to the ramparts, whence he knew a pathway descended to the high road and along which he could make good his escape to one of the other little towns that lay to the northward, and so to the railway.

But first he paused and gazed out over the scene at his feet where the great plain lay like a silver map of some dream country. The still beauty of it entered his heart, increasing his sense of bewilderment and unreality. No air stirred, the leaves of the plane trees stood motionless, the near details were defined with the sharpness of day against dark shadows, and in the distance the fields and woods melted away into haze and shimmering mistiness.

But the breath caught in his throat and he stood stockstill as though transfixed when his gaze passed from the horizon and fell upon the near prospect in the depth of the valley at his feet. The whole lower slopes of the hill, that lay hid from the brightness of the moon, were aglow, and through the glare he saw countless moving forms, shifting thick and fast between the openings of the trees; while overhead, like leaves driven by the wind, he discerned flying shapes that hovered darkly one moment against the sky and then settled down with cries and weird singing through the branches into the region that was aflame.

Spellbound, he stood and stared for a time that he could not measure. And then, moved by one of the terrible impulses that seemed to control the whole adventure, he climbed swiftly upon the top of the broad coping, and balanced a moment where the valley gaped at his feet. But in that very instant, as he stood hovering, a sudden movement among the shadows of the houses caught his eye, and he turned to see the outline of a large animal dart swiftly across the open space behind him, and land with a flying leap upon the top of the wall a little lower down. It ran like the wind to his feet and then rose up beside him upon the ramparts. A shiver seemed to run through the moonlight, and his sight trembled for a second. His heart pulsed fearfully. Ilsé stood beside him, peering into his face.

Some dark substance, he saw, stained the girl's face and skin, shining in the moonlight as she stretched her hands towards him; she was dressed in wretched tattered garments that yet became her mightily; rue and vervain twined about her temples; her eyes glittered with unholy light. He only just controlled the wild impulse to take her in his arms and leap with her from their giddy perch into the valley below.

"See!" she cried, pointing with an arm on which the rags fluttered in the rising wind towards the forest aglow in the distance. "See where they await us! The woods are alive! Already the Great Ones are there, and the dance will soon begin! The salve is here! Anoint yourself and come!"

Though a moment before the sky was clear and cloudless, yet even while she spoke the face of the moon grew dark and the wind began to toss in the crests of the plane trees at his feet. Stray gusts brought the sounds of hoarse singing and crying from the lower slopes of the hill, and the pungent odour he had already noticed about the courtyard of the inn rose about him in the air.

"Transform, transform!" she cried again, her voice rising like a song. "Rub well your skin before you fly. Come! Come with me to the Sabbath, to the madness of its furious delight, to the sweet abandonment of its evil worship! See! The Great Ones are there, and the terrible Sacraments prepared. The Throne is occupied. Anoint and come! Anoint and come!"

She grew to the height of a tree beside him, leaping upon the wall with flaming eyes and hair strewn upon the night. He too began to change swiftly. Her hands touched the skin of his face and neck, streaking him with the burning salve that sent the old magic into his blood with the power before which fades all that is good.

A wild roar came up to his ears from the heart of the wood, and the girl, when she heard it, leaped upon the wall in the frenzy of her wicked joy.

"Satan is there!" she screamed, rushing upon him and striving to draw him with her to the edge of the wall. "Satan has come. The Sacraments call us! Come, with your dear apostate soul, and we will worship and dance till the moon dies and the world is forgotten!"

Just saving himself from the dreadful plunge, Vezin struggled to release himself from her grasp, while the passion tore at his reins and all but mastered him. He shrieked aloud, not knowing what he said, and then he shrieked again. It was the old impulses, the old awful habits instinctively finding voice; for though it seemed to him that he merely shrieked nonsense, the words he uttered really had meaning in them, and were intelligible. It was the ancient call. And it was heard below. It was answered.

The wind whistled at the skirts of his coat as the air round him darkened with many flying forms crowding upwards out of the valley. The crying of hoarse voices smote upon his ears, coming closer. Strokes of wind buffeted him, tearing him this way and that along the crumbling top of the stone wall; and Ilsé clung to him with her long shining arms, smooth and bare, holding him fast about the neck. But not Ilsé alone, for a dozen of them surrounded him, dropping out of the air. The pungent odour of the anointed bodies stifled him, exciting him to the old madness of the Sabbath, the dance of the witches and sorcerers doing honour to the personified Evil of the world.

"Anoint and away! Anoint and away!" they cried in wild chorus about him. "To the Dance that never dies! To the sweet and fearful fantasy of evil!"

Another moment and he would have yielded and gone, for his will turned soft and the flood of passionate memory all but overwhelmed him, when – so can a small thing alter the whole course of an adventure – he caught his foot upon a loose stone in the edge of the wall, and then fell with a sudden crash on to the ground below. But he fell towards the houses, in the open space of dust and cobblestones, and fortunately not into the gaping depth of the valley on the farther side.

And they, too, came in a tumbling heap about him, like flies upon a piece of food, but as they fell he was released for a moment from the power of their touch, and in that brief instant of freedom there flashed into his mind the sudden intuition that saved him. Before he could regain his feet he saw them scrabbling awkwardly back upon the wall, as though bat-like they could only fly by dropping from a height, and had no hold upon him in the open. Then, seeing them perched there in a row like cats upon a roof, all dark and singularly shapeless, their eyes like lamps, the sudden memory came back to him of Ilsé's terror at the sight of fire.

Quick as a flash he found his matches and lit the dead leaves that lay under the wall.

Dry and withered, they caught fire at once, and the wind carried the flame in a long line down the length of the wall, licking upwards as it ran; and with shrieks and wailings, the crowded row of forms upon the top melted away into the air on the other side, and were gone with a great rush and whirring of their bodies down into the heart of the haunted valley, leaving Vezin breathless and shaken in the middle of the deserted ground.

"Ilsé!" he called feebly; "Ilsé!" for his heart ached to think that she was really gone to the great Dance without him, and that he had lost the opportunity of its fearful joy. Yet at the same time his relief was so great, and he was so dazed and troubled in mind with the whole thing, that he hardly knew what he was saying, and only cried aloud in the fierce storm of his emotion....

The fire under the wall ran its course, and the moonlight came out again, soft and clear, from its temporary eclipse. With one last shuddering look at the ruined ramparts, and a feeling of horrid wonder for the haunted valley beyond, where the shapes still crowded and flew, he turned his face towards the town and slowly made his way in the direction of the hotel.

And as he went, a great wailing of cries, and a sound of howling, followed him from the gleaming forest below, growing fainter and fainter with the bursts of wind as he disappeared between the houses.

## Chapter VI

"IT MAY SEEM rather abrupt to you, this sudden tame ending," said Arthur Vezin, glancing with flushed face and timid eyes at Dr. Silence sitting there with his notebook, "but the fact is – er – from that moment my memory seems to have failed rather. I have no distinct recollection of how I got home or what precisely I did.

"It appears I never went back to the inn at all. I only dimly recollect racing down a long white road in the moonlight, past woods and villages, still and deserted, and then the dawn came up, and I saw the towers of a biggish town and so came to a station.

"But, long before that, I remember pausing somewhere on the road and looking back to where the hill-town of my adventure stood up in the moonlight, and thinking how exactly like a great monstrous cat it lay there upon the plain, its huge front paws lying down the two main streets, and the twin and broken towers of the cathedral marking its torn ears against the sky. That picture stays in my mind with the utmost vividness to this day.

"Another thing remains in my mind from that escape – namely, the sudden sharp reminder that I had not paid my bill, and the decision I made, standing there on the dusty highroad, that the small baggage I had left behind would more than settle for my indebtedness.

"For the rest, I can only tell you that I got coffee and bread at a café on the outskirts of this town I had come to, and soon after found my way to the station and caught a train later in the day. That same evening I reached London."

"And how long altogether," asked John Silence quietly, "do you think you stayed in the town of the adventure?"

Vezin looked up sheepishly.

"I was coming to that," he resumed, with apologetic wrigglings of his body. "In London I found that I was a whole week out in my reckoning of time. I had stayed over a week in the town, and it ought to have been September 15th – instead of which it was only September 10th!"

"So that, in reality, you had only stayed a night or two in the inn?" queried the doctor.

Vezin hesitated before replying. He shuffled upon the mat.

"I must have gained time somewhere," he said at length – "somewhere or somehow. I certainly had a week to my credit. I can't explain it. I can only give you the fact."

"And this happened to you last year, since when you have never been back to the place?"

"Last autumn, yes," murmured Vezin; "and I have never dared to go back. I think I never want to."

"And, tell me," asked Dr. Silence at length, when he saw that the little man had evidently come to the end of his words and had nothing more to say, "had you ever read up the subject of the old witchcraft practices during the Middle Ages, or been at all interested in the subject?"

"Never!" declared Vezin emphatically. "I had never given a thought to such matters so far as I know—"

"Or to the question of reincarnation, perhaps?"

"Never – before my adventure; but I have since," he replied significantly.

There was, however, something still on the man's mind that he wished to relieve himself of by confession, yet could only with difficulty bring himself to mention; and it was only after the sympathetic tactfulness of the doctor had provided numerous openings that he at length availed himself of one of them, and stammered that he would like to show him the marks he still had on his neck where, he said, the girl had touched him with her anointed hands.

He took off his collar after infinite fumbling hesitation, and lowered his shirt a little for the doctor to see. And there, on the surface of the skin, lay a faint reddish line across the shoulder and extending a little way down the back towards the spine. It certainly indicated exactly the position an arm might have taken in the act of embracing. And on the other side of the neck, slightly higher up, was a similar mark, though not quite so clearly defined.

"That was where she held me that night on the ramparts," he whispered, a strange light coming and going in his eyes.

* * *

It was some weeks later when I again found occasion to consult John Silence concerning another extraordinary case that had come under my notice, and we fell to discussing Vezin's story. Since hearing it, the doctor had made investigations on his own account, and one of his secretaries had discovered that Vezin's ancestors had actually lived for generations in the very town where the adventure came to him. Two of them, both women, had been tried and convicted as witches, and had been burned alive at the stake. Moreover, it had not been difficult to prove that the very inn where Vezin stayed was built about 1700 upon the spot where the funeral pyres stood and the executions took place. The town was a sort of headquarters for all the sorcerers and witches of the entire region, and after conviction they were burnt there literally by scores.

"It seems strange," continued the doctor, "that Vezin should have remained ignorant of all this; but, on the other hand, it was not the kind of history that successive generations would have been anxious to keep alive, or to repeat to their children. Therefore I am inclined to think he still knows nothing about it.

"The whole adventure seems to have been a very vivid revival of the memories of an earlier life, caused by coming directly into contact with the living forces still intense enough to hang about the place, and, by a most singular chance, too, with the very souls who had taken part with him in the events of that particular life. For the mother and daughter who impressed him so strangely must have been leading actors, with himself, in the scenes and practices of witchcraft which at that period dominated the imaginations of the whole country.

"One has only to read the histories of the times to know that these witches claimed the power of transforming themselves into various animals, both for the purposes of disguise and also to convey themselves swiftly to the scenes of their imaginary orgies. Lycanthropy, or the power to change themselves into wolves, was everywhere believed in, and the ability to transform themselves into cats by rubbing their bodies with a special salve or ointment provided by Satan himself, found equal credence. The witchcraft trials abound in evidences of such universal beliefs."

Dr. Silence quoted chapter and verse from many writers on the subject, and showed how every detail of Vezin's adventure had a basis in the practices of those dark days.

"But that the entire affair took place subjectively in the man's own consciousness, I have no doubt," he went on, in reply to my questions; "for my secretary who has been to the town to investigate, discovered his signature in the visitors' book, and proved by it that he had arrived on September 8th, and left suddenly without paying his bill. He left two days later, and they still were in possession of his dirty brown bag and some tourist clothes. I paid a few francs in settlement of his debt, and have sent his luggage on to him. The daughter was absent from home, but the proprietress, a large woman very much as he described her, told my secretary that he had seemed a very strange, absent-minded kind of gentleman, and after his disappearance she had feared for a long time that he had met with a violent end in the neighbouring forest where he used to roam about alone.

"I should like to have obtained a personal interview with the daughter so as to ascertain how much was subjective and how much actually took place with her as Vezin told it. For her dread of fire and the sight of burning must, of course, have been the intuitive memory of her former painful death at the stake, and have thus explained why he fancied more than once that he saw her through smoke and flame."

"And that mark on his skin, for instance?" I inquired.

"Merely the marks produced by hysterical brooding," he replied, "like the stigmata of the *religieuses*, and the bruises which appear on the bodies of hypnotised subjects who have been told to expect them. This is very common and easily explained. Only it seems curious that these marks should have remained so long in Vezin's case. Usually they disappear quickly."

"Obviously he is still thinking about it all, brooding, and living it all over again," I ventured.

"Probably. And this makes me fear that the end of his trouble is not yet. We shall hear of him again. It is a case, alas! I can do little to alleviate."

Dr. Silence spoke gravely and with sadness in his voice.

"And what do you make of the Frenchman in the train?" I asked further – "the man who warned him against the place, *à cause du sommeil et à cause des chats*? Surely a very singular incident?"

"A very singular incident indeed," he made answer slowly, "and one I can only explain on the basis of a highly improbable coincidence—"

"Namely?"

"That the man was one who had himself stayed in the town and undergone there a similar experience. I should like to find this man and ask him. But the crystal is useless here, for I have no slightest clue to go upon, and I can only conclude that some singular psychic affinity, some force still active in his being out of the same past life, drew him thus to the personality of Vezin, and enabled him to fear what might happen to him, and thus to warn him as he did.

"Yes," he presently continued, half talking to himself, "I suspect in this case that Vezin was swept into the vortex of forces arising out of the intense activities of a past life, and that he lived over again a scene in which he had often played a leading part centuries before. For strong actions set up forces that are so slow to exhaust themselves, they may be said in a sense never to die. In this case they were not vital enough to render the illusion complete, so that the little man found himself caught in a very distressing confusion of the present and the past; yet he was sufficiently sensitive to recognise that it was true, and to fight against the degradation of returning, even in memory, to a former and lower state of development.

"Ah yes!" he continued, crossing the floor to gaze at the darkening sky, and seemingly quite oblivious of my presence, "subliminal up-rushes of memory like this can be exceedingly painful, and sometimes exceedingly dangerous. I only trust that this gentle soul may soon escape from this obsession of a passionate and tempestuous past. But I doubt it, I doubt it."

His voice was hushed with sadness as he spoke, and when he turned back into the room again there was an expression of profound yearning upon his face, the yearning of a soul whose desire to help is sometimes greater than his power.

**If you enjoyed this, you might also like…**
Secret Worship, see page 275
The Sea Fit, see page 41

# Secret Worship

HARRIS, the silk merchant, was in South Germany on his way home from a business trip when the idea came to him suddenly that he would take the mountain railway from Strassbourg and run down to revisit his old school after an interval of something more than thirty years. And it was to this chance impulse of the junior partner in Harris Brothers of St. Paul's Churchyard that John Silence owed one of the most curious cases of his whole experience, for at that very moment he happened to be tramping these same mountains with a holiday knapsack, and from different points of the compass the two men were actually converging towards the same inn.

Now, deep down in the heart that for thirty years had been concerned chiefly with the profitable buying and selling of silk, this school had left the imprint of its peculiar influence, and, though perhaps unknown to Harris, had strongly coloured the whole of his subsequent existence. It belonged to the deeply religious life of a small Protestant community (which it is unnecessary to specify), and his father had sent him there at the age of fifteen, partly because he would learn the German requisite for the conduct of the silk business, and partly because the discipline was strict, and discipline was what his soul and body needed just then more than anything else.

The life, indeed, had proved exceedingly severe, and young Harris benefited accordingly; for though corporal punishment was unknown, there was a system of mental and spiritual correction which somehow made the soul stand proudly erect to receive it, while it struck at the very root of the fault and taught the boy that his character was being cleaned and strengthened, and that he was not merely being tortured in a kind of personal revenge.

That was over thirty years ago, when he was a dreamy and impressionable youth of fifteen; and now, as the train climbed slowly up the winding mountain gorges, his mind travelled back somewhat lovingly over the intervening period, and forgotten details rose vividly again before him out of the shadows. The life there had been very wonderful, it seemed to him, in that remote mountain village, protected from the tumults of the world by the love and worship of the devout Brotherhood that ministered to the needs of some hundred boys from every country in Europe. Sharply the scenes came back to him. He smelt again the long stone corridors, the hot pinewood rooms, where the sultry hours of summer study were passed with bees droning through open windows in the sunshine, and German characters struggling in the mind with dreams of English lawns – and then the sudden awful cry of the master in German –

"Harris, stand up! You sleep!"

And he recalled the dreadful standing motionless for an hour, book in hand, while the knees felt like wax and the head grew heavier than a cannon-ball.

The very smell of the cooking came back to him – the daily *Sauerkraut*, the watery chocolate on Sundays, the flavour of the stringy meat served twice a week at *Mittagessen*; and he smiled to think again of the half-rations that was the punishment for speaking English. The very odour of the milk-bowls – the hot sweet aroma that rose from the soaking peasant-bread at the six-o'clock breakfast – came back to him pungently, and he saw the huge *Speisesaal* with the hundred boys in their school uniform, all eating sleepily in silence, gulping down the coarse bread and scalding milk in terror of the bell that would presently cut them short – and, at the far end where the masters sat, he saw the narrow slit windows with the vistas of enticing field and forest beyond.

And this, in turn, made him think of the great barnlike room on the top floor where all slept together in wooden cots, and he heard in memory the clamour of the cruel bell that woke them on winter mornings at five o'clock and summoned them to the stone-flagged *Waschkammer*, where boys and masters alike, after scanty and icy washing, dressed in complete silence.

From this his mind passed swiftly, with vivid picture-thoughts, to other things, and with a passing shiver he remembered how the loneliness of never being alone had eaten into him, and how everything – work, meals, sleep, walks, leisure – was done with his 'division' of twenty other boys and under the eyes of at least two masters. The only solitude possible was by asking for half an hour's practice in the cell-like music rooms, and Harris smiled to himself as he recalled the zeal of his violin studies.

Then, as the train puffed laboriously through the great pine forests that cover these mountains with a giant carpet of velvet, he found the pleasanter layers of memory giving up their dead, and he recalled with admiration the kindness of the masters, whom all addressed as Brother, and marvelled afresh at their devotion in burying themselves for years in such a place, only to leave it, in most cases, for the still rougher life of missionaries in the wild places of the world.

He thought once more of the still, religious atmosphere that hung over the little forest community like a veil, barring the distressful world; of the picturesque ceremonies at Easter, Christmas, and New Year; of the numerous feast-days and charming little festivals. The *Beschehr-Fest*, in particular, came back to him – the feast of gifts at Christmas – when the entire community paired off and gave presents, many of which had taken weeks to make or the savings of many days to purchase. And then he saw the midnight ceremony in the church at New Year, with the shining face of the *Prediger* in the pulpit – the village preacher who, on the last night of the old year, saw in the empty gallery beyond the organ loft the faces of all who were to die in the ensuing twelve months, and who at last recognised himself among them, and, in the very middle of his sermon, passed into a state of rapt ecstasy and burst into a torrent of praise.

Thickly the memories crowded upon him. The picture of the small village dreaming its unselfish life on the mountain-tops, clean, wholesome, simple, searching vigorously for its God, and training hundreds of boys in the grand way, rose up in his mind with all the power of an obsession. He felt once more the old mystical enthusiasm, deeper than the sea and more wonderful than the stars; he heard again the winds sighing from leagues of forest over the red roofs in the moonlight; he heard the Brothers' voices talking of the things beyond this life as though they had actually experienced them in the body; and, as he sat in the jolting train, a spirit of unutterable longing passed over his seared and tired soul, stirring in the depths of him a sea of emotions that he thought had long since frozen into immobility.

And the contrast pained him – the idealistic dreamer then, the man of business now – so that a spirit of unworldly peace and beauty known only to the soul in meditation laid its feathered finger upon his heart, moving strangely the surface of the waters.

Harris shivered a little and looked out of the window of his empty carriage. The train had long passed Hornberg, and far below the streams tumbled in white foam down the limestone rocks. In front of him, dome upon dome of wooded mountain stood against the sky. It was October, and the air was cool and sharp, woodsmoke and damp moss exquisitely mingled in it with the subtle odours of the pines. Overhead, between the tips of the highest firs, he saw the first stars peeping, and the sky was a clean, pale amethyst that seemed exactly the colour all these memories clothed themselves with in his mind.

He leaned back in his corner and sighed. He was a heavy man, and he had not known sentiment for years; he was a big man, and it took much to move him, literally and figuratively; he was a man in whom the dreams of God that haunt the soul in youth, though overlaid by the scum that gathers in the fight for money, had not, as with the majority, utterly died the death.

He came back into this little neglected pocket of the years, where so much fine gold had collected and lain undisturbed, with all his semispiritual emotions aquiver; and, as he watched the mountain-tops come nearer, and smelt the forgotten odours of his boyhood, something melted on the surface of his soul and left him sensitive to a degree he had not known since, thirty years before, he had lived here with his dreams, his conflicts, and his youthful suffering.

A thrill ran through him as the train stopped with a jolt at a tiny station and he saw the name in large black lettering on the grey stone building, and below it, the number of metres it stood above the level of the sea.

"The highest point on the line!" he exclaimed. "How well I remember it – Sommerau – Summer Meadow. The very next station is mine!"

And, as the train ran downhill with brakes on and steam shut off, he put his head out of the window and one by one saw the old familiar landmarks in the dusk. They stared at him like dead faces in a dream. Queer, sharp feelings, half poignant, half sweet, stirred in his heart.

"There's the hot, white road we walked along so often with the two Brüder always at our heels," he thought; "and there, by Jove, is the turn through the forest to '*Die Galgen*', the stone gallows where they hanged the witches in olden days!"

He smiled a little as the train slid past.

"And there's the copse where the Lilies of the Valley powdered the ground in spring; and, I swear," – he put his head out with a sudden impulse – "if that's not the very clearing where Calame, the French boy, chased the swallow-tail with me, and Bruder Pagel gave us half-rations for leaving the road without permission, and for shouting in our mother tongues!" And he laughed again as the memories came back with a rush, flooding his mind with vivid detail.

The train stopped, and he stood on the grey gravel platform like a man in a dream. It seemed half a century since he last waited there with corded wooden boxes, and got into the train for Strassbourg and home after the two years' exile. Time dropped from him like an old garment and he felt a boy again. Only, things looked so much smaller than his memory of them; shrunk and dwindled they looked, and the distances seemed on a curiously smaller scale.

He made his way across the road to the little Gasthaus, and, as he went, faces and figures of former schoolfellows – German, Swiss, Italian, French, Russian – slipped out of the shadowy woods and silently accompanied him. They flitted by his side, raising their eyes questioningly, sadly, to his. But their names he had forgotten. Some of the

Brothers, too, came with them, and most of these he remembered by name – Bruder Röst, Bruder Pagel, Bruder Schliemann, and the bearded face of the old preacher who had seen himself in the haunted gallery of those about to die – Bruder Gysin. The dark forest lay all about him like a sea that any moment might rush with velvet waves upon the scene and sweep all the faces away. The air was cool and wonderfully fragrant, but with every perfumed breath came also a pallid memory....

Yet, in spite of the underlying sadness inseparable from such an experience, it was all very interesting, and held a pleasure peculiarly its own, so that Harris engaged his room and ordered supper feeling well pleased with himself, and intending to walk up to the old school that very evening. It stood in the centre of the community's village, some four miles distant through the forest, and he now recollected for the first time that this little Protestant settlement dwelt isolated in a section of the country that was otherwise Catholic. Crucifixes and shrines surrounded the clearing like the sentries of a beleaguering army. Once beyond the square of the village, with its few acres of field and orchard, the forest crowded up in solid phalanxes, and beyond the rim of trees began the country that was ruled by the priests of another faith. He vaguely remembered, too, that the Catholics had showed sometimes a certain hostility towards the little Protestant oasis that flourished so quietly and benignly in their midst. He had quite forgotten this. How trumpery it all seemed now with his wide experience of life and his knowledge of other countries and the great outside world. It was like stepping back, not thirty years, but three hundred.

There were only two others besides himself at supper. One of them, a bearded, middle-aged man in tweeds, sat by himself at the far end, and Harris kept out of his way because he was English. He feared he might be in business, possibly even in the silk business, and that he would perhaps talk on the subject. The other traveller, however, was a Catholic priest. He was a little man who ate his salad with a knife, yet so gently that it was almost inoffensive, and it was the sight of 'the cloth' that recalled his memory of the old antagonism. Harris mentioned by way of conversation the object of his sentimental journey, and the priest looked up sharply at him with raised eyebrows and an expression of surprise and suspicion that somehow piqued him. He ascribed it to his difference of belief.

"Yes," went on the silk merchant, pleased to talk of what his mind was so full, "and it was a curious experience for an English boy to be dropped down into a school of a hundred foreigners. I well remember the loneliness and intolerable Heimweh of it at first." His German was very fluent.

The priest opposite looked up from his cold veal and potato salad and smiled. It was a nice face. He explained quietly that he did not belong here, but was making a tour of the parishes of Wurttemberg and Baden.

"It was a strict life," added Harris. "We English, I remember, used to call it *Gefängnisleben* – prison life!"

The face of the other, for some unaccountable reason, darkened. After a slight pause, and more by way of politeness than because he wished to continue the subject, he said quietly –

"It was a flourishing school in those days, of course. Afterwards, I have heard—" He shrugged his shoulders slightly, and the odd look – it almost seemed a look of alarm – came back into his eyes. The sentence remained unfinished.

Something in the tone of the man seemed to his listener uncalled for – in a sense reproachful, singular. Harris bridled in spite of himself.

"It has changed?" he asked. "I can hardly believe—"

"You have not heard, then?" observed the priest gently, making a gesture as though to cross himself, yet not actually completing it. "You have not heard what happened there before it was abandoned—?"

It was very childish, of course, and perhaps he was overtired and overwrought in some way, but the words and manner of the little priest seemed to him so offensive – so disproportionately offensive – that he hardly noticed the concluding sentence. He recalled the old bitterness and the old antagonism, and for a moment he almost lost his temper.

"Nonsense," he interrupted with a forced laugh, "*Unsinn*! You must forgive me, sir, for contradicting you. But I was a pupil there myself. I was at school there. There was no place like it. I cannot believe that anything serious could have happened to – to take away its character. The devotion of the Brothers would be difficult to equal anywhere—"

He broke off suddenly, realising that his voice had been raised unduly and that the man at the far end of the table might understand German; and at the same moment he looked up and saw that this individual's eyes were fixed upon his face intently. They were peculiarly bright. Also they were rather wonderful eyes, and the way they met his own served in some way he could not understand to convey both a reproach and a warning. The whole face of the stranger, indeed, made a vivid impression upon him, for it was a face, he now noticed for the first time, in whose presence one would not willingly have said or done anything unworthy. Harris could not explain to himself how it was he had not become conscious sooner of its presence.

But he could have bitten off his tongue for having so far forgotten himself. The little priest lapsed into silence. Only once he said, looking up and speaking in a low voice that was not intended to be overheard, but that evidently *was* overheard, "You will find it different." Presently he rose and left the table with a polite bow that included both the others.

And, after him, from the far end rose also the figure in the tweed suit, leaving Harris by himself.

He sat on for a bit in the darkening room, sipping his coffee and smoking his fifteen-pfennig cigar, till the girl came in to light the oil lamps. He felt vexed with himself for his lapse from good manners, yet hardly able to account for it. Most likely, he reflected, he had been annoyed because the priest had unintentionally changed the pleasant character of his dream by introducing a jarring note. Later he must seek an opportunity to make amends. At present, however, he was too impatient for his walk to the school, and he took his stick and hat and passed out into the open air.

And, as he crossed before the Gasthaus, he noticed that the priest and the man in the tweed suit were engaged already in such deep conversation that they hardly noticed him as he passed and raised his hat.

He started off briskly, well remembering the way, and hoping to reach the village in time to have a word with one of the Brüder. They might even ask him in for a cup of coffee. He felt sure of his welcome, and the old memories were in full possession once more. The hour of return was a matter of no consequence whatever.

It was then just after seven o'clock, and the October evening was drawing in with chill airs from the recesses of the forest. The road plunged straight from the railway clearing into its depths, and in a very few minutes the trees engulfed him and the clack of his boots fell dead and echoless against the serried stems of a million firs. It was very black; one trunk was hardly distinguishable from another. He walked smartly, swinging his holly stick. Once or twice he passed a peasant on his way to bed, and the guttural "Gruss Gott," unheard for so long, emphasised the passage of time, while yet making it seem as nothing. A fresh group of pictures crowded his mind. Again the figures of former schoolfellows flitted out of the forest and kept pace by his side, whispering of the doings of long ago. One reverie stepped hard upon the heels of another. Every turn in the road, every clearing of the forest, he knew, and each in turn brought forgotten associations to life. He enjoyed himself thoroughly.

He marched on and on. There was powdered gold in the sky till the moon rose, and then a wind of faint silver spread silently between the earth and stars. He saw the tips of the fir trees shimmer, and heard them whisper as the breeze turned their needles towards the light. The mountain air was indescribably sweet. The road shone like the foam of a river through the gloom. White moths flitted here and there like silent thoughts across his path, and a hundred smells greeted him from the forest caverns across the years.

Then, when he least expected it, the trees fell away abruptly on both sides, and he stood on the edge of the village clearing.

He walked faster. There lay the familiar outlines of the houses, sheeted with silver; there stood the trees in the little central square with the fountain and small green lawns; there loomed the shape of the church next to the Gasthof der Brüdergemeinde; and just beyond, dimly rising into the sky, he saw with a sudden thrill the mass of the huge school building, blocked castlelike with deep shadows in the moonlight, standing square and formidable to face him after the silences of more than a quarter of a century.

He passed quickly down the deserted village street and stopped close beneath its shadow, staring up at the walls that had once held him prisoner for two years – two unbroken years of discipline and homesickness. Memories and emotions surged through his mind; for the most vivid sensations of his youth had focused about this spot, and it was here he had first begun to live and learn values. Not a single footstep broke the silence, though lights glimmered here and there through cottage windows; but when he looked up at the high walls of the school, draped now in shadow, he easily imagined that well-known faces crowded to the windows to greet him – closed windows that really reflected only moonlight and the gleam of stars.

This, then, was the old school building, standing foursquare to the world, with its shuttered windows, its lofty, tiled roof, and the spiked lightning-conductors pointing like black and taloned fingers from the corners. For a long time he stood and stared. Then, presently, he came to himself again, and realised to his joy that a light still shone in the windows of the Bruderstube.

He turned from the road and passed through the iron railings; then climbed the twelve stone steps and stood facing the black wooden door with the heavy bars of iron, a door he had once loathed and dreaded with the hatred and passion of an imprisoned soul, but now looked upon tenderly with a sort of boyish delight.

Almost timorously he pulled the rope and listened with a tremor of excitement to the clanging of the bell deep within the building. And the long-forgotten sound brought the past before him with such a vivid sense of reality that he positively shivered. It was like the magic bell in the fairy-tale that rolls back the curtain of Time and summons the figures from the shadows of the dead. He had never felt so sentimental in his life. It was like being young again. And, at the same time, he began to bulk rather large in his own eyes with a certain spurious importance. He was a big man from the world of strife and action. In this little place of peaceful dreams would he, perhaps, not cut something of a figure?

"I'll try once more," he thought after a long pause, seizing the iron bell-rope, and was just about to pull it when a step sounded on the stone passage within, and the huge door slowly swung open.

A tall man with a rather severe cast of countenance stood facing him in silence.

"I must apologise – it is somewhat late," he began a trifle pompously, "but the fact is I am an old pupil. I have only just arrived and really could not restrain myself." His German seemed not quite so fluent as usual. "My interest is so great. I was here in '70."

The other opened the door wider and at once bowed him in with a smile of genuine welcome.

"I am Bruder Kalkmann," he said quietly in a deep voice. "I myself was a master here about that time. It is a great pleasure always to welcome a former pupil." He looked at him very keenly for a few seconds, and then added, "I think, too, it is splendid of you to come – very splendid."

"It is a very great pleasure," Harris replied, delighted with his reception.

The dimly lighted corridor with its flooring of grey stone, and the familiar sound of a German voice echoing through it – with the peculiar intonation the Brothers always used in speaking – all combined to lift him bodily, as it were, into the dream-atmosphere of long-forgotten days. He stepped gladly into the building and the door shut with the familiar thunder that completed the reconstruction of the past. He almost felt the old sense of imprisonment, of aching nostalgia, of having lost his liberty.

Harris sighed involuntarily and turned towards his host, who returned his smile faintly and then led the way down the corridor.

"The boys have retired," he explained, "and, as you remember, we keep early hours here. But, at least, you will join us for a little while in the *Bruderstube* and enjoy a cup of coffee." This was precisely what the silk merchant had hoped, and he accepted with an alacrity that he intended to be tempered by graciousness. "And tomorrow," continued the Bruder, "you must come and spend a whole day with us. You may even find acquaintances, for several pupils of your day have come back here as masters."

For one brief second there passed into the man's eyes a look that made the visitor start. But it vanished as quickly as it came. It was impossible to define. Harris convinced himself it was the effect of a shadow cast by the lamp they had just passed on the wall. He dismissed it from his mind.

"You are very kind, I'm sure," he said politely. "It is perhaps a greater pleasure to me than you can imagine to see the place again. Ah," – he stopped short opposite a door with the upper half of glass and peered in – "surely there is one of the music rooms where I used to practise the violin. How it comes back to me after all these years!"

Bruder Kalkmann stopped indulgently, smiling, to allow his guest a moment's inspection.

"You still have the boys' orchestra? I remember I used to play 'zweite Geige' in it. Bruder Schliemann conducted at the piano. Dear me, I can see him now with his long black hair and – and—" He stopped abruptly. Again the odd, dark look passed over the stern face of his companion. For an instant it seemed curiously familiar.

"We still keep up the pupils' orchestra," he said, "but Bruder Schliemann, I am sorry to say—" he hesitated an instant, and then added, "Bruder Schliemann is dead."

"Indeed, indeed," said Harris quickly. "I am sorry to hear it." He was conscious of a faint feeling of distress, but whether it arose from the news of his old music teacher's death, or – from something else – he could not quite determine. He gazed down the corridor that lost itself among shadows. In the street and village everything had seemed so much smaller than he remembered, but here, inside the school building, everything seemed so much bigger. The corridor was loftier and longer, more spacious and vast, than the mental picture he had preserved. His thoughts wandered dreamily for an instant.

He glanced up and saw the face of the Bruder watching him with a smile of patient indulgence.

"Your memories possess you," he observed gently, and the stern look passed into something almost pitying.

"You are right," returned the man of silk, "they do. This was the most wonderful period of my whole life in a sense. At the time I hated it—" He hesitated, not wishing to hurt the Brother's feelings.

"According to English ideas it seemed strict, of course," the other said persuasively, so that he went on.

" – Yes, partly that; and partly the ceaseless nostalgia, and the solitude which came from never being really alone. In English schools the boys enjoy peculiar freedom, you know."

Bruder Kalkmann, he saw, was listening intently.

"But it produced one result that I have never wholly lost," he continued self-consciously, "and am grateful for."

"*Ach! Wie so, denn?*"

"The constant inner pain threw me headlong into your religious life, so that the whole force of my being seemed to project itself towards the search for a deeper satisfaction – a real resting-place for the soul. During my two years here I yearned for God in my boyish way as perhaps I have never yearned for anything since. Moreover, I have never quite lost that sense of peace and inward joy which accompanied the search. I can never quite forget this school and the deep things it taught me."

He paused at the end of his long speech, and a brief silence fell between them. He feared he had said too much, or expressed himself clumsily in the foreign language, and when Bruder Kalkmann laid a hand upon his shoulder, he gave a little involuntary start.

"So that my memories perhaps do possess me rather strongly," he added apologetically; "and this long corridor, these rooms, that barred and gloomy front door, all touch chords that – that—" His German failed him and he glanced at his companion with an explanatory smile and gesture. But the Brother had removed the hand from his shoulder and was standing with his back to him, looking down the passage.

"Naturally, naturally so," he said hastily without turning round. "*Es ist doch selbstverständlich.* We shall all understand."

Then he turned suddenly, and Harris saw that his face had turned most oddly and disagreeably sinister. It may only have been the shadows again playing their tricks with the wretched oil lamps on the wall, for the dark expression passed instantly as they retraced their steps down the corridor, but the Englishman somehow got the impression that he had said something to give offence, something that was not quite to the other's taste. Opposite the door of the *Bruderstube* they stopped. Harris realised that it was late and he had possibly stayed talking too long. He made a tentative effort to leave, but his companion would not hear of it.

"You must have a cup of coffee with us," he said firmly as though he meant it, "and my colleagues will be delighted to see you. Some of them will remember you, perhaps."

The sound of voices came pleasantly through the door, men's voices talking together. Bruder Kalkmann turned the handle and they entered a room ablaze with light and full of people.

"Ah – but your name?" he whispered, bending down to catch the reply; "you have not told me your name yet."

"Harris," said the Englishman quickly as they went in. He felt nervous as he crossed the threshold, but ascribed the momentary trepidation to the fact that he was breaking the strictest rule of the whole establishment, which forbade a boy under severest penalties to come near this holy of holies where the masters took their brief leisure.

"Ah, yes, of course – Harris," repeated the other as though he remembered it. "Come in, Herr Harris, come in, please. Your visit will be immensely appreciated. It is really very fine, very wonderful of you to have come in this way."

The door closed behind them and, in the sudden light which made his sight swim for a moment, the exaggeration of the language escaped his attention. He heard the voice of Bruder Kalkmann introducing him. He spoke very loud, indeed, unnecessarily, – absurdly loud, Harris thought.

"Brothers," he announced, "it is my pleasure and privilege to introduce to you Herr Harris from England. He has just arrived to make us a little visit, and I have already expressed to him on behalf of us all the satisfaction we feel that he is here. He was, as you remember, a pupil in the year '70."

It was a very formal, a very German introduction, but Harris rather liked it. It made him feel important and he appreciated the tact that made it almost seem as though he had been expected.

The black forms rose and bowed; Harris bowed; Kalkmann bowed. Everyone was very polite and very courtly. The room swam with moving figures; the light dazzled him after the gloom of the corridor, there was thick cigar smoke in the atmosphere. He took the chair that was offered to him between two of the Brothers, and sat down, feeling vaguely that his perceptions were not quite as keen and accurate as usual. He felt a trifle dazed perhaps, and the spell of the past came strongly over him, confusing the immediate present and making everything dwindle oddly to the dimensions of long ago. He seemed to pass under the mastery of a great mood that was a composite reproduction of all the moods of his forgotten boyhood.

Then he pulled himself together with a sharp effort and entered into the conversation that had begun again to buzz round him. Moreover, he entered into it with keen pleasure, for the Brothers – there were perhaps a dozen of them in the little room – treated him with a charm of manner that speedily made him feel one of themselves. This, again, was a very subtle delight to him. He felt that he had stepped out of the greedy, vulgar, self-seeking world, the world of silk and markets and profit-making – stepped into the cleaner atmosphere where spiritual ideals were paramount and life was simple and devoted. It all charmed him inexpressibly, so that he realised – yes, in a sense – the degradation of his twenty years' absorption in business. This keen atmosphere under the stars where men thought only of their souls, and of the souls of others, was too rarefied for the world he was now associated with. He found himself making comparisons to his own disadvantage – comparisons with the mystical little dreamer that had stepped thirty years before from the stern peace of this devout community, and the man of the world that he had since become – and the contrast made him shiver with a keen regret and something like self-contempt.

He glanced round at the other faces floating towards him through tobacco smoke – this acrid cigar smoke he remembered so well: how keen they were, how strong, placid, touched with the nobility of great aims and unselfish purposes. At one or two he looked particularly. He hardly knew why. They rather fascinated him. There was something so very stern and uncompromising about them, and something, too, oddly, subtly, familiar, that yet just eluded him. But whenever their eyes met his own they held undeniable welcome in them; and some held more – a kind of perplexed admiration, he thought, something that was between esteem and deference. This note of respect in all the faces was very flattering to his vanity.

Coffee was served presently, made by a black-haired Brother who sat in the corner by the piano and bore a marked resemblance to Bruder Schliemann, the musical director of thirty years ago. Harris exchanged bows with him when he took the cup from his white hands, which he noticed were like the hands of a woman. He lit a cigar, offered to him by his neighbour, with whom he was chatting delightfully, and who, in the glare of the lighted match, reminded him sharply for a moment of Bruder Pagel, his former room-master.

"*Es ist wirklich merkwürdig*," he said, "how many resemblances I see, or imagine. It is really *very* curious!"

"Yes," replied the other, peering at him over his coffee cup, "the spell of the place is wonderfully strong. I can well understand that the old faces rise before your mind's eye – almost to the exclusion of ourselves perhaps."

They both laughed presently. It was soothing to find his mood understood and appreciated. And they passed on to talk of the mountain village, its isolation, its remoteness from worldly life, its peculiar fitness for meditation and worship, and for spiritual development – of a certain kind.

"And your coming back in this way, Herr Harris, has pleased us all so much," joined in the Bruder on his left. "We esteem you for it most highly. We honour you for it."

Harris made a deprecating gesture. "I fear, for my part, it is only a very selfish pleasure," he said a trifle unctuously.

"Not all would have had the courage," added the one who resembled Bruder Pagel.

"You mean," said Harris, a little puzzled, "the disturbing memories—?"

Bruder Pagel looked at him steadily, with unmistakable admiration and respect. "I mean that most men hold so strongly to life, and can give up so little for their beliefs," he said gravely.

The Englishman felt slightly uncomfortable. These worthy men really made too much of his sentimental journey. Besides, the talk was getting a little out of his depth. He hardly followed it.

"The worldly life still has *some* charms for me," he replied smilingly, as though to indicate that sainthood was not yet quite within his grasp.

"All the more, then, must we honour you for so freely coming," said the Brother on his left; "so unconditionally!"

A pause followed, and the silk merchant felt relieved when the conversation took a more general turn, although he noted that it never travelled very far from the subject of his visit and the wonderful situation of the lonely village for men who wished to develop their spiritual powers and practise the rites of a high worship. Others joined in, complimenting him on his knowledge of the language, making him feel utterly at his ease, yet at the same time a little uncomfortable by the excess of their admiration. After all, it was such a very small thing to do, this sentimental journey.

The time passed along quickly; the coffee was excellent, the cigars soft and of the nutty flavour he loved. At length, fearing to outstay his welcome, he rose reluctantly to take his leave. But the others would not hear of it. It was not often a former pupil returned to visit them in this simple, unaffected way. The night was young. If necessary they could even find him a corner in the great *Schlafzimmer* upstairs. He was easily persuaded to stay a little longer. Somehow he had become the centre of the little party. He felt pleased, flattered, honoured.

"And perhaps Bruder Schliemann will play something for us – now."

It was Kalkmann speaking, and Harris started visibly as he heard the name, and saw the black-haired man by the piano turn with a smile. For Schliemann was the name of his old music director, who was dead. Could this be his son? They were so exactly alike.

"If Bruder Meyer has not put his Amati to bed, I will accompany him," said the musician suggestively, looking across at a man whom Harris had not yet noticed, and who, he now saw, was the very image of a former master of that name.

Meyer rose and excused himself with a little bow, and the Englishman quickly observed that he had a peculiar gesture as though his neck had a false join on to the body just below the collar and feared it might break. Meyer of old had this trick of movement. He remembered how the boys used to copy it.

He glanced sharply from face to face, feeling as though some silent, unseen process were changing everything about him. All the faces seemed oddly familiar. Pagel, the Brother he had been talking with, was of course the image of Pagel, his former room-master, and Kalkmann, he now realised for the first time, was the very twin of another master whose name he had quite forgotten, but whom he used to dislike intensely in the old days. And, through the smoke, peering at him from the corners of the room, he saw that all the Brothers about him had the faces he had known and lived with long ago – Röst, Fluheim, Meinert, Rigel, Gysin.

He stared hard, suddenly grown more alert, and everywhere saw, or fancied he saw, strange likenesses, ghostly resemblances, – more, the identical faces of years ago. There was something queer about it all, something not quite right, something that made him feel uneasy. He shook himself, mentally and actually, blowing the smoke from before his eyes with a long breath, and as he did so he noticed to his dismay that everyone was fixedly staring. They were watching him.

This brought him to his senses. As an Englishman, and a foreigner, he did not wish to be rude, or to do anything to make himself foolishly conspicuous and spoil the harmony of the evening. He was a guest, and a privileged guest at that. Besides, the music had already begun. Bruder Schliemann's long white fingers were caressing the keys to some purpose.

He subsided into his chair and smoked with half-closed eyes that yet saw everything.

But the shudder had established itself in his being, and, whether he would or not, it kept repeating itself. As a town, far up some inland river, feels the pressure of the distant sea, so he became aware that mighty forces from somewhere beyond his ken were urging themselves up against his soul in this smoky little room. He began to feel exceedingly ill at ease.

And as the music filled the air his mind began to clear. Like a lifted veil there rose up something that had hitherto obscured his vision. The words of the priest at the railway inn flashed across his brain unbidden: "You will find it different." And also, though why he could not tell, he saw mentally the strong, rather wonderful eyes of that other guest at the supper-table, the man who had overheard his conversation, and had later got into earnest talk with the priest. He took out his watch and stole a glance at it. Two hours had slipped by. It was already eleven o'clock.

Schliemann, meanwhile, utterly absorbed in his music, was playing a solemn measure. The piano sang marvellously. The power of a great conviction, the simplicity of great art, the vital spiritual message of a soul that had found itself – all this, and more, were in the chords, and yet somehow the music was what can only be described as impure – atrociously and diabolically impure. And the piece itself, although Harris did not recognise it as anything familiar, was surely the music of a Mass – huge, majestic, sombre? It stalked through the smoky room with slow power, like the passage of something that was mighty, yet profoundly intimate, and as it went there stirred into each and every face about him the signature of the enormous forces of which it was the audible symbol. The countenances round him turned sinister, but not idly, negatively sinister: they grew dark with purpose. He suddenly recalled the face of Bruder Kalkmann in the corridor earlier in the evening. The motives of their secret souls rose to the eyes, and mouths, and foreheads, and hung there for all to see like the black banners of an assembly of ill-starred and fallen creatures. Demons – was the horrible word that flashed through his brain like a sheet of fire.

When this sudden discovery leaped out upon him, for a moment he lost his self-control. Without waiting to think and weigh his extraordinary impression, he did a very foolish but a very natural thing. Feeling himself irresistibly driven by the sudden stress to some kind of action, he sprang to his feet – and screamed! To his own utter amazement he stood up and shrieked aloud!

But no one stirred. No one, apparently, took the slightest notice of his absurdly wild behaviour. It was almost as if no one but himself had heard the scream at all – as though the music had drowned it and swallowed it up – as though after all perhaps he had not really screamed as loudly as he imagined, or had not screamed at all.

Then, as he glanced at the motionless, dark faces before him, something of utter cold passed into his being, touching his very soul.... All emotion cooled suddenly, leaving him like a receding tide. He sat down again, ashamed, mortified, angry with himself for behaving like a fool and a boy. And the music, meanwhile, continued to issue from the white and snakelike fingers of Bruder Schliemann, as poisoned wine might issue from the weirdly fashioned necks of antique phials.

And, with the rest of them, Harris drank it in.

Forcing himself to believe that he had been the victim of some kind of illusory perception, he vigorously restrained his feelings. Then the music presently ceased, and everyone applauded and began to talk at once, laughing, changing seats, complimenting the player, and behaving naturally and easily as though nothing out of the way had happened. The faces appeared normal once more. The Brothers crowded round their visitor, and he joined in their talk and even heard himself thanking the gifted musician.

But, at the same time, he found himself edging towards the door, nearer and nearer, changing his chair when possible, and joining the groups that stood closest to the way of escape.

"I must thank you all *tausendmal* for my little reception and the great pleasure – the very great honour you have done me," he began in decided tones at length, "but I fear I have trespassed far too long already on your hospitality. Moreover, I have some distance to walk to my inn."

A chorus of voices greeted his words. They would not hear of his going – at least not without first partaking of refreshment. They produced pumpernickel from one cupboard, and rye-bread and sausage from another, and all began to talk again and eat. More coffee was made, fresh cigars lighted, and Bruder Meyer took out his violin and began to tune it softly.

"There is always a bed upstairs if Herr Harris will accept it," said one.

"And it is difficult to find the way out now, for all the doors are locked," laughed another loudly.

"Let us take our simple pleasures as they come," cried a third. "Bruder Harris will understand how we appreciate the honour of this last visit of his."

They made a dozen excuses. They all laughed, as though the politeness of their words was but formal, and veiled thinly – more and more thinly – a very different meaning.

"And the hour of midnight draws near," added Bruder Kalkmann with a charming smile, but in a voice that sounded to the Englishman like the grating of iron hinges.

Their German seemed to him more and more difficult to understand. He noted that they called him 'Bruder' too, classing him as one of themselves.

And then suddenly he had a flash of keener perception, and realised with a creeping of his flesh that he had all along misinterpreted – grossly misinterpreted all they had been saying. They had talked about the beauty of the place, its isolation and remoteness from the world, its peculiar fitness for certain kinds of spiritual development and worship – yet hardly, he now grasped, in the sense in which he had taken the words. They had meant something different. Their spiritual powers, their desire for loneliness, their passion for worship, were not the powers, the solitude, or the worship that *he* meant and understood. He was playing a part in some horrible masquerade; he was among men who cloaked their lives with religion in order to follow their real purposes unseen of men.

What did it all mean? How had he blundered into so equivocal a situation? Had he blundered into it at all? Had he not rather been led into it, deliberately led? His thoughts grew dreadfully confused, and his confidence in himself began to fade. And why, he suddenly thought again, were they so impressed by the mere fact of his coming to revisit his old school? What was it they so admired and wondered at in his simple act? Why did they set such store upon his having the courage to come, to 'give himself so freely', 'unconditionally' as one of them had expressed it with such a mockery of exaggeration?

Fear stirred in his heart most horribly, and he found no answer to any of his questionings. Only one thing he now understood quite clearly: it was their purpose to keep him here. They did not intend that he should go. And from this moment he realised that they were sinister, formidable and, in some way he had yet to discover, inimical to himself, inimical to his life. And the phrase one of them had used a moment ago – "this *last* visit of his" – rose before his eyes in letters of flame.

Harris was not a man of action, and had never known in all the course of his career what it meant to be in a situation of real danger. He was not necessarily a coward, though, perhaps, a man of untried nerve. He realised at last plainly that he was in a very awkward predicament indeed, and that he had to deal with men who were utterly in earnest. What their intentions were he only vaguely guessed. His mind, indeed, was too confused for definite ratiocination, and he was only able to follow blindly the strongest instincts that moved in him. It never occurred to him that the Brothers might all be mad, or that he himself might have temporarily lost his senses and be suffering under some terrible delusion. In fact, nothing occurred to him – he realised nothing – except that he meant to escape – and the quicker the better. A tremendous revulsion of feeling set in and overpowered him.

Accordingly, without further protest for the moment, he ate his pumpernickel and drank his coffee, talking meanwhile as naturally and pleasantly as he could, and when a suitable interval had passed, he rose to his feet and announced once more that he must now take his leave. He spoke very quietly, but very decidedly. No one hearing him could doubt that he meant what he said. He had got very close to the door by this time.

"I regret," he said, using his best German, and speaking to a hushed room, "that our pleasant evening must come to an end, but it is now time for me to wish you all goodnight." And then, as no one said anything, he added, though with a trifle less assurance, "And I thank you all most sincerely for your hospitality."

"On the contrary," replied Kalkmann instantly, rising from his chair and ignoring the hand the Englishman had stretched out to him, "it is we who have to thank you; and we do so most gratefully and sincerely."

And at the same moment at least half a dozen of the Brothers took up their position between himself and the door.

"You are very good to say so," Harris replied as firmly as he could manage, noticing this movement out of the corner of his eye, "but really I had no conception that – my little chance visit could have afforded you so much pleasure." He moved another step nearer the door, but Bruder Schliemann came across the room quickly and stood in front of him. His attitude was uncompromising. A dark and terrible expression had come into his face.

"But it was *not* by chance that you came, Bruder Harris," he said so that all the room could hear; "surely we have not misunderstood your presence here?" He raised his black eyebrows.

"No, no," the Englishman hastened to reply, "I was – I am delighted to be here. I told you what pleasure it gave me to find myself among you. Do not misunderstand me, I beg." His voice faltered a little, and he had difficulty in finding the words. More and more, too, he had difficulty in understanding *their* words.

"Of course," interposed Bruder Kalkmann in his iron bass, "*we* have not misunderstood. You have come back in the spirit of true and unselfish devotion. You offer yourself freely, and we all appreciate it. It is your willingness and nobility that have so completely won our veneration and respect." A faint murmur of applause ran round the room. "What we all delight in – what our great Master will especially delight in – is the value of your spontaneous and voluntary—"

He used a word Harris did not understand. He said "*Opfer.*" The bewildered Englishman searched his brain for the translation, and searched in vain. For the life of him he could not remember what it meant. But the word, for all his inability to translate it, touched his soul with ice. It was worse, far worse, than anything he had imagined. He felt like a lost, helpless creature, and all power to fight sank out of him from that moment.

"It is magnificent to be such a willing—" added Schliemann, sidling up to him with a dreadful leer on his face. He made use of the same word – "*Opfer.*"

God! What could it all mean? 'Offer himself!' 'True spirit of devotion!' 'Willing', 'unselfish', 'magnificent!' *Opfer, Opfer, Opfer!* What in the name of heaven did it mean, that strange, mysterious word that struck such terror into his heart?

He made a valiant effort to keep his presence of mind and hold his nerves steady. Turning, he saw that Kalkmann's face was a dead white. Kalkmann! He understood that well enough. *Kalkmann* meant 'Man of Chalk': he knew that. But what did '*Opfer*' mean? That was the real key to the situation. Words poured through his disordered mind in an endless stream – unusual, rare words he had perhaps heard but once in his life – while '*Opfer*', a word in common use, entirely escaped him. What an extraordinary mockery it all was!

Then Kalkmann, pale as death, but his face hard as iron, spoke a few low words that he did not catch, and the Brothers standing by the walls at once turned the lamps down so that the room became dim. In the half light he could only just discern their faces and movements.

"It is time," he heard Kalkmann's remorseless voice continue just behind him. "The hour of midnight is at hand. Let us prepare. He comes! He comes; Bruder Asmodelius comes!" His voice rose to a chant.

And the sound of that name, for some extraordinary reason, was terrible – utterly terrible; so that Harris shook from head to foot as he heard it. Its utterance filled the air like soft thunder, and a hush came over the whole room. Forces rose all about him, transforming the normal into the horrible, and the spirit of craven fear ran through all his being, bringing him to the verge of collapse.

*Asmodelius! Asmodelius!* The name was appalling. For he understood at last to whom it referred and the meaning that lay between its great syllables. At the same instant, too, he suddenly understood the meaning of that unremembered word. The import of the word '*Opfer*' flashed upon his soul like a message of death.

He thought of making a wild effort to reach the door, but the weakness of his trembling knees, and the row of black figures that stood between, dissuaded him at once. He would have screamed for help, but remembering the emptiness of the vast building, and the loneliness of the situation, he understood that no help could come that way, and he kept his lips closed. He stood still and did nothing. But he knew now what was coming.

Two of the Brothers approached and took him gently by the arm.

"Bruder Asmodelius accepts you," they whispered; "are you ready?"

Then he found his tongue and tried to speak. "But what have I to do with this Bruder Asm – Asmo—?" he stammered, a desperate rush of words crowding vainly behind the halting tongue.

The name refused to pass his lips. He could not pronounce it as they did. He could not pronounce it at all. His sense of helplessness then entered the acute stage, for this inability to speak the name produced a fresh sense of quite horrible confusion in his mind, and he became extraordinarily agitated.

"I came here for a friendly visit," he tried to say with a great effort, but, to his intense dismay, he heard his voice saying something quite different, and actually making use of that very word they had all used: "I came here as a willing *Opfer*," he heard his own voice say, "and *I am quite ready*."

He was lost beyond all recall now! Not alone his mind, but the very muscles of his body had passed out of control. He felt that he was hovering on the confines of a phantom or demon-world – a world in which the name they had spoken constituted the Master-name, the word of ultimate power.

What followed he heard and saw as in a nightmare.

"In the half light that veils all truth, let us prepare to worship and adore," chanted Schliemann, who had preceded him to the end of the room.

"In the mists that protect our faces before the Black Throne, let us make ready the willing victim," echoed Kalkmann in his great bass.

They raised their faces, listening expectantly, as a roaring sound, like the passing of mighty projectiles, filled the air, far, far away, very wonderful, very forbidding. The walls of the room trembled.

"He comes! He comes! He comes!" chanted the Brothers in chorus.

The sound of roaring died away, and an atmosphere of still and utter cold established itself over all. Then Kalkmann, dark and unutterably stern, turned in the dim light and faced the rest.

"Asmodelius, our *Hauptbruder*, is about us," he cried in a voice that even while it shook was yet a voice of iron; "Asmodelius is about us. Make ready."

There followed a pause in which no one stirred or spoke. A tall Brother approached the Englishman; but Kalkmann held up his hand.

"Let the eyes remain uncovered," he said, "in honour of so freely giving himself." And to his horror Harris then realised for the first time that his hands were already fastened to his sides.

The Brother retreated again silently, and in the pause that followed all the figures about him dropped to their knees, leaving him standing alone, and as they dropped, in voices hushed with mingled reverence and awe, they cried, softly, odiously, appallingly, the name of the Being whom they momentarily expected to appear.

Then, at the end of the room, where the windows seemed to have disappeared so that he saw the stars, there rose into view far up against the night sky, grand and terrible, the outline of a man. A kind of grey glory enveloped it so that it resembled a steel-cased statue, immense, imposing, horrific in its distant splendour; while, at the same time, the face was so spiritually mighty, yet so proudly, so austerely sad, that Harris felt as he stared, that the sight was more than his eyes could meet, and that in another moment the power of vision would fail him altogether, and he must sink into utter nothingness.

So remote and inaccessible hung this figure that it was impossible to gauge anything as to its size, yet at the same time so strangely close, that when the grey radiance from its mightily broken visage, august and mournful, beat down upon his soul, pulsing like some dark star with the powers of spiritual evil, he felt almost as though he were looking into a face no farther removed from him in space than the face of any one of the Brothers who stood by his side.

And then the room filled and trembled with sounds that Harris understood full well were the failing voices of others who had preceded him in a long series down the years. There came first a plain, sharp cry, as of a man in the last anguish, choking for his breath, and yet, with the very final expiration of it, breathing the name of the Worship – of the dark Being who rejoiced to hear it. The cries of the strangled; the short, running gasp of the suffocated; and the smothered gurgling of the tightened throat, all these, and more, echoed back and forth between the walls, the very walls in which he now stood a prisoner, a sacrificial victim. The cries, too, not alone of the broken bodies, but – far worse – of beaten, broken souls. And as the ghastly chorus rose and fell, there came also the faces of the lost and unhappy creatures to whom they belonged, and, against that curtain of pale grey light, he saw float past him in the air, an array of white and piteous human countenances that seemed to beckon and gibber at him as though he were already one of themselves.

Slowly, too, as the voices rose, and the pallid crew sailed past, that giant form of grey descended from the sky and approached the room that contained the worshippers and their prisoner. Hands rose and sank about him in the darkness, and he felt that he was being draped in other garments than his own; a circlet of ice seemed to run about his head, while round the waist, enclosing the fastened arms, he felt a girdle tightly drawn. At last, about his very throat, there ran a soft and silken touch which, better than if there had been full light, and a mirror held to his face, he understood to be the cord of sacrifice – and of death.

At this moment the Brothers, still prostrate upon the floor, began again their mournful, yet impassioned chanting, and as they did so a strange thing happened. For, apparently without moving or altering its position, the huge Figure seemed, at once and suddenly, to be inside the room, almost beside him, and to fill the space around him to the exclusion of all else.

He was now beyond all ordinary sensations of fear, only a drab feeling as of death – the death of the soul – stirred in his heart. His thoughts no longer even beat vainly for escape. The end was near, and he knew it.

The dreadfully chanting voices rose about him in a wave: "We worship! We adore! We offer!" The sounds filled his ears and hammered, almost meaningless, upon his brain.

Then the majestic grey face turned slowly downwards upon him, and his very soul passed outwards and seemed to become absorbed in the sea of those anguished eyes. At the same moment a dozen hands forced him to his knees, and in the air before him he saw the arm of Kalkmann upraised, and felt the pressure about his throat grow strong.

It was in this awful moment, when he had given up all hope, and the help of gods or men seemed beyond question, that a strange thing happened. For before his fading and terrified vision there slid, as in a dream of light – yet without apparent rhyme or reason – wholly unbidden and unexplained – the face of that other man at the supper table of the railway inn. And the sight, even mentally, of that strong, wholesome, vigorous English face, inspired him suddenly with a new courage.

It was but a flash of fading vision before he sank into a dark and terrible death, yet, in some inexplicable way, the sight of that face stirred in him unconquerable hope and the certainty of deliverance. It was a face of power, a face, he now realised, of simple goodness such as might have been seen by men of old on the shores of Galilee; a face, by heaven, that could conquer even the devils of outer space.

And, in his despair and abandonment, he called upon it, and called with no uncertain accents. He found his voice in this overwhelming moment to some purpose; though the words he actually used, and whether they were in German or English, he could never remember. Their effect, nevertheless, was instantaneous. The Brothers understood, and that grey Figure of evil understood.

For a second the confusion was terrific. There came a great shattering sound. It seemed that the very earth trembled. But all Harris remembered afterwards was that voices rose about him in the clamour of terrified alarm –

"A man of power is among us! A man of God!"

The vast sound was repeated – the rushing through space as of huge projectiles – and he sank to the floor of the room, unconscious. The entire scene had vanished, vanished like smoke over the roof of a cottage when the wind blows.

And, by his side, sat down a slight un-German figure, – the figure of the stranger at the inn – the man who had the 'rather wonderful eyes'.

* * *

When Harris came to himself he felt cold. He was lying under the open sky, and the cool air of field and forest was blowing upon his face. He sat up and looked about him. The memory of the late scene was still horribly in his mind, but no vestige of it remained. No walls or ceiling enclosed him; he was no longer in a room at all. There were no lamps turned low, no cigar smoke, no black forms of sinister worshippers, no tremendous grey Figure hovering beyond the windows.

Open space was about him, and he was lying on a pile of bricks and mortar, his clothes soaked with dew, and the kind stars shining brightly overhead. He was lying, bruised and shaken, among the heaped-up débris of a ruined building.

He stood up and stared about him. There, in the shadowy distance, lay the surrounding forest, and here, close at hand, stood the outline of the village buildings. But, underfoot, beyond question, lay nothing but the broken heaps of stones that betokened a building long since crumbled to dust. Then he saw that the stones were blackened, and that great wooden beams, half burnt, half rotten, made lines through the general débris. He stood, then, among the ruins of a burnt and shattered building, the weeds and nettles proving conclusively that it had lain thus for many years.

The moon had already set behind the encircling forest, but the stars that spangled the heavens threw enough light to enable him to make quite sure of what he saw. Harris, the silk merchant, stood among these broken and burnt stones and shivered.

Then he suddenly became aware that out of the gloom a figure had risen and stood beside him. Peering at him, he thought he recognised the face of the stranger at the railway inn.

"Are *you* real?" he asked in a voice he hardly recognised as his own.

"More than real – I'm friendly," replied the stranger; "I followed you up here from the inn."

Harris stood and stared for several minutes without adding anything. His teeth chattered. The least sound made him start; but the simple words in his own language, and the tone in which they were uttered, comforted him inconceivably.

"You're English too, thank God," he said inconsequently. "These German devils—" He broke off and put a hand to his eyes. "But what's become of them all – and the room – and – and—" The hand travelled down to his throat and moved nervously round his neck. He drew a long, long breath of relief. "Did I dream everything – everything?" he said distractedly.

He stared wildly about him, and the stranger moved forward and took his arm. "Come," he said soothingly, yet with a trace of command in the voice, "we will move away from here. The high-road, or even the woods will be more to your taste, for we are standing now on one of the most haunted – and most terribly haunted – spots of the whole world."

He guided his companion's stumbling footsteps over the broken masonry until they reached the path, the nettles stinging their hands, and Harris feeling his way like a man in a dream. Passing through the twisted iron railing they reached the path, and thence made their way to the road, shining white in the night. Once safely out of the ruins, Harris collected himself and turned to look back.

"But, how is it possible?" he exclaimed, his voice still shaking. "How can it be possible? When I came in here I saw the building in the moonlight. They opened the door. I saw the figures and heard the voices and touched, yes touched their very hands, and saw their damned black faces, saw them far more plainly than I see you now." He was deeply bewildered. The glamour was still upon his eyes with a degree of reality stronger than the reality even of normal life. "Was I so utterly deluded?"

Then suddenly the words of the stranger, which he had only half heard or understood, returned to him.

"Haunted?" he asked, looking hard at him; "haunted, did you say?" He paused in the roadway and stared into the darkness where the building of the old school had first appeared to him. But the stranger hurried him forward.

"We shall talk more safely farther on," he said. "I followed you from the inn the moment I realised where you had gone. When I found you it was eleven o'clock—"

"Eleven o'clock," said Harris, remembering with a shudder.

" – I saw you drop. I watched over you till you recovered consciousness of your own accord, and now – now I am here to guide you safely back to the inn. I have broken the spell – the glamour—"

"I owe you a great deal, sir," interrupted Harris again, beginning to understand something of the stranger's kindness, "but I don't understand it all. I feel dazed and shaken." His teeth still chattered, and spells of violent shivering passed over him from head to foot. He found that he was clinging to the other's arm. In this way they passed beyond the deserted and crumbling village and gained the high-road that led homewards through the forest.

"That school building has long been in ruins," said the man at his side presently; "it was burnt down by order of the Elders of the community at least ten years ago. The village has been uninhabited ever since. But the simulacra of certain ghastly events that took place under that roof in past days still continue. And the 'shells' of the chief participants still enact there the dreadful deeds that led to its final destruction, and to the desertion of the whole settlement. They were devil-worshippers!"

Harris listened with beads of perspiration on his forehead that did not come alone from their leisurely pace through the cool night. Although he had seen this man but once before in his life, and had never before exchanged so much as a word with him, he felt a degree of confidence and a subtle sense of safety and well-being in his presence that were the most healing influences he could possibly have wished after the experience he had been through. For all that, he still felt as if he were walking in a dream, and though he heard every word that fell from his companion's lips, it was only the next day that the full import of all he said became fully clear to him. The presence of this quiet stranger, the man with the wonderful eyes which he felt now, rather than saw, applied a soothing anodyne to his shattered spirit that healed him through and through. And this healing influence, distilled from the dark figure at his side, satisfied his first imperative need, so that he almost forgot to realise how strange and opportune it was that the man should be there at all.

It somehow never occurred to him to ask his name, or to feel any undue wonder that one passing tourist should take so much trouble on behalf of another. He just walked by his side, listening to his quiet words, and allowing himself to enjoy the very wonderful experience after his recent ordeal, of being helped, strengthened, blessed. Only once, remembering vaguely something of his reading of years ago, he turned to the man beside him, after some more than usually remarkable words, and heard himself, almost involuntarily it seemed, putting the question: "Then are you a Rosicrucian, sir, perhaps?" But the stranger had ignored the words, or possibly not heard them, for he continued with his talk as though unconscious of any interruption, and Harris became aware that another somewhat unusual picture had taken possession of his mind, as they walked there side by side through the cool reaches of the forest, and that he had found his imagination suddenly charged with the childhood memory of Jacob wrestling with an angel – wrestling all night with a being of superior quality whose strength eventually became his own.

"It was your abrupt conversation with the priest at supper that first put me upon the track of this remarkable occurrence," he heard the man's quiet voice beside him in the darkness, "and it was from him I learned after you left the story of the devil-worship that became secretly established in the heart of this simple and devout little community."

"Devil-worship! Here—!" Harris stammered, aghast.

"Yes – here; – conducted secretly for years by a group of Brothers before unexplained disappearances in the neighbourhood led to its discovery. For where could they have found a safer place in the whole wide world for their ghastly traffic and perverted powers than here, in the very precincts – under cover of the very shadow of saintliness and holy living?"

"Awful, awful!" whispered the silk merchant, "and when I tell you the words they used to me—"

"I know it all," the stranger said quietly. "I saw and heard everything. My plan first was to wait till the end and then to take steps for their destruction, but in the interest of your personal safety," – he spoke with the utmost gravity and conviction – "in the interest of the safety of your soul, I made my presence known when I did, and before the conclusion had been reached—"

"My safety! The danger, then, was real. They were alive and—" Words failed him. He stopped in the road and turned towards his companion, the shining of whose eyes he could just make out in the gloom.

"It was a concourse of the shells of violent men, spiritually developed but evil men, seeking after death – the death of the body – to prolong their vile and unnatural existence. And had they accomplished their object you, in turn, at the death of your body, would have passed into their power and helped to swell their dreadful purposes."

Harris made no reply. He was trying hard to concentrate his mind upon the sweet and common things of life. He even thought of silk and St. Paul's Churchyard and the faces of his partners in business.

"For you came all prepared to be caught," he heard the other's voice like someone talking to him from a distance; "your deeply introspective mood had already reconstructed the past so vividly, so intensely, that you were *en rapport* at once with any forces of those days that chanced still to be lingering. And they swept you up all unresistingly."

Harris tightened his hold upon the stranger's arm as he heard. At the moment he had room for one emotion only. It did not seem to him odd that this stranger should have such intimate knowledge of his mind.

"It is, alas, chiefly the evil emotions that are able to leave their photographs upon surrounding scenes and objects," the other added, "and who ever heard of a place haunted by a noble deed, or of beautiful and lovely ghosts revisiting the glimpses of the moon? It is unfortunate. But the wicked passions of men's hearts alone seem strong enough to leave pictures that persist; the good are ever too lukewarm."

The stranger sighed as he spoke. But Harris, exhausted and shaken as he was to the very core, paced by his side, only half listening. He moved as in a dream still. It was very wonderful to him, this walk home under the stars in the early hours of the October morning, the peaceful forest all about them, mist rising here and there over the small clearings, and the sound of water from a hundred little invisible streams filling in the pauses of the talk. In after life he always looked back to it as something magical and impossible, something that had seemed too beautiful, too curiously beautiful, to have been quite true. And, though at the time he heard and understood but a quarter of what the stranger said, it came back to him afterwards, staying with him till the end of his days, and always with a curious, haunting sense of unreality, as though he had enjoyed a wonderful dream of which he could recall only faint and exquisite portions.

But the horror of the earlier experience was effectually dispelled; and when they reached the railway inn, somewhere about three o'clock in the morning, Harris shook the stranger's hand gratefully, effusively, meeting the look of those rather wonderful eyes with a full heart, and went up to his room, thinking in a hazy, dream-like way of the words with which the stranger had brought their conversation to an end as they left the confines of the forest –

"And if thought and emotion can persist in this way so long after the brain that sent them forth has crumbled into dust, how vitally important it must be to control their very birth in the heart, and guard them with the keenest possible restraint."

But Harris, the silk merchant, slept better than might have been expected, and with a soundness that carried him half-way through the day. And when he came downstairs and learned that the stranger had already taken his departure, he realised with keen regret that he had never once thought of asking his name.

"Yes, he signed the visitors' book," said the girl in reply to his question.

And he turned over the blotted pages and found there, the last entry, in a very delicate and individual handwriting –

*John Silence, London*

**If you enjoyed this, you might also like…**
Smith: An Episode in a Lodging House, see page 235
The Pikestaffe Case, see page 331

# The Man Who Found Out

## Chapter I

**PROFESSOR** Mark Ebor, the scientist, led a double life, and the only persons who knew it were his assistant, Dr. Laidlaw, and his publishers. But a double life need not always be a bad one, and, as Dr. Laidlaw and the gratified publishers well knew, the parallel lives of this particular man were equally good, and indefinitely produced would certainly have ended in a heaven somewhere that can suitably contain such strangely opposite characteristics as his remarkable personality combined.

For Mark Ebor, F.R.S., etc., etc., was that unique combination hardly ever met with in actual life, a man of science and a mystic.

As the first, his name stood in the gallery of the great, and as the second – but there came the mystery! For under the pseudonym of 'Pilgrim' (the author of that brilliant series of books that appealed to so many), his identity was as well concealed as that of the anonymous writer of the weather reports in a daily newspaper. Thousands read the sanguine, optimistic, stimulating little books that issued annually from the pen of 'Pilgrim', and thousands bore their daily burdens better for having read; while the Press generally agreed that the author, besides being an incorrigible enthusiast and optimist, was also – a woman; but no one ever succeeded in penetrating the veil of anonymity and discovering that 'Pilgrim' and the biologist were one and the same person.

Mark Ebor, as Dr. Laidlaw knew him in his laboratory, was one man; but Mark Ebor, as he sometimes saw him after work was over, with rapt eyes and ecstatic face, discussing the possibilities of 'union with God' and the future of the human race, was quite another.

"I have always held, as you know," he was saying one evening as he sat in the little study beyond the laboratory with his assistant and intimate, "that Vision should play a large part in the life of the awakened man – not to be regarded as infallible, of course, but to be observed and made use of as a guide-post to possibilities—"

"I am aware of your peculiar views, sir," the young doctor put in deferentially, yet with a certain impatience.

"For Visions come from a region of the consciousness where observation and experiment are out of the question," pursued the other with enthusiasm, not noticing the interruption, "and, while they should be checked by reason afterwards, they should not be laughed at or ignored. All inspiration, I hold, is of the nature of interior Vision, and all our best knowledge has come – such is my confirmed belief – as a sudden revelation to the brain prepared to receive it—"

"Prepared by hard work first, by concentration, by the closest possible study of ordinary phenomena," Dr. Laidlaw allowed himself to observe.

"Perhaps," sighed the other; "but by a process, none the less, of spiritual illumination. The best match in the world will not light a candle unless the wick be first suitably prepared."

It was Laidlaw's turn to sigh. He knew so well the impossibility of arguing with his chief when he was in the regions of the mystic, but at the same time the respect he felt for his tremendous attainments was so sincere that he always listened with attention and deference, wondering how far the great man would go and to what end this curious combination of logic and 'illumination' would eventually lead him.

"Only last night," continued the elder man, a sort of light coming into his rugged features, "the vision came to me again – the one that has haunted me at intervals ever since my youth, and that will not be denied."

Dr. Laidlaw fidgeted in his chair.

"About the Tablets of the Gods, you mean – and that they lie somewhere hidden in the sands," he said patiently. A sudden gleam of interest came into his face as he turned to catch the professor's reply.

"And that I am to be the one to find them, to decipher them, and to give the great knowledge to the world—"

"Who will not believe," laughed Laidlaw shortly, yet interested in spite of his thinly-veiled contempt.

"Because even the keenest minds, in the right sense of the word, are hopelessly – unscientific," replied the other gently, his face positively aglow with the memory of his vision. "Yet what is more likely," he continued after a moment's pause, peering into space with rapt eyes that saw things too wonderful for exact language to describe, "than that there should have been given to man in the first ages of the world some record of the purpose and problem that had been set him to solve? In a word," he cried, fixing his shining eyes upon the face of his perplexed assistant, "that God's messengers in the far-off ages should have given to His creatures some full statement of the secret of the world, of the secret of the soul, of the meaning of life and death – the explanation of our being here, and to what great end we are destined in the ultimate fullness of things?"

Dr. Laidlaw sat speechless. These outbursts of mystical enthusiasm he had witnessed before. With any other man he would not have listened to a single sentence, but to Professor Ebor, man of knowledge and profound investigator, he listened with respect, because he regarded this condition as temporary and pathological, and in some sense a reaction from the intense strain of the prolonged mental concentration of many days.

He smiled, with something between sympathy and resignation as he met the other's rapt gaze.

"But you have said, sir, at other times, that you consider the ultimate secrets to be screened from all possible—"

"The *ultimate* secrets, yes," came the unperturbed reply; "but that there lies buried somewhere an indestructible record of the secret meaning of life, originally known to men in the days of their pristine innocence, I am convinced. And, by this strange vision so often vouchsafed to me, I am equally sure that one day it shall be given to me to announce to a weary world this glorious and terrific message."

And he continued at great length and in glowing language to describe the species of vivid dream that had come to him at intervals since earliest childhood, showing in detail how he discovered these very Tablets of the Gods, and proclaimed their splendid contents – whose precise nature was always, however, withheld from him in the vision – to a patient and suffering humanity.

"The *Scrutator*, sir, well described 'Pilgrim' as the Apostle of Hope," said the young doctor gently, when he had finished; "and now, if that reviewer could hear you speak and realise from what strange depths comes your simple faith—"

The professor held up his hand, and the smile of a little child broke over his face like sunshine in the morning.

"Half the good my books do would be instantly destroyed," he said sadly; "they would say that I wrote with my tongue in my cheek. But wait," he added significantly; "wait till I find these Tablets of the Gods! Wait till I hold the solutions of the old world-problems in my hands! Wait till the light of this new revelation breaks upon confused humanity, and it wakes to find its bravest hopes justified! Ah, then, my dear Laidlaw—"

He broke off suddenly; but the doctor, cleverly guessing the thought in his mind, caught him up immediately.

"Perhaps this very summer," he said, trying hard to make the suggestion keep pace with honesty; "in your explorations in Assyria – your digging in the remote civilisation of what was once Chaldea, you may find – what you dream of—"

The professor held up his hand, and the smile of a fine old face.

"Perhaps," he murmured softly, "perhaps!"

And the young doctor, thanking the gods of science that his leader's aberrations were of so harmless a character, went home strong in the certitude of his knowledge of externals, proud that he was able to refer his visions to self-suggestion, and wondering complaisantly whether in his old age he might not after all suffer himself from visitations of the very kind that afflicted his respected chief.

And as he got into bed and thought again of his master's rugged face, and finely shaped head, and the deep lines traced by years of work and self-discipline, he turned over on his pillow and fell asleep with a sigh that was half of wonder, half of regret.

## Chapter II

**IT WAS** in February, nine months later, when Dr. Laidlaw made his way to Charing Cross to meet his chief after his long absence of travel and exploration. The vision about the so-called Tablets of the Gods had meanwhile passed almost entirely from his memory.

There were few people in the train, for the stream of traffic was now running the other way, and he had no difficulty in finding the man he had come to meet. The shock of white hair beneath the low-crowned felt hat was alone enough to distinguish him by easily.

"Here I am at last!" exclaimed the professor, somewhat wearily, clasping his friend's hand as he listened to the young doctor's warm greetings and questions. "Here I am – a little older, and *much* dirtier than when you last saw me!" He glanced down laughingly at his travel-stained garments.

"And *much* wiser," said Laidlaw, with a smile, as he bustled about the platform for porters and gave his chief the latest scientific news.

At last they came down to practical considerations.

"And your luggage – where is that? You must have tons of it, I suppose?" said Laidlaw.

"Hardly anything," Professor Ebor answered. "Nothing, in fact, but what you see."

"Nothing but this hand-bag?" laughed the other, thinking he was joking.

"And a small portmanteau in the van," was the quiet reply. "I have no other luggage."

"You have no other luggage?" repeated Laidlaw, turning sharply to see if he were in earnest.

"Why should I need more?" the professor added simply.

Something in the man's face, or voice, or manner – the doctor hardly knew which – suddenly struck him as strange. There was a change in him, a change so profound – so little on the surface, that is – that at first he had not become aware of it. For a moment it was as though an utterly alien personality stood before him in that noisy, bustling throng. Here, in all the homely, friendly turmoil of a Charing Cross crowd, a curious feeling of cold passed over his heart, touching his life with icy finger, so that he actually trembled and felt afraid.

He looked up quickly at his friend, his mind working with startled and unwelcome thoughts.

"Only this?" he repeated, indicating the bag. "But where's all the stuff you went away with? And – have you brought nothing home – no treasures?"

"This is all I have," the other said briefly. The pale smile that went with the words caused the doctor a second indescribable sensation of uneasiness. Something was very wrong, something was very queer; he wondered now that he had not noticed it sooner.

"The rest follows, of course, by slow freight," he added tactfully, and as naturally as possible. "But come, sir, you must be tired and in want of food after your long journey. I'll get a taxi at once, and we can see about the other luggage afterwards."

It seemed to him he hardly knew quite what he was saying; the change in his friend had come upon him so suddenly and now grew upon him more and more distressingly. Yet he could not make out exactly in what it consisted. A terrible suspicion began to take shape in his mind, troubling him dreadfully.

"I am neither very tired, nor in need of food, thank you," the professor said quietly. "And this is all I have. There is no luggage to follow. I have brought home nothing – nothing but what you see."

His words conveyed finality. They got into a taxi, tipped the porter, who had been staring in amazement at the venerable figure of the scientist, and were conveyed slowly and noisily to the house in the north of London where the laboratory was, the scene of their labours of years.

And the whole way Professor Ebor uttered no word, nor did Dr. Laidlaw find the courage to ask a single question.

It was only late that night, before he took his departure, as the two men were standing before the fire in the study – that study where they had discussed so many problems of vital and absorbing interest – that Dr. Laidlaw at last found strength to come to the point with direct questions. The professor had been giving him a superficial and desultory account of his travels, of his journeys by camel, of his encampments among the mountains and in the desert, and of his explorations among the buried temples, and, deeper, into the waste of the pre-historic sands, when suddenly the doctor came to the desired point with a kind of nervous rush, almost like a frightened boy.

"And you found—" he began stammering, looking hard at the other's dreadfully altered face, from which every line of hope and cheerfulness seemed to have been obliterated as a sponge wipes markings from a slate – "you found—"

"I found," replied the other, in a solemn voice, and it was the voice of the mystic rather than the man of science – "I found what I went to seek. The vision never once failed me. It led me straight to the place like a star in the heavens. I found – the Tablets of the Gods."

Dr. Laidlaw caught his breath, and steadied himself on the back of a chair. The words fell like particles of ice upon his heart. For the first time the professor had uttered the well-known phrase without the glow of light and wonder in his face that always accompanied it.

"You have – brought them?" he faltered.

"I have brought them home," said the other, in a voice with a ring like iron; "and I have – deciphered them."

Profound despair, the bloom of outer darkness, the dead sound of a hopeless soul freezing in the utter cold of space seemed to fill in the pauses between the brief sentences. A silence followed, during which Dr. Laidlaw saw nothing but the white face before him alternately fade and return. And it was like the face of a dead man.

"They are, alas, indestructible," he heard the voice continue, with its even, metallic ring.

"Indestructible," Laidlaw repeated mechanically, hardly knowing what he was saying.

Again a silence of several minutes passed, during which, with a creeping cold about his heart, he stood and stared into the eyes of the man he had known and loved so long – aye, and worshipped, too; the man who had first opened his own eyes when they were blind, and had led him to the gates of knowledge, and no little distance along the difficult path beyond; the man who, in another direction, had passed on the strength of his faith into the hearts of thousands by his books.

"I may see them?" he asked at last, in a low voice he hardly recognised as his own. "You will let me know – their message?"

Professor Ebor kept his eyes fixedly upon his assistant's face as he answered, with a smile that was more like the grin of death than a living human smile.

"When I am gone," he whispered; "when I have passed away. Then you shall find them and read the translation I have made. And then, too, in your turn, you must try, with the latest resources of science at your disposal to aid you, to compass their utter destruction." He paused a moment, and his face grew pale as the face of a corpse. "Until that time," he added presently, without looking up, "I must ask you not to refer to the subject again – and to keep my confidence meanwhile – *ab – so – lute – ly*."

## Chapter III

**A YEAR** passed slowly by, and at the end of it Dr. Laidlaw had found it necessary to sever his working connexion with his friend and one-time leader. Professor Ebor was no longer the same man. The light had gone out of his life; the laboratory was closed; he no longer put pen to paper or applied his mind to a single problem. In the short space of a few months he had passed from a hale and hearty man of late middle life to the condition of old age – a man collapsed and on the edge of dissolution. Death, it was plain, lay waiting for him in the shadows of any day – and he knew it.

To describe faithfully the nature of this profound alteration in his character and temperament is not easy, but Dr. Laidlaw summed it up to himself in three words: *Loss of Hope*. The splendid mental powers remained indeed undimmed, but the incentive to use them – to use them for the help of others – had gone. The character still held to its fine and unselfish habits of years, but the far goal to which they had been the leading strings had faded away. The desire for knowledge – knowledge for its own sake – had died, and the passionate hope which hitherto had animated with tireless energy the heart and brain of this splendidly equipped intellect had suffered total eclipse. The central fires had gone out. Nothing was worth doing, thinking, working for. There *was* nothing to work for any longer!

The professor's first step was to recall as many of his books as possible; his second to close his laboratory and stop all research. He gave no explanation, he invited no questions. His whole personality crumbled away, so to speak, till his daily life became a mere mechanical process of clothing the body, feeding the body, keeping it in good health so as to avoid physical discomfort, and, above all, doing nothing that could interfere with sleep. The professor did everything he could to lengthen the hours of sleep, and therefore of forgetfulness.

It was all clear enough to Dr. Laidlaw. A weaker man, he knew, would have sought to lose himself in one form or another of sensual indulgence – sleeping-draughts, drink, the first pleasures that came to hand. Self-destruction would have been the method of a little bolder type; and deliberate evil-doing, poisoning with his awful knowledge all he could, the means of still another kind of man. Mark Ebor was none of these. He held himself under fine control, facing silently and without complaint the terrible facts he honestly believed himself to have been unfortunate enough to discover. Even to his intimate friend and assistant, Dr. Laidlaw, he vouchsafed no word of true explanation or lament. He went straight forward to the end, knowing well that the end was not very far away.

And death came very quietly one day to him, as he was sitting in the arm-chair of the study, directly facing the doors of the laboratory – the doors that no longer opened. Dr. Laidlaw, by happy chance, was with him at the time, and just able to reach his side in response to the sudden painful efforts for breath; just in time, too, to catch the murmured words that fell from the pallid lips like a message from the other side of the grave.

"Read them, if you must; and, if you can – destroy. But" – his voice sank so low that Dr. Laidlaw only just caught the dying syllables – "but – never, never – give them to the world."

And like a grey bundle of dust loosely gathered up in an old garment the professor sank back into his chair and expired.

But this was only the death of the body. His spirit had died two years before.

## Chapter IV

**THE ESTATE** of the dead man was small and uncomplicated, and Dr. Laidlaw, as sole executor and residuary legatee, had no difficulty in settling it up. A month after the funeral he was sitting alone in his upstairs library, the last sad duties completed, and his mind full of poignant memories and regrets for the loss of a friend he had revered and loved, and to whom his debt was so incalculably great. The last two years, indeed, had been for him terrible. To watch the swift decay of the greatest combination of heart and brain he had ever known, and to realise he was powerless to help, was a source of profound grief to him that would remain to the end of his days.

At the same time an insatiable curiosity possessed him. The study of dementia was, of course, outside his special province as a specialist, but he knew enough of it to understand how small a matter might be the actual cause of how great an illusion, and he had been devoured from the very beginning by a ceaseless and increasing anxiety to know what the professor had found in the sands of 'Chaldea', what these precious Tablets of the Gods might be, and particularly – for this was the real cause that had sapped the man's sanity and hope – what the inscription was that he had believed to have deciphered thereon.

The curious feature of it all to his own mind was, that whereas his friend had dreamed of finding a message of glorious hope and comfort, he had apparently found (so far as he had found anything intelligible at all, and not invented the whole thing in his dementia) that the secret of the world, and the meaning of life and death, was of so terrible a nature that it robbed the heart of courage and the soul of hope. What, then, could be the contents of the little brown parcel the professor had bequeathed to him with his pregnant dying sentences?

Actually his hand was trembling as he turned to the writing-table and began slowly to unfasten a small old-fashioned desk on which the small gilt initials 'M.E.' stood forth as a melancholy memento. He put the key into the lock and half turned it. Then, suddenly, he stopped and looked about him. Was that a sound at the back of the room? It was just as though someone had laughed and then tried to smother the laugh with a cough. A slight shiver ran over him as he stood listening.

"This is absurd," he said aloud; "too absurd for belief – that I should be so nervous! It's the effect of curiosity unduly prolonged." He smiled a little sadly and his eyes wandered to the blue summer sky and the plane trees swaying in the wind below his window. "It's the reaction," he continued. "The curiosity of two years to be quenched in a single moment! The nervous tension, of course, must be considerable."

He turned back to the brown desk and opened it without further delay. His hand was firm now, and he took out the paper parcel that lay inside without a tremor. It was heavy. A moment later there lay on the table before him a couple of weather-worn plaques of grey stone – they looked like stone, although they felt like metal – on which he saw markings of a curious character that might have been the mere tracings of natural forces through the ages, or, equally well, the half-obliterated hieroglyphics cut upon their surface in past centuries by the more or less untutored hand of a common scribe.

He lifted each stone in turn and examined it carefully. It seemed to him that a faint glow of heat passed from the substance into his skin, and he put them down again suddenly, as with a gesture of uneasiness.

"A very clever, or a very imaginative man," he said to himself, "who could squeeze the secrets of life and death from such broken lines as those!"

Then he turned to a yellow envelope lying beside them in the desk, with the single word on the outside in the writing of the professor – the word *Translation*.

"Now," he thought, taking it up with a sudden violence to conceal his nervousness, "now for the great solution. Now to learn the meaning of the worlds, and why mankind was made, and why discipline is worthwhile, and sacrifice and pain the true law of advancement."

There was the shadow of a sneer in his voice, and yet something in him shivered at the same time. He held the envelope as though weighing it in his hand, his mind pondering many things. Then curiosity won the day, and he suddenly tore it open with the gesture of an actor who tears open a letter on the stage, knowing there is no real writing inside at all.

A page of finely written script in the late scientist's handwriting lay before him. He read it through from beginning to end, missing no word, uttering each syllable distinctly under his breath as he read.

The pallor of his face grew ghastly as he neared the end. He began to shake all over as with ague. His breath came heavily in gasps. He still gripped the sheet of paper, however, and deliberately, as by an intense effort of will, read it through a second time from beginning to end. And this time, as the last syllable dropped from his lips, the whole face of the man flamed with a sudden and terrible anger. His skin became deep, deep red, and he clenched his teeth. With all the strength of his vigorous soul he was struggling to keep control of himself.

For perhaps five minutes he stood there beside the table without stirring a muscle. He might have been carved out of stone. His eyes were shut, and only the heaving of the chest betrayed the fact that he was a living being. Then, with a strange quietness, he lit a match and applied it to the sheet of paper he held in his hand. The ashes fell slowly about him, piece by piece, and he blew them from the window-sill into the air, his eyes following them as they floated away on the summer wind that breathed so warmly over the world.

He turned back slowly into the room. Although his actions and movements were absolutely steady and controlled, it was clear that he was on the edge of violent action. A hurricane might burst upon the still room any moment. His muscles were tense and rigid. Then, suddenly, he whitened, collapsed, and sank backwards into a chair, like a tumbled bundle of inert matter. He had fainted.

In less than half an hour he recovered consciousness and sat up. As before, he made no sound. Not a syllable passed his lips. He rose quietly and looked about the room.

Then he did a curious thing.

Taking a heavy stick from the rack in the corner he approached the mantlepiece, and with a heavy shattering blow he smashed the clock to pieces. The glass fell in shivering atoms.

"Cease your lying voice for ever," he said, in a curiously still, even tone. "There is no such thing as *time*!"

He took the watch from his pocket, swung it round several times by the long gold chain, smashed it into smithereens against the wall with a single blow, and then walked into his laboratory next door, and hung its broken body on the bones of the skeleton in the corner of the room.

"Let one damned mockery hang upon another," he said smiling oddly. "Delusions, both of you, and cruel as false!"

He slowly moved back to the front room. He stopped opposite the bookcase where stood in a row the 'Scriptures of the World', choicely bound and exquisitely printed, the late professor's most treasured possession, and next to them several books signed 'Pilgrim'.

One by one he took them from the shelf and hurled them through the open window.

"A devil's dreams! A devil's foolish dreams!" he cried, with a vicious laugh.

Presently he stopped from sheer exhaustion. He turned his eyes slowly to the wall opposite, where hung a weird array of Eastern swords and daggers, scimitars and spears, the collections of many journeys. He crossed the room and ran his finger along the edge. His mind seemed to waver.

"No," he muttered presently; "not that way. There are easier and better ways than that." He took his hat and passed downstairs into the street.

## Chapter V

**IT WAS** five o'clock, and the June sun lay hot upon the pavement. He felt the metal door-knob burn the palm of his hand.

"Ah, Laidlaw, this is well met," cried a voice at his elbow; "I was in the act of coming to see you. I've a case that will interest you, and besides, I remembered that you flavoured your tea with orange leaves! – and I admit—"

It was Alexis Stephen, the great hypnotic doctor.

"I've had no tea today," Laidlaw said, in a dazed manner, after staring for a moment as though the other had struck him in the face. A new idea had entered his mind.

"What's the matter?" asked Dr. Stephen quickly. "Something's wrong with you. It's this sudden heat, or overwork. Come, man, let's go inside."

A sudden light broke upon the face of the younger man, the light of a heaven-sent inspiration. He looked into his friend's face, and told a direct lie.

"Odd," he said, "I myself was just coming to see you. I have something of great importance to test your confidence with. But in *your* house, please," as Stephen urged him towards his own door – "in your house. It's only round the corner, and I – I cannot go back there – to my rooms – till I have told you.

"I'm your patient – for the moment," he added stammeringly as soon as they were seated in the privacy of the hypnotist's sanctum, "and I want – er—"

"My dear Laidlaw," interrupted the other, in that soothing voice of command which had suggested to many a suffering soul that the cure for its pain lay in the powers of its own reawakened will, "I am always at your service, as you know. You have only to tell me what I can do for you, and I will do it." He showed every desire to help him out. His manner was indescribably tactful and direct.

Dr. Laidlaw looked up into his face.

"I surrender my will to you," he said, already calmed by the other's healing presence, "and I want you to treat me hypnotically – and at once. I want you to suggest to me" – his voice became very tense – "that I shall forget – forget till I die – everything that has occurred to me during the last two hours; till I die, mind," he added, with solemn emphasis, "till I die."

He floundered and stammered like a frightened boy. Alexis Stephen looked at him fixedly without speaking.

"And further," Laidlaw continued, "I want you to ask me no questions. I wish to forget for ever something I have recently discovered – something so terrible and yet so obvious that I can hardly understand why it is not patent to every mind in the world – for I have had a moment of absolute *clear vision* – of merciless clairvoyance. But I want no one else in the whole world to know what it is – least of all, old friend, yourself."

He talked in utter confusion, and hardly knew what he was saying. But the pain on his face and the anguish in his voice were an instant passport to the other's heart.

"Nothing is easier," replied Dr. Stephen, after a hesitation so slight that the other probably did not even notice it. "Come into my other room where we shall not be disturbed. I can heal you. Your memory of the last two hours shall be wiped out as though it had never been. You can trust me absolutely."

"I know I can," Laidlaw said simply, as he followed him in.

## Chapter VI

**AN HOUR LATER** they passed back into the front room again. The sun was already behind the houses opposite, and the shadows began to gather.

"I went off easily?" Laidlaw asked.

"You were a little obstinate at first. But though you came in like a lion, you went out like a lamb. I let you sleep a bit afterwards."

Dr. Stephen kept his eyes rather steadily upon his friend's face.

"What were you doing by the fire before you came here?" he asked, pausing, in a casual tone, as he lit a cigarette and handed the case to his patient.

"I? Let me see. Oh, I know; I was worrying my way through poor old Ebor's papers and things. I'm his executor, you know. Then I got weary and came out for a whiff of air." He spoke lightly and with perfect naturalness. Obviously he was telling the truth. "I prefer specimens to papers," he laughed cheerily.

"I know, I know," said Dr. Stephen, holding a lighted match for the cigarette. His face wore an expression of content. The experiment had been a complete success. The memory of the last two hours was wiped out utterly. Laidlaw was already chatting gaily and easily about a dozen other things that interested him. Together they went out into the street, and at his door Dr. Stephen left him with a joke and a wry face that made his friend laugh heartily.

"Don't dine on the professor's old papers by mistake," he cried, as he vanished down the street.

Dr. Laidlaw went up to his study at the top of the house. Half way down he met his housekeeper, Mrs. Fewings. She was flustered and excited, and her face was very red and perspiring.

"There've been burglars here," she cried excitedly, "or something funny! All your things is just any'ow, sir. I found everything all about everywhere!" She was very confused. In this orderly and very precise establishment it was unusual to find a thing out of place.

"Oh, my specimens!" cried the doctor, dashing up the rest of the stairs at top speed. "Have they been touched or—"

He flew to the door of the laboratory. Mrs. Fewings panted up heavily behind him.

"The labatry ain't been touched," she explained, breathlessly, "but they smashed the libry clock and they've 'ung your gold watch, sir, on the skelinton's hands. And the books that weren't no value they flung out er the window just like so much rubbish. They must have been wild drunk, Dr. Laidlaw, sir!"

The young scientist made a hurried examination of the rooms. Nothing of value was missing. He began to wonder what kind of burglars they were. He looked up sharply at Mrs. Fewings standing in the doorway. For a moment he seemed to cast about in his mind for something.

"Odd," he said at length. "I only left here an hour ago and everything was all right then."

"Was it, sir? Yes, sir." She glanced sharply at him. Her room looked out upon the courtyard, and she must have seen the books come crashing down, and also have heard her master leave the house a few minutes later.

"And what's this rubbish the brutes have left?" he cried, taking up two slabs of worn grey stone, on the writing-table. "Bath brick, or something, I do declare."

He looked very sharply again at the confused and troubled housekeeper.

"Throw them on the dust heap, Mrs. Fewings, and – and let me know if anything is missing in the house, and I will notify the police this evening."

When she left the room he went into the laboratory and took his watch off the skeleton's fingers. His face wore a troubled expression, but after a moment's thought it cleared again. His memory was a complete blank.

"I suppose I left it on the writing-table when I went out to take the air," he said. And there was no one present to contradict him.

He crossed to the window and blew carelessly some ashes of burned paper from the sill, and stood watching them as they floated away lazily over the tops of the trees.

**If you enjoyed this, you might also like...**
The Sea Fit, see page 41
H.S.H., see page 108

# A Victim of Higher Space

"THERE'S a hextraordinary gentleman to see you, sir," said the new man.

"Why 'extraordinary'?" asked Dr. Silence, drawing the tips of his thin fingers through his brown beard. His eyes twinkled pleasantly. "Why 'extraordinary', Barker?" he repeated encouragingly, noticing the perplexed expression in the man's eyes.

"He's so – so thin, sir. I could hardly see 'im at all – at first. He was inside the house before I could ask the name," he added, remembering strict orders.

"And who brought him here?"

"He come alone, sir, in a closed cab. He pushed by me before I could say a word – making no noise not what I could hear. He seemed to move so soft like—"

The man stopped short with obvious embarrassment, as though he had already said enough to jeopardise his new situation, but trying hard to show that he remembered the instructions and warnings he had received with regard to the admission of strangers not properly accredited.

"And where is the gentleman now?" asked Dr. Silence, turning away to conceal his amusement.

"I really couldn't exactly say, sir. I left him standing in the 'all—"

The doctor looked up sharply. "But why in the hall, Barker? Why not in the waiting-room?" He fixed his piercing though kindly eyes on the man's face. "Did he frighten you?" he asked quickly.

"I think he did, sir, if I may say so. I seemed to lose sight of him, as it were—" The man stammered, evidently convinced by now that he had earned his dismissal. "He come in so funny, just like a cold wind," he added boldly, setting his heels at attention and looking his master full in the face.

The doctor made an internal note of the man's halting description; he was pleased that the slight signs of psychic intuition which had induced him to engage Barker had not entirely failed at the first trial. Dr. Silence sought for this qualification in all his assistants, from secretary to serving man, and if it surrounded him with a somewhat singular crew, the drawbacks were more than compensated for on the whole by their occasional flashes of insight.

"So the gentleman made you feel queer, did he?"

"That was it, I think, sir," repeated the man stolidly.

"And he brings no kind of introduction to me – no letter or anything?" asked the doctor, with feigned surprise, as though he knew what was coming.

The man fumbled, both in mind and pockets, and finally produced an envelope.

"I beg pardon, sir," he said, greatly flustered; "the gentleman handed me this for you."

It was a note from a discerning friend, who had never yet sent him a case that was not vitally interesting from one point or another.

"Please see the bearer of this note," the brief message ran, "though I doubt if even you can do much to help him."

John Silence paused a moment, so as to gather from the mind of the writer all that lay behind the brief words of the letter. Then he looked up at his servant with a graver expression than he had yet worn.

"Go back and find this gentleman," he said, "and show him into the green study. Do not reply to his question, or speak more than actually necessary; but think kind, helpful, sympathetic thoughts as strongly as you can, Barker. You remember what I told you about the importance of *thinking*, when I engaged you. Put curiosity out of your mind, and think gently, sympathetically, affectionately, if you can."

He smiled, and Barker, who had recovered his composure in the doctor's presence, bowed silently and went out.

There were two different reception-rooms in Dr. Silence's house. One (intended for persons who imagined they needed spiritual assistance when really they were only candidates for the asylum) had padded walls, and was well supplied with various concealed contrivances by means of which sudden violence could be instantly met and overcome. It was, however, rarely used. The other, intended for the reception of genuine cases of spiritual distress and out-of-the-way afflictions of a psychic nature, was entirely draped and furnished in a soothing deep green, calculated to induce calmness and repose of mind. And this room was the one in which Dr. Silence interviewed the majority of his 'queer' cases, and the one into which he had directed Barker to show his present caller.

To begin with, the arm-chair in which the patient was always directed to sit, was nailed to the floor, since its immovability tended to impart this same excellent characteristic to the occupant. Patients invariably grew excited when talking about themselves, and their excitement tended to confuse their thoughts and to exaggerate their language. The inflexibility of the chair helped to counteract this. After repeated endeavours to drag it forward, or push it back, they ended by resigning themselves to sitting quietly. And with the futility of fidgeting there followed a calmer state of mind.

Upon the floor, and at intervals in the wall immediately behind, were certain tiny green buttons, practically unnoticeable, which on being pressed permitted a soothing and persuasive narcotic to rise invisibly about the occupant of the chair. The effect upon the excitable patient was rapid, admirable, and harmless. The green study was further provided with a secret spy-hole; for John Silence liked when possible to observe his patient's face before it had assumed that mask the features of the human countenance invariably wear in the presence of another person. A man sitting alone wears a psychic expression; and this expression is the man himself. It disappears the moment another person joins him. And Dr. Silence often learned more from a few moments' secret observation of a face than from hours of conversation with its owner afterwards.

A very light, almost a dancing, step followed Barker's heavy tread towards the green room, and a moment afterwards the man came in and announced that the gentleman was waiting. He was still pale and his manner nervous.

"Never mind, Barker," the doctor said kindly; "if you were not psychic the man would have had no effect upon you at all. You only need training and development. And when you have learned to interpret these feelings and sensations better, you will feel no fear, but only a great sympathy."

"Yes, sir; thank you, sir!" And Barker bowed and made his escape, while Dr. Silence, an amused smile lurking about the corners of his mouth, made his way noiselessly down the passage and put his eye to the spy-hole in the door of the green study.

This spy-hole was so placed that it commanded a view of almost the entire room, and, looking through it, the doctor saw a hat, gloves, and umbrella lying on a chair by the table, but searched at first in vain for their owner.

The windows were both closed and a brisk fire burned in the grate. There were various signs – signs intelligible at least to a keenly intuitive soul – that the room was occupied, yet so far as human beings were concerned, it was empty, utterly empty. No one sat in the chairs; no one stood on the mat before the fire; there was no sign even that a patient was anywhere close against the wall, examining the Böcklin reproductions – as patients so often did when they thought they were alone – and therefore rather difficult to see from the spy-hole. Ordinarily speaking, there was no one in the room. It was undeniable.

Yet Dr. Silence was quite well aware that a human being *was* in the room. His psychic apparatus never failed in letting him know the proximity of an incarnate or discarnate being. Even in the dark he could tell that. And he now knew positively that his patient – the patient who had alarmed Barker, and had then tripped down the corridor with that dancing footstep – was somewhere concealed within the four walls commanded by his spy-hole. He also realised – and this was most unusual – that this individual whom he desired to watch knew that he was being watched. And, further, that the stranger himself was also watching! In fact, that it was he, the doctor, who was being observed – and by an observer as keen and trained as himself.

An inkling of the true state of the case began to dawn upon him, and he was on the verge of entering – indeed, his hand already touched the door-knob – when his eye, still glued to the spy-hole, detected a slight movement. Directly opposite, between him and the fireplace, something stirred. He watched very attentively and made certain that he was not mistaken. An object on the mantelpiece – it was a blue vase – disappeared from view. It passed out of sight together with the portion of the marble mantelpiece on which it rested. Next, that part of the fire and grate and brass fender immediately below it vanished entirely, as though a slice had been taken clean out of them.

Dr. Silence then understood that something between him and these objects was slowly coming into being, something that concealed them and obstructed his vision by inserting itself in the line of sight between them and himself.

He quietly awaited further results before going in.

First he saw a thin perpendicular line tracing itself from just above the height of the clock and continuing downwards till it reached the woolly fire-mat. This line grew wider, broadened, grew solid. It was no shadow; it was something substantial. It defined itself more and more. Then suddenly, at the top of the line, and about on a level with the face of the clock, he saw a round luminous disc gazing steadily at him. It was a human eye, looking straight into his own, pressed there against the spy-hole. And it was bright with intelligence. Dr. Silence held his breath for a moment – and stared back at it.

Then, like someone moving out of deep shadow into light, he saw the figure of a man come sliding sideways into view, a whitish face following the eye, and the perpendicular line he had first observed broadening out and developing into the complete figure of a human being. It was the patient. He had apparently been standing there in front of the fire all the time. A second eye had followed the first, and both of them stared steadily at the spy-hole, sharply concentrated, yet with a sly twinkle of humour and amusement that made it impossible for the doctor to maintain his position any longer.

He opened the door and went in quickly. As he did so he noticed for the first time the sound of a German band coming in gaily through the open ventilators. In some intuitive, unaccountable fashion the music connected itself with the patient he was about to interview. This sort of prevision was not unfamiliar to him. It always explained itself later.

The man, he saw, was of middle age and of very ordinary appearance; so ordinary, in fact, that he was difficult to describe – his only peculiarity being his extreme thinness. Pleasant – that is, good – vibrations issued from his atmosphere and met Dr. Silence as he advanced to greet him, yet vibrations alive with currents and discharges betraying the perturbed and disordered condition of his mind and brain. There was evidently something wholly out of the usual in the state of his thoughts. Yet, though strange, it was not altogether distressing; it was not the impression that the broken and violent atmosphere of the insane produces upon the mind. Dr. Silence realised in a flash that here was a case of absorbing interest that might require all his powers to handle properly.

"I was watching you through my little peep-hole – as you saw," he began, with a pleasant smile, advancing to shake hands. "I find it of the greatest assistance sometimes—"

But the patient interrupted him at once. His voice was hurried and had odd, shrill changes in it, breaking from high to low in unexpected fashion. One moment it thundered, the next it almost squeaked.

"I understand without explanation," he broke in rapidly. "You get the true note of a man in this way – when he thinks himself unobserved. I quite agree. Only, in my case, I fear, you saw very little. My case, as you of course grasp, Dr. Silence, is extremely peculiar, uncomfortably peculiar. Indeed, unless Sir William had positively assured me—"

"My friend has sent you to me," the doctor interrupted gravely, with a gentle note of authority, "and that is quite sufficient. Pray, be seated, Mr.—"

"Mudge – Racine Mudge," returned the other.

"Take this comfortable one, Mr. Mudge," leading him to the fixed chair, "and tell me your condition in your own way and at your own pace. My whole day is at your service if you require it."

Mr. Mudge moved towards the chair in question and then hesitated.

"You will promise me not to use the narcotic buttons," he said, before sitting down. "I do not need them. Also I ought to mention that anything you think of vividly will reach my mind. That is apparently part of my peculiar case." He sat down with a sigh and arranged his thin legs and body into a position of comfort. Evidently he was very sensitive to the thoughts of others, for the picture of the green buttons had only entered the doctor's mind for a second, yet the other had instantly snapped it up. Dr. Silence noticed, too, that Mr. Mudge held on tightly with both hands to the arms of the chair.

"I'm rather glad the chair is nailed to the floor," he remarked, as he settled himself more comfortably. "It suits me admirably. The fact is – and this is my case in a nutshell – which is all that a doctor of your marvellous development requires – the fact is, Dr. Silence, I am a victim of Higher Space. That's what's the matter with me – Higher Space!"

The two looked at each other for a space in silence, the little patient holding tightly to the arms of the chair which 'suited him admirably', and looking up with staring eyes, his atmosphere positively trembling with the waves of some unknown activity; while the doctor smiled kindly and sympathetically, and put his whole person as far as possible into the mental condition of the other.

"Higher Space," repeated Mr. Mudge, "that's what it is. Now, do you think you can help me with *that*?"

There was a pause during which the men's eyes steadily searched down below the surface of their respective personalities. Then Dr. Silence spoke.

"I am quite sure I can help," he answered quietly; "sympathy must always help, and suffering always owns my sympathy. I see you have suffered cruelly. You must tell me all about your case, and when I hear the gradual steps by which you reached this strange condition, I have no doubt I can be of assistance to you."

He drew a chair up beside his interlocutor and laid a hand on his shoulder for a moment. His whole being radiated kindness, intelligence, desire to help.

"For instance," he went on, "I feel sure it was the result of no mere chance that you became familiar with the terrors of what you term Higher Space; for Higher Space is no mere external measurement. It is, of course, a spiritual state, a spiritual condition, an inner development, and one that we must recognise as abnormal, since it is beyond the reach of the world at the present stage of evolution. Higher Space is a mythical state."

"Oh!" cried the other, rubbing his birdlike hands with pleasure, "the relief it is to be to talk to someone who can understand! Of course what you say is the utter truth. And you are right that no mere chance led me to my present condition, but, on the other hand, prolonged and deliberate study. Yet chance in a sense now governs it. I mean, my entering the condition of Higher Space seems to depend upon the chance of this and that circumstance. For instance, the mere sound of that German band sent me off. Not that all music will do so, but certain sounds, certain vibrations, at once key me up to the requisite pitch, and off I go. Wagner's music always does it, and that band must have been playing a stray bit of Wagner. But I'll come to all that later. Only, first, I must ask you to send away your man from the spy-hole."

John Silence looked up with a start, for Mr. Mudge's back was to the door, and there was no mirror. He saw the brown eye of Barker glued to the little circle of glass, and he crossed the room without a word and snapped down the black shutter provided for the purpose, and then heard Barker shuffle away along the passage.

"Now," continued the little man in the chair, "I can begin. You have managed to put me completely at my ease, and I feel I may tell you my whole case without shame or reserve. You will understand. But you must be patient with me if I go into details that are already familiar to you – details of Higher Space, I mean – and if I seem stupid when I have to describe things that transcend the power of language and are really therefore indescribable."

"My dear friend," put in the other calmly, "that goes without saying. To know Higher Space is an experience that defies description, and one is obliged to make use of more or less intelligible symbols. But, pray, proceed. Your vivid thoughts will tell me more than your halting words."

An immense sigh of relief proceeded from the little figure half lost in the depths of the chair. Such intelligent sympathy meeting him half-way was a new experience to him, and it touched his heart at once. He leaned back, relaxing his tight hold of the arms, and began in his thin, scale-like voice.

"My mother was a Frenchwoman, and my father an Essex bargeman," he said abruptly. "Hence my name – Racine and Mudge. My father died before I ever saw him. My mother inherited money from her Bordeaux relations, and when she died soon after, I was left alone with wealth and a strange freedom. I had no guardian, trustees, sisters, brothers, or any connection in the world to look after me. I grew up, therefore, utterly without education. This much was to my advantage; I learned none of that deceitful rubbish taught in schools, and so had nothing to unlearn when I awakened to my true love – mathematics, higher mathematics and higher geometry. These, however, I seemed to know instinctively. It was like the memory of what I had deeply studied before; the principles were in my blood, and I simply raced through the ordinary stages, and beyond, and then did the same with geometry. Afterwards, when I read the books on these subjects, I understood how swift and undeviating the knowledge had come back to me. It was simply memory. It was simply *re-collecting* the memories of what I had known before in a previous existence and required no books to teach me."

In his growing excitement, Mr. Mudge attempted to drag the chair forward a little nearer to his listener, and then smiled faintly as he resigned himself instantly again to its immovability, and plunged anew into the recital of his singular 'disease'.

"The audacious speculations of Bolyai, the amazing theories of Gauss – that through a point more than one line could be drawn parallel to a given line; the possibility that the angles of a triangle are together *greater* than two right angles, if drawn upon immense curvatures – the breathless intuitions of Beltrami and Lobatchewsky – all these I hurried through, and emerged, panting but unsatisfied, upon the verge of my – my new world, my Higher Space possibilities – in a word, my disease!

"How I got there," he resumed after a brief pause, during which he appeared to be listening intently for an approaching sound, "is more than I can put intelligibly into words. I can only hope to leave your mind with an intuitive comprehension of the possibility of what I say.

"Here, however, came a change. At this point I was no longer absorbing the fruits of studies I had made before; it was the beginning of new efforts to learn for the first time, and I had to go slowly and laboriously through terrible work. Here I sought for the theories and speculations of others. But books were few and far between, and with the exception of one man – a 'dreamer', the world called him – whose audacity and piercing intuition amazed and delighted me beyond description, I found no one to guide or help.

"You, of course, Dr. Silence, understand something of what I am driving at with these stammering words, though you cannot perhaps yet guess what depths of pain my new knowledge brought me to, nor why an acquaintance with a new development of space should prove a source of misery and terror."

Mr. Racine Mudge, remembering that the chair would not move, did the next best thing he could in his desire to draw nearer to the attentive man facing him, and sat forward upon the very edge of the cushions, crossing his legs and gesticulating with both hands as though he saw into this region of new space he was attempting to describe, and might any moment tumble into it bodily from the edge of the chair and disappear from view. John Silence, separated from him by three paces, sat with his eyes fixed upon the thin white face opposite, noting every word and every gesture with deep attention.

"This room we now sit in, Dr. Silence, has one side open to space – to Higher Space. A closed box only *seems* closed. There is a way in and out of a soap bubble without breaking the skin."

"You tell me no new thing," the doctor interposed gently.

"Hence, if Higher Space exists and our world borders upon it and lies partially in it, it follows necessarily that we see only portions of all objects. We never see their true and complete shape. We see their three measurements, but not their fourth. The new direction is concealed from us, and when I hold this book and move my hand all round it I have not really made a complete circuit. We only perceive those portions of any object which exist in our three dimensions; the rest escapes us. But, once we learn to see in Higher Space, and objects will appear as they actually are. Only they will thus be hardly recognisable!

"Now, you may begin to grasp something of what I am coming to."

"I am beginning to understand something of what you must have suffered," observed the doctor soothingly, "for I have made similar experiments myself, and only stopped just in time—"

"You are the one man in all the world who can hear and understand, *and* sympathise," exclaimed Mr. Mudge, grasping his hand and holding it tightly while he spoke. The nailed chair prevented further excitability.

"Well," he resumed, after a moment's pause, "I procured the implements and the coloured blocks for practical experiment, and I followed the instructions carefully till I had arrived at a working conception of four-dimensional space. The tessaract, the figure whose boundaries are cubes, I knew by heart. That is to say, I knew it and saw it mentally, for my eye, of course, could never take in a new measurement, or my hands and feet handle it.

"So, at least, I thought," he added, making a wry face. "I had reached the stage, you see, when I could *imagine* in a new dimension. I was able to conceive the shape of that new figure which is intrinsically different to all we know – the shape of the tessaract. I could perceive in four dimensions. When, therefore, I looked at a cube I could see all its sides at once. Its top was not foreshortened, nor its farther side and base invisible. I saw the whole thing out flat, so to speak. And this tessaract was bounded by cubes! Moreover, I also saw its content – its insides."

"You were not yourself able to enter this new world," interrupted Dr. Silence.

"Not then. I was only able to conceive intuitively what it was like and how exactly it must look. Later, when I slipped in there and saw objects in their entirety, unlimited by the paucity of our poor three measurements, I very nearly lost my life. For, you see, space does not stop at a single new dimension, a fourth. It extends in all possible new ones, and we must conceive it as containing any number of new dimensions. In other words, there is no space at all, but only a spiritual condition. But, meanwhile, I had come to grasp the strange fact that the objects in our normal world appear to us only partially."

Mr. Mudge moved farther forward till he was balanced dangerously on the very edge of the chair. "From this starting point," he resumed, "I began my studies and experiments, and continued them for years. I had money, and I was without friends. I lived in solitude and experimented. My intellect, of course, had little part in the work, for intellectually it was all unthinkable. Never was the limitation of mere reason more plainly demonstrated. It was mystically, intuitively, spiritually that I began to advance. And what I learnt, and knew, and did is all impossible to put into language, since it all describes experiences transcending the experiences of men. It is only some of the results – what you would call the symptoms of my disease – that I can give you, and even these must often appear absurd contradictions and impossible paradoxes.

"I can only tell you, Dr. Silence" – his manner became exceedingly impressive – "that I reached sometimes a point of view whence all the great puzzle of the world became plain to me, and I understood what they call in the Yoga books 'The Great Heresy of Separateness'; why all great teachers have urged the necessity of man loving his neighbour as himself; how men are all really *one*; and why the utter loss of self is necessary to salvation and the discovery of the true life of the soul."

He paused a moment and drew breath.

"Your speculations have been my own long ago," the doctor said quietly. "I fully realise the force of your words. Men are doubtless not separate at all – in the sense they imagine—"

"All this about the very much Higher Space I only dimly, very dimly, conceived, of course," the other went on, raising his voice again by jerks; "but what did happen to me was the humbler accident of – the simpler disaster – oh, dear, how shall I put it—?"

He stammered and showed visible signs of distress.

"It was simply this," he resumed with a sudden rush of words, "that, accidentally, as the result of my years of experiment, I one day slipped bodily into the next world, the world of four dimensions, yet without knowing precisely how I got there, or how I could get back again. I discovered, that is, that my ordinary three-dimensional body was but an expression – a projection – of my higher four-dimensional body!

"Now you understand what I meant much earlier in our talk when I spoke of chance. I cannot control my entrance or exit. Certain people, certain human atmospheres, certain wandering forces, thoughts, desires even – the radiations of certain combinations of colour, and above all, the vibrations of certain kinds of music, will suddenly throw me into a state of what I can only describe as an intense and terrific inner vibration – and behold I am off! Off in the direction at right angles to all our known directions! Off in the direction the cube takes when it begins to trace the outlines of the new figure! Off into my breathless and semi-divine Higher Space! Off, *inside myself*, into the world of four dimensions!"

He gasped and dropped back into the depths of the immovable chair.

"And there," he whispered, his voice issuing from among the cushions, "there I have to stay until these vibrations subside, or until they do something which I cannot find words to describe properly or intelligibly to you – and then, behold, I am back again. First, that is, I disappear. Then I reappear."

"Just so," exclaimed Dr. Silence, "and that is why a few—"

"Why a few moments ago," interrupted Mr. Mudge, taking the words out of his mouth, "you found me gone, and then saw me return. The music of that wretched German band sent me off. Your intense thinking about me brought me back – when the band had stopped its Wagner. I saw you approach the peep-hole and I saw Barker's intention of doing so later. For me no interiors are hidden. I see inside. When in that state the content of your mind, as of your body, is open to me as the day. Oh, dear, oh, dear, oh, dear!"

Mr. Mudge stopped and again mopped his brow. A light trembling ran over the surface of his small body like wind over grass. He still held tightly to the arms of the chair.

"At first," he presently resumed, "my new experiences were so vividly interesting that I felt no alarm. There was no room for it. The alarm came a little later."

"Then you actually penetrated far enough into that state to experience yourself as a normal portion of it?" asked the doctor, leaning forward, deeply interested.

Mr. Mudge nodded a perspiring face in reply.

"I did," he whispered, "undoubtedly I did. I am coming to all that. It began first at night, when I realised that sleep brought no loss of consciousness—"

"The spirit, of course, can never sleep. Only the body becomes unconscious," interposed John Silence.

"Yes, we know that – theoretically. At night, of course, the spirit is active elsewhere, and we have no memory of where and how, simply because the brain stays behind and receives no record. But I found that, while remaining conscious, I also retained memory. I had attained to the state of continuous consciousness, for at night I regularly, with the first approaches of drowsiness, entered *nolens volens* the four-dimensional world.

"For a time this happened regularly, and I could not control it; though later I found a way to regulate it better. Apparently sleep is unnecessary in the higher – the four-dimensional – body. Yes, perhaps. But I should infinitely have preferred dull sleep to the knowledge. For, unable to control my movements, I wandered to and fro, attracted, owing to my partial development and premature arrival, to parts of this new world that alarmed me more and more. It was the awful waste and drift of a monstrous world, so utterly different to all we know and see that I cannot even hint at the nature of the sights and objects and beings in it. More than that, I cannot even remember them. I cannot now picture them to myself even, but can recall only the *memory of the impression* they made upon me, the horror and devastating terror of it all. To be in several places at once, for instance—"

"Perfectly," interrupted John Silence, noticing the increase of the other's excitement, "I understand exactly. But now, please, tell me a little more of this alarm you experienced, and how it affected you."

"It's not the disappearing and reappearing *per se* that I mind," continued Mr. Mudge, "so much as certain other things. It's seeing people and objects in their weird entirety, in their true and complete shapes, that is so distressing. It introduces me to a world of monsters. Horses, dogs, cats, all of which I loved; people, trees, children; all that I have considered beautiful in life – everything, from a human face to a cathedral – appear to me in a different shape and aspect to all I have known before. I cannot perhaps convince you why this should be terrible, but I assure you that it is so. To hear the human voice proceeding from this novel appearance which I scarcely recognise as a human body is ghastly, simply ghastly. To see inside everything and everybody is a form of insight peculiarly distressing. To be so confused in geography as to find myself one moment at the North Pole, and the next at Clapham Junction – or possibly at both places simultaneously – is absurdly terrifying. Your imagination will readily furnish other details without my multiplying my experiences now. But you have no idea what it all means, and how I suffer."

Mr. Mudge paused in his panting account and lay back in his chair. He still held tightly to the arms as though they could keep him in the world of sanity and three measurements, and only now and again released his left hand in order to mop his face. He looked very thin and white and oddly unsubstantial, and he stared about him as though he saw into this other space he had been talking about.

John Silence, too, felt warm. He had listened to every word and had made many notes. The presence of this man had an exhilarating effect upon him. It seemed as if Mr. Racine Mudge still carried about with him something of that breathless Higher-Space condition he had been describing. At any rate, Dr. Silence had himself advanced sufficiently far along the legitimate paths of spiritual and psychic transformations to realise that the visions of this extraordinary little person had a basis of truth for their origin.

After a pause that prolonged itself into minutes, he crossed the room and unlocked a drawer in a bookcase, taking out a small book with a red cover. It had a lock to it, and he produced a key out of his pocket and proceeded to open the covers. The bright eyes of Mr. Mudge never left him for a single second.

"It almost seems a pity," he said at length, "to cure you, Mr. Mudge. You are on the way to discovery of great things. Though you may lose your life in the process – that is, your life here in the world of three dimensions – you would lose thereby nothing of great value – you will pardon my apparent rudeness, I know – and you might gain what is infinitely greater. Your suffering, of course, lies in the fact that you alternate between the two worlds and are never wholly in one or the other. Also, I rather imagine, though I cannot be certain of this from any personal experiments, that you have here and there penetrated even into space of more than four dimensions, and have hence experienced the terror you speak of."

The perspiring son of the Essex bargeman and the woman of Normandy bent his head several times in assent, but uttered no word in reply.

"Some strange psychic predisposition, dating no doubt from one of your former lives, has favoured the development of your 'disease'; and the fact that you had no normal training at school or college, no leading by the poor intellect into the culs-de-sac falsely called knowledge, has further caused your exceedingly rapid movement along the lines of direct inner experience. None of the knowledge you have foreshadowed has come to you through the senses, of course."

Mr. Mudge, sitting in his immovable chair, began to tremble slightly. A wind again seemed to pass over his surface and again to set it curiously in motion like a field of grass.

"You are merely talking to gain time," he said hurriedly, in a shaking voice. "This thinking aloud delays us. I see ahead what you are coming to, only please be quick, for something is going to happen. A band is again coming down the street, and if it plays – if it plays Wagner – I shall be off in a twinkling."

"Precisely. I will be quick. I was leading up to the point of how to effect your cure. The way is this: You must simply learn to *block the entrances*."

"True, true, utterly true!" exclaimed the little man, dodging about nervously in the depths of the chair. "But how, in the name of space, is that to be done?"

"By concentration. They are all within you, these entrances, although outer cases such as colour, music and other things lead you towards them. These external things you cannot hope to destroy, but once the entrances are blocked, they will lead you only to bricked walls and closed channels. You will no longer be able to find the way."

"Quick, quick!" cried the bobbing figure in the chair. "How is this concentration to be effected?"

"This little book," continued Dr. Silence calmly, "will explain to you the way." He tapped the cover. "Let me now read out to you certain simple instructions, composed, as I see you divine, entirely from my own personal experiences in the same direction. Follow these instructions and you will no longer enter the state of Higher Space. The entrances will be blocked effectively."

Mr. Mudge sat bolt upright in his chair to listen, and John Silence cleared his throat and began to read slowly in a very distinct voice.

But before he had uttered a dozen words, something happened. A sound of street music entered the room through the open ventilators, for a band had begun to play in the stable mews at the back of the house – the March from *Tannhäuser*. Odd as it may seem that a German band should twice within the space of an hour enter the same mews and play Wagner, it was nevertheless the fact.

Mr. Racine Mudge heard it. He uttered a sharp, squeaking cry and twisted his arms with nervous energy round the chair. A piteous look that was not far from tears spread over his white face. Grey shadows followed it – the grey of fear. He began to struggle convulsively.

"Hold me fast! Catch me! For God's sake, keep me here! I'm on the rush already. Oh, it's frightful!" he cried in tones of anguish, his voice as thin as a reed.

Dr. Silence made a plunge forward to seize him, but in a flash, before he could cover the space between them, Mr. Racine Mudge, screaming and struggling, seemed to shoot past him into invisibility. He disappeared like an arrow from a bow propelled at infinite speed, and his voice no longer sounded in the external air, but seemed in some curious way to make itself heard somewhere within the depths of the doctor's own being. It was almost like a faint singing cry in his head, like a voice of dream, a voice of vision and unreality.

"Alcohol, alcohol!" it cried, "give me alcohol! It's the quickest way. Alcohol, before I'm out of reach!"

The doctor, accustomed to rapid decisions and even more rapid action, remembered that a brandy flask stood upon the mantelpiece, and in less than a second he had seized it and was holding it out towards the space above the chair recently occupied by the visible Mudge. Then, before his very eyes, and long ere he could unscrew the metal stopper, he saw the contents of the closed glass phial sink and lessen as though someone were drinking violently and greedily of the liquor within.

"Thanks! Enough! It deadens the vibrations!" cried the faint voice in his interior, as he withdrew the flask and set it back upon the mantelpiece. He understood that in Mudge's present condition one side of the flask was open to space and he could drink without removing the stopper. He could hardly have had a more interesting proof of what he had been hearing described at such length.

But the next moment – the very same moment it almost seemed – the German band stopped midway in its tune – and there was Mr. Mudge back in his chair again, gasping and panting!

"Quick!" he shrieked, "stop that band! Send it away! Catch hold of me! Block the entrances! Block the entrances! Give me the red book! Oh, oh, oh-h-h-h!!!"

The music had begun again. It was merely a temporary interruption. The *Tannhäuser* March started again, this time at a tremendous pace that made it sound like a rapid two-step as though the instruments played against time.

But the brief interruption gave Dr. Silence a moment in which to collect his scattering thoughts, and before the band had got through half a bar, he had flung forward upon the chair and held Mr. Racine Mudge, the struggling little victim of Higher Space, in a grip of iron. His arms went all round his diminutive person, taking in a good part of the chair at the same time. He was not a big man, yet he seemed to smother Mudge completely.

Yet, even as he did so, and felt the wriggling form underneath him, it began to melt and slip away like air or water. The wood of the arm-chair somehow disentangled itself from between his own arms and those of Mudge. The phenomenon known as the passage of matter through matter took place. The little man seemed actually to get mixed up in his own being. Dr. Silence could just see his face beneath him. It puckered and grew dark as though from some great internal effort. He heard the thin, reedy voice cry in his ear to "Block the entrances, block the entrances!" and then – but how in the world describe what is indescribable?

John Silence half rose up to watch. Racine Mudge, his face distorted beyond all recognition, was making a marvellous inward movement, as though doubling back upon himself. He turned funnel-wise like water in a whirling vortex, and then appeared to break up somewhat as a reflection breaks up and divides in a distorting convex mirror. He went neither forward nor backwards, neither to the right nor the left, neither up nor down. But he went. He went utterly. He simply flashed away out of sight like a vanishing projectile.

All but one leg! Dr. Silence just had the time and the presence of mind to seize upon the left ankle and boot as it disappeared, and to this he held on for several seconds like grim death. Yet all the time he knew it was a foolish and useless thing to do.

The foot was in his grasp one moment, and the next it seemed – this was the only way he could describe it – inside his own skin and bones, and at the same time outside his hand

and all round it. It seemed mixed up in some amazing way with his own flesh and blood. Then it was gone, and he was tightly grasping a draught of heated air.

"Gone! Gone! Gone!" cried a thick, whispering voice, somewhere deep within his own consciousness. "Lost! Lost! Lost!" it repeated, growing fainter and fainter till at length it vanished into nothing and the last signs of Mr. Racine Mudge vanished with it.

John Silence locked his red book and replaced it in the cabinet, which he fastened with a click, and when Barker answered the bell he inquired if Mr. Mudge had left a card upon the table. It appeared that he had, and when the servant returned with it, Dr. Silence read the address and made a note of it. It was in North London.

"Mr. Mudge has gone," he said quietly to Barker, noticing his expression of alarm.

"He's not taken his 'at with him, sir."

"Mr. Mudge requires no hat where he is now," continued the doctor, stooping to poke the fire. "But he may return for it—"

"And the humbrella, sir."

"And the umbrella."

"He didn't go out *my* way, sir, if you please," stuttered the amazed servant, his curiosity overcoming his nervousness.

"Mr. Mudge has his own way of coming and going, and prefers it. If he returns by the door at any time remember to bring him instantly to me, and be kind and gentle with him and ask no questions. Also, remember, Barker, to think pleasantly, sympathetically, affectionately of him while he is away. Mr. Mudge is a very suffering gentleman."

Barker bowed and went out of the room backwards, gasping and feeling round the inside of his collar with three very hot fingers of one hand.

It was two days later when he brought in a telegram to the study. Dr. Silence opened it, and read as follows:

> Bombay. Just slipped out again. All safe. Have blocked entrances. Thousand thanks. Address Cooks, London. – Mudge.

Dr. Silence looked up and saw Barker staring at him bewilderingly. It occurred to him that somehow he knew the contents of the telegram.

"Make a parcel of Mr. Mudge's things," he said briefly, "and address them Thomas Cook & Sons, Ludgate Circus. And send them there exactly a month from today and marked 'To be called for.'"

"Yes, sir," said Barker, leaving the room with a deep sigh and a hurried glance at the waste-paper basket where his master had dropped the pink paper.

**If you enjoyed this, you might also like…**
The Pikestaffe Case, see page 331
Ancient Sorceries, see page 246

# The Other Wing

## Chapter I

**IT USED TO** puzzle him that, after dark, someone would look in round the edge of the bedroom door, and withdraw again too rapidly for him to see the face. When the nurse had gone away with the candle this happened: "Good night, Master Tim," she said usually, shading the light with one hand to protect his eyes; "dream of me and I'll dream of you." She went out slowly. The sharp-edged shadow of the door ran across the ceiling like a train. There came a whispered colloquy in the corridor outside, about himself, of course, and – he was alone. He heard her steps going deeper and deeper into the bosom of the old country house; they were audible for a moment on the stone flooring of the hall; and sometimes the dull thump of the baize door into the servants' quarters just reached him, too – then silence. But it was only when the last sound, as well as the last sign of her had vanished, that the face emerged from its hiding-place and flashed in upon him round the corner. As a rule, too, it came just as he was saying, "Now I'll go to sleep. I won't think any longer. Good night, Master Tim, and happy dreams." He loved to say this to himself; it brought a sense of companionship, as though there were two persons speaking.

The room was on the top of the old house, a big, high-ceilinged room, and his bed against the wall had an iron railing round it; he felt very safe and protected in it. The curtains at the other end of the room were drawn. He lay watching the firelight dancing on the heavy folds, and their pattern, showing a spaniel chasing a long-tailed bird towards a bushy tree, interested and amused him. It was repeated over and over again. He counted the number of dogs, and the number of birds, and the number of trees, but could never make them agree. There was a plan somewhere in that pattern; if only he could discover it, the dogs and birds and trees would 'come out right'. Hundreds and hundreds of times he had played this game, for the plan in the pattern made it possible to take sides, and the bird and dog were against him. They always won, however; Tim usually fell asleep just when the advantage was on his own side. The curtains hung steadily enough most of the time, but it seemed to him once or twice that they stirred – hiding a dog or bird on purpose to prevent his winning. For instance, he had eleven birds and eleven trees, and, fixing them in his mind by saying, "that's eleven birds and eleven trees, but only ten dogs," his eyes darted back to find the eleventh dog, when – the curtain moved and threw all his calculations into confusion again. The eleventh dog was hidden. He did not quite like the movement; it gave him questionable feelings, rather, for the curtain did not move of itself. Yet, usually, he was too intent upon counting the dogs to feel positive alarm.

Opposite to him was the fireplace, full of red and yellow coals; and, lying with his head sideways on the pillow, he could see directly in between the bars. When the coals settled with a soft and powdery crash, he turned his eyes from the curtains to the grate, trying to discover exactly which bits had fallen. So long as the glow was there the sound seemed pleasant enough, but sometimes he awoke later in the night, the room huge with darkness, the fire almost out – and the sound was not so pleasant then. It startled him. The coals did not fall of themselves. It seemed that someone poked them cautiously. The shadows were very thick before the bars. As with the curtains, moreover, the morning aspect of the extinguished fire, the ice-cold cinders that made a clinking sound like tin, caused no emotion whatever in his soul.

And it was usually while he lay waiting for sleep, tired both of the curtain and the coal games, on the point, indeed, of saying, "I'll go to sleep now," that the puzzling thing took place. He would be staring drowsily at the dying fire, perhaps counting the stockings and flannel garments that hung along the high fender-rail when, suddenly, a person looked in with lightning swiftness through the door and vanished again before he could possibly turn his head to see. The appearance and disappearance were accomplished with amazing rapidity always.

It was a head and shoulders that looked in, and the movement combined the speed, the lightness and the silence of a shadow. Only it was not a shadow. A hand held the edge of the door. The face shot round, saw him, and withdrew like lightning. It was utterly beyond him to imagine anything more quick and clever. It darted. He heard no sound. It went. But – it had seen him, looked him all over, examined him, noted what he was doing with that lightning glance. It wanted to know if he were awake still, or asleep. And though it went off, it still watched him from a distance; it waited somewhere; it knew all about him. Where it waited no one could ever guess. It came probably, he felt, from beyond the house, possibly from the roof, but most likely from the garden or the sky. Yet, though strange, it was not terrible. It was a kindly and protective figure, he felt. And when it happened he never called for help, because the occurrence simply took his voice away.

"It comes from the Nightmare Passage," he decided; "but it's not a nightmare." It puzzled him.

Sometimes, moreover, it came more than once in a single night. He was pretty sure – not quite positive – that it occupied his room as soon as he was properly asleep. It took possession, sitting perhaps before the dying fire, standing upright behind the heavy curtains, or even lying down in the empty bed his brother used when he was home from school. Perhaps it played the curtain game, perhaps it poked the coals; it knew, at any rate, where the eleventh dog had lain concealed. It certainly came in and out; certainly, too, it did not wish to be seen. For, more than once, on waking suddenly in the midnight blackness, Tim knew it was standing close beside his bed and bending over him. He felt, rather than heard, its presence. It glided quietly away. It moved with marvellous softness, yet he was positive it moved. He felt the difference, so to speak. It had been near him, now it was gone. It came back, too – just as he was falling into sleep again. Its midnight coming and going, however, stood out sharply different from its first shy, tentative approach. For in the firelight it came alone; whereas in the black and silent hours, it had with it – others.

And it was then he made up his mind that its swift and quiet movements were due to the fact that it had wings. It flew. And the others that came with it in the darkness were 'its little ones'. He also made up his mind that all were friendly, comforting, protective, and that while positively not a Nightmare, it yet came somehow along the Nightmare Passage before it reached him. "You see, it's like this," he explained to the nurse: "The big one comes to visit me alone, but it only brings its little ones when I'm quite asleep."

"Then the quicker you get to sleep the better, isn't it, Master Tim?"

He replied: "Rather! I always do. Only I wonder where they come from!" He spoke, however, as though he had an inkling.

But the nurse was so dull about it that he gave her up and tried his father. "Of course," replied this busy but affectionate parent; "it's either nobody at all, or else it's Sleep coming to carry you away to the land of dreams." He made the statement kindly but somewhat briskly, for he was worried just then about the extra taxes on his land, and the effort to fix his mind on Tim's fanciful world was beyond him at the moment. He lifted the boy on to his knee, kissed and patted him as though he were a favourite dog, and planted him on the rug again with a flying sweep. "Run and ask your mother," he added; "she knows all that kind of thing. Then come back and tell me all about it – another time."

Tim found his mother in an armchair before the fire of another room; she was knitting and reading at the same time – a wonderful thing the boy could never understand. She raised her head as he came in, pushed her glasses on to her forehead, and held her arms out. He told her everything, ending up with what his father said.

"You see, it's not Jackman, or Thompson, or any one like that," he exclaimed. "It's someone real."

"But nice," she assured him, "someone who comes to take care of you and see that you're all safe and cosy."

"Oh, yes, I know that. But—"

"I think your father's right," she added quickly. "It's Sleep, I'm sure, who pops in round the door like that. Sleep has got wings, I've always heard."

"Then the other thing – the little ones?" he asked. "Are they just sorts of dozes, you think?"

Mother did not answer for a moment. She turned down the page of her book, closed it slowly, put it on the table beside her. More slowly still she put her knitting away, arranging the wool and needles with some deliberation.

"Perhaps," she said, drawing the boy closer to her and looking into his big eyes of wonder, "they're dreams!"

Tim felt a thrill run through him as she said it. He stepped back a foot or so and clapped his hands softly. "Dreams!" he whispered with enthusiasm and belief; "of course! I never thought of that."

His mother, having proved her sagacity, then made a mistake. She noted her success, but instead of leaving it there, she elaborated and explained. As Tim expressed it she 'went on about it'. Therefore he did not listen. He followed his train of thought alone. And presently, he interrupted her long sentences with a conclusion of his own:

"Then I know where She hides," he announced with a touch of awe. "Where She lives, I mean." And without waiting to be asked, he imparted the information: "It's in the Other Wing."

"Ah!" said his mother, taken by surprise. "How clever of you, Tim!" – and thus confirmed it.

Thenceforward this was established in his life – that Sleep and her attendant Dreams hid during the daytime in that unused portion of the great Elizabethan mansion called the Other Wing. This other wing was unoccupied, its corridors untrodden, its windows shuttered and its rooms all closed. At various places green baize doors led into it, but no one ever opened them. For many years this part had been shut up; and for the children, properly speaking, it was out of bounds. They never mentioned it as a possible place, at any rate; in hide-and-seek it was not considered, even; there was a hint of the inaccessible about the Other Wing. Shadows, dust, and silence had it to themselves.

But Tim, having ideas of his own about everything, possessed special information about the Other Wing. He believed it was inhabited. Who occupied the immense series of empty rooms, who trod the spacious corridors, who passed to and fro behind the shuttered windows, he had not known exactly. He had called these occupants 'they', and the most important among them was 'The Ruler'. The Ruler of the Other Wing was a kind of deity, powerful, far away, ever present yet never seen.

And about this Ruler he had a wonderful conception for a little boy; he connected her, somehow, with deep thoughts of his own, the deepest of all. When he made up adventures to the moon, to the stars, or to the bottom of the sea, adventures that he lived inside himself, as it were – to reach them he must invariably pass through the chambers of the Other Wing. Those corridors and halls, the Nightmare Passage among them, lay along the route; they were the first stage of the journey. Once the green baize doors swung to behind him and the long dim passage stretched ahead, he was well on his way into the adventure of the moment; the Nightmare Passage once passed, he was safe from capture; but once the shutters of a window had been flung open, he was free of the gigantic world that lay beyond. For then light poured in and he could see his way.

The conception, for a child, was curious. It established a correspondence between the mysterious chambers of the Other Wing and the occupied, but unguessed chambers of his Inner Being. Through these chambers, through these darkened corridors, along a passage, sometimes dangerous, or at least of questionable repute, he must pass to find all adventures that were real. The light – when he pierced far enough to take the shutters down – was discovery. Tim did not actually think, much less say, all this. He was aware of it, however. He felt it. The Other Wing was inside himself as well as through the green baize doors. His inner map of wonder included both of them.

But now, for the first time in his life, he knew who lived there and who the Ruler was. A shutter had fallen of its own accord; light poured in; he made a guess, and Mother had confirmed it. Sleep and her Little Ones, the host of dreams, were the daylight occupants. They stole out when the darkness fell. All adventures in life began and ended by a dream – discoverable by first passing through the Other Wing.

## Chapter II

**AND**, having settled this, his one desire now was to travel over the map upon journeys of exploration and discovery. The map inside himself he knew already, but the map of the Other Wing he had not seen. His mind knew it, he had a clear mental picture of rooms and halls and passages, but his feet had never trod the silent floors where dust and shadows hid the flock of dreams by day. The mighty chambers where Sleep ruled he longed to stand in, to see the Ruler face to face. He made up his mind to get into the Other Wing.

To accomplish this was difficult; but Tim was a determined youngster, and he meant to try; he meant, also, to succeed. He deliberated. At night he could not possibly manage it; in any case, the Ruler and her host all left it after dark, to fly about the world; the Wing would be empty, and the emptiness would frighten him. Therefore he must make a daylight visit; and it was a daylight visit he decided on. He deliberated more. There were rules and risks involved: it meant going out of bounds, the danger of being seen, the certainty of being questioned by some idle and inquisitive grown-up: "Where in the world have you been all this time" – and so forth. These things he thought out carefully, and though he arrived at no solution, he felt satisfied that it would be all right. That is, he recognised the risks. To be prepared was half the battle, for nothing then could take him by surprise.

The notion that he might slip in from the garden was soon abandoned; the red bricks showed no openings; there was no door; from the courtyard, also, entrance was impracticable; even on tiptoe he could barely reach the broad windowsills of stone. When playing alone, or walking with the French governess, he examined every outside possibility. None offered. The shutters, supposing he could reach them, were thick and solid.

Meanwhile, when opportunity offered, he stood against the outside walls and listened, his ear pressed against the tight red bricks; the towers and gables of the Wing rose overhead; he heard the wind go whispering along the eaves; he imagined tiptoe movements and a sound of wings inside. Sleep and her Little Ones were busily preparing for their journeys after dark; they hid, but they did not sleep; in this unused Wing, vaster alone than any other country house he had ever seen, Sleep taught and trained her flock of feathered Dreams. It was very wonderful. They probably supplied the entire county. But more wonderful still was the thought that the Ruler herself should take the trouble to come to his particular room and personally watch over him all night long. That was amazing. And it flashed across his imaginative, inquiring mind: "Perhaps they take me with them! The moment I'm asleep! That's why she comes to see me!"

Yet his chief preoccupation was, how Sleep got out. Through the green baize doors, of course! By a process of elimination he arrived at a conclusion: he, too, must enter through a green baize door and risk detection.

Of late, the lightning visits had ceased. The silent, darting figure had not peeped in and vanished as it used to do. He fell asleep too quickly now, almost before Jackman reached the hall, and long before the fire began to die. Also, the dogs and birds upon the curtains always matched the trees exactly, and he won the curtain game quite easily; there was never a dog or bird too many; the curtain never stirred. It had been thus ever since his talk with Mother and Father. And so he came to make a second discovery: His parents did not really believe in his Figure. She kept away on that account. They doubted her; she hid. Here was still another incentive to go and find her out. He ached for her, she was so kind, she gave herself so much trouble – just for his little self in the big and lonely bedroom. Yet his parents spoke of her as though she were of no account. He longed to see her, face to face, and tell her that he believed in her and loved her. For he was positive she would like to hear it. She cared. Though he had fallen asleep of late too quickly for him to see her flash in at the door, he had known nicer dreams than ever in his life before – travelling dreams. And it was she who sent them. More – he was sure she took him out with her.

One evening, in the dusk of a March day, his opportunity came; and only just in time, for his brother Jack was expected home from school on the morrow, and with Jack in the other bed, no Figure would ever care to show itself. Also it was Easter, and after Easter, though Tim was not aware of it at the time, he was to say goodbye finally to governesses and become a day-boarder at a preparatory school for Wellington. The opportunity offered itself so naturally, moreover, that Tim took it without hesitation. It never occurred to him to question, much less to refuse it. The thing was obviously meant to be. For he found himself unexpectedly in front of a green baize door; and the green baize door was – swinging! Somebody, therefore, had just passed through it.

It had come about in this wise. Father, away in Scotland, at Inglemuir, the shooting place, was expected back next morning; Mother had driven over to the church upon some Easter business or other; and the governess had been allowed her holiday at home in France. Tim, therefore, had the run of the house, and in the hour between tea and bedtime he made good use of it. Fully able to defy such second-rate obstacles as nurses and butlers, he explored all manner of forbidden places with ardent thoroughness, arriving finally in the sacred precincts of his father's study. This wonderful room was the very heart and centre of the whole big house; he had been birched here long ago; here, too, his father had told him with a grave yet smiling face: "You've got a new companion, Tim, a little sister; you must be very kind to her." Also, it was the place where all the money was kept. What he called 'father's jolly smell' was strong in it – papers, tobacco, books, flavoured by hunting crops and gunpowder.

At first he felt awed, standing motionless just inside the door; but presently, recovering equilibrium, he moved cautiously on tiptoe towards the gigantic desk where important papers were piled in untidy patches. These he did not touch; but beside them his quick eye noted the jagged piece of iron shell his father brought home from his Crimean campaign and now used as a letter-weight. It was difficult to lift, however. He climbed into the comfortable chair and swung round and round. It was a swivel-chair, and he sank down among the cushions in it, staring at the strange things on the great desk before him, as if fascinated. Next he turned away and saw the stick-rack in the corner – this, he knew, he was allowed to touch. He had played with these sticks before. There were twenty, perhaps, all told, with curious carved handles, brought from every corner of the world; many of them cut by his father's own hand in queer and distant places. And, among them, Tim fixed his eye upon a cane with an ivory handle, a slender, polished cane that he had always coveted tremendously. It was the kind he meant to use when he was a man. It bent, it quivered, and when he swished it through the air it trembled like a riding-whip, and made a whistling noise. Yet it was very strong in spite of its elastic qualities. A family treasure, it was also an old-fashioned relic; it had been his grandfather's walking stick. Something of another century clung visibly about it still. It had dignity and grace and leisure in its very aspect. And it suddenly occurred to him: "How grandpapa must miss it! Wouldn't he just love to have it back again!"

How it happened exactly, Tim did not know, but a few minutes later he found himself walking about the deserted halls and passages of the house with the air of an elderly gentleman of a hundred years ago, proud as a courtier, flourishing the stick like an eighteenth-century dandy in the Mall. That the cane reached to his shoulder made no difference; he held it accordingly, swaggering on his way. He was off upon an adventure. He dived down through the byways of the Other Wing, inside himself, as though the stick transported him to the days of the old gentleman who had used it in another century.

It may seem strange to those who dwell in smaller houses, but in this rambling Elizabethan mansion there were whole sections that, even to Tim, were strange and unfamiliar. In his mind the map of the Other Wing was clearer by far than the geography of the part he travelled daily. He came to passages and dim-lit halls, long corridors of stone beyond the Picture Gallery; narrow, wainscoted connecting-channels with four steps down and a little later two steps up; deserted chambers with arches guarding them – all hung with the soft March twilight and all bewilderingly unrecognised. With a sense of adventure born of naughtiness he went carelessly along, farther and farther into the heart of this unfamiliar country, swinging the cane, one thumb stuck into the armpit of his blue serge suit, whistling softly to himself, excited yet keenly on the alert – and suddenly found himself opposite a door that checked all further advance. It was a green baize door. And it was swinging.

He stopped abruptly, facing it. He stared, he gripped his cane more tightly, he held his breath. "The Other Wing!" he gasped in a swallowed whisper. It was an entrance, but an entrance he had never seen before. He thought he knew every door by heart; but this one was new. He stood motionless for several minutes, watching it; the door had two halves, but one half only was swinging, each swing shorter than the one before; he heard the little puffs of air it made; it settled finally, the last movements very short and rapid; it stopped. And the boy's heart, after similar rapid strokes, stopped also – for a moment.

"Someone's just gone through," he gulped. And even as he said it he knew who the someone was. The conviction just dropped into him. "It's Grandfather; he knows I've got his stick. He wants it!" On the heels of this flashed instantly another amazing certainty. "He sleeps in there. He's having dreams. That's what being dead means."

His first impulse, then, took the form of, "I must let Father know; it'll make him burst for joy"; but his second was for himself – to finish his adventure. And it was this, naturally enough, that gained the day. He could tell his father later. His first duty was plainly to go through the door into the Other Wing. He must give the stick back to its owner. He must hand it back.

The test of will and character came now. Tim had imagination, and so knew the meaning of fear; but there was nothing craven in him. He could howl and scream and stamp like any other person of his age when the occasion called for such behaviour, but such occasions were due to temper roused by a thwarted will, and the histrionics were half 'pretended' to produce a calculated effect. There was no one to thwart his will at present. He also knew how to be afraid of Nothing, to be afraid without ostensible cause, that is – which was merely 'nerves'. He could have 'the shudders' with the best of them.

But, when a real thing faced him, Tim's character emerged to meet it. He would clench his hands, brace his muscles, set his teeth – and wish to heaven he was bigger. But he would not flinch. Being imaginative, he lived the worst a dozen times before it happened, yet in the final crash he stood up like a man. He had that highest pluck – the courage of a sensitive temperament. And at this particular juncture, somewhat ticklish for a boy of eight or nine, it did not fail him. He lifted the cane and pushed the swinging door wide open. Then he walked through it – into the Other Wing.

## Chapter III

**THE GREEN** baize door swung to behind him; he was even sufficiently master of himself to turn and close it with a steady hand, because he did not care to hear the series of muffled thuds its lessening swings would cause. But he realised clearly his position, knew he was doing a tremendous thing.

Holding the cane between fingers very tightly clenched, he advanced bravely along the corridor that stretched before him. And all fear left him from that moment, replaced, it seemed, by a mild and exquisite surprise. His footsteps made no sound, he walked on air; instead of darkness, or the twilight he expected, a diffused and gentle light that seemed like the silver on the lawn when a half-moon sails a cloudless sky, lay everywhere. He knew his way, moreover, knew exactly where he was and whither he was going. The corridor was as familiar to him as the floor of his own bedroom; he recognised the shape and length of it; it agreed exactly with the map he had constructed long ago. Though he had never, to the best of his knowledge, entered it before, he knew with intimacy its every detail.

And thus the surprise he felt was mild and far from disconcerting. "I'm here again!" was the kind of thought he had. It was how he got here that caused the faint surprise, apparently. He no longer swaggered, however, but walked carefully, and half on tiptoe, holding the ivory handle of the cane with a kind of affectionate respect. And as he advanced, the light closed softly up behind him, obliterating the way by which he had come. But this he did not know, because he did not look behind him. He only looked in front, where the corridor stretched its silvery length towards the great chamber where he knew the cane must be surrendered. The person who had preceded him down this ancient corridor, passing through the green baize door just before he reached it, this person, his father's father, now stood in that great chamber, waiting to receive his own. Tim knew it as surely as he knew he breathed. At the far end he even made out the larger patch of silvery light which marked its gaping doorway.

There was another thing he knew as well – that this corridor he moved along between rooms with fast-closed doors, was the Nightmare Corridor; often and often he had traversed it; each room was occupied. "This is the Nightmare Passage," he whispered to himself, "but I know the Ruler – it doesn't matter. None of them can get out or do anything." He heard them, none the less, inside, as he passed by; he heard them scratching to get out. The feeling of security made him reckless; he took unnecessary risks; he brushed the panels as he passed. And the love of keen sensation for its own sake, the desire to feel 'an awful thrill', tempted him once so sharply that he raised his stick and poked a fast-shut door with it!

He was not prepared for the result, but he gained the sensation and the thrill. For the door opened with instant swiftness half an inch, a hand emerged, caught the stick and tried to draw it in. Tim sprang back as if he had been struck. He pulled at the ivory handle with all his strength, but his strength was less than nothing. He tried to shout, but his voice had gone. A terror of the moon came over him, for he was unable to loosen his hold of the handle; his fingers had become a part of it. An appalling weakness turned him helpless. He was dragged inch by inch towards the fearful door. The end of the stick was already through the narrow, crack. He could not see the hand that pulled, but he knew it was terrific. He understood now why the world was strange, why horses galloped furiously, and why trains whistled as they raced through stations. All the comedy and terror of nightmare gripped his heart with pincers made of ice. The disproportion was abominable. The final collapse rushed over him when, without a sign of warning, the door slammed silently, and between the jamb and the wall the cane was crushed as flat as if it were a bulrush. So irresistible was the force behind the door that the solid stick just went flat as a stalk of a bulrush.

He looked at it. It was a bulrush.

He did not laugh; the absurdity was so distressingly unnatural. The horror of finding a bulrush where he had expected a polished cane – this hideous and appalling detail held the nameless horror of the nightmare. It betrayed him utterly. Why had he not always known really that the stick was not a stick, but a thin and hollow reed...?

Then the cane was safely in his hand, unbroken. He stood looking at it. The Nightmare was in full swing. He heard another door opening behind his back, a door he had not touched. There was just time to see a hand thrusting and waving dreadfully, familiarly, at him through the narrow crack – just time to realise that this was another Nightmare acting in atrocious concert with the first, when he saw closely beside him, towering to the ceiling, the protective, kindly Figure that visited his bedroom. In the turning movement he made to meet the attack, he became aware of her. And his terror passed. It was a nightmare terror merely. The infinite horror vanished. Only the comedy remained. He smiled.

He saw her dimly only, she was so vast, but he saw her, the Ruler of the Other Wing at last, and knew that he was safe again. He gazed with a tremendous love and wonder, trying to see her clearly; but the face was hidden far aloft and seemed to melt into the sky beyond the roof. He discerned that she was larger than the Night, only far, far softer, with wings that folded above him more tenderly even than his mother's arms; that there were points of light like stars among the feathers, and that she was vast enough to cover millions and millions of people all at once. Moreover, she did not fade or go, so far as he could see, but spread herself in such a way that he lost sight of her. She spread over the entire Wing…

And Tim remembered that this was all quite natural really. He had often and often been down this corridor before; the Nightmare Corridor was no new experience; it had to be faced as usual. Once knowing what hid inside the rooms, he was bound to tempt them out. They drew, enticed, attracted him; this was their power. It was their special strength that they could suck him helplessly towards them, and that he was obliged to go. He understood exactly why he was tempted to tap with the cane upon their awful doors, but, having done so, he had accepted the challenge and could now continue his journey quietly and safely. The Ruler of the Other Wing had taken him in charge.

A delicious sense of carelessness came on him. There was softness as of water in the solid things about him, nothing that could hurt or bruise. Holding the cane firmly by its ivory handle, he went forward along the corridor, walking as on air.

The end was quickly reached: He stood upon the threshold of the mighty chamber where he knew the owner of the cane was waiting; the long corridor lay behind him, in front he saw the spacious dimensions of a lofty hall that gave him the feeling of being in the Crystal Palace, Euston Station, or St. Paul's. High, narrow windows, cut deeply into the wall, stood in a row upon the other side; an enormous open fireplace of burning logs was on his right; thick tapestries hung from the ceiling to the floor of stone; and in the centre of the chamber was a massive table of dark, shining wood, great chairs with carved stiff backs set here and there beside it. And in the biggest of these throne-like chairs there sat a figure looking at him gravely – the figure of an old, old man.

Yet there was no surprise in the boy's fast-beating heart; there was a thrill of pleasure and excitement only, a feeling of satisfaction. He had known quite well the figure would be there, known also it would look like this exactly. He stepped forward on to the floor of stone without a trace of fear or trembling, holding the precious cane in two hands now before him, as though to present it to its owner. He felt proud and pleased. He had run risks for this.

And the figure rose quietly to meet him, advancing in a stately manner over the hard stone floor. The eyes looked gravely, sweetly down at him, the aquiline nose stood out. Tim knew him perfectly: the knee-breeches of shining satin, the gleaming buckles on the shoes, the neat dark stockings, the lace and ruffles about neck and wrists, the coloured waistcoat opening so widely – all the details of the picture over father's mantelpiece, where it hung between two Crimean bayonets, were reproduced in life before his eyes at last. Only the polished cane with the ivory handle was not there.

Tim went three steps nearer to the advancing figure and held out both his hands with the cane laid crosswise on them.

"I've brought it, Grandfather," he said, in a faint but clear and steady tone; "here it is."

And the other stooped a little, put out three fingers half concealed by falling lace, and took it by the ivory handle. He made a courtly bow to Tim. He smiled, but though there was pleasure, it was a grave, sad smile. He spoke then: the voice was slow and very deep. There was a delicate softness in it, the suave politeness of an older day.

"Thank you," he said; "I value it. It was given to me by my grandfather. I forgot it when I—" His voice grew indistinct a little.

"Yes?" said Tim.

"When I – left," the old gentleman repeated.

"Oh," said Tim, thinking how beautiful and kind the gracious figure was.

The old man ran his slender fingers carefully along the cane, feeling the polished surface with satisfaction. He lingered specially over the smoothness of the ivory handle. He was evidently very pleased.

"I was not quite myself – er – at the moment," he went on gently; "my memory failed me somewhat." He sighed, as though an immense relief was in him.

"I forget things, too – sometimes," Tim mentioned sympathetically. He simply loved his grandfather. He hoped – for a moment – he would be lifted up and kissed. "I'm awfully glad I brought it," he faltered – "that you've got it again."

The other turned his kind grey eyes upon him; the smile on his face was full of gratitude as he looked down.

"Thank you, my boy. I am truly and deeply indebted to you. You courted danger for my sake. Others have tried before, but the Nightmare Passage – er—" He broke off. He tapped the stick firmly on the stone flooring, as though to test it. Bending a trifle, he put his weight upon it. "Ah!" he exclaimed with a short sigh of relief, "I can now—"

His voice again grew indistinct; Tim did not catch the words.

"Yes?" he asked again, aware for the first time that a touch of awe was in his heart.

"—get about again," the other continued very low. "Without my cane," he added, the voice failing with each word the old lips uttered, "I could not…possibly…allow myself… to be seen. It was indeed…deplorable…unpardonable of me…to forget in such a way. Zounds, sir…! I – I…"

His voice sank away suddenly into a sound of wind. He straightened up, tapping the iron ferrule of his cane on the stones in a series of loud knocks. Tim felt a strange sensation creep into his legs. The queer words frightened him a little.

The old man took a step towards him. He still smiled, but there was a new meaning in the smile. A sudden earnestness had replaced the courtly, leisurely manner. The next words seemed to blow down upon the boy from above, as though a cold wind brought them from the sky outside.

Yet the words, he knew, were kindly meant, and very sensible. It was only the abrupt change that startled him. Grandfather, after all, was but a man! The distant sound recalled something in him to that outside world from which the cold wind blew.

"My eternal thanks to you," he heard, while the voice and face and figure seemed to withdraw deeper and deeper into the heart of the mighty chamber. "I shall not forget your kindness and your courage. It is a debt I can, fortunately, one day repay…But now you had best return and with dispatch. For your head and arm lie heavily on the table, the documents are scattered, there is a cushion fallen…and my son is in the house…

Farewell! You had best leave me quickly. See! She stands behind you, waiting. Go with her! Go now...!"

The entire scene had vanished even before the final words were uttered. Tim felt empty space about him. A vast, shadowy Figure bore him through it as with mighty wings. He flew, he rushed, he remembered nothing more – until he heard another voice and felt a heavy hand upon his shoulder.

"Tim, you rascal! What are you doing in my study? And in the dark, like this!"

He looked up into his father's face without a word. He felt dazed. The next minute his father had caught him up and kissed him.

"Ragamuffin! How did you guess I was coming back tonight?" He shook him playfully and kissed his tumbling hair. "And you've been asleep, too, into the bargain. Well – how's everything at home – eh? Jack's coming back from school tomorrow, you know, and..."

## Chapter IV

**JACK** came home, indeed, the following day, and when the Easter holidays were over, the governess stayed abroad and Tim went off to adventures of another kind in the preparatory school for Wellington. Life slipped rapidly along with him; he grew into a man; his mother and his father died; Jack followed them within a little space; Tim inherited, married, settled down into his great possessions – and opened up the Other Wing. The dreams of imaginative boyhood all had faded; perhaps he had merely put them away, or perhaps he had forgotten them. At any rate, he never spoke of such things now, and when his Irish wife mentioned her belief that the old country house possessed a family ghost, even declaring that she had met an eighteenth-century figure of a man in the corridors, "an old, old man who bends down upon a stick" – Tim only laughed and said:

"That's as it ought to be! And if these awful land-taxes force us to sell some day, a respectable ghost will increase the market value."

But one night he woke and heard a tapping on the floor. He sat up in bed and listened. There was a chilly feeling down his back. Belief had long since gone out of him; he felt uncannily afraid. The sound came nearer and nearer; there were light footsteps with it. The door opened – it opened a little wider, that is, for it already stood ajar – and there upon the threshold stood a figure that it seemed he knew. He saw the face as with all the vivid sharpness of reality. There was a smile upon it, but a smile of warning and alarm. The arm was raised. Tim saw the slender hand, lace falling down upon the long, thin fingers, and in them, tightly gripped, a polished cane. Shaking the cane twice to and fro in the air, the face thrust forward, spoke certain words, and – vanished. But the words were inaudible; for, though the lips distinctly moved, no sound, apparently, came from them.

And Tim sprang out of bed. The room was full of darkness. He turned the light on. The door, he saw, was shut as usual. He had, of course, been dreaming. But he noticed a curious odour in the air. He sniffed it once or twice – then grasped the truth. It was a smell of burning!

Fortunately, he awoke just in time...

He was acclaimed a hero for his promptitude. After many days, when the damage was repaired, and nerves had settled down once more into the calm routine of country life, he told the story to his wife – the entire story. He told the adventure of his imaginative boyhood with it. She asked to see the old family cane. And it was this request of hers that brought back to memory a detail Tim had entirely forgotten all these years. He remembered it suddenly again – the loss of the cane, the hubbub his father kicked up about it, the endless, futile search. For the stick had never been found, and Tim, who was questioned very closely concerning it, swore with all his might that he had not the smallest notion where it was. Which was, of course, the truth.

**If you enjoyed this, you might also like...**
The Wings of Horus, see page 192
Keeping His Promise, see page 361

# The Pikestaffe Case

## Chapter I

**THE VITALITY** of old governesses deserves an explanatory memorandum by a good physiologist. It is remarkable. They tend to survive the grown-up married men and women they once taught as children. They hang on forever, as a man might put it crudely, a man, that is, who, taught by one of them in his earliest schoolroom days, would answer enquiries fifty years later without enthusiasm: "Oh, we keep her going, yes. She doesn't want for anything!"

Miss Helena Speke had taught the children of a distinguished family, and these distinguished children, with expensive progeny of their own now, still kept her going. They had clubbed together, seeing that Miss Speke retained her wonderful health, and had established her in a nice little house where she could take respectable lodgers – men for preference – giving them the three B's – bed, bath, and breakfast. Being a capable woman, Miss Speke more than made both ends meet. She wanted for nothing. She kept going.

Applicants for her rooms, especially for the first-floor suite, had to be recommended. She had a stern face for those who rang the bell without a letter in their pockets. She never advertised. Indeed, there was no need to do so. The two upper floors had been occupied by the same tenants for many years – a chief clerk in a branch bank and a retired clergyman respectively. It was only the best suite that sometimes "happened to be vacant at the moment." From two guineas inclusive before the war, her price for this had been raised, naturally, to four, the tenant paying his gas-stove, light, and bath extra. Breakfast – she prided herself legitimately on her good breakfasts – was included.

For a long time now this first-floor suite had been unoccupied. The cost of living worried Miss Speke, as it worried most other people. Her servant was cheap but incompetent, and once she could let the suite she meant to engage a better one. The distinguished children were scattered out of reach about the world; the eldest had been killed in the war; a married one, a woman, lived in India; another married one was in the throes of divorce – an expensive business; and the fourth, the most generous and last, found himself in the Bankruptcy Court, and so was unable to help.

It was in these conditions that Miss Speke, her vitality impaired, decided to advertise. Although she inserted the words 'references essential', she meant in her heart to use her own judgment, and if a likely gentleman presented himself and agreed to pay her price, she might accept him. The clergyman and the bank official upstairs were a protection, she felt. She invariably mentioned them to applicants: "I have a clergyman of the Church of England on the top floor. He's been with me for eleven years. And a banker has the floor below. Mine is a very quiet house, you see." These words formed part of the ritual she recited in the hall, facing her proposed tenants on the linoleum by the hat-rack; and it was these words she addressed to the tall, thin, pale-faced man with scanty hair and spotless linen, who informed her that he was a tutor, a teacher of higher mathematics to the sons of various families – he mentioned some first-class names where references could be obtained – a student besides and something of an author in his leisure hours. His pupils he taught, of course, in their respective houses, one being in Belgrave Square, another in The Albany; it was only after tea, or in the evenings, that he did his own work. All this he explained briefly, but with great courtesy of manner.

Mr. Thorley was well spoken, with a gentle voice, kind, farseeing eyes, and an air of being lonely and uncared for that touched some forgotten, dried-up spring in Miss Speke's otherwise rather cautious heart. He looked every inch a scholar – "and a gentleman," as she explained afterwards to everybody who was interested in him, these being numerous, of unexpected kinds, and all very close, not to say unpleasantly close, questioners indeed. But what chiefly influenced her in his favour was the fact, elicited in conversation, that years ago he had been a caller at the house in Portman Square where she was governess to the distinguished family. She did not exactly remember him, but he had certainly known Lady Araminta, the mother of her charges.

Thus it was that Mr. Thorley – John Laking Thorley, M.A., of Jesus College, Cambridge – was accepted by Miss Speke as tenant of her best suite on the first floor at the price mentioned, breakfast included, winning her confidence so fully that she never went to the trouble even of taking up the references he gave her. She liked him, she felt safe with him, she pitied him. He had not bargained, nor tried to beat her down. He just reflected a moment, then agreed. He proved, indeed, an exemplary lodger, early to bed and not too early to rise, of regular habits, thoughtful of the expensive new servant, careful with towels, electric light, and ink-stains, prompt in his payments, and never once troubling her with complaints or requests, as other lodgers did, not excepting the banker and the clergyman. Moreover, he was a tidy man, who never lost anything, because he invariably put everything in its proper place and thus knew exactly where to look for it. She noticed this tidiness at once.

Miss Speke, especially in the first days of his tenancy, studied him, as she studied all her lodgers. She studied his room when he was out 'of a morning'. At her leisure she did this, knowing he would never break in and disturb her unexpectedly. She was neither prying nor inquisitive, she assured herself, but she was curious. "I have a right to know something about the gentlemen who sleep under my roof with me," was the way she put it in her own mind. His clothes, she found, were ample, including evening dress, white gloves, and an opera hat. He had plenty of boots and shoes. His linen was good. His wardrobe, indeed, though a trifle uncared for, especially his socks, was a gentleman's wardrobe. Only one thing puzzled her. The full-length mirror, standing on mahogany legs – a present from the generous 'child', now in the Bankruptcy Court, and, a handsome thing, a special attraction in the best suite – this fine mirror Mr. Thorley evidently did not like. The second or third morning he was with her she went to his bedroom before the servant had done it up, and saw, to her surprise, that this full-length glass stood with its back to the room. It had been placed close against the wall in a corner, its unattractive back turned outward.

"It gave me quite a shock to see it," as she said afterwards. "And such a handsome piece, too!"

Her first thought, indeed, sent a cold chill down her energetic spine. "He's cracked it!" But it was not cracked. She paused in some amazement, wondering why her new lodger had done this thing; then she turned the mirror again into its proper position, and left the room. Next morning she found it again with its face close against the wall.

The following day it was the same – she turned it round, only to find it the next morning again with its back to the room.

She asked the servant, but the servant knew nothing about it.

"He likes it that way, I suppose, mum," was all Sarah said. "I never laid a 'and on it once."

Miss Speke, after much puzzled consideration, decided it must be something to do with the light. Mr. Thorley, she remembered, wore horn-rimmed spectacles for reading. She scented a mystery. It caused her a slight – oh, a very slight – feeling of discomfort. Well, if he did not like the handsome mirror, she could perhaps use it in her own room. To see it neglected hurt her a little. Not many furnished rooms could boast a full-length glass, she reflected. A few days later, meeting Mr. Thorley on the linoleum before the hat-rack, she enquired if he was quite comfortable, and if the breakfast was to his liking. He was polite and even cordial. Everything was perfect, he assured her. He had never been so well looked after. And the house was so quiet.

"And the bed, Mr. Thorley? You sleep well, I hope." She drew nearer to the subject of the mirror, but with caution. For some reason she found a difficulty in actually broaching it. It suddenly dawned upon her that there was something queer about his treatment of that full-length glass. She was by no means fanciful, Miss Speke, retired governess; only the faintest suspicion of something odd brushed her mind and vanished. But she did feel something. She found it impossible to mention the handsome thing outright.

"There's nothing you would like changed in the room, or altered?" she enquired with a smile, "or – in any way put different – perhaps?"

Mr. Thorley hesitated for a moment. A curious expression, half sad, half yearning, she thought, lit on his thoughtful face for one second and was gone. The idea of moving anything seemed distasteful to him.

"Nothing, Miss Speke, I thank you," he replied courteously, but without delay. "Everything is really as I like it." Then, with a little bow, he asked: "I trust my typewriter disturbs nobody. Please let me know if it does."

Miss Speke assured him that nobody minded the typewriter in the least, nor even heard it, and, with another charming little bow and a smile, Mr. Thorley went out to give his lessons in the higher mathematics.

"There!" she reflected, "and I never even asked him!" It had been impossible.

From the window she watched him going down the street, his head bent, evidently in deep thought, his books beneath his arm, looking, she thought, every inch the gentleman and the scholar that he undoubtedly was. His personality left a very strong impression on her mind. She found herself rather wondering about him. As he turned the corner Miss Speke owned to two things that rose simultaneously in her mind: first, the relief that the lodger was out for the day and could be counted upon not to return unexpectedly; secondly, that it would interest her to slip up and see what kind of books he read. A minute later she was in his sitting-room. It was already swept and dusted, the breakfast cleared away, and the books, she saw, lay partly on the table where he had just left them and partly on the broad mantelpiece he used as a shelf. She was alone, the servant was downstairs in the kitchen. She examined Mr. Thorley's books.

The examination left her bewildered and uninspired. "I couldn't make them out at all," she put it. But they were evidently what she called costly volumes, and that she liked. "Something to do with his work, I suppose – mathematics, and all that," she decided, after turning over pages covered with some kind of hieroglyphics, symbols being a word she did not know in that connection. There was no printing, there were no sentences, there was nothing she could lay hold of, and the diagrams she thought perhaps were Euclid, or possibly astronomical. Most of the names were odd and quite unknown to her. Gauss! Minowski! Lobatchewski! And it affronted her that some of these were German. A writer named Einstein was popular with her lodger and that, she felt, was a pity, as well as a mistake in taste. It all alarmed her a little; or, rather she felt that touch of respect, almost of awe, pertaining to some world entirely beyond her ken. She was rather glad when the search – it was a duty – ended.

"There's nothing there," she reflected, meaning there was nothing that explained his dislike of the full-length mirror. And, disappointed, yet with a faint relief, she turned to his private papers. These, since he was a tidy man, were in a drawer. Mr. Thorley never left anything lying about. Now, a letter Miss Speke would not have thought of reading, but papers, especially learned papers, were another matter. Conscience, nevertheless, did prick her faintly as she cautiously turned over sheaf after sheaf of large white foolscap, covered with designs, and curves, and diagrams in ink, the ink he never spilt, and assuredly in his recent handwriting. And it was among these foolscap sheets that she suddenly came upon one sheet in particular that caught her attention and even startled her. In the centre, surrounded by scriggly hierglyphics, numbers, curves and lines meaningless to her, she saw a drawing of the full-length mirror. Some of the curves ran into it and through it, emerging on the other side. She knew it was *the* mirror because its exact measurements were indicated in red ink.

This, as mentioned, startled her. What could it mean? she asked herself, staring intently at the curious sheet, as though it must somehow yield its secret to prolonged even if unintelligent enquiry. "It looks like an experiment or something," was the furthest her mind could probe into the mystery, though this, she admitted, was not very far. Holding the paper at various angles, even upside down, she examined it with puzzled curiosity, then slowly laid it down again in the exact place whence she had taken it. That faint breath of alarm had again suddenly brushed her soul, as though she approached a mystery she had better leave unsolved.

"It's very strange" she began, carefully closing the drawer, but unable to complete the sentence even in her mind. "I don't think I like it – quite," and she turned to go out. It was just then that something touched her face tickling one cheek, something fine as a cobweb, something in the air. She picked it away. It was a thread of silk, extremely fine, so fine, indeed, that it might almost have been a spider's web of gossamer such as one sees floating over the garden lawn on a sunny morning. Miss Speke brushed it away, giving it no further thought, and went about her usual daily duties.

## Chapter II

**BUT** in her mind was established now a vague uneasiness, though so vague that at first she did not recognise it. Her thought would suddenly pause. "Now, what is it?" she would ask herself. "Something's on my mind. What is it I've forgotten?" The picture of her first-floor lodger appeared, and she knew at once. "Oh, yes, it's that mirror and the diagrams, of course." Some taut wire of alarm was quivering at the back of her mind. It was akin to those childhood alarms that pertain to the big unexplained mysteries no parent can elucidate because no parent knows. "Only God can tell that," says the parent, evading the insoluble problem. "I'd better not think about it," was the analogous conclusion reached by Miss Speke. Meanwhile the impression the new lodger's personality made upon her mind perceptibly deepened. He seemed to her full of power, above little things, a man of intense and mysterious mental life. He was constantly and somewhat possessingly in her thoughts. The mere thought of him, she found, stimulated her.

It was just before luncheon, as she returned from her morning marketing, that the servant drew her attention to certain marks upon the carpet of Mr. Thorley's sitting-room. She had discovered them as she handled the vacuum cleaner – faint, short lines drawn by dark chalk or crayons, in shape like the top or bottom right-angle of a square bracket, and sometimes with a tiny arrow shown as well. There were occasional other marks, too, that Miss Speke recognised as the hieroglyphics she called squiggles. Mistress and servant examined them together in a stooping position. They found others on the bedroom carpet, too, only these were not straight; they were small curved lines; and about the feet of the full-length mirror they clustered in a quantity, segments of circles, some large, some small. They looked as if someone had snipped off curly hair, or pared his fingernails with sharp scissors, only considerably larger, and they were so faint that they were only visible when the sunlight fell upon them.

"I knew they was drawn on," said Sarah, puzzled, yet proud that she had found them, "because they didn't come up with the dust and fluff."

"I'll – speak to Mr. Thorley," was the only comment Miss Speke made. "I'll tell him." Her voice was not quite steady, but the girl apparently noticed nothing.

"There's all this too, please, mum." She pointed to a number of fine silk threads she had collected upon a bit of newspaper, preparatory to the dustbin. "They was stuck on the cupboard door and the walls, stretched all across the room, but rather 'igh up. I only saw them by chance. One caught on my face."

Miss Speke stared, touched, examined for some seconds without speaking. She remembered the thread that had tickled her own cheek. She looked enquiringly round the room, and the servant, following her suggestion, indicated where the threads had been attached to walls and furniture. No marks, however, were left; there was no damage done.

"I'll mention it to Mr. Thorley," said her mistress briefly, unwilling to discuss the matter with the new servant, much less to admit that she was uncomfortably at sea. "Mr. Thorley," she added, as though there was nothing unusual, "is a high mathematician. He makes – measurements and – calculations of that sort." She had not sufficient control of her voice to be more explicit, and she went from the room aware that, unaccountably, she was trembling. She had first gathered up the threads, meaning to show them to her lodger when she demanded an explanation. But the explanation was delayed, for – to state it bluntly – she was afraid to ask him for it. She put it off till the following morning, then till the day after, and, finally, she decided to say nothing about the matter at all. "I'd better leave it, perhaps, after all," she persuaded herself. "There's no damage done, anyhow. I'd better not enquire." All the same she did not like it. By the end of the week, however, she was able to pride herself upon her restraint and tact; the marks on the carpet, rubbed out by the girl, were not renewed, and the fine threads of silk were never again found stretching through the air from wall to furniture. Mr. Thorley had evidently noticed their removal and had discontinued what he had observed was an undesirable performance. He was a scholar and a gentleman. But he was more. He was frank and straight-dealing. One morning he asked to see his landlady and told her all about it himself.

"Oh," he said in his pleasantest, easiest manner when she came into the room, "I wanted to tell you, Miss Speke – indeed, I meant to do so long before this – about the marks I made on your carpets" – he smiled apologetically – "and the silk threads I stretched. I use them for measurements – for problems I set my pupils, and one morning I left them there by mistake. The marks easily rub out. But I will use scraps of paper instead another time. I can pin these on – if you will kindly tell your excellent servant not to touch them – er – they're rather important to me." He smiled again charmingly, and his face wore the wistful, rather yearning expression that had already appealed to her. The eyes, it struck her, were very brilliant. "Any damage," he added – "though, I assure you, none is possible really – I would, of course, make good to you, Miss Speke."

"Thank you, Mr. Thorley," was all Miss Speke could find to say, so confused was her mind by troubling thoughts and questions she dared not express. "Of course – this is my best suite, you see."

It was all most amicable and pleasant between them.

"I wonder – have my books come?" he asked, as he went out. "Ah, there they are, I do believe!" he exclaimed, for through the open front door a van was seen discharging a very large packing-case.

"Your books, Mr. Thorley—?" Miss Speke murmured, noting the size of the package with dismay. "But I'm afraid – you'll hardly find space to put them in," she stammered. "The rooms – er" – she did not wish to disparage them – "are so small, aren't they?"

Mr. Thorley smiled delightfully. "Oh, please do not trouble on that account," he said. "I shall find space all right, I assure you. It's merely a question of knowing where and how to put them," and he proceeded to give the men instructions.

A few days later a second case arrived.

"I'm expecting some instruments, too," he mentioned casually, "mathematical instruments," and he again assured her with his confident smile that she need have no anxiety on the score of space. Nor would he dent the walls or scrape the furniture the least little bit. There was always room, he reminded her gently again, provided one knew how to stow things away. Both books and instruments were necessary to his work. Miss Speke need feel no anxiety at all.

But Miss Speke felt more than anxiety, she felt uneasiness, she felt a singular growing dread. There lay in her a seed of distress that began to sprout rapidly. Everything arrived as Mr. Thorley has announced, case upon case was unpacked in his room by his own hands. The straw and wood she used for firing purposes, there was no mess, no litter, no untidiness, nor were walls and furniture injured in any way. What caused her dread to deepen into something bordering upon actual alarm was the fact that, on searching Mr. Thorley's rooms when he was out, she could discover no trace of any of the things that had arrived. There was no sign of either books or instruments. Where had he stored them? Where could they lie concealed? She asked herself innumerable questions, but found no answer to them. These stores, enough to choke and block the room, had been brought in through the sitting-room door. They could not possibly have been taken out again. They had not been taken out. Yet no trace of them was anywhere to be seen. It was very strange, she thought; indeed, it was more than strange. She felt excited. She felt a touch of hysterical alarm.

Meanwhile, thin strips of white paper, straight, angled, curved, were pinned upon the carpet; threads of finest silk again stretched overhead connecting the top of the door lintel with the window, the high cupboard with the curtain rods – yet too high to be brushed away merely by the head of anyone moving in the room. And the full-length mirror still stood with its face close against the wall.

The mystery of these aerial entanglements increased Miss Speke's alarm considerably. What could their purpose be? "Thank God," she thought, "this isn't war time!" She knew enough to realise their meaning was not 'wireless'. That they bore some relation to the lines on the carpet and to the diagrams and curves upon the paper, she grasped vaguely. But what it all meant baffled her and made her feel quite stupid. Where all the books and instruments had disappeared added to her bewilderment. She felt more and more perturbed. A vague, uncertain fear was worse than something definite she could face and deal with. Her fear increased. Then, suddenly, yet with a reasonable enough excuse, Sarah gave notice.

For some reason Miss Speke did not argue with the girl. She preferred to let the real meaning of her leaving remain unexpressed. She just let her go. But the fact disturbed her extraordinarily. Sarah had given every satisfaction, there had been no sign of a grievance, no complaint, the work was not hard, the pay was good. It was simply that the girl preferred to leave. Miss Speke attributed it to Mr. Thorley. She became more and more disturbed in mind. Also she found herself, more and more, avoiding her lodger, whose regular habits made such avoidance an easy matter. Knowing his hours of exit and entrance, she took care to be out of the way. At the mere sound of his step she flew to cover. The new servant, a stupid, yet not inefficient country girl, betrayed no reaction of any sort, no unfavourable reaction at at any rate. Having received her instructions, Lizzie did her work without complaint from either side. She did not remove the paper and the thread, nor did she mention them. She seemed just the country clod she was. Miss Speke, however, began to have restless nights. She contracted an unpleasant habit: she lay awake – listening.

## Chapter III

**AS THE RESULT** of one of these sleepless nights she came to the abrupt conclusion that she would be happier without Mr. Thorley in the house – only she had not the courage to ask him to leave. The truth was she had not the courage to speak to him at all, much less to give him notice, however nicely.

After much cogitation she hit upon a plan that promised well: she sent him a carefully worded letter explaining that, owing to increased cost of living, she found herself compelled to raise his terms. The 'raise' was more than considerable, it was unreasonable, but he paid what she demanded, sending down a cheque for three months in advance with his best compliments. The letter somehow made her tremble. It was at this stage she first became aware of the existence in her of other feelings than discomfort, uneasiness, and alarm. These other feelings, being in contradiction of her dread, were difficult to describe, but their result was plain – she did not really wish Mr. Thorley to go after all. His friendly 'compliments', his refusal of her hint, caused her a secret pleasure. It was not the cheque at the increased rate that pleased her – it was simply the fact that her lodger meant to stay.

It might be supposed that some delayed sense of romance had been stirred in her, but this really was not the case at all. Her pleasure was due to another source, but to a source uncommonly obscure and very strange. She feared him, feared his presence, above all, feared going into his room, while yet there was something about the mere idea of

Mr. Thorley that entranced her. Another thing may as well be told at once – she herself faced it boldly – she would enter his dreaded room, when he was out, and would deliberately linger there. There was an odd feeling in the room that gave her pleasure, and more than pleasure – happiness. Surrounded by the enigmas of his personality, by the lines and curves of white paper pinned upon her carpet, by the tangle of silken threads above her head, by the mysterious books, the more than mysterious diagrams in his drawer – yet all these, even the dark perplexity of the rejected mirror and the vanished objects, were forgotten in the curious sense of happiness she derived from merely sitting in his room. Her fear contained this other remarkable ingredient – an uncommon sense of joy, of liberty, of freedom. She felt *exaltée*.

She could not explain it, she did not attempt to do so. She would go shaking and trembling into his room, and a few minutes later this sense of uncommon happiness – of release, almost of escape, she felt it – would steal over her as though in her dried-up frozen soul spring had burst upon midwinter, as though something that crawled had suddenly most gloriously found wings. An indescribable exhilaration caught her.

Under this influence the dingy street turned somehow radiant, and the front door of her poor lodging-house opened upon blue seas, yellow sands, and mountains carpeted with flowers. Her whole life, painfully repressed and crushed down in the dull service of convential nonentities, flashed into colour, movement, and adventure. Nothing confined her. She was no longer limited. She knew advance in all possible directions. She knew the stars. She knew escape!

An attempt has been made to describe for her what she never could have described herself.

The reaction, upon coming out again, was painful. Her life in the past as a governess, little better than a servant; her life in the present as lodging-house keeper; her struggle with servants, with taxes, with daily expenses; her knowledge that no future but a mere 'living' lay in front of her until the grave was reached – these overwhelmed her with an intense depression that the contrast rendered almost insupportable. Whereas in his room she had perfume, freedom, liberty, and wonder – the wonder of some entirely new existence.

Thus, briefly, while Miss Speke longed for Mr. Thorley to leave her house, she became obsessed with the fear that one day he really would go. Her mind, it is seen, became uncommonly disturbed; her lodger's presence being undoubtedly the cause. Her nights were now more than restless, they were sleepless. Whence came, she asked herself repeatedly in the dark watches, her fear? Whence came, too, her strange enchantment?

It was at this juncture, then, that a further item of perplexity was added to her mind. Miss Speke, as has been seen, was honourably disposed; she respected the rights of others, their property as well. Yet, included in the odd mood of elation the room and its atmosphere caused her, was also a vagrant, elusive feeling that the intimate, the personal – above all, the personal – had lost their original rigidity. Small individual privacies, secrecy, no longer held their familiar meaning quite. The idea that most things in life were to be shared slipped into her. A 'secret', to this expansive mood, was a childish attitude.

At any rate, it was while lingering in her lodger's attractive room one day – a habit now – that she did something that caused her surprise, yet did not shock her. She saw an open letter lying on his table – and she read it.

Rather than an actual letter, however, it seemed a note, a memorandum. It began: *To J.L.T.*

In a boyish writing, the meaning of the language escaped her entirely. She understood the strange words as little as she understood the phases of the moon, while yet she derived from their perusal a feeling of mysterious beauty, similar to the emotions the changes of that lovely satellite stirred in her:

> To J.L.T.
> I followed your instructions, though with intense effort and difficulty. I woke at 4 o'clock. About ten minutes later, as you said might happen, I woke a second time. The change into the second state was as great as the change from sleeping to waking, in the ordinary meaning of these words. But I could not remain 'awake'. I fell asleep again in about a minute – back into the usual waking state, I mean. Description in words is impossible, as you know. What I felt was too terrific to feel for long. The new energy must presently have burned me up. It frightened me – as you warned me it would. And this fear, no doubt, was the cause of my 'falling asleep' again so quickly.
> Cannot we arrange a Call for Help for similar occasions in future?
> G.P.

Against this note Mr. Thorley had written various strangest 'squiggles'; higher mathematics, Miss Speke supposed. In the opposite margin, also in her lodger's writing, were these words:

> *We must agree on a word to use when frightened.* Help, *or* Help me, *seems the best. To be uttered with the whole being.*

Mr. Thorley had added a few other notes. She read them without the faintest prick of conscience. Though she understood no single sentence, a thrill of deep delight ran through her:

> *It amounts, of course, to a new direction; a direction at right angles to all we know, a new direction in oneself, a new direction – in living. But it can, perhaps, be translated into mathematical terms by the intellect. This, however, only a simile at best. Cannot be experienced that way. Actual experience possible only to changed consciousness. But good to become mathematically accustomed to it. The mathematical experiments are worth it. They induce the mind, at any rate, to dwell upon the new direction. This helps...*

Miss Speke laid down the letter exactly where she had found it. No shame was in her. 'G.P.' she knew, meant Gerald Pikestaffe; he was one of her lodger's best pupils, the one in Belgrave Square. Her feeling of mysterious elation, as already mentioned, seemed above all such matters as small secrecies or petty personal privacies. She had read a 'private' letter without remorse. One feeling only caused in her a certain commonplace emotion: the feeling that, while she read the letter, her lodger was present, watching her. He seemed close behind her, looking over her shoulder almost, observing her acts, her mood, her very thoughts – yet not objecting. He was aware, at any rate, of what she did...

It was under these circumstances that she bethought herself of her old tenant, the retired clergyman on the top floor, and sought his aid. The consolation of talking to another would be something, yet when the interview began all she could manage to say was that her mind was troubled and her heart not quite as it should be, and that she "didn't know what to do about it all." For the life of her she could not find more definite words. To mention Mr. Thorley she found suddenly utterly impossible.

"Prayer," the old man interrupted her halfway, "prayer, my dear lady. Prayer, I find," he repeated smoothly, "is always the best course in all one's troubles and perplexities. Leave it to God. He knows. And in His good time He will answer." He advised her to read the Bible and Longfellow. She added Florence Barclay to the list and followed his advice. The books, however, comforted her very little.

After some hesitation she then tried her other tenant. But the 'banker' stopped her even sooner than the clergyman had done. MacPherson was very prompt:

"I can give you another ten shillings or maybe half a guinea," he said briskly. "Times are deeficult, I know. But I can't do more. If that's suffeecient I shall be delighted to stay on" and, with a nod and a quick smile that settled the matter then and there, he was through the door and down the steps on the way to his office.

It was evident that Miss Speke must face her troubles alone, a fact, for the rest, life had already taught her. The loyal, courageous spirit in her accepted the situation. The alternate moods of happiness and depression, meanwhile, began to wear her out. "If only Mr. Thorley would go! If only Mr. Thorley will not go!" For some weeks now she had successfully avoided him. He made no requests nor complaints. His habits were as regular as sunrise, his payments likewise. Not even the servant mentioned him. He became a shadow in the house.

Then, with the advent of summertime, he came home, as it were, an hour earlier than usual. He invariably worked from 5:30 to 7:30, when he went out for his dinner. Tea he always had at a pupil's house. It was a light evening, caused by the advance of the clock, and Miss Speke, mending her underwear at the window, suddenly perceived his figure coming down the street.

She watched, fascinated. Of two instincts – to hide herself, or to wait there and catch his eye – she obeyed the latter. She had not seen him for several weeks, and a deep thrill of happiness ran through her. His walk was peculiar, she noticed at once; he did not walk in a straight line. His tall, thin outline flowed down the pavement in long, sweeping curves, yet quite steadily. He was not drunk. He came nearer; he was not twenty feet away; at ten feet she saw his face clearly, and received a shock. It was worn, and thin, and wasted, but a light of happiness, of something more than happiness indeed, shone in it. He reached the area railings. He looked up. His face seemed ablaze. Their eyes met, his with no start of recognition, hers with a steady stare of wonder. She ran into the passage, and before Mr. Thorley had time to use his latchkey she had opened the door for him herself. Little she knew, as she stood there trembling, that she stood also upon the threshold of an amazing adventure.

Face to face with him her presence of mind deserted her. She could only look up into that worn and wasted face, into those happy, severe, and brilliant eyes, where yet burned a strange expression of wistful yearning, of uncommon wonder, of something that seemed not of this world quite. Such an expression she had never seen before upon any human countenance. Its light dazzled her. There was uncommon fire in the eyes. It enthralled her. The same instant, as she stood there gazing at him without a single word, either of welcome or enquiry, it flashed across her that he needed something from her. He needed help, her help. It was a farfetched notion, she was well aware, but it came to her irresistibly. The conviction was close to her, closer than her skin.

It was this knowledge, doubtless, that enabled her to hear without resentment the strange words he at once made use of:

"Ah, I thank you. Miss Speke, I thank you," the thin lips parting in a smile, the shining eyes lit with an emotion of more than ordinary welcome. "You cannot know what a relief it is to me to see you. You are so sound, so wholesome, so ordinary, so – forgive me, I beg – so commonplace."

He was gone past her and upstairs into his sitting-room. She heard the key turn softly. She was aware that she had not shut the front door. She did so, then went back, trembling, happy, frightened, into her own room. She had a curious, rushing feeling, both frightful and bewildering, that the room did not contain her... She was still sitting there two hours later, when she heard Mr. Thorley's step come down the stairs and leave the house. She was still sitting there when she heard him return, open the door with his key, and go up to his sitting-room. The interval might have been two minutes or two weeks, instead of two hours merely. And all this time she had the wondrous sensation that the room did not contain her. The walls and ceilings did not shut her in. She was out of the room. Escape had come very close to her. She was out of the house... out of herself as well...

## Chapter IV

**SHE WENT** early to bed, taking this time the Bible with her. Her strange sensations had passed, they had left her gradually. She had made herself a cup of tea and had eaten a soft-boiled egg and some bread-and-butter. She felt more normal again, but her nerves were unusually sensitive. It was a comfort to know there were two men in the house with her, two worthy men, a clergyman and a banker. The Bible, the banker, the clergyman, with Mrs. Barclay and Longfellow not far from her bed, were certainly a source of comfort to her.

The traffic died away, the rumbling of the distant motorbuses ceased, and, with the passing of the hours, the night became intensely still.

It was April. Her window was opened at the top and she could smell the cool, damp air of coming spring. Soothed by the books she began to feel drowsy. She glanced at the clock – it was just on two – then blew out the candle and prepared to sleep. Her thoughts turned automatically to Mr. Thorley, lying asleep on the floor above, his threads and paper strips and mysterious diagrams all about him – when, suddenly, a voice broke through the silence with a cry for help. It was a man's voice, and it sounded a long way off. But she recognised it instantly, and she sprang out of bed without a trace of fear. It was Mr. Thorley calling, and in the voice was anguish.

"He's in trouble? In danger! He needs help? I knew it!" ran rapidly through her mind, as she lit the candle with fingers that did not tremble. The clock showed three. She had slept a full hour. She opened the door and peered into the passage, but saw no one there; the stairs, too, were empty. The call was not repeated.

"Mr. Thorley!" she cried aloud. "Mr. Thorley! Do you want anything?" And by the sound of her voice she realised how distant and muffled his own had been. "I'm coming!"

She stood there waiting, but no answer came. There was no sound. She realised the uncommon stillness of the night.

"Did you call me?" she tried again, but with less confidence. "Can I do anything for you?"

Again there was no answer; nothing stirred; the house was silent as the grave. The linoleum felt cold against her bare feet, and she stole back to get her slippers and a dressing-gown, while a hundred possibilities flashed through her mind at once. Oddly enough, she never once thought of burglars, nor of fire, nor, indeed, of any ordinary situation that required ordinary help. Why this was so she could not say. No ordinary fear, at any rate, assailed her in that moment, nor did she feel the smallest touch of nervousness about her own safety.

"Was it – I wonder – a dream?" she asked herself as she pulled the dressing-gown about her. "Did I dream that voice?" when the thrilling cry broke forth again, startling her so that she nearly dropped the candle:

"Help! Help! Help me!"

Very distinct, yet muffled as by distance, it was beyond all question the voice of Mr. Thorley. What she had taken for anguish in it she now recognised was terror. It sounded on the floor above, it was the closed door doubtless that caused the muffled effect of distance.

Miss Speke ran along the passage instantly, and with extraordinary speed for an elderly woman; she was halfway up the stairs in a moment, when, just as she reached the first little landing by the bathroom and turned to begin the second flight, the voice came again: "Help! Help!" but this time with a difference that, truth to tell, did set her nerves unpleasantly aquiver. For there were two voices instead of one, and they were not upstairs at all. Both were below her in the passage she had just that moment left. Close they were behind her. One, moreover, was not the voice of Mr. Thorley. It was a boy's clear soprano. Both called for help together, and both held a note of terror that made her heart shake.

Under these conditions it may be forgiven to Miss Speke that she lost her balance and reeled against the wall, clutching the banisters for a moment's support. Yet her courage did not fail her. She turned instantly and quickly went downstairs again – to find the passage empty of any living figure. There was no one visible. There was only silence, a motionless hat-rack, the door of her own room slightly ajar, and shadows.

"Mr. Thorley!" she called. "Mr. Thorley!" her voice not quite so loud and confident as before. It had a whisper in it. No answer came. She repeated the words, her tone with still less volume. Only faint echoes that seemed to linger unduly came in response. Peering into her own room she found it exactly as she had left it. The dining-room, facing it, was likewise empty. Yet a moment before she had plainly heard two voices calling for help within a few yards of where she stood. Two voices! What could it mean? She noticed now for the first time a peculiar freshness in the air a sharpness, almost a perfume, as though all the windows were wide open, and the air of coming spring was in the house.

Terror, though close, had not yet actually gripped her. That she had gone crazy occurred to her, but only to be dismissed. She was quite sane and self-possessed. The changing direction of the sounds lay beyond all explanation, but an explanation, she was positive, there must be. The odd freshness in the air was heartening, and seemed to brace her. No, terror had not yet really gripped her. Ideas of summoning the servant, the clergyman, the banker, these she equally dismissed. It was no ordinary help that was needed, not theirs at any rate. She went boldly upstairs again and knocked at

Mr. Thorley's bedroom door. She knocked again and again, loud enough to waken him, if he had perchance called out in sleep, but not loud enough to disturb her other tenants. No answer came. There was no sound within. No light shone through the cracks. With his sitting-room the same conditions held.

It was the strangeness of the second voice that now stole over her with a deadly fear. She found herself cold and shivering. As she, at length, went slowly downstairs again the cries were suddenly audible once more. She heard both voices; "Help! Help! Help me!" Then silence. They were fainter this time. Far away, they sounded, withdrawn curiously into some remote distance, yet ever with the same anguish, the same terror in them as before. The direction, however, this time she could not tell at all. In a sense they seemed both close and far, both above her and below; they seemed – it was the only way she could describe the astounding thing – in any direction, or in all directions.

Miss Speke was really terrified at last. The strange, full horror of it gripped her, turning her heart suddenly to ice. The two voices, the terror in them, the extraordinary impression that they had withdrawn further into some astounding distance – this overcame her. She became appalled. Staggering into her room, she reached the bed and fell upon it in a senseless heap. She had fainted.

## Chapter V

**SHE SLEPT LATE**, owing probably to exhausted nerves. Though usually up and about by 7:30, it was after nine when the servant woke her. She sprawled half in the bed, half out; the candle, which luckily had extinguished itself in falling, lay upon the carpet. The events of the night came slowly back to her as she watched the servant's face. The girl was white and shaking.

"Are you ill, mum?" Lizzie asked anxiously in a whisper; then, without waiting for an answer, blurted out what she had really come in to say: "Mr. Thorley, mum! I can't get into his room. There's no answer." The girl was very frightened.

Mr. Thorley invariably had breakfast at 8 o'clock, and was out of the house punctually at 8:45.

"Was he ill in the night – perhaps – do you think?" Miss Speke said. It was the nearest she could get to asking if the girl had heard the voices. She had admirable control of herself by this time. She got up, still in her dressing-gown and slippers.

"Not that I know of, mum," was the reply.

"Come" said her mistress firmly. "We'll go in." And they went upstairs together.

The bedroom door, as the girl had said, was closed, but the sitting-room was open. Miss Speke led the way. The freshness of the night before lay still in the air, she noticed, though the windows were all closed tightly. There was an exhilarating sharpness, a delightful tang as of open space. She particularly mentions this. On the carpet, as usual, lay the strips of white paper, fastened with small pins, and the silk threads, also as usual, stretched across from lintel to cupboard, from window to bracket. Miss Speke brushed several of them from her face.

The door into the bedroom she opened, and went boldly in, followed more cautiously by the girl. "There's nothing to be afraid of," said her mistress firmly. The bed, she saw, had not been slept in. Everything was neat and tidy. The long mirror stood close against the wall, showing its ugly back as usual, while about its four feet clustered the curved strips of paper Miss Speke had grown accustomed to.

"Pull the blinds up, Lizzie," she said in a quiet voice.

The light now enabled her to see everything quite clearly. There were silken threads, she noticed distinctly, stretching from bed to window, and though both windows were closed there was this strange sweetness in the air as of a flowering spring garden. She sniffed it with a curious feeling of pleasure, of freedom, of, release, though Lizzie, apparently, noticed nothing of all this.

"There's his 'at and mackintosh," the girl whispered in a frightened voice, pointing to the hooks on the door. "And the umbrella in the corner. But I don't see 'is boots, mum. They weren't put out to be cleaned."

Miss Speke turned and looked at her, voice and manner under full command. "What do you mean?" she asked.

"Mr. Thorley ain't gone out, mum," was the reply in a tremulous tone.

At that very moment a faint, distant cry was audible in a man's voice: "Help! Help!" Immediately after it a soprano, fainter still, called from what seemed even greater distance: "Help me!" The direction was not ascertainable. It seemed both in the room, yet far away outside in space above the roofs. A glance at the girl convinced Miss Speke that she had heard nothing.

"Mr. Thorley is not *here*," whispered Miss Speke, one hand upon the brass bed-rail for support.

The room was undeniably empty.

"Leave everything exactly as it is," ordered her mistress as they went out. Tears stood in her eyes, she lingered a moment on the threshold, but the sounds were not repeated. "Exactly as it is," she repeated, closing the bedroom and then the sitting-room door behind her. She locked the latter, putting the key in her pocket. Two days later, as Mr. Thorley had not returned, she informed the police. But Mr. Thorley never returned. He had disappeared completely. He left no trace. He was never heard of again, though – once – he was seen.

Yet, this is not entirely accurate perhaps, for he was seen twice, in the sense that he was seen by two persons, and though he was not 'heard of', he was certainly heard. Miss Speke heard his voice from time to time. She heard it in the daytime and at night; calling for help and always with the same words she had first heard: "Help! Help! Help me!" It sounded very far away, withdrawn into immense distance, the distance ever increasing. Occasionally she heard the boy's voice with it; they called together sometimes; she never heard the soprano voice alone. But the anguish and terror she had first noticed were no longer present. Alarm had gone out of them. It was more like an echo that she heard. Through all the hubbub, confusion and distressing annoyance of the police search and enquiry, the voice and voices came to her, though she never mentioned them to a single living soul, not even to her old tenants, the clergyman and the banker. They kept their rooms on – which was about all she could have asked of them. The best suite was never let again. It was kept locked and empty. The dust accumulated. The mirror remained untouched, its face against the wall.

The voices, meanwhile, grew more and more faint; the distance seemed to increase; soon the voice of the boy was no longer heard at all, only the cry of Mr. Thorley, her mysterious but perfect lodger, sang distantly from time to time, both in the sunshine and in the still darkness of the night hours. The direction whence it came, too, remained, as before, undeterminable. It came from anywhere and everywhere – from above, below, on all sides. It had become, too, a pleasant, even a happy sound; no dread belonged to it any more. The intervals grew longer then; days first, then weeks passed without a sound; and invariably, after these increasing intervals, the voice had become fainter, weaker, withdrawn into ever greater and greater distance. With the coming of the warm spring days it grew almost inaudible. Finally, with the great summer heats, it died away completely.

## Chapter VI

**THE DISAPPEARANCE** of Mr. Thorley, however, had caused no public disturbance on its own account, nor until it was bracketed with another disappearance, that of one of his pupils, Sir Mark Pikestaffe's son. The Pikestaffe Case then became a daily mystery that filled the papers. Mr. Thorley was of no consequence, whereas Sir Mark was a figure in the public eye.

Mr. Thorley's life, as enquiry proved, held no mystery. He had left everything in order. He did not owe a penny. He owned, indeed, considerable property, both in land and securities, and teaching mathematics, especially to promising pupils, seemed to have been a hobby merely. A half-brother called eventually to take away his few possessions, but the books and instruments he had brought into the lodging-house were never traced. He was a scholar and a gentleman to the last, a man, too, it appeared, of immense attainments and uncommon ability, one of the greatest mathematical brains, if the modest obituaries were to be believed, the world has ever known. His name now passed into oblivion. He left no record of his researches or achievements. Out of some mysterious sense of loyalty and protection Miss Speke never mentioned his peculiar personal habits. The strips of paper, as the silken threads, she had carefully removed and destroyed long before the police came to make their search of his rooms...

But the disappearance of young Gerald Pikestaffe raised a tremendous hubbub. It was some days before the two disappearances were connected, both having occurred on the same night, it was then proved. The boy, a lad of great talent, promising a brilliant future, and the favourite pupil of the older man, his tutor, had not even left the house. His room was empty – and that was all. He left no clue, no trace. Terrible hints and suggestions were, of course, spread far and wide, but there was not a scrap of evidence forthcoming to support them, Gerald Pikestaffe and Mr. Thorley, at the same moment of the same night, vanished from the face of the earth and were no more seen. The matter ended there. The one link between them appeared to have been an amazing, an exceptional gift for higher mathematics. The Pikestaffe Case merely added one more to the insoluble mysteries with which commonplace daily life is sprinkled.

\* \* \*

It was some six weeks to a month after the event that Miss Speke received a letter from one of her former charges, the most generous one, now satisfactorily finished with the Bankruptcy Court. He had honourably discharged his obligations; he was doing well; he wrote and asked Miss Speke to put him up for a week or two. "And do please give me Mr. Thorley's room," he asked. "The case thrilled me, and I should like to sleep in that room. I always loved mysteries, you remember... There's something very mysterious about this thing. Besides, I knew the P. boy a little – an astounding genius, if ever there was one."

Though it cost her much effort and still more hesitation, she consented finally. She prepared the rooms herself. There was a new servant, Lizzie having given notice the day after the disappearance, and the older woman who now waited upon the clergyman and the banker was not quite to be trusted with the delicate job. Miss Speke, entering the empty rooms on tiptoe, a strange trepidation in her heart, but that same heart firm with courage, drew up the blinds, swept the floors, dusted the furniture, and made the bed. All she did with her own hands. Only the full-length mirror she did not touch. What terror still was in her clung to that handsome piece. It was haunted by memories. For her it was still both wonderful and somehow awful. The ghost of her strange experience hid invisibly in its polished, if now unseen, depths. She dared not handle it, far less move it from the resting-place where it rested in peace. *His* hands had placed it there. To her it was sacred.

It had been given to her by Colonel Lyle, who would now occupy the room, stand on the wondrous carpet, move through the air where once the mysterious silks had floated, sleep in the very bed itself. All this he could do, but the mirror he must not touch.

"I'll explain to him a little. I'll beg him not to move it. He's very understanding," she said to herself, as she went out to buy some flowers for the sitting-room. Colonel Lyle was expected that very afternoon. Lilac, she remembered, was what he always liked. It took her longer than she expected to find really fresh bunches, of the colour that he preferred, and when she got back it was time to be thinking about his tea. The sun's rays fell slanting down the dingy street, touching it with happy gold. This, with thoughts of the teakettle and what vase would suit the flowers best, filled her mind as she passed along the linoleum in the narrow hall – then noticed suddenly a new hat and coat hanging on the usually empty pegs. Colonel Lyle had arrived before his time.

"He's already come," she said to herself with a little gasp. A heavy dread settled instantly on her spirit. She stood a moment motionless in the passage, the lilac blossoms in her hand. She was listening.

"The gentleman's come, mum," she heard the servant say, and at the same moment saw her at the top of the kitchen stairs in the hall. "He went up to his room, mum."

Miss Speke held out the flowers. With an effort to make her voice sound ordinary she gave an order about them. "Put them in water, Mary, please. The double vase will do." She watched the woman take them slowly, oh, so slowly, from her. But her mind was elsewhere. It was still listening. And after the woman had gone down to the kitchen again slowly, oh, so slowly, she stood motionless for some minutes, listening, still intently listening. But no sound broke the quiet of the afternoon. She heard only the blundering noises made by the woman in the kitchen below. On the floor above was – silence.

Miss Speke then turned and went upstairs.

Now, Miss Speke admits frankly that she was 'in a state', meaning thereby, doubtless, that her nerves were tightly strung. Her heart was thumping, her ears and eyes strained to their utmost capacity; her hands, she remembers, felt a little cold, and her legs moved uncertainly. She denies, however, that her 'state', though it may be described as nervous, could have betrayed her into either invention or delusion. What she saw she saw, and nothing can shake her conviction. Colonel Lyle, besides, is there to support her in the main outline, and Colonel Lyle, when first he had entered the room, was certainly not 'in a state', whatever excuses he may have offered later to comfort her. Moreover, to counteract her trepidation, she says that, as she pushed the door wide open – it was already ajar – the original mood of elation met her in the face with its lift of wonder and release. This modified her dread. She declares that joy rushed upon her, and that her 'nerves' were on the instant entirely forgotten.

"What I saw, I saw," remains her emphatic and unshakable verdict. "I saw – everything."

The first thing she saw admitted certainly of no doubt. Colonel Lyle lay huddled up against the further wall, half upon the carpet and half-leaning on the wainscoting. He was unconscious. One arm was stretched towards the mirror, the hand still clutching one of its mahogany feet. And the mirror had been moved. It turned now slightly more towards the room.

The picture, indeed, told its own story, a story Colonel Lyle himself repeated afterwards when he had recovered. He was surprised to find the mirror – his mirror – with its face to the wall; he went forward to put it in its proper position; in doing this he looked into it; he saw something, and – the next thing he knew – Miss Speke was bringing him round.

She explains, further, that her overmastering curiosity to look into the mirror, as Colonel Lyle had evidently looked himself, prevented her from immediately rendering first-aid to that gentleman, as she unquestionably should have done. Instead, she crossed the room, stepped over his huddled form, turned the mirror a little further round towards her, and looked straight into it.

The eye, apparently, takes in a great deal more than the mind is consciously aware of having 'seen' at the moment. Miss Speke saw everything, she claims. But details certainly came back to her later, details she had not been aware of at the time. At the moment, however, her impressions, though extremely vivid, were limited to certain outstanding items. These items were – that her own reflection was not visible, no picture of herself being there; that Mr. Thorley and a boy – she recognised the Pikestaffe lad from the newspaper photographs she had seen – were plainly there, and that books and instruments in great quantity filled all the nearer space, blocking up the foreground. Beyond, behind, stretching in all directions, she affirms, was empty space that produced upon her the effect of the infinite heavens as seen in a clear night sky. This space was prodigious, yet in some way not alarming. It did not terrify; rather it comforted, and, in a sense, uplifted. A diffused soft light pervaded the huge panorama. There were no shadows, there were no high lights.

Curiously enough, however, the absence of any reproduction of herself did not at first strike her as at all out of the way; she noticed the fact, no more than that; it was, perhaps, naturally, the deep shock of seeing Mr. Thorley and the boy that held her absolutely spellbound, arresting her faculties as though they had been frozen.

Mr. Thorley was moving to and fro, his body bent, his hand thrown forward. He looked as natural as in life. He moved steadily, as with a purpose, now nearer, now further, but his figure always bent as though he were intent upon something in his hands. The boy moved, too, but with a more gentle, less vigorous, motion that suggested floating. He followed the larger figure, keeping close, his face raised from time to time as though his companion spoke to him. The expression that he wore was quiet, peaceful, happy, and intent. He was absorbed in what he was doing at the moment. Then, suddenly, Mr. Thorley straightened himself up. He turned. Miss Speke saw his face for the first time. He looked into her eyes. The face blazed with light. The gaze was straight, and full, and clear. It betrayed recognition. Mr. Thorley smiled at her.

In a very few seconds she was aware of all this, of its main outlines, at any rate. She saw the moving, living figures in the midst of this stupendous and amazing space. The overwhelming surprise it caused her prevented, apparently, the lesser emotion of personal alarm; fear she certainly did not feel at first. It was when Mr. Thorley looked at her with his brilliant eyes and blazing smile that her heart gave its violent jump, missed a beat or two, then began hammering against her ribs like released machinery that has gone beyond control. She was aware of the happy glory in the face, a face that was thin to emaciation, almost transparent, yet wearing an expression that was no longer earthly. Then, as he smiled, he came towards her; he beckoned; he stretched both hands out, while the boy looked up and watched.

Mr. Thorley's advance, however, had two distracting peculiarities – that as he drew nearer he moved not in a straight line, but in a curve. As a skater performing 'edges', though on both feet instead of on one, he swept gracefully and with incredible speed in her direction. The other peculiarity was that with each step nearer his figure grew smaller. It lessened in height. He seemed, indeed, to be moving in two directions at once. He became diminutive.

The sight ought by rights to have paralysed her, yet it produced again, instead of terror, an effect of exhilaration she could not possibly account for. There came once again that fine elation to her mind. Not only did all desire to resist die away almost before it was born, but more, she felt its opposite – an overpowering wish to join him. The tiny hands were still stretched out to greet her, to draw her in, to welcome her; the smile upon the diminutive face, as it came nearer and nearer, was enchanting. She heard his voice then:

"Come, come to us! Here reality is nearer, and there is liberty...!"

The voice was very close and loud as in life, but it was not in front. It was behind her. Against her very ear it sounded in the air behind her back. She moved one foot forward; she raised her arms. She felt herself being sucked in – into that glorious space. There was an indescribable change in her whole being.

The cumulative effect of so many amazing happenings, all of them contrary to nature, should have been destructive to her reason. Their combined shock should have dislocated her system somewhere and have laid her low. But with every individual, it seems, the breaking-point is different. Her system, indeed, was dislocated, and a moment later and she was certainly laid low, yet it was not the effect of the figure, the voice, the gliding approach of Mr. Thorley that produced this. It was the flaw of little human egoism that brought her down. For it was in this instant that she first realised the absence of her own reflection in the mirror. The fact, though noticed before, had not entered her consciousness as such. It now definitely did so. The arms she lifted in greeting had no reflected counterpart. Her figure, she realised with a shock of terror, was not there. She dropped, then, like a stricken animal, one outstretched hand clutching the frame of the mirror as she did so.

"Gracious God!" she heard herself scream as she collapsed. She heard, too, the crash of the falling mirror which she overturned and brought down with her.

Whether the noise brought Colonel Lyle round, or whether it was the combined weight of Miss Speke and the handsome piece upon his legs that roused him, is of no consequence. He stirred, opened his eyes, disentangled himself and proceeded, not without astonishment, to render first-aid to the unconscious lady.

The explanations that followed are, equally, of little consequence. His own attack, he considered, was chiefly due to fatigue, to violent indigestion, and to the aftereffects of his protracted bankruptcy proceedings. Thus, at any rate, he assured Miss Speke. He added, however, that he had received rather a shock from the handsome piece, for, surprised at finding it turned to the wall, he had replaced it and looked into it, but had not seen himself reflected. This had amazed him a good deal, yet what amazed him still more was that he had seen something moving in the depths of the glass. "I saw a face," he said, "and it was a face I knew. It was Gerald Pikestaffe. Behind him was another figure, the figure of a man, whose face I could not see." A mist rose before his eyes, his head swam a bit, and he evidently swayed for some unaccountable reason. It was a blow received in falling that stunned him momentarily.

He stood over her, while he fanned her face; her swoon was of brief duration; she recovered quickly; she listened to his story with a quiet mind. The aftereffect of too great wonder leaves no room for pettier emotions, and traces of the exhilaration she had experienced were still about her heart and soul.

"Is it smashed?" was the first thing she asked, to which Colonel Lyle made no answer at first, merely pointing to the carpet where the frame of the long mirror lay in broken fragments.

"There was no glass, you see," he said presently. He, too, was quiet, his manner very earnest; his voice, though subdued as by a hint of awe, betrayed the glow of some intense inner excitement that lit fire in his eyes as well. "He had cut it out long ago, of course. He used the empty framework, merely."

"Eh?" said Miss Speke, looking down incredulously, but finding no sign of splinters on the floor.

Her companion smiled. "We shall find it about somewhere if we look," he said calmly, which, indeed, proved later true – lying flat beneath the carpet under the bed. "His measurements and calculations led – probably by chance – towards the mirror" – he seemed speaking to himself more than to his bewildered listener – "perhaps by chance, perhaps by knowledge," he continued, "up to the mirror – and then *through* it." He looked down at Miss Speke and laughed a little. "So, like Alice, he went through it, too, taking his books and instruments, the boy as well, all with him. The boy, that is, had the knowledge too."

"I only know one thing," said Miss Speke, unable to follow him or find meaning in his words, "I shall never let these rooms again. I shall lock them up."

Her companion collected the broken pieces and made a little heap of them.

"And I shall pray for him," added Miss Speke, as he led her presently downstairs to her own quarters. "I shall never cease to pray for him as long as I live."

"He hardly needs that," murmured Colonel Lyle, but to himself. "The first terror has long since left him. He's found the new direction – and moved along it."

**If you enjoyed this, you might also like…**
A Victim of Higher Space, see page 307
The Other Wing, see page 319

# Ghostly Visitations

# A Haunted Island

**THE FOLLOWING** events occurred on a small island of isolated position in a large Canadian lake, to whose cool waters the inhabitants of Montreal and Toronto flee for rest and recreation in the hot months. It is only to be regretted that events of such peculiar interest to the genuine student of the psychical should be entirely uncorroborated. Such unfortunately, however, is the case.

Our own party of nearly twenty had returned to Montreal that very day, and I was left in solitary possession for a week or two longer, in order to accomplish some important 'reading' for the law which I had foolishly neglected during the summer.

It was late in September, and the big trout and maskinonge were stirring themselves in the depths of the lake, and beginning slowly to move up to the surface waters as the north winds and early frosts lowered their temperature. Already the maples were crimson and gold, and the wild laughter of the loons echoed in sheltered bays that never knew their strange cry in the summer.

With a whole island to oneself, a two-storey cottage, a canoe, and only the chipmunks, and the farmer's weekly visit with eggs and bread, to disturb one, the opportunities for hard reading might be very great. It all depends!

The rest of the party had gone off with many warnings to beware of Indians, and not to stay late enough to be the victim of a frost that thinks nothing of forty below zero. After they had gone, the loneliness of the situation made itself unpleasantly felt. There were no other islands within six or seven miles, and though the mainland forests lay a couple of miles behind me, they stretched for a very great distance unbroken by any signs of human habitation. But, though the island was completely deserted and silent, the rocks and trees that had echoed human laughter and voices almost every hour of the day for two months could not fail to retain some memories of it all; and I was not surprised to fancy I heard a shout or a cry as I passed from rock to rock, and more than once to imagine that I heard my own name called aloud.

In the cottage there were six tiny little bedrooms divided from one another by plain unvarnished partitions of pine. A wooden bedstead, a mattress, and a chair, stood in each room, but I only found two mirrors, and one of these was broken.

The boards creaked a good deal as I moved about, and the signs of occupation were so recent that I could hardly believe I was alone. I half expected to find someone left behind, still trying to crowd into a box more than it would hold. The door of one room was stiff, and refused for a moment to open, and it required very little persuasion to imagine someone was holding the handle on the inside, and that when it opened I should meet a pair of human eyes.

A thorough search of the floor led me to select as my own sleeping quarters a little room with a diminutive balcony over the verandah roof. The room was very small, but the bed was large, and had the best mattress of them all. It was situated directly over the sitting-room where I should live and do my 'reading', and the miniature window looked out to the rising sun. With the exception of a narrow path which led from the front door and verandah through the trees to the boat-landing, the island was densely covered with maples, hemlocks, and cedars. The trees gathered in round the cottage so closely that the slightest wind made the branches scrape the roof and tap the wooden walls. A few moments after sunset the darkness became impenetrable, and ten yards beyond the glare of the lamps that shone through the sitting-room windows – of which there were four – you could not see an inch before your nose, nor move a step without running up against a tree.

The rest of that day I spent moving my belongings from my tent to the sitting-room, taking stock of the contents of the larder, and chopping enough wood for the stove to last me for a week. After that, just before sunset, I went round the island a couple of times in my canoe for precaution's sake. I had never dreamed of doing this before, but when a man is alone he does things that never occur to him when he is one of a large party.

How lonely the island seemed when I landed again! The sun was down, and twilight is unknown in these northern regions. The darkness comes up at once. The canoe safely pulled up and turned over on her face, I groped my way up the little narrow pathway to the verandah. The six lamps were soon burning merrily in the front room; but in the kitchen, where I 'dined', the shadows were so gloomy, and the lamplight was so inadequate, that the stars could be seen peeping through the cracks between the rafters.

I turned in early that night. Though it was calm and there was no wind, the creaking of my bedstead and the musical gurgle of the water over the rocks below were not the only sounds that reached my ears. As I lay awake, the appalling emptiness of the house grew upon me. The corridors and vacant rooms seemed to echo innumerable footsteps, shufflings, the rustle of skirts, and a constant undertone of whispering. When sleep at length overtook me, the breathings and noises, however, passed gently to mingle with the voices of my dreams.

A week passed by, and the 'reading' progressed favourably. On the tenth day of my solitude, a strange thing happened. I awoke after a good night's sleep to find myself possessed with a marked repugnance for my room. The air seemed to stifle me. The more I tried to define the cause of this dislike, the more unreasonable it appeared. There was something about the room that made me afraid. Absurd as it seems, this feeling clung to me obstinately while dressing, and more than once I caught myself shivering, and conscious of an inclination to get out of the room as quickly as possible. The more I tried to laugh it away, the more real it became; and when at last I was dressed, and went out into the passage, and downstairs into the kitchen, it was with feelings of relief, such as I might imagine would accompany one's escape from the presence of a dangerous contagious disease.

While cooking my breakfast, I carefully recalled every night spent in the room, in the hope that I might in some way connect the dislike I now felt with some disagreeable incident that had occurred in it. But the only thing I could recall was one stormy night when I suddenly awoke and heard the boards creaking so loudly in the corridor that I was convinced there were people in the house. So certain was I of this, that I had descended the stairs, gun in hand, only to find the doors and windows securely fastened, and the mice and black-beetles in sole possession of the floor. This was certainly not sufficient to account for the strength of my feelings.

The morning hours I spent in steady reading; and when I broke off in the middle of the day for a swim and luncheon, I was very much surprised, if not a little alarmed, to find that my dislike for the room had, if anything, grown stronger. Going upstairs to get a book, I experienced the most marked aversion to entering the room, and while within I was conscious all the time of an uncomfortable feeling that was half uneasiness and half apprehension. The result of it was that, instead of reading, I spent the afternoon on the water paddling and fishing, and when I got home about sundown, brought with me half a dozen delicious black bass for the supper-table and the larder.

As sleep was an important matter to me at this time, I had decided that if my aversion to the room was so strongly marked on my return as it had been before, I would move my bed down into the sitting-room, and sleep there. This was, I argued, in no sense a concession to an absurd and fanciful fear, but simply a precaution to ensure a good night's sleep. A bad night involved the loss of the next day's reading, – a loss I was not prepared to incur.

I accordingly moved my bed downstairs into a corner of the sitting-room facing the door, and was moreover uncommonly glad when the operation was completed, and the door of the bedroom closed finally upon the shadows, the silence, and the strange *fear* that shared the room with them.

The croaking stroke of the kitchen clock sounded the hour of eight as I finished washing up my few dishes, and closing the kitchen door behind me, passed into the front room. All the lamps were lit, and their reflectors, which I had polished up during the day, threw a blaze of light into the room.

Outside the night was still and warm. Not a breath of air was stirring; the waves were silent, the trees motionless, and heavy clouds hung like an oppressive curtain over the heavens. The darkness seemed to have rolled up with unusual swiftness, and not the faintest glow of colour remained to show where the sun had set. There was present in the atmosphere that ominous and overwhelming silence which so often precedes the most violent storms.

I sat down to my books with my brain unusually clear, and in my heart the pleasant satisfaction of knowing that five black bass were lying in the ice-house, and that tomorrow morning the old farmer would arrive with fresh bread and eggs. I was soon absorbed in my books.

As the night wore on the silence deepened. Even the chipmunks were still; and the boards of the floors and walls ceased creaking. I read on steadily till, from the gloomy shadows of the kitchen, came the hoarse sound of the clock striking nine. How loud the strokes sounded! They were like blows of a big hammer. I closed one book and opened another, feeling that I was just warming up to my work.

This, however, did not last long. I presently found that I was reading the same paragraphs over twice, simple paragraphs that did not require such effort. Then I noticed that my mind began to wander to other things, and the effort to recall my thoughts became harder with each digression. Concentration was growing momentarily more difficult. Presently I discovered that I had turned over two pages instead of one, and had not noticed my mistake until I was well down the page. This was becoming serious. What was the disturbing influence? It could not be physical fatigue. On the contrary, my mind was unusually alert, and in a more receptive condition than usual. I made a new and determined effort to read, and for a short time succeeded in giving my whole attention to my subject. But in a very few moments again I found myself leaning back in my chair, staring vacantly into space.

Something was evidently at work in my sub-consciousness. There was something I had neglected to do. Perhaps the kitchen door and windows were not fastened. I accordingly went to see, and found that they were! The fire perhaps needed attention. I went in to see, and found that it was all right! I looked at the lamps, went upstairs into every bedroom in turn, and then went round the house, and even into the ice-house. Nothing was wrong; everything was in its place. Yet something *was* wrong! The conviction grew stronger and stronger within me.

When I at length settled down to my books again and tried to read, I became aware, for the first time, that the room seemed growing cold. Yet the day had been oppressively warm, and evening had brought no relief. The six big lamps, moreover, gave out heat enough to warm the room pleasantly. But a chilliness, that perhaps crept up from the lake, made itself felt in the room, and caused me to get up to close the glass door opening on to the verandah.

For a brief moment I stood looking out at the shaft of light that fell from the windows and shone some little distance down the pathway, and out for a few feet into the lake.

As I looked, I saw a canoe glide into the pathway of light, and immediately crossing it, pass out of sight again into the darkness. It was perhaps a hundred feet from the shore, and it moved swiftly.

I was surprised that a canoe should pass the island at that time of night, for all the summer visitors from the other side of the lake had gone home weeks before, and the island was a long way out of any line of water traffic.

My reading from this moment did not make very good progress, for somehow the picture of that canoe, gliding so dimly and swiftly across the narrow track of light on the black waters, silhouetted itself against the background of my mind with singular vividness. It kept coming between my eyes and the printed page. The more I thought about it the more surprised I became. It was of larger build than any I had seen during the past summer months, and was more like the old Indian war canoes with the high curving bows and stern and wide beam. The more I tried to read, the less success attended my efforts; and finally I closed my books and went out on the verandah to walk up and down a bit, and shake the chilliness out of my bones.

The night was perfectly still, and as dark as imaginable. I stumbled down the path to the little landing wharf, where the water made the very faintest of gurgling under the timbers. The sound of a big tree falling in the mainland forest, far across the lake, stirred echoes in the heavy air, like the first guns of a distant night attack. No other sound disturbed the stillness that reigned supreme.

As I stood upon the wharf in the broad splash of light that followed me from the sitting-room windows, I saw another canoe cross the pathway of uncertain light upon the water, and disappear at once into the impenetrable gloom that lay beyond. This time I saw more distinctly than before. It was like the former canoe, a big birch-bark, with high-crested bows and stern and broad beam. It was paddled by two Indians, of whom the one in the stern – the steerer – appeared to be a very large man. I could see this very plainly; and though the second canoe was much nearer the island than the first, I judged that they were both on their way home to the Government Reservation, which was situated some fifteen miles away upon the mainland.

I was wondering in my mind what could possibly bring any Indians down to this part of the lake at such an hour of the night, when a third canoe, of precisely similar build, and also occupied by two Indians, passed silently round the end of the wharf. This time the canoe was very much nearer shore, and it suddenly flashed into my mind that the three canoes were in reality one and the same, and that only one canoe was circling the island!

This was by no means a pleasant reflection, because, if it were the correct solution of the unusual appearance of the three canoes in this lonely part of the lake at so late an hour, the purpose of the two men could only reasonably be considered to be in some way connected with myself. I had never known of the Indians attempting any violence upon the settlers who shared the wild, inhospitable country with them; at the same time, it was not beyond the region of possibility to suppose… But then I did not care even to think of such hideous possibilities, and my imagination immediately sought relief in all manner of other solutions to the problem, which indeed came readily enough to my mind, but did not succeed in recommending themselves to my reason.

Meanwhile, by a sort of instinct, I stepped back out of the bright light in which I had hitherto been standing, and waited in the deep shadow of a rock to see if the canoe would again make its appearance. Here I could see, without being seen, and the precaution seemed a wise one.

After less than five minutes the canoe, as I had anticipated, made its fourth appearance. This time it was not twenty yards from the wharf, and I saw that the Indians meant to land. I recognised the two men as those who had passed before, and the steerer was certainly an immense fellow. It was unquestionably the same canoe. There could be no longer any doubt that for some purpose of their own the men had been going round and round the island for some time, waiting for an opportunity to land. I strained my eyes to follow them in the darkness, but the night had completely swallowed them up, and not even the faintest swish of the paddles reached my ears as the Indians plied their long and powerful strokes. The canoe would be round again in a few moments, and this time it was possible that the men might land. It was well to be prepared. I knew nothing of their intentions, and two to one (when the two are big Indians!) late at night on a lonely island was not exactly my idea of pleasant intercourse.

In a corner of the sitting-room, leaning up against the back wall, stood my Marlin rifle, with ten cartridges in the magazine and one lying snugly in the greased breech. There was just time to get up to the house and take up a position of defence in that corner. Without an instant's hesitation I ran up to the verandah, carefully picking my way among the trees, so as to avoid being seen in the light. Entering the room, I shut the door leading to the verandah, and as quickly as possible turned out every one of the six lamps. To be in a room so brilliantly lighted, where my every movement could be observed from outside, while I could see nothing but impenetrable darkness at every window, was by all laws of warfare an unnecessary concession to the enemy. And this enemy, if enemy it was to be, was far too wily and dangerous to be granted any such advantages.

I stood in the corner of the room with my back against the wall, and my hand on the cold rifle-barrel. The table, covered with my books, lay between me and the door, but for the first few minutes after the lights were out the darkness was so intense that nothing could be discerned at all. Then, very gradually, the outline of the room became visible, and the framework of the windows began to shape itself dimly before my eyes.

After a few minutes the door (its upper half of glass), and the two windows that looked out upon the front verandah, became specially distinct; and I was glad that this was so, because if the Indians came up to the house I should be able to see their approach, and gather something of their plans. Nor was I mistaken, for there presently came to my ears the peculiar hollow sound of a canoe landing and being carefully dragged up over the rocks. The paddles I distinctly heard being placed underneath, and the silence that ensued thereupon I rightly interpreted to mean that the Indians were stealthily approaching the house...

While it would be absurd to claim that I was not alarmed – even frightened – at the gravity of the situation and its possible outcome, I speak the whole truth when I say that I was not overwhelmingly afraid for myself. I was conscious that even at this stage of the night I was passing into a psychical condition in which my sensations seemed no longer normal. Physical fear at no time entered into the nature of my feelings; and though I kept my hand upon my rifle the greater part of the night, I was all the time conscious that its assistance could be of little avail against the terrors that I had to face. More than once I seemed to feel most curiously that I was in no real sense a part of the proceedings, nor actually involved in them, but that I was playing the part of a spectator – a spectator, moreover, on a psychic rather than on a material plane. Many of my sensations that night were too vague for definite description and analysis, but the main feeling that will stay with me to the end of my days is the awful horror of it all, and the miserable sensation that if the strain had lasted a little longer than was actually the case my mind must inevitably have given way.

Meanwhile I stood still in my corner, and waited patiently for what was to come. The house was as still as the grave, but the inarticulate voices of the night sang in my ears, and I seemed to hear the blood running in my veins and dancing in my pulses.

If the Indians came to the back of the house, they would find the kitchen door and window securely fastened. They could not get in there without making considerable noise, which I was bound to hear. The only mode of getting in was by means of the door that faced me, and I kept my eyes glued on that door without taking them off for the smallest fraction of a second.

My sight adapted itself every minute better to the darkness. I saw the table that nearly filled the room, and left only a narrow passage on each side. I could also make out the straight backs of the wooden chairs pressed up against it, and could even distinguish my papers and inkstand lying on the white oilcloth covering. I thought of the gay faces that had gathered round that table during the summer, and I longed for the sunlight as I had never longed for it before.

Less than three feet to my left the passage-way led to the kitchen, and the stairs leading to the bedrooms above commenced in this passage-way, but almost in the sitting-room itself. Through the windows I could see the dim motionless outlines of the trees: not a leaf stirred, not a branch moved.

A few moments of this awful silence, and then I was aware of a soft tread on the boards of the verandah, so stealthy that it seemed an impression directly on my brain rather than upon the nerves of hearing. Immediately afterwards a black figure darkened the glass door, and I perceived that a face was pressed against the upper panes. A shiver ran down my back, and my hair was conscious of a tendency to rise and stand at right angles to my head.

It was the figure of an Indian, broad-shouldered and immense; indeed, the largest figure of a man I have ever seen outside of a circus hall. By some power of light that seemed to generate itself in the brain, I saw the strong dark face with the aquiline nose and high cheek-bones flattened against the glass. The direction of the gaze I could not determine; but faint gleams of light as the big eyes rolled round and showed their whites, told me plainly that no corner of the room escaped their searching.

For what seemed fully five minutes the dark figure stood there, with the huge shoulders bent forward so as to bring the head down to the level of the glass; while behind him, though not nearly so large, the shadowy form of the other Indian swayed to and fro like a bent tree. While I waited in an agony of suspense and agitation for their next movement little currents of icy sensation ran up and down my spine and my heart seemed alternately to stop beating and then start off again with terrifying rapidity. They must have heard its thumping and the singing of the blood in my head! Moreover, I was conscious, as I felt a cold stream of perspiration trickle down my face, of a desire to scream, to shout, to bang the walls like a child, to make a noise, or do anything that would relieve the suspense and bring things to a speedy climax.

It was probably this inclination that led me to another discovery, for when I tried to bring my rifle from behind my back to raise it and have it pointed at the door ready to fire, I found that I was powerless to move. The muscles, paralysed by this strange fear, refused to obey the will. Here indeed was a terrifying complication!

\* \* \*

There was a faint sound of rattling at the brass knob, and the door was pushed open a couple of inches. A pause of a few seconds, and it was pushed open still further. Without a sound of footsteps that was appreciable to my ears, the two figures glided into the room, and the man behind gently closed the door after him.

They were alone with me between the four walls. Could they see me standing there, so still and straight in my corner? Had they, perhaps, already seen me? My blood surged and sang like the roll of drums in an orchestra; and though I did my best to suppress my breathing, it sounded like the rushing of wind through a pneumatic tube.

My suspense as to the next move was soon at an end – only, however, to give place to a new and keener alarm. The men had hitherto exchanged no words and no signs, but there were general indications of a movement across the room, and whichever way they went they would have to pass round the table. If they came my way they would have to pass within six inches of my person. While I was considering this very disagreeable possibility, I perceived that the smaller Indian (smaller by comparison) suddenly raised his arm and pointed to the ceiling. The other fellow raised his head and followed the direction of his companion's arm. I began to understand at last. They were going upstairs, and the room directly overhead to which they pointed had been until this night my bedroom. It was the room in which I had experienced that very morning so strange a sensation of fear, and but for which I should then have been lying asleep in the narrow bed against the window.

The Indians then began to move silently around the room; they were going upstairs, and they were coming round my side of the table. So stealthy were their movements that, but for the abnormally sensitive state of the nerves, I should never have heard them. As it was, their cat-like tread was distinctly audible. Like two monstrous black cats they came round the table toward me, and for the first time I perceived that the smaller of the two dragged something along the floor behind him. As it trailed along over the floor with a soft, sweeping sound, I somehow got the impression that it was a large dead thing with outstretched wings, or a large, spreading cedar branch. Whatever it was, I was unable to see it even in outline, and I was too terrified, even had I possessed the power over my muscles, to move my neck forward in the effort to determine its nature.

Nearer and nearer they came. The leader rested a giant hand upon the table as he moved. My lips were glued together, and the air seemed to burn in my nostrils. I tried to close my eyes, so that I might not see as they passed me; but my eyelids had stiffened, and refused to obey. Would they never get by me? Sensation seemed also to have left my legs, and it was as if I were standing on mere supports of wood or stone. Worse still, I was conscious that I was losing the power of balance, the power to stand upright, or even to lean backwards against the wall. Some force was drawing me forward, and a dizzy terror seized me that I should lose my balance, and topple forward against the Indians just as they were in the act of passing me.

Even moments drawn out into hours must come to an end some time, and almost before I knew it the figures had passed me and had their feet upon the lower step of the stairs leading to the upper bedrooms. There could not have been six inches between us, and yet I was conscious only of a current of cold air that followed them. They had not touched me, and I was convinced that they had not seen me. Even the trailing thing on the floor behind them had not touched my feet, as I had dreaded it would, and on such an occasion as this I was grateful even for the smallest mercies.

The absence of the Indians from my immediate neighbourhood brought little sense of relief. I stood shivering and shuddering in my corner, and, beyond being able to breathe more freely, I felt no whit less uncomfortable. Also, I was aware that a certain light, which, without apparent source or rays, had enabled me to follow their every gesture and movement, had gone out of the room with their departure. An unnatural darkness now filled the room, and pervaded its every corner so that I could barely make out the positions of the windows and the glass doors.

As I said before, my condition was evidently an abnormal one. The capacity for feeling surprise seemed, as in dreams, to be wholly absent. My senses recorded with unusual accuracy every smallest occurrence, but I was able to draw only the simplest deductions.

The Indians soon reached the top of the stairs, and there they halted for a moment. I had not the faintest clue as to their next movement. They appeared to hesitate. They were listening attentively. Then I heard one of them, who by the weight of his soft tread must have been the giant, cross the narrow corridor and enter the room directly overhead – my own little bedroom. But for the insistence of that unaccountable dread I had experienced there in the morning, I should at that very moment have been lying in the bed with the big Indian in the room standing beside me.

For the space of a hundred seconds there was silence, such as might have existed before the birth of sound. It was followed by a long quivering shriek of terror, which rang out into the night, and ended in a short gulp before it had run its full course. At the same moment the other Indian left his place at the head of the stairs, and joined his companion in the bedroom. I heard the 'thing' trailing behind him along the floor. A thud followed, as of something heavy falling, and then all became as still and silent as before.

It was at this point that the atmosphere, surcharged all day with the electricity of a fierce storm, found relief in a dancing flash of brilliant lightning simultaneously with a crash of loudest thunder. For five seconds every article in the room was visible to me with amazing distinctness, and through the windows I saw the tree trunks standing in solemn rows. The thunder pealed and echoed across the lake and among the distant islands, and the flood-gates of heaven then opened and let out their rain in streaming torrents.

The drops fell with a swift rushing sound upon the still waters of the lake, which leaped up to meet them, and pattered with the rattle of shot on the leaves of the maples and the roof of the cottage. A moment later, and another flash, even more brilliant and of longer duration than the first, lit up the sky from zenith to horizon, and bathed the room momentarily in dazzling whiteness. I could see the rain glistening on the leaves and branches outside. The wind rose suddenly, and in less than a minute the storm that had been gathering all day burst forth in its full fury.

Above all the noisy voices of the elements, the slightest sounds in the room overhead made themselves heard, and in the few seconds of deep silence that followed the shriek of terror and pain I was aware that the movements had commenced again. The men were leaving the room and approaching the top of the stairs. A short pause, and they began to descend. Behind them, tumbling from step to step, I could hear that trailing 'thing' being dragged along. It had become ponderous!

I awaited their approach with a degree of calmness, almost of apathy, which was only explicable on the ground that after a certain point Nature applies her own anaesthetic, and a merciful condition of numbness supervenes. On they came, step by step, nearer and nearer, with the shuffling sound of the burden behind growing louder as they approached.

They were already half-way down the stairs when I was galvanised afresh into a condition of terror by the consideration of a new and horrible possibility. It was the reflection that if another vivid flash of lightning were to come when the shadowy procession was in the room, perhaps when it was actually passing in front of me, I should see everything in detail, and worse, be seen myself! I could only hold my breath and wait – wait while the minutes lengthened into hours, and the procession made its slow progress round the room.

The Indians had reached the foot of the staircase. The form of the huge leader loomed in the doorway of the passage, and the burden with an ominous thud had dropped from the last step to the floor. There was a moment's pause while I saw the Indian turn and stoop to assist his companion. Then the procession moved forward again, entered the room close on my left, and began to move slowly round my side of the table. The leader was already beyond me, and his companion, dragging on the floor behind him the burden, whose confused outline I could dimly make out, was exactly in front of me, when the cavalcade came to a dead halt. At the same moment, with the strange suddenness of thunderstorms, the splash of the rain ceased altogether, and the wind died away into utter silence.

For the space of five seconds my heart seemed to stop beating, and then the worst came. A double flash of lightning lit up the room and its contents with merciless vividness.

The huge Indian leader stood a few feet past me on my right. One leg was stretched forward in the act of taking a step. His immense shoulders were turned toward his companion, and in all their magnificent fierceness I saw the outline of his features. His gaze was directed upon the burden his companion was dragging along the floor; but his profile, with the big aquiline nose, high cheek-bone, straight black hair and bold chin, burnt itself in that brief instant into my brain, never again to fade.

Dwarfish, compared with this gigantic figure, appeared the proportions of the other Indian, who, within twelve inches of my face, was stooping over the thing he was dragging in a position that lent to his person the additional horror of deformity. And the burden, lying upon a sweeping cedar branch which he held and dragged by a long stem, was the body of a white man. The scalp had been neatly lifted, and blood lay in a broad smear upon the cheeks and forehead.

Then, for the first time that night, the terror that had paralysed my muscles and my will lifted its unholy spell from my soul. With a loud cry I stretched out my arms to seize the big Indian by the throat, and, grasping only air, tumbled forward unconscious upon the ground.

I had recognised the body, and *the face was my own...!*

It was bright daylight when a man's voice recalled me to consciousness. I was lying where I had fallen, and the farmer was standing in the room with the loaves of bread in his hands. The horror of the night was still in my heart, and as the bluff settler helped me to my feet and picked up the rifle which had fallen with me, with many questions and expressions of condolence, I imagine my brief replies were neither self-explanatory nor even intelligible.

That day, after a thorough and fruitless search of the house, I left the island, and went over to spend my last ten days with the farmer; and when the time came for me to leave, the necessary reading had been accomplished, and my nerves had completely recovered their balance.

On the day of my departure the farmer started early in his big boat with my belongings to row to the point, twelve miles distant, where a little steamer ran twice a week for the accommodation of hunters. Late in the afternoon I went off in another direction in my canoe, wishing to see the island once again, where I had been the victim of so strange an experience.

In due course I arrived there, and made a tour of the island. I also made a search of the little house, and it was not without a curious sensation in my heart that I entered the little upstairs bedroom. There seemed nothing unusual.

Just after I re-embarked, I saw a canoe gliding ahead of me around the curve of the island. A canoe was an unusual sight at this time of the year, and this one seemed to have sprung from nowhere. Altering my course a little, I watched it disappear around the next projecting point of rock. It had high curving bows, and there were two Indians in it. I lingered with some excitement, to see if it would appear again round the other side of the island; and in less than five minutes it came into view. There were less than two hundred yards between us, and the Indians, sitting on their haunches, were paddling swiftly in my direction.

I never paddled faster in my life than I did in those next few minutes. When I turned to look again, the Indians had altered their course, and were again circling the island.

The sun was sinking behind the forests on the mainland, and the crimson-coloured clouds of sunset were reflected in the waters of the lake, when I looked round for the last time, and saw the big bark canoe and its two dusky occupants still going round the island. Then the shadows deepened rapidly; the lake grew black, and the night wind blew its first breath in my face as I turned a corner, and a projecting bluff of rock hid from my view both island and canoe.

**If you enjoyed this, you might also like...**
The Willows, see page 11
The Camp of the Dog, see page 132

# Keeping His Promise

**IT WAS** eleven o'clock at night, and young Marriott was locked into his room, cramming as hard as he could cram. He was a 'Fourth Year Man' at Edinburgh University and he had been ploughed for this particular examination so often that his parents had positively declared they could no longer supply the funds to keep him there.

His rooms were cheap and dingy, but it was the lecture fees that took the money. So Marriott pulled himself together at last and definitely made up his mind that he would pass or die in the attempt, and for some weeks now he had been reading as hard as mortal man can read. He was trying to make up for lost time and money in a way that showed conclusively he did not understand the value of either. For no ordinary man – and Marriott was in every sense an ordinary man – can afford to drive the mind as he had lately been driving his, without sooner or later paying the cost.

Among the students he had few friends or acquaintances, and these few had promised not to disturb him at night, knowing he was at last reading in earnest. It was, therefore, with feelings a good deal stronger than mere surprise that he heard his door-bell ring on this particular night and realised that he was to have a visitor. Some men would simply have muffled the bell and gone on quietly with their work. But Marriott was not this sort. He was nervous. It would have bothered and pecked at his mind all night long not to know who the visitor was and what he wanted. The only thing to do, therefore, was to let him in – and out again – as quickly as possible.

The landlady went to bed at ten o'clock punctually, after which hour nothing would induce her to pretend she heard the bell, so Marriott jumped up from his books with an exclamation that augured ill for the reception of his caller, and prepared to let him in with his own hand.

The streets of Edinburgh town were very still at this late hour – it was late for Edinburgh – and in the quiet neighbourhood of F— Street, where Marriott lived on the third floor, scarcely a sound broke the silence. As he crossed the floor, the bell rang a second time, with unnecessary clamour, and he unlocked the door and passed into the little hallway with considerable wrath and annoyance in his heart at the insolence of the double interruption.

"The fellows all know I'm reading for this exam. Why in the world do they come to bother me at such an unearthly hour?"

The inhabitants of the building, with himself, were medical students, general students, poor Writers to the Signet, and some others whose vocations were perhaps not so obvious. The stone staircase, dimly lighted at each floor by a gas-jet that would not turn above a certain height, wound down to the level of the street with no pretence at carpet or railing. At some levels it was cleaner than at others. It depended on the landlady of the particular level.

The acoustic properties of a spiral staircase seem to be peculiar. Marriott, standing by the open door, book in hand, thought every moment the owner of the footsteps would come into view. The sound of the boots was so close and so loud that they seemed to travel disproportionately in advance of their cause. Wondering who it could be, he stood ready with all manner of sharp greetings for the man who dared thus to disturb his work. But the man did not appear. The steps sounded almost under his nose, yet no one was visible.

A sudden queer sensation of fear passed over him – a faintness and a shiver down the back. It went, however, almost as soon as it came, and he was just debating whether he would call aloud to his invisible visitor, or slam the door and return to his books, when the cause of the disturbance turned the corner very slowly and came into view.

It was a stranger. He saw a youngish man short of figure and very broad. His face was the colour of a piece of chalk and the eyes, which were very bright, had heavy lines underneath them. Though the cheeks and chin were unshaven and the general appearance unkempt, the man was evidently a gentleman, for he was well dressed and bore himself with a certain air. But, strangest of all, he wore no hat, and carried none in his hand; and although rain had been falling steadily all the evening, he appeared to have neither overcoat nor umbrella.

A hundred questions sprang up in Marriott's mind and rushed to his lips, chief among which was something like "Who in the world are you?" and "What in the name of heaven do you come to me for?" But none of these questions found time to express themselves in words, for almost at once the caller turned his head a little so that the gas light in the hall fell upon his features from a new angle. Then in a flash Marriott recognised him.

"Field! Man alive! Is it you?" he gasped.

The Fourth Year Man was not lacking in intuition, and he perceived at once that here was a case for delicate treatment. He divined, without any actual process of thought, that the catastrophe often predicted had come at last, and that this man's father had turned him out of the house. They had been at a private school together years before, and though they had hardly met once since, the news had not failed to reach him from time to time with considerable detail, for the family lived near his own and between certain of the sisters there was great intimacy. Young Field had gone wild later, he remembered hearing about it all – drink, a woman, opium, or something of the sort – he could not exactly call to mind.

"Come in," he said at once, his anger vanishing. "There's been something wrong, I can see. Come in, and tell me all about it and perhaps I can help—" He hardly knew what to say, and stammered a lot more besides. The dark side of life, and the horror of it, belonged to a world that lay remote from his own select little atmosphere of books and dreamings. But he had a man's heart for all that.

He led the way across the hall, shutting the front door carefully behind him, and noticed as he did so that the other, though certainly sober, was unsteady on his legs, and evidently much exhausted. Marriott might not be able to pass his examinations, but he at least knew the symptoms of starvation – acute starvation, unless he was much mistaken – when they stared him in the face.

"Come along," he said cheerfully, and with genuine sympathy in his voice. "I'm glad to see you. I was going to have a bite of something to eat, and you're just in time to join me."

The other made no audible reply, and shuffled so feebly with his feet that Marriott took his arm by way of support. He noticed for the first time that the clothes hung on him with pitiful looseness. The broad frame was literally hardly more than a frame.

He was as thin as a skeleton. But, as he touched him, the sensation of faintness and dread returned. It only lasted a moment, and then passed off, and he ascribed it not unnaturally to the distress and shock of seeing a former friend in such a pitiful plight.

"Better let me guide you. It's shamefully dark – this hall. I'm always complaining," he said lightly, recognising by the weight upon his arm that the guidance was sorely needed, "but the old cat never does anything except promise." He led him to the sofa, wondering all the time where he had come from and how he had found out the address. It must be at least seven years since those days at the private school when they used to be such close friends.

"Now, if you'll forgive me for a minute," he said, "I'll get supper ready – such as it is. And don't bother to talk. Just take it easy on the sofa. I see you're dead tired. You can tell me about it afterwards, and we'll make plans."

The other sat down on the edge of the sofa and stared in silence, while Marriott got out the brown loaf, scones, and huge pot of marmalade that Edinburgh students always keep in their cupboards. His eyes shone with a brightness that suggested drugs, Marriott thought, stealing a glance at him from behind the cupboard door. He did not like yet to take a full square look. The fellow was in a bad way, and it would have been so like an examination to stare and wait for explanations. Besides, he was evidently almost too exhausted to speak. So, for reasons of delicacy – and for another reason as well which he could not exactly formulate to himself – he let his visitor rest apparently unnoticed, while he busied himself with the supper. He lit the spirit lamp to make cocoa, and when the water was boiling he drew up the table with the good things to the sofa, so that Field need not have even the trouble of moving to a chair.

"Now, let's tuck in," he said, "and afterwards we'll have a pipe and a chat. I'm reading for an exam, you know, and I always have something about this time. It's jolly to have a companion."

He looked up and caught his guest's eyes directed straight upon his own. An involuntary shudder ran through him from head to foot. The face opposite him was deadly white and wore a dreadful expression of pain and mental suffering.

"By Gad!" he said, jumping up, "I quite forgot. I've got some whisky somewhere. What an ass I am. I never touch it myself when I'm working like this."

He went to the cupboard and poured out a stiff glass which the other swallowed at a single gulp and without any water. Marriott watched him while he drank it, and at the same time noticed something else as well – Field's coat was all over dust, and on one shoulder was a bit of cobweb. It was perfectly dry; Field arrived on a soaking wet night without hat, umbrella, or overcoat, and yet perfectly dry, even dusty. Therefore he had been under cover. What did it all mean? Had he been hiding in the building?

It was very strange. Yet he volunteered nothing; and Marriott had pretty well made up his mind by this time that he would not ask any questions until he had eaten and slept. Food and sleep were obviously what the poor devil needed most and first – he was pleased with his powers of ready diagnosis – and it would not be fair to press him till he had recovered a bit.

They ate their supper together while the host carried on running a one-sided conversation, chiefly about himself and his exams and his 'old cat' of a landlady, so that the guest need not utter a single word unless he really wished to – which he evidently did not! But, while he toyed with his food, feeling no desire to eat, the other ate voraciously. To see a hungry man devour cold scones, stale oatcake, and brown bread laden with marmalade was a revelation to this inexperienced student who had never known what it was to be without at least three meals a day. He watched in spite of himself, wondering why the fellow did not choke in the process.

But Field seemed to be as sleepy as he was hungry. More than once his head dropped and he ceased to masticate the food in his mouth. Marriott had positively to shake him before he would go on with his meal. A stronger emotion will overcome a weaker, but this struggle between the sting of real hunger and the magical opiate of overpowering sleep was a curious sight to the student, who watched it with mingled astonishment and alarm. He had heard of the pleasure it was to feed hungry men, and watch them eat, but he had never actually witnessed it, and he had no idea it was like this. Field ate like an animal – gobbled, stuffed, gorged. Marriott forgot his reading, and began to feel something very much like a lump in his throat.

"Afraid there's been awfully little to offer you, old man," he managed to blurt out when at length the last scone had disappeared, and the rapid, one-sided meal was at an end. Field still made no reply, for he was almost asleep in his seat. He merely looked up wearily and gratefully.

"Now you must have some sleep, you know," he continued, "or you'll go to pieces. I shall be up all night reading for this blessed exam. You're more than welcome to my bed. Tomorrow we'll have a late breakfast and – and see what can be done – and make plans – I'm awfully good at making plans, you know," he added with an attempt at lightness.

Field maintained his 'dead sleepy' silence, but appeared to acquiesce, and the other led the way into the bedroom, apologising as he did so to this half-starved son of a baronet – whose own home was almost a palace – for the size of the room. The weary guest, however, made no pretence of thanks or politeness. He merely steadied himself on his friend's arm as he staggered across the room, and then, with all his clothes on, dropped his exhausted body on the bed. In less than a minute he was to all appearances sound asleep.

For several minutes Marriott stood in the open door and watched him; praying devoutly that he might never find himself in a like predicament, and then fell to wondering what he would do with his unbidden guest on the morrow. But he did not stop long to think, for the call of his books was imperative, and happen what might, he must see to it that he passed that examination.

Having again locked the door into the hall, he sat down to his books and resumed his notes on *materia medica* where he had left off when the bell rang. But it was difficult for some time to concentrate his mind on the subject. His thoughts kept wandering to the picture of that white-faced, strange-eyed fellow, starved and dirty, lying in his clothes and boots on the bed. He recalled their schooldays together before they had drifted apart, and how they had vowed eternal friendship – and all the rest of it. And now! What horrible straits to be in. How could any man let the love of dissipation take such hold upon him?

But one of their vows together Marriott, it seemed, had completely forgotten. Just now, at any rate, it lay too far in the background of his memory to be recalled.

Through the half-open door – the bedroom led out of the sitting-room and had no other door – came the sound of deep, long-drawn breathing, the regular, steady breathing of a tired man, so tired that, even to listen to it made Marriott almost want to go to sleep himself.

"He needed it," reflected the student, "and perhaps it came only just in time!"

Perhaps so; for outside the bitter wind from across the Forth howled cruelly and drove the rain in cold streams against the window-panes, and down the deserted streets. Long before Marriott settled down again properly to his reading, he heard distantly, as it were, through the sentences of the book, the heavy, deep breathing of the sleeper in the next room.

A couple of hours later, when he yawned and changed his books, he still heard the breathing, and went cautiously up to the door to look round.

At first the darkness of the room must have deceived him, or else his eyes were confused and dazzled by the recent glare of the reading lamp. For a minute or two he could make out nothing at all but dark lumps of furniture, the mass of the chest of drawers by the wall, and the white patch where his bath stood in the centre of the floor.

Then the bed came slowly into view. And on it he saw the outline of the sleeping body gradually take shape before his eyes, growing up strangely into the darkness, till it stood out in marked relief – the long black form against the white counterpane.

He could hardly help smiling. Field had not moved an inch. He watched him a moment or two and then returned to his books. The night was full of the singing voices of the wind and rain. There was no sound of traffic; no hansoms clattered over the cobbles, and it was still too early for the milk carts. He worked on steadily and conscientiously, only stopping now and again to change a book, or to sip some of the poisonous stuff that kept him awake and made his brain so active, and on these occasions Field's breathing was always distinctly audible in the room. Outside, the storm continued to howl, but inside the house all was stillness. The shade of the reading lamp threw all the light upon the littered table, leaving the other end of the room in comparative darkness. The bedroom door was exactly opposite him where he sat. There was nothing to disturb the worker, nothing but an occasional rush of wind against the windows, and a slight pain in his arm.

This pain, however, which he was unable to account for, grew once or twice very acute. It bothered him; and he tried to remember how, and when, he could have bruised himself so severely, but without success.

At length the page before him turned from yellow to grey, and there were sounds of wheels in the street below. It was four o'clock. Marriott leaned back and yawned prodigiously. Then he drew back the curtains. The storm had subsided and the Castle Rock was shrouded in mist. With another yawn he turned away from the dreary outlook and prepared to sleep the remaining four hours till breakfast on the sofa. Field was still breathing heavily in the next room, and he first tip-toed across the floor to take another look at him.

Peering cautiously round the half-opened door his first glance fell upon the bed now plainly discernible in the grey light of morning. He stared hard. Then he rubbed his eyes. Then he rubbed his eyes again and thrust his head farther round the edge of the door. With fixed eyes he stared harder still, and harder.

But it made no difference at all. He was staring into an empty room.

The sensation of fear he had felt when Field first appeared upon the scene returned suddenly, but with much greater force. He became conscious, too, that his left arm was throbbing violently and causing him great pain. He stood wondering, and staring, and trying to collect his thoughts. He was trembling from head to foot.

By a great effort of the will he left the support of the door and walked forward boldly into the room.

There, upon the bed, was the impress of a body, where Field had lain and slept. There was the mark of the head on the pillow, and the slight indentation at the foot of the bed where the boots had rested on the counterpane. And there, plainer than ever – for he was closer to it – was *the breathing*!

Marriott tried to pull himself together. With a great effort he found his voice and called his friend aloud by name!

"Field! Is that you? Where are you?"

There was no reply; but the breathing continued without interruption, coming directly from the bed. His voice had such an unfamiliar sound that Marriott did not care to repeat his questions, but he went down on his knees and examined the bed above and below, pulling the mattress off finally, and taking the coverings away separately one by one. But though the sounds continued there was no visible sign of Field, nor was there any space in which a human being, however small, could have concealed itself. He pulled the bed out from the wall, but the sound *stayed where it was*. It did not move with the bed.

Marriott, finding self-control a little difficult in his weary condition, at once set about a thorough search of the room. He went through the cupboard, the chest of drawers, the little alcove where the clothes hung – everything. But there was no sign of anyone. The small window near the ceiling was closed; and, anyhow, was not large enough to let a cat pass. The sitting-room door was locked on the inside; he could not have got out that way. Curious thoughts began to trouble Marriott's mind, bringing in their train unwelcome sensations. He grew more and more excited; he searched the bed again till it resembled the scene of a pillow fight; he searched both rooms, knowing all the time it was useless, – and then he searched again. A cold perspiration broke out all over his body; and the sound of heavy breathing, all this time, never ceased to come from the corner where Field had lain down to sleep.

Then he tried something else. He pushed the bed back exactly into its original position – and himself lay down upon it just where his guest had lain. But the same instant he sprang up again in a single bound. The breathing was close beside him, almost on his cheek, and between him and the wall! Not even a child could have squeezed into the space.

He went back into his sitting-room, opened the windows, welcoming all the light and air possible, and tried to think the whole matter over quietly and clearly. Men who read too hard, and slept too little, he knew were sometimes troubled with very vivid hallucinations. Again he calmly reviewed every incident of the night; his accurate sensations; the vivid details; the emotions stirred in him; the dreadful feast – no single hallucination could ever combine all these and cover so long a period of time. But with less satisfaction he thought of the recurring faintness, and curious sense of horror that had once or twice come over him, and then of the violent pains in his arm. These were quite unaccountable.

Moreover, now that he began to analyse and examine, there was one other thing that fell upon him like a sudden revelation: *During the whole time Field had not actually uttered a single word!* Yet, as though in mockery upon his reflections, there came ever from that inner room the sound of the breathing, long-drawn, deep, and regular. The thing was incredible. It was absurd.

Haunted by visions of brain fever and insanity, Marriott put on his cap and macintosh and left the house. The morning air on Arthur's Seat would blow the cobwebs from his brain; the scent of the heather, and above all, the sight of the sea. He roamed over the wet slopes above Holyrood for a couple of hours, and did not return until the exercise had shaken some of the horror out of his bones, and given him a ravening appetite into the bargain.

As he entered he saw that there was another man in the room, standing against the window with his back to the light. He recognised his fellow-student Greene, who was reading for the same examination.

"Read hard all night, Marriott," he said, "and thought I'd drop in here to compare notes and have some breakfast. You're out early?" he added, by way of a question. Marriott said he had a headache and a walk had helped it, and Greene nodded and said "Ah!" But when the girl had set the steaming porridge on the table and gone out again, he went on with rather a forced tone, "Didn't know you had any friends who drank, Marriott?"

This was obviously tentative, and Marriott replied drily that he did not know it either.

"Sounds just as if some chap were 'sleeping it off' in there, doesn't it, though?" persisted the other, with a nod in the direction of the bedroom, and looking curiously at his friend. The two men stared steadily at each other for several seconds, and then Marriott said earnestly –

"Then you hear it too, thank God!"

"Of course I hear it. The door's open. Sorry if I wasn't meant to."

"Oh, I don't mean that," said Marriott, lowering his voice. "But I'm awfully relieved. Let me explain. Of course, if you hear it too, then it's all right; but really it frightened me more than I can tell you. I thought I was going to have brain fever, or something, and you know what a lot depends on this exam. It always begins with sounds, or visions, or some sort of beastly hallucination, and I—"

"Rot!" ejaculated the other impatiently. "What *are* you talking about?"

"Now, listen to me, Greene," said Marriott, as calmly as he could, for the breathing was still plainly audible, "and I'll tell you what I mean, only don't interrupt." And thereupon he related exactly what had happened during the night, telling everything, even down to the pain in his arm. When it was over he got up from the table and crossed the room.

"You hear the breathing now plainly, don't you?" he said. Greene said he did. "Well, come with me, and we'll search the room together." The other, however, did not move from his chair.

"I've been in already," he said sheepishly; "I heard the sounds and thought it was you. The door was ajar – so I went in."

Marriott made no comment, but pushed the door open as wide as it would go. As it opened, the sound of breathing grew more and more distinct.

"*Someone* must be in there," said Greene under his breath.

"*Someone* is in there, but *where*?" said Marriott. Again he urged his friend to go in with him. But Greene refused point-blank; said he had been in once and had searched the room and there was nothing there. He would not go in again for a good deal.

They shut the door and retired into the other room to talk it all over with many pipes. Greene questioned his friend very closely, but without illuminating result, since questions cannot alter facts.

"The only thing that ought to have a proper, a logical, explanation is the pain in my arm," said Marriott, rubbing that member with an attempt at a smile. "It hurts so infernally and aches all the way up. I can't remember bruising it, though."

"Let me examine it for you," said Greene. "I'm awfully good at bones in spite of the examiners' opinion to the contrary." It was a relief to play the fool a bit, and Marriott took his coat off and rolled up his sleeve.

"By George, though, I'm bleeding!" he exclaimed. "Look here! What on earth's this?"

On the forearm, quite close to the wrist, was a thin red line. There was a tiny drop of apparently fresh blood on it. Greene came over and looked closely at it for some minutes. Then he sat back in his chair, looking curiously at his friend's face.

"You've scratched yourself without knowing it," he said presently.

"There's no sign of a bruise. It must be something else that made the arm ache."

Marriott sat very still, staring silently at his arm as though the solution of the whole mystery lay there actually written upon the skin.

"What's the matter? I see nothing very strange about a scratch," said Greene, in an unconvincing sort of voice. "It was your cuff links probably. Last night in your excitement—"

But Marriott, white to the very lips, was trying to speak. The sweat stood in great beads on his forehead. At last he leaned forward close to his friend's face.

"Look," he said, in a low voice that shook a little. "Do you see that red mark? I mean *underneath* what you call the scratch?"

Greene admitted he saw something or other, and Marriott wiped the place clean with his handkerchief and told him to look again more closely.

"Yes, I see," returned the other, lifting his head after a moment's careful inspection. "It looks like an old scar."

"It *is* an old scar," whispered Marriott, his lips trembling. "*Now* it all comes back to me."

"All what?" Greene fidgeted on his chair. He tried to laugh, but without success. His friend seemed bordering on collapse.

"Hush! Be quiet, and – I'll tell you," he said. "*Field made that scar.*"

For a whole minute the two men looked each other full in the face without speaking.

"Field made that scar!" repeated Marriott at length in a louder voice.

"Field! You mean – last night?"

"No, not last night. Years ago – at school, with his knife. And I made a scar in his arm with mine." Marriott was talking rapidly now.

"We exchanged drops of blood in each other's cuts. He put a drop into my arm and I put one into his—"

"In the name of heaven, what for?"

"It was a boys' compact. We made a sacred pledge, a bargain. I remember it all perfectly now. We had been reading some dreadful book and we swore to appear to one another – I mean, whoever died first swore to show himself to the other. And we sealed the compact with each other's blood. I remember it all so well – the hot summer afternoon in the playground, seven years ago – and one of the masters caught us and confiscated the knives – and I have never thought of it again to this day—"

"And you mean—" stammered Greene.

But Marriott made no answer. He got up and crossed the room and lay down wearily upon the sofa, hiding his face in his hands.

Greene himself was a bit non-plussed. He left his friend alone for a little while, thinking it all over again. Suddenly an idea seemed to strike him. He went over to where Marriott still lay motionless on the sofa and roused him. In any case it was better to face the matter, whether there was an explanation or not. Giving in was always the silly exit.

"I say, Marriott," he began, as the other turned his white face up to him. "There's no good being so upset about it. I mean – if it's all an hallucination we know what to do. And if it isn't – well, we know what to think, don't we?"

"I suppose so. But it frightens me horribly for some reason," returned his friend in a hushed voice. "And that poor devil—"

"But, after all, if the worst is true and – and that chap *has* kept his promise – well, he has, that's all, isn't it?"

Marriott nodded.

"There's only one thing that occurs to me," Greene went on, "and that is, are you quite sure that – that he really ate like that – I mean that he actually *ate anything at all*?" he finished, blurting out all his thought.

Marriott stared at him for a moment and then said he could easily make certain. He spoke quietly. After the main shock no lesser surprise could affect him.

"I put the things away myself," he said, "after we had finished. They are on the third shelf in that cupboard. No one's touched 'em since."

He pointed without getting up, and Greene took the hint and went over to look.

"Exactly," he said, after a brief examination; "just as I thought. It was partly hallucination, at any rate. The things haven't been touched. Come and see for yourself."

Together they examined the shelf. There was the brown loaf, the plate of stale scones, the oatcake, all untouched. Even the glass of whisky Marriott had poured out stood there with the whisky still in it.

"You were feeding – no one," said Greene. "Field ate and drank nothing. He was not there at all!"

"But the breathing?" urged the other in a low voice, staring with a dazed expression on his face.

Greene did not answer. He walked over to the bedroom, while Marriott followed him with his eyes. He opened the door, and listened. There was no need for words. The sound of deep, regular breathing came floating through the air. There was no hallucination about that, at any rate. Marriott could hear it where he stood on the other side of the room.

Greene closed the door and came back. "There's only one thing to do," he declared with decision. "Write home and find out about him, and meanwhile come and finish your reading in my rooms. I've got an extra bed."

"Agreed," returned the Fourth Year Man; "there's no hallucination about that exam; I must pass that whatever happens."

And this was what they did.

It was about a week later when Marriott got the answer from his sister. Part of it he read out to Greene –

"It is curious," she wrote, "that in your letter you should have enquired after Field. It seems a terrible thing, but you know only a short while ago Sir John's patience became exhausted, and he turned him out of the house, they say without a penny. Well, what do you think? He has killed himself. At least, it looks like suicide. Instead of leaving the house, he went down into the cellar and simply starved himself to death.... They're trying to suppress it, of course, but I heard it all from my maid, who got it from their footman.... They found the body on the 14th and the doctor said he had died about twelve hours before.... He was dreadfully thin...."

"Then he died on the 13th," said Greene.

Marriott nodded.

"That's the very night he came to see you."

Marriott nodded again.

**If you enjoyed this, you might also like...**
The Occupant of the Room, see page 408
Tongues of Fire, see page 206

# The Empty House

**CERTAIN HOUSES**, like certain persons, manage somehow to proclaim at once their character for evil. In the case of the latter, no particular feature need betray them; they may boast an open countenance and an ingenuous smile; and yet a little of their company leaves the unalterable conviction that there is something radically amiss with their being: that they are evil. Willy nilly, they seem to communicate an atmosphere of secret and wicked thoughts which makes those in their immediate neighbourhood shrink from them as from a thing diseased.

And, perhaps, with houses the same principle is operative, and it is the aroma of evil deeds committed under a particular roof, long after the actual doers have passed away, that makes the gooseflesh come and the hair rise. Something of the original passion of the evil-doer, and of the horror felt by his victim, enters the heart of the innocent watcher, and he becomes suddenly conscious of tingling nerves, creeping skin, and a chilling of the blood. He is terror-stricken without apparent cause.

There was manifestly nothing in the external appearance of this particular house to bear out the tales of the horror that was said to reign within. It was neither lonely nor unkempt. It stood, crowded into a corner of the square, and looked exactly like the houses on either side of it. It had the same number of windows as its neighbours; the same balcony overlooking the gardens; the same white steps leading up to the heavy black front door; and, in the rear, there was the same narrow strip of green, with neat box borders, running up to the wall that divided it from the backs of the adjoining houses. Apparently, too, the number of chimney pots on the roof was the same; the breadth and angle of the eaves; and even the height of the dirty area railings.

And yet this house in the square, that seemed precisely similar to its fifty ugly neighbours, was as a matter of fact entirely different – horribly different.

Wherein lay this marked, invisible difference is impossible to say. It cannot be ascribed wholly to the imagination, because persons who had spent some time in the house, knowing nothing of the facts, had declared positively that certain rooms were so disagreeable they would rather die than enter them again, and that the atmosphere of the whole house produced in them symptoms of a genuine terror; while the series of innocent tenants who had tried to live in it and been forced to decamp at the shortest possible notice, was indeed little less than a scandal in the town.

When Shorthouse arrived to pay a 'week-end' visit to his Aunt Julia in her little house on the sea-front at the other end of the town, he found her charged to the brim with mystery and excitement. He had only received her telegram that morning, and he had come anticipating boredom; but the moment he touched her hand and kissed her apple-skin wrinkled cheek, he caught the first wave of her electrical condition. The impression deepened when he learned that there were to be no other visitors, and that he had been telegraphed for with a very special object.

Something was in the wind, and the 'something' would doubtless bear fruit; for this elderly spinster aunt, with a mania for psychical research, had brains as well as will power, and by hook or by crook she usually managed to accomplish her ends. The revelation was made soon after tea, when she sidled close up to him as they paced slowly along the sea-front in the dusk.

"I've got the keys," she announced in a delighted, yet half awesome voice. "Got them till Monday!"

"The keys of the bathing-machine, or—?" he asked innocently, looking from the sea to the town. Nothing brought her so quickly to the point as feigning stupidity.

"Neither," she whispered. "I've got the keys of the haunted house in the square – and I'm going there tonight."

Shorthouse was conscious of the slightest possible tremor down his back. He dropped his teasing tone. Something in her voice and manner thrilled him. She was in earnest.

"But you can't go alone—" he began.

"That's why I wired for you," she said with decision.

He turned to look at her. The ugly, lined, enigmatical face was alive with excitement. There was the glow of genuine enthusiasm round it like a halo. The eyes shone. He caught another wave of her excitement, and a second tremor, more marked than the first, accompanied it.

"Thanks, Aunt Julia," he said politely; "thanks awfully."

"I should not dare to go quite alone," she went on, raising her voice; "but with you I should enjoy it immensely. You're afraid of nothing, I know."

"Thanks *so* much," he said again. "Er – is anything likely to happen?"

"A great deal *has* happened," she whispered, "though it's been most cleverly hushed up. Three tenants have come and gone in the last few months, and the house is said to be empty for good now."

In spite of himself Shorthouse became interested. His aunt was so very much in earnest.

"The house is very old indeed," she went on, "and the story – an unpleasant one – dates a long way back. It has to do with a murder committed by a jealous stableman who had some affair with a servant in the house. One night he managed to secrete himself in the cellar, and when everyone was asleep, he crept upstairs to the servants' quarters, chased the girl down to the next landing, and before anyone could come to the rescue threw her bodily over the banisters into the hall below."

"And the stableman—?"

"Was caught, I believe, and hanged for murder; but it all happened a century ago, and I've not been able to get more details of the story."

Shorthouse now felt his interest thoroughly aroused; but, though he was not particularly nervous for himself, he hesitated a little on his aunt's account.

"On one condition," he said at length.

"Nothing will prevent my going," she said firmly; "but I may as well hear your condition."

"That you guarantee your power of self-control if anything really horrible happens. I mean – that you are sure you won't get too frightened."

"Jim," she said scornfully, "I'm not young, I know, nor are my nerves; but *with you* I should be afraid of nothing in the world!"

This, of course, settled it, for Shorthouse had no pretensions to being other than a very ordinary young man, and an appeal to his vanity was irresistible. He agreed to go.

Instinctively, by a sort of sub-conscious preparation, he kept himself and his forces well in hand the whole evening, compelling an accumulative reserve of control by that nameless inward process of gradually putting all the emotions away and turning the key upon them – a process difficult to describe, but wonderfully effective, as all men who have lived through severe trials of the inner man well understand. Later, it stood him in good stead.

But it was not until half-past ten, when they stood in the hall, well in the glare of friendly lamps and still surrounded by comforting human influences, that he had to make the first call upon this store of collected strength. For, once the door was closed, and he saw the deserted silent street stretching away white in the moonlight before them, it came to him clearly that the real test that night would be in dealing with *two fears* instead of one. He would have to carry his aunt's fear as well as his own. And, as he glanced down at her sphinx-like countenance and realised that it might assume no pleasant aspect in a rush of real terror, he felt satisfied with only one thing in the whole adventure – that he had confidence in his own will and power to stand against any shock that might come.

Slowly they walked along the empty streets of the town; a bright autumn moon silvered the roofs, casting deep shadows; there was no breath of wind; and the trees in the formal gardens by the sea-front watched them silently as they passed along. To his aunt's occasional remarks Shorthouse made no reply, realising that she was simply surrounding herself with mental buffers – saying ordinary things to prevent herself thinking of extraordinary things. Few windows showed lights, and from scarcely a single chimney came smoke or sparks. Shorthouse had already begun to notice everything, even the smallest details. Presently they stopped at the street corner and looked up at the name on the side of the house full in the moonlight, and with one accord, but without remark, turned into the square and crossed over to the side of it that lay in shadow.

"The number of the house is thirteen," whispered a voice at his side; and neither of them made the obvious reference, but passed across the broad sheet of moonlight and began to march up the pavement in silence.

It was about half-way up the square that Shorthouse felt an arm slipped quietly but significantly into his own, and knew then that their adventure had begun in earnest, and that his companion was already yielding imperceptibly to the influences against them. She needed support.

A few minutes later they stopped before a tall, narrow house that rose before them into the night, ugly in shape and painted a dingy white. Shutterless windows, without blinds, stared down upon them, shining here and there in the moonlight. There were weather streaks in the wall and cracks in the paint, and the balcony bulged out from the first floor a little unnaturally. But, beyond this generally forlorn appearance of an unoccupied house, there was nothing at first sight to single out this particular mansion for the evil character it had most certainly acquired.

Taking a look over their shoulders to make sure they had not been followed, they went boldly up the steps and stood against the huge black door that fronted them forbiddingly. But the first wave of nervousness was now upon them, and Shorthouse fumbled a long time with the key before he could fit it into the lock at all. For a moment, if truth were told, they both hoped it would not open, for they were a prey to various unpleasant emotions as they stood there on the threshold of their ghostly adventure. Shorthouse, shuffling with the key and hampered by the steady weight on his arm, certainly felt the solemnity of the moment. It was as if the whole world – for all experience seemed at that instant concentrated in his own consciousness – were listening to the grating noise of that key. A stray puff of wind wandering down the empty street woke a momentary rustling in the trees behind them, but otherwise this rattling of the key was the only sound audible; and at last it turned in the lock and the heavy door swung open and revealed a yawning gulf of darkness beyond.

With a last glance at the moonlit square, they passed quickly in, and the door slammed behind them with a roar that echoed prodigiously through empty halls and passages. But, instantly, with the echoes, another sound made itself heard, and Aunt Julia leaned suddenly so heavily upon him that he had to take a step backwards to save himself from falling.

A man had coughed close beside them – so close that it seemed they must have been actually by his side in the darkness.

With the possibility of practical jokes in his mind, Shorthouse at once swung his heavy stick in the direction of the sound; but it met nothing more solid than air. He heard his aunt give a little gasp beside him.

"There's someone here," she whispered; "I heard him."

"Be quiet!" he said sternly. "It was nothing but the noise of the front door."

"Oh! get a light – quick!" she added, as her nephew, fumbling with a box of matches, opened it upside down and let them all fall with a rattle on to the stone floor.

The sound, however, was not repeated; and there was no evidence of retreating footsteps. In another minute they had a candle burning, using an empty end of a cigar case as a holder; and when the first flare had died down he held the impromptu lamp aloft and surveyed the scene. And it was dreary enough in all conscience, for there is nothing more desolate in all the abodes of men than an unfurnished house dimly lit, silent, and forsaken, and yet tenanted by rumour with the memories of evil and violent histories.

They were standing in a wide hall-way; on their left was the open door of a spacious dining-room, and in front the hall ran, ever narrowing, into a long, dark passage that led apparently to the top of the kitchen stairs. The broad uncarpeted staircase rose in a sweep before them, everywhere draped in shadows, except for a single spot about half-way up where the moonlight came in through the window and fell on a bright patch on the boards. This shaft of light shed a faint radiance above and below it, lending to the objects within its reach a misty outline that was infinitely more suggestive and ghostly than complete darkness. Filtered moonlight always seems to paint faces on the surrounding gloom, and as Shorthouse peered up into the well of darkness and thought of the countless empty rooms and passages in the upper part of the old house, he caught himself longing again for the safety of the moonlit square, or the cosy, bright drawing-room they had left an hour before. Then realising that these thoughts were dangerous, he thrust them away again and summoned all his energy for concentration on the present.

"Aunt Julia," he said aloud, severely, "we must now go through the house from top to bottom and make a thorough search."

The echoes of his voice died away slowly all over the building, and in the intense silence that followed he turned to look at her. In the candle-light he saw that her face was already ghastly pale; but she dropped his arm for a moment and said in a whisper, stepping close in front of him –

"I agree. We must be sure there's no one hiding. That's the first thing."

She spoke with evident effort, and he looked at her with admiration.

"You feel quite sure of yourself? It's not too late—"

"I think so," she whispered, her eyes shifting nervously toward the shadows behind. "Quite sure, only one thing—"

"What's that?"

"You must never leave me alone for an instant."

"As long as you understand that any sound or appearance must be investigated at once, for to hesitate means to admit fear. That is fatal."

"Agreed," she said, a little shakily, after a moment's hesitation. "I'll try—"

Arm in arm, Shorthouse holding the dripping candle and the stick, while his aunt carried the cloak over her shoulders, figures of utter comedy to all but themselves, they began a systematic search.

Stealthily, walking on tip-toe and shading the candle lest it should betray their presence through the shutterless windows, they went first into the big dining-room. There was not a stick of furniture to be seen. Bare walls, ugly mantel-pieces and empty grates stared at them. Everything, they felt, resented their intrusion, watching them, as it were, with veiled eyes; whispers followed them; shadows flitted noiselessly to right and left; something seemed ever at their back, watching, waiting an opportunity to do them injury. There was the inevitable sense that operations which went on when the room was empty had been temporarily suspended till they were well out of the way again. The whole dark interior of the old building seemed to become a malignant Presence that rose up, warning them to desist and mind their own business; every moment the strain on the nerves increased.

Out of the gloomy dining-room they passed through large folding doors into a sort of library or smoking-room, wrapt equally in silence, darkness, and dust; and from this they regained the hall near the top of the back stairs.

Here a pitch black tunnel opened before them into the lower regions, and – it must be confessed – they hesitated. But only for a minute. With the worst of the night still to come it was essential to turn from nothing. Aunt Julia stumbled at the top step of the dark descent, ill lit by the flickering candle, and even Shorthouse felt at least half the decision go out of his legs.

"Come on!" he said peremptorily, and his voice ran on and lost itself in the dark, empty spaces below.

"I'm coming," she faltered, catching his arm with unnecessary violence.

They went a little unsteadily down the stone steps, a cold, damp air meeting them in the face, close and mal-odorous. The kitchen, into which the stairs led along a narrow passage, was large, with a lofty ceiling. Several doors opened out of it – some into cupboards with empty jars still standing on the shelves, and others into horrible little ghostly back offices, each colder and less inviting than the last. Black beetles scurried over the floor, and once, when they knocked against a deal table standing in a corner, something about the size of a cat jumped down with a rush and fled, scampering across the stone floor into the darkness. Everywhere there was a sense of recent occupation, an impression of sadness and gloom.

Leaving the main kitchen, they next went towards the scullery. The door was standing ajar, and as they pushed it open to its full extent Aunt Julia uttered a piercing scream, which she instantly tried to stifle by placing her hand over her mouth. For a second Shorthouse stood stock-still, catching his breath. He felt as if his spine had suddenly become hollow and someone had filled it with particles of ice.

Facing them, directly in their way between the doorposts, stood the figure of a woman. She had dishevelled hair and wildly staring eyes, and her face was terrified and white as death.

She stood there motionless for the space of a single second. Then the candle flickered and she was gone – gone utterly – and the door framed nothing but empty darkness.

"Only the beastly jumping candle-light," he said quickly, in a voice that sounded like someone else's and was only half under control. "Come on, aunt. There's nothing there."

He dragged her forward. With a clattering of feet and a great appearance of boldness they went on, but over his body the skin moved as if crawling ants covered it, and he knew by the weight on his arm that he was supplying the force of locomotion for two. The scullery was cold, bare, and empty; more like a large prison cell than anything else. They went round it, tried the door into the yard, and the windows, but found them all fastened securely. His aunt moved beside him like a person in a dream. Her eyes were tightly shut, and she seemed merely to follow the pressure of his arm. Her courage filled him with amazement. At the same time he noticed that a certain odd change had come over her face, a change which somehow evaded his power of analysis.

"There's nothing here, aunty," he repeated aloud quickly. "Let's go upstairs and see the rest of the house. Then we'll choose a room to wait up in."

She followed him obediently, keeping close to his side, and they locked the kitchen door behind them. It was a relief to get up again. In the hall there was more light than before, for the moon had travelled a little further down the stairs. Cautiously they began to go up into the dark vault of the upper house, the boards creaking under their weight.

On the first floor they found the large double drawing-rooms, a search of which revealed nothing. Here also was no sign of furniture or recent occupancy; nothing but dust and neglect and shadows. They opened the big folding doors between front and back drawing-rooms and then came out again to the landing and went on upstairs.

They had not gone up more than a dozen steps when they both simultaneously stopped to listen, looking into each other's eyes with a new apprehension across the flickering candle flame. From the room they had left hardly ten seconds before came the sound of doors quietly closing. It was beyond all question; they heard the booming noise that accompanies the shutting of heavy doors, followed by the sharp catching of the latch.

"We must go back and see," said Shorthouse briefly, in a low tone, and turning to go downstairs again.

Somehow she managed to drag after him, her feet catching in her dress, her face livid.

When they entered the front drawing-room it was plain that the folding doors had been closed – half a minute before. Without hesitation Shorthouse opened them. He almost expected to see someone facing him in the back room; but only darkness and cold air met him. They went through both rooms, finding nothing unusual. They tried in every way to make the doors close of themselves, but there was not wind enough even to set the candle flame flickering. The doors would not move without strong pressure. All was silent as the grave. Undeniably the rooms were utterly empty, and the house utterly still.

"It's beginning," whispered a voice at his elbow which he hardly recognised as his aunt's.

He nodded acquiescence, taking out his watch to note the time. It was fifteen minutes before midnight; he made the entry of exactly what had occurred in his notebook, setting the candle in its case upon the floor in order to do so. It took a moment or two to balance it safely against the wall.

Aunt Julia always declared that at this moment she was not actually watching him, but had turned her head towards the inner room, where she fancied she heard something moving; but, at any rate, both positively agreed that there came a sound of rushing feet, heavy and very swift – and the next instant the candle was out!

But to Shorthouse himself had come more than this, and he has always thanked his fortunate stars that it came to him alone and not to his aunt too. For, as he rose from the stooping position of balancing the candle, and before it was actually extinguished, a face thrust itself forward so close to his own that he could almost have touched it with his lips. It was a face working with passion; a man's face, dark, with thick features, and angry, savage eyes. It belonged to a common man, and it was evil in its ordinary normal expression, no doubt, but as he saw it, alive with intense, aggressive emotion, it was a malignant and terrible human countenance.

There was no movement of the air; nothing but the sound of rushing feet – stockinged or muffled feet; the apparition of the face; and the almost simultaneous extinguishing of the candle.

In spite of himself, Shorthouse uttered a little cry, nearly losing his balance as his aunt clung to him with her whole weight in one moment of real, uncontrollable terror. She made no sound, but simply seized him bodily. Fortunately, however, she had seen nothing, but had only heard the rushing feet, for her control returned almost at once, and he was able to disentangle himself and strike a match.

The shadows ran away on all sides before the glare, and his aunt stooped down and groped for the cigar case with the precious candle. Then they discovered that the candle had not been *blown* out at all; it had been *crushed* out. The wick was pressed down into the wax, which was flattened as if by some smooth, heavy instrument.

How his companion so quickly overcame her terror, Shorthouse never properly understood; but his admiration for her self-control increased tenfold, and at the same time served to feed his own dying flame – for which he was undeniably grateful. Equally inexplicable to him was the evidence of physical force they had just witnessed. He at once suppressed the memory of stories he had heard of 'physical mediums' and their dangerous phenomena; for if these were true, and either his aunt or himself was unwittingly a physical medium, it meant that they were simply aiding to focus the forces of a haunted house already charged to the brim. It was like walking with unprotected lamps among uncovered stores of gun-powder.

So, with as little reflection as possible, he simply relit the candle and went up to the next floor. The arm in his trembled, it is true, and his own tread was often uncertain, but they went on with thoroughness, and after a search revealing nothing they climbed the last flight of stairs to the top floor of all.

Here they found a perfect nest of small servants' rooms, with broken pieces of furniture, dirty cane-bottomed chairs, chests of drawers, cracked mirrors, and decrepit bedsteads. The rooms had low sloping ceilings already hung here and there with cobwebs, small windows, and badly plastered walls – a depressing and dismal region which they were glad to leave behind.

It was on the stroke of midnight when they entered a small room on the third floor, close to the top of the stairs, and arranged to make themselves comfortable for the remainder of their adventure. It was absolutely bare, and was said to be the room – then used as a clothes closet – into which the infuriated groom had chased his victim and finally caught her. Outside, across the narrow landing, began the stairs leading up to the floor above, and the servants' quarters where they had just searched.

In spite of the chilliness of the night there was something in the air of this room that cried for an open window. But there was more than this. Shorthouse could only describe it by saying that he felt less master of himself here than in any other part of the house. There was something that acted directly on the nerves, tiring the resolution, enfeebling the will. He was conscious of this result before he had been in the room five minutes, and it was in the short time they stayed there that he suffered the wholesale depletion of his vital forces, which was, for himself, the chief horror of the whole experience.

They put the candle on the floor of the cupboard, leaving the door a few inches ajar, so that there was no glare to confuse the eyes, and no shadow to shift about on walls and ceiling. Then they spread the cloak on the floor and sat down to wait, with their backs against the wall.

Shorthouse was within two feet of the door on to the landing; his position commanded a good view of the main staircase leading down into the darkness, and also of the beginning of the servants' stairs going to the floor above; the heavy stick lay beside him within easy reach.

The moon was now high above the house. Through the open window they could see the comforting stars like friendly eyes watching in the sky. One by one the clocks of the town struck midnight, and when the sounds died away the deep silence of a windless night fell again over everything. Only the boom of the sea, far away and lugubrious, filled the air with hollow murmurs.

Inside the house the silence became awful; awful, he thought, because any minute now it might be broken by sounds portending terror. The strain of waiting told more and more severely on the nerves; they talked in whispers when they talked at all, for their voices aloud sounded queer and unnatural. A chilliness, not altogether due to the night air, invaded the room, and made them cold. The influences against them, whatever these might be, were slowly robbing them of self-confidence, and the power of decisive action; their forces were on the wane, and the possibility of real fear took on a new and terrible meaning. He began to tremble for the elderly woman by his side, whose pluck could hardly save her beyond a certain extent.

He heard the blood singing in his veins. It sometimes seemed so loud that he fancied it prevented his hearing properly certain other sounds that were beginning very faintly to make themselves audible in the depths of the house. Every time he fastened his attention on these sounds, they instantly ceased. They certainly came no nearer. Yet he could not rid himself of the idea that movement was going on somewhere in the lower regions of the house. The drawing-room floor, where the doors had been so strangely closed, seemed too near; the sounds were further off than that. He thought of the great kitchen, with the scurrying black-beetles, and of the dismal little scullery; but, somehow or other, they did not seem to come from there either. Surely they were not *outside* the house!

Then, suddenly, the truth flashed into his mind, and for the space of a minute he felt as if his blood had stopped flowing and turned to ice.

The sounds were not downstairs at all; they were *upstairs* – upstairs, somewhere among those horrid gloomy little servants' rooms with their bits of broken furniture, low ceilings, and cramped windows – upstairs where the victim had first been disturbed and stalked to her death.

And the moment he discovered where the sounds were, he began to hear them more clearly. It was the sound of feet, moving stealthily along the passage overhead, in and out among the rooms, and past the furniture.

He turned quickly to steal a glance at the motionless figure seated beside him, to note whether she had shared his discovery. The faint candle-light coming through the crack in the cupboard door, threw her strongly-marked face into vivid relief against the white of the wall. But it was something else that made him catch his breath and stare again. An extraordinary something had come into her face and seemed to spread over her features like a mask; it smoothed out the deep lines and drew the skin everywhere a little tighter so that the wrinkles disappeared; it brought into the face – with the sole exception of the old eyes – an appearance of youth and almost of childhood.

He stared in speechless amazement – amazement that was dangerously near to horror. It was his aunt's face indeed, but it was her face of forty years ago, the vacant innocent face of a girl. He had heard stories of that strange effect of terror which could wipe a human countenance clean of other emotions, obliterating all previous expressions; but he had never realised that it could be literally true, or could mean anything so simply horrible as what he now saw. For the dreadful signature of overmastering fear was written plainly in that utter vacancy of the girlish face beside him; and when, feeling his intense gaze, she turned to look at him, he instinctively closed his eyes tightly to shut out the sight.

Yet, when he turned a minute later, his feelings well in hand, he saw to his intense relief another expression; his aunt was smiling, and though the face was deathly white, the awful veil had lifted and the normal look was returning.

"Anything wrong?" was all he could think of to say at the moment. And the answer was eloquent, coming from such a woman.

"I feel cold – and a little frightened," she whispered.

He offered to close the window, but she seized hold of him and begged him not to leave her side even for an instant.

"It's upstairs, I know," she whispered, with an odd half laugh; "but I can't possibly go up."

But Shorthouse thought otherwise, knowing that in action lay their best hope of self-control.

He took the brandy flask and poured out a glass of neat spirit, stiff enough to help anybody over anything. She swallowed it with a little shiver. His only idea now was to get out of the house before her collapse became inevitable; but this could not safely be done by turning tail and running from the enemy. Inaction was no longer possible; every minute he was growing less master of himself, and desperate, aggressive measures were imperative without further delay. Moreover, the action must be taken *towards* the enemy, not away from it; the climax, if necessary and unavoidable, would have to be faced boldly. He could do it now; but in ten minutes he might not have the force left to act for himself, much less for both!

Upstairs, the sounds were meanwhile becoming louder and closer, accompanied by occasional creaking of the boards. Someone was moving stealthily about, stumbling now and then awkwardly against the furniture.

Waiting a few moments to allow the tremendous dose of spirits to produce its effect, and knowing this would last but a short time under the circumstances, Shorthouse then quietly got on his feet, saying in a determined voice –

"Now, Aunt Julia, we'll go upstairs and find out what all this noise is about. You must come too. It's what we agreed."

He picked up his stick and went to the cupboard for the candle. A limp form rose shakily beside him breathing hard, and he heard a voice say very faintly something about being "ready to come". The woman's courage amazed him; it was so much greater than his own; and, as they advanced, holding aloft the dripping candle, some subtle force exhaled from this trembling, white-faced old woman at his side that was the true source of his inspiration. It held something really great that shamed him and gave him the support without which he would have proved far less equal to the occasion.

They crossed the dark landing, avoiding with their eyes the deep black space over the banisters. Then they began to mount the narrow staircase to meet the sounds which, minute by minute, grew louder and nearer. About half-way up the stairs Aunt Julia stumbled and Shorthouse turned to catch her by the arm, and just at that moment there came a terrific crash in the servants' corridor overhead. It was instantly followed by a shrill, agonised scream that was a cry of terror and a cry for help melted into one.

Before they could move aside, or go down a single step, someone came rushing along the passage overhead, blundering horribly, racing madly, at full speed, three steps at a time, down the very staircase where they stood. The steps were light and uncertain; but close behind them sounded the heavier tread of another person, and the staircase seemed to shake.

Shorthouse and his companion just had time to flatten themselves against the wall when the jumble of flying steps was upon them, and two persons, with the slightest possible interval between them, dashed past at full speed. It was a perfect whirlwind of sound breaking in upon the midnight silence of the empty building.

The two runners, pursuer and pursued, had passed clean through them where they stood, and already with a thud the boards below had received first one, then the other. Yet they had seen absolutely nothing – not a hand, or arm, or face, or even a shred of flying clothing.

There came a second's pause. Then the first one, the lighter of the two, obviously the pursued one, ran with uncertain footsteps into the little room which Shorthouse and his aunt had just left. The heavier one followed. There was a sound of scuffling, gasping, and smothered screaming; and then out on to the landing came the step – of a single person *treading weightily*.

A dead silence followed for the space of half a minute, and then was heard a rushing sound through the air. It was followed by a dull, crashing thud in the depths of the house below – on the stone floor of the hall.

Utter silence reigned after. Nothing moved. The flame of the candle was steady. It had been steady the whole time, and the air had been undisturbed by any movement whatsoever. Palsied with terror, Aunt Julia, without waiting for her companion, began fumbling her way downstairs; she was crying gently to herself, and when Shorthouse put his arm round her and half carried her he felt that she was trembling like a leaf. He went into the little room and picked up the cloak from the floor, and, arm in arm, walking very slowly, without speaking a word or looking once behind them, they marched down the three flights into the hall.

In the hall they saw nothing, but the whole way down the stairs they were conscious that someone followed them; step by step; when they went faster *it* was left behind, and when they went more slowly *it* caught them up. But never once did they look behind to see; and at each turning of the staircase they lowered their eyes for fear of the following horror they might see upon the stairs above.

With trembling hands Shorthouse opened the front door, and they walked out into the moonlight and drew a deep breath of the cool night air blowing in from the sea.

**If you enjoyed this, you might also like…**
The Listener, see page 382
The Decoy, see page 463

# The Listener

*Sept. 4.* – I have hunted all over London for rooms suited to my income – £120 a year – and have at last found them. Two rooms, without modern conveniences, it is true, and in an old, ramshackle building, but within a stone's throw of P— Place and in an eminently respectable street. The rent is only £25 a year. I had begun to despair when at last I found them by chance.

The chance was a mere chance, and unworthy of record. I had to sign a lease for a year, and I did so willingly. The furniture from our old place in Hampshire, which has been stored so long, will just suit them.

*Oct. 1.* – Here I am in my two rooms, in the centre of London, and not far from the offices of the periodicals, where occasionally I dispose of an article or two. The building is at the end of a cul-de-sac. The alley is well paved and clean, and lined chiefly with the backs of sedate and institutional-looking buildings. There is a stable in it. My own house is dignified with the title of 'Chambers'. I feel as if one day the honour must prove too much for it, and it will swell with pride – and fall asunder. It is very old. The floor of my sitting-room has valleys and low hills on it, and the top of the door slants away from the ceiling with a glorious disregard of what is usual.

They must have quarrelled – fifty years ago – and have been going apart ever since.

*Oct. 2.* – My landlady is old and thin, with a faded, dusty face. She is uncommunicative. The few words she utters seem to cost her pain. Probably her lungs are half choked with dust. She keeps my rooms as free from this commodity as possible, and has the assistance of a strong girl who brings up the breakfast and lights the fire. As I have said already, she is not communicative.

In reply to pleasant efforts on my part she informed me briefly that I was the only occupant of the house at present. My rooms had not been occupied for some years. There had been other gentlemen upstairs, but they had left.

She never looks straight at me when she speaks, but fixes her dim eyes on my middle waistcoat button, till I get nervous and begin to think it isn't on straight, or is the wrong sort of button altogether.

*Oct. 8.* – My week's book is nicely kept, and so far is reasonable. Milk and sugar 7d., bread 6d., butter 8d., marmalade 6d., eggs 1s. 8d., laundress 2s. 9d., oil 6d., attendance 5s.; total 12s. 2d.

The landlady has a son who, she told me, is "somethink on a homnibus". He comes occasionally to see her. I think he drinks, for he talks very loud, regardless of the hour of the day or night, and tumbles about over the furniture downstairs.

All the morning I sit indoors writing – articles; verses for the comic papers; a novel I've been 'at' for three years, and concerning which I have dreams; a children's book, in which the imagination has free rein; and another book which is to last as long as myself, since it is an honest record of my soul's advance or retreat in the struggle of life. Besides these, I keep a book of poems which I use as a safety valve, and concerning which I have no dreams whatsoever.

Between the lot I am always occupied. In the afternoons I generally try to take a walk for my health's sake, through Regent's Park, into Kensington Gardens, or farther afield to Hampstead Heath.

*Oct. 10.* – Everything went wrong today. I have two eggs for breakfast. This morning one of them was bad. I rang the bell for Emily. When she came in I was reading the paper, and, without looking up, I said, "Egg's bad." "Oh, is it, sir?" she said; "I'll get another one," and went out, taking the egg with her. I waited my breakfast for her return, which was in five minutes. She put the new egg on the table and went away. But, when I looked down, I saw that she had taken away the good egg and left the bad one – all green and yellow – in the slop basin. I rang again.

"You've taken the wrong egg," I said.

"Oh!" she exclaimed; "I thought the one I took down didn't smell so very bad." In due time she returned with the good egg, and I resumed my breakfast with two eggs, but less appetite. It was all very trivial, to be sure, but so stupid that I felt annoyed. The character of that egg influenced everything I did. I wrote a bad article, and tore it up. I got a bad headache. I used bad words – to myself. Everything was bad, so I 'chucked' work and went for a long walk.

I dined at a cheap chop-house on my way back, and reached home about nine o'clock.

Rain was just beginning to fall as I came in, and the wind was rising. It promised an ugly night. The alley looked dismal and dreary, and the hall of the house, as I passed through it, felt chilly as a tomb. It was the first stormy night I had experienced in my new quarters. The draughts were awful. They came criss-cross, met in the middle of the room, and formed eddies and whirlpools and cold silent currents that almost lifted the hair of my head. I stuffed up the sashes of the windows with neckties and odd socks, and sat over the smoky fire to keep warm. First I tried to write, but found it too cold. My hand turned to ice on the paper.

What tricks the wind did play with the old place! It came rushing up the forsaken alley with a sound like the feet of a hurrying crowd of people who stopped suddenly at the door. I felt as if a lot of curious folk had arranged themselves just outside and were staring up at my windows.

Then they took to their heels again and fled whispering and laughing down the lane, only, however, to return with the next gust of wind and repeat their impertinence. On the other side of my room a single square window opens into a sort of shaft, or well, that measures about six feet across to the back wall of another house. Down this funnel the wind dropped, and puffed and shouted. Such noises I never heard before. Between these two entertainments I sat over the fire in a great-coat, listening to the deep booming in the chimney. It was like being in a ship at sea, and I almost looked for the floor to rise in undulations and rock to and fro.

*Oct. 12.* – I wish I were not quite so lonely – and so poor. And yet I love both my loneliness and my poverty. The former makes me appreciate the companionship of the wind and rain, while the latter preserves my liver and prevents me wasting time in dancing attendance upon women.

Poor, ill-dressed men are not acceptable 'attendants'.

My parents are dead, and my only sister is – no, not dead exactly, but married to a very rich man. They travel most of the time, he to find his health, she to lose herself. Through sheer neglect on her part she has long passed out of my life. The door closed when, after an absolute silence of five years, she sent me a cheque for £50 at Christmas. It was signed by her husband! I returned it to her in a thousand pieces and in an unstamped envelope. So at least I had the satisfaction of knowing that it cost her something! She wrote back with a broad quill pen that covered a whole page with three lines, "You are evidently as cracked as ever, and rude and ungrateful into the bargain." It had always been my special terror lest the insanity of my father's family should leap across the generations and appear in me. This thought haunted me, and she knew it. So after this little exchange of civilities the door slammed, never to open again. I heard the crash it made, and, with it, the falling from the walls of my heart of many little bits of china with their own peculiar value – rare china, some of it, that only needed dusting. The same walls, too, carried mirrors in which I used sometimes to see reflected the misty lawns of childhood, the daisy chains, the wind-torn blossoms scattered through the orchard by warm rains, the robbers' cave in the long walk, and the hidden store of apples in the hayloft. She was my inseparable companion then – but, when the door slammed, the mirrors cracked across their entire length, and the visions they held vanished for ever. Now I am quite alone. At forty one cannot begin all over again to build up careful friendships, and all others are comparatively worthless.

Oct. 14. – My bedroom is 10 by 10. It is below the level of the front room, and a step leads down into it. Both rooms are very quiet on calm nights, for there is no traffic down this forsaken alley-way. In spite of the occasional larks of the wind, it is a most sheltered strip. At its upper end, below my windows, all the cats of the neighbourhood congregate as soon as darkness gathers. They lie undisturbed on the long ledge of a blind window of the opposite building, for after the postman has come and gone at 9.30, no footsteps ever dare to interrupt their sinister conclave, no step but my own, or sometimes the unsteady footfall of the son who 'is somethink on a homnibus'.

Oct. 15. – I dined at an 'A.B.C.' shop on poached eggs and coffee, and then went for a stroll round the outer edge of Regent's Park. It was ten o'clock when I got home.1 counted no less than thirteen cats, all of a dark colour, crouching under the lee side of the alley walls. It was a cold night, and the stars shone like points of ice in a blue-black sky. The cats turned their heads and stared at me in silence as I passed. An odd sensation of shyness took possession of me under the glare of so many pairs of unblinking eyes. As I fumbled with the latch-key they jumped noiselessly down and pressed against my legs, as if anxious to be let in. But I slammed the door in their faces and ran quickly upstairs. The front room, as I entered to grope for the matches, felt as cold as a stone vault, and the air held an unusual dampness.

Oct. 17. – For several days I have been working on a ponderous article that allows no play for the fancy. My imagination requires a judicious rein; I am afraid to let it loose, for it carries me sometimes into appalling places beyond the stars and beneath the world. No one realises the danger more than I do. But what a foolish thing to write here – for there is no one to know, no one to realise! My mind of late has held unusual thoughts,

thoughts I have never had before, about medicines and drugs and the treatment of strange illnesses. I cannot imagine their source.

At no time in my life have I dwelt upon such ideas now constantly throng my brain. I have had no exercise lately, for the weather has been shocking; and all my afternoons have been spent in the reading-room of the British Museum, where I have a reader's ticket.

I have made an unpleasant discovery: there are rats in the house. At night from my bed I have heard them scampering across the hills and valleys of the front room, and my sleep has been a good deal disturbed in consequence.

*Oct. 19.* – The landlady, I find, has a little boy with her, probably her son's child. In fine weather he plays in the alley, and draws a wooden cart over the cobbles. One of the wheels is off, and it makes a most distracting noise. After putting up with it as long as possible, I found it was getting on my nerves, and I could not write. So I rang the bell. Emily answered it.

"Emily, will you ask the little fellow to make less noise? It's impossible to work."

The girl went downstairs, and soon afterwards the child was called in by the kitchen door. I felt rather a brute for spoiling his play. In a few minutes, however, the noise began again, and I felt that he was the brute. He dragged the broken toy with a string over the stones till the rattling noise jarred every nerve in my body. It became unbearable, and I rang the bell a second time.

"That noise must be put a stop to!" I said to the girl, with decision.

"Yes, sir," she grinned, "I know; but one of the wheels is hoff. The men in the stable offered to mend it for 'im, but he wouldn't let them. He says he likes it that way."

"I can't help what he likes. The noise must stop. I can't write."

"Yes, sir; I'll tell Mrs. Monson."

The noise stopped for the day then.

*Oct. 23.* – Every day for the past week that cart has rattled over the stones, till I have come to think of it as a huge carrier's van with four wheels and two horses; and every morning I have been obliged to ring the bell and have it stopped. The last time Mrs. Monson herself came up, and said she was sorry I had been annoyed; the sounds should not occur again. With rare discursiveness she went on to ask if I was comfortable, and how I liked the rooms. I replied cautiously. I mentioned the rats. She said they were mice. I spoke of the draughts. She said, "Yes, it were a draughty 'ouse." I referred to the cats, and she said they had been as long as she could remember. By way of conclusion, she informed me that the house was over two hundred years old, and that the last gentleman who had occupied my rooms was a painter who "'ad real Jimmy Bueys and Raffles 'anging all hover the walls". It took me some moments to discern that Cimabue and Raphael were in the woman's mind.

*Oct. 24.* – Last night the son who is 'somethink on a homnibus' came in. He had evidently been drinking, for I heard loud and angry voices below in the kitchen long after I had gone to bed. Once, too, I caught the singular words rising up to me through the floor, "Burning from top to bottom is the only thing that'll ever make this 'ouse right." I knocked on the floor, and the voices ceased suddenly, though later I again heard their clamour in my dreams.

These rooms are very quiet, almost too quiet sometimes. On windless nights they are silent as the grave, and the house might be miles in the country. The roar of London's traffic reaches me only in heavy, distant vibrations. It holds an ominous note sometimes, like that of an approaching army, or an immense tidal-wave very far away thundering in the night.

*Oct. 27.* – Mrs. Monson, though admirably silent, is a foolish, fussy woman. She does such stupid things. In dusting the room she puts all my things in the wrong places. The ashtrays, which should be on the writing-table, she sets in a silly row on the mantelpiece. The pen-tray, which should be beside the inkstand, she hides away cleverly among the books on my reading-desk.

My gloves she arranges daily in idiotic array upon a half-filled bookshelf, and I always have to rearrange them on the low table by the door. She places my armchair at impossible angles between the fire and the light, and the tablecloth – the one with Trinity Hall stains – she puts on the table in such a fashion that when I look at it I feel as if my tie and all my clothes were on crooked and awry. She exasperates me. Her very silence and meekness are irritating.

Sometimes I feel inclined to throw the inkstand at her, just to bring an expression into her watery eyes and a squeak from those colourless lips. Dear me! What violent expressions I am making use of! How very foolish of me! And yet it almost seems as if the words were not my own, but had been spoken into my ear – I mean, I never make use of such terms naturally.

*Oct. 30.* – I have been here a month. The place does not agree with me, I think. My headaches are more frequent and violent, and my nerves are a perpetual source of discomfort and annoyance.

I have conceived a great dislike for Mrs. Monson, a feeling I am certain she reciprocates.

Somehow, the impression comes frequently to me that there are goings on in this house of which I know nothing, and which she is careful to hide from me.

Last night her son slept in the house, and this morning as I was standing at the window I saw him go out. He glanced up and caught my eye. It was a loutish figure and a singularly repulsive face that I saw, and he gave me the benefit of a very unpleasant leer. At least, so I imagined.

Evidently I am getting absurdly sensitive to trifles, and I suppose it is my disordered nerves making themselves felt. In the British Museum this afternoon I noticed several people at the readers' table staring at me and watching every movement I made. Whenever I looked up from my books I found their eyes upon me. It seemed to me unnecessary and unpleasant, and I left earlier than was my custom. When I reached the door I threw back a last look into the room, and saw every head at the table turned in my direction. It annoyed me very much, and yet I know it is foolish to take note of such things. When I am well they pass me by. I must get more regular exercise. Of late I have had next to none.

*Nov. 2.* – The utter stillness of this house is beginning to oppress me. I wish there were other fellows living upstairs. No footsteps ever sound overhead, and no tread ever passes my door to go up the next flight of stairs. I am beginning to feel some curiosity to go up myself and see what the upper rooms are like. I feel lonely here and isolated, swept into a deserted corner of the world and forgotten... Once I actually caught myself gazing into the long, cracked mirrors, trying to see the sunlight dancing beneath the trees in the orchard. But only deep shadows seemed to congregate there now, and I soon desisted.

It has been very dark all day, and no wind stirring. The fogs have begun. I had to use a reading-lamp all this morning. There was no cart to be heard today. I actually missed it. This morning, in the gloom and silence, I think I could almost have welcomed it. After all, the sound is a very human one, and this empty house at the end of the alley holds other noises that are not quite so satisfactory.

I have never once seen a policeman in the lane, and the postmen always hurry out with no evidence of a desire to loiter.

*10 p.m.* – As I write this I hear no sound but the deep murmur of the distant traffic and the low sighing of the wind. The two sounds melt into one another. Now and again a cat raises its shrill, uncanny cry upon the darkness. The cats are always there under my windows when the darkness falls. The wind is dropping into the funnel with a noise like the sudden sweeping of immense distant wings. It is a dreary night. I feel lost and forgotten.

*Nov. 3.* – From my windows I can see arrivals. When anyone comes to the door I can just see the hat and shoulders and the hand on the bell. Only two fellows have been to see me since I came here two months ago. Both of them I saw from the window before they came up, and heard their voices asking if I was in. Neither of them ever came back.

I have finished the ponderous article. On reading it through, however, I was dissatisfied with it, and drew my pencil through almost every page. There were strange expressions and ideas in it that I could not explain, and viewed with amazement, not to say alarm. They did not sound like my very own, and I could not remember having written them. Can it be that my memory is beginning to be affected?

My pens are never to be found. That stupid old woman puts them in a different place each day. I must give her due credit for finding so many new hiding places; such ingenuity is wonderful. I have told her repeatedly, but she always says, "I'll speak to Emily, sir." Emily always says, "I'll tell Mrs. Monson, sir." Their foolishness makes me irritable and scatters all my thoughts. I should like to stick the lost pens into them and turn them out, blind-eyed, to be scratched and mauled by those thousand hungry cats. Whew! What a ghastly thought! Where in the world did it come from? Such an idea is no more my own than it is the policeman's. Yet I felt I had to write it. It was like a voice singing in my head, and my pen wouldn't stop till the last word was finished. What ridiculous nonsense! I must and will restrain myself. I must take more regular exercise; my nerves and liver plague me horribly.

*Nov. 4.* – I attended a curious lecture in the French quarter on 'Death', but the room was so hot and I was so weary that I fell asleep. The only part I heard, however, touched my imagination vividly. Speaking of suicides, the lecturer said that self-murder was no escape from the miseries of the present, but only a preparation of greater sorrow for the future. Suicides, he declared, cannot shirk their responsibilities so easily. They must return to take up life exactly where they laid it so violently down, but with the added pain and punishment of their weakness. Many of them wander the earth in unspeakable misery till they can reclothe themselves in the body of someone else

– generally a lunatic, or weak-minded person, who cannot resist the hideous obsession. This is their only means of escape. Surely a weird and horrible idea! I wish I had slept all the time and not heard it at all. My mind is morbid enough without such ghastly fancies. Such mischievous propaganda should be stopped by the police. I'll write to the *Times* and suggest it.

Good idea!

I walked home through Greek Street, Soho, and imagined that a hundred years had slipped back into place and De Quincey was still there, haunting the night with invocations to his 'just, subtle, and mighty' drug. His vast dreams seemed to hover not very far away. Once started in my brain, the pictures refused to go away; and I saw him sleeping in that cold, tenantless mansion with the strange little waif who was afraid of its ghosts, both together in the shadows under a single horseman's cloak; or wandering in the companionship of the spectral Anne; or, later still, on his way to the eternal rendezvous at the foot of Great Titchfield Street, the rendezvous she never was able to keep. What an unutterable gloom, what an untold horror of sorrow and suffering comes over me as I try to realise something of what that man – boy he then was – must have taken into his lonely heart.

As I came up the alley I saw a light in the top window, and a head and shoulders thrown in an exaggerated shadow upon the blind. I wondered what the son could be doing up there at such an hour.

*Nov. 5.* – This morning, while writing, someone came up the creaking stairs and knocked cautiously at my door. Thinking it was the landlady, I said, "Come in!" The knock was repeated, and I cried louder, "Come in, come in!" But no one turned the handle, and I continued my writing with a vexed "Well, stay out, then!" under my breath. Went on writing? I tried to, but my thoughts had suddenly dried up at their source. I could not set down a single word. It was a dark, yellow-fog morning, and there was little enough inspiration in the air as it was, but that stupid woman standing just outside my door waiting to be told again to come in roused a spirit of vexation that filled my head to the exclusion of all else. At last I jumped up and opened the door myself.

"What do you want, and why in the world don't you come in?" I cried out. But the words dropped into empty air. There was no one there. The fog poured up the dingy staircase in deep yellow coils, but there was no sign of a human being anywhere.

I slammed the door, with imprecations upon the house and its noises, and went back to my work. A few minutes later Emily came in with a letter.

"Were you or Mrs. Monson outside a few minutes ago knocking at my door?"

"No, sir."

"Are you sure?

"Mrs. Monson's gone to market, and there's no one but me and the child in the 'ole 'ouse, and I've been washing the dishes for the last hour, sir."

I fancied the girl's face turned a shade paler. She fidgeted towards the door with a glance over her shoulder.

"Wait, Emily," I said, and then told her what I had heard. She stared stupidly at me, though her eyes shifted now and then over the articles in the room.

"Who was it? "I asked when I had come to the end. "Mrs. Monson says it's honly mice," she said, as if repeating a learned lesson.

"Mice!" I exclaimed; "it's nothing of the sort. Someone was feeling about outside my door. Who was it? Is the son in the house?"

Her whole manner changed suddenly, and she became earnest instead of evasive. She seemed anxious to tell the truth.

"Oh no, sir; there's no one in the house at all but you and me and the child, and there couldn't 'ave been nobody at your door. As for them knocks—" She stopped abruptly, as though she had said too much.

"Well, what about the knocks?" I said more gently.

"Of course," she stammered, "the knocks isn't mice, nor the footsteps neither, but then—"

Again she came to a full halt.

"Anything wrong with the house?"

"Lor', no, sir; the drains is splendid!"

"I don't mean drains, girl. I mean, did anything – anything bad ever happen here?"

She flushed up to the roots of her hair, and then turned suddenly pale again. She was obviously in considerable distress, and there was something she was anxious, yet afraid to tell – some forbidden thing she was not allowed to mention.

"I don't mind what it was, only I should like to know," I said encouragingly.

Raising her frightened eyes to my face, she began to blurt out something about "that which 'appened once to a gentleman that lived hupstairs", when a shrill voice calling her name sounded below.

"Emily, Emily!" It was the returning landlady, and the girl tumbled downstairs as if pulled backwards by a rope, leaving me full of conjectures as to what in the world could have happened to a gentleman upstairs that could in so curious a manner affect my ears downstairs.

*Nov. 10.* – I have done capital work; have finished the ponderous article and had it accepted for the Review, and another one ordered. I feel well and cheerful, and have had regular exercise and good sleep; no headaches, no nerves, no liver! Those pills the chemist recommended are wonderful. I can watch the child playing with his cart and feel no annoyance; sometimes I almost feel inclined to join him. Even the grey-faced landlady rouses pity in me; I am sorry for her: so worn, so weary, so oddly put together, just like the building. She looks as if she had once suffered some shock of terror, and was momentarily dreading another. When I spoke to her today very gently about not putting the pens in the ash-tray and the gloves on the hook-shelf she raised her faint eyes to mine for the first time, and said with the ghost of a smile, "I'll try and remember, sir." I felt inclined to pat her on the back and say, "Come, cheer up and be jolly. Life's not so bad after all." Oh! I am much better. There's nothing like open air and success and good sleep. They build up as if by magic the portions of the heart eaten down by despair and unsatisfied yearnings. Even to the cats I feel friendly. When I came in at eleven o'clock tonight they followed me to the door in a stream, and I stooped down to stroke the one nearest to me.

Bah! The brute hissed and spat, and struck at me with her paws. The claw caught my hand and drew blood in a thin line. The others danced sideways into the darkness, screeching, as though I had done them an injury. I believe these cats really hate me. Perhaps they are only waiting to be reinforced. Then they will attack me. Ha, ha! In spite of the momentary annoyance, this fancy sent me laughing upstairs to my room.

The fire was out, and the room seemed unusually cold. As I groped my way over to the mantelpiece to find the matches I realised all at once that there was another person standing beside me in the darkness. I could, of course, see nothing, but my fingers, feeling along the ledge, came into forcible contact with something that was at once withdrawn. It was cold and moist. I could have sworn it was somebody's hand. My flesh began to creep instantly.

"Who's that?" I exclaimed in a loud voice.

My voice dropped into the silence like a pebble into a deep well. There was no answer, but at the same moment I heard someone moving away from me across the room in the direction of the door. It was a confused sort of footstep, and the sound of garments brushing the furniture on the way. The same second my hand stumbled upon the matchbox, and I struck a light. I expected to see Mrs. Monson, or Emily, or perhaps the son who is something on an omnibus. But the flare of the gas-jet illumined an empty room; there was not a sign of a person anywhere. I felt the hair stir upon my head, and instinctively I backed up against the wall, lest something should approach me from behind. I was distinctly alarmed. But the next minute I recovered myself. The door was open on to the landing, and I crossed the room, not without some inward trepidation, and went out. The light from the room fell upon the stairs, but there was no one to be seen anywhere, nor was there any sound on the creaking wooden staircase to indicate a departing creature.

I was in the act of turning to go in again when a sound overhead caught my ear. It was a very faint sound, not unlike the sigh of wind; yet it could not have been the wind, for the night was still as the grave. Though it was not repeated, I resolved to go upstairs and see for myself what it all meant. Two senses had been affected – touch and hearing – and I could not believe that I had been deceived. So, with a lighted candle, I went stealthily forth on my unpleasant journey into the upper regions of this queer little old house.

On the first landing there was only one door, and it was locked. On the second there was also only one door, but when I turned the handle it opened. There came forth to meet me the chill musty air that is characteristic of a long unoccupied room. With it there came an indescribable odour. I use the adjective advisedly. Though very faint, diluted as it were, it was nevertheless an odour that made my gorge rise. I had never smelt anything like it before, and I cannot describe it.

The room was small and square, close under the roof, with a sloping ceiling and two tiny windows. It was cold as the grave, without a shred of carpet or a stick of furniture. The icy atmosphere and the nameless odour combined to make the room abominable to me, and, after lingering a moment to see that it contained no cupboards or corners into which a person might have crept for concealment, I made haste to shut the door, and went downstairs again to bed.

Evidently I had been deceived after all as to the noise.

In the night I had a foolish but very vivid dream. I dreamed that the landlady and another person, dark and not properly visible, entered my room on all fours, followed by a horde of immense cats. They attacked me as I lay in bed, and murdered me, and then dragged my body upstairs and deposited it on the floor of that cold little square room under the roof.

*Nov. 11.* – Since my talk with Emily – the unfinished talk – I have hardly once set eyes on her. Mrs. Monson now attends wholly to my wants. As usual, she does everything exactly as I don't like it done. It is all too utterly trivial to mention, but it is exceedingly irritating. Like small doses of morphine often repeated, she has finally a cumulative effect.

*Nov. 12.* – This morning I woke early, and came into the front room to get a book, meaning to read in bed till it was time to get up. Emily was laying the fire.

"Good morning!" I said cheerfully. "Mind you make a good fire. It's very cold."

The girl turned and showed me a startled face. It was not Emily at all!

"Where's Emily? " I exclaimed.

"You mean the girl as was 'ere before me?"

"Has Emily left?"

"I came on the 6th," she replied sullenly, "and she'd gone then." I got my book and went back to bed. Emily must have been sent away almost immediately after our conversation. This reflection kept coming between me and the printed page. I was glad when it was time to get up.

Such prompt energy, such merciless decision, seemed to argue something of importance – to somebody.

*Nov. 13.* – The wound inflicted by the cat's claw has swollen, and causes me annoyance and some pain. It throbs and itches. I'm afraid my blood must be in poor condition, or it would have healed by now. I opened it with a penknife soaked in an antiseptic solution, and cleansed it thoroughly. I have heard unpleasant stories of the results of wounds inflicted by cats.

*Nov. 14.* – In spite of the curious effect this house certainly exercises upon my nerves, I like it. It is lonely and deserted in the very heart of London, but it is also for that reason quiet to work in. I wonder why it is so cheap. Some people might be suspicious, but I did not even ask the reason. No answer is better than a lie. If only I could remove the cats from the outside and the rats from the inside. I feel that I shall grow accustomed more and more to its peculiarities, and shall die here. Ah, that expression reads queerly and gives a wrong impression: I meant live and die here. I shall renew the lease from year to year till one of us crumbles to pieces. From present indications the building will be the first to go.

*Nov. 16.* – It is abominable the way my nerves go up and down with me – and rather discouraging. This morning I woke to find my clothes scattered about the room, and a cane chair overturned beside the bed. My coat and waistcoat looked just as if they had been tried on by someone in the night. I had horribly vivid dreams, too, in which someone covering his face with his hands kept coming close up to me, crying out as if in pain. "Where can I find covering? Oh, who will clothe me?" How silly, and yet it frightened me a little. It was so dreadfully real. It is now over a year since I last walked in my sleep and woke up with such a shock on the cold pavement of Earl's Court Road, where I then lived. I thought I was cured, but evidently not. This discovery has rather a disquieting effect upon me. Tonight I shall resort to the old trick of tying my toe to the bed-post.

*Nov. 17.* – Last night I was again troubled by most oppressive dreams. Someone seemed to be moving in the night up and down my room, sometimes passing into the front room, and then returning to stand beside the bed and stare intently down upon me. I was being watched by this person all night long. I never actually awoke, though I was often very near it. I suppose it was a nightmare from indigestion, for this morning I have one of my old vile headaches. Yet all my clothes lay about the floor when I awoke, where they had evidently been flung (had I so tossed them?) during the dark hours, and my trousers trailed over the step into the front room.

Worse than this, though – I fancied I noticed about the room in the morning that strange, fetid odour. Though very faint, its mere suggestion is foul and nauseating. What in the world can it be, I wonder?... In future I shall lock my door.

*Nov. 26.* – I have accomplished a lot of good work during this past week, and have also managed to get regular exercise. I have felt well and in an equable state of mind. Only two things have occurred to disturb my equanimity. The first is trivial in itself, and no doubt to be easily explained. The upper window where I saw the light on the night of November 4, with the shadow of a large head and shoulders upon the blind, is one of the windows in the square room under the roof. In reality it has no blind at all!

Here is the other thing. I was coming home last night in a fresh fall of snow about eleven o'clock, my umbrella low down over my head. Half-way up the alley, where the snow was wholly untrodden, I saw a man's legs in front of me. The umbrella hid the rest of his figure, but on raising it I saw that he was tall and broad and was walking, as I was, towards the door of my house. He could not have been four feet ahead of me. I had thought the alley was empty when I entered it, but might of course have been mistaken very easily.

A sudden gust of wind compelled me to lower the umbrella, and when I raised it again, not half a minute later, there was no longer any man to be seen. With a few more steps I reached the door. It was closed as usual. I then noticed with a sudden sensation of dismay that the surface of the freshly fallen snow was unbroken. My own foot-marks were the only ones to be seen anywhere, and though I retraced my way to the point where I had first seen the man, I could find no slightest impression of any other boots. Feeling creepy and uncomfortable, I went upstairs, and was glad to get into bed.

*Nov. 28.* – With the fastening of my bedroom door the disturbances ceased. I am convinced that I walked in my sleep. Probably I untied my toe and then tied it up again. The fancied security of the locked door would alone have been enough to restore sleep to my troubled spirit and enable me to rest quietly.

Last night, however, the annoyance was suddenly renewed in another and more aggressive form. I woke in the darkness with the impression that someone was standing outside my bedroom door listening. As I became more awake the impression grew into positive knowledge.

Though there was no appreciable sound of moving or breathing, I was so convinced of the propinquity of a listener that I crept out of bed and approached the door. As I did so there came faintly from the next room the unmistakable sound of someone retreating stealthily across the floor. Yet, as I heard it, it was neither the tread of a man nor a regular footstep, but rather, it seemed to me, a confused sort of crawling, almost as of someone on his hands and knees.

I unlocked the door in less than a second, and passed quickly into the front room, and I could feel, as by the subtlest imaginable vibrations upon my nerves, that the spot I was standing in had just that instant been vacated! The Listener had moved; he was now behind the other door, standing in the passage. Yet this door was also closed. I moved swiftly, and as silently as possible, across the floor, and turned the handle. A cold rush of air met me from the passage and sent shiver after shiver down my back. There was no one in the doorway; there was no one on the little landing; there was no one moving down the staircase. Yet I had been so quick that this midnight Listener could not be very far away, and I felt that if I persevered I should eventually come face to face with him. And the courage that came so opportunely to overcome my nervousness and horror seemed born of the unwelcome conviction that it was somehow necessary for my safety as well as my sanity that I should find this intruder and force his secret from him. For was it not the intent action of his mind upon my own, in concentrated listening, that had awakened me with such a vivid realisation of his presence?

Advancing across the narrow landing, I peered down into the well of the little house. There was nothing to be seen; no one was moving in the darkness. How cold the oilcloth was to my bare feet.

I cannot say what it was that suddenly drew my eyes upwards. I only know that, without apparent reason, I looked up and saw a person about half-way up the next turn of the stairs, leaning forward over the balustrade and staring straight into my face. It was a man. He appeared to be clinging to the rail rather than standing on the stairs. The gloom made it impossible to see much beyond the general outline, but the head and shoulders were seemingly enormous, and stood sharply silhouetted against the skylight in the roof immediately above. The idea flashed into my brain in a moment that I was looking into the visage of something monstrous. The huge skull, the mane-like hair, the wide-humped shoulders, suggested, in a way I did not pause to analyse, that which was scarcely human; and for some seconds, fascinated by horror, I returned the gaze and stared into the dark, inscrutable countenance above me, without knowing exactly where I was or what I was doing.

Then I realised in quite a new way that I was face to face with the secret midnight Listener, and I steeled myself as best I could for what was about to come.

The source of the rash courage that came to me at this awful moment will ever be to me an inexplicable mystery. Though shivering with fear, and my forehead wet with an unholy dew, I resolved to advance. Twenty questions leaped to my lips: What are you? What do you want? Why do you listen and watch? Why do you come into my room? But none of them found articulate utterance.

I began forthwith to climb the stairs, and with the first signs of my advance he drew himself back into the shadows and began to move. He retreated as swiftly as I advanced. I heard the sound of his crawling motion a few steps ahead of me, ever maintaining the same distance. When I reached the landing he was half-way up the next flight, and when I was half-way up the next flight he had already arrived at the top landing. I then heard him open the door of the little square room under the roof and go in. Immediately, though the door did not close after him, the sound of his moving entirely ceased.

At this moment I longed for a light, or a stick, or any weapon whatsoever; but I had none of these things, and it was impossible to go back. So I marched steadily up the rest of the stairs, and in less than a minute found myself standing in the gloom face to face with the door through which this creature had just entered.

For a moment I hesitated. The door was about half-way open, and the Listener was standing evidently in his favourite attitude just behind it – listening. To search through that dark room for him seemed hopeless; to enter the same small space where he was seemed horrible. The very idea filled me with loathing, and I almost decided to turn back.

It is strange at such times how trivial things impinge on the consciousness with a shock as of something important and immense. Something – it may have been a beetle or a mouse – scuttled over the bare boards behind me. The door moved a quarter of an inch, closing. My decision came back with a sudden rush, as it were, and thrusting out a foot, I kicked the door so that it swung sharply back to its full extent, and permitted me to walk forward slowly into the aperture of profound blackness beyond. What a queer soft sound my bare feet made on the boards! How the blood sang and buzzed in my head!

I was inside. The darkness closed over me, hiding even the windows. I began to grope my way round the walls in a thorough search; but in order to prevent all possibility of the other's escape, I first of all closed the door.

There we were, we two, shut in together between four walls, within a few feet of one another.

But with what, with whom, was I thus momentarily imprisoned? A new light flashed suddenly over the affair with a swift, illuminating brilliance – and I knew I was a fool, an utter fool! I was wide awake at last, and the horror was evaporating. My cursed nerves again; a dream, a nightmare, and the old result – walking in my sleep. The figure was a dream-figure. Many a time before had the actors in my dreams stood before me for some moments after I was awake…

There was a chance match in my pyjamas' pocket, and I struck it on the wall. The room was utterly empty. It held not even a shadow. I went quickly down to bed, cursing my wretched nerves and my foolish, vivid dreams. But as soon as ever I was asleep again, the same uncouth figure of a man crept back to my bedside, and bending over me with his immense head close to my ear, whispered repeatedly in my dreams, "I want your body; I want its covering. I'm waiting for it, and listening always." Words scarcely less foolish than the dream.

But I wonder what that queer odour was up in the square room. I noticed it again, and stronger than ever before, and it seemed to be also in my bedroom when I woke this morning.

*Nov. 29.* – Slowly, as moonbeams rise over a misty sea in June, the thought is entering my mind that my nerves and somnambulistic dreams do not adequately account for the influence this house exercises upon me. It holds me as with a fine, invisible net. I cannot escape if I would. It draws me, and it means to keep me.

*Nov. 30.* – The post this morning brought me a letter from Aden, forwarded from my old rooms in Earl's Court. It was from Chapter, my former Trinity chum, who is on his way home from the East, and asks for my address. I sent it to him at the hotel he mentioned, 'to await arrival'.

As I have already said, my windows command a view of the alley, and I can see an arrival without difficulty. This morning, while I was busy writing, the sound of footsteps coming up the alley filled me with a sense of vague alarm that I could in no way account for. I went over to the window, and saw a man standing below waiting for the door to be opened. His shoulders were broad, his top-hat glossy, and his overcoat fitted beautifully round the collar. All this I could see, but no more. Presently the door was opened, and the shock to my nerves was unmistakable when I heard a man's voice ask, "Is Mr.— still here?" mentioning my name. I could not catch the answer, but it could only have been in the affirmative, for the man entered the hall and the door shut to behind him. But I waited in vain for the sound of his steps on the stairs. There was no sound of any kind. It seemed to me so strange that I opened my door and looked out. No one was anywhere to be seen. I walked across the narrow landing, and looked through the window that commands the whole length of the alley. There was no sign of a human being, coming or going.

The lane was deserted. Then I deliberately walked downstairs into the kitchen, and asked the grey-faced landlady if a gentleman had just that minute called for me.

The answer, given with an odd, weary sort of smile, was "No!"

*Dec. 1.* – I feel genuinely alarmed and uneasy over the state of my nerves. Dreams are dreams, but never before have I had dreams in broad daylight.

I am looking forward very much to Chapter's arrival. He is a capital fellow, vigorous, healthy, with no nerves, and even less imagination; and he has £2,000 a year into the bargain.

Periodically he makes me offers – the last was to travel round the world with him as secretary, which was a delicate way of paying my expenses and giving me some pocket-money – offers, however, which I invariably decline. I prefer to keep his friendship. Women could not come between us; money might – therefore I give it no opportunity. Chapter always laughed at what he called my 'fancies', being himself possessed only of that thin-blooded quality of imagination which is ever associated with the prosaic-minded man. Yet, if taunted with this obvious lack, his wrath is deeply stirred. His psychology is that of the crass materialist – always a rather funny article. It will afford me genuine relief, none the less, to hear the cold judgment his mind will have to pass upon the story of this house as I shall have it to tell.

*Dec. 2.* – The strangest part of it all I have not referred to in this brief diary. Truth to tell, I have been afraid to set it down in black and white. I have kept it in the background of my thoughts, preventing it as far as possible from taking shape. In spite of my efforts, however, it has continued to grow stronger.

Now that I come to face the issue squarely it is harder to express than I imagined. Like a half-remembered melody that trips in the head but vanishes the moment you try to sing it, these thoughts form a group in the background of my mind, behind my mind, as it were, and refuse to come forward. They are crouching ready to spring, but the actual leap never takes place.

In these rooms, except when my mind is strongly concentrated on my own work, I find myself suddenly dealing in thoughts and ideas that are not my own! New, strange conceptions, wholly foreign to my temperament, are for ever cropping up in my head. What precisely they are is of no particular importance. The point is that they are entirely apart from the channel in which my thoughts have hitherto been accustomed to flow. Especially they come when my mind is at rest, unoccupied; when I'm dreaming over the fire, or sitting with a book which fails to hold my attention. Then these thoughts which are not mine spring into life and make me feel exceedingly uncomfortable. Sometimes they are so strong that I almost feel as if someone were in the room beside me, thinking aloud.

Evidently my nerves and liver are shockingly out of order. I must work harder and take more vigorous exercise. The horrid thoughts never come when my mind is much occupied. But they are always there – waiting and as it were alive.

What I have attempted to describe above came first upon me gradually after I had been some days in the house, and then grew steadily in strength. The other strange thing has come to me only twice in all these weeks. It appals me. It is the consciousness of the propinquity of some deadly and loathsome disease. It comes over me like a wave of fever heat, and then passes off, leaving me cold and trembling. The air seems for a few seconds to become tainted. So penetrating and convincing is the thought of this sickness, that on both occasions my brain has turned momentarily dizzy, and through my mind, like flames of white heat, have flashed the ominous names of all the dangerous illnesses I know. I can no more explain these visitations than I can fly, yet I know there is no dreaming about the clammy skin and palpitating heart which they always leave as witnesses of their brief visit.

Most strongly of all was I aware of this nearness of a mortal sickness when, on the night of the 28th, I went upstairs in pursuit of the listening figure. When we were shut in together in that little square room under the roof, I felt that I was face to face with the actual essence of this invisible and malignant disease. Such a feeling never entered my heart before, and I pray to God it never may again.

There! Now I have confessed. I have given some expression at least to the feelings that so far I have been afraid to see in my own writing. For – since I can no longer deceive myself – the experiences of that night (28th) were no more a dream than my daily breakfast is a dream; and the trivial entry in this diary by which I sought to explain away an occurrence that caused me unutterable horror was due solely to my desire not to acknowledge in words what I really felt and believed to be true. The increase that would have accrued to my horror by so doing might have been more than I could stand.

*Dec. 3.* – I wish Chapter would come. My facts are all ready marshalled, and I can see his cool, grey eyes fixed incredulously on my face as I relate them: the knocking at my door, the well-dressed caller, the light in the upper window and the shadow upon the blind, the man who preceded me in the snow, the scattering of my clothes at night, Emily's arrested confession, the landlady's suspicious reticence, the midnight listener on the stairs, and those awful subsequent words in my sleep; and above all, and hardest to tell, the presence of the abominable sickness, and the stream of thoughts and ideas that are not my own.

I can see Chapter's face, and I can almost hear his deliberate words, "You've been at the tea again, and underfeeding, I expect, as usual. Better see my nerve doctor, and then come with me to the south of France." For this fellow, who knows nothing of disordered liver or high-strung nerves, goes regularly to a great nerve specialist with the periodical belief that his nervous system is beginning to decay.

*Dec. 5.* – Ever since the incident of the Listener, I have kept a night-light burning in my bedroom, and my sleep has been undisturbed. Last night, however, I was subjected to a far worse annoyance. I woke suddenly, and saw a man in front of the dressing-table regarding himself in the mirror. The door was locked, as usual. I knew at once it was the Listener, and the blood turned to ice in my veins. Such a wave of horror and dread swept over me that it seemed to turn me rigid in the bed, and I could neither move nor speak. I noted, however, that the odour I so abhorred was strong in the room.

The man seemed to be tall and broad. He was stooping forward over the mirror. His back was turned to me, but in the glass I saw the reflection of a huge head and face illumined fitfully by the flicker of the night-light. The spectral grey of very early morning stealing in round the edges of the curtains lent an additional horror to the picture, for it fell upon hair that was tawny and mane-like, hanging loosely about a face whose swollen, rugose features bore the once seen never forgotten leonine expression of – I dare not write down that awful word. But, by way of corroborative proof, I saw in the faint mingling of the two lights that there were several bronze-coloured blotches on the cheeks which the man was evidently examining with great care in the glass. The lips were pale and very thick and large. One hand I could not see, but the other rested on the ivory back of my hair-brush. Its muscles were strangely contracted, the fingers thin to emaciation, the back of the hand closely puckered up. It was like a big grey spider crouching to spring, or the claw of a great bird.

The full realisation that I was alone in the room with this nameless creature, almost within arm's reach of him, overcame me to such a degree that, when he suddenly turned and regarded me with small beady eyes, wholly out of proportion to the grandeur of their massive setting, I sat bolt upright in bed, uttered a loud cry, and then fell back in a dead swoon of terror upon the bed.

*Dec. 5.* – When I came to this morning, the first thing I noticed was that my clothes were strewn all over the floor... I find it difficult to put my thoughts together, and have sudden accesses of violent trembling. I determined that I would go at once to Chapter's hotel and find out when he is expected. I cannot refer to what happened in the night; it is too awful, and I have to keep my thoughts rigorously away from it. I feel light-headed and queer, couldn't eat any breakfast, and have twice vomited with blood. While dressing to go out, a hansom rattled up noisily over the cobbles, and a minute later the door opened, and to my great joy in walked the very subject of my thoughts.

The sight of his strong face and quiet eyes had an immediate effect upon me, and I grew calmer again. His very handshake was a sort of tonic. But, as I listened eagerly to the deep tones of his reassuring voice, and the visions of the night-time paled a little, I began to realise how very hard it was going to be to tell him my wild intangible tale. Some men radiate an animal vigour that destroys the delicate woof of a vision and effectually prevents its reconstruction.

Chapter was one of these men.

We talked of incidents that had filled the interval since we last met, and he told me something of his travels. He talked and I listened. But, so full was I of the horrid thing I had to tell, that I made a poor listener. I was for ever watching my opportunity to leap in and explode it all under his nose.

Before very long, however, it was borne in upon me that he too was merely talking for time.

He too held something of importance in the background of his mind, something too weighty to let fall till the right moment presented itself. So that during the whole of the first half-hour we were both waiting for the psychological moment in which properly to release our respective bombs; and the intensity of our minds' action set up opposing forces that merely sufficed to hold one another in check – and nothing more. As soon as I realised this, therefore, I resolved to yield.

I renounced for the time my purpose of telling my story, and had the satisfaction of seeing that his mind, released from the restraint of my own, at once began to make preparations for the discharge of its momentous burden. The talk grew less and less magnetic; the interest waned; the descriptions of his travels became less alive. There were pauses between his sentences. Presently he repeated himself. His words clothed no living thoughts. The pauses grew longer. Then the interest dwindled altogether and went out like a candle in the wind. His voice ceased, and he looked up squarely into my face with serious and anxious eyes.

The psychological moment had come at last!

"I say—" he began, and then stopped short.

I made an unconscious gesture of encouragement, but said no word. I dreaded the impending disclosure exceedingly. A dark shadow seemed to precede it.

"I say," he blurted out at last, "what in the world made you ever come to this place – to these rooms, I mean?"

"They're cheap, for one thing," I began, "and central and—"

"They're too cheap," he interrupted. "Didn't you ask what made 'em so cheap?"

"It never occurred to me at the time."

There was a pause in which he avoided my eyes.

"For God's sake, go on, man, and tell it!" I cried, for the suspense was getting more than I could stand in my nervous condition.

"This was where Blount lived so long," he said quietly, "and where he – died. You know, in the old days I often used to come here and see him, and do what I could to alleviate his—" He stuck fast again.

"Well!" I said with a great effort. "Please go on – faster."

"But," Chapter went on, turning his face to the window with a perceptible shiver, "he finally got so terrible I simply couldn't stand it, though I always thought I could stand anything. It got on my nerves and made me dream, and haunted me day and night."

I stared at him, and said nothing. I had never heard of Blount in my life, and didn't know what he was talking about. But, all the same, I was trembling, and my mouth had become strangely dry.

"This is the first time I've been back here since," he said almost in a whisper, "and, 'pon my word, it gives me the creeps. I swear it isn't fit for a man to live in. I never saw you look so bad, old man."

"I've got it for a year," I jerked out, with a forced laugh; "signed the lease and all. I thought it was rather a bargain."

Chapter shuddered, and buttoned his overcoat up to his neck. Then he spoke in a low voice, looking occasionally behind him as though he thought someone was listening. I too could have sworn someone else was in the room with us.

"He did it himself, you know, and no one blamed him a bit; his sufferings were awful. For the last two years he used to wear a veil when he went out, and even then it was always in a closed carriage. Even the attendant who had nursed him for so long was at length obliged to leave. The extremities of both the lower limbs were gone, dropped off, and he moved about the ground on all fours with a sort of crawling motion. The odour, too, was—"

I was obliged to interrupt him here. I could hear no more details of that sort. My skin was moist, I felt hot and cold by turns, for at last I was beginning to understand.

"Poor devil," Chapter went on; "I used to keep my eyes closed as much as possible. He always begged to be allowed to take his veil off, and asked if I minded very much. I used to stand by the open window. He never touched me, though. He rented the whole house. Nothing would induce him to leave it."

"Did he occupy – these very rooms?"

"No. He had the little room on the top floor, the square one just under the roof. He preferred it because it was dark. These rooms were too near the ground, and he was afraid people might see him through the windows. A crowd had been known to follow him up to the very door, and then stand below the windows in the hope of catching a glimpse of his face."

"But there were hospitals."

"He wouldn't go near one, and they didn't like to force him. You know, they say it's not contagious, so there was nothing to prevent his staying here if he wanted to. He spent all his time reading medical books, about drugs and so on. His head and face were something appalling, just like a lion's."

I held up my hand to arrest further description.

"He was a burden to the world, and he knew it. One night I suppose he realised it too keenly to wish to live. He had the free use of drugs – and in the morning he was found dead on the floor. Two years ago, that was, and they said then he had still several years to live."

"Then, in Heaven's name!" I cried, unable to bear the suspense any longer, "tell me what it was he had, and be quick about it."

"I thought you knew!" he exclaimed, with genuine surprise. "I thought you knew!"

He leaned forward and our eyes met. In a scarcely audible whisper I caught the words his lips seemed almost afraid to utter:

"He was a leper!"

**If you enjoyed this, you might also like…**
The Occupant of the Room, see page 408
The Damned, see page 414

# The Kit-Bag

**WHEN THE WORDS** "Not Guilty" sounded through the crowded courtroom that dark December afternoon, Arthur Wilbraham, the great criminal KC, and leader for the triumphant defence, was represented by his junior; but Johnson, his private secretary, carried the verdict across to his chambers like lightning.

"It's what we expected, I think," said the barrister, without emotion; "and, personally, I am glad the case is over." There was no particular sign of pleasure that his defence of John Turk, the murderer, on a plea of insanity, had been successful, for no doubt he felt, as everybody who had watched the case felt, that no man had ever better deserved the gallows.

"I'm glad too," said Johnson. He had sat in the court for ten days watching the face of the man who had carried out with callous detail one of the most brutal and cold-blooded murders of recent years.

The counsel glanced up at his secretary. They were more than employer and employed; for family and other reasons, they were friends. "Ah, I remember; yes," he said with a kind smile, "and you want to get away for Christmas? You're going to skate and ski in the Alps, aren't you? If I was your age I'd come with you."

Johnson laughed shortly. He was a young man of twenty-six, with a delicate face like a girl's. "I can catch the morning boat now," he said; "but that's not the reason I'm glad the trial is over. I'm glad it's over because I've seen the last of that man's dreadful face. It positively haunted me. That white skin, with the black hair brushed low over the forehead, is a thing I shall never forget, and the description of the way the dismembered body was crammed and packed with lime into that—"

"Don't dwell on it, my dear fellow," interrupted the other, looking at him curiously out of his keen eyes, "don't think about it. Such pictures have a trick of coming back when one least wants them." He paused a moment. "Now go," he added presently, "and enjoy your holiday. I shall want all your energy for my Parliamentary work when you get back. And don't break your neck skiing."

Johnson shook hands and took his leave. At the door he turned suddenly.

"I knew there was something I wanted to ask you," he said. "Would you mind lending me one of your kit-bags? It's too late to get one tonight, and I leave in the morning before the shops are open."

"Of course; I'll send Henry over with it to your rooms. You shall have it the moment I get home."

"I promise to take great care of it," said Johnson gratefully, delighted to think that within thirty hours he would be nearing the brilliant sunshine of the high Alps in winter. The thought of that criminal court was like an evil dream in his mind.

He dined at his club and went on to Bloomsbury, where he occupied the top floor in one of those old, gaunt houses in which the rooms are large and lofty. The floor below his own was vacant and unfurnished, and below that were other lodgers whom he did not know. It was cheerless, and he looked forward heartily to a change. The night was even more cheerless: it was miserable, and few people were about. A cold, sleety rain was driving down the streets before the keenest east wind he had ever felt. It howled dismally among the big, gloomy houses of the great squares, and when he reached his rooms he heard it whistling and shouting over the world of black roofs beyond his windows.

In the hall he met his landlady, shading a candle from the draughts with her thin hand. "This come by a man from Mr. Wilbr'im's, sir."

She pointed to what was evidently the kit-bag, and Johnson thanked her and took it upstairs with him. "I shall be going abroad in the morning for ten days, Mrs. Monks," he said. "I'll leave an address for letters."

"And I hope you'll 'ave a merry Christmas, sir," she said, in a raucous, wheezy voice that suggested spirits, "and better weather than this."

"I hope so too," replied her lodger, shuddering a little as the wind went roaring down the street outside.

When he got upstairs he heard the sleet volleying against the window panes. He put his kettle on to make a cup of hot coffee, and then set about putting a few things in order for his absence. "And now I must pack – such as my packing is," he laughed to himself, and set to work at once.

He liked the packing, for it brought the snow mountains so vividly before him, and made him forget the unpleasant scenes of the past ten days. Besides, it was not elaborate in nature. His friend had lent him the very thing – a stout canvas kit-bag, sack-shaped, with holes round the neck for the brass bar and padlock. It was a bit shapeless, true, and not much to look at, but its capacity was unlimited, and there was no need to pack carefully. He shoved in his waterproof coat, his fur cap and gloves, his skates and climbing boots, his sweaters, snow-boots, and ear-caps; and then on the top of these he piled his woollen shirts and underwear, his thick socks, puttees, and knickerbockers. The dress suit came next, in case the hotel people dressed for dinner, and then, thinking of the best way to pack his white shirts, he paused a moment to reflect. "That's the worst of these kit-bags," he mused vaguely, standing in the centre of the sitting-room, where he had come to fetch some string.

It was after ten o'clock. A furious gust of wind rattled the windows as though to hurry him up, and he thought with pity of the poor Londoners whose Christmas would be spent in such a climate, whilst he was skimming over snowy slopes in bright sunshine, and dancing in the evening with rosy-cheeked girls – Ah! that reminded him; he must put in his dancing-pumps and evening socks. He crossed over from his sitting-room to the cupboard on the landing where he kept his linen.

And as he did so he heard someone coming softly up the stairs.

He stood still a moment on the landing to listen. It was Mrs. Monks's step, he thought; she must be coming up with the last post. But then the steps ceased suddenly, and he heard no more. They were at least two flights down, and he came to the conclusion they were too heavy to be those of his bibulous landlady. No doubt they belonged to a late lodger who had mistaken his floor. He went into his bedroom and packed his pumps and dress-shirts as best he could.

The kit-bag by this time was two-thirds full, and stood upright on its own base like a sack of flour. For the first time he noticed that it was old and dirty, the canvas faded and worn, and that it had obviously been subjected to rather rough treatment. It was not a very nice bag to have sent him – certainly not a new one, or one that his chief valued. He gave the matter a passing thought, and went on with his packing. Once or twice, however, he caught himself wondering who it could have been wandering down below, for Mrs. Monks had not come up with letters, and the floor was empty and unfurnished. From time to time, moreover, he was almost certain he heard a soft tread of someone padding about over the bare boards – cautiously, stealthily, as silently as possible – and, further, that the sounds had been lately coming distinctly nearer.

For the first time in his life he began to feel a little creepy. Then, as though to emphasise this feeling, an odd thing happened: as he left the bedroom, having just packed his recalcitrant white shirts, he noticed that the top of the kit-bag lopped over towards him with an extraordinary resemblance to a human face. The canvas fell into a fold like a nose and forehead, and the brass rings for the padlock just filled the position of the eyes. A shadow – or was it a travel stain? for he could not tell exactly – looked like hair. It gave him rather a turn, for it was so absurdly, so outrageously, like the face of John Turk the murderer.

He laughed, and went into the front room, where the light was stronger.

"That horrid case has got on my mind," he thought; "I shall be glad of a change of scene and air." In the sitting-room, however, he was not pleased to hear again that stealthy tread upon the stairs, and to realise that it was much closer than before, as well as unmistakably real. And this time he got up and went out to see who it could be creeping about on the upper staircase at so late an hour.

But the sound ceased; there was no one visible on the stairs. He went to the floor below, not without trepidation, and turned on the electric light to make sure that no one was hiding in the empty rooms of the unoccupied suite. There was not a stick of furniture large enough to hide a dog. Then he called over the banisters to Mrs. Monks, but there was no answer, and his voice echoed down into the dark vault of the house, and was lost in the roar of the gale that howled outside. Everyone was in bed and asleep – everyone except himself and the owner of this soft and stealthy tread.

"My absurd imagination, I suppose," he thought. "It must have been the wind after all, although – it seemed so *very* real and close, I thought." He went back to his packing. It was by this time getting on towards midnight. He drank his coffee up and lit another pipe – the last before turning in.

It is difficult to say exactly at what point fear begins, when the causes of that fear are not plainly before the eyes. Impressions gather on the surface of the mind, film by film, as ice gathers upon the surface of still water, but often so lightly that they claim no definite recognition from the consciousness. Then a point is reached where the accumulated impressions become a definite emotion, and the mind realises that something has happened. With something of a start, Johnson suddenly recognised that he felt nervous – oddly nervous; also, that for some time past the causes of this feeling had been gathering slowly in his mind, but that he had only just reached the point where he was forced to acknowledge them.

It was a singular and curious malaise that had come over him, and he hardly knew what to make of it. He felt as though he were doing something that was strongly objected to by another person, another person, moreover, who had some right to object. It was a most disturbing and disagreeable feeling, not unlike the persistent promptings of conscience: almost, in fact, as if he were doing something he knew to be wrong. Yet, though he searched vigorously and honestly in his mind, he could nowhere lay his finger upon the secret of this growing uneasiness, and it perplexed him. More, it distressed and frightened him.

"Pure nerves, I suppose," he said aloud with a forced laugh. "Mountain air will cure all that! Ah," he added, still speaking to himself, "and that reminds me – my snow-glasses."

He was standing by the door of the bedroom during this brief soliloquy, and as he passed quickly towards the sitting-room to fetch them from the cupboard he saw out of the corner of his eye the indistinct outline of a figure standing on the stairs, a few feet from the top. It was someone in a stooping position, with one hand on the banisters, and the face peering up towards the landing. And at the same moment he heard a shuffling footstep. The person who had been creeping about below all this time had at last come up to his own floor. Who in the world could it be? And what in the name of Heaven did he want?

Johnson caught his breath sharply and stood stock still. Then, after a few seconds' hesitation, he found his courage, and turned to investigate. The stairs, he saw to his utter amazement, were empty; there was no one. He felt a series of cold shivers run over him, and something about the muscles of his legs gave a little and grew weak. For the space of several minutes he peered steadily into the shadows that congregated about the top of the staircase where he had seen the figure, and then he walked fast – almost ran, in fact – into the light of the front room; but hardly had he passed inside the doorway when he heard someone come up the stairs behind him with a quick bound and go swiftly into his bedroom. It was a heavy, but at the same time a stealthy footstep – the tread of somebody who did not wish to be seen. And it was at this precise moment that the nervousness he had hitherto experienced leaped the boundary line, and entered the state of fear, almost of acute, unreasoning fear. Before it turned into terror there was a further boundary to cross, and beyond that again lay the region of pure horror. Johnson's position was an unenviable one.

"By Jove! That *was* someone on the stairs, then," he muttered, his flesh crawling all over; "and whoever it was has now gone into my bedroom." His delicate, pale face turned absolutely white, and for some minutes he hardly knew what to think or do. Then he realised intuitively that delay only set a premium upon fear; and he crossed the landing boldly and went straight into the other room, where, a few seconds before, the steps had disappeared.

"Who's there? Is that you, Mrs. Monks?" he called aloud, as he went, and heard the first half of his words echo down the empty stairs, while the second half fell dead against the curtains in a room that apparently held no other human figure than his own.

"Who's there?" he called again, in a voice unnecessarily loud and that only just held firm. "What do you want here?"

The curtains swayed very slightly, and, as he saw it, his heart felt as if it almost missed a beat; yet he dashed forward and drew them aside with a rush. A window, streaming with rain, was all that met his gaze. He continued his search, but in vain; the cupboards held nothing but rows of clothes, hanging motionless; and under the bed there was no sign of anyone hiding. He stepped backwards into the middle of the room, and, as he did so, something all but tripped him up. Turning with a sudden spring of alarm he saw – the kit-bag.

"Odd!" he thought. "That's not where I left it!" A few moments before it had surely been on his right, between the bed and the bath; he did not remember having moved it. It was very curious. What in the world was the matter with everything? Were all his senses gone queer? A terrific gust of wind tore at the windows, dashing the sleet against the glass with the force of a small gunshot, and then fled away howling dismally over the waste of

Bloomsbury roofs. A sudden vision of the Channel next day rose in his mind and recalled him sharply to realities.

"There's no one here at any rate; that's quite clear!" he exclaimed aloud. Yet at the time he uttered them he knew perfectly well that his words were not true and that he did not believe them himself. He felt exactly as though someone was hiding close about him, watching all his movements, trying to hinder his packing in some way. "And two of my senses," he added, keeping up the pretence, "have played me the most absurd tricks: the steps I heard and the figure I saw were both entirely imaginary."

He went back to the front room, poked the fire into a blaze, and sat down before it to think. What impressed him more than anything else was the fact that the kit-bag was no longer where he had left it. It had been dragged nearer to the door.

What happened afterwards that night happened, of course, to a man already excited by fear, and was perceived by a man that had not the full and proper control, therefore, of the senses. Outwardly, Johnson remained calm and master of himself to the end, pretending to the very last that everything he witnessed had a natural explanation, or was merely delusions of his tired nerves. But inwardly, in his very heart, he knew all along that someone had been hiding downstairs in the empty suite when he came in, that this person had watched his opportunity and then stealthily made his way up to the bedroom, and that all he saw and heard afterwards, from the moving of the kit-bag to – well, to the other things this story has to tell – were caused directly by the presence of this invisible person.

And it was here, just when he most desired to keep his mind and thoughts controlled, that the vivid pictures received day after day upon the mental plates exposed in the courtroom of the Old Bailey, came strongly to light and developed themselves in the dark room of his inner vision. Unpleasant, haunting memories have a way of coming to life again just when the mind least desires them – in the silent watches of the night, on sleepless pillows, during the lonely hours spent by sick and dying beds. And so now, in the same way, Johnson saw nothing but the dreadful face of John Turk, the murderer, lowering at him from every corner of his mental field of vision; the white skin, the evil eyes, and the fringe of black hair low over the forehead. All the pictures of those ten days in court crowded back into his mind unbidden, and very vivid.

"This is all rubbish and nerves," he exclaimed at length, springing with sudden energy from his chair. "I shall finish my packing and go to bed. I'm overwrought, overtired. No doubt, at this rate I shall hear steps and things all night!"

But his face was deadly white all the same. He snatched up his field-glasses and walked across to the bedroom, humming a music-hall song as he went – a trifle too loud to be natural; and the instant he crossed the threshold and stood within the room something turned cold about his heart, and he felt that every hair on his head stood up.

The kit-bag lay close in front of him, several feet nearer to the door than he had left it, and just over its crumpled top he saw a head and face slowly sinking down out of sight as though someone were crouching behind it to hide, and at the same moment a sound like a long-drawn sigh was distinctly audible in the still air about him between the gusts of the storm outside.

Johnson had more courage and will-power than the girlish indecision of his face indicated; but at first such a wave of terror came over him that for some seconds he could do nothing but stand and stare. A violent trembling ran down his back and legs, and he was conscious of a foolish, almost a hysterical, impulse to scream aloud. That sigh seemed in his very ear, and the air still quivered with it. It was unmistakably a human sigh.

"Who's there?" he said at length, finding his voice; but though he meant to speak with loud decision, the tones came out instead in a faint whisper, for he had partly lost the control of his tongue and lips.

He stepped forward, so that he could see all round and over the kit-bag. Of course there was nothing there, nothing but the faded carpet and the bulging canvas sides. He put out his hands and threw open the mouth of the sack where it had fallen over, being only three parts full, and then he saw for the first time that round the inside, some six inches from the top, there ran a broad smear of dull crimson. It was an old and faded blood stain. He uttered a scream, and drew back his hands as if they had been burnt. At the same moment the kit-bag gave a faint, but unmistakable, lurch forward towards the door.

Johnson collapsed backwards, searching with his hands for the support of something solid, and the door, being further behind him than he realised, received his weight just in time to prevent his falling, and shut to with a resounding bang. At the same moment the swinging of his left arm accidentally touched the electric switch, and the light in the room went out.

It was an awkward and disagreeable predicament, and if Johnson had not been possessed of real pluck he might have done all manner of foolish things. As it was, however, he pulled himself together, and groped furiously for the little brass knob to turn the light on again. But the rapid closing of the door had set the coats hanging on it a-swinging, and his fingers became entangled in a confusion of sleeves and pockets, so that it was some moments before he found the switch. And in those few moments of bewilderment and terror two things happened that sent him beyond recall over the boundary into the region of genuine horror – he distinctly heard the kit-bag shuffling heavily across the floor in jerks, and close in front of his face sounded once again the sigh of a human being.

In his anguished efforts to find the brass button on the wall he nearly scraped the nails from his fingers, but even then, in those frenzied moments of alarm – so swift and alert are the impressions of a man keyed-up by a vivid emotion – he had time to realise that he dreaded the return of the light, and that it might be better for him to stay hidden in the merciful screen of darkness. It was but the impulse of a moment, however, and before he had time to act upon it he had yielded automatically to the original desire, and the room was flooded again with light.

But the second instinct had been right. It would have been better for him to have stayed in the shelter of the kind darkness. For there, close before him, bending over the half-packed kit-bag, clear as life in the merciless glare of the electric light, stood the figure of John Turk, the murderer. Not three feet from him the man stood, the fringe of black hair marked plainly against the pallor of the forehead, the whole horrible presentment of the scoundrel, as vivid as he had seen him day after day in the Old Bailey, when he stood there in the dock, cynical and callous, under the very shadow of the gallows.

In a flash Johnson realised what it all meant: the dirty and much-used bag; the smear of crimson within the top; the dreadful stretched condition of the bulging sides. He remembered how the victim's body had been stuffed into a canvas bag for burial, the ghastly, dismembered fragments forced with lime into this very bag; and the bag itself produced as evidence – it all came back to him as clear as day...

Very softly and stealthily his hand groped behind him for the handle of the door, but before he could actually turn it the very thing that he most of all dreaded came about, and John Turk lifted his devil's face and looked at him. At the same moment that heavy sigh passed through the air of the room, formulated somehow into words: "It's my bag. And I want it."

Johnson just remembered clawing the door open, and then falling in a heap upon the floor of the landing, as he tried frantically to make his way into the front room.

He remained unconscious for a long time, and it was still dark when he opened his eyes and realised that he was lying, stiff and bruised, on the cold boards. Then the memory of what he had seen rushed back into his mind, and he promptly fainted again. When he woke the second time the wintry dawn was just beginning to peep in at the windows, painting the stairs a cheerless, dismal grey, and he managed to crawl into the front room, and cover himself with an overcoat in the armchair, where at length he fell asleep.

A great clamour woke him. He recognised Mrs. Monks's voice, loud and voluble.

"What! You ain't been to bed, sir! Are you ill, or has anything 'appened? And there's an urgent gentleman to see you, though it ain't seven o'clock yet, and—"

"Who is it?" he stammered. "I'm all right, thanks. Fell asleep in my chair, I suppose."

"Someone from Mr. Wilb'rim's, and he says he ought to see you quick before you go abroad, and I told him—"

"Show him up, please, at once," said Johnson, whose head was whirling, and his mind was still full of dreadful visions.

Mr. Wilbraham's man came in with many apologies, and explained briefly and quickly that an absurd mistake had been made, and that the wrong kit-bag had been sent over the night before.

"Henry somehow got hold of the one that came over from the courtoom, and Mr. Wilbraham only discovered it when he saw his own lying in his room, and asked why it had not gone to you," the man said.

"Oh!" said Johnson stupidly.

"And he must have brought you the one from the murder case instead, sir, I'm afraid," the man continued, without the ghost of an expression on his face. "The one John Turk packed the dead both in. Mr. Wilbraham's awful upset about it, sir, and told me to come over first thing this morning with the right one, as you were leaving by the boat."

He pointed to a clean-looking kit-bag on the floor, which he had just brought. "And I was to bring the other one back, sir," he added casually.

For some minutes Johnson could not find his voice. At last he pointed in the direction of his bedroom. "Perhaps you would kindly unpack it for me. Just empty the things out on the floor."

The man disappeared into the other room, and was gone for five minutes. Johnson heard the shifting to and fro of the bag, and the rattle of the skates and boots being unpacked.

"Thank you, sir," the man said, returning with the bag folded over his arm. "And can I do anything more to help you, sir?"

"What is it?" asked Johnson, seeing that he still had something he wished to say.

The man shuffled and looked mysterious. "Beg pardon, sir, but knowing your interest in the Turk case, I thought you'd maybe like to know what's happened—"

"Yes."

"John Turk killed hisself last night with poison immediately on getting his release, and he left a note for Mr. Wilbraham saying as he'd be much obliged if they'd have him put away, same as the woman he murdered, in the old kit-bag."

"What time – did he do it?" asked Johnson.

"Ten o'clock last night, sir, the warder says."

**If you enjoyed this, you might also like...**
The Doll, see page 213
The Decoy, see page 463

# The Occupant of the Room

**HE ARRIVED** late at night by the yellow diligence, stiff and cramped after the toilsome ascent of three slow hours. The village, a single mass of shadow, was already asleep. Only in front of the little hotel was there noise and light and bustle – for a moment. The horses, with tired, slouching gait, crossed the road and disappeared into the stable of their own accord, their harness trailing in the dust; and the lumbering diligence stood for the night where they had dragged it – the body of a great yellow-sided beetle with broken legs.

In spite of his physical weariness the schoolmaster, revelling in the first hours of his ten-guinea holiday, felt exhilarated. For the high Alpine valley was marvellously still; stars twinkled over the torn ridges of the Dent du Midi where spectral snows gleamed against rocks that looked like solid ink; and the keen air smelt of pine forests, dew-soaked pastures, and freshly sawn wood. He took it all in with a kind of bewildered delight for a few minutes, while the other three passengers gave directions about their luggage and went to their rooms. Then he turned and walked over the coarse matting into the glare of the hall, only just able to resist stopping to examine the big mountain map that hung upon the wall by the door.

And, with a sudden disagreeable shock, he came down from the ideal to the actual. For at the inn – the only inn – there was no vacant room. Even the available sofas were occupied...

How stupid he had been not to write! Yet it had been impossible, he remembered, for he had come to the decision suddenly that morning in Geneva, enticed by the brilliance of the weather after a week of rain.

They talked endlessly, this gold-braided porter and the hard-faced old woman – her face was hard, he noticed – gesticulating all the time, and pointing all about the village with suggestions that he ill understood, for his French was limited and their *patois* was fearful.

"*There!*" – he might find a room, "or *there*! But we are, *hélas* full – more full than we care about. Tomorrow, perhaps – if So-and-So give up their rooms—!" And then, with much shrugging of shoulders, the hard-faced old woman stared at the gold-braided porter, and the porter stared sleepily at the schoolmaster.

At length, however, by some process of hope he did not himself understand, and following directions given by the old woman that were utterly unintelligible, he went out into the street and walked towards a dark group of houses she had pointed out to him. He only knew that he meant to thunder at a door and ask for a room. He was too weary to think out details. The porter half made to go with him, but turned back at the last moment to speak with the old woman. The houses sketched themselves dimly in the general blackness. The air was cold. The whole valley was filled with the rush and thunder of falling water. He was thinking vaguely that the dawn could not be very far away, and that he might even spend the night wandering in the woods, when there was a sharp noise behind him and he turned to see a figure hurrying after him. It was the porter – running.

And in the little hall of the inn there began again a confused three-cornered conversation, with frequent muttered colloquy and whispered asides in *patois* between the woman and the porter – the net result of which was that, "If Monsieur did not object – there *was* a room, after all, on the first floor – only it was in a sense 'engaged'. That is to say—"

But the schoolmaster took the room without inquiring too closely into the puzzle that had somehow provided it so suddenly. The ethics of hotel-keeping had nothing to do with him. If the woman offered him quarters it was not for him to argue with her whether the said quarters were legitimately hers to offer.

But the porter, evidently a little thrilled, accompanied the guest up to the room and supplied in a mixture of French and English details omitted by the landlady – and Minturn, the schoolmaster, soon shared the thrill with him, and found himself in the atmosphere of a possible tragedy.

All who know the peculiar excitement that belongs to high mountain valleys where dangerous climbing is a chief feature of the attractions, will understand a certain faint element of high alarm that goes with the picture. One looks up at the desolate, soaring ridges and thinks involuntarily of the men who find their pleasure for days and nights together scaling perilous summits among the clouds, and conquering inch by inch the icy peaks that for ever shake their dark terror in the sky. The atmosphere of adventure, spiced with the possible horror of a very grim order of tragedy, is inseparable from any imaginative contemplation of the scene; and the idea Minturn gleaned from the half-frightened porter lost nothing by his ignorance of the language. This Englishwoman, the real occupant of the room, had insisted on going without a guide. She had left just before daybreak two days before – the porter had seen her start – and… she had not returned! The route was difficult and dangerous, yet not impossible for a skilled climber, even a solitary one. And the Englishwoman was an experienced mountaineer. Also, she was self-willed, careless of advice, bored by warnings, self-confident to a degree. Queer, moreover; for she kept entirely to herself, and sometimes remained in her room with locked doors, admitting no one, for days together: a 'crank', evidently, of the first water.

This much Minturn gathered clearly enough from the porter's talk while his luggage was brought in and the room set to rights; further, too, that the search party had gone out and *might*, of course, return at any moment. In which case— Thus the room was empty, yet still hers. "If Monsieur did not object – if the risk he ran of having to turn out suddenly in the night—" It was the loquacious porter who furnished the details that made the transaction questionable; and Minturn dismissed the loquacious porter as soon as possible, and prepared to get into the hastily arranged bed and snatch all the hours of sleep he could before he was turned out.

At first, it must be admitted, he felt uncomfortable – distinctly uncomfortable. He was in someone else's room. He had really no right to be there. It was in the nature of an unwarrantable intrusion; and while he unpacked he kept looking over his shoulder as though someone were watching him from the corners. Any moment, it seemed, he would hear a step in the passage, a knock would come at the door, the door would open, and there he would see this vigorous Englishwoman looking him up and down with anger. Worse still – he would hear her voice asking him what he was doing in her room – her bedroom. Of course, he had an adequate explanation, but still—!

Then, reflecting that he was already half undressed, the humour of it flashed for a second across his mind, and he laughed – *quietly*. And at once, after that laughter, under his breath, came the sudden sense of tragedy he had felt before. Perhaps, even while he smiled, her body lay broken and cold upon those awful heights, the wind of snow playing over her hair, her glazed eyes staring sightless up to the stars.... It made him shudder. The sense of this woman whom he had never seen, whose name even he did not know, became extraordinarily real. Almost he could imagine that she was somewhere in the room with him, hidden, observing all he did.

He opened the door softly to put his boots outside, and when he closed it again he turned the key. Then he finished unpacking and distributed his few things about the room. It was soon done; for, in the first place, he had only a small Gladstone and a knapsack, and secondly, the only place where he could spread his clothes was the sofa. There was no chest of drawers, and the cupboard, an unusually large and solid one, was locked. The Englishwoman's things had evidently been hastily put away in it. The only sign of her recent presence was a bunch of faded *Alpenrosen* standing in a glass jar upon the washhand stand. This, and a certain faint perfume, were all that remained. In spite, however, of these very slight evidences, the whole room was pervaded with a curious sense of occupancy that he found exceedingly distasteful. One moment the atmosphere seemed subtly charged with a 'just left' feeling; the next it was a queer awareness of 'still here' that made him turn cold and look hurriedly behind him.

Altogether, the room inspired him with a singular aversion, and the strength of this aversion seemed the only excuse for his tossing the faded flowers out of the window, and then hanging his mackintosh upon the cupboard door in such a way as to screen it as much as possible from view. For the sight of that big, ugly cupboard, filled with the clothing of a woman who might then be beyond any further need of covering – thus his imagination insisted on picturing it – touched in him a startled sense of the Incongruous that did not stop there, but crept through his mind gradually till it merged somehow into a sense of a rather grotesque horror. At any rate, the sight of that cupboard was offensive, and he covered it almost instinctively. Then, turning out the electric light, he got into bed.

But the instant the room was dark he realised that it was more than he could stand; for, with the blackness, there came a sudden rush of cold that he found it hard to explain. And the odd thing was that, when he lit the candle beside his bed, he noticed that his hand trembled.

This, of course, was too much. His imagination was taking liberties and must be called to heel. Yet the way he called it to order was significant, and its very deliberateness betrayed a mind that has already admitted fear. And fear, once in, is difficult to dislodge. He lay there upon his elbow in bed and carefully took note of all the objects in the room – with the intention, as it were, of taking an inventory of everything his senses perceived, then drawing a line, adding them up finally, and saying with decision, "That's all the room contains! I've counted every single thing. There is nothing more. *Now* – I may sleep in peace!"

And it was during this absurd process of enumerating the furniture of the room that the dreadful sense of distressing lassitude came over him that made it difficult even to finish counting. It came swiftly, yet with an amazing kind of violence that overwhelmed him softly and easily with a sensation of enervating weariness hard to describe. And its first effect was to banish fear. He no longer possessed enough energy to feel really afraid or nervous. The cold remained, but the alarm vanished. And into every corner of his usually vigorous personality crept the insidious poison of a *muscular* fatigue – at first – that in a few seconds, it seemed, translated itself into *spiritual* inertia. A sudden consciousness of the foolishness, the crass futility, of life, of effort, of fighting – of all that makes life worth living, shot into every fibre of his being, and left him utterly weak. A spirit of black pessimism that was not even vigorous enough to assert itself, invaded the secret chambers of his heart…

Every picture that presented itself to his mind came dressed in grey shadows: those bored and sweating horses toiling up the ascent to – nothing! That hard-faced landlady taking so much trouble to let her desire for gain conquer her sense of morality – for a few francs! That gold-braided porter, so talkative, fussy, energetic, and so anxious to tell all he knew! What was the use of them all? And for himself, what in the world was the good of all the labour and drudgery he went through in that preparatory school where he was junior master? What could it lead to? Wherein lay the value of so much uncertain toil, when the ultimate secrets of life were hidden and no one knew the final goal? How foolish was effort, discipline, work! How vain was pleasure! How trivial the noblest life!

With a fearful jump that nearly upset the candle Minturn pulled himself together. Such vicious thoughts were usually so remote from his normal character that the sudden vile invasion produced a swift reaction. Yet, only for a moment. Instantly, again, the black depression descended upon him like a wave. His work – it could lead to nothing but the dreary labour of a small headmastership after all – seemed as vain and foolish as his holiday in the Alps. What an idiot he had been, to be sure, to come out with a knapsack merely to work himself into a state of exhaustion climbing over toilsome mountains that led to nowhere – resulted in nothing. A dreariness of the grave possessed him. Life was a ghastly fraud! Religion childish humbug! Everything was merely a trap – a trap of death; a coloured toy that Nature used as a decoy! But a decoy for what? For nothing! There was no meaning in anything. The only *real* thing was – DEATH. And the happiest people were those who found it soonest.

*Then why wait for it to come?*

He sprang out of bed, thoroughly frightened. This was horrible. Surely mere physical fatigue could not produce a world so black, an outlook so dismal, a cowardice that struck with such sudden hopelessness at the very roots of life? For, normally, he was cheerful and strong, full of the tides of healthy living; and this appalling lassitude swept the very basis of his personality into Nothingness and the desire for death. It was like the development of a Secondary Personality. He had read, of course, how certain persons who suffered shocks developed thereafter entirely different characteristics, memory, tastes, and so forth. It had all rather frightened him. Though scientific men vouched for it, it was hardly to be believed. Yet here was a similar thing taking place in his own consciousness. He was, beyond question, experiencing all the mental variations of – *someone else*! It was un-moral. It was awful. It was – well, after all, at the same time, it was uncommonly interesting.

And this interest he began to feel was the first sign of his returning normal Self. For to feel interest is to live, and to love life.

He sprang into the middle of the room – then switched on the electric light. And the first thing that struck his eye was – the big cupboard.

"Hallo! There's that – beastly cupboard!" he exclaimed to himself, involuntarily, yet aloud. It held all the clothes, the swinging skirts and coats and summer blouses of the dead woman. For he knew now – somehow or other – that she *was* dead.…

At that moment, through the open windows, rushed the sound of falling water, bringing with it a vivid realisation of the desolate, snow-swept heights. He saw her – positively *saw* her! – lying where she had fallen, the frost upon her cheeks, the snow-dust eddying about her hair and eyes, her broken limbs pushing against the lumps of ice. For a moment the sense of spiritual lassitude – of the emptiness of life – vanished before this picture of broken effort – of a small human force battling pluckily, yet in vain, against the impersonal and pitiless Potencies of Inanimate Nature – and he found himself again, his normal self. Then, instantly, returned again that terrible sense of cold, nothingness, emptiness....

And he found himself standing opposite the big cupboard where her clothes were. He wanted to see those clothes – things she had used and worn. Quite close he stood, almost touching it. The next second he had touched it. His knuckles struck upon the wood.

Why he knocked is hard to say. It was an instinctive movement probably. Something in his deepest self dictated it – ordered it. He knocked at the door. And the dull sound upon the wood into the stillness of that room brought – horror. Why it should have done so he found it as hard to explain to himself as why he should have felt impelled to knock. The fact remains that when he heard the faint reverberation inside the cupboard, it brought with it so vivid a realisation of the woman's presence that he stood there shivering upon the floor with a dreadful sense of anticipation: he almost expected to hear an answering knock from within – the rustling of the hanging skirts perhaps – or, worse still, to see the locked door slowly open towards him.

And from that moment, he declares that in some way or other he must have partially lost control of himself, or at least of his better judgment; for he became possessed by such an overmastering desire to tear open that cupboard door and see the clothes within, that he tried every key in the room in the vain effort to unlock it, and then, finally, before he quite realised what he was doing – rang the bell!

But, having rung the bell for no obvious or intelligent reason at two o'clock in the morning, he then stood waiting in the middle of the floor for the servant to come, conscious for the first time that something outside his ordinary self had pushed him towards the act. It was almost like an internal voice that directed him... and thus, when at last steps came down the passage and he faced the cross and sleepy chambermaid, amazed at being summoned at such an hour, he found no difficulty in the matter of what he should say. For the same power that insisted he should open the cupboard door also impelled him to utter words over which he apparently had no control.

"It's not *you* I rang for!" he said with decision and impatience, "I want a man. Wake the porter and send him up to me at once – hurry! I tell you, hurry—!"

And when the girl had gone, frightened at his earnestness, Minturn realised that the words surprised himself as much as they surprised her. Until they were out of his mouth he had not known what exactly he was saying. But now he understood that some force foreign to his own personality was using his mind and organs. The black depression that had possessed him a few moments before was also part of it. The powerful mood of this vanished woman had somehow momentarily taken possession of him – communicated, possibly, by the atmosphere of things in the room still belonging to her. But even now, when the porter, without coat or collar, stood beside him in the room, he did not understand *why* he insisted, with a positive fury admitting no denial, that the key of that cupboard must be found and the door instantly opened.

The scene was a curious one. After some perplexed whispering with the chambermaid at the end of the passage, the porter managed to find and produce the key in question. Neither he nor the girl knew clearly what this excited Englishman was up to, or why he was so passionately intent upon opening the cupboard at two o'clock in the morning. They watched him with an air of wondering what was going to happen next. But something of his curious earnestness, even of his late fear, communicated itself to them, and the sound of the key grating in the lock made them both jump.

They held their breath as the creaking door swung slowly open. All heard the clatter of that other key as it fell against the wooden floor – within. The cupboard had been locked *from the inside*. But it was the scared housemaid, from her position in the corridor, who first saw – and with a wild scream fell crashing against the bannisters.

The porter made no attempt to save her. The schoolmaster and himself made a simultaneous rush towards the door, now wide open. They, too, had seen.

There were no clothes, skirts or blouses on the pegs, but, all by itself, from an iron hook in the centre, they saw the body of the Englishwoman hanging by the neck, the head bent horribly forwards, the tongue protruding. Jarred by the movement of unlocking, the body swung slowly round to face them. ... Pinned upon the inside of the door was a hotel envelope with the following words pencilled in straggling writing:

> *Tired – unhappy – hopelessly depressed... I cannot face life any longer... All is black. I must put an end to it... I meant to do it on the mountains, but was afraid. I slipped back to my room unobserved. This way is easiest and best...*

**If you enjoyed this, you might also like...**
The Damned, see page 414
The Listener, see page 382

# The Damned

## Chapter I

"I'M OVER FORTY, Frances, and rather set in my ways," I said good-naturedly, ready to yield if she insisted that our going together on the visit involved her happiness. "My work is rather heavy just now too, as you know. The question is, could I work there – with a lot of unassorted people in the house?"

"Mabel doesn't mention any other people, Bill," was my sister's rejoinder. "I gather she's alone – as well as lonely."

By the way she looked sideways out of the window at nothing, it was obvious she was disappointed, but to my surprise she did not urge the point; and as I glanced at Mrs. Franklyn's invitation lying upon her sloping lap, the neat, childish handwriting conjured up a mental picture of the banker's widow, with her timid, insignificant personality, her pale grey eyes and her expression as of a backward child. I thought, too, of the roomy country mansion her late husband had altered to suit his particular needs, and of my visit to it a few years ago when its barren spaciousness suggested a wing of Kensington Museum fitted up temporarily as a place to eat and sleep in. Comparing it mentally with the poky Chelsea flat where I and my sister kept impecunious house, I realised other points as well. Unworthy details flashed across me to entice: the fine library, the organ, the quiet work-room I should have, perfect service, the delicious cup of early tea, and hot baths at any moment of the day – without a geyser!

"It's a longish visit, a month – isn't it?" I hedged, smiling at the details that seduced me, and ashamed of my man's selfishness, yet knowing that Frances expected it of me. "There are points about it, I admit. If you're set on my going with you, I could manage it all right."

I spoke at length in this way because my sister made no answer. I saw her tired eyes gazing into the dreariness of Oakley Street and felt a pang strike through me. After a pause, in which again she said no word, I added: "So, when you write the letter, you might hint, perhaps, that I usually work all the morning, and – er – am not a very lively visitor! Then she'll understand, you see." And I half-rose to return to my diminutive study, where I was slaving, just then, at an absorbing article on Comparative Aesthetic Values in the Blind and Deaf.

But Frances did not move. She kept her grey eyes upon Oakley Street where the evening mist from the river drew mournful perspectives into view. It was late October. We heard the omnibuses thundering across the bridge. The monotony of that broad, characterless street seemed more than usually depressing. Even in June sunshine it was dead, but with autumn its melancholy soaked into every house between King's Road and the Embankment. It washed thought into the past, instead of inviting it hopefully towards the future. For me, its easy width was an avenue through which nameless slums across the river sent creeping messages of depression, and I always regarded it as Winter's main entrance into London – fog, slush, gloom trooped down it every November, waving their forbidding banners till March came to rout them.

Its one claim upon my love was that the south wind swept sometimes unobstructed up it, soft with suggestions of the sea. These lugubrious thoughts I naturally kept to myself, though I never ceased to regret the little flat whose cheapness had seduced us. Now, as I watched my sister's impassive face, I realised that perhaps she, too, felt as I felt, yet, brave woman, without betraying it.

"And, look here, Fanny," I said, putting a hand upon her shoulder as I crossed the room, "it would be the very thing for you. You're worn out with catering and housekeeping. Mabel is your oldest friend, besides, and you've hardly seen her since he died—"

"She's been abroad for a year, Bill, and only just came back," my sister interposed. "She came back rather unexpectedly, though I never thought she would go there to live—" She stopped abruptly. Clearly, she was only speaking half her mind. "Probably," she went on, "Mabel wants to pick up old links again."

"Naturally," I put in, "yourself chief among them." The veiled reference to the house I let pass.

It involved discussing the dead man for one thing.

"I feel I ought to go anyhow," she resumed, "and of course it would be jollier if you came too. You'd get in such a muddle here by yourself, and eat wrong things, and forget to air the rooms, and – oh, everything!" She looked up laughing. "Only," she added, "there's the British Museum—?"

"But there's a big library there," I answered, "and all the books of reference I could possibly want. It was of you I was thinking. You could take up your painting again; you always sell half of what you paint. It would be a splendid rest too, and Sussex is a jolly country to walk in. By all means, Fanny, I advise—"

Our eyes met, as I stammered in my attempts to avoid expressing the thought that hid in both our minds. My sister had a weakness for dabbling in the various 'new' theories of the day, and Mabel, who before her marriage had belonged to foolish societies for investigating the future life to the neglect of the present one, had fostered this undesirable tendency. Her amiable, impressionable temperament was open to every psychic wind that blew. I deplored, detested the whole business. But even more than this I abhorred the later influence that Mr. Franklyn had steeped his wife in, capturing her body and soul in his sombre doctrines. I had dreaded lest my sister also might be caught.

"Now that she is alone again—"

I stopped short. Our eyes now made pretence impossible, for the truth had slipped out inevitably, stupidly, although unexpressed in definite language. We laughed, turning our faces a moment to look at other things in the room. Frances picked up a book and examined its cover as though she had made an important discovery, while I took my case out and lit a cigarette I did not want to smoke. We left the matter there. I went out of the room before further explanation could cause tension. Disagreements grow into discord from such tiny things – wrong adjectives, or a chance inflection of the voice. Frances had a right to her views of life as much as I had. At least, I reflected comfortably, we had separated upon an agreement this time, recognised mutually, though not actually stated.

And this point of meeting was, oddly enough, our way of regarding someone who was dead.

For we had both disliked the husband with a great dislike, and during his three years' married life had only been to the house once – for a weekend visit; arriving late on Saturday, we had left after an early breakfast on Monday morning. Ascribing my sister's dislike to a natural jealousy at losing her old friend, I said merely that he displeased me.

Yet we both knew that the real emotion lay much deeper. Frances, loyal, honourable creature, had kept silence; and beyond saying that house and grounds – he altered one and laid out the other – distressed her as an expression of his personality somehow ('distressed' was the word she used), no further explanation had passed her lips.

Our dislike of his personality was easily accounted for – up to a point, since both of us shared the artist's point of view that a creed, cut to measure and carefully dried, was an ugly thing, and that a dogma to which believers must subscribe or perish everlastingly was a barbarism resting upon cruelty. But while my own dislike was purely due to an abstract worship of Beauty, my sister's had another twist in it, for with her 'new' tendencies, she believed that all religions were an aspect of truth and that no one, even the lowest wretch, could escape 'heaven' in the long run.

Samuel Franklyn, the rich banker, was a man universally respected and admired, and the marriage, though Mabel was fifteen years his junior, won general applause; his bride was an heiress in her own right – breweries – and the story of her conversion at a revivalist meeting where Samuel Franklyn had spoken fervidly of heaven, and terrifyingly of sin, hell and damnation, even contained a touch of genuine romance. She was a brand snatched from the burning; his detailed eloquence had frightened her into heaven; salvation came in the nick of time; his words had plucked her from the edge of that lake of fire and brimstone where their worm dieth not and the fire is not quenched. She regarded him as a hero, sighed her relief upon his saintly shoulder, and accepted the peace he offered her with a grateful resignation.

For her husband was a 'religious man' who successfully combined great riches with the glamour of winning souls. He was a portly figure, though tall, with masterful, big hands, his fingers rather thick and red; and his dignity, that just escaped being pompous, held in it something that was implacable. A convinced assurance, almost remorseless, gleamed in his eyes when he preached especially, and his threats of hell fire must have scared souls stronger than the timid, receptive Mabel whom he married. He clad himself in long frock-coats hat buttoned unevenly, big square boots, and trousers that invariably bagged at the knee and were a little short; he wore low collars, spats occasionally, and a tall black hat that was not of silk. His voice was alternately hard and unctuous; and he regarded theatres, ballrooms, and racecourses as the vestibule of that brimstone lake of whose geography he was as positive as of his great banking offices in the City. A philanthropist up to the hilt, however, no one ever doubted his complete sincerity; his convictions were ingrained, his faith borne out by his life – as witness his name upon so many admirable Societies, as treasurer, patron, or heading the donation list. He bulked large in the world of doing good, a broad and stately stone in the rampart against evil. And his heart was genuinely kind and soft for others – who believed as he did.

Yet, in spite of this true sympathy with suffering and his desire to help, he was narrow as a telegraph wire and unbending as a church pillar; he was intensely selfish; intolerant as an officer of the Inquisition, his bourgeois soul constructed a revolting scheme of heaven that was reproduced in miniature in all he did and planned. Faith was the *sine qua non* of salvation, and by 'faith' he meant belief in his own particular view of things – "which faith, except every one do keep whole and undefiled, without doubt he shall perish everlastingly." All the world but his own small, exclusive sect must be damned eternally – a pity, but alas, inevitable. He was right.

Yet he prayed without ceasing, and gave heavily to the poor – the only thing he could not give being big ideas to his provincial and suburban deity. Pettier than an insect, and more obstinate than a mule, he had also the superior, sleek humility of a 'chosen one'. He was churchwarden too. He read the lesson in a 'place of worship', either chilly or overheated, where neither organ, vestments, nor lighted candles were permitted, but where the odour of hair-wash on the boys' heads in the back rows pervaded the entire building.

This portrait of the banker, who accumulated riches both on earth and in heaven, may possibly be overdrawn, however, because Frances and I were 'artistic temperaments' that viewed the type with a dislike and distrust amounting to contempt. The majority considered Samuel Franklyn a worthy man and a good citizen. The majority, doubtless, held the saner view. A few years more, and he certainly would have been made a baronet. He relieved much suffering in the world, as assuredly as he caused many souls the agonies of torturing fear by his emphasis upon damnation.

Had there been one point of beauty in him, we might have been more lenient; only we found it not, and, I admit, took little pains to search. I shall never forget the look of dour forgiveness with which he heard our excuses for missing Morning Prayers that Sunday morning of our single visit to The Towers. My sister learned that a change was made soon afterwards, prayers being 'conducted' after breakfast instead of before.

The Towers stood solemnly upon a Sussex hill amid park-like modern grounds, but the house cannot better be described – it would be so wearisome for one thing – than by saying that it was a cross between an overgrown, pretentious Norwood villa and one of those saturnine Institutes for cripples the train passes as it slinks ashamed through South London into Surrey. It was 'wealthily' furnished and at first sight imposing, but on closer acquaintance revealed a meager personality, barren and austere. One looked for Rules and Regulations on the walls, all signed By Order. The place was a prison that shut out 'the world'. There was, of course, no billiard-room, no smoking-room, no room for play of any kind, and the great hall at the back, once a chapel, which might have been used for dancing, theatricals, or other innocent amusements, was consecrated in his day to meetings of various kinds, chiefly brigades, temperance or missionary societies. There was a harmonium at one end – on the level floor – a raised dais or platform at the other, and a gallery above for the servants, gardeners, and coachmen. It was heated with hot-water pipes, and hung with Doré's pictures, though these latter were soon removed and stored out of sight in the attics as being too unspiritual. In polished, shiny wood, it was a representation in miniature of that poky exclusive Heaven he took about with him, externalising it in all he did and planned, even in the grounds about the house.

Changes in The Towers, Frances told me, had been made during Mabel's year of widowhood abroad – an organ put into the big hall, the library made livable and re-catalogued – when it was permissible to suppose she had found her soul again and returned to her normal, healthy views of life, which included enjoyment and play, literature, music and the arts, without, however, a touch of that trivial thoughtlessness usually termed worldliness. Mrs. Franklyn, as I remembered her, was a quiet little woman, shallow, perhaps, and easily influenced, but sincere as a dog and thorough in her faithful Friendship. Her tastes at heart were catholic, and that heart was simple and unimaginative. That she took up with the various movements of the day was sign merely that she was searching in her limited way for a belief that should bring her peace. She was, in fact, a very ordinary woman, her caliber a little less than that of Frances. I knew they used to discuss all kinds of theories together, but as these discussions never resulted in action, I had come to regard her as harmless. Still, I was not sorry when she married, and I did not welcome now a renewal of the former intimacy. The philanthropist she had given no children, or she would have made a good and sensible mother. No doubt she would marry again.

"Mabel mentions that she's been alone at The Towers since the end of August," Frances told me at teatime; "and I'm sure she feels out of it and lonely. It would be a kindness to go. Besides, I always liked her."

I agreed. I had recovered from my attack of selfishness. I expressed my pleasure.

"You've written to accept," I said, half statement and half question.

Frances nodded. "I thanked for you," she added quietly, "explaining that you were not free at the moment, but that later, if not inconvenient, you might come down for a bit and join me."

I stared. Frances sometimes had this independent way of deciding things. I was convicted, and punished into the bargain.

Of course there followed argument and explanation, as between brother and sister who were affectionate, but the recording of our talk could be of little interest. It was arranged thus, Frances and I both satisfied. Two days later she departed for The Towers, leaving me alone in the flat with everything planned for my comfort and good behaviour – she was rather a tyrant in her quiet way – and her last words as I saw her off from Charing Cross rang in my head for a long time after she was gone:

"I'll write and let you know, Bill. Eat properly, mind, and let me know if anything goes wrong."

She waved her small gloved hand, nodded her head till the feather brushed the window, and was gone.

## Chapter II

**AFTER** the note announcing her safe arrival a week of silence passed, and then a letter came; there were various suggestions for my welfare, and the rest was the usual rambling information and description Frances loved, generously italicised.

"...and we are quite alone," she went on in her enormous handwriting that seemed such a waste of space and labour, "though some others are coming presently, I believe. You could work here to your heart's content. Mabel quite understands, and says she would love to have you when you feel free to come. She has changed a bit – back to her old natural self: she never mentions him. The place has changed too in certain ways: it has more cheerfulness, I think. She has put it in, this cheerfulness, spaded it in, if you know what I mean; but it lies about uneasily and is not natural – quite. The organ is a beauty. She must be very rich now, but she's as gentle and sweet as ever. Do you know, Bill, I think he must have frightened her into marrying him. I get the impression she was afraid of him." This last sentence was inked out, but I read it through the scratching; the letters being too big to hide. "He had an inflexible will beneath all that oily kindness which passed for spiritual. He was a real personality, I mean. I'm sure he'd have sent you and me cheerfully to the stake in another century – for our own good. Isn't it odd she never speaks of him, even to me?" This, again, was stroked through, though without the intention to obliterate – merely because it was repetition, probably. "The only reminder of him in the house now is a big copy of the presentation portrait that stands on the stairs of the Multitechnic Institute at Peckham – you know – that life-size one with his fat hand sprinkled with rings resting on a thick Bible and the other slipped between the buttons of a tight frock-coat. It hangs in the dining room and rather dominates our meals. I wish Mabel would take it down. I think she'd like to, if she dared. There's not a single photograph of him anywhere, even in her own room. Mrs. Marsh is here – you remember her, his housekeeper, the wife of the man who got penal servitude for killing a baby or something – you said she robbed him and justified her stealing because the story of the unjust steward was in the Bible! How we laughed over that! She's just the same too, gliding about all over the house and turning up when least expected."

Other reminiscences filled the next two sides of the letter, and ran, without a trace of punctuation, into instructions about a Salamander stove for heating my work-room in the flat; these were followed by things I was to tell the cook, and by requests for several articles she had forgotten and would like sent after her, two of them blouses, with descriptions so lengthy and contradictory that I sighed as I read them – "unless you come down soon, in which case perhaps you wouldn't mind bringing them; not the mauve one I wear in the evening sometimes, but the pale blue one with lace round the collar and the crinkly front. They're in the cupboard – or the drawer, I'm not sure which – of my bedroom. Ask Annie if you're in doubt. Thanks most awfully. Send a telegram, remember, and we'll meet you in the motor any time. I don't quite know if I shall stay the whole month – alone. It all depends...." And she closed the letter, the italicised words increasing recklessly towards the end, with a repetition that Mabel would love to have me "for myself", as also to have a "man in the house", and that I only had to telegraph the day and the train.... This letter, coming by the second post, interrupted me in a moment of absorbing work, and, having read it through to make sure there was nothing requiring instant attention, I threw it aside and went on with my notes and reading. Within five minutes, however, it was back at me again. That restless thing called 'between the lines' fluttered about my mind. My interest in the Balkan States – political article that had been 'ordered' – faded. Somewhere, somehow I felt disquieted, disturbed. At first I persisted in my work, forcing myself to concentrate, but soon found that a layer of new impressions floated between the article and my attention. It was like a shadow, though a shadow that dissolved upon inspection. Once or twice I glanced up, expecting to find someone in the room, that the door had opened unobserved and Annie was waiting for instructions. I heard the buses thundering across the bridge. I was aware of Oakley Street.

Montenegro and the blue Adriatic melted into the October haze along that depressing Embankment that aped a riverbank, and sentences from the letter flashed before my eyes and stung me. Picking it up and reading it through more carefully, I rang the bell and told Annie to find the blouses and pack them for the post, showing her finally the written description, and resenting the superior smile with which she at once interrupted. "I know them, sir," and disappeared.

But it was not the blouses: it was that exasperating thing 'between the lines' that put an end to my work with its elusive teasing nuisance. The first sharp impression is alone of value in such a case, for once analysis begins the imagination constructs all kinds of false interpretation. The more I thought, the more I grew fuddled. The letter, it seemed to me, wanted to say another thing; instead the eight sheets conveyed it merely. It came to the edge of disclosure, then halted.

There was something on the writer's mind, and I felt uneasy. Studying the sentences brought, however, no revelation, but increased confusion only; for while the uneasiness remained, the first clear hint had vanished. In the end I closed my books and went out to look up another matter at the British Museum library. Perhaps I should discover it that way – by turning the mind in a totally new direction. I lunched at the Express Dairy in Oxford Street close by, and telephoned to Annie that I would be home to tea at five.

And at tea, tired physically and mentally after breathing the exhausted air of the Rotunda for five hours, my mind suddenly delivered up its original impression, vivid and clear-cut; no proof accompanied the revelation; it was mere presentiment, but convincing. Frances was disturbed in her mind, her orderly, sensible, housekeeping mind; she was uneasy, even perhaps afraid; something in the house distressed her, and she had need of me. Unless I went down, her time of rest and change, her quite necessary holiday, in fact, would be spoilt. She was too unselfish to say this, but it ran everywhere between the lines. I saw it clearly now. Mrs. Franklyn, moreover – and that meant Frances too – would like a 'man in the house'. It was a disagreeable phrase, a suggestive way of hinting something she dared not state definitely. The two women in that great, lonely barrack of a house were afraid.

My sense of duty, affection, unselfishness, whatever the composite emotion may be termed, was stirred; also my vanity. I acted quickly, lest reflection should warp clear, decent judgment.

"Annie," I said, when she answered the bell, "you need not send those blouses by the post. I'll take them down tomorrow when I go. I shall be away a week or two, possibly longer." And, having looked up a train, I hastened out to telegraph before I could change my fickle mind.

But no desire came that night to change my mind. I was doing the right, the necessary thing. I was even in something of a hurry to get down to The Towers as soon as possible. I chose an early afternoon train.

## Chapter III

**A TELEGRAM** had told me to come to a town ten miles from the house, so I was saved the crawling train to the local station, and travelled down by an express. As soon as we left London the fog cleared off, and an autumn sun, though without heat in it, painted the landscape with golden browns and yellows. My spirits rose as I lay back in the luxurious motor and sped between the woods and hedges. Oddly enough, my anxiety of overnight had disappeared. It was due, no doubt, to that exaggeration of detail which reflection in loneliness brings. Frances and I had not been separated for over a year, and her letters from The Towers told so little. It had seemed unnatural to be deprived of those intimate particulars of mood and feeling I was accustomed to. We had such confidence in one another, and our affection was so deep. Though she was but five years younger than myself, I regarded her as a child. My attitude was fatherly.

In return, she certainly mothered me with a solicitude that never cloyed. I felt no desire to marry while she was still alive. She painted in watercolours with a reasonable success, and kept house for me; I wrote, reviewed books and lectured on aesthetics; we were a humdrum couple of quasi-artists, well satisfied with life, and all I feared for her was that she might become a suffragette or be taken captive by one of these wild theories that caught her imagination sometimes, and that Mabel, for one, had fostered. As for myself, no doubt she deemed me a trifle solid or stolid – I forget which word she preferred – but on the whole there was just sufficient difference of opinion to make intercourse suggestive without monotony, and certainly without quarrelling.

Drawing in deep draughts of the stinging autumn air, I felt happy and exhilarated. It was like going for a holiday, with comfort at the end of the journey instead of bargaining for centimes.

But my heart sank noticeably the moment the house came into view. The long drive, lined with hostile monkey trees and formal wellingtonias that were solemn and sedate, was mere extension of the miniature approach to a thousand semidetached suburban 'residences'; and the appearance of The Towers, as we turned the corner with a rush, suggested a commonplace climax to a story that had begun interestingly, almost thrillingly. A villa had escaped from the shadow of the Crystal Palace, thumped its way down by night, grown suddenly monstrous in a shower of rich rain, and settled itself insolently to stay. Ivy climbed about the opulent red-brick walls, but climbed neatly and with disfiguring effect, sham as on a prison or – the simile made me smile – an orphan asylum. There was no hint of the comely roughness of untidy ivy on a ruin. Clipped, trained, and precise it was, as on a brand-new protestant church. I swear there was not a bird's nest nor a single earwig in it anywhere. About the porch it was particularly thick, smothering a seventeenth-century lamp with a contrast that was quite horrible. Extensive glass-houses spread away on the farther side of the house; the numerous towers to which the building owed its name seemed made to hold school bells; and the windowsills, thick with potted flowers, made me think of the desolate suburbs of Brighton or Bexhill. In a commanding position upon the crest of a hill, it overlooked miles of undulating, wooded country southwards to the Downs, but behind it, to the north, thick banks of ilex, holly, and privet protected it from the cleaner and more stimulating winds. Hence, though highly placed, it was shut in. Three years had passed since I last set eyes upon, it, but the unsightly memory I had retained was justified by the reality. The place was deplorable.

It is my habit to express my opinions audibly sometimes, when impressions are strong enough to warrant it; but now I only sighed "Oh, dear," as I extricated my legs from many rugs and went into the house. A tall parlour-maid, with the bearing of a grenadier, received me, and standing behind her was Mrs. Marsh, the housekeeper, whom I remembered because her untidy back hair had suggested to me that it had been burnt. I went at once to my room, my hostess already dressing for dinner, but Frances came in to see me just as I was struggling with my black tie that had got tangled like a bootlace. She fastened it for me in a neat, effective bow, and while I held my chin up for the operation, staring blankly at the ceiling, the impression came – I wondered, was it her touch that caused it? – that something in her trembled. Shrinking perhaps is the truer word. Nothing in her face or manner betrayed it, nor in her pleasant, easy talk while she tidied my things and scolded my slovenly packing, as her habit was, questioning me about the servants at the flat. The blouses, though right, were crumpled, and my scolding was deserved. There was no impatience even. Yet somehow or other the suggestion of a shrinking reserve and holding back reached my mind. She had been lonely, of course, but it was more than that; she was glad that I had come, yet for some reason unstated she could have wished that I had stayed away. We discussed the news that had accumulated during our brief separation, and in doing so the impression, at best exceedingly slight, was forgotten. My chamber was large and beautifully furnished; the hall and dining room of our flat would have gone into it with a good remainder; yet it was not a place I could settle down in for work. It conveyed the idea of impermanence, making me feel transient as in a hotel bedroom. This, of course, was the fact. But some rooms convey a settled, lasting hospitality even in a hotel; this one did not; and as I was accustomed to work in the room I slept in, at least when visiting, a slight frown must have crept between my eyes.

"Mabel has fitted a work-room for you just out of the library," said the clairvoyant Frances. "No one will disturb you there, and you'll have fifteen thousand books all catalogued within easy reach. There's a private staircase too. You can breakfast in your room and slip down in your dressing gown if you want to." She laughed. My spirits took a turn upwards as absurdly as they had gone down.

"And how are you?" I asked, giving her a belated kiss. "It's jolly to be together again. I did feel rather lost without you, I'll admit."

"That's natural," she laughed. "I'm so glad."

She looked well and had country colour in her cheeks. She informed me that she was eating and sleeping well, going out for little walks with Mabel, painting bits of scenery again, and enjoying a complete change and rest; and yet, for all her brave description, the word somehow did not quite ring true. Those last words in particular did not ring true. There lay in her manner, just out of sight, I felt, this suggestion of the exact reverse – of unrest, shrinking, almost of anxiety. Certain small strings in her seemed over-tight. 'Keyed-up' was the slang expression that crossed my mind. I looked rather searchingly into her face as she was telling me this.

"Only – the evenings," she added, noticing my query, yet rather avoiding my eyes, "the evenings are – well, rather heavy sometimes, and I find it difficult to keep awake."

"The strong air after London makes you drowsy," I suggested, "and you like to get early to bed."

Frances turned and looked at me for a moment steadily. "On the contrary, Bill, I dislike going to bed – here. And Mabel goes so early." She said it lightly enough, fingering the disorder upon my dressing table in such a stupid way that I saw her mind was working in another direction altogether. She looked up suddenly with a kind of nervousness from the brush and scissors.

"Billy," she said abruptly, lowering her voice, "isn't it odd, but I hate sleeping alone here? I can't make it out quite; I've never felt such a thing before in my life. Do you – think it's all nonsense?"

And she laughed, with her lips but not with her eyes; there was a note of defiance in her I failed to understand.

"Nothing a nature like yours feels strongly is nonsense, Frances," I replied soothingly.

But I, too, answered with my lips only, for another part of my mind was working elsewhere, and among uncomfortable things. A touch of bewilderment passed over me. I was not certain how best to continue. If I laughed she would tell me no more, yet if I took her too seriously the strings would tighten further. Instinctively, then, this flashed rapidly across me: that something of what she felt, I had also felt, though interpreting it differently. Vague it was, as the coming of rain or storm that announce themselves hours in advance with their hint of faint, unsettling excitement in the air. I had been but a short hour in the house – big, comfortable, luxurious house – but had experienced this sense of being unsettled, unfixed, fluctuating – a kind of impermanence that transient lodgers in hotels must feel, but that a guest in a friend's home ought not to feel, be the visit short or long. To Frances, an impressionable woman, the feeling had come in the terms of alarm. She disliked sleeping alone, while yet she longed to sleep. The precise idea in my mind evaded capture, merely brushing through me, three-quarters out of sight; I realised only that we both felt the same thing, and that neither of us could get at it clearly.

Degrees of unrest we felt, but the actual thing did not disclose itself. It did not happen.

I felt strangely at sea for a moment. Frances would interpret hesitation as endorsement, and encouragement might be the last thing that could help her.

"Sleeping in a strange house," I answered at length, "is often difficult at first, and one feels lonely. After fifteen months in our tiny flat one feels lost and uncared-for in a big house. It's an uncomfortable feeling – I know it well. And this is a barrack, isn't it? The masses of furniture only make it worse. One feels in storage somewhere underground – the furniture doesn't furnish. One must never yield to fancies, though—"

Frances looked away towards the windows; she seemed disappointed a little.

"After our thickly-populated Chelsea," I went on quickly, "it seems isolated here."

But she did not turn back, and clearly I was saying the wrong thing. A wave of pity rushed suddenly over me. Was she really frightened, perhaps? She was imaginative, I knew, but never moody; common sense was strong in her, though she had her times of hypersensitiveness. I caught the echo of some unreasoning, big alarm in her. She stood there, gazing across my balcony towards the sea of wooded country that spread dim and vague in the obscurity of the dusk. The deepening shadows entered the room, I fancied, from the grounds below. Following her abstracted gaze a moment, I experienced a curious sharp desire to leave, to escape. Out yonder was wind and space and freedom. This enormous building was oppressive, silent, still.

Great catacombs occurred to me, things beneath the ground, imprisonment and capture. I believe I even shuddered a little.

I touched her shoulder. She turned round slowly, and we looked with a certain deliberation into each other's eyes.

"Fanny," I asked, more gravely than I intended, "you are not frightened, are you? Nothing has happened, has it?"

She replied with emphasis, "Of course not! How could it – I mean, why should I?" She stammered, as though the wrong sentence flustered her a second. "It's simply – that I have this ter – this dislike of sleeping alone."

Naturally, my first thought was how easy it would be to cut our visit short. But I did not say this. Had it been a true solution, Frances would have said it for me long ago.

"Wouldn't Mabel double-up with you?" I said instead, "or give you an adjoining room, so that you could leave the door between you open? There's space enough, heaven knows."

And then, as the gong sounded in the hall below for dinner, she said, as with an effort, this thing:

"Mabel did ask me – on the third night – after I had told her. But I declined."

"You'd rather be alone than with her?" I asked, with a certain relief.

Her reply was so gravely given, a child would have known there was more behind it: "Not that; but that she did not really want it."

I had a moment's intuition and acted on it impulsively. "She feels it too, perhaps, but wishes to face it by herself – and get over it?"

My sister bowed her head, and the gesture made me realise of a sudden how grave and solemn our talk had grown, as though some portentous thing were under discussion. It had come of itself – indefinite as a gradual change of temperature. Yet neither of us knew its nature, for apparently neither of us could state it plainly. Nothing happened, even in our words.

"That was my impression," she said, " – that if she yields to it she encourages it. And a habit forms so easily. Just think," she added with a faint smile that was the first sign of lightness she had yet betrayed, "what a nuisance it would be – everywhere – if everybody was afraid of being alone – like that."

I snatched readily at the chance. We laughed a little, though it was a quiet kind of laughter that seemed wrong. I took her arm and led her towards the door.

"Disastrous, in fact," I agreed.

She raised her voice to its normal pitch again, as I had done. "No doubt it will pass," she said, "now that you have come. Of course, it's chiefly my imagination." Her tone was lighter, though nothing could convince me that the matter itself was light – just then. "And in any case," tightening her grip on my arm as we passed into the bright enormous corridor and caught sight of Mrs. Franklyn waiting in the cheerless hall below, "I'm very glad you're here, Bill, and Mabel, I know, is too."

"If it doesn't pass," I just had time to whisper with a feeble attempt at jollity, "I'll come at night and snore outside your door. After that you'll be so glad to get rid of me that you won't mind being alone."

"That's a bargain," said Frances.

I shook my hostess by the hand, made a banal remark about the long interval since last we met, and walked behind them into the great dining room, dimly lit by candles, wondering in my heart how long my sister and I should stay, and why in the world we had ever left our cozy little flat to enter this desolation of riches and false luxury at all. The unsightly picture of the late Samuel Franklyn, Esq., stared down upon me from the farther end of the room above the mighty mantelpiece.

He looked, I thought, like some pompous Heavenly Butler who denied to all the world, and to us in particular, the right of entry without presentation cards signed by his hand as proof that we belonged to his own exclusive set. The majority, to his deep grief, and in spite of all his prayers on their behalf, must burn and 'perish everlastingly'.

## Chapter IV

**WITH** the instinct of the healthy bachelor I always try to make myself a nest in the place I live in, be it for long or short. Whether visiting, in lodging-house, or in hotel, the first essential is this nest – one's own things built into the walls as a bird builds in its feathers. It may look desolate and uncomfortable enough to others, because the central detail is neither bed nor wardrobe, sofa nor armchair, but a good solid writing-table that does not wriggle, and that has wide elbowroom.

And The Towers is vividly described for me by the single fact that I could not 'nest' there.

I took several days to discover this, but the first impression of impermanence was truer than I knew. The feathers of the mind refused here to lie one way. They ruffled, pointed, and grew wild.

Luxurious furniture does not mean comfort; I might as well have tried to settle down in the sofa and armchair department of a big shop. My bedroom was easily managed; it was the private workroom, prepared especially for my reception, that made me feel alien and outcast.

Externally, it was all one could desire: an antechamber to the great library, with not one, but two generous oak tables, to say nothing of smaller ones against the walls with capacious drawers.

There were reading desks, mechanical devices for holding books, perfect light, quiet as in a church, and no approach but across the huge adjoining room. Yet it did not invite.

"I hope you'll be able to work here," said my little hostess the next morning, as she took me in – her only visit to it while I stayed in the house – and showed me the ten-volume Catalogue.

"It's absolutely quiet and no one will disturb you."

"If you can't, Bill, you're not much good," laughed Frances, who was on her arm. "Even I could write in a study like this!"

I glanced with pleasure at the ample tables, the sheets of thick blotting paper, the rulers, sealing wax, paper knives, and all the other immaculate paraphernalia. "It's perfect," I answered with a secret thrill, yet feeling a little foolish. This was for Gibbon or Carlyle, rather than for my potboiling insignificancies. "If I can't write masterpieces here, it's certainly not your fault," and I turned with gratitude to Mrs. Franklyn. She was looking straight at me, and there was a question in her small pale eyes I did not understand. Was she noting the effect upon me, I wondered?

"You'll write here – perhaps a story about the house," she said, "Thompson will bring you anything you want; you only have to ring." She pointed to the electric bell on the central table, the wire running neatly down the leg. "No one has ever worked here before, and the library has been hardly used since it was put in. So there's no previous atmosphere to affect your imagination – er – adversely."

We laughed. "Bill isn't that sort," said my sister; while I wished they would go out and leave me to arrange my little nest and set to work.

I thought, of course, it was the huge listening library that made me feel so inconsiderable – the fifteen thousand silent, staring books, the solemn aisles, the deep, eloquent shelves. But when the women had gone and I was alone, the beginning of the truth crept over me, and I felt that first hint of disconsolateness which later became an imperative No. The mind shut down, images ceased to rise and flow. I read, made copious notes, but I wrote no single line at The Towers.

Nothing completed itself there. Nothing happened.

The morning sunshine poured into the library through ten long narrow windows; birds were singing; the autumn air, rich with a faint aroma of November melancholy that stung the imagination pleasantly, filled my antechamber. I looked out upon the undulating wooded landscape, hemmed in by the sweep of distant Downs, and I tasted a whiff of the sea. Rooks cawed as they floated above the elms, and there were lazy cows in the nearer meadows. A dozen times I tried to make my nest and settle down to work, and a dozen times, like a turning fastidious dog upon a hearth rug, I rearranged my chair and books and papers. The temptation of the Catalogue and shelves, of course, was accountable for much, yet not, I felt, for all. That was a manageable seduction. My work, moreover, was not of the creative kind that requires absolute absorption; it was the mere readable presentation of data I had accumulated. My notebooks were charged with facts ready to tabulate – facts, too, that interested me keenly. A mere effort of the will was necessary, and concentration of no difficult kind. Yet, somehow, it seemed beyond me: something forever pushed the facts into disorder… and in the end I sat in the sunshine, dipping into a dozen books selected from the shelves outside, vexed with myself and only half-enjoying it. I felt restless. I wanted to be elsewhere.

And even while I read, attention wandered. Frances, Mabel, her late husband, the house and grounds, each in turn and sometimes all together, rose uninvited into the stream of thought, hindering any consecutive flow of work. In disconnected fashion came these pictures that interrupted concentration, yet presenting themselves as broken fragments of a bigger thing my mind already groped for unconsciously. They fluttered round this hidden thing of which they were aspects, fugitive interpretations, no one of them bringing complete revelation. There was no adjective, such as pleasant or unpleasant, that I could attach to what I felt, beyond that the result was unsettling. Vague as the atmosphere of a dream, it yet persisted, and I could not dissipate it.

Isolated words or phrases in the lines I read sent questions scouring across my mind, sure sign that the deeper part of me was restless and ill at ease.

Rather trivial questions too – half-foolish interrogations, as of a puzzled or curious child: Why was my sister afraid to sleep alone, and why did her friend feel a similar repugnance, yet seek to conquer it? Why was the solid luxury of the house without comfort, its shelter without the sense of permanence? Why had Mrs. Franklyn asked us to come, artists, unbelieving vagabonds, types at the farthest possible remove from the saved sheep of her husband's household? Had a reaction set in against the hysteria of her conversion? I had seen no signs of religious fervour in her; her atmosphere was that of an ordinary, high-minded woman, yet a woman of the world. Lifeless, though, a little, perhaps, now that I came to think about it: she had made no definite impression upon me of any kind. And my thoughts ran vaguely after this fragile clue.

Closing my book, I let them run. For, with this chance reflection came the discovery that I could not see her clearly – could not feel her soul, her personality. Her face, her small pale eyes, her dress and body and walk, all these stood before me like a photograph; but her Self evaded me. She seemed not there, lifeless, empty, a shadow – nothing. The picture was disagreeable, and I put it by. Instantly she melted out, as though light thought had conjured up a phantom that had no real existence. And at that very moment, singularly enough, my eye caught sight of her moving past the window, going silently along the gravel path. I watched her, a sudden new sensation gripping me. "There goes a prisoner," my thought instantly ran, "one who wishes to escape, but cannot."

What brought the outlandish notion, heaven only knows. The house was of her own choice, she was twice an heiress, and the world lay open at her feet. Yet she stayed – unhappy, frightened, caught. All this flashed over me, and made a sharp impression even before I had time to dismiss it as absurd. But a moment later explanation offered itself, though it seemed as far-fetched as the original impression. My mind, being logical, was obliged to provide something, apparently. For Mrs. Franklyn, while dressed to go out, with thick walking-boots, a pointed stick, and a motor-cap tied on with a veil as for the windy lanes, was obviously content to go no farther than the little garden paths. The costume was a sham and a pretence. It was this, and her lithe, quick movements that suggested a caged creature – a creature tamed by fear and cruelty that cloaked themselves in kindness – pacing up and down, unable to realise why it got no farther, but always met the same bars in exactly the same place. The mind in her was barred.

I watched her go along the paths and down the steps from one terrace to another, until the laurels hid her altogether; and into this mere imagining of a moment came a hint of something slightly disagreeable, for which my mind, search as it would, found no explanation at all. I remembered then certain other little things. They dropped into the picture of their own accord. In a mind not deliberately hunting for clues, pieces of a puzzle sometimes come together in this way, bringing revelation, so that for a second there flashed across me, vanishing instantly again before I could consider it, a large, distressing thought. I can only describe vaguely as a Shadow.

Dark and ugly, oppressive certainly it might be described, with something torn and dreadful about the edges that suggested pain and strife and terror. The interior of a prison with two rows of occupied condemned cells, seen years ago in New York, sprang to memory after it – the connection between the two impossible to surmise even. But the 'certain other little things' mentioned above were these: that Mrs. Franklyn, in last night's dinner talk, had always referred to 'this house', but never called it 'home'; and had emphasised unnecessarily, for a well-bred woman, our 'great kindness' in coming down to stay so long with her. Another time, in answer to my futile compliment about the 'stately rooms', she said quietly, "It is an enormous house for so small a party; but I stay here very little, and only till I get it straight again." The three of us were going up the great staircase to bed as this was said, and, not knowing quite her meaning, I dropped the subject. It edged delicate ground, I felt. Frances added no word of her own. It now occurred to me abruptly that 'stay' was the word made use of, when 'live' would have been more natural. How insignificant to recall! Yet why did they suggest themselves just at this moment…?

And, on going to Frances's room to make sure she was not nervous or lonely, I realised abruptly, that Mrs. Franklyn, of course, had talked with her in a confidential sense that I, as a mere visiting brother, could not share. Frances had told me nothing. I might easily have wormed it out of her, had I not felt that for us to discuss further our hostess and her house merely because we were under the roof together, was not quite nice or loyal.

"I'll call you, Bill, if I'm scared," she had laughed as we parted, my room being just across the big corridor from her own. I had fallen asleep, thinking what in the world was meant by 'getting it straight again'.

And now in my antechamber to the library, on the second morning, sitting among piles of foolscap and sheets of spotless blotting-paper, all useless to me, these slight hints came back and helped to frame the big, vague Shadow I have mentioned. Up to the neck in this Shadow, almost drowned, yet just treading water, stood the figure of my hostess in her walking costume. Frances and I seemed swimming to her aid. The Shadow was large enough to include both house and grounds, but farther than that I could not see…. Dismissing it, I fell to reading my purloined book again. Before I turned another page, however, another startling detail leaped out at me: the figure of Mrs. Franklyn in the Shadow was not living. It floated helplessly, like a doll or puppet that has no life in it. It was both pathetic and dreadful.

Any one who sits in reverie thus, of course, may see similar ridiculous pictures when the will no longer guides construction. The incongruities of dreams are thus explained. I merely record the picture as it came. That it remained by me for several days, just as vivid dreams do, is neither here nor there. I did not allow myself to dwell upon it. The curious thing, perhaps, is that from this moment I date my inclination, though not yet my desire, to leave. I purposely say 'to leave'.

I cannot quite remember when the word changed to that aggressive, frantic thing which is escape.

## Chapter V

**WE WERE LEFT** delightfully to ourselves in this pretentious country mansion with the soul of a villa. Frances took up her painting again, and, the weather being propitious, spent hours out of doors, sketching flowers, trees and nooks of woodland, garden, even the house itself where bits of it peered suggestively across the orchards. Mrs. Franklyn seemed always busy about something or other, and never interfered with us except to propose motoring, tea in another part of the lawn, and so forth. She flitted everywhere, preoccupied, yet apparently doing nothing. The house engulfed her rather. No visitor called. For one thing, she was not supposed to be back from abroad yet; and for another, I think, the neighbourhood – her husband's neighbourhood – was puzzled by her sudden cessation from good works. Brigades and temperance societies did not ask to hold their meetings in the big hall, and the vicar arranged the school-treats in another's field without explanation. The full-length portrait in the dining room, and the presence of the housekeeper with the 'burnt' back hair, indeed, were the only reminders of the man who once had lived here. Mrs. Marsh retained her place in silence, well-paid sinecure as it doubtless was, yet with no hint of that suppressed disapproval one might have expected from her. Indeed there was nothing positive to disapprove, since nothing 'worldly' entered grounds or building. In her master's lifetime she had been another 'brand snatched from the burning', and it had then been her custom to give vociferous 'testimony' at the revival meetings where he adorned the platform and led in streams of prayer. I saw her sometimes on the stairs, hovering, wandering, half-watching and half-listening, and the idea came to me once that this woman somehow formed a link with the departed influence of her bigoted employer. She, alone among us, belonged to the house, and looked at home there. When I saw her talking – oh, with such correct and respectful mien – to Mrs. Franklyn, I had the feeling that for all her unaggressive attitude, she yet exerted some influence that sought to make her mistress stay in the building forever – live there. She would prevent her escape, prevent 'getting it straight again', thwart somehow her will to freedom, if she could. The idea in me was of the most fleeting kind. But another time, when I came down late at night to get a book from the library antechamber, and found her sitting in the hall – alone – the impression left upon me was the reverse of fleeting. I can never forget the vivid, disagreeable effect it produced upon me. What was she doing there at half-past eleven at night, all alone in the darkness? She was sitting upright, stiff, in a big chair below the clock. It gave me a turn. It was so incongruous and odd. She rose quietly as I turned the corner of the stairs, and asked me respectfully, her eyes cast down as usual, whether I had finished with the library, so that she might lock up. There was no more to it than that; but the picture stayed with me – unpleasantly.

These various impressions came to me at odd moments, of course, and not in a single sequence as I now relate them. I was hard at work before three days were past, not writing, as explained, but reading, making notes, and gathering material from the library for future use. It was in chance moments that these curious flashes came, catching me unawares with a touch of surprise that sometimes made me start. For they proved that my under-mind was still conscious of the Shadow, and that far away out of sight lay the cause of it that left me with a vague unrest, unsettled, seeking to 'nest' in a place that did not want me. Only when this deeper part knows harmony, perhaps, can good brainwork result, and my inability to write was thus explained.

Certainly, I was always seeking for something here I could not find – an explanation that continually evaded me. Nothing but these trivial hints offered themselves. Lumped together, however, they had the effect of defining the Shadow a little. I became more and more aware of its very real existence. And, if I have made little mention of Frances and my hostess in this connection, it is because they contributed at first little or nothing towards the discovery of what this story tries to tell. Our life was wholly external, normal, quiet, and uneventful; conversation banal – Mrs. Franklyn's conversation in particular. They said nothing that suggested revelation.

Both were in this Shadow, and both knew that they were in it, but neither betrayed by word or act a hint of interpretation. They talked privately, no doubt, but of that I can report no details.

And so it was that, after ten days of a very commonplace visit, I found myself looking straight into the face of a Strangeness that defied capture at close quarters. "There's something here that never happens," were the words that rose in my mind, "and that's why none of us can speak of it."

And as I looked out of the window and watched the vulgar blackbirds, with toes turned in, boring out their worms, I realised sharply that even they, as indeed everything large and small in the house and grounds, shared this strangeness, and were twisted out of normal appearance because of it. Life, as expressed in the entire place, was crumpled, dwarfed, emasculated. God's meanings here were crippled, His love of joy was stunted. Nothing in the garden danced or sang.

There was hate in it. "The Shadow," my thought hurried on to completion, "is a manifestation of hate; and hate is the Devil." And then I sat back frightened in my chair, for I knew that I had partly found the truth.

Leaving my books I went out into the open. The sky was overcast, yet the day by no means gloomy, for a soft, diffused light oozed through the clouds and turned all things warm and almost summery. But I saw the grounds now in their nakedness because I understood. Hate means strife, and the two together weave the robe that terror wears. Having no so-called religious beliefs myself, nor belonging to any set of dogmas called a creed, I could stand outside these feelings and observe. Yet they soaked into me sufficiently for me to grasp sympathetically what others, with more cabined souls (I flattered myself), might feel. That picture in the dining room stalked everywhere, hid behind every tree, peered down upon me from the peaked ugliness of the bourgeois towers, and left the impress of its powerful hand upon every bed of flowers. "You must not do this, you must not do that," went past me through the air. "You must not leave these narrow paths," said the rigid iron railings of black. "You shall not walk here," was written on the lawns. "Keep to the steps," "Don't pick the flowers; make no noise of laughter, singing, dancing," was placarded all over the rose-garden, and "Trespassers will be – not prosecuted but – destroyed" hung from the crest of monkey tree and holly. Guarding the ends of each artificial terrace stood gaunt, implacable policemen, warders, jailers. "Come with us," they chanted, "or be damned eternally."

I remember feeling quite pleased with myself that I had discovered this obvious explanation of the prison feeling the place breathed out. That the posthumous influence of heavy old Samuel Franklyn might be an inadequate solution did not occur to me. By 'getting the place straight again', his widow, of course, meant forgetting the glamour of fear and foreboding his depressing creed had temporarily forced upon her; and Frances, delicately minded being, did not speak of it because it was the influence of the man her friend had loved. I felt lighter; a load was lifted from me. "To trace the unfamiliar to the familiar," came back a sentence I had read somewhere, "is to understand." It was a real relief. I could talk with Frances now, even with my hostess, no danger of treading clumsily. For the key was in my hands. I might even help to dissipate the Shadow, 'to get it straight again'. It seemed, perhaps, our long invitation was explained!

I went into the house laughing – at myself a little. "Perhaps after all the artist's outlook, with no hard and fast dogmas, is as narrow as the others! How small humanity is! And why is there no possible and true combination of all outlooks?"

The feeling of 'unsettling' was very strong in me just then, in spite of my big discovery which was to clear everything up. And at the moment I ran into Frances on the stairs, with a portfolio of sketches under her arm.

It came across me then abruptly that, although she had worked a great deal since we came, she had shown me nothing. It struck me suddenly as odd, unnatural. The way she tried to pass me now confirmed my newborn suspicion that – well, that her results were hardly what they ought to be.

"Stand and deliver!" I laughed, stepping in front of her. "I've seen nothing you've done since you've been here, and as a rule you show me all your things. I believe they are atrocious and degrading!" Then my laughter froze.

She made a sly gesture to slip past me, and I almost decided to let her go, for the expression that flashed across her face shocked me. She looked uncomfortable and ashamed; the colour came and went a moment in he cheeks, making me think of a child detected in some secret naughtiness. It was almost fear.

"It's because they're not finished then?" I said, dropping the tone of banter, "or because they're too good for me to understand?" For my criticism of painting, she told me, was crude and ignorant sometimes. "But you'll let me see them later, won't you?"

Frances, however, did not take the way of escape I offered. She changed her mind. She drew the portfolio from beneath her arm instead. "You can see them if you really want to, Bill," she said quietly, and her tone reminded me of a nurse who says to a boy just grown out of childhood, "you are old enough now to look upon horror and ugliness – only I don't advise it."

"I do want to," I said, and made to go downstairs with her. But, instead, she said in the same low voice as before, "Come up to my room, we shall be undisturbed there." So I guessed that she had been on her way to show the paintings to our hostess, but did not care for us all three to see them together. My mind worked furiously.

"Mabel asked me to do them," she explained in a tone of submissive horror, once the door was shut, "in fact, she begged it of me. You know how persistent she is in her quiet way. I – er – had to."

She flushed and opened the portfolio on the little table by the window, standing behind me as I turned the sketches over – sketches of the grounds and trees and garden. In the first moment of inspection, however, I did not take in clearly why my sister's sense of modesty had been offended. For my attention flashed a second elsewhere. Another bit of the puzzle had dropped into place, defining still further the nature of what I called 'the Shadow'. Mrs. Franklyn, I now remembered, had suggested to me in the library that I might perhaps write something about the place, and I had taken it for one of her banal sentences and paid no further attention. I realised now that it was said in earnest. She wanted our interpretations, as expressed in our respective 'talents', painting and writing. Her invitation was explained. She left us to ourselves on purpose.

"I should like to tear them up," Frances was whispering behind me with a shudder, "only I promised—" She hesitated a moment.

"Promised not to?" I asked with a queer feeling of distress, my eyes glued to the papers.

"Promised always to show them to her first," she finished so low I barely caught it.

I have no intuitive, immediate grasp of the value of paintings; results come to me slowly, and though everyone believes his own judgment to be good, I dare not claim that mine is worth more than that of any other layman, Frances had too often convicted me of gross ignorance and error. I can only say that I examined these sketches with a feeling of amazement that contained revulsion, if not actually horror and disgust. They were outrageous. I felt hot for my sister, and it was a relief to know she had moved across the room on some pretence or other, and did not examine them with me. Her talent, of course, is mediocre, yet she has her moments of inspiration – moments, that is to say, when a view of Beauty not normally her own flames divinely through her. And these interpretations struck me forcibly as being thus 'inspired' – not her own. They were uncommonly well done; they were also atrocious. The meaning in them, however, was never more than hinted. There the unholy skill and power came in: they suggested so abominably, leaving most to the imagination. To find such significance in a bourgeois villa garden, and to interpret it with such delicate yet legible certainty, was a kind of symbolism that was sinister, even diabolical. The delicacy was her own, but the point of view was another's.

And the word that rose in my mind was not the gross description of 'impure', but the more fundamental qualification – 'un-pure'.

In silence I turned the sketches over one by one, as a boy hurries through the pages of an evil book lest he be caught.

"What does Mabel do with them?" I asked presently in a low tone, as I neared the end. "Does she keep them?"

"She makes notes about them in a book and then destroys them," was the reply from the end of the room. I heard a sigh of relief. "I'm glad you've seen them, Bill. I wanted you to – but was afraid to show them. You understand?"

"I understand," was my reply, though it was not a question intended to be answered. All I understood really was that Mabel's mind was as sweet and pure as my sister's, and that she had some good reason for what she did. She destroyed the sketches, but first made notes! It was an interpretation of the place she sought. Brother-like, I felt resentment, though, that Frances should waste her time and talent, when she might be doing work that she could sell. Naturally, I felt other things as well....

"Mabel pays me five guineas for each one," I heard. "Absolutely insists."

I stared at her stupidly a moment, bereft of speech or wit. "I must either accept, or go away," she went on calmly, but a little white. "I've tried everything. There was a scene the third day I was here – when I showed her my first result. I wanted to write to you, but hesitated—"

"It's unintentional, then, on your part – forgive my asking it, Frances, dear?" I blundered, hardly knowing what to think or say. 'Between the lines' of her letter came back to me. "I mean, you make the sketches in your ordinary way and – the result comes out of itself, so to speak?"

She nodded, throwing her hands out like a Frenchman. "We needn't keep the money for ourselves, Bill. We can give it away, but – I must either accept or leave," and she repeated the shrugging gesture. She sat down on the chair facing me, staring helplessly at the carpet.

"You say there was a scene?" I went on presently, "She insisted?"

"She begged me to continue," my sister replied very quietly. "She thinks – that is, she has an idea or theory that there's something about the place – something she can't get at quite." Frances stammered badly. She knew I did not encourage her wild theories.

"Something she feels – yes," I helped her, more than curious.

"Oh, you know what I mean, Bill," she said desperately. "That the place is saturated with some influence that she is herself too positive or too stupid to interpret. She's trying to make herself negative and receptive, as she calls it, but can't, of course, succeed. Haven't you noticed how dull and impersonal and insipid she seems, as though she had no personality? She thinks impressions will come to her that way. But they don't—"

"Naturally."

"So she's trying me – us – what she calls the sensitive and impressionable artistic temperament. She says that until she is sure exactly what this influence is, she can't fight it, turn it out, 'get the house straight', as she phrases it."

Remembering my own singular impressions, I felt more lenient than I might otherwise have done. I tried to keep impatience out of my voice.

"And this influence, what – whose is it?"

We used the pronoun that followed in the same breath, for I answered my own question at the same moment as she did:

"His." Our heads nodded involuntarily towards the floor, the dining room being directly underneath.

And my heart sank, my curiosity died away on the instant; I felt bored. A commonplace haunted house was the last thing in the world to amuse or interest me. The mere thought exasperated, with its suggestions of imagination, overwrought nerves, hysteria, and the rest.

Mingled with my other feelings was certainly disappointment. To see a figure or feel a 'presence', and report from day to day strange incidents to each other would be a form of weariness I could never tolerate.

"But really, Frances," I said firmly, after a moment's pause, "it's too far-fetched, this explanation. A curse, you know, belongs to the ghost stories of early Victorian days." And only my positive conviction that there was something after all worth discovering, and that it most certainly was not this, prevented my suggesting that we terminate our visit forthwith, or as soon as we decently could. "This is not a haunted house, whatever it is," I concluded somewhat vehemently, bringing my hand down upon her odious portfolio.

My sister's reply revived my curiosity sharply.

"I was waiting for you to say that. Mabel says exactly the same. He is in it – but it's something more than that alone, something far bigger and more complicated." Her sentence seemed to indicate the sketches, and though I caught the inference I did not take it up, having no desire to discuss them with her just them indeed, if ever.

I merely stared at her and listened. Questions, I felt sure, would be of little use. It was better she should say her thought in her own way.

"He is one influence, the most recent," she went on slowly, and always very calmly, "but there are others – deeper layers, as it were – underneath. If his were the only one, something would happen. But nothing ever does happen. The others hinder and prevent – as though each were struggling to predominate."

I had felt it already myself. The idea was rather horrible. I shivered.

"That's what is so ugly about it – that nothing ever happens," she said. "There is this endless anticipation – always on the dry edge of a result that never materialises. It is torture. Mabel is at her wits' end, you see. And when she begged me – what I felt about my sketches – I mean—"

She stammered badly as before.

I stopped her. I had judged too hastily. That queer symbolism in her paintings, pagan and yet not innocent, was, I understood, the result of mixture. I did not pretend to understand, but at least I could be patient. I consequently held my peace. We did talk on a little longer, but it was more general talk that avoided successfully our hostess, the paintings, wild theories, and him – until at length the emotion Frances had hitherto so successfully kept under burst vehemently forth again.

It had hidden between her calm sentences, as it had hidden between the lines of her letter. It swept her now from head to foot, packed tight in the thing she then said.

"Then, Bill, if it is not an ordinary haunted house," she asked, "what is it?"

The words were commonplace enough. The emotion was in the tone of her voice that trembled; in the gesture she made, leaning forward and clasping both hands upon her knees, and in the slight blanching of her cheeks as her brave eyes asked the question and searched my own with anxiety that bordered upon panic. In that moment she put herself under my protection. I winced.

"And why," she added, lowering her voice to a still and furtive whisper, "does nothing ever happen? If only," – this with great emphasis – "something would happen – break this awful tension – bring relief. It's the waiting I cannot stand." And she shivered all over as she said it, a touch of wildness in her eyes.

I would have given much to have made a true and satisfactory answer. My mind searched frantically for a moment, but in vain. There lay no sufficient answer in me. I felt what she felt, though with differences. No conclusive explanation lay within reach. Nothing happened. Eager as I was to shoot the entire business into the rubbish heap where ignorance and superstition discharge their poisonous weeds, I could not honestly accomplish this. To treat Frances as a child, and merely 'explain away' would be to strain her confidence in my protection, so affectionately claimed. It would further be dishonest to myself – weak, besides – to deny that I had also felt the strain and tension even as she did. While my mind continued searching, I returned her stare in silence; and Frances then, with more honesty and insight than my own, gave suddenly the answer herself – an answer whose truth and adequacy, so far as they went, I could not readily gainsay:

"I think, Bill, because it is too big to happen here – to happen anywhere, indeed, all at once – and too awful!"

To have tossed the sentence aside as nonsense, argued it away, proved that it was really meaningless, would have been easy – at any other time or in any other place; and, had the past week brought me none of the vivid impressions it had brought me, this is doubtless what I should have done. My narrowness again was proved. We understand in others only what we have in ourselves. But her explanation, in a measure, I knew was true. It hinted at the strife and struggle that my notion of a Shadow had seemed to cover thinly.

"Perhaps," I murmured lamely, waiting in vain for her to say more. "But you said just now that you felt the thing was 'in layers', as it were. Do you mean each one – each influence – fighting for the upper hand?"

I used her phraseology to conceal my own poverty. Terminology, after all, was nothing, provided we could reach the idea itself.

Her eyes said yes. She had her clear conception, arrived at independently, as was her way.

And, unlike her sex, she kept it clear, unsmothered by too many words.

"One set of influences gets at me, another gets at you. It's according to our temperaments, I think." She glanced significantly at the vile portfolio. "Sometimes they are mixed – and therefore false. There has always been in me, more than in you, the pagan thing, perhaps, though never, thank God, like that."

The frank confession of course invited my own, as it was meant to do. Yet it was difficult to find the words.

"What I have felt in this place, Frances, I honestly can hardly tell you, because – er – my impressions have not arranged themselves in any definite form I can describe. The strife, the agony of vainly-sought escape, and the unrest – a sort of prison atmosphere – this I have felt at different times and with varying degrees of strength. But I find, as yet, no final label to attach. I couldn't say pagan, Christian, or anything like that, I mean, as you do. As with the blind and deaf, you may have an intensification of certain senses denied to me, or even another sense altogether in embryo—"

"Perhaps," she stopped me, anxious to keep to the point, "you feel it as Mabel does. She feels the whole thing complete."

"That also is possible," I said very slowly. I was thinking behind my words. Her odd remark that it was 'big and awful' came back upon me as true. A vast sensation of distress and discomfort swept me suddenly. Pity was in it, and a fierce contempt, a savage, bitter anger as well. Fury against some sham authority was part of it.

"Frances," I said, caught unawares, and dropping all pretence, "what in the world can it be?" I looked hard at her. For some minutes neither of us spoke.

"Have you felt no desire to interpret it?" she asked presently, "Mabel did suggest my writing something about the house," was my reply, "but I've felt nothing imperative. That sort of writing is not my line, you know. My only feeling," I added, noticing that she waited for more, "is the impulse to explain, discover, get it out of me somehow, and so get rid of it. Not by writing, though – as yet." And again I repeated my former question:

"What in the world do you think it is?" My voice had become involuntarily hushed. There was awe in it. Her answer, given with slow emphasis, brought back all my reserve: the phraseology provoked me rather: – "Whatever it is, Bill, it is not of God."

I got up to go downstairs. I believe I shrugged my shoulders. "Would you like to leave, Frances? Shall we go back to town?" I suggested this at the door, and hearing no immediate reply, I turned back to look. Frances was sitting with her head bowed over and buried in her hands. The attitude horribly suggested tears. No woman, I realised, can keep back the pressure of strong emotion as long as Frances had done, without ending in a fluid collapse. I waited a moment uneasily, longing to comfort, yet afraid to act – and in this way discovered the existence of the appalling emotion in myself, hitherto but half guessed. At all costs a scene must be prevented: it would involve such exaggeration and overstatement. Brutally, such is the weakness of the ordinary man, I turned the handle to go out, but my sister then raised her head. The sunlight caught her face, framed untidily in its auburn hair, and I saw her wonderful expression with a start. Pity, tenderness, and sympathy shone in it like a flame. It was undeniable. There shone through all her features the imperishable love and yearning to sacrifice self for others which I have seen in only one type of human being. It was the great mother look.

"We must stay by Mabel and help her get it straight," she whispered, making the decision for us both.

I murmured agreement. Abashed and half ashamed, I stole softly from the room and went out into the grounds. And the first thing clearly realised when alone was this: that the long scene between us was without definite result. The exchange of confidence was really nothing but hints and vague suggestion. We had decided to stay, but it was a negative decision not to leave rather than a positive action. All our words and questions, our guesses, inferences, explanations, our most subtle allusions and insinuations, even the odious paintings themselves, were without definite result. Nothing had happened.

## Chapter VI

**AND INSTINCTIVELY**, once alone, I made for the places where she had painted her extraordinary pictures; I tried to see what she had seen. Perhaps, now that she had opened my mind to another view, I should be sensitive to some similar interpretation – and possibly by way of literary expression. If I were to write about the place, I asked myself, how should I treat it? I deliberately invited an interpretation in the way that came easiest to me – writing.

But in this case there came no such revelation. Looking closely at the trees and flowers, the bits of lawn and terrace, the rose-garden and corner of the house where the flaming creeper hung so thickly, I discovered nothing of the odious, unpure thing her colour and grouping had unconsciously revealed. At first, that is, I discovered nothing. The reality stood there, commonplace and ugly, side by side with her distorted version of it that lay in my mind. It seemed incredible. I tried to force it, but in vain. My imagination, ploughed less deeply than hers, or to another pattern, grew different seed. Where I saw the gross soul of an overgrown suburban garden, inspired by the spirit of a vulgar, rich revivalist who loved to preach damnation, she saw this rush of pagan liberty and joy, this strange license of primitive flesh which, tainted by the other, produced the adulterated, vile result.

Certain things, however, gradually then became apparent, forcing themselves upon me, willy-nilly. They came slowly, but overwhelmingly. Not that facts had changed, or natural details altered in the grounds – this was impossible – but that I noticed for the first time various aspects I had not noticed before – trivial enough, yet for me, just then, significant. Some I remembered from previous days; others I saw now as I wandered to and fro, uneasy, uncomfortable, – almost, it seemed, watched by some one who took note of my impressions. The details were so foolish, the total result so formidable. I was half aware that others tried hard to make me see. It was deliberate.

My sister's phrase, "one layer got at me, another gets at you," flashed, undesired, upon me.

For I saw, as with the eyes of a child, what I can only call a goblin garden – house, grounds, trees, and flowers belonged to a goblin world that children enter through the pages of their fairy tales. And what made me first aware of it was the whisper of the wind behind me, so that I turned with a sudden start, feeling that something had moved closer. An old ash tree, ugly and ungainly, had been artificially trained to form an arbor at one end of the terrace that was a tennis lawn, and the leaves of it now went rustling together, swishing as they rose and fell. I looked at the ash tree, and felt as though I had passed that moment between doors into this goblin garden that crouched behind the real one. Below, at a deeper layer perhaps, lay hidden the one my sister had entered.

To deal with my own, however, I call it goblin, because an odd aspect of the quaint in it yet never quite achieved the picturesque. Grotesque, probably, is the truer word, for everywhere I noticed, and for the first time, this slight alteration of the natural due either to the exaggeration of some detail, or to its suppression, generally, I think, to the latter. Life everywhere appeared to me as blocked from the full delivery of its sweet and lovely message. Some counter influence stopped it – suppression; or sent it awry – exaggeration. The house itself, mere expression, of course, of a narrow, limited mind, was sheer ugliness; it required no further explanation. With the grounds and garden, so far as shape and general plan were concerned, this was also true; but that trees and flowers and other natural details should share the same deficiency perplexed my logical soul, and even dismayed it. I stood and stared, then moved about, and stood and stared again. Everywhere was this mockery of a sinister, unfinished aspect. I sought in vain to recover my normal point of view. My mind had found this goblin garden and wandered to and fro in it, unable to escape.

The change was in myself, of course, and so trivial were the details which illustrated it, that they sound absurd, thus mentioned one by one. For me, they proved it, is all I can affirm. The goblin touch lay plainly everywhere: in the forms of the trees, planted at neat intervals along the lawns; in this twisted ash that rustled just behind me; in the shadow of the gloomy wellingtonias, whose sweeping skirts obscured the grass; but especially, I noticed, in the tops and crests of them. For here, the delicate, graceful curves of last year's growth seemed to shrink back into themselves. None of them pointed upwards. Their life had failed and turned aside just when it should have become triumphant. The character of a tree reveals itself chiefly at the extremities, and it was precisely here that they all drooped and achieved this hint of goblin distortion – in the growth, that is, of the last few years. What ought to have been fairy, joyful, natural, was instead uncomely to the verge of the grotesque. Spontaneous expression was arrested. My mind perceived a goblin garden, and was caught in it. The place grimaced at me.

With the flowers it was similar, though far more difficult to detect in detail for description. I saw the smaller vegetable growth as impish, half-malicious. Even the terraces sloped ill, as though their ends had sagged since they had been so lavishly constructed; their varying angles gave a queerly bewildering aspect to their sequence that was unpleasant to the eye. One might wander among their deceptive lengths and get lost – lost among open terraces! – with the house quite close at hand. Unhomely seemed the entire garden, unable to give repose, restlessness in it everywhere, almost strife, and discord certainly.

Moreover, the garden grew into the house, the house into the garden, and in both was this idea of resistance to the natural – the spirit that says No to joy. All over it I was aware of the effort to achieve another end, the struggle to burst forth and escape into free, spontaneous expression that should be happy and natural, yet the effort forever frustrated by the weight of this dark shadow that rendered it abortive. Life crawled aside into a channel that was a cul-de-sac, then turned horribly upon itself. Instead of blossom and fruit, there were weeds. This approach of life I was conscious of – then dismal failure. There was no fulfillment. Nothing happened.

And so, through this singular mood, I came a little nearer to understand the unpure thing that had stammered out into expression through my sister's talent. For the unpure is merely negative; it has no existence; it is but the cramped expression of what is true, stammering its way brokenly over false boundaries that seek to limit and confine. Great, full expression of anything is pure, whereas here was only the incomplete, unfinished, and therefore ugly. There was a strife and pain and desire to escape. I found myself shrinking from house and grounds as one shrinks from the touch of the mentally arrested, those in whom life has turned awry. There was almost mutilation in it.

Past items, too, now flocked to confirm this feeling that I walked, liberty captured and half-maimed, in a monstrous garden. I remembered days of rain that refreshed the countryside, but left these grounds, cracked with the summer heat, unsatisfied and thirsty; and how the big winds, that cleaned the woods and fields elsewhere, crawled here with difficulty through the dense foliage that protected The Towers from the North and West and East. They were ineffective, sluggish currents. There was no real wind. Nothing happened. I began to realise – far more clearly than in my sister's fanciful explanation about 'layers' – that here were many contrary influences at work, mutually destructive of one another. House and grounds were not haunted merely; they were the arena of past thinking and feeling, perhaps of terrible, impure beliefs, each striving to suppress the others, yet no one of them achieving supremacy because no one of them was strong enough, no one of them was true. Each, moreover, tried to win me over, though only one was able to reach my mind at all. For some obscure reason – possibly because my temperament had a natural bias towards the grotesque – it was the goblin layer. With me, it was the line of least resistance....

In my own thoughts this 'goblin garden' revealed, of course, merely my personal interpretation. I felt now objectively what long ago my mind had felt subjectively. My work, essential sign of spontaneous life with me, had stopped dead; production had become impossible.

I stood now considerably closer to the cause of this sterility. The Cause, rather, turned bolder, had stepped insolently nearer. Nothing happened anywhere; house, garden, mind alike were barren, abortive, torn by the strife of frustrate impulse, ugly, hateful, sinful. Yet behind it all was still the desire of life – desire to escape – accomplish. Hope – an intolerable hope – I became startlingly aware – crowned torture.

And, realising this, though in some part of me where Reason lost her hold, there rose upon me then another and a darker thing that caught me by the throat and made me shrink with a sense of revulsion that touched actual loathing. I knew instantly whence it came, this wave of abhorrence and disgust, for even while I saw red and felt revolt rise in me, it seemed that I grew partially aware of the layer next below the goblin. I perceived the existence of this deeper stratum. One opened the way for the other, as it were. There were so many, yet all inter-related; to admit one was to clear the way for all. If I lingered I should be caught – horribly. They struggled with such violence for supremacy among themselves, however, that this latest uprising was instantly smothered and crushed back, though not before a glimpse had been revealed to me, and the redness in my thoughts transferred itself to colour my surroundings thickly and appallingly – with blood. This lurid aspect drenched the garden, smeared the terraces, lent to the very soil a tinge as of sacrificial rites, that choked the breath in me, while it seemed to fix me to the earth my feet so longed to leave. It was so revolting that at the same time I felt a dreadful curiosity as of fascination – I wished to stay. Between these contrary impulses I think I actually reeled a moment, transfixed by a fascination of the Awful. Through the lighter goblin veil I felt myself sinking down, down, down into this turgid layer that was so much more violent and so much more ancient. The upper layer, indeed, seemed fairy by comparison with this terror born of the lust for blood, thick with the anguish of human sacrificial victims.

Upper! Then I was already sinking; my feet were caught; I was actually in it! What atavistic strain, hidden deep within me, had been touched into vile response, giving this flash of intuitive comprehension, I cannot say. The coatings laid on by civilisation are probably thin enough in all of us. I made a supreme effort. The sun and wind came back. I could almost swear I opened my eyes. Something very atrocious surged back into the depths, carrying with it a thought of tangled woods, of big stones standing in a circle, motionless, white figures, the one form bound with ropes, and the ghastly gleam of the knife. Like smoke upon a battlefield, it rolled away....

I was standing on the gravel path below the second terrace when the familiar goblin garden danced back again, doubly grotesque now, doubly mocking, yet, by way of contrast, almost welcome. My glimpse into the depths was momentary, it seems, and had passed utterly away.

The common world rushed back with a sense of glad relief, yet ominous now forever, I felt, for the knowledge of what its past had built upon. In street, in theatre, in the festivities of friends, in music-room or playing field, even indeed in church – how could the memory of what I had seen and felt leave its hideous trace? The very structure of my Thought, it seemed to me, was stained.

What has been thought by others can never be obliterated until....

With a start my reverie broke and fled, scattered by a violent sound that I recognised for the first time in my life as wholly desirable. The returning motor meant that my hostess was back.

Yet, so urgent had been my temporary obsession, that my first presentation of her was – well, not as I knew her now. Floating along with a face of anguished torture I saw Mabel, a mere effigy captured by others' thinking, pass down into those depths of fire and blood that only just had closed beneath my feet. She dipped away. She vanished, her fading eyes turned to the last towards some saviour who had failed her. And that strange intolerable hope was in her face.

The mystery of the place was pretty thick about me just then. It was the fall of dusk, and the ghost of slanting sunshine was as unreal as though badly painted. The garden stood at attention all about me. I cannot explain it, but I can tell it, I think, exactly as it happened, for it remains vivid in me forever – that, for the first time, something almost happened, myself apparently the combining link through which it pressed towards delivery:

I had already turned towards the house. In my mind were pictures – not actual thoughts – of the motor, tea on the verandah, my sister, Mabel – when there came behind me this tumultuous, awful rush – as I left the garden. The ugliness, the pain, the striving to escape, the whole negative and suppressed agony that was the Place, focused that second into a concentrated effort to produce a result. It was a blinding tempest of long-frustrate desire that heaved at me, surging appallingly behind me like an anguished mob. I was in the act of crossing the frontier into my normal self again, when it came, catching fearfully at my skirts. I might use an entire dictionary of descriptive adjectives yet come no nearer to it than this – the conception of a huge assemblage determined to escape with me, or to snatch me back among themselves. My legs trembled for an instant, and I caught my breath – then turned and ran as fast as possible up the ugly terraces.

At the same instant, as though the clanging of an iron gate cut short the unfinished phrase, I thought the beginning of an awful thing:

"The Damned..."

Like this it rushed after me from that goblin garden that had sought to keep me:

"The Damned!"

For there was sound in it. I know full well it was subjective, not actually heard at all; yet somehow sound was in it – a great volume, roaring and booming thunderously, far away, and below me. The sentence dipped back into the depths that gave it birth, unfinished. Its completion was prevented. As usual, nothing happened. But it drove behind me like a hurricane as I ran towards the house, and the sound of it I can only liken to those terrible undertones you may hear standing beside Niagara. They lie behind the mere crash of the falling flood, within it somehow, not audible to all – felt rather than definitely heard.

It seemed to echo back from the surface of those sagging terraces as I flew across their sloping ends, for it was somehow underneath them. It was in the rustle of the wind that stirred the skirts of the drooping wellingtonias. The beds of formal flowers passed it on to the creepers, red as blood, that crept over the unsightly building. Into the structure of the vulgar and forbidding house it sank away; The Towers took it home. The uncomely doors and windows seemed almost like mouths that had uttered the words themselves, and on the upper floors at that very moment I saw two maids in the act of closing them again.

And on the verandah, as I arrived breathless, and shaken in my soul, Frances and Mabel, standing by the tea table, looked up to greet me. In the faces of both were clearly legible the signs of shock. They watched me coming, yet so full of their own distress that they hardly noticed the state in which I came. In the face of my hostess, however, I read another and a bigger thing than in the face of Frances. Mabel knew. She had experienced what I had experienced. She had heard that awful sentence I had heard but heard it not for the first time; heard it, moreover, I verily believe, complete and to its dreadful end.

"Bill, did you hear that curious noise just now?" Frances asked it sharply before I could say a word. Her manner was confused; she looked straight at me; and there was a tremor in her voice she could not hide.

"There's wind about," I said, "wind in the trees and sweeping round the walls. It's risen rather suddenly." My voice faltered rather.

"No. It wasn't wind," she insisted, with a significance meant for me alone, but badly hidden. "It was more like distant thunder, we thought. How you ran too!" she added. "What a pace you came across the terraces!"

I knew instantly from the way she said it that they both had already heard the sound before and were anxious to know if I had heard it, and how. My interpretation was what they sought.

"It was a curiously deep sound, I admit. It may have been big guns at sea," I suggested, "forts or cruisers practicing. The coast isn't so very far, and with the wind in the right direction—"

The expression on Mabel's face stopped me dead.

"Like huge doors closing," she said softly in her colourless voice, "enormous metal doors shutting against a mass of people clamoring to get out." The gravity, the note of hopelessness in her tones, was shocking.

Frances had gone into the house the instant Mabel began to speak. "I'm cold," she had said; "I think I'll get a shawl." Mabel and I were alone. I believe it was the first time we had been really alone since I arrived. She looked up from the teacups, fixing her pallid eyes on mine. She had made a question of the sentence.

"You hear it like that?" I asked innocently. I purposely used the present tense.

She changed her stare from one eye to the other; it was absolutely expressionless. My sister's step sounded on the floor of the room behind us.

"If only—" Mabel began, then stopped, and my own feelings leaping out instinctively completed the sentence I felt was in her mind:

"—something would happen."

She instantly corrected me. I had caught her thought, yet somehow phrased it wrongly.

"We could escape!" She lowered her tone a little, saying it hurriedly. The 'we' amazed and horrified me; but something in her voice and manner struck me utterly dumb. There was ice and terror in it. It was a dying woman speaking – a lost and hopeless soul.

In that atrocious moment I hardly noticed what was said exactly, but I remember that my sister returned with a grey shawl about her shoulders, and that Mabel said, in her ordinary voice again, "It is chilly, yes; let's have tea inside," and that two maids, one of them the grenadier, speedily carried the loaded trays into the morning-room and put a match to the logs in the great open fireplace. It was, after all, foolish to risk the sharp evening air, for dusk was falling steadily, and even the sunshine of the day just fading could not turn autumn into summer. I was the last to come in. Just as I left the verandah a large black bird swooped down in front of me past the pillars; it dropped from overhead, swerved abruptly to one side as it caught sight of me, and flapped heavily towards the shrubberies on the left of the terraces, where it disappeared into the gloom. It flew very low, very close. And it startled me, I think because in some way it seemed like my Shadow materialised – as though the dark horror that was rising everywhere from house and garden, then settling back so thickly yet so imperceptibly upon us all, were incarnated in that whirring creature that passed between the daylight and the coming night.

I stood a moment, wondering if it would appear again, before I followed the others indoors, and as I was in the act of closing the windows after me, I caught a glimpse of a figure on the lawn. It was some distance away, on the other side of the shrubberies, in fact where the bird had vanished. But in spite of the twilight that half magnified, half obscured it, the identity was unmistakable. I knew the housekeeper's stiff walk too well to be deceived. "Mrs. Marsh taking the air," I said to myself. I felt the necessity of saying it, and I wondered why she was doing so at this particular hour. If I had other thoughts they were so vague, and so quickly and utterly suppressed, that I cannot recall them sufficiently to relate them here.

And, once indoors, it was to be expected that there would come explanation, discussion, conversation, at any rate, regarding the singular noise and its cause, some uttered evidence of the mood that had been strong enough to drive us all inside. Yet there was none. Each of us purposely, and with various skill, ignored it. We talked little, and when we did it was of anything in the world but that. Personally, I experienced a touch of that same bewilderment which had come over me during my first talk with Frances on the evening of my arrival, for I recall now the acute tension, and the hope, yet dread, that one or other of us must sooner or later introduce the subject. It did not happen, however; no reference was made to it even remotely. It was the presence of Mabel, I felt positive, that prohibited. As soon might we have discussed Death in the bedroom of a dying woman.

The only scrap of conversation I remember, where all was ordinary and commonplace, was when Mabel spoke casually to the grenadier asking why Mrs. Marsh had omitted to do something or other – what it was I forget – and that the maid replied respectfully that "Mrs. Marsh was very sorry, but her 'and still pained her." I enquired, though so casually that I scarcely know what prompted the words, whether she had injured herself severely, and the reply, "She upset a lamp and burnt herself," was said in a tone that made me feel my curiosity was indiscreet, "but she always has an excuse for not doing things she ought to do." The little bit of conversation remained with me, and I remember particularly the quick way Frances interrupted and turned the talk upon the delinquencies of servants in general, telling incidents of her own at our flat with a volubility that perhaps seemed forced, and that certainly did not encourage general talk as it may have been intended to do. We lapsed into silence immediately she finished.

But for all our care and all our calculated silence, each knew that something had, in these last moments, come very close; it had brushed us in passing; it had retired; and I am inclined to think now that the large dark thing I saw, riding the dusk, probably bird of prey, was in some sense a symbol of it in my mind – that actually there had been no bird at all, I mean, but that my mood of apprehension and dismay had formed the vivid picture in my thoughts. It had swept past us, it had retreated, but it was now, at this moment, in hiding very close. And it was watching us.

Perhaps, too, it was mere coincidence that I encountered Mrs. Marsh, his housekeeper, several times that evening in the short interval between tea and dinner, and that on each occasion the sight of this gaunt, half-saturnine woman fed my prejudice against her. Once, on my way to the telephone, I ran into her just where the passage is somewhat jammed by a square table carrying the Chinese gong, a grandfather's clock and a box of croquet mallets. We both gave way, then both advanced, then again gave way – simultaneously. It seemed, impossible to pass. We stepped with decision to the same side, finally colliding in the middle, while saying those futile little things, half apology, half excuse, that are inevitable at such times. In the end she stood upright against the wall for me to pass, taking her place against the very door I wished to open. It was ludicrous.

"Excuse me – I was just going in – to telephone," I explained. And she sidled off, murmuring apologies, but opening the door for me while she did so. Our hands met a moment on the handle.

There was a second's awkwardness – it was too stupid. I remembered her injury, and by way of something to say, I enquired after it. She thanked me; it was entirely healed now, but it might have been much worse; and there was something about the "mercy of the Lord" that I didn't quite catch. While telephoning, however – London call, and my attention focused on it – realised sharply that this was the first time I had spoken with her; also, that I had – touched her.

It happened to be a Sunday, and the lines were clear. I got my connection quickly, and the incident was forgotten while my thoughts went up to London. On my way upstairs, then, the woman came back into my mind, so that I recalled other things about her – how she seemed all over the house, in unlikely places often; how I had caught her sitting in the hall alone that night; how she was forever coming and going with her lugubrious visage and that untidy hair at the back that had made me laugh three years ago with the idea that it looked singed or burnt; and how the impression on my first arrival at The Towers was that this woman somehow kept alive, though its evidence was outwardly suppressed, the influence of her late employer and of his sombre teachings. Somewhere with her was associated the idea of punishment, vindictiveness, revenge. I remembered again suddenly my odd notion that she sought to keep her present mistress here, a prisoner in this bleak and comfortless house, and that really, in spite of her obsequious silence, she was intensely opposed to the change of thought that had reclaimed Mabel to a happier view of life.

All this in a passing second flashed in review before me, and I discovered, or at any rate reconstructed, the real Mrs. Marsh. She was decidedly in the Shadow. More, she stood in the forefront of it, stealthily leading an assault, as it were, against The Towers and its occupants, as though, consciously or unconsciously, she laboured incessantly to this hateful end.

I can only judge that some state of nervousness in me permitted the series of insignificant thoughts to assume this dramatic shape, and that what had gone before prepared the way and led her up at the head of so formidable a procession. I relate it exactly as it came to me. My nerves were doubtless somewhat on edge by now. Otherwise I should hardly have been a prey to the exaggeration at all. I seemed open to so many strange, impressions.

Nothing else, perhaps, can explain my ridiculous conversation with her, when, for the third time that evening, I came suddenly upon the woman half-way down the stairs, standing by an open window as if in the act of listening. She was dressed in black, a black shawl over her square shoulders and black gloves on her big, broad hands. Two black objects, prayer books apparently, she clasped, and on her head she wore a bonnet with shaking beads of jet. At first I did not know her, as I came running down upon her from the landing; it was only when she stood aside to let me pass that I saw her profile against the tapestry and recognised Mrs. Marsh. And to catch her on the front stairs, dressed like this, struck me as incongruous – impertinent. I paused in my dangerous descent. Through the opened window came the sound of bells – church bells – a sound more depressing to me than superstition, and as nauseating. Though the action was ill judged, I obeyed the sudden prompting – was it a secret desire to attack, perhaps? – and spoke to her.

"Been to church, I suppose, Mrs. Marsh?" I said. "Or just going, perhaps?"

Her face, as she looked up a second to reply, was like an iron doll that moved its lips and turned its eyes, but made no other imitation of life at all.

"Some of us still goes, sir," she said unctuously.

It was respectful enough, yet the implied judgment of the rest of the world made me almost angry. A deferential insolence lay behind the affected meekness.

"For those who believe no doubt it is helpful," I smiled. "True religion brings peace and happiness, I'm sure – joy, Mrs. Marsh, joy!" I found keen satisfaction in the emphasis.

She looked at me like a knife. I cannot describe the implacable thing that shone in her fixed, stern eyes, nor the shadow of felt darkness that stole across her face. She glittered. I felt hate in her. I knew – she knew too – who was in the thoughts of us both at that moment.

She replied softly, never forgetting her place for an instant:

"There is joy, sir – in 'eaven – over one sinner that repenteth, and in church there goes up prayer to Gawd for those 'oo – well, for the others, sir, 'oo—"

She cut short her sentence thus. The gloom about her as she said it was like the gloom about a hearse, a tomb, a darkness of great hopeless dungeons. My tongue ran on of itself with a kind of bitter satisfaction:

"We must believe there are no others, Mrs. Marsh. Salvation, you know, would be such a failure if there were. No merciful, all-foreseeing God could ever have devised such a fearful plan—"

Her voice, interrupting me, seemed to rise out of the bowels of the earth:

"They rejected the salvation when it was offered to them, sir, on earth."

"But you wouldn't have them tortured forever because of one mistake in ignorance," I said, fixing her with my eye. "Come now, would you, Mrs. Marsh? No God worth worshipping could permit such cruelty. Think a moment what it means."

She stared at me, a curious expression in her stupid eyes. It seemed to me as though the 'woman' in her revolted, while yet she dared not suffer her grim belief to trip. That is, she would willingly have had it otherwise but for a terror that prevented.

"We may pray for them, sir, and we do – we may 'ope." She dropped her eyes to the carpet.

"Good, good!" I put in cheerfully, sorry now that I had spoken at all. "That's more hopeful, at any rate isn't it?"

She murmured something about Abraham's bosom, and the "time of salvation not being forever," as I tried to pass her. Then a half gesture that she made stopped me. There was something more she wished to say – to ask. She looked up furtively. In her eyes I saw the 'woman' peering out through fear.

"Per'aps, sir." she faltered, as though lightning must strike her dead, "per'aps, would you think, a drop of cold water, given in His name, might moisten—?"

But I stopped her, for the foolish talk had lasted long enough. "Of course," I exclaimed, "of course. For God is love, remember, and love means charity, tolerance, sympathy, and sparing others pain," and I hurried past her, determined to end the outrageous conversation for which yet I knew myself entirely to blame. Behind me, she stood stock-still for several minutes, half bewildered, half alarmed, as I suspected. I caught the fragment of another sentence, one word of it, rather – "punishment" – but the rest escaped me. Her arrogance and condescending tolerance exasperated me, while I was at the same time secretly pleased that I might have touched some string of remorse or sympathy in her after all. Her belief was iron; she dared not let it go; yet somewhere underneath there lurked the germ of a wholesome revulsion. She would help 'them' – if she dared. Her question proved it.

Half ashamed of myself, I turned and crossed the hail quickly lest I should be tempted to say more, and in me was a disagreeable sensation as though I had just left the Incurable Ward of some great hospital. A reaction caught me as of nausea. Ugh! I wanted such people cleansed by fire. They seemed to me as centers of contamination whose vicious thoughts flowed out to stain God's glorious world. I saw myself, Frances, Mabel too especially, on the rack, while that odious figure of cruelty and darkness stood over us and ordered the awful handles turned in order that we might be 'saved' – forced, that is, to think and believe exactly as she thought and believed.

I found relief for my somewhat childish indignation by letting myself loose upon the organ then. The flood of Bach and Beethoven brought back the sense of proportion. It proved, however, at the same time that there had been this growth of distortion in me, and that it had been provided apparently by my closer contact – for the first time – with that funereal personality, the woman who, like her master, believed that all holding views of God that differed from her own, must be damned eternally. It gave me, moreover, some faint clue perhaps, though a clue I was unequal of following up, to the nature of the strife and terror and frustrate influence in the house. That housekeeper had to do with it. She kept it alive. Her thought was like a spell she waved above her mistress's head.

## Chapter VII

**THAT NIGHT** I was wakened by a hurried tapping at my door, and before I could answer, Frances stood beside my bed. She had switched on the light as she came in. Her hair fell straggling over her dressing gown. Her face was deathly pale, its expression so distraught it was almost haggard.

The eyes were very wide. She looked almost like another woman.

She was whispering at a great pace: "Bill, Bill, wake up, quick!"

"I am awake. What is it?" I whispered too. I was startled.

"Listen!" was all she said. Her eyes stared into vacancy.

There was not a sound in the great house. The wind had dropped, and all was still. Only the tapping seemed to continue endlessly in my brain. The clock on the mantelpiece pointed to half-past two.

"I heard nothing, Frances. What is it?" I rubbed my eyes; I had been very deeply asleep.

"Listen!" she repeated very softly, holding up one finger and turning her eyes towards the door she had left ajar. Her usual calmness had deserted her. She was in the grip of some distressing terror.

For a full minute we held our breath and listened. Then her eyes rolled round again and met my own, and her skin went even whiter than before.

"It woke me," she said beneath her breath, and moving a step nearer to my bed. "It was the Noise." Even her whisper trembled.

"The Noise!" The word repeated itself dully of its own accord. I would rather it had been anything in the world but that – earthquake, foreign cannon, collapse of the house above our heads! "The Noise, Frances! Are you sure?" I was playing really for a little time.

"It was like thunder. At first I thought it was thunder. But a minute later it came again – from underground. It's appalling." She muttered the words, her voice not properly under control.

There was a pause of perhaps a minute, and then we both spoke at once. We said foolish, obvious things that neither of us believed in for a second. The roof had fallen in, there were burglars downstairs, the safes had been blown open. It was to comfort each other as children do that we said these things; also it was to gain further time.

"There's someone in the house, of course," I heard my voice say finally, as I sprang out of bed and hurried into dressing gown and slippers. "Don't be alarmed. I'll go down and see," and from the drawer I took a pistol it was my habit to carry everywhere with me. I loaded it carefully while Frances stood stock-still beside the bed and watched. I moved towards the open door.

"You stay here, Frances," I whispered, the beating of my heart making the words uneven, "while I go down and make a search. Lock yourself in, girl. Nothing can happen to you. It was downstairs, you said?"

"Underneath," she answered faintly, pointing through the floor.

She moved suddenly between me and the door.

"Listen! Hark!" she said, the eyes in her face quite fixed; "it's coming again," and she turned her head to catch the slightest sound. I stood there watching her, and while I watched her, shook.

But nothing stirred. From the halls below rose only the whirr and quiet ticking of the numerous clocks. The blind by the open window behind us flapped out a little into the room as the draught caught it.

"I'll come with you, Bill – to the next floor," she broke the silence. "Then I'll stay with Mabel – till you come up again." The blind sank down with a long sigh as she said it.

The question jumped to my lips before I could repress it:

"Mabel is awake. She heard it too?"

I hardly know why horror caught me at her answer. All was so vague and terrible as we stood there playing the great game of this sinister house where nothing ever happened.

"We met in the passage. She was on her way to me."

What shook in me, shook inwardly. Frances, I mean, did not see it. I had the feeling just that the Noise was upon us, that any second it would boom and roar about our ears. But the deep silence held. I only heard my sister's little whisper coming across the room in answer to my question:

"Then what is Mabel doing now?"

And her reply proved that she was yielding at last beneath the dreadful tension, for she spoke at once, unable longer to keep up the pretence. With a kind of relief, as it were, she said it out, looking helplessly at me like a child:

"She is weeping and gna—"

My expression must have stopped her. I believe I clapped both hands upon her mouth, though when I realised things clearly again, I found they were covering my own ears instead. It was a moment of unutterable horror. The revulsion I felt was actually physical. It would have given me pleasure to fire off all the five chambers of my pistol into the air above my head; the sound – a definite, wholesome sound that explained itself – would have been a positive relief. Other feelings, though, were in me too, all over me, rushing to and fro. It was vain to seek their disentanglement; it was impossible. I confess that I experienced, among them, a touch of paralysing fear – though for a moment only; it passed as sharply as it came, leaving me with a violent flush of blood to the face such as bursts of anger bring, followed abruptly by an icy perspiration over the entire body. Yet I may honestly avow that it was not ordinary personal fear I felt, nor any common dread of physical injury. It was, rather, a vast, impersonal shrinking – a sympathetic shrinking – from the agony and terror that countless others, somewhere, somehow, felt for themselves. The first sensation of a prison overwhelmed me in that instant, of bitter strife and frenzied suffering, and the fiery torture of the yearning to escape that was yet hopelessly uttered.... It was of incredible power. It was real. The vain, intolerable hope swept over me.

I mastered myself, though hardly knowing how, and took my sister's hand. It was as cold as ice, as I led her firmly to the door and out into the passage. Apparently she noticed nothing of my so near collapse, for I caught her whisper as we went. "You are brave, Bill; splendidly brave."

The upper corridors of the great sleeping house were brightly lit; on her way to me she had turned on every electric switch her hand could reach; and as we passed the final flight of stairs to the floor below, I heard a door shut softly and knew that Mabel had been listening – waiting for us. I led my sister up to it. She knocked, and the door was opened cautiously an inch or so. The room was pitch black. I caught no glimpse of Mabel standing there. Frances turned to me with a hurried whisper, "Billy, you will be careful, won't you?" and went in. I just had time to answer that I would not be long, and Frances to reply, "You'll find us here—" when the door closed and cut her sentence short before its end.

But it was not alone the closing door that took the final words. Frances – by the way she disappeared I knew it – had made a swift and violent movement into the darkness that was as though she sprang. She leaped upon that other woman who stood back among the shadows, for, simultaneously with the clipping of the sentence, another sound was also stopped – stifled, smothered, choked back lest I should also hear it. Yet not in time. I heard it – a hard and horrible sound that explained both the leap and the abrupt cessation of the whispered words.

I stood irresolute a moment. It was as though all the bones had been withdrawn from my body, so that I must sink and fall. That sound plucked them out, and plucked out my self-possession with them. I am not sure that it was a sound I had ever heard before, though children, I half remembered, made it sometimes in blind rages when they knew not what they did. In a grown-up person certainly I had never known it. I associated it with animals rather – horribly. In the history of the world, no doubt, it has been common enough, alas, but fortunately today there can be but few who know it, or would recognise it even when heard. The bones shot back into my body the same instant, but red-hot and burning; the brief instant of irresolution passed; I was torn between the desire to break down the door and enter, and to run – run for my life from a thing I dared not face.

Out of the horrid tumult, then, I adopted neither course. Without reflection, certainly without analysis of what was best to do for my sister, myself or Mabel, I took up my action where it had been interrupted. I turned from the awful door and moved slowly towards the head of the stairs.

But that dreadful little sound came with me. I believe my own teeth chattered. It seemed all over the house – in the empty halls that opened into the long passages towards the music-room, and even in the grounds outside the building. From the lawns and barren garden, from the ugly terraces themselves, it rose into the night, and behind it came a curious driving sound, incomplete, unfinished, as of wailing for deliverance, the wailing of desperate souls in anguish, the dull and dry beseeching of hopeless spirits in prison.

That I could have taken the little sound from the bedroom where I actually heard it, and spread it thus over the entire house and grounds, is evidence, perhaps, of the state my nerves were in.

The wailing assuredly was in my mind alone. But the longer I hesitated, the more difficult became my task, and, gathering up my dressing gown, lest I should trip in the darkness, I passed slowly down the staircase into the hall below. I carried neither candle nor matches; every switch in room and corridor was known to me. The covering of darkness was indeed rather comforting than otherwise, for if it prevented seeing, it also prevented being seen. The heavy pistol, knocking against my thigh as I moved, made me feel I was carrying a child's toy, foolishly. I experienced in every nerve that primitive vast dread which is the Thrill of darkness. Merely the child in me was comforted by that pistol.

The night was not entirely black; the iron bars across the glass front door were visible, and, equally, I discerned the big, stiff wooden chairs in the hall, the gaping fireplace, the upright pillars supporting the staircase, the round table in the center with its books and flower-vases, and the basket that held visitors' cards. There, too, was the stick and umbrella stand and the shelf with railway guides, directory, and telegraph forms. Clocks ticked everywhere with sounds like quiet footfalls. Light fell here and there in patches from the floor above. I stood a moment in the hall, letting my eyes grow more accustomed to the gloom, while deciding on a plan of search. I made out the ivy trailing outside over one of the big windows... and then the tall clock by the front door made a grating noise deep down inside its body – it was the Presentation clock, large and hideous, given by the congregation of his church – and, dreading the booming strike it seemed to threaten, I made a quick decision. If others beside myself were about in the night, the sound of that striking might cover their approach.

So I tiptoed to the right, where the passage led towards the dining room. In the other direction were the morning- and drawing rooms, both little used, and various other rooms beyond that had been his, generally now kept locked. I thought of my sister, waiting upstairs with that frightened woman for my return. I went quickly, yet stealthily.

And, to my surprise, the door of the dining room was open. It had been opened. I paused on the threshold, staring about me. I think I fully expected to see a figure blocked in the shadows against the heavy sideboard, or looming on the other side beneath his portrait. But the room was empty; I felt it empty. Through the wide bow-windows that gave on to the verandah came an uncertain glimmer that even shone reflected in the polished surface of the dinner-table, and again I perceived the stiff outline of chairs, waiting tenantless all round it, two larger ones with high carved backs at either end. The monkey trees on the upper terrace, too, were visible outside against the sky, and the solemn crests of the wellingtonias on the terraces below. The enormous clock on the mantelpiece ticked very slowly, as though its machinery were running down, and I made out the pale round patch that was its face. Resisting my first inclination to turn the lights up – my hand had gone so far as to finger the friendly knob – I crossed the room so carefully that no single board creaked, nor a single chair, as I rested a hand upon its back, moved on the parquet flooring. I turned neither to the right nor left, nor did I once look back.

I went towards the long corridor filled with priceless *objets d'art*, that led through various antechambers into the spacious music-room, and only at the mouth of this corridor did I next halt a moment in uncertainty. For this long corridor, lit faintly by high windows on the left from the verandah, was very narrow, owing to the mass of shelves and fancy tables it contained. It was not that I feared to knock over precious things as I went, but, that, because of its ungenerous width, there would be no room to pass another person – if I met one. And the certainty had suddenly come upon me that somewhere in this corridor another person at this actual moment stood. Here, somehow, amid all this dead atmosphere of furniture and impersonal emptiness, lay the hint of a living human presence; and with such conviction did it come upon me, that my hand instinctively gripped the pistol in my pocket before I could even think. Either someone had passed along this corridor just before me, or someone lay waiting at its farther end – withdrawn or flattened into one of the little recesses, to let me pass. It was the person who had opened the door. And the blood ran from my heart as I realised it.

It was not courage that sent me on, but rather a strong impulsion from behind that made it impossible to retreat: the feeling that a throng pressed at my back, drawing nearer and nearer; that I was already half surrounded, swept, dragged, coaxed into a vast prison-house where there was wailing and gnashing of teeth, where their worm dieth not and their fire is not quenched. I can neither explain nor justify the storm of irrational emotion that swept me as I stood in that moment, staring down the length of the silent corridor towards the music-room at the far end, I can only repeat that no personal bravery sent me down it, but that the negative emotion of fear was swamped in this vast sea of pity and commiseration for others that surged upon me.

My senses, at least, were no whit confused; if anything, my brain registered impressions with keener accuracy than usual. I noticed, for instance, that the two swinging doors of baize that cut the corridor into definite lengths, making little rooms of the spaces between them, were both wide-open – in the dim light no mean achievement. Also that the fronds of a palm plant, some ten feet in front of me, still stirred gently from the air of someone who had recently gone past them. The long green leaves waved to and fro like hands. Then I went stealthily forward down the narrow space, proud even that I had this command of myself, and so carefully that my feet made no sound upon the Japanese matting on the floor.

It was a journey that seemed timeless. I have no idea how fast or slow I went, but I remember that I deliberately examined articles on each side of me, peering with particular closeness into the recesses of wall and window. I passed the first baize doors, and the passage beyond them widened out to hold shelves of books; there were sofas and small reading-tables against the wall.

It narrowed again presently, as I entered the second stretch. The windows here were higher and smaller, and marble statuettes of classical subject lined the walls, watching me like figures of the dead. Their white and shining faces saw me, yet made no sign. I passed next between the second baize doors. They, too, had been fastened back with hooks against the wall. Thus all doors were open – had been recently opened.

And so, at length, I found myself in the final widening of the corridor which formed an antechamber to the music-room itself. It had been used formerly to hold the overflow of meetings. No door separated it from the great hall beyond, but heavy curtains hung usually to close it off, and these curtains were invariably drawn. They now stood wide. And here – I can merely state the impression that came upon me – I knew myself at last surrounded. The throng that pressed behind me, also surged in front: facing me in the big room, and waiting for my entry, stood a multitude; on either side of me, in the very air above my head, the vast assemblage paused upon my coming. The pause, however, was momentary, for instantly the deep, tumultuous movement was resumed that yet was silent as a cavern underground. I felt the agony that was in it, the passionate striving, the awful struggle to escape. The semi-darkness held beseeching faces that fought to press themselves upon my vision, yearning yet hopeless eyes, lips scorched and dry, mouths that opened to implore but found no craved delivery in actual words, and a fury of misery and hate that made the life in me stop dead, frozen by the horror of vain pity. That intolerable, vain Hope was everywhere.

And the multitude, it came to me, was not a single multitude, but many; for, as soon as one huge division pressed too close upon the edge of escape, it was dragged back by another and prevented. The wild host was divided against itself. Here dwelt the Shadow I had 'imagined' weeks ago, and in it struggled armies of lost souls as in the depths of some bottomless pit whence there is no escape. The layers mingled, fighting against themselves in endless torture. It was in this great Shadow I had clairvoyantly seen Mabel, but about its fearful mouth, I now was certain, hovered another figure of darkness, a figure who sought to keep it in existence, since to her thought were due those lampless depths of woe without escape.... Towards me the multitudes now surged.

It was a sound and a movement that brought me back into myself. The great dock at the farther end of the room just then struck the hour of three. That was the sound. And the movement—? I was aware that a figure was passing across the distant center of the floor. Instantly I dropped back into the arena of my little human terror. My hand again clutched stupidly at the pistol butt. I drew back into the folds of the heavy curtain. And the figure advanced.

I remember every detail. At first it seemed to me enormous – this advancing shadow – far beyond human scale; but as it came nearer, I measured it, though not consciously, by the organ pipes that gleamed in faint colours, just above its gradual soft approach.

It passed them, already halfway across the great room. I saw then that its stature was that of ordinary men. The prolonged booming of the clock died away. I heard the footfall, shuffling upon the polished boards. I heard another sound – a voice, low and monotonous, droning as in prayer. The figure was speaking. It was a woman. And she carried in both hands before her a small object that faintly shimmered – a glass of water. And then I recognised her.

There was still an instant's time before she reached me, and I made use of it. I shrank back, flattening myself against the wall. Her voice ceased a moment, as she turned and carefully drew the curtains together behind her, closing them with one hand. Oblivious of my presence, though she actually touched my dressing gown with the hand that pulled the cords, she resumed her dreadful, solemn march, disappearing at length down the long vista of the corridor like a shadow.

But as she passed me, her voice began again, so that I heard each word distinctly as she uttered it, her head aloft, her figure upright, as though she moved at the head of a procession:

"A drop of cold water, given in His name, shall moisten their burning tongues."

It was repeated monotonously over and over again, droning down into the distance as she went, until at length both voice and figure faded into the shadows at the farther end.

For a time, I have no means of measuring precisely, I stood in that dark corner, pressing my back against the wall, and would have drawn the curtains down to hide me had I dared to stretch an arm out. The dread that presently the woman would return passed gradually away. I realised that the air had emptied, the crowd her presence had stirred into activity had retreated; I was alone in the gloomy under-space of the odious building.... Then I remembered suddenly again the terrified women waiting for me on that upper landing; and realised that my skin was wet and freezing cold after a profuse perspiration. I prepared to retrace my steps. I remember the effort it cost me to leave the support of the wall and covering darkness of my corner, and step out into the grey light of the corridor. At first I sidled, then, finding this mode of walking impossible, turned my face boldly and walked quickly, regardless that my dressing gown set the precious objects shaking as I passed. A wind that sighed mournfully against the high, small windows seemed to have got inside the corridor as well; it felt so cold; and every moment I dreaded to see the outline of the woman's figure as she waited in recess or angle against the wall for me to pass.

Was there another thing I dreaded even more? I cannot say. I only know that the first baize doors had swung to behind me, and the second ones were close at hand, when the great dim thunder caught me, pouring up with prodigious volume so that it, seemed to roll out from another world. It shook the very bowels of the building. I was closer to it than that other time, when it had followed me from the goblin garden. There was strength and hardness in it, as of metal reverberation. Some touch of numbness, almost of paralysis, must surely have been upon me that I felt no actual terror, for I remember even turning and standing still to hear it better. "That is the Noise," my thought ran stupidly, and I think I whispered it aloud; "the Doors are closing." The wind outside against the windows was audible, so it cannot have been really loud, yet to me it was the biggest, deepest sound I have ever heard, but so far away, with such awful remoteness in it, that I had to doubt my own ears at the same time. It seemed underground – the rumbling of earthquake gates that shut remorselessly within the rocky Earth – stupendous ultimate thunder. They were shut off from help again. The doors had closed.

I felt a storm of pity, an agony of bitter, futile hate sweep through me. My memory of the figure changed then. The Woman with the glass of cooling water had stepped down from Heaven; but the Man – or was it Men? – who smeared this terrible layer of belief and Thought upon the world…!

I crossed the dining room – it was fancy, of course, that held my eyes from glancing at the portrait for fear I should see it smiling approval – and so finally reached the hall, where the light from the floor above seemed now quite bright in comparison. All the doors I closed carefully behind me; but first I had to open them. The woman had closed every one. Up the stairs, then, I actually ran, two steps at a time. My sister was standing outside Mabel's door. By her face I knew that she had also heard. There was no need to ask. I quickly made my mind up.

"There's nothing," I said, and detailed briefly my tour of search. "All is quiet and undisturbed downstairs." May God forgive me!

She beckoned to me, closing the door softly behind her. My heart beat violently a moment, then stood still.

"Mabel," she said aloud.

It was like the sentence of a judge, that one short word.

I tried to push past her and go in, but she stopped me with her arm. She was wholly mistress of herself, I saw.

"Hush!" she said in a lower voice. "I've got her round again with brandy. She's sleeping quietly now. We won't disturb her."

She drew me farther out into the landing, and as she did so, the clock in the hall below struck half-past three. I had stood, then, thirty minutes in the corridor below. "You've been such a long time," she said simply. "I feared for you," and she took my hand in her own that was cold and clammy.

## Chapter VIII

**AND THEN**, while that dreadful house stood listening about us in the early hours of this chill morning upon the edge of winter, she told me, with laconic brevity, things about Mabel that I heard as from a distance. There was nothing so unusual or tremendous in the short recital, nothing indeed I might not have already guessed for myself. It was the time and scene, the inference, too, that made it so afflicting: the idea that Mabel believed herself so utterly and hopelessly lost – beyond recovery damned.

That she had loved him with so passionate a devotion that she had given her soul into his keeping, this certainly I had not divined – probably because I had never thought about it one way or the other. He had 'converted' her, I knew, but that she had subscribed whole-heartedly to that most cruel and ugly of his dogmas – this was new to me, and came with a certain shock as I heard it. In love, of course, the weaker nature is receptive to all manner of suggestion. This man had 'suggested' his pet brimstone lake so vividly that she had listened and believed. He had frightened her into heaven; and his heaven, a definite locality in the skies, had its foretaste here on earth in miniature – The Towers, house, and garden. Into his dolorous scheme of a handful saved and millions damned, his enclosure, as it were, of sheep and goats, he had swept her before she was aware of it. Her mind no longer was her own. And it was Mrs. Marsh who kept the thought-stream open, though tempered, as she deemed, with that touch of craven, superstitious mercy.

But what I found it difficult to understand, and still more difficult to accept, was that, during her year abroad, she had been so haunted with a secret dread of that hideous after-death that she had finally revolted and tried to recover that clearer state of mind she had enjoyed before the religious bully had stunned her – yet had tried in vain. She had returned to The Towers to find her soul again, only to realise that it was lost eternally. The cleaner state of mind lay then beyond recovery. In the reaction that followed the removal of his terrible 'suggestion', she felt the crumbling of all that he had taught her, but searched in vain for the peace and beauty his teachings had destroyed. Nothing came to replace these. She was empty, desolate, hopeless; craving her former joy and carelessness, she found only hate and diabolical calculation. This man, whom she had loved to the point of losing her soul for him, had bequeathed to her one black and fiery thing – the terror of the damned. His thinking wrapped her in this iron garment that held her fast.

All this Frances told me, far more briefly than I have here repeated it. In her eyes and gestures and laconic sentences lay the conviction of great beating issues and of menacing drama my own description fails to recapture. It was all so incongruous and remote from the world I lived in that more than once a smile, though a smile of pity, fluttered to my lips; but a glimpse of my face in the mirror showed rather the leer of a grimace. There was no real laughter anywhere that night.

The entire adventure seemed so incredible, here, in this twentieth century – but yet delusion, that feeble word, did not occur once in the comments my mind suggested though did not utter. I remembered that forbidding Shadow too; my sister's watercolours; the vanished personality of our hostess; the inexplicable, thundering Noise, and the figure of Mrs. Marsh in her midnight ritual that was so childish yet so horrible. I shivered in spite of my own 'emancipated' cast of mind.

"There is no Mabel," were the words with which my sister sent another shower of ice down my spine. "He has killed her in his lake of fire and brimstone."

I stared at her blankly, as in a nightmare where nothing true or possible ever happened.

"He killed her in his lake of fire and brimstone," she repeated more faintly.

A desperate effort was in me to say the strong, sensible thing which should destroy the oppressive horror that grew so stiflingly about us both, but again the mirror drew the attempted smile into the merest grin, betraying the distortion that was everywhere in the place.

"You mean," I stammered beneath my breath, "that her faith has gone, but that the terror has remained?" I asked it, dully groping. I moved out of the line of the reflection in the glass.

She bowed her head as though beneath a weight; her skin was the pallor of grey ashes.

"You mean," I said louder, "that she has lost her – mind?"

"She is terror incarnate," was the whispered answer. "Mabel has lost her soul. Her soul is – there!" She pointed horribly below. "She is seeking it…?"

The word 'soul' stung me into something of my normal self again.

"But her terror, poor thing, is not – cannot be – transferable to us!" I exclaimed more vehemently. "It certainly is not convertible into feelings, sights and – even sounds!"

She interrupted me quickly, almost impatiently, speaking with that conviction by which she conquered me so easily that night.

"It is her terror that revived 'the Others'. It has brought her into touch with them. They are loose and driving after her. Her efforts at resistance have given them also hope – that escape, after all, is possible. Day and night they strive."

"Escape! Others!" The anger fast rising in me dropped of its own accord at the moment of birth. It shrank into a shuddering beyond my control. In that moment, I think, I would have believed in the possibility of anything and everything she might tell me. To argue or contradict seemed equally futile.

"His strong belief, as also the beliefs of others who have preceded him," she replied, so sure of herself that I actually turned to look over my shoulder, "have left their shadow like a thick deposit over the house and grounds. To them, poor souls imprisoned by thought, it was hopeless as granite walls – until her resistance, her effort to dissipate it – let in light. Now, in their thousands, they are flocking to this little light, seeking escape. Her own escape, don't you see, may release them all!"

It took my breath away. Had his predecessors, former occupants of this house, also preached damnation of all the world but their own exclusive sect? Was this the explanation of her obscure talk of 'layers', each striving against the other for domination? And if men are spirits, and these spirits survive, could strong Thought thus determine their condition even afterwards?

So many questions flooded into me that I selected no one of them, but stared in uncomfortable silence, bewildered, out of my depth, and acutely, painfully distressed. There was so odd a mixture of possible truth and incredible, unacceptable explanation in it all; so much confirmed, yet so much left darker than before. What she said did, indeed, offer a quasi-interpretation of my own series of abominable sensations – strife, agony, pity, hate, escape – but so far-fetched that only the deep conviction in her voice and attitude made it tolerable for a second even. I found myself in a curious state of mind. I could neither think clearly nor say a word to refute her amazing statements, whispered there beside me in the shivering hours of the early morning with only a wall between ourselves and – Mabel. Close behind her words I remember this singular thing, however – that an atmosphere as of the Inquisition seemed to rise and stir about the room, beating awful wings of black above my head.

Abruptly, then, a moment's common sense returned to me. I faced her.

"And the Noise?" I said aloud, more firmly, "the roar of the closing doors? We have all heard that! Is that subjective too?"

Frances looked sideways about her in a queer fashion that made my flesh creep again. I spoke brusquely, almost angrily. I repeated the question, and waited with anxiety for her reply.

"What noise?" she asked, with the frank expression of an innocent child. "What closing doors?"

But her face turned from grey to white, and I saw that drops of perspiration glistened on her forehead. She caught at the back of a chair to steady herself, then glanced about her again with that sidelong look that made my blood run cold. I understood suddenly then. She did not take in what I said. I knew now. She was listening – for something else.

And the discovery revived in me a far stronger emotion than any mere desire for immediate explanation. Not only did I not insist upon an answer, but I was actually terrified lest she would answer. More, I felt in me a terror lest I should be moved to describe my own experiences below-stairs, thus increasing their reality and so the reality of all. She might even explain them too!

Still listening intently, she raised her head and looked me in the eyes. Her lips opened to speak. The words came to me from a great distance, it seemed, and her voice had a sound like a stone that drops into a deep well, its fate though hidden, known.

"We are in it with her, too, Bill. We are in it with her. Our interpretations vary – because we are – in parts of it only. Mabel is in it – all."

The desire for violence came over me. If only she would say a definite thing in plain King's English! If only I could find it in me to give utterance to what shouted so loud within me! If only – the same old cry – something would happen! For all this elliptic talk that dazed my mind left obscurity everywhere. Her atrocious meaning, nonetheless, flashed through me, though vanishing before it wholly divulged itself.

It brought a certain reaction with it. I found my tongue. Whether I actually believed what I said is more than I can swear to; that it seemed to me wise at the moment is all I remember. My mind was in a state of obscure perception less than that of normal consciousness.

"Yes, Frances, I believe that what you say is the truth, and that we are in it with her" – I meant to say I with loud, hostile emphasis, but instead I whispered it lest she should hear the trembling of my voice – "and for that reason, my dear sister, we leave tomorrow, you and I – today, rather, since it is long past midnight – we leave this house of the damned. We go back to London."

Frances looked up, her face distraught almost beyond recognition. But it was not my words that caused the tumult in her heart. It was a sound – the sound she had been listening for – so faint I barely caught it myself, and had she not pointed I could never have known the direction whence it came. Small and terrible it rose again in the stillness of the night, the sound of gnashing teeth. And behind it came another – the tread of stealthy footsteps. Both were just outside the door.

The room swung round me for a second. My first instinct to prevent my sister going out – she had dashed past me frantically to the door – gave place to another when I saw the expression in her eyes. I followed her lead instead; it was surer than my own. The pistol in my pocket swung uselessly against my thigh. I was flustered beyond belief and ashamed that I was so.

"Keep close to me, Frances," I said huskily, as the door swung wide and a shaft of light fell upon a figure moving rapidly. Mabel was going down the corridor. Beyond her, in the shadows on the staircase, a second figure stood beckoning, scarcely visible.

"Before they get her! Quick!" was screamed into my ears, and our arms were about her in the same moment. It was a horrible scene. Not that Mabel struggled in the least, but that she collapsed as we caught her and fell with her dead weight, as of a corpse, limp, against us. And her teeth began again. They continued, even beneath the hand that Frances clapped upon her lips....

We carried her back into her own bedroom, where she lay down peacefully enough. It was so soon over.... The rapidity of the whole thing robbed it of reality almost. It had the swiftness of something remembered rather than of something witnessed. She slept again so quickly that it was almost as if we had caught her sleepwalking. I cannot say. I asked no questions at the time; I have asked none since; and my help was needed as little as the protection of my pistol. Frances was strangely competent and collected.... I lingered for some time uselessly by the door, till at length, looking up with a sigh, she made a sign for me to go.

"I shall wait in your room next door," I whispered, "till you come." But, though going out, I waited in the corridor instead, so as to hear the faintest call for help. In that dark corridor upstairs I waited, but not long. It may have been fifteen minutes when Frances reappeared, locking the door softly behind her. Leaning over the banisters, I saw her.

"I'll go in again about six o'clock," she whispered, "as soon as it gets light. She is sound asleep now. Please don't wait. If anything happens I'll call – you might leave your door ajar, perhaps."

And she came up, looking like a ghost.

But I saw her first safely into bed, and the rest of the night I spent in an armchair close to my opened door, listening for the slightest sound. Soon after five o'clock I heard Frances fumbling with the key, and, peering over the railing again, I waited till she reappeared and went back into her own room. She closed her door. Evidently she was satisfied that all was well.

Then, and then only, did I go to bed myself, but not to sleep. I could not get the scene out of my mind, especially that odious detail of it which I hoped and believed my sister had not seen – the still, dark figure of the housekeeper waiting on the stairs below – waiting, of course, for Mabel.

## Chapter IX

IT SEEMS I became a mere spectator after that; my sister's lead was so assured for one thing, and, for another, the responsibility of leaving Mabel alone – Frances laid it bodily upon my shoulders – was a little more than I cared about. Moreover, when we all three met later in the day, things went on so exactly as before, so absolutely without friction or distress, that to present a sudden, obvious excuse for cutting our visit short seemed ill-judged. And on the lowest grounds it would have been desertion. At any rate, it was beyond my powers, and Frances was quite firm that she must stay. We therefore did stay. Things that happen in the night always seem exaggerated and distorted when the sun shines brightly next morning; no one can reconstruct the terror of a nightmare afterwards, nor comprehend why it seemed so overwhelming at the time.

I slept till ten o'clock, and when I rang for breakfast, a note from my sister lay upon the tray, its message of counsel couched in a calm and comforting strain. Mabel, she assured me, was herself again and remembered nothing of what had happened; there was no need of any violent measures; I was to treat her exactly as if I knew nothing. "And, if you don't mind, Bill, let us leave the matter unmentioned between ourselves as well. Discussion exaggerates; such things are best not talked about. I'm sorry I disturbed you so unnecessarily; I was stupidly excited. Please forget all the things I said at the moment." She had written 'nonsense' first instead of 'things', then scratched it out. She wished to convey that hysteria had been abroad in the night, and I readily gulped the explanation down, though it could not satisfy me in the smallest degree.

There was another week of our visit still, and we stayed it out to the end without disaster. My desire to leave at times became that frantic thing, desire to escape; but I controlled it, kept silent, watched and wondered. Nothing happened. As before, and everywhere, there was no sequence of development, no connection between cause and effect; and climax, none whatever. The thing swayed up and down, backwards and forwards like a great loose curtain in the wind, and I could only vaguely surmise what caused the draught or why there was a curtain at all. A novelist might mould the queer material into coherent sequence that would be interesting but could not be true.

It remains, therefore, not a story but a history. Nothing happened.

Perhaps my intense dislike of the fall of darkness was due wholly to my stirred imagination, and perhaps my anger when I learned that Frances now occupied a bed in our hostess's room was unreasonable. Nerves were unquestionably on edge. I was forever on the lookout for some event that should make escape imperative, but yet that never presented itself. I slept lightly, left my door ajar to catch the slightest sound, even made stealthy tours of the house below-stairs while everybody dreamed in their beds. But I discovered nothing; the doors were always locked; I neither saw the housekeeper again in unreasonable times and places, nor heard a footstep in the passages and halls. The Noise was never once repeated. That horrible, ultimate thunder, my intensest dread of all, lay withdrawn into the abyss whence it had twice arisen. And though in my thoughts it was sternly denied existence, the great black reason for the fact afflicted me unbelievably. Since Mabel's fruitless effort to escape, the Doors kept closed remorselessly. She had failed; they gave up hope. For this was the explanation that haunted the region of my mind where feelings stir and hint before they clothe themselves in actual language. Only I firmly kept it there; it never knew expression.

But, if my ears were open, my eyes were opened too, and it were idle to pretend that I did not notice a hundred details that were capable of sinister interpretation had I been weak enough to yield. Some protective barrier had fallen into ruins round me, so that Terror stalked behind the general collapse, feeling for me through all the gaping fissures. Much of this, I admit, must have been merely the elaboration of those sensations I had first vaguely felt, before subsequent events and my talks with Frances had dramatised them into living thoughts. I therefore leave them unmentioned in this history, just as my mind left them unmentioned in that interminable final week. Our life went on precisely as before – Mabel unreal and outwardly so still; Frances, secretive, anxious, tactful to the point of slyness, and keen to save to the point of self-forgetfulness.

There were the same stupid meals, the same wearisome long evenings, the stifling ugliness of house and grounds, the Shadow settling in so thickly that it seemed almost a visible, tangible thing. I came to feel the only friendly things in all this hostile, cruel place were the robins that hopped boldly over the monstrous terraces and even up to the windows of the unsightly house itself. The robins alone knew joy; they danced, believing no evil thing was possible in all God's radiant world. They believed in everybody; their god's plan of life had no room in it for hell, damnation, and lakes of brimstone. I came to love the little birds. Had Samuel Franklyn known them, he might have preached a different sermon, bequeathing love in place of terror!

Most of my time I spent writing; but it was a pretence at best, and rather a dangerous one besides. For it stirred the mind to production, with the result that other things came pouring in as well. With reading it was the same. In the end I found an aggressive, deliberate resistance to be the only way of feasible defence. To walk far afield was out of the question, for it meant leaving my sister too long alone, so that my exercise was confined to nearer home. My saunters in the grounds, however, never surprised the goblin garden again. It was close at hand, but I seemed unable to get wholly into it. Too many things assailed my mind for any one to hold exclusive possession, perhaps.

Indeed, all the interpretations, all the 'layers', to use my sister's phrase, slipped in by turns and lodged there for a time. They came day and night, and though my reason denied them entrance they held their own as by a kind of squatter's right. They stirred moods already in me, that is, and did not introduce entirely new ones; for every mind conceals ancestral deposits that have been cultivated in turn along the whole line of its descent. Any day a chance shower may cause this one or that to blossom. Thus it came to me, at any rate. After darkness the Inquisition paced the empty corridors and set up ghastly apparatus in the dismal halls; and once, in the library, there swept over me that easy and delicious conviction that by confessing my wickedness I could resume it later, since Confession is expression, and expression brings relief and leaves one ready to accumulate again. And in such mood I felt bitter and unforgiving towards all others who thought differently. Another time it was a Pagan thing that assaulted me – so trivial yet oh, so significant at the time – when I dreamed that a herd of centaurs rolled up with a great stamping of hoofs round the house to destroy it, and then woke to hear the horses tramping across the field below the lawns; they neighed ominously and their noisy panting was audible as if it were just outside my windows.

But the tree episode, I think, was the most curious of all – except, perhaps, the incident with the children which I shall mention in a moment – for its closeness to reality was so unforgettable.

Outside the east window of my room stood a giant wellingtonia on the lawn, its head rising level with the upper sash. It grew some twenty feet away, planted on the highest terrace, and I often saw it when closing my curtains for the night, noticing how it drew its heavy skirts about it, and how the light from other windows threw glimmering streaks and patches that turned it into the semblance of a towering, solemn image. It stood there then so strikingly, somehow like a great old-world idol, that it claimed attention. Its appearance was curiously formidable. Its branches rustled without visibly moving and it had a certain portentous, forbidding air, so grand and dark and monstrous in the night that I was always glad when my curtains shut it out. Yet, once in bed, I had never thought about it one way or the other, and by day had certainly never sought it out.

One night, then, as I went to bed and closed this window against a cutting easterly wind, I saw – that there were two of these trees. A brother wellingtonia rose mysteriously beside it, equally huge, equally towering, equally monstrous. The menacing pair of them faced me there upon the lawn. But in this new arrival lay a strange suggestion that frightened me before I could argue it away. Exact counterpart of its giant companion, it revealed also that gross, odious quality that all my sister's paintings held. I got the odd impression that the rest of these trees, stretching away dimly in a troop over the farther lawns, were similar, and that, led by this enormous pair, they had all moved boldly closer to my windows. At the same moment a blind was drawn down over an upper room; the second tree disappeared into the surrounding darkness.

It was, of course, this chance light that had brought it into the field of vision, but when the black shutter dropped over it, hiding it from view, the manner of its vanishing produced the queer effect that it had slipped into its companion – almost that it had been an emanation of the one I so disliked, and not really a tree at all! In this way the garden turned vehicle for expressing what lay behind it all...!

The behaviour of the doors, the little, ordinary doors, seems scarcely worth mention at all, their queer way of opening and shutting of their own accord; for this was accountable in a hundred natural ways, and to tell the truth, I never caught one in the act of moving. Indeed, only after frequent repetitions did the detail force itself upon me, when, having noticed one, I noticed all. It produced, however, the unpleasant impression of a continual coming and going in the house, as though, screened cleverly and purposely from actual sight, someone in the building held constant invisible intercourse with – others.

Upon detailed descriptions of these uncertain incidents I do not venture, individually so trivial, but taken all together so impressive and so insolent. But the episode of the children, mentioned above, was different. And I give it because it showed how vividly the intuitive child-mind received the impression – one impression, at any rate – of what was in the air. It may be told in a very few words. I believe they were the coachman's children, and that the man had been in Mr. Franklyn's service; but of neither point am I quite positive.

I heard screaming in the rose-garden that runs along the stable walls – it was one afternoon not far from the tea-hour – and on hurrying up I found a little girl of nine or ten fastened with ropes to a rustic seat, and two other children – boys, one about twelve and one much younger – gathering sticks beneath the climbing rose trees. The girl was white and frightened, but the others were laughing and talking among themselves so busily while they picked that they did not notice my abrupt arrival. Some game, I understood, was in progress, but a game that had become too serious for the happiness of the prisoner, for there was a fear in the girl's eyes that was a very genuine fear indeed. I unfastened her at once; the ropes were so loosely and clumsily knotted that they had not hurt her skin; it was not that which made her pale. She collapsed a moment upon the bench, then picked up her tiny skirts and dived away at full speed into the safety of the stable-yard.

There was no response to my brief comforting, but she ran as though for her life, and I divined that some horrid boys' cruelty had been afoot. It was probably mere thoughtlessness, as cruelty with children usually is, but something in me decided to discover exactly what it was.

And the boys, not one whit alarmed at my intervention, merely laughed shyly when I explained that their prisoner had escaped, and told me frankly what their "gime" had been. There was no vestige of shame in them, nor any idea, of course, that they aped a monstrous reality.

That it was mere pretence was neither here nor there. To them, though make-believe, it was a make-believe of something that was right and natural and in no sense cruel. Grown-ups did it too. It was necessary for her good.

"We was going to burn her up, sir," the older one informed me, answering my "Why?" with the explanation, "Because she wouldn't believe what we wanted 'er to believe."

And, game though it was, the feeling of reality about the little episode was so arresting, so terrific in some way, that only with difficulty did I confine my admonitions on this occasion to mere words. The boys slunk off, frightened in their turn, yet not, I felt, convinced that they had erred in principle. It was their inheritance. They had breathed it in with the atmosphere of their bringing-up. They would renew the salutary torture when they could – till she 'believed' as they did.

I went back into the house, afflicted with a passion of mingled pity and distress impossible to describe, yet on my short way across the garden was attacked by other moods in turn, each more real and bitter than its predecessor. I received the whole series, as it were, at once. I felt like a diver rising to the surface through layers of water at different temperatures, though here the natural order was reversed, and the cooler strata were uppermost, the heated ones below. Thus, I was caught by the goblin touch of the willows that fringed the field; by the sensuous curving of the twisted ash that formed a gateway to the little grove of sapling oaks where fauns and satyrs lurked to play in the moonlight before Pagan altars; and by the cloaking darkness, next, of the copse of stunted pines, close gathered each to each, where hooded figures stalked behind an awful cross. The episode with the children seemed to have opened me like a knife. The whole Place rushed at me.

I suspect this synthesis of many moods produced in me that climax of loathing and disgust which made me feel the limit of bearable emotion had been reached, so that I made straight to find Frances in order to convince her that at any rate I must leave. For, although this was our last day in the house, and we had arranged to go next day, the dread was in me that she would still find some persuasive reason for staying on. And an unexpected incident then made my dread unnecessary. The front door was open and a cab stood in the drive; a tall, elderly man was gravely talking in the hall with the parlour maid we called the Grenadier. He held a piece of paper in his hand. "I have called to see the house," I heard him say, as I ran up the stairs to Frances, who was peering like an inquisitive child over the banisters....

"Yes," she told me with a sigh, I know not whether of resignation or relief, "the house is to be let or sold. Mabel has decided. Some Society or other, I believe—"

I was overjoyed: this made our leaving right and possible. "You never told me, Frances!"

"Mabel only heard of it a few days ago. She told me herself this morning. It is a chance, she says. Alone she cannot get it 'straight'."

"Defeat?" I asked, watching her closely.

"She thinks she has found a way out. It's not a family, you see, it's a Society, a sort of Community – they go in for thought—"

"A Community!" I gasped. "You mean religious?"

She shook her head. "Not exactly," she said smiling, "but some kind of association of men and women who want a headquarters in the country – a place where they can write and meditate – think – mature their plans and all the rest – I don't know exactly what."

"Utopian dreamers?" I asked, yet feeling an immense relief come over me as I heard. But I asked in ignorance, not cynically. Frances would know. She knew all this kind of thing.

"No, not that exactly," she smiled. "Their teachings are grand and simple – old as the world too, really – the basis of every religion before men's minds perverted them with their manufactured creeds—"

Footsteps on the stairs, and the sound of voices, interrupted our odd impromptu conversation, as the Grenadier came up, followed by the tall, grave gentleman who was being shown over the house. My sister drew me along the corridor towards her room, where she went in and closed the door behind me, yet not before I had stolen a good look at the caller – long enough, at least, for his face and general appearance to have made a definite impression on me. For something strong and peaceful emanated from his presence; he moved with such quiet dignity; the glance of his eyes was so steady and reassuring, that my mind labeled him instantly as a type of man one would turn to in an emergency and not be disappointed. I had seen him but for a passing moment, but I had seen him twice, and the way he walked down the passage, looking competently about him, conveyed the same impression as when I saw him standing at the door – fearless, tolerant, wise. "A sincere and kindly character," I judged instantly, "a man whom some big kind of love has trained in sweetness towards the world; no hate in him anywhere." A great deal, no doubt, to read in so brief a glance! Yet his voice confirmed my intuition, a deep and very gentle voice, great firmness in it too.

"Have I become suddenly sensitive to people's atmospheres in this extraordinary fashion?" I asked myself, smiling, as I stood in the room and heard the door close behind me. "Have I developed some clairvoyant faculty here?" At any other time I should have mocked.

And I sat down and faced my sister, feeling strangely comforted and at peace for the first time since I had stepped beneath The Towers' roof a month ago. Frances, I then saw, was smiling a little as she watched me.

"You know him?" I asked.

"You felt it too?" was her question in reply. "No," she added, "I don't know him – beyond the fact that he is a leader in the Movement and has devoted years and money to its objects. Mabel felt the same thing in him that you have felt – and jumped at it."

"But you've seen him before?" I urged, for the certainty was in me that he was no stranger to her.

She shook her head. "He called one day early this week, when you were out. Mabel saw him. I believe—" she hesitated a moment, as though expecting me to stop her with my usual impatience of such subjects – "I believe he has explained everything to her – the beliefs he embodies, she declares, are her salvation – might be, rather, if she could adopt them."

"Conversion again!" For I remembered her riches, and how gladly a Society would gobble them.

"The layers I told you about," she continued calmly, shrugging her shoulders slightly – "the deposits that are left behind by strong thinking and real belief – but especially by ugly, hateful belief, because, you see – unfortunately there's more vital passion in that sort—"

"Frances, I don't understand a bit," I said out loud, but said it a little humbly, for the impression the man had left was still strong upon me and I was grateful for the steady sense of peace and comfort he had somehow introduced. The horrors had been so dreadful. My nerves, doubtless, were more than a little overstrained. Absurd as it must sound, I classed him in my mind with the robins, the happy, confiding robins who believed in everybody and thought no evil! I laughed a moment at my ridiculous idea, and my sister, encouraged by this sign of patience in me, continued more fluently.

"Of course you don't understand, Bill? Why should you? You've never thought about such things. Needing no creed yourself, you think all creeds are rubbish."

"I'm open to conviction – I'm tolerant," I interrupted.

"You're as narrow as Sam Franklyn, and as crammed with prejudice," she answered, knowing that she had me at her mercy.

"Then, pray, what may be his, or his Society's beliefs?" I asked, feeling no desire to argue, "and how are they going to prove your Mabel's salvation? Can they bring beauty into all this aggressive hate and ugliness?"

"Certain hope and peace," she said, "that peace which is understanding, and that understanding which explains all creeds and therefore tolerates them."

"Toleration! The one word a religious man loathes above all others! His pet word is damnation—"

"Tolerates them," she repeated patiently, unperturbed by my explosion, "because it includes them all."

"Fine, if true," I admitted, "very fine. But how, pray, does it include them all?"

"Because the key-word, the motto, of their Society is, 'There is no religion higher than Truth', and it has no single dogma of any kind. Above all," she went on, "because it claims that no individual can be 'lost'. It teaches universal salvation. To damn outsiders is uncivilised, childish, impure. Some take longer than others – it's according to the way they think and live – but all find peace, through development, in the end. What the creeds call a hopeless soul, it regards as a soul having further to go. There is no damnation—"

"Well, well," I exclaimed, feeling that she rode her hobby horse too wildly, too roughly over me, "but what is the bearing of all this upon this dreadful place, and upon Mabel? I'll admit that there is this atmosphere – this – er – inexplicable horror in the house and grounds, and that if not of damnation exactly, it is certainly damnable. I'm not too prejudiced to deny that, for I've felt it myself."

To my relief she was brief. She made her statement, leaving me to take it or reject it as I would.

"The thought and belief its former occupants – have left behind. For there has been coincidence here, a coincidence that must be rare. The site on which this modern house now stands was Roman, before that Early Britain, with burial mounds, before that again, Druid – the Druid stones still lie in that copse below the field, the Tumuli among the ilexes behind the drive. The older building Sam Franklyn altered and practically pulled down was a monastery; he changed the chapel into a meeting hall, which is now the music room; but, before he came here, the house was occupied by Manetti, a violent Catholic without tolerance or vision; and in the interval between these two, Julius Weinbaum had it, Hebrew of most rigid orthodox type imaginable – so they all have left their—"

"Even so," I repeated, yet interested to hear the rest, "what of it?"

"Simply this," said Frances with conviction, "that each in turn has left his layer of concentrated thinking and belief behind him; because each believed intensely, absolutely, beyond the least weakening of any doubt – the kind of strong belief and thinking that is rare anywhere today, the kind that wills, impregnates objects, saturates the atmosphere, haunts, in a word. And each, believing he was utterly and finally right, damned with equally positive conviction the rest of the world. One and all preached that implicitly if not explicitly. It's the root of every creed. Last of the bigoted, grim series came Samuel Franklyn."

I listened in amazement that increased as she went on. Up to this point her explanation was so admirable. It was, indeed, a pretty study in psychology if it were true.

"Then why does nothing ever happen?" I enquired mildly. "A place so thickly haunted ought to produce a crop of no ordinary results!"

"There lies the proof," she went on in a lowered voice, "the proof of the horror and the ugly reality. The thought and belief of each occupant in turn kept all the others under. They gave no sign of life at the time. But the results of thinking never die. They crop out again the moment there's an opening. And, with the return of Mabel in her negative state, believing nothing positive herself the place for the first time found itself free to reproduce its buried stores.

"Damnation, hell-fire, and the rest – the most permanent and vital thought of all those creeds, since it was applied to the majority of the world – broke loose again, for there was no restraint to hold it back. Each sought to obtain its former supremacy. None conquered. There results a pandemonium of hate and fear, of striving to escape, of agonised, bitter warring to find safety, peace – salvation. The place is saturated by that appalling stream of thinking – the terror of the damned. It concentrated upon Mabel, whose negative attitude furnished the channel of deliverance. You and I, according to our sympathy with her, were similarly involved. Nothing happened, because no one layer could ever gain the supremacy."

I was so interested – I dare not say amused – that I stared in silence while she paused a moment, afraid that she would draw rein and end the fairy tale too soon.

"The beliefs of this man, of his Society rather, vigorously thought and therefore vigorously given out here, will put the whole place straight. It will act as a solvent. These vitriolic layers actively denied, will fuse and disappear in the stream of gentle, tolerant sympathy which is love. For each member, worthy of the name, loves the world, and all creeds go into the melting-pot; Mabel, too, if she joins them out of real conviction, will find salvation—"

"Thinking, I know, is of the first importance," I objected, "but don't you, perhaps, exaggerate the power of feeling and emotion which in religion are au fond always hysterical?"

"What is the world," she told me, "but thinking and feeling? An individual's world is entirely what that individual thinks and believes – interpretation. There is no other. And unless he really thinks and really believes, he has no permanent world at all. I grant that few people think, and still fewer believe, and that most take ready-made suits and make them do. Only the strong make their own things; the lesser fry, Mabel among them, are merely swept up into what has been manufactured for them. They get along somehow. You and I have made for ourselves, Mabel has not. She is a nonentity, and when her belief is taken from her, she goes with it."

It was not in me just then to criticise the evasion, or pick out the sophistry from the truth. I merely waited for her to continue.

"None of us have Truth, my dear Frances," I ventured presently, seeing that she kept silent.

"Precisely," she answered, "but most of us have beliefs. And what one believes and thinks affects the world at large. Consider the legacy of hatred and cruelty involved in the doctrines men have built into their creeds where the *sine qua non* of salvation is absolute acceptance of one particular set of views or else perishing everlastingly – for only by repudiating history can they disavow it—"

"You're not quite accurate," I put in. "Not all the creeds teach damnation, do they? Franklyn did, of course, but the others are a bit modernised now surely?"

"Trying to get out of it," she admitted, "perhaps they are, but damnation of unbelievers – of most of the world, that is – is their rather favourite idea if you talk with them."

"I never have."

She smiled. "But I have," she said significantly, "so, if you consider what the various occupants of this house have so strongly held and thought and believed, you need not be surprised that the influence they have left behind them should be a dark and dreadful legacy. For thought, you know, does leave—"

The opening of the door, to my great relief, interrupted her, as the Grenadier led in the visitor to see the room. He bowed to both of us with a brief word of apology, looked round him, and withdrew, and with his departure the conversation between us came naturally to an end. I followed him out. Neither of us in any case, I think, cared to argue further.

And, so far as I am aware, the curious history of The Towers ends here too. There was no climax in the story sense. Nothing ever really happened. We left next morning for London. I only know that the Society in question took the house and have since occupied it to their entire satisfaction, and that Mabel, who became a member shortly afterwards, now stays there frequently when in need of repose from the arduous and unselfish labours she took upon herself under its aegis. She dined with us only the other night, here in our tiny Chelsea flat, and a jollier, saner, more interesting and happy guest I could hardly wish for. She was vital – in the best sense; the lay figure had come to life. I found it difficult to believe she was the same woman whose fearful effigy had floated down those dreary corridors and almost disappeared in the depths of that atrocious Shadow.

What her beliefs were now I was wise enough to leave unquestioned, and Frances, to my great relief, kept the conversation well away from such inappropriate topics. It was clear, however, that the woman had in herself some secret source of joy, that she was now an aggressive, positive force, sure of herself, and apparently afraid of nothing in heaven or hell. She radiated something very like hope and courage about her, and talked as though the world were a glorious place and everybody in it kind and beautiful. Her optimism was certainly infectious.

The Towers were mentioned only in passing. The name of Marsh came up – not the Marsh, it so happened, but a name in some book that was being discussed – and I was unable to restrain myself. Curiosity was too strong. I threw out a casual enquiry Mabel could leave unanswered if she wished. But there was no desire to avoid it. Her reply was frank and smiling.

"Would you believe it? She married," Mabel told me, though obviously surprised that I remembered the housekeeper at all; "and is happy as the day is long. She's found her right niche in life. A sergeant—"

"The army!" I ejaculated.

"Salvation Army," she explained merrily.

Frances exchanged a glance with me. I laughed too, for the information took me by surprise. I cannot say why exactly, but I expected at least to hear that the woman had met some dreadful end, not impossibly by burning.

"And The Towers, now called the Rest House," Mabel chattered on, "seems to me the most peaceful and delightful spot in England—"

"Really," I said politely.

"When I lived there in the old days – while you were there, perhaps, though I won't be sure."

Mabel went on, "the story got abroad that it was haunted. Wasn't it odd? A less likely place for a ghost I've never seen. Why, it had no atmosphere at all." She said this to Frances, glancing up at me with a smile that apparently had no hidden meaning. "Did you notice anything queer about it when you were there?"

This was plainly addressed to me.

"I found it – er – difficult to settle down to anything," I said, after an instant's hesitation. "I couldn't work there—"

"But I thought you wrote that wonderful book on the Deaf and Blind while you stayed with me," she asked innocently.

I stammered a little. "Oh no, not then. I only made a few notes – er – at The Towers. My mind, oddly enough, refused to produce at all down there. But – why do you ask? Did anything – was anything supposed to happen there?"

She looked searchingly into my eyes a moment before she answered:

"Not that I know of," she said simply.

**If you enjoyed this, you might also like…**
The Empty House, see page 371
Smith: An Episode in a Lodging House, see page 235

# The Decoy

IT BELONGED to the category of unlovely houses about which an ugly superstition clings, one reason being, perhaps, its inability to inspire interest in itself without assistance. It seemed too ordinary to possess individuality, much less to exert an influence. Solid and ungainly, its huge bulk dwarfing the park timber, its best claim to notice was a negative one – it was unpretentious.

From the little hill its expressionless windows stared across the Kentish Weald, indifferent to weather, dreary in winter, bleak in spring, unblessed in summer. Some colossal hand had tossed it down, then let it starve to death, a country mansion that might well strain the adjectives of advertisers and find inheritors with difficulty. Its soul had fled, said some; it had committed suicide, thought others; and it was an inheritor, before he killed himself in the library, who thought this latter, yielding, apparently, to an hereditary taint in the family. For two other inheritors followed suit, with an interval of twenty years between them, and there was no clear reason to explain the three disasters. Only the first owner, indeed, lived permanently in the house, the others using it in the summer months and then deserting it with relief. Hence, when John Burley, present inheritor, assumed possession, he entered a house about which clung an ugly superstition, based, nevertheless, upon a series of undeniably ugly facts.

This century deals harshly with superstitious folk, deeming them fools or charlatans; but John Burley, robust, contemptuous of half lights, did not deal harshly with them, because he did not deal with them at all. He was hardly aware of their existence. He ignored them as he ignored, say, the Esquimaux, poets, and other human aspects that did not touch his scheme of life. A successful business man, he concentrated on what was real; he dealt with business people. His philanthropy, on a big scale, was also real; yet, though he would have denied it vehemently, he had his superstition as well. No man exists without some taint of superstition in his blood; the racial heritage is too rich to be escaped entirely. Burley's took this form – that unless he gave his tithe to the poor he would not prosper. This ugly mansion, he decided, would make an ideal Convalescent Home.

"Only cowards or lunatics kill themselves," he declared flatly, when his use of the house was criticised. "I'm neither one nor t'other." He let out his gusty, boisterous laugh. In his invigorating atmosphere such weakness seemed contemptible, just as superstition in his presence seemed feeblest ignorance. Even its picturesqueness faded. "I can't conceive," he boomed, "can't even imagine to myself," he added emphatically, "the state of mind in which a man can think of suicide, much less do it." He threw his chest out with a challenging air. "I tell you, Nancy, it's either cowardice or mania. And I've no use for either."

Yet he was easy-going and good-humoured in his denunciation. He admitted his limitations with a hearty laugh his wife called noisy. Thus he made allowances for the fairy fears of sailorfolk, and had even been known to mention haunted ships his companies owned. But he did so in the terms of tonnage and £ s. d. His scope was big; details were made for clerks.

His consent to pass a night in the mansion was the consent of a practical business man and philanthropist who dealt condescendingly with foolish human nature. It was based on the common-sense of tonnage and £ s. d. The local newspapers had revived the silly story of the suicides, calling attention to the effect of the superstition upon the fortunes of the house, and so, possibly, upon the fortunes of its present owner. But the mansion, otherwise a white elephant, was precisely ideal for his purpose, and so trivial a matter as spending a night in it should not stand in the way. "We must take people as we find them, Nancy."

His young wife had her motive, of course, in making the proposal, and, if she was amused by what she called 'spook-hunting', he saw no reason to refuse her the indulgence. He loved her, and took her as he found her – late in life. To allay the superstitions of prospective staff and patients and supporters, all, in fact, whose goodwill was necessary to success, he faced this boredom of a night in the building before its opening was announced. "You see, John, if you, the owner, do this, it will nip damaging talk in the bud. If anything went wrong later it would only be put down to this suicide idea, this haunting influence. The Home will have a bad name from the start. There'll be endless trouble. It will be a failure."

"You think my spending a night there will stop the nonsense?" he inquired.

"According to the old legend it breaks the spell," she replied. "That's the condition, anyhow."

"But somebody's sure to die there sooner or later," he objected. "We can't prevent that."

"We can prevent people whispering that they died unnaturally." She explained the working of the public mind.

"I see," he replied, his lip curling, yet quick to gauge the truth of what she told him about collective instinct.

"Unless *you* take poison in the hall," she added laughingly, "or elect to hang yourself with your braces from the hat peg."

"I'll do it," he agreed, after a moment's thought. "I'll sit up with you. It will be like a honeymoon over again, you and I on the spree – eh?" He was even interested now; the boyish side of him was touched perhaps; but his enthusiasm was less when she explained that three was a better number than two on such an expedition.

"I've often done it before, John. We were always three."

"Who?" he asked bluntly. He looked wonderingly at her, but she answered that if anything went wrong a party of three provided a better margin for help. It was sufficiently obvious. He listened and agreed. "I'll get young Mortimer," he suggested. "Will he do?"

She hesitated. "Well – he's cheery; he'll be interested, too. Yes, he's as good as another." She seemed indifferent.

"And he'll make the time pass with his stories," added her husband.

So Captain Mortimer, late officer on a T.B.D., a 'cheery lad', afraid of nothing, cousin of Mrs. Burley, and now filling a good post in the company's London offices, was engaged as third hand in the expedition. But Captain Mortimer was young and ardent, and Mrs. Burley was young and pretty and ill-mated, and John Burley was a neglectful, and self-satisfied husband.

Fate laid the trap with cunning, and John Burley, blind-eyed, careless of detail, floundered into it. He also floundered out again, though in a fashion none could have expected of him.

The night agreed upon eventually was as near to the shortest in the year as John Burley could contrive – June 18th – when the sun set at 8:18 and rose about a quarter to four. There would be barely three hours of true darkness. "You're the expert," he admitted, as she explained that sitting through the actual darkness only was required, not necessarily from sunset to sunrise. "We'll do the thing properly. Mortimer's not very keen, he had a dance or something," he added, noticing the look of annoyance that flashed swiftly in her eyes; "but he got out of it. He's coming." The pouting expression of the spoilt woman amused him. "Oh, no, he didn't need much persuading really," he assured her. "Some girl or other, of course. He's young, remember." To which no comment was forthcoming, though the implied comparison made her flush.

They motored from South Audley Street after an early tea, in due course passing Sevenoaks and entering the Kentish Weald; and, in order that the necessary advertisement should be given, the chauffeur, warned strictly to keep their purpose quiet, was to put up at the country inn and fetch them an hour after sunrise; they would breakfast in London. "He'll tell everybody," said his practical and cynical master; "the local newspaper will have it all next day. A few hours' discomfort is worth while if it ends the nonsense. We'll read and smoke, and Mortimer shall tell us yarns about the sea." He went with the driver into the house to superintend the arrangement of the room, the lights, the hampers of food, and so forth, leaving the pair upon the lawn.

"Four hours isn't much, but it's something," whispered Mortimer, alone with her for the first time since they started. "It's simply ripping of you to have got me in. You look divine tonight. You're the most wonderful woman in the world." His blue eyes shone with the hungry desire he mistook for love. He looked as if he had blown in from the sea, for his skin was tanned and his light hair bleached a little by the sun. He took her hand, drawing her out of the slanting sunlight towards the rhododendrons.

"I didn't, you silly boy. It was John suggested your coming." She released her hand with an affected effort. "Besides, you overdid it – pretending you had a dance."

"You could have objected," he said eagerly, "and didn't. Oh, you're too lovely, you're delicious!" He kissed her suddenly with passion. There was a tiny struggle, in which she yielded too easily, he thought.

"Harry, you're an idiot!" she cried breathlessly, when he let her go. "I really don't know how you dare! And John's your friend. Besides, you know" – she glanced round quickly – "it isn't safe here." Her eyes shone happily, her cheeks were flaming. She looked what she was, a pretty, young, lustful animal, false to ideals, true to selfish passion only. "Luckily," she added, "he trusts me too fully to think anything."

The young man, worship in his eyes, laughed gaily. "There's no harm in a kiss," he said. "You're a child to him, he never thinks of you as a woman. Anyhow, his head's full of ships and kings and sealing-wax," he comforted her, while respecting her sudden instinct which warned him not to touch her again, "and he never sees anything. Why, even at ten yards—"

From twenty yards away a big voice interrupted him, as John Burley came round a corner of the house and across the lawn towards them. The chauffeur, he announced, had left the hampers in the room on the first floor and gone back to the inn. "Let's take a walk round," he added, joining them, "and see the garden. Five minutes before sunset we'll go in and feed." He laughed. "We must do the thing faithfully, you know, mustn't we, Nancy? Dark to dark, remember. Come on, Mortimer" – he took the young man's arm – "a last look round before we go in and hang ourselves from adjoining hooks in the matron's room!" He reached out his free hand towards his wife.

"Oh, hush, John!" she said quickly. "I don't like – especially now the dusk is coming." She shivered, as though it were a genuine little shiver, pursing her lips deliciously as she did so; whereupon he drew her forcibly to him, saying he was sorry, and kissed her exactly where she had been kissed two minutes before, while young Mortimer looked on. "We'll take care of you between us," he said. Behind a broad back the pair exchanged a swift but meaning glance, for there was that in his tone which enjoined wariness, and perhaps after all he was not so blind as he appeared. They had their code, these two. "All's well," was signalled; "but another time be more careful!"

There still remained some minutes' sunlight before the huge red ball of fire would sink behind the wooded hills, and the trio, talking idly, a flutter of excitement in two hearts certainly, walked among the roses. It was a perfect evening, windless, perfumed, warm. Headless shadows preceded them gigantically across the lawn as they moved, and one side of the great building lay already dark; bats were flitting, moths darted to and fro above the azalea and rhododendron clumps. The talk turned chiefly on the uses of the mansion as a Convalescent Home, its probable running cost, suitable staff, and so forth.

"Come along," John Burley said presently, breaking off and turning abruptly, "we must be inside, actually inside, before the sun's gone. We must fulfil the conditions faithfully," he repeated, as though fond of the phrase. He was in earnest over everything in life, big or little, once he set his hand to it.

They entered, this incongruous trio of ghost-hunters, no one of them really intent upon the business in hand, and went slowly upstairs to the great room where the hampers lay. Already in the hall it was dark enough for three electric torches to flash usefully and help their steps as they moved with caution, lighting one corner after another. The air inside was chill and damp. "Like an unused museum," said Mortimer. "I can smell the specimens." They looked about them, sniffing. "That's humanity," declared his host, employer, friend, "with cement and whitewash to flavour it"; and all three laughed as Mrs. Burley said she wished they had picked some roses and brought them in. Her husband was again in front on the broad staircase, Mortimer just behind him, when she called out. "I don't like being last," she exclaimed. "It's so black behind me in the hall. I'll come between you two," and the sailor took her outstretched hand, squeezing it, as he passed her up. "There's a figure, remember," she said hurriedly, turning to gain her husband's attention, as when she touched wood at home. "A figure is seen; that's part of the story. The figure of a man." She gave a tiny shiver of pleasurable, half-imagined alarm as she took his arm.

"I hope we shall see it," he mentioned prosaically.

"I hope we shan't," she replied with emphasis. "It's only seen before – something happens." Her husband said nothing, while Mortimer remarked facetiously that it would be a pity if they had their trouble for nothing. "Something can hardly happen to all three of us," he said lightly, as they entered a large room where the paper-hangers had conveniently left a rough table of bare planks. Mrs. Burley, busy with her own thoughts, began to unpack the sandwiches and wine. Her husband strolled over to the window. He seemed restless.

"So this," his deep voice startled her, "is where one of us" – he looked round him – "is to—"

"John!" She stopped him sharply, with impatience. "Several times already I've begged you." Her voice rang rather shrill and querulous in the empty room, a new note in it.

She was beginning to feel the atmosphere of the place, perhaps. On the sunny lawn it had not touched her, but now, with the fall of night, she was aware of it, as shadow called to shadow and the kingdom of darkness gathered power. Like a great whispering gallery, the whole house listened.

"Upon my word, Nancy," he said with contrition, as he came and sat down beside her, "I quite forgot again. Only I cannot take it seriously. It's so utterly unthinkable to me that a man—"

"But why evoke the idea at all?" she insisted in a lowered voice, that snapped despite its faintness. "Men, after all, don't do such things for nothing."

"We don't know everything in the universe, do we?" Mortimer put in, trying clumsily to support her. "All I know just now is that I'm famished and this veal and ham pie is delicious." He was very busy with his knife and fork. His foot rested lightly on her own beneath the table; he could not keep his eyes off her face; he was continually passing new edibles to her.

"No," agreed John Burley, "not everything. You're right there."

She kicked the younger man gently, flashing a warning with her eyes as well, while her husband, emptying his glass, his head thrown back, looked straight at them over the rim, apparently seeing nothing. They smoked their cigarettes round the table, Burley lighting a big cigar. "Tell us about the figure, Nancy?" he inquired. "At least there's no harm in that. It's new to me. I hadn't heard about a figure." And she did so willingly, turning her chair sideways from the dangerous, reckless feet. Mortimer could now no longer touch her. "I know very little," she confessed; "only what the paper said. It's a man.... And he changes."

"How changes?" asked her husband. "Clothes, you mean, or what?"

Mrs. Burley laughed, as though she was glad to laugh. Then she answered: "According to the story, he shows himself each time to the man—"

"The man who—?"

"Yes, yes, of course. He appears to the man who dies – as himself."

"H'm," grunted her husband, naturally puzzled. He stared at her.

"Each time the chap saw his own double" – Mortimer came this time usefully to the rescue – "before he did it."

Considerable explanation followed, involving much psychic jargon from Mrs. Burley, which fascinated and impressed the sailor, who thought her as wonderful as she was lovely, showing it in his eyes for all to see. John Burley's attention wandered. He moved over to the window, leaving them to finish the discussion between them; he took no part in it, made no comment even, merely listening idly and watching them with an air of absent-mindedness through the cloud of cigar smoke round his head. He moved from window to window, ensconcing himself in turn in each deep embrasure, examining the fastenings, measuring the thickness of the stonework with his handkerchief. He seemed restless, bored, obviously out of place in this ridiculous expedition. On his big massive face lay a quiet, resigned expression his wife had never seen before. She noticed it now as, the discussion ended, the pair tidied away the *débris* of dinner, lit the spirit lamp for coffee and laid out a supper which would be very welcome with the dawn. A draught passed through the room, making the papers flutter on the table. Mortimer turned down the smoking lamps with care.

"Wind's getting up a bit – from the south," observed Burley from his niche, closing one half of the casement window as he said it. To do this, he turned his back a moment, fumbling for several seconds with the latch, while Mortimer, noting it, seized his sudden opportunity with the foolish abandon of his age and temperament. Neither he nor his victim perceived that, against the outside darkness, the interior of the room was plainly reflected in the window-pane. One reckless, the other terrified, they snatched the fearful joy, which might, after all, have been lengthened by another full half-minute, for the head they feared, followed by the shoulders, pushed through the side of the casement still open, and remained outside, taking in the night.

"A grand air," said his deep voice, as the head drew in again, "I'd like to be at sea a night like this." He left the casement open and came across the room towards them. "Now," he said cheerfully, arranging a seat for himself, "let's get comfortable for the night. Mortimer, we expect stories from you without ceasing, until dawn or the ghost arrives. Horrible stories of chains and headless men, remember. Make it a night we shan't forget in a hurry." He produced his gust of laughter.

They arranged their chairs, with other chairs to put their feet on, and Mortimer contrived a footstool by means of a hamper for the smallest feet; the air grew thick with tobacco smoke; eyes flashed and answered, watched perhaps as well; ears listened and perhaps grew wise; occasionally, as a window shook, they started and looked round; there were sounds about the house from time to time, when the entering wind, using broken or open windows, set loose objects rattling.

But Mrs. Burley vetoed horrible stories with decision. A big, empty mansion, lonely in the country, and even with the comfort of John Burley and a lover in it, has its atmosphere. Furnished rooms are far less ghostly. This atmosphere now came creeping everywhere, through spacious halls and sighing corridors, silent, invisible, but all-pervading, John Burley alone impervious to it, unaware of its soft attack upon the nerves. It entered possibly with the summer night wind, but possibly it was always there.... And Mrs. Burley looked often at her husband, sitting near her at an angle; the light fell on his fine strong face; she felt that, though apparently so calm and quiet, he was really very restless; something about him was a little different; she could not define it; his mouth seemed set as with an effort; he looked, she thought curiously to herself, patient and very dignified; he was rather a dear after all. Why did she think the face inscrutable? Her thoughts wandered vaguely, unease, discomfort among them somewhere, while the heated blood – she had taken her share of wine – seethed in her.

Burley turned to the sailor for more stories. "Sea and wind in them," he asked. "No horrors, remember!" and Mortimer told a tale about the shortage of rooms at a Welsh seaside place where spare rooms fetched fabulous prices, and one man alone refused to let – a retired captain of a South Seas trader, very poor, a bit crazy apparently. He had two furnished rooms in his house worth twenty guineas a week. The rooms faced south; he kept them full of flowers; but he would not let. An explanation of his unworldly obstinacy was not forthcoming until Mortimer – they fished together – gained his confidence. "The South Wind lives in them," the old fellow told him. "I keep them free for her."

"For *her*?"

"It was on the South Wind my love came to me," said the other softly; "and it was on the South Wind that she left—"

It was an odd tale to tell in such company, but he told it well.

"Beautiful," thought Mrs. Burley. Aloud she said a quiet, "Thank you. By 'left', I suppose he meant she died or ran away?"

John Burley looked up with a certain surprise. "We ask for a story," he said, "and you give us a poem." He laughed. "You're in love, Mortimer," he informed him, "and with my wife probably."

"Of course I am, sir," replied the young man gallantly. "A sailor's heart, you know," while the face of the woman turned pink, then white. She knew her husband more intimately than Mortimer did, and there was something in his tone, his eyes, his words, she did not like. Harry was an idiot to choose such a tale. An irritated annoyance stirred in her, close upon dislike. "Anyhow, it's better than horrors," she said hurriedly.

"Well," put in her husband, letting forth a minor gust of laughter, "it's possible, at any rate. Though one's as crazy as the other." His meaning was not wholly clear. "If a man really loved," he added in his blunt fashion, "and was tricked by her, I could almost conceive his—"

"Oh, don't preach, John, for Heaven's sake. You're so dull in the pulpit." But the interruption only served to emphasise the sentence which, otherwise, might have been passed over.

"Could conceive his finding life so worthless," persisted the other, "that—" He hesitated. "But there, now, I promised I wouldn't," he went on, laughing good-humouredly. Then, suddenly, as though in spite of himself, driven it seemed: "Still, under such conditions, he might show his contempt for human nature and for life by—"

It was a tiny stifled scream that stopped him this time.

"John, I hate, I loathe you, when you talk like that. And you've broken your word again." She was more than petulant; a nervous anger sounded in her voice. It was the way he had said it, looking from them towards the window, that made her quiver. She felt him suddenly as a man; she felt afraid of him.

Her husband made no reply; he rose and looked at his watch, leaning sideways towards the lamp, so that the expression of his face was shaded. "Two o'clock," he remarked. "I think I'll take a turn through the house. I may find a workman asleep or something. Anyhow, the light will soon come now." He laughed; the expression of his face, his tone of voice, relieved her momentarily. He went out. They heard his heavy tread echoing down the carpetless long corridor.

Mortimer began at once. "Did he mean anything?" he asked breathlessly. "He doesn't love you the least little bit, anyhow. He never did. I do. You're wasted on him. You belong to me." The words poured out. He covered her face with kisses. "Oh, I didn't mean *that*," he caught between the kisses.

The sailor released her, staring. "What then?" he whispered. "Do you think he saw us on the lawn?" He paused a moment, as she made no reply. The steps were audible in the distance still. "I know!" he exclaimed suddenly. "It's the blessed house he feels. That's what it is. He doesn't like it."

A wind sighed through the room, making the papers flutter; something rattled; and Mrs. Burley started. A loose end of rope swinging from the paperhanger's ladder caught her eye. She shivered slightly.

"He's different," she replied in a low voice, nestling very close again, "and so restless. Didn't you notice what he said just now – that under certain conditions he could understand a man" – she hesitated – "doing it," she concluded, a sudden drop in her voice. "Harry," she looked full into his eyes, "that's not like him. He didn't say that for nothing."

"Nonsense! He's bored to tears, that's all. And the house is getting on your nerves, too." He kissed her tenderly. Then, as she responded, he drew her nearer still and held her passionately, mumbling incoherent words, among which "nothing to be afraid of" was distinguishable. Meanwhile, the steps were coming nearer. She pushed him away. "You must behave yourself. I insist. You shall, Harry," then buried herself in his arms, her face hidden against his neck – only to disentangle herself the next instant and stand clear of him. "I hate you, Harry," she exclaimed sharply, a look of angry annoyance flashing across her face. "And I *hate* myself. Why do you treat me—?" She broke off as the steps came closer, patted her hair straight, and stalked over to the open window.

"I believe after all you're only playing with me," he said viciously. He stared in surprised disappointment, watching her. "It's him you really love," he added jealously. He looked and spoke like a petulant spoilt boy.

She did not turn her head. "He's always been fair to me, kind and generous. He never blames me for anything. Give me a cigarette and don't play the stage hero. My nerves are on edge, to tell you the truth." Her voice jarred harshly, and as he lit her cigarette he noticed that her lips were trembling; his own hand trembled too. He was still holding the match, standing beside her at the window-sill, when the steps crossed the threshold and John Burley came into the room. He went straight up to the table and turned the lamp down. "It was smoking," he remarked. "Didn't you see?"

"I'm sorry, sir," and Mortimer sprang forward, too late to help him. "It was the draught as you pushed the door open." The big man said, "Ah!" and drew a chair over, facing them. "It's just *the* very house," he told them. "I've been through every room on this floor. It will make a splendid Home, with very little alteration, too." He turned round in his creaking wicker chair and looked up at his wife, who sat swinging her legs and smoking in the window embrasure. "Lives will be saved inside these old walls. It's a good investment," he went on, talking rather to himself it seemed. "People will die here, too—"

"Hark!" Mrs. Burley interrupted him. "That noise – what is it?" A faint thudding sound in the corridor or in the adjoining room was audible, making all three look round quickly, listening for a repetition, which did not come. The papers fluttered on the table, the lamps smoked an instant.

"Wind," observed Burley calmly, "our little friend, the South Wind. Something blown over again, that's all." But, curiously, the three of them stood up. "I'll go and see," he continued. "Doors and windows are all open to let the paint dry." Yet he did not move; he stood there watching a white moth that dashed round and round the lamp, flopping heavily now and again upon the bare deal table.

"Let me go, sir," put in Mortimer eagerly. He was glad of the chance; for the first time he, too, felt uncomfortable. But there was another who, apparently, suffered a discomfort greater than his own and was accordingly even more glad to get away. "I'll go," Mrs. Burley announced, with decision. "I'd like to. I haven't been out of this room since we came. I'm not an atom afraid."

It was strange that for a moment she did not make a move either; it seemed as if she waited for something. For perhaps fifteen seconds no one stirred or spoke. She knew by the look in her lover's eyes that he had now become aware of the slight, indefinite change in her husband's manner, and was alarmed by it. The fear in him woke her contempt; she suddenly despised the youth, and was conscious of a new, strange yearning towards her husband; against her worked nameless pressures, troubling her being. There was an alteration in the room, she thought; something had come in. The trio stood listening to the gentle wind outside, waiting for the sound to be repeated; two careless, passionate young lovers and a man stood waiting, listening, watching in that room; yet it seemed there were five persons altogether and not three, for two guilty consciences stood apart and separate from their owners. John Burley broke the silence.

"Yes, you go, Nancy. Nothing to be afraid of – there. It's only wind." He spoke as though he meant it.

Mortimer bit his lips. "I'll come with you," he said instantly. He was confused. "Let's all three go. I don't think we ought to be separated." But Mrs. Burley was already at the door. "I insist," she said, with a forced laugh. "I'll call if I'm frightened," while her husband, saying nothing, watched her from the table.

"Take this," said the sailor, flashing his electric torch as he went over to her. "Two are better than one." He saw her figure exquisitely silhouetted against the black corridor beyond; it was clear she wanted to go; any nervousness in her was mastered by a stronger emotion still; she was glad to be out of their presence for a bit. He had hoped to snatch a word of explanation in the corridor, but her manner stopped him. Something else stopped him, too.

"First door on the left," he called out, his voice echoing down the empty length. "That's the room where the noise came from. Shout if you want us."

He watched her moving away, the light held steadily in front of her, but she made no answer, and he turned back to see John Burley lighting his cigar at the lamp chimney, his face thrust forward as he did so. He stood a second, watching him, as the lips sucked hard at the cigar to make it draw; the strength of the features was emphasised to sternness. He had meant to stand by the door and listen for the least sound from the adjoining room, but now found his whole attention focused on the face above the lamp. In that minute he realised that Burley had wished – had meant – his wife to go. In that minute also he forgot his love, his shameless, selfish little mistress, his worthless, caddish little self. For John Burley looked up. He straightened slowly, puffing hard and quickly to make sure his cigar was lit, and faced him. Mortimer moved forward into the room, self-conscious, embarrassed, cold.

"Of course it was only wind," he said lightly, his one desire being to fill the interval while they were alone with commonplaces. He did not wish the other to speak, "Dawn wind, probably." He glanced at his wrist-watch. "It's half-past two already, and the sun gets up at a quarter to four. It's light by now, I expect. The shortest night is never quite dark." He rambled on confusedly, for the other's steady, silent stare embarrassed him. A faint sound of Mrs. Burley moving in the next room made him stop a moment. He turned instinctively to the door, eager for an excuse to go.

"That's nothing," said Burley, speaking at last and in a firm quiet voice. "Only my wife, glad to be alone – my young and pretty wife. She's all right. I know her better than you do. Come in and shut the door."

Mortimer obeyed. He closed the door and came close to the table, facing the other, who at once continued.

"If I thought," he said, in that quiet deep voice, "that you two were serious" – he uttered his words very slowly, with emphasis, with intense severity – "do you know what I should do? I will tell you, Mortimer. I should like one of us two – you or myself – to remain in this house, dead."

His teeth gripped his cigar tightly; his hands were clenched; he went on through a half-closed mouth. His eyes blazed steadily.

"I trust her so absolutely – understand me? – that my belief in women, in human beings, would go. And with it the desire to live. Understand me?"

Each word to the young careless fool was a blow in the face, yet it was the softest blow, the flash of a big deep heart, that hurt the most. A dozen answers – denial, explanation, confession, taking all guilt upon himself – crowded his mind, only to be dismissed. He stood motionless and silent, staring hard into the other's eyes. No word passed his lips; there was no time in any case. It was in this position that Mrs. Burley, entering at that moment, found them. She saw her husband's face; the other man stood with his back to her. She came in with a little nervous laugh. "A bell-rope swinging in the wind and hitting a sheet of metal before the fireplace," she informed them. And all three laughed together then, though each laugh had a different sound. "But I hate this house," she added. "I wish we had never come."

"The moment there's light in the sky," remarked her husband quietly, "we can leave. That's the contract; let's see it through. Another half-hour will do it. Sit down, Nancy, and have a bite of something." He got up and placed a chair for her. "I think I'll take another look round." He moved slowly to the door. "I may go out on to the lawn a bit and see what the sky is doing."

It did not take half a minute to say the words, yet to Mortimer it seemed as though the voice would never end. His mind was confused and troubled. He loathed himself, he loathed the woman through whom he had got into this awkward mess.

The situation had suddenly become extremely painful; he had never imagined such a thing; the man he had thought blind had after all seen everything – known it all along, watched them, waited. And the woman, he was now certain, loved her husband; she had fooled him, Mortimer, all along, amusing herself.

"I'll come with you, sir. Do let me," he said suddenly. Mrs. Burley stood pale and uncertain between them. She looked scared. What has happened, she was clearly wondering.

"No, no, Harry" – he called him 'Harry' for the first time – "I'll be back in five minutes at most. My wife mustn't be alone either." And he went out.

The young man waited till the footsteps sounded some distance down the corridor, then turned, but he did not move forward; for the first time he let pass unused what he called 'an opportunity'. His passion had left him; his love, as he once thought it, was gone. He looked at the pretty woman near him, wondering blankly what he had ever seen there to attract him so wildly. He wished to Heaven he was out of it all. He wished he were dead. John Burley's words suddenly appalled him.

One thing he saw plainly – she was frightened. This opened his lips.

"What's the matter?" he asked, and his hushed voice shirked the familiar Christian name. "Did you see anything?" He nodded his head in the direction of the adjoining room. It was the sound of his own voice addressing her coldly that made him abruptly see himself as he really was, but it was her reply, honestly given, in a faint even voice, that told him she saw her own self too with similar clarity. God, he thought, how revealing a tone, a single word can be!

"I saw – nothing. Only I feel uneasy – dear." That 'dear' was a call for help.

"Look here," he cried, so loud that she held up a warning finger, "I'm – I've been a damned fool, a cad! I'm most frightfully ashamed. I'll do anything – *anything* to get it right." He felt cold, naked, his worthlessness laid bare; she felt, he knew, the same. Each revolted suddenly from the other. Yet he knew not quite how or wherefore this great change had thus abruptly come about, especially on her side. He felt that a bigger, deeper emotion than he could understand was working on them, making mere physical relationships seem empty, trivial, cheap and vulgar. His cold increased in face of this utter ignorance.

"Uneasy?" he repeated, perhaps hardly knowing exactly why he said it. "Good Lord, but he can take care of himself—"

"Oh, *he* is a man," she interrupted; "yes."

Steps were heard, firm, heavy steps, coming back along the corridor. It seemed to Mortimer that he had listened to this sound of steps all night, and would listen to them till he died. He crossed to the lamp and lit a cigarette, carefully this time, turning the wick down afterwards. Mrs. Burley also rose, moving over towards the door, away from him. They listened a moment to these firm and heavy steps, the tread of a man, John Burley. A man… and a philanderer, flashed across Mortimer's brain like fire, contrasting the two with fierce contempt for himself. The tread became less audible. There was distance in it. It had turned in somewhere.

"There!" she exclaimed in a hushed tone. "He's gone in."

"Nonsense! It passed us. He's going out on to the lawn."

The pair listened breathlessly for a moment, when the sound of steps came distinctly from the adjoining room, walking across the boards, apparently towards the window.

"There!" she repeated. "He did go in." Silence of perhaps a minute followed, in which they heard each other's breathing. "I don't like his being alone – in there," Mrs. Burley said in a thin faltering voice, and moved as though to go out. Her hand was already on the knob of the door, when Mortimer stopped her with a violent gesture.

"Don't! For God's sake, don't!" he cried, before she could turn it. He darted forward. As he laid a hand upon her arm a thud was audible through the wall. It was a heavy sound, and this time there was no wind to cause it.

"It's only that loose swinging thing," he whispered thickly, a dreadful confusion blotting out clear thought and speech.

"There was no loose swaying thing at all," she said in a failing voice, then reeled and swayed against him. "I invented that. There was nothing." As he caught her, staring helplessly, it seemed to him that a face with lifted lids rushed up at him. He saw two terrified eyes in a patch of ghastly white. Her whisper followed, as she sank into his arms. "It's John. He's—"

At which instant, with terror at its climax, the sound of steps suddenly became audible once more – the firm and heavy tread of John Burley coming out again into the corridor. Such was their amazement and relief that they neither moved nor spoke. The steps drew nearer. The pair seemed petrified; Mortimer did not remove his arms, nor did Mrs. Burley attempt to release herself. They stared at the door and waited. It was pushed wider the next second, and John Burley stood beside them. He was so close he almost touched them – there in each other's arms.

"Jack, dear!" cried his wife, with a searching tenderness that made her voice seem strange.

He gazed a second at each in turn. "I'm going out on to the lawn for a moment," he said quietly. There was no expression on his face; he did not smile, he did not frown; he showed no feeling, no emotion – just looked into their eyes, and then withdrew round the edge of the door before either could utter a word in answer. The door swung to behind him. He was gone.

"He's going to the lawn. He said so." It was Mortimer speaking, but his voice shook and stammered. Mrs. Burley had released herself. She stood now by the table, silent, gazing with fixed eyes at nothing, her lips parted, her expression vacant. Again she was aware of an alteration in the room; something had gone out.... He watched her a second, uncertain what to say or do. It was the face of a drowned person, occurred to him. Something intangible, yet almost visible stood between them in that narrow space. Something had ended, there before his eyes, definitely ended. The barrier between them rose higher, denser. Through this barrier her words came to him with an odd whispering remoteness.

"Harry.... You saw? You noticed?"

"What d'you mean?" he said gruffly. He tried to feel angry, contemptuous, but his breath caught absurdly.

"Harry – he was different. The eyes, the hair, the" – her face grew like death – "the twist in his face—"

"What on earth are you saying? Pull yourself together." He saw that she was trembling down the whole length of her body, as she leaned against the table for support. His own legs shook. He stared hard at her.

"Altered, Harry... altered." Her horrified whisper came at him like a knife. For it was true. He, too, had noticed something about the husband's appearance that was not quite normal. Yet, even while they talked, they heard him going down the carpetless stairs; the sounds ceased as he crossed the hall; then came the noise of the front door banging, the reverberation even shaking the room a little where they stood.

Mortimer went over to her side. He walked unevenly.

"My dear! For God's sake – this is sheer nonsense. Don't let yourself go like this. I'll put it straight with him – it's all my fault." He saw by her face that she did not understand his words; he was saying the wrong thing altogether; her mind was utterly elsewhere. "He's all right," he went on hurriedly. "He's out on the lawn now—"

He broke off at the sight of her. The horror that fastened on her brain plastered her face with deathly whiteness.

"That was not John at all!" she cried, a wail of misery and terror in her voice. She rushed to the window and he followed. To his immense relief a figure moving below was plainly visible. It was John Burley. They saw him in the faint grey of the dawn, as he crossed the lawn, going away from the house. He disappeared.

"There you are! See?" whispered Mortimer reassuringly. "He'll be back in—" when a sound in the adjoining room, heavier, louder than before, cut appallingly across his words, and Mrs. Burley, with that wailing scream, fell back into his arms. He caught her only just in time, for she stiffened into ice, daft with the uncomprehended terror of it all, and helpless as a child.

"Darling, my darling – oh, God!" He bent, kissing her face wildly. He was utterly distraught.

"Harry! Jack – oh, oh!" she wailed in her anguish. "It took on his likeness. It deceived us... to give him time. He's done it."

She sat up suddenly. "Go," she said, pointing to the room beyond, then sank fainting, a dead weight in his arms.

He carried her unconscious body to a chair, then entering the adjoining room he flashed his torch upon the body of her husband hanging from a bracket in the wall. He cut it down five minutes too late.

**If you enjoyed this, you might also like…**
The Empty House, see page 371
The Terror of the Twins, see page 176

# Biographies

**Algernon Blackwood**
Algernon Henry Blackwood (1869–1951) was a writer who crafted his tales with extraordinary vision. Born in Kent but working at numerous careers in America and Canada in his youth, he eventually settled back in England in his thirties. He wrote many novels and short stories including 'The Willows', which was rated by Lovecraft as one of his favourite stories, and he is credited by many scholars as a real master of imagery who wrote at a consistently high standard.

**Ramsey Campbell**
*Foreword: Algernon Blackwood Horror Stories*
Ramsey Campbell has been given more awards than any other writer in the field, including the Grand Master Award of the World Horror Convention, the Lifetime Achievement Award of the Horror Writers Association, the Living Legend Award of the International Horror Guild and the World Fantasy Lifetime Achievement Award. In 2015 he was made an Honorary Fellow of Liverpool John Moores University for outstanding services to literature. Among his novels available from Flame Tree Press are *Thirteen Days by Sunset Beach*, *The Wise Friend*, *Somebody's Voice*, *Fellstones*, *The Lonely Lands*, and his *Three Births of Daoloth* trilogy: *The Searching Dead*, *Born to the Dark* and *The Way of the Worm*.

# Sources

## Nature & The Wilderness

**The Willows**
Originally Published in *The Listener and Other Stories*, 1907

**The Sea Fit**
Originally Published in *Country Life*, June 25, 1910

**The Wendigo**
Originally Published in *The Lost Valley and Other Stories*, 1910

**The Glamour of the Snow**
Originally Published in *The Pall Mall Magazine*, December 1911

**Ancient Lights**
Originally Published in *The Eye-Witness*, Vol. 3 No. 4, 11 July 1912

**Special Delivery**
Originally Published in *Pan's Garden: A Volume of Nature Stories*, 1912

**By Water**
Originally Published in *The Westminster Gazette*, April 18, 1914

**H.S.H.**
Originally Published in *Day and Night Stories*, 1917

## Tales of Transformation

**May Day Eve**
Originally Published in *The Listener and Other Stories*, 1907

**The Camp of the Dog**
Originally Published in *John Silence, Physician Extraordinary*, 1908

**The Terror of the Twins**
Originally Published in *The Westminster Gazette*, November 6, 1909

**The Transfer**
Originally Published in *Country Life*, Dec 9, 1911

**Strange Disappearance of a Baronet**
Originally Published in *Ten Minute Stories*, 1914

**The Wings of Horus**
Originally Published in *The Century Magazine*, v. 89, November 1914

**Tongues of Fire**
Originally Published in *Tongues of Fire and Other Sketches*, 1924

**The Doll**
Originally Published in *The Doll and One Other*, 1946

## Weird Realities

**Smith: An Episode in a Lodging House**
Originally Published in *The Empty House and Other Ghost Stories*, 1906

**Ancient Sorceries**
Originally Published in *John Silence, Physician Extraordinary*, 1908

**Secret Worship**
Originally Published in *John Silence, Physician Extraordinary*, 1908

**The Man Who Found Out**
Originally Published in *The Canadian Magazine*, December 1912

**A Victim of Higher Space**
Originally Published in *The Occult Review*, December 1914

**The Other Wing**
Originally Published in *McBride's*, November 1915

**The Pikestaffe Case**
Originally Published in *Cassell's Magazine*, serialised between July and September 1923

## Ghostly Visitations

**A Haunted Island**
Originally Published in *The Pall Mall Magazine*, April 1899

**Keeping His Promise**
Originally Published in *The Empty House and Other Ghost Stories*, 1906

**The Empty House**
Originally Published in *The Empty House and Other Ghost Stories*, 1906

**The Listener**
Originally Published in *The Listener and Other Stories*, 1907

**The Kit-Bag**
Originally Published in *Pall Mall Magazine*, December 1908

**The Occupant of the Room**
Originally Published in *Nash's Magazine*, December 1909

**The Damned**
Originally Published in *Incredible Adventures*, 1914

**The Decoy**
Originally Published in *The Wolves of God and Other Fey Stories*, 1921

# FLAME TREE PUBLISHING
# Epic, Dark, Thrilling & Gothic

*New & Classic Writing*

**Flame Tree's Gothic Fantasy books offer a carefully curated series of new titles, each with combinations of original and classic writing:**

*Chilling Horror • Chilling Ghost • Asian Ghost • Science Fiction • Murder Mayhem
Crime & Mystery • Swords & Steam • Dystopia Utopia • Supernatural Horror
Lost Worlds • Time Travel • Heroic Fantasy • Pirates & Ghosts • Agents & Spies
Endless Apocalypse • Alien Invasion • Robots & AI • Lost Souls • Haunted House
Cosy Crime • American Gothic • Urban Crime • Epic Fantasy • Detective Mysteries
Detective Thrillers • A Dying Planet • Footsteps in the Dark • Bodies in the Library
Strange Lands • Weird Horror • Lost Atlantis • Lovecraft Mythos • Terrifying Ghosts
Black Sci-Fi • Chilling Crime • Compelling Science Fiction • Christmas Gothic
First Peoples Shared Stories • Alternate History • Hidden Realms
Immigrant Sci-Fi • Spirits & Ghouls*

**Also, new companion titles offer rich collections of classic fiction, myths and tales in the gothic fantasy tradition:**

*Charles Dickens Supernatural • George Orwell Visions of Dystopia • H.G. Wells
Sherlock Holmes • Edgar Allan Poe • Bram Stoker Horror • Mary Shelley Horror
Lovecraft • M.R. James Ghost Stories • Algernon Blackwood Horror Stories
Robert Louis Stevenson Collection • The Divine Comedy • The Age of Queen Victoria
Brothers Grimm Fairy Tales • Hans Christian Andersen Fairy Tales • Moby Dick
Alice's Adventures in Wonderland • King Arthur & The Knights of the Round Table
The Wonderful Wizard of Oz • Ramayana • The Odyssey and the Iliad • The Aeneid
Paradise Lost • The Decameron • One Thousand and One Arabian Nights
Persian Myths & Tales • African Myths & Tales • Celtic Myths & Tales
Greek Myths & Tales • Norse Myths & Tales • Chinese Myths & Tales • Japanese Myths & Tales
Native American Myths & Tales • Aztec Myths & Tales • Egyptian Myths & Tales
Irish Fairy Tales • Scottish Folk & Fairy Tales • Viking Folk & Fairy Tales
Heroes & Heroines Myths & Tales • Gods & Monsters Myths & Tales
Beasts & Creatures Myths & Tales • Witches, Wizards, Seers & Healers Myths & Tales*

Available from all good bookstores, worldwide, and online at
*flametreepublishing.com*

**See our new fiction imprint**
FLAME TREE PRESS | FICTION WITHOUT FRONTIERS
New and original writing in Horror, Crime, SF and Fantasy

And join our monthly newsletter with offers and more stories:
FLAME TREE FICTION NEWSLETTER

*flametreepress.com*

For our books, calendars, blog
and latest special offers please see:
*flametreepublishing.com*